Afterwife

Afterwife

POLLY WILLIAMS

BERKLEY BOOKS, NEW YORK

BERKLEY BOOKS
Published by the Penguin Group
Penguin Group (USA) Inc.
375 Hudson Street, New York, New York 10014, USA
Penguin Group (Canada), 90 Eglinton Avenue East, Suite 700, Toronto, Ontario M4P 2Y3, Canada
(a division of Pearson Penguin Canada Inc.) • Penguin Books Ltd., 80 Strand, London WC2R 0RL,
England • Penguin Group Ireland, 25 St. Stephen's Green, Dublin 2, Ireland (a division of Penguin
Books Ltd.) • Penguin Group (Australia), 250 Camberwell Road, Camberwell, Victoria 3124, Australia
(a division of Pearson Australia Group Pty. Ltd.) • Penguin Books India Pvt. Ltd., 11 Community
Centre, Panchsheel Park, New Delhi—110 017, India • Penguin Group (NZ), 67 Apollo Drive,
Rosedale, Auckland 0632, New Zealand (a division of Pearson New Zealand Ltd.) • Penguin Books
(South Africa) (Pty.) Ltd., 24 Sturdee Avenue, Rosebank, Johannesburg 2196, South Africa

Penguin Books Ltd., Registered Offices: 80 Strand, London WC2R 0RL, England

This is a work of fiction. Names, characters, places, and incidents either are the product of the author's imagination or are used fictitiously, and any resemblance to actual persons, living or dead, business establishments, events, or locales is entirely coincidental. The publisher does not have any control over and does not assume any responsibility for author or third-party websites or their content

This book is an original publication of The Berkley Publishiing Group.

PUBLISHING HISTORY
Previously published in the UK as *Angel at No. 33*
Berkley trade paperback edition / January 2013

Library of Congress Cataloging-in-Publication Data

Williams, Polly, date.
[Angel at no. 33]
Afterwife / Polly Williams. — 1st ed.
p. cm.
ISBN 978-0-425-25943-6
1. Motherless families—Fiction. 2. Traffic accident victims—Family relationships—
Fiction. 3. Widowers—Fiction. 4. Female friendship—Fiction. 5. Man-woman relationships—
Fiction. 6. Domestic fiction. I. Title.
PR6123.I5527A83 2013
823'.92—dc23
2012010305

PRINTED IN THE UNITED STATES OF AMERICA

10 9 8 7 6 5 4 3 2 1

For my husband, Ben, with love

Acknowledgments

A big thank-you to Jackie Cantor, Kim Witherspoon, Allison Hunter, Lizzy Kremer, Amanda Ng, Katina Doyle, Andrea Chase, Julia Williams, and, as always, Ben, Oscar, Jago, and Alice.

One

So I get run over by a bus and I am wearing my worst knickers. Huge banana-yellow knickers. I lay there in Regent Street, skirt hitched up around my waist like one of those binge drinkers you see on the news. As a crowd clustered, I panned back from the indignity of that crumpled body, fast, shakily, until the figure receded to a lump on the road, surrounded by a circus of flashing lights. Still, you could have seen those knickers from space.

Am I dead? Not sure actually. Don't *feel* dead. Maybe it's that I don't feel dead in the way that an old person doesn't feel old. Or I have a phantom self, much like an amputee has a phantom limb. Either way, totally weird. I am a christened nonbeliever who never goes to church apart from midnight mass at Christmas—soft spot for carols and candles—but I don't believe. Not in that stuff. I believe in a bit of yoga (lapsed). The healing power of cold white wine of an evening (unlapsed). But I don't believe in heaven. I don't believe in ghosts. Or angels.

And yet.

I am at my own funeral! Look up. I am here, high near the rafters, where pigeons poo and virulent woodworm has set in, unbeknownst to the gay rev. (Colin. He would be called Colin.) There is a drone, shuffling damp shoes on cold dry stone. It's my Facebook page sprung to life. Heads down, frowning, they walk solemnly through the church's heavy wooden doors. They all look at least ten years older than their Facebook profile photographs, ashen faced, wearing charcoal and black and sunglasses, like an army of glum fashionistas. Some I haven't seen in the flesh for years—can't quite believe my ex Don Adderson has the nerve to show up after screwing Iris, also here, shameless—and I watch as they sing, cry and, yes, yawn. (True to form, Danny Brixham taps out an email on his BlackBerry during the prayer.)

Among the throng I spot the tight cluster of my Muswell Hill friends, neighbors, school mums, the people who've populated my daily life since I had Freddie and moved out to the burbs, the people who make up my favorite coffee circuit in the world. Yep, there's Tash, cutting a dash in black with red shoes. (Red shoes at a funeral? Me neither.) Lydia, the loudest sobber in church. There's always one, and if you knew Lydia you'd know it absolutely would have to be Lydia. And Suze, dear old Suze with her wild blonde fro, twitching her speech notes, raring to go. She loves public speaking of any kind (entirely wasted on the PTA—should be running a small nation) and I can see she has written reams of absolute tosh about my role in the school community, the volunteering that she's repeatedly bamboozled and guilt-tripped me into at the school gates: cake sales, international evenings, Christmas fairs, let's-make-bunting parties, the 5K I ran in a red polka dot fifties ball gown for the twin school in Bolivia. Standing in the same block, directly in front of them, is my poor darling family. Mum, broken. Dad, disbelieving. Mad Aunt Pat, on the other hand, looking like she's rather enjoying the drama, certainly the opportunity to wear what looks like a giant Oreo cookie on her head. And then there's my little sister, Mary. If ever anyone needed a bit of privacy. Poor sis. And Jenny. There's my best mate, Jenny, just behind her, who looks like she's been breakfasting on crystal meth and has put on her makeup in the dark. There is so much I want to say to my dearest Jenny, not least that she always used to say that I'd be late for my own funeral. (Wrong!)

Funeral. That means I'm really dead, doesn't it? I'm presuming someone's actually checked my pulse. Damn. What if they haven't? What if there's been some terrible *error*?

Ollie's handsome face says that something terrible has happened. His eyes are puffy, slitty, unlit windows. He is cloaked in a cold blue aura like a surgical overall. While Freddie . . . No, I can't go there. My darling, beautiful little Freddie.

Whenever I think about either of them living even one minute longer without me I hear a whistling sound, a terrible hiss, like a vicious wind howling across a featureless moor, and it fills me with darkness.

There are no words.

Five days ago I was alive enough to get riled by the way Ollie stacked the plates in the dishwasher. Alive enough to worry about the six pounds that I'd put on over Christmas and vowing to start the Dukan diet. Alive enough to make a New Year's resolution, assuming I'd make one the year after that, and that, and that, and . . .

Okay, let's rewind. Forget my funeral, here's how my curtain fell.

Five days ago

It's only a damp Tuesday night but after the hungover drear of New Year's Day I am really quite keen to get out of the house, to see someone who isn't my immediate family. But I am late. I am always bloody late. This time I've lost a boot, and this is slowing my progress out of the house. My husband is not helping.

"You love me how much out of ten?" Ollie asks, sitting on the bottom step of the stairs, head resting on his knees, watching me with those heavy-lidded black eyes of his. They are the eyes of a young Italian lover, even though he's not that young, nor Italian. He's originally from Wigan.

"Nine and a half."

"When we first met it was eleven."

"That was before we shared a bathroom." I hop down the hall on my solo boot. Daft Punk blasts. "Turn it down, Ol, seriously. Where the hell is my other boot?"

Ollie shrugs, pulls Freddie onto his lap. "We have means of stopping Mummy from going out in sexy boots, don't we, Freddie?" Ollie and Freddie. Their faces repeat the same features in a different color palette. They look at each other and grin an identical Brady-patented grin.

"Ollie, I haven't seen Jenny in yonks!"

"Must be at least twenty-four hours."

"Not since Christmas actually."

"Sweetheart, it's January the sixth."

I ignore him and dementedly start pulling things out of the wicker basket in the hall: gloves, trapper hats, fleecy Wellie Warmers, umbrellas, remnants of Christmas wrapping paper that survived my hungover New Year's Day cleaning purge. Ping Pong, north London's least affectionate tabby, pounces on a glove and kills it, shaking her head from side to side with the glove in her jaws. "How can a boot just disappear into thin air? How is this *possible*?"

"Mummy's boot has made a break for it." Ollie laughs and nuzzles his nose into Freddie's blond brush of hair. "It's passed through the portal into that world of lost things never to be found again."

"Like Doctor Who." Freddie nods gravely.

"Like my sunglasses. Did you ever find those flash snowboarding sunglasses that your sis gave me for Christmas, Soph?"

I give him an exasperated look—he is constantly losing things, which is why I suspect him of playing a key role in the disappearance of the boot—and hop into the living room. "No, I didn't."

"What's for me and Freddie's dinner?"

Annoyed by this assumption—albeit a correct assumption—that I am in charge of all things fridge, cupboard and supermarket, I say nothing and bend down to look beneath our gray velvet sofa, the underworld where Lego bricks and hair balls breed.

"Soph? What's for supper?"

"Last night's lentil and hock soup in the fridge."

"Aww. Can't we have fish and chips?" asks Freddie. Ollie winks at him. And I know that they will have fish and chips, probably with an artery-fuzzing battered sausage and one of those pickled eggs that looks like a rude body part preserved in a jar.

"Aha!" Lost object found. I grab a plastic segment of Hot Wheels track and determinedly prod my boot into my reach, then tug it on. My foot collides with something hard and sharp. Transformer. I zip the boot up over my skinny jean and it feels tight, too tight, like the waistline of my jeans, which have also miraculously shrunk. I know that my legs have been stuffed like a Christmas stocking with brandy cream, champagne truffles and mince pies. I know that some long, hard weeks of denial lie ahead of me and this is depressing. I hate dieting. It's not in my nature. I'd like more of everything, more food, sex, sleep, shoes—and more time. Why am I always running out of time?

My phone beeps.

It's a text from Jenny in the new tapas bar on Beak Street where we've only got a table because swanky London is still drinking mulled wine beside log fires in their bolt-holes in the Cotswolds. "Pitying look from waiter. Where r u?"

"On way!" I fib back, yanking on a shaggy black fake fur coat. (Like to think that it gives me a slutty Hollywood glamour. Ollie says it makes me look like a giant goatee and is only acceptable if I go nudie underneath.) Freddie sinks back against Ollie's chest, drinking me in, studying me intently, as he always does when I'm dressed up, as if I'm morphing into someone who isn't just his mum—which is about the size of it.

"You've dropped something, Soph. Behind you," says Ollie.

I bend down, nothing. "What?"

"Just wanted to see what you looked like when you bent over." Ollie grins. It's his filthy rock star grin.

"Ollie!" I roll my eyes, enjoying that after all this time my bottom still rocks his world. I blow them puff-puff kisses like the movie star I was certain I'd be when I was a kid, before I got booted out of the Saturday club, aged fifteen, for snogging my drama teacher. "Boys, be good."

"What time you back, beautiful?"

"Won't be late." I step out of the warm hug of number thirty-three into the exhilarating possibilities of the London night. "Love you," I call over my shoulder, as I always do, but meaning it all the same.

Forward three hours, Jenny and I are at the tapas place, second bottle of white wine almost finished. I can no longer feel the blister on my left pinkie toe caused by those damn boots—is it possible to put weight on one's toes?—and the evening is beginning to fray pleasantly at the edges. I am probably talking too much because I've spent too long brooding on things over Christmas and am feeling the need to unburden myself, dropping my sticky, undigested gripes onto the restaurant table like the remains of the figgy pudding in my fridge.

"Do you want the hard, bitter January truth?" Jenny is refusing to indulge me.

I peek out at her from between my fingers. "If you must."

"Most people would kill for your problems." Satisfied by this decree, Jenny slumps back into her wooden chair as the waiter uncorks another bottle of wine and pours it into our lipstick-smudged glasses. "And . . ." she says, wiggling her finger, "most women would kill for a man like Ollie, and you know it, Soph."

"They would change their mind once they'd tried living with him for longer than it takes to finish a *Mad Men* box set."

She laughs, eyes me fondly. Her eyes are pink rimmed because she's a little drunk. We both are. "You're a hard woman, Sophie Brady."

"Nocturnal, totally unpractical. He's less domesticated than Freddie."

She gives me a sharp look.

"Yeah, yeah. Obviously, I wouldn't have him any other way."

"So the problem is . . . ?"

"No problem. It's just rubbishy life stuff." I sip my wine, not really tasting it now. It's got to that stage of the night. "Not something to be *solved*, Jenny. Not everything can be solved. Life is not a Sudoku puzzle."

"Hmm," she says, unconvinced. Jenny is an optimistic skeptical pragmatist. She believes there is a global conspiracy to make us all worry too much so that we buy newspapers and insurance "and comfort products like Babybel cheese, the world's weirdest food." Her words, not mine. I like Babybel. The color of that red wax is the same as the lippy that I wear every day, naked without it.

"If you've been with someone since you were twenty-two and . . . Oh, I don't know. I'm sure it's the same for him. He only ever got to have two other girlfriends before I came along. We were both so young! And now we've been together longer than Blair was in government! Or Thatcher!" I sluice my wine around the glass. "The truth is, and God, I'd never say this to Ollie, so swear on your life not to repeat this, but I miss how it used to be, Jen. You know, in the early days. It's sad knowing that I will never feel that adrenaliney lust rush thing again. That, you know"—I assume a bad cockney accent—"me and Ollie is for keeps, like."

"That's actually a far sweeter sentiment than you realize, Soph." Jenny looks a bit wistful.

I feel bad for having what everyone wants and not being grateful enough. I've brought us down. I must bring us up again. "But what about the *grrr*?"

"The what?"

I growl again. "The *GRRR*. Come 'ere! That feeling."

Jenny laughs. A couple at the adjacent table who don't look like they have much *grrr* going on pretend they're not listening in. The woman's feet curl around her chair legs. She frowns.

"Overrated." Jenny's eyes dance. I love the way her eyes dance. She's one of those rare women who looks prettier drunk, loosened up a little.

"I think it's just that I'd like to feel that *grrr* one more time before—" I slam my hands on the table. Jenny is glazing over. "Sorry! I'll shut up. Clearly I'm going through some kind of horribly clichéd midlife crisis. It's boring and I apologize."

"Don't apologize," she laughs. "Just tell me when it peaks. Because we've not even started, Soph."

"Actually I think it might have peaked already."

"When?" She laughs.

"Supermarket this afternoon." I gulp back some wine, warming to my theme. "You know those self-service tills that never work and you always end up having to wait for a real live human being to come and unlock the damn thing because it malfunctions if you use your own bag? 'Unidentified object in the bagging area!' Fuck, I hate them. I hate supermarkets. And no, I don't have a Nectar loyalty card! No, I *don't* want a Nectar card!"

"Don't be poncy."

"The day I get a supermarket loyalty card, it's all over, Jenny." I gulp back more wine. "See, a clear case of midlife crisis."

Jenny leans back in her chair and studies me in that scrutinizing way of hers. "You're not old enough for a midlife crisis, Soph. You have to be *forty*. You're thirty-five." Jenny is very exact. She has an ordered walk-in wardrobe of a mind. Mine is more like an overstuffed knicker drawer.

"I could die when I am seventy and that would make me midlife exactly." (Posthumous note: no discernible shiver of irony felt at the time.) I scoop a spoonful of crème caramel into my mouth and its sweetness is like a kiss.

"Women don't die at seventy anymore. We die at eighty-two or something." Jenny breaks into the crust of her chocolate torte with the edge of her spoon, releasing a river of sweet goo. It looks better than my crème caramel. "The blokes go first."

"Just as well. Ollie would confuse the laundry rack with his Zimmer frame and hang underpants on it."

"This is amazing. Taste?"

I reach across the table and attack her torte with my spoon. (Calories don't count if they belong to someone else.) It *is* better than my custard. "But isn't the really tragic thing that we'll be too old to enjoy our freedom when we finally get it?"

"No! I'm looking forward to us being old."

I try to imagine us old, like, proper old. It is hard. We've been young forever. I still buy polka dot tights at Topshop. Last year I rolled around in the mud at Glastonbury, naked.

"I don't want to be one of those exhausting women who try to stay thirtysomething forever. I want to wear different shades of beige and write letters of complaint about bad language to the BBC. I'll feel cheated otherwise."

"Why is it you always order the better dessert, Jenny?"

"I just go for the most calorific option. Simple tactic." She wipes her mouth with her napkin. It takes off the last bit of her pink lipstick. She looks about ten without makeup, like a frighteningly intelligent schoolgirl with her pretty, soft baby face, wide blue eyes and permanent little frown of studied comprehension. Jenny is my only girlfriend who tackles the weekend newspaper comment pages before the magazine supplements. She devours all the big, heavy books you're meant to read, rather than the fun ones. She actually finished *Wolf Hall*! That said, Jenny knows all the lyrics to Dolly Parton's back catalog too. "I intend to eat more dessert all year," she adds cheerfully. "My New Year's resolution is not to beat myself up for being over ten stone. I've thought about it, and I've come to the conclusion that I'd rather eat pudding than be skinny."

"Me too, me too." I reach across for another spoonful.

"Fat, happy and gobby."

I pick up my wineglass with camp flourish. "My New Year's resolution was not to drink in January."

Jenny raises her glass and we giggle.

"Fat faces age bloody well, you know," I reflect with my drunk puzzler.

"True, true."

"The brilliant thing is fat people don't have to choose between their face and their ass. They say, I'll have both, please! Like in a restaurant."

"Good point." Jenny licks her spoon. "And you know what, Soph? When we're old, like, proper old, we will eat pudding for every meal because . . . who gives a toss?"

"All the men will be dead, anyway! And all the skinnies will have died of carb deficiency." I rest my chin on my hand and reflect on the happy gluttony awaiting me. "For the record, Jenny, when I'm old I'm going to wear one of those see-through plastic headscarves to keep the rain off my blow-dried bouff. And I'll be rocking those orthopedic shoes with padded soles. I've always fancied those."

"We can go on cruises together. I've always wanted to go on a cruise, one of those really cheesy ones with a songstress in red sequins on a white grand piano belting out Shirley Bassey."

"Me too! Me too!" I raise my glass. It wobbles in my hand. "We can cruise to the Galápagos. I've always wanted to go to the Galápagos."

"To see turtles and those giant spooky stones."

"That's Easter Island."

"Okay, Easter Island too."

"And St. Barts. I will dreadlock my pubes and smoke psychotropic skunk on the beach because, hell, why not?"

"Shall we do Vegas too? We could gamble our pensions."

"Fuck yeah."

We laugh and sit in easy silence for a few moments, scraping the last smears of sweetness off the dessert plates, enjoying the crushed, happy hubbub of the restaurant and being away from the dog end of the Christmas holidays. We devour the remains of the bread basket and chortle childishly when a waiter drops a tray beside us in a slapstick manner. The tea light is at the end of its wax, smoking and spluttering a salty blue. It is in this happy drunken blur I decide that this is the moment to bring the subject up. "Dare I ask, Jenny?"

Something flickers across her eyes. She doesn't want me to ask. "The answer's no."

I sloppily lean over the table, warming my hands on the dying tea light. "But I thought you were going to have the Big Conversation."

"It shrank. It became a conversation about the best way to cook the rack of lamb," she says briskly, looking away from me into the restaurant.

"I guess you've got to set a wedding date at some point," I say carefully. "I mean, you don't want to end up walking down the aisle in your seventies looking like Vivienne Westwood."

She doesn't laugh like she's meant to. Instead she sniffs. "It's perfectly normal to be engaged for one year."

"I was joking, Jenny." This is my cue to tell her. My mouth opens then closes. Nothing comes out. I can talk absolute nonsense until my larynx bleeds but I can't talk about *this*. Best friends, no secrets? True. But I don't want to ruin our supper, or worse. Anyway, I'm probably too drunk. So I promise myself that I'll call round to her apartment next week, during the day, while Sam's out, and we'll have coffee and passion fruit cheesecake and we'll talk then. She loves cheesecake. The cheesecake will help.

She looks at me, narrows her eyes. "I know you don't approve of him, Soph."

"That's not true."

Silence. We both know that the conversation has hit a protrusion like a speed bump in the road. We do the same thing, look away from each other and around the restaurant, smiling hazily, women who've drunk too much and know each other well enough to drop the topic before we start whacking each other over the head with our handbags. Some diners are beginning to leave now, picking up bills, bustling to the loo, while the late-night crowd, flushed from a theater or bar, take their tables and overorder tapas.

A waiter asks us if we want to order anything else, like he wants us to leave. I glance at my watch. "Where has the evening gone? I feel like I only got here five minutes ago. I should get home."

Jenny looks disappointed. "But we haven't dissected Sarah's affair yet."

"I know, nor Maxine's new teeth. They file the real teeth to Shane MacGowan pegs before they put veneers on. Isn't that totally gross?"

"I've heard that the veneers drop off all the time. Imagine, you'd never want to bite into an apple again."

Giggles snort through my nose. "Do you remember when my hair extension blew off on Primrose Hill and landed on that labradoodle?" I don't know why I suddenly remember this but I can see it vividly. That gorgeous gusty day on top of Primrose Hill, London unrolling before us, Freddie, a baby then, sitting on the picnic blanket, squashing strawberries into his mouth with his fist. A lifetime ago, literally.

"And the dog humped the bouff!"

I catch the time on the oversized watch face of the woman sitting adjacent to us. It really is getting late.

Jenny catches me looking. She knows what I am thinking. "Isn't it bad karma to leave so much wine?" She draws a finger down the bottle's label. "Good wine too."

"It would be a bit studenty to ask to take it home, wouldn't it?"

"It would, Soph. Yes."

"It does seem rather a shame."

"And you *were* late, Sophie. Had you been on time then we would have finished the bottle by now."

"Excellent point. What do you suggest, then?"

Jenny fills our glasses. "Rude not to."

"I hold you fully responsible, Jenny." I hiccup. "And I want you to know that I will put all the blame on you when Ollie's on my case about me coming home rat arsed."

Jenny raises her glass. "Deal. That is what unmarried friends are for, isn't it? To get their married friends off the hook with their husbands."

When we finally leave the restaurant it is raining outside, hard rain that comes at you at an angle. It is icy cold, threatening sleet. The street is splashy and full of people who've drunk too much, have not got an umbrella and want to get home, people like us, desperately trying to get cabs. We give up trying to hire a cab on Beak Street and wander toward the promising river of traffic on Regent Street, the leather soles of my boots skiddy on the wet pavement. Occupied cab after occupied cab zooms by, some maddeningly clicking their lights off just as they pass, others commandeered by new groups of revelers filtering in from Great Marlborough Street and Foubert's Place, nicking cabs that are rightfully ours, seeing as we've waited for years already. A newly stolen cab throws a wash of dirty puddle over our feet.

"This is rubbish, Jenny. Time to get a dodgy cab."

"Minicab drivers all look like criminal photo fits."

"I'm not doing the flippin' Tube at this time."

"Yay!" Jenny grabs my hand. "O ye of little faith. Look. There's one. Just behind that bus."

We watch as a yellow light, a warm, happy smudge in the wet darkness, moves toward us, slowly getting brighter.

"Right," I say, jaw set, arm outstretched. "Watch *this*! I'm going to get this cab if it kills me."

Two

The coffin was white, decorated with a trembling bunch of marsh-mallow pink lilies. To Jenny it seemed pitifully insubstantial. The idea that Sophie's body—beautiful, funny, larger-than-life Sophie—was inside, dead five days, cold as clay, was almost unbelievable. She squeezed Sam's hand harder, feeling the stiff rim of his shirt cuff push into her wrist.

A sob echoed around the overcrowded church. Each time a sob erupted, which was frequently—every four or five breaths; she'd counted—Jenny's teeth ground together and her fillings twanged. Not knowing where to look, she kept her gaze on the forlorn figure of Ollie standing in the front pew. He had a new stoop in his coathanger shoulders and his face was full of shadows. It was as if all his energy had pooled into his left hand, the hand knitted tightly to Freddie's. No wonder. Freddie looked so heartbreakingly tiny, shrunk to Lilliputian proportions by the soar of the stained-glass windows and the yawning width of the church.

Ollie and Freddie, the two great loves of Sophie's life, were flanked by Ollie's formidable-looking mother, Vicki, and, holding Freddie's other hand, Soph's mother, Sally, slighter than ever, all angles and elbows in a black skirt suit, the lone black feather on her hat shaking. Mike, Soph's dad, had one arm belted tight around her shoulder—squishing the jacket's shoulder pad up oddly—and his other around Sophie's sister, Mary. Poor Mary, whose normally pretty face was puffy as a mushroom from crying and given a strange pallor by light streaming through a yellow pane of stained glass.

She had no doubt that they must wish it were her, Jenny, who'd stepped out in front of the bus instead of their beautiful daughter. She wasn't a mother, a wife; she didn't and never would burn as brightly as Sophie. If she could have taken her place she would. But it had all happened in an instant. A hand outstretched, a slip of leather sole, a knuckle crunch of metal and bone. She could still see Sophie lying in the road. The image was imprinted in her brain forever, like a bright lightbulb after you close your eyes.

"Deal." That was her word. And it kept coming back to haunt her. She'd selfishly cajoled Sophie into drinking more wine when she should have realized that Sophie was a mother, they weren't twenty-somethings anymore. Sophie had responsibilities: most women their age did. Jenny was the oddity, needily trying to squeeze more out of Sophie, unable to let go. If she'd let Sophie return home earlier, then it wouldn't have been raining and the road wouldn't have been slippery and that particular bus wouldn't be on Regent Street, it would have been somewhere else on its route. And so would they.

As requested by the rev—Colin, she thought how much Sophie would appreciate the fact he was called Colin—she held up the photocopied hymn sheet. Sophie's beautiful face was stamped at the top, so that it resembled a newsletter. The paper shook and the ink smudged beneath her sweating fingers. Could she sing? She was amazed that a song was coming out of her mouth, not a scream. "Jerusalem." She and Soph had sung this many times over the years at weddings. Some couples had worked out; others hadn't. None of them were ever as glamorous and besotted as Ollie and Sophie were. Had been. Oh, God. The hymn sheet shook harder in her hand. So, so wrong. She looked up at the sweeping church rafters, eyes prickling with tears. Sophie, where are you? Please stop being dead. It's not big and it's not funny. No one's bloody laughing.

All she wanted to do was lie down in bed with a pillow over her head and listen to Sophie's answer machine message over and over—"*Soph's phone, don't you dare hang up before leaving a message!*"—and pretend none of this was happening.

"You alright, babes?" whispered Sam, looking down at her from his six-foot height.

She nodded, mouth dry. She could sing but not speak. Which did not bode well for her speech. (Unless she sang it?) The service continued, painfully slowly. It was like Sophie's wedding, she thought, but in reverse.

Oh, God, speeches. They'd started! She was nowhere near ready. She needed another six months of prep. Sophie's little sister, Mary, was the first to go. Never lifting her swollen eyes from her notes, she attempted some anecdotes about Sophie as a child—how she'd once found a kitten, which she named Sock, in the street and, fearing that she wouldn't be allowed to keep it, had nurtured Sock in her knicker drawer for three days on milk-sodden digestive biscuits before anyone realized he was there—and then tried to articulate what a wonderful mother she had been. At that point Mary's voice crumpled like a brown paper bag and she had to be led back to her pew.

Not her yet. Not her yet. She had a few minutes to pull herself together. Come on, Jenny.

A new speaker started to walk purposefully down the aisle. She checked the service notes. Suze. Suze Wilson. She vaguely remembered Sophie mentioning her name. A school mum? Yes, she was pretty sure she was a school mum. Suze. Long on the z.

Suze had a rubbery face beneath an extraordinary helmet of frizzy hair, the hair oddly fascinating in its extreme of unflattery. (How could Jenny still notice unflattering hair in the depths of grief? What was wrong with her?) Suze tilted her chin upward, revealing a large mole resembling a squashed raisin beneath her jaw, and started to speak, her thunderous voice submitting the congregation into still, respectful silence like an evangelical pastor's. She rhapsodized about Sophie's contribution to school life and the community, her volunteering, her cake baking, her quiz night organizing, the fact that she was the most glamorous mother at the school gates. How the other mothers used to joke that she never wore the same shoes twice. Then, minutes later, the frizzy orator had finished. Colin was looking at Jenny expectantly, one bushy eye brow raised.

"Sure you're up to it?" Sam looked doubtful.

Jenny started the long walk to the podium, her hard-soled shoes clattering unpleasantly on the stone floor. Her new black trousers, bought in haste online for the occasion, dug into her hips as she walked. They were a size too small, she realized—she was a twelve, not a ten, kidding nobody—and frumpy in their bland formality, like a campaigning regional politician. She wished she'd worn something more flamboyant in homage. Sophie would have worn black and leopard print, a vintage fifties full-skirted suit. Something like that. The walk went on forever, and the trousers shifted around her waist with every step so by the time she finally stood up on the podium and raised her eyes to the congregation, the zipper was twisted and pulled up inside her crotch. Camel hoof. Great. Sophie would be laughing.

All eyes were on her now. The tension in the church pulsed. She could hear it. Tick, tick, tick. Like an electric fence.

Notes. She just needed to read her notes and she'd be fine. But the handwriting swam before her. She gulped, refocused. The words she'd written and practiced reading aloud to Sam over the porridge she couldn't eat this morning suddenly seemed wrong, written about someone who wasn't Sophie. She looked up helplessly at the rows and rows of expectant, flushed, strained faces, then quickly down again. Sweat dripped down her nose and splodged onto the paper. I'm going to fuck up. I'm going to fuck up explosively.

The pause stretched, taut, painful, like a doctor pulling a stitch from a wound. She glanced at Sam. His face was knotted with embarrassment. She looked at Ollie and his wounded black eyes surprised her by their softness. He was the one person who should hate her and didn't. "I've written these notes . . ." she began, taking courage from Ollie. If he could be brave, so could she. The microphone amplified her voice. She didn't sound like herself. "And they're all about what a wonderful person Sophie . . ." She couldn't say "was." She couldn't. "But you all know that. That's why this church is crammed. So I'm going to go off trail with this, please bear with me." Sam was biting his fist now, shaking his head and looking at her like she'd completely lost the plot. "I was the last person to see Sophie alive." A collective intake of breath. "And for this I am hugely privileged. We had fun that night, the night she died. Apart from anything, Soph, my oldest, dearest friend, was the best laugh. And she found humor in the blackest places—she'd find it here today." Ollie cracked a small, surprised smile. The rest of the congregation looked stony faced, like she'd said something terrible. "And that night, she was more alive than most of us will ever be. She was one of those people, full of . . . light and dazzle, the central point in any room. And she had the rudest, loudest laugh. We used to call it the Honk." She choked up then. Her mouth made an involuntary pop-pop noise, as if her heart was exploding like space candy on her tongue. It was unimaginable that she'd never hear the Honk again. "Whenever I think of Sophie, I think of Sophie dancing. She loved to dance and she never gave a sh—" She caught herself. ". . . a hoot what anyone thought. She didn't have hang-ups like the rest of us. In fact, she loved people looking at her. Which I guess brings me to . . ." She paused, suddenly unsure what to say next. ". . . *hats!* Sophie loved hats, especially vintage ones with plumes. And swirly skirted dresses. Sequins and shoes. She was the high priestess of shoes." There was a ripple of laughter, a sense of people finally relaxing. "Sophie could get away with anything because she was beautiful but also because she was happy. She made happiness glamorous. And it was her family who made her so very happy, so secure in who she was." Ollie was wiping away tears on the sleeve of his crumpled black jacket. "She was madly in love with Ollie. And Freddie . . ." Freddie was staring down at the floor, as if willing himself to disappear. "Freddie made her just the proudest mother on earth." Her voice broke. She sniffed, collected herself. "I guess all I want to say is that I will miss Sophie forever. As a girlfriend, as a human being, she is totally irreplaceable." She looked down at her unused notes, a wave of doubt crashing down on her. What on earth was she thinking? Wrap, wrap! "That's it, um, thanks."

As she began the excruciating walk back to her pew, eyes boring into her navy Marks and Spencer shirt, Neil Young's "Harvest Moon" started to crackle through the church's ancient speakers. Rows of people—the friends, the cousins, the exes, Freddie's teacher, Sophie's hairdresser, her cleaner, the music industry friends of Ollie's, all the people who'd ever known and loved Sophie, for to know her was to love her, Jenny realized, wishing she'd said that too—dissolved into tears. Jenny wondered how many of them recognized the song. It was Sophie and Ollie's first dance song at their wedding reception. *"Because I'm so in love with you, I want to see you dance again,"* Young sang, filling the belly of the church. Sucking the tears down her throat, she joined the mass shuffle to the throng in the graveyard. The light was yellowy and dark clouds were boiling over the steeple of the church. The air smelled of rain.

"Why did you change your speech at the last minute?" asked Sam. "Was it rubbish?"

Sam pulled her toward his dark blue suit. His second best suit. "No, your speech was . . ." He hesitated. "Sweet, really sweet, Jenny. Don't worry about it."

She fisted her hands deep in her jacket pockets. All she wanted to do was go home, pour herself a humongous glass of wine and phone Sophie. That was what she always did after a bad day. And this was the baddest of days. She turned to Sam and saw him being pulled back into the crowd by Crispin, the bisexual gardener with the gold tooth who Sophie had recommended for their flower boxes. Without Sam sandwiched next to her, she felt exposed, watched, the last person to have seen Sophie alive, the bad influence. She wished she could scoot away like the other guests, sink back into the north London streets, into her altered life. She checked her watch. Not long now. The burial in Highgate Cemetery was to be just a small, immediate family affair, thank goodness. She didn't have the stomach for it. Her job was to take Freddie back to Ollie's and make him supper. She was glad she had a job, a use. Yes, she must find Freddie. Where was he? Peering over the obfuscating hats and feather fascinators in the crowd, she noticed a woman determinedly plowing toward her. "Jenny!"

She froze. It was the woman who was being eaten by her own hair.

"Suze Wilson." An extended purple-gloved hand. The handshake crunched her fingers. "I've heard so much about you."

"You have?" she said, taken aback.

"From Sophie," Suze explained.

She felt the heat rise on her cheeks. "Yes, of course."

Suze moved closer conspiratorially, biscuit breath on Jenny's cheek. "You were brave speaking off-the-cuff like that, really brave."

"Thanks." She smiled back, not knowing what to say. Sophie's death had left a smoldering gap in her conversation. Yet it was all anyone wanted to talk about.

Suze persevered. "You must feel terrible. Being there." She paused, giving Jenny the space to fill in the gory details. "Seeing the accident and everything," she added when no details were forthcoming.

Jenny looked away. She could still see Sophie's body in the road. Hear the crunch and thump.

"Look, sorry, anytime you want to talk."

"Thank you." I don't want to talk. I don't want to talk to you, she thought. And I don't like your purple gloves.

"And if you don't mind I may get in contact anyway."

"Yeah?" Could she perhaps climb up and over Suze's hill of hair and flee over the shoulders of the crowd?

"Ollie will need all the help he can get now, won't he?"

"Yes, yes, he will." She smiled, feeling a stab of guilt for her earlier irritation. Suze was clearly a nice, practically minded woman. She was Sophie's friend. Making a renewed effort to be friendly, she rifled in her handbag and found a curly-edged business card. "Here's my number."

Suze looked down at the white card—*Jenny Vale, copy editor*—with a glint of triumph. "Brill!"

Jenny sidled away, faking an obligation somewhere else in the crowd.

Before she could get very far Ollie touched her lightly on the arm. "Hey, Jenny." His voice was barely audible.

"I'm sorry, I'm just so sorry, Ollie." The dark gray cloud had engulfed the steeple. It started to rain suddenly, pinprick-sore against the raw skin around her eyes.

He glanced at his watch. "We're going to . . ." He hesitated for an eternity. He couldn't say bury. She took Ollie's hand because it felt like the right thing to do. But once she had it she didn't know what to do with it. "Go to the cemetery now."

"I'll take Freddie back."

They stood for a moment, transfixed by the back of Freddie's tousled blond head, neither of them moving, not wanting to take him away from his mother's body. And Jenny was still holding Ollie's hand. She needed to drop it.

"Jenny, there's something I need to ask you."

"Yes?" She had a bad feeling about what he was about to say next. She dropped his hand.

He fixed her with sleepless baggy eyes. "Did Sophie talk about us, about me and her, our marriage, the night she died?"

The bad feeling got badder. What could she say? If she told him the truth he might take the words Sophie had uttered in a drunken, restless mood and hold them against his heart forever. And she'd promised Sophie she wouldn't repeat them.

"I need to know if—"

Colin the rev interrupted them. "Ollie," he whispered, a pink, beringed hand on the sleeve of Ollie's black wool suit, "it is time."

Three

I can't bring myself to peek inside the coffin. Not going to be a good look, is it? So I leave my beloved family scattering chocolaty Highgate soil into the hole, soak away past the graves of George Eliot and Henry Moore, the Gothic avenues of tombs, the guarding stone angels, through the damp, dark, ivy-cloaked trees of Highgate woods into the drizzly January morning air. I follow Jenny as she drives back to number thirty-three in her little yellow Mini with Freddie in the backseat staring, puzzled, silent, out the window. I follow them through the gray front door—*hours* of my short life I wasted locating that exact shade of cloud gray—past the surprisingly tidy hall. Clearly, mother-in-law has been busy and her gray felt slippers sit neatly, incongruously, beside my old knitted moccasin boots. I skirt along the stripped pine floor and into our kitchen, always my favorite room with its wooden units that nearly bankrupted us, the red KitchenAid cake mixer, the big range oven, the Dualit toaster, things I loved so much in a way that Ollie never understood but being Ollie indulged anyway because he'd do pretty much anything

to make me happy. Ping Pong hisses as I pass and bolts out through
the cat flap. Charming. Missed you too.

After the cold and damp of the church, the smell of Jenny burning fish fingers is immensely comforting. (Jenny has many talents
but cooking is not one of them. She would happily survive on Marmite toast, Minstrels and precut packaged carrot sticks.) Freddie eats
it all up, which makes me curdle with maternal pleasure. It's good
to know that he's not lost his appetite, that nature's hardwired imper-
ative for his six-year-old body to run and eat and grow overrides his
grief. After some warmed rice pudding topped with half a jar of
honey on top—Freddie tells her that's how much I used to put on,
the monkey—they curl up together on the velvet sofa. Freddie's lids
slowly shut as Jenny reads *Tintin in Tibet*, her Captain Haddock
voice a dead ringer for Billy Connolly. While he sleeps Jenny cries,
stroking his unbrushed mop of curls. I move closer to them, not
wanting to frighten her, hoping that somehow, if I wish it hard
enough, I will radiate some heat, something that will comfort them,
let them know that I am here.

Ollie and the grannies come back. Jenny does her big bright smile
thing that she always does when she's trying to pretend she's not
been crying, and fools nobody. Freddie doesn't want her to go. She
hesitates, unsure of the protocol, not wanting to disappoint Freddie,
not wanting to intrude. Granny Vicki crushes Freddie to that
bosom—it's the Thames flood barrier of bosoms—and Jenny leaves
for the apartment she shares with Sam in Camden. I become the
dust in the dusty shadows, only brightening again as a button moon
rises above the slate rooftops and London's insomniac skyline glows
acid orange. Restless to be back where I belong, I feather down the
hall, shaken by the tectonic rumble of my mother-in-law snoring in
the spare bedroom, sinus problems having taken a turn for the worse.

It's midnight. I want to get back to my side of the bed, the side
nearest the bathroom because ever since I had Freddie I've needed

to go in the night. (No, didn't do my pelvic floors. Does anyone?) My side of the bed is oddly empty. Odd because I normally go to bed before Ollie, who is prone to watching MTV with a beer in his hand late into the night. But nothing's normal now, is it? Everything is the same but different, like one of those pictures in Freddie's puzzle books where you have to spot things that are wrong, like the dog with five legs, the lady with a teapot poking out of her handbag.

Ollie is not sleeping like he usually does, either, which is like a hibernating grizzly, but twisting and turning, ruching up the bedsheets—the same bedsheets that we slept on together last week—asleep but talking indecipherably, then sitting bolt upright, flicking the light on, getting up, walking to the kitchen, pouring himself a large whiskey, downing it, then staggering through to Freddie's room, crawling under Freddie's pirate duvet and, with Freddie stirring slightly in his arms, finally falling asleep. I hover a few inches above them, rising and falling on the valleys of their warm breath like a bird. The night is over in a millisecond. Dawn breaks, Ollie breaks wind, Freddie unfurls from sleep in his green pajamas like a new shoot and Vicki starts bustling around the kitchen and begins, I kid you not, to reorganize my spice cupboard.

Nothing is sacred.

Hours shuffle like cards. Suddenly it's Monday. Ollie doesn't look like he's slept at all. He can't be arsed to shower and when I get near him, laminating his body as close as I can, he smells of scalp and skin and sweat. He's been sweating a lot even though it's cold. It's as if he's carried a stash of drugs through Dubai customs in the sole of his sneaker. He needs to shave, but doesn't. He attempts to pack Vicki off to the local supermarket while he gets Freddie ready for school. But she won't budge. She's fussing. No, Ollie mumbles. He wants to do this himself, he's got to be able to do it himself. Finally, Vicki takes the sledgehammer hint and is successfully banished to buy a pint of milk. Ollie rummages through the kitchen cupboards, looking for Freddie's lunchbox. It's on the shelf above the sink, as it always is, but, maddeningly, he looks everywhere but there. He curses, gives up. He puts two Penguin bars in an old plastic bag—two?—alongside one of Jenny's cold burned fish fingers, which he wraps in cellophane—impressed by the cellophane bit—and a Marmite sandwich made from bread that has outlived me. He does not brush Freddie's hair, which sticks out like wings. And he does not notice that Freddie is wearing his Superman pajama top beneath his gray school shirt. Freddie has been trying to wear this Superman top to school for at least a year.

Ollie, one of the hungriest men alive, forgets to feed himself and, more cataclysmically, forgets to feed the mightily disgruntled Ping Pong. He can't find the school bag, which is on a hook in the utility cupboard, the same hook it's been hung on for the last two years.

I'm beginning to realize how much I did. How much I micromanaged our lives. And I'm worrying about how Ollie is going to cope. Because there is the domesticated man. And there's Ollie. This is a man who once watered a houseplant for a year before realizing it was plastic. This is a man who only last week put washing powder tablets in the tumble dryer. Yes, Ollie is a brilliant music producer. His brain can organize an infinite variation of bars and chords and breaks. But it cannot compute how many pints of milk a family of three drinks in a week. (Five.)

Ollie and Freddie finally leave for school, hands knotted together. How much I want to slip my hands into that tight little knot. How much I want to run my fingers through Freddie's hair and feel his hot boy's neck. How I want to yank up Ollie back to his full height to stop that gorgeous body from collapsing in on itself like a wonky old deck chair. He is normally so reassuringly solid—wide shouldered, barrel chested, male and bulky like a hunk of roughly hewn oak—but day by day he looks whittled down. His twisted-fit Levi's are slipping down his hips. His face is newly angular, unshaven and angry; his jaw is jutting because his teeth are constantly clenched. He reminds me of how he used to look in his twenties when he'd spent too many sleepless weekends on the coke that made him so elated then so utterly miserable, before "his angel of Harpenden," as he used to call me back then, rescued him and made him drink Chablis instead. But I can't rescue him now. It seems I'm merely watching them rather than watching over them, more CCTV than celestial being.

At the school gates there's a throng of mothers, milling with muted excitement as if waiting for some sale doors to fling open. Freddie and Ollie walk down the street toward them. The hushed talking immediately stops. They part to make room for his passing, buggies are swiftly jerked out of his way, fevered looks are exchanged. Eyes fill with tears.

My husband, the *pope*!

Ollie blanks them, walking determinedly toward the cheerful red door of class 2A to the left on the playground, the farthest class from the gate, and therefore the one with the longest public parade. The crowd's ventriloquist whispers sound like a distant storm at sea. The mothers discuss protocol beneath their breath. There is no consensus and a few are now breaking ranks and gamely stepping forward to smile sympathetically at Freddie—he looks down, hates being singled out at the best of times—and offer condolences to Ollie, who scuffs his trainer against the painted yellow lines on the concrete playground like a schoolboy. Resisting the urge to hug Freddie—he is still mine, still someone else's child—the women reach instead for Ollie, maternally patting his arm or hand or, rather less maternally in Tash's case, the small of his back, near the waistband of his jeans. Even those who are tearful and tongue-tied want to touch Ollie, as if they need to know what a bereaved dad actually feels like. Perhaps touching one makes them feel it won't happen to them too. I guess we've all wondered: having children makes you ponder your mortality, ghoulishly hypothesize the what-ifs. Funny thing is that before this happened I did that too, idly, indulgently. Comfortable that things like this didn't happen to people like us.

The school bell rings. There is a twitch in Ollie's lower lip now, barely perceptible but a sign to me who knows that lower lip as well as I know my own that he is fighting tears.

If Ollie cries now I swear someone will try to breastfeed him.

Mrs. Simpson, Freddie's teacher, greets them at class 2A's door. She is professional and kind and does not make a fuss—much to Ollie's and Freddie's obvious relief—and takes Freddie's hand and leads him inside his old classroom, which, I hope, will be mercifully the same as it always was, unlike everything else in his life. The door closes. Ollie stands there for a moment, facing the shut door, lost, his face blank like a man who has woken up and no longer has the first clue who he is. His features reconfigure and he takes a deep breath, then walks back to the tall iron school gates, his black eyes drilling into the ground.

This is not a good enough defense. Oh, no. Without Freddie to shield him, Ollie is open season. Some of the women have been waiting for him to return: I know their migratory patterns and I know that normally they would have flocked to Starbucks by now. Instead, they're hovering by the gate. Suze. Tash. Lydia. Liz. The usual suspects.

"Is there anything, anything at all we can do to help?" implores Suze. Her giant breasts quiver in the deep V of her gaping blue blouse as if they are domed conductors for the group's electrical storm of pent-up emotion.

Ollie shakes his head and tries to smile. "No. Thanks." He starts to walk away.

Lydia bars him with her sheepskin Ugg boot. "Washing?"

"Washing?" repeats Ollie, puzzled.

"Would you like us to do your washing, Ollie?" Lydia speaks

slowly as if addressing a small child, even though Ollie towers over her fairy frame.

"Washing," he repeats, as if it were something he hadn't ever considered before, and probably hasn't. "My mother . . ."

"Or shopping?" Liz agitates her foot on her son's blue scooter.

"I . . . I . . ." Ollie is a man of few words but is never normally lost for them. He stares blankly at the scooter.

"Would Freddie like to sleep over?" Tash jumps into his hesitation, stepping closer so that he can smell the perfume caught within the soft pelt of her white fake fur stole. (Even I can smell the perfume and I'm near the school hall guttering.)

A lemony sun breaks through the cloud. Ollie's pupils shrink to pencil points. In the last three weeks he's spent a lot of time alone in the dark, like a miner. His olive skin is pale and flaky. "I'm trying to keep Freddie close. Just at the moment."

"As normal as possible. Of course, of course," gushes Tash apologetically. "But if you ever need me to take Freddie to school, when, er, you go back to work." She blushes, wondering if she's said the wrong thing. "Not that I want to . . ."

I feel for him. Normally, at this juncture I'd read the signs, swoop into the conversation and pluck him out, the sunny, social one to counterbalance his northern, Heathcliffian tendencies. "Thanks. That would be great," he mumbles, giving them what they want, waiting to be released.

Tash looks around at the other women with a look of unmistakable triumph.

Ollie digs his hands into his jeans pockets, attempts to walk away again.

Not so fast, buster! "You will let *us* know, won't you?" says Suze. She's somehow standing in front of him without anyone being sure how she got there. It's social kung fu. "If you need anything, Ollie, anything at all? Just pick up the phone. You've got my number, haven't you? Let me write it out for you just in case. Oh, bollocks. Anyone got a pen?"

Ollie grunts, like he always grunts when he begins to feel obligated. Ollie is one of the world's kindest men, the best of men, but he hates obligation. He likes to think he can be selfish if he wants to. It's an adolescent thing that lots of wives of music producers have to contend with. Most of the time his main selfishness, apart from nicking my moisturizer and refusing to cook, manifests itself merely in putting on headphones and sinking into his music, annoying but not up there in the great pantheon of male selfishness, clearly. I complained about this in the past but now wish I hadn't, firstly because I knew about his antisocial solipsistic tendencies from the beginning—I'd wake up in bed to find him wearing these big fat headphones over his long hair and I thought it quite the sexiest thing ever—and also because the flaw, if it is a flaw, is just Ollie. I should have realized I'd have been bored to tears with the man I often complained he wasn't, the domesticated, fully socialized, Muswell Hill thirtysomething dad behind the cake stall. Why did I not tell him more often that I just loved him as he was?

Like secrets, words that are left unsaid get buried with you.

Four

"Firecracker." Sam rolled off Jenny with a skin-sucking squelch. "I needed that."

Jenny flopped back into the slightly sinister microclimate of their Tempur-Pedic mattress. She did not feel like a firecracker. Since Sophie had died—three weeks, three days, fourteen hours ago—sex didn't work, not for her at any rate. Sometimes she wondered if she'd ever orgasm again. Part of her hoped she wouldn't. Sophie couldn't. Why should she? She'd grown a giant retro bush. She'd stopped shaving under her arms. Yes, she was morphing into the world's unsexiest creature. And she didn't give a damn.

She just wished her heart would stop slamming, that's all. It was a frantic tattoo. She'd ditched coffee after one p.m., forced herself to bathe by candlelight before bed—setting fire to a tinderstick loofah in the process—but still her heart jumped about inside her chest like someone who'd snorted a kilo of amphetamine and was prancing about on a speaker in a nightclub.

Sam yawned, releasing a mist of morning breath. Inside his

mouth his uvula looked pink and animate, like it might have an opinion. It probably did. Later, she knew that he'd brush his tongue. He was the only person she'd ever met who brushed his tongue. She watched him fiddle with his omnipresent iPhone; Mumford & Sons poured out from a hidden speaker in the bedpost. The apartment was full of hidden speakers. Music suddenly blasting out of cabinets and walls and baths like raucous ghosts, making her jump. It was a boy's apartment, home to families of remote controls, gleaming with hard, aeronautical steel surfaces, smelling of freshly ground coffee. It was like waking up in Business Class every morning.

He trailed a finger down her shoulder. "Shall we ambulate down to the greasy spoon?" He didn't look up, back on the phone again. Tap tap tap. "I need trans fats."

"No, I'm taking Freddie out, remember?" She smiled as brightly as she could manage, trying to look normal. But nothing was normal. Sophie being alive was normal. This wasn't.

You've got to find a way of moving on, that was what Sam kept saying. But, damn, move on *where*? For the last fifteen-odd years of her life she and Sophie had been on the same train, Sophie sitting beside her, her favorite apple green boxy handbag on her lap, shopping bags at her feet, body tilted toward Jenny at an angle so that their shoulders touched and sometimes she'd get a mouthful of Sophie's luscious long dark hair, which always tasted of expensive, honey-scented shampoo. Even a train journey with Sophie was a hoot. She was one of those women who would cheerfully chat loudly and unself-consciously in a crowded carriage about anything: gossip, politics, the shoes of the woman down the carriage, the headlines on the man opposite's newspaper and sex. Sophie loved talking about sex. ("Okay. Sex in a tent. Boris Johnson or David Cameron? No, no, no! You have to choose one, you *have* to, Jenny. My God, you're blushing! You've thought about this before, haven't you? I reckon you're a Boris bonker. Fess up. No, I'm not going to shush.") What she wouldn't do now for just one more journey from Oxford Circus to King's Cross with her. One more gossip. One more chat. There were so many more things they still had to say.

Sam looked up and eyed her with a mixture of wariness and concern. "You alright, babes?"

She snapped back to the bedroom, to the present. "Fine!"

Sam started doing one of the morning stretches that Big Eric, his trainer, had taught him last month for an extortionate sum, something weird and painful looking involving his arm being bent back over his shoulders and a fair amount of clicking. "Stiff as a corpse this morning," he muttered through the exertion. "I told Big Eric no more fucking weights. Masochist."

Wishing he hadn't said "corpse," she watched his arms bulge. They'd certainly gotten bigger. Secretly she preferred them before, sinewy but strong, the way he was naturally meant to be. Funnily enough, out of all of his handsome frame it was his head she loved best, the only thing he couldn't work out in the gym. His head was like Bruce Willis's, closely shaved to hide the spreading bald patch, symmetrical, satisfying, like a slightly furry pet. She liked to place her palm across it and feel its alive heat. And she liked that it flowed seamlessly into his smooth, unusual face without the interruption of hair. Sam's good looks were architectural, vulpine. He had a face that could have been designed by the architect Norman Foster.

She'd noticed him instantly at the small book launch in a Marylebone bookshop all those years ago. He'd been smartly dressed, swaggery—red socks!—not the usual publishing type, no surprise, as he wasn't. She'd felt the burn of those bright LED blue eyes following her around the room. Shyness had prevented her from returning that confrontational gaze. Of course she'd had no idea at the time that this shyness would be misinterpreted as hard-to-get hauteur. That he'd see getting his fingers into her pants as the ultimate challenge. (She would have said yes please if he'd asked politely.) Sam loved a challenge. He liked his women "slightly difficult, chewy like hard toffee," he'd once said, qualifying it with, "it was only afterwards I discovered you were more like fudge." That had made her laugh. He used to make her laugh a lot.

Sam released his biceps and lay heavily back onto the bed, his jaw cracking as he yawned. "RoboCop, I am not."

"You've been working late all week." She meant this nicely but it came out wrong, more like an accusation. This kept happening, words coming out wrong.

He looked up at her sharply. "It's good that I'm this busy, bloody brilliant in the current climate."

"I know, I know." Had she made Sam defensive about his career? That wasn't her intention. He had once dreamed of being a human rights lawyer and had grown up to be a divorce lawyer. This was what happened in life to most people, a gradual distillation of intent. One had to be pragmatic. She'd once dreamed of being a gardener, and she was a copy editor. How did that happen? Well, the rent happened. London happened. Her "career" happened while she was thinking about other things. Like nights out with the girls in karaoke bars in town. Chris. Tim. Sam. Chelsea Flower Show. Her highlights. Her waxing schedule. How to avoid going home for lunch every Sunday. Dolly at Wembley Arena. The demanding full-time vocation of being Sophie's best friend. Her love of books.

So she dotted the i's and crossed the t's and realigned paragraphs. She was good at it. Although sometimes it felt like her pastime was copyediting and her real job was trying to get her printer to work. Her specialty, her passion, although she would take on anything, was the kind of sumptuous gardening and house books that few bought, much less read. She'd always loved detail, the antlike march of letters across a page, the excitement of undressing a manuscript from its large padded envelope. But she'd made some embarrassing mistakes recently. Only last week she'd not spotted that a manuscript had three chapter fives. If there were a disacknowledgments section for people who'd made the production of the book infinitely more difficult she'd take pride of place.

"Let's go somewhere fancy soon. I don't know, Barcelona? Rome? Business is good, all good, babes," Sam added, rubbing a hand along her thigh.

She smiled. "As long as you're not one of the divorcing couples."

"As long as you're not the husband! Some of the payouts. Woowee!" He whistled, stared up at the ceiling. "It's a miracle anyone gets married."

The elephant in the room swished its tail. She remembered Sophie asking her about the wedding date that fateful night. Pushing the conversation out of her head, she quickly sat up and slipped her feet into her sheepskin slippers. She didn't want to think about that.

"Interesting look." He smiled, glancing down.

"Oh!" She'd put the slippers on the wrong feet. Yesterday she'd gone out to buy a newspaper with her jumper inside out. How she missed her old brain, her tidy, organized, optimistic brain. Where had it gone? It was as if someone had crept in the night Sophie died and emptied all her boxes, books and files all over the floor, like a demented ex-employee sabotaging the boss's office.

"Chuck over the lighter. Thanks, darling."

She handed him the bullet-cold weight of the Zippo and gazed out the window at the poised row of grubby Georgian houses on the opposite side of the Camden street. They looked different since Sophie had died, in a way she couldn't quite put her finger on. She felt the faint vibration of a Silverlink train, heard its rumble, then the deaf bloke's telly next door. Again, these familiar noises now sounded foreign, like something outside a hotel window the first morning in a new city.

Sam exhaled a curl of smoke. "Where you taking Freddie, then?"

"Thinking zoo, but it's a bit arctic, isn't it?" The freezing February sky looked heavy and white. "I remember being dragged to the zoo as a child when it was like this. The only thing you get to see are llamas and rare breed pigs."

"Nothing wrong with a rare breed. Preferably between two slices of bread with a dollop of ketchup."

She bit down on her bottom lip, where she had developed a permanent dent like the pothole Camden Council wouldn't mend outside the apartment. "Why don't you come?"

"Don't do zoos, babes."

Sam didn't do north of London or easyJet or rubber-soled shoes. The zoo thing was a new one. "Huh?"

"The sight of animals in cages freaks me out."

"You know you really should have become an animal rights lawyer." It was meant to be a joke. But he shot her a dark look over his coffee cup. "Aquarium?"

"A tank is a cage."

"So is an apartment. Oh, go on, darling. Come."

He shook his head, serious suddenly. "You know what I'm like with kids, Jen. I never know what to say at the best of times. Let alone . . ."

"Forget it."

"Why don't I take you for lunch first?" he said, trying to appease her for refusing to play zoos with Freddie. "Then I can drive you up to Muswell Hill."

"Thanks, but I'm having lunch with Ollie first."

Sam's face clouded. He ground out the cigarette with a long stub and got out of bed. Led Zeppelin's "Whole Lotta Love" started to crash out of the speakers. He turned it up and mouthed along to it.

"What?"

"You've spent more time with Ollie than you have with me recently."

"Come on, Sam." She shook her head at the futility of explanation.

They'd been here before. "He's no good on his own. I owe it to Soph to be there now."

He rolled his eyes. "You make it all sound like a country and western track. Sweetheart, Ollie's a *man*. He just needs the space to drink himself into oblivion and shag himself stupid."

"Sam!" She felt everything tense between them again. It had been building over the last few weeks. Like an electrical storm about to break.

"You can't make it better, Jenny, don't you get it?" His voice was higher now, that odd pitch he used when he was angry but tried to hide it. "You can't bring Sophie back." He took her hand, pressed the tips of her fingertips to his soft morning mouth. They would smell of cigarettes all day.

"Sophie would have looked out for you had I died," she said gently.

He made a scoff noise in the back of his throat.

She yanked her hand away. Rage was starting to build in perfect synchronicity with Jimmy Page's guitar solo. "Did you even *like* Sophie, Sam?"

He visibly started, paling beneath his smooth skin. "What are you saying?"

"You don't seem that affected, that's all. It's like everything is the same as it was."

"What do you want me to do, wear a T-shirt?"

No, grief had made neither of them better people. It was almost banal. This bickering. The way she'd put on seven pounds. That constant feeling that something was lost. Her keys? Her phone? She'd scrabble around in her handbag before realizing that the lost thing was Sophie.

"She was a beautiful woman who died too young. But she wasn't my wife, Jenny. I'm not going to phonily pretend my life is decimated by her dying." Sam pulled on his white underpants, rearranged his balls. "I refuse to emote on call."

"I'm not asking you to emote, I'm asking you . . . to . . . to give a bit more of a shit, that's all!"

He looked at her in disbelief. "You think I don't give a shit? Bloody hell. You really don't know me at all, do you, Jenny?"

At Sam's persuasion—exercise is a mood enhancer!—she'd gone to a punishing class of Legs, Bums and Tums with a Leo Sayer lookalike instructor who'd shouted, "Hey, you at the back with the hair!" when she could go no further with the star jumps that were making her tits ache. (And what was wrong with her hair? Pots and bloody kettles.) Hamstrings singing with pain, ears ringing with Girls Aloud, she'd reversed badly out of the gym parking space beneath the gaze of three sniggering teenage girls; and now here she was, still a bit BOish, sitting in a snarl of traffic on route to Muswell Hill, London's tightly packed heart now behind her, pulsing beneath its gray layer of grimy snow.

She wondered if Ollie's mother, Vicki, would be at Ollie's today, and hoped not. Sophie used to call her "Joan Collins's long-lost sister from Basingstoke." Still, rather Joan Collins's long-lost sister than Soph's poor mum, Sally, who was a sodden tangle of tears, hurt and neediness. She'd called Jenny every night the week before, wanting to go over the fateful evening in detail. What had Sophie drunk? Eaten? What had they talked about? As she spoke her pain was audible, like nails scraping a blackboard. A mother's pain, no less-ened by her daughter's age. Sophie may as well have been five.

Stopping at the traffic lights, she glanced about her and exhaled the tension of crowded inner London.

Trees. That was the thing she first noticed about Muswell Hill.

All the trees, skeletal now but in summer shivers of green. Yes, trees, wider roads, lots of white people, and a lovely view. From different points in the neighborhood you could see the whole of London spread out below you like a meal on a plate. Jenny pulled up outside Ollie's house. A typical suburban Edwardian house, it had a fashionable circus-style number thirty-three transfer on the upper windowpane, a soft gray door, and a recycle box alarmingly full of empty wine bottles and beer cans next to the pathway. The blinds were shut and the frosted front path was unscuffed by footprints. She knocked, waited for a few minutes before Freddie opened the front door, wearing his Superman pajamas and clutching a battered stack of Match Attax cards.

"Hey, Freddie!" She hugged him, sniffed his hair. It didn't smell how it usually smelled, fresh and boyish, like wind and soil. No, he smelled sockish today and his angelic curls were matted at the back. "You alright?" Stupid question.

"Yes, thank you." Freddie smiled politely, as Sophie had taught him, but he didn't maintain eye contact for long. She wondered if the horrible truth—his mother wasn't coming back—had dawned yet. A notably slimmed-down Ping Pong curled around his ankles and mewed pitifully.

Inside the hall it was chaotic, more chaotic than the previous week. Not just mess, but layers of mess, stratified in the manner of an archaeological dump, Monday's mess on Tuesday's and so on. Coats. Boots everywhere. An empty chip tray nestled inside Freddie's bicycle helmet. It was as if Sophie's death had frozen it in situ like petrifying volcanic mud. The television was on in the living room, frozen to a Sky menu. The potted palm in front of the bay window was drooping pathetically, its leaves curling and yellowing at the edges. A duvet was balled into the corner of the velvet sofa. It didn't contain Ollie. "Where's Daddy, sweetheart?"

"Kitchen," said Freddie matter-of-factly.

She put her hand lightly on his soft cheek, still as adorably con-
vex as a baby's. But he shrugged her hand off and ran upstairs.

Ollie, or a man who vaguely resembled Ollie, was hunched pathetically beneath the huge Sex Pistols' *No Future* original print in the
kitchen, staring at a small, crumpled sheet of white paper. He was
wearing the same black jeans he'd been wearing the last time she saw
him, as well as the same navy cashmere jumper with the giant hole on
the left elbow. "Ollie?"

He looked up with puffy eyes and tried to smile. "Hey, Jenny."
His voice rasped, like the throat of a forty-a-day smoker. She swore
he had peppercorns of gray on his temples where he didn't a week
earlier. She wanted to put her arms around him and hug him close
but still felt as if she didn't quite have permission, or familiarity. The
truth was she'd actually always felt quite shy around Ollie—he was
too good-looking—and she had only known him through the prism
of Sophie. Sophie had been her best friend. Ollie was Sophie's husband. If they'd divorced—always the test—she'd have been in the
Sophie camp. And now, here they were, thrust together in the most
unlikely of circumstances.

"You've got a starter beard."

He ran his fingers through it. "Bit Bin Laden?"

"No, sort of Jim Morrison."

"Rider on the storm."

A pop cultural reference! A good sign! He was functioning. Feeling a wave of relief, she smiled properly for the first time that day.
She liked it at number thirty-three. Apart from anything else, her
misery paled against his and this made her feel like the sane one.
"Any grannies in the house?"

"Sent Mum home."

"Really?"

"Don't worry. She's still phoning every couple of hours. Like a
speaking clock." He pushed the bit of white paper up beneath his

fingernail and put on a high woman's voice. "'It's four o'clock, Oliver. Have you got dressed yet? Have you canceled Sophie's bank accounts? It's five o'clock, Oliver, has Freddie had his tea? Have you spoken to the lawyers? When is the case coming to court?' And on and on." He shook his head. "Bless her. She's driving me nuts."

"Er, I guess there's a lot of stuff to sort out." She could only imagine.

"We die and do you know what we leave behind?" Ollie kicked back in his chair angrily. "Admin. We leave admin. Fucking great."

"Maybe it's too soon to send your mum home, Ol," she said, wondering when she'd slipped into calling him Ol rather than Ollie and whether this was overfamiliar. Sophie had called him Ol. "How about Soph's sister? Would . . ."

"I need to do this on my own." Eerie choral medieval chanting music started to pour out of his speakers. It reminded her of churches and crypts. No, it was not going to help. He needed Emmylou Harris.

He glanced at her, reading her mind. "It's this or replaying Sophie's voice on the answer machine."

Déjà vu suddenly hit her with such force she stepped backward. Two years before. A dark winter's afternoon. Walking up the path of number thirty-three, hearing music, loud music, soft, smooth, old soul. The lights were on in the house, the curtains open, and she saw Sophie and Ollie clutching each other, dancing around the living room, oblivious to anything but each other, his arm tight around her waist, her eyes fixed hungrily on his face. Like Taylor and Burton, she'd thought. Shocked by the erotic intensity and not wanting to intrude, she'd turned right round and walked twice around the block, realizing that she'd never danced like that with anyone. From that to this. It was pitiful. "You can't be alone," she said quietly. "Not right now."

"I'm not alone. I've got Fred." He looked out the window, eyes focused on something invisible in the middle distance. "It was airless in the house with everyone here, Jenny, all of us choking on grief. Believe me, this is easier." He shook his head. "A few days ago, I had this energy surge and ran about sorting everything out, phoning the idiots at Orange, calling her building society, some twat at London transport, and feeling almost positive, even though that sounds mad, and then . . . I . . . I just crashed."

"Oh, Ollie." This big, wonderful chunk of a man as vulnerable as a little boy, it wasn't right. But he'd get through this. He had to. She was going to make sure of it.

"It keeps going round and round my head. If you'd both left the restaurant thirty seconds earlier . . . If you'd got a cab . . ." His face crumpled. "The what-ifs of it all make me want to rip my skin off. Fuck. Fuck. I can't explain." He looked up at her desperately. "I can't *be*, Jenny. I can't just be anymore. Tell me how. Please."

She leaned toward him then, needing to be close to him. He smelled different from Sam. Saltier. She recognized the smell from Sophie, who'd always smelled slightly of Ollie in the way other people smelled of their houses.

"I don't want to be here, Jen," he said so quietly, she could barely hear him.

"Don't even say that, Ollie. Freddie needs you." She noticed that there was a Coco Pop trapped in his beard.

His eyes darkened. "I need him more. And I hate that. It should be the other way round."

"I think you're holding up really well, Ollie. I do, really." Should she tell him about the Coco Pop?

"Every day I wake up knowing not only that she's gone but that I've got to face another day missing her. Then I spend the whole day waiting for her to come back, expecting her to be late."

The medieval monks started chanting more incessantly, the same Latin words, over and over. "Ollie, bereavement is a process." She wished desperately that she could offer less trite words of comfort. "It's not always going to feel like this."

He snorted. "You believe that, do you?"

"Yes, yes, I do. I have to." It just hadn't happened yet. And in a weird way, part of her didn't want it to happen. Her grief was all she had left of Sophie. She wondered if Ollie felt the same. Or were there different types of grief, Jenny wondered, different strains and hybrids? So that the grief a mother who lost a child suffered was fundamentally different from the pain of losing a friend or wife? Or was everyone stuck in the same long, dark tunnel, maybe just in different places, some closer to the light than others?

Ollie rolled himself a cigarette, licking the paper with the efficiency of someone who did it all the time, rather than someone who had supposedly stopped smoking when Sophie was pregnant with Freddie. The blue-gray smoke curled out of his mouth, over his beard, into the room like a Scooby-Doo spirit. "I woke up yesterday and I swear I couldn't remember what she looked like. The past is fading, Jen."

Jenny bit her lip, trying not to cry. Hopeless. She'd come here to comfort Ollie. She didn't want him comforting her. She had to be strong. Strong and organized and helpful.

"No one else was there, you see. It was our world, the two of us. She was the witness. Now it's gone. All fucking gone."

I was there, thought Jenny. I saw it. I saw you two fall in love. I saw how happy you made Sophie. You two were the yardstick by which I measured every relationship, *my* relationship. You two were the real deal. She saw them dancing again, dancers on their private stage, the look in Ollie's eyes as he gazed at Sophie, a gaze of wonderment and ball-busting lust.

Freddie barreled into the room. "Hungry."

"Are you? Um . . ." Ollie scratched his head, as if trying to make sense of the meaning of the word. "Fancy some toast?"

"We had that already today. Daddy, you have something in your beard. Euch." He picked out the Coco Pop that Jenny had been longing to pick out and flicked it to the floor.

Ollie walked over to the fridge and surveyed it blankly. The open fridge door released a stale cheesy waft into the kitchen.

"I'll pop out to the deli," she said. Now this *was* something practical she could do. Something maternal. "You've got a nice one, haven't you, up on the high street?"

"Can you get some chocolate cake?" Freddie asked.

"Sure. Whatever you fancy." She winked at Ollie. "Chocolate cake for breakfast, lunch and dinner."

Freddie pulled on Ollie's hand. "Can I watch *Deadly 60*?"

Ollie shook his head. "Too much telly already, Fred."

"*Strictly Come Dancing*?"

Jenny smiled. "You like *Strictly*, Freddie?"

"Freddie *loves Strictly*." Ollie grinned. "Soph got him into it. She had it all ramped up on the Sky Plus." He looked down at the floor. "It's still there. He watches it over and over."

"I wish I was allowed to watch *Strictly*. Sam won't let me," she whispered to Freddie. "You and I must have a secret *Strictly* sesh together, Freddie."

A smile lit up Freddie's face. "Now?"

"Not right now, Fred," said Ollie quickly. "I'm talking to Jenny."

"Daddy . . ."

"Oh, okay, *Deadly 60*." Freddie ran out of the room before Ollie had a chance to change his mind. Ollie rolled his eyes. "Can't refuse him anything."

"Totally understandable."

"He's my little warrior. He doesn't deserve this shit." Ollie took one more pull on his cigarette and stubbed it out, half smoked. He looked out the window. A cream puff of snow was settling on the sill, airy and solid at the same time. Like love, Jenny suddenly thought. Like how true love is meant to be. Like what Soph and Ollie had. Airy but solid, like meringue. "How has Freddie been?"

"Nightmares." Ollie rested his square jaw in his hands. She noticed a crescent of grime beneath his fingernails. "Although he's better when he sleeps in my bed. He dreamed of Ben Ten last night. Progress?"

"Definitely progress." Jenny tried to stop her eyes from filling by blinking really fast. She could cope with most things, just not the idea of Freddie losing his mother. "And the counseling?"

"Nice lady, says he's doing okay. Well mothered, she says." He raised his eyebrows at the irony. "It helps."

"Well fathered too."

Ollie turned to her, dark eyes blazing. "Jenny, he thinks that Sophie is still *here*. That she talks to him. That she's in the room."

Jenny felt the hairs prickle on the back of her neck. "I sometimes feel Sophie is still here," she confessed quietly. She'd never tell Sam that. Sam would tell her to get a grip. "Do you?"

Silence. He looked at her long and hard before speaking. "Yes."

She felt a wave of relief. It wasn't just her. "Do you talk to her?"

"Doesn't talk back" was all he said, turning to face the window despondently. The sky was a cushiony blue above the rooftops now, framing the crow's-wing black of his shoulder-length hair. "But the bond between her and Freddie was so close, so . . . so umbilical that maybe she can connect with him." He shook his head, closing his eyes again. "I'm going back to the studio Monday."

It took a moment to sink in. "Already?"

"I need to do something." Ollie started rolling another cigarette. "Anyway, there's no one else who's going to do it."

"What about Freddie's pickup times and stuff?" Jenny didn't really know what childcare was involved but she'd heard Sophie talk about it often enough, the endless deadlines. It had always struck her as an enormously complicated business requiring military planning. The reason Sophie hadn't been able to go back to work was because Ollie worked such erratic and long hours, sometimes not leaving the studio until late evening. How on earth would Ollie, not the most practical of men, fill her shoes?

"Don't worry, Jenny. I'll sort it."

"I'll help you all I can. Happy to take him swimming, whatever. I mean, I'd love to, if you want me to," she stuttered, suddenly worried that she might be intruding. "I wish I could do more, Ollie. I wish I lived closer."

Ollie got up and walked slowly to the fridge and pulled out a beer.

Should she say anything about the drinking? No, no, she shouldn't. Not now. Let it go. "Is there anything I can help you with today? Like now, as I'm here? I feel like I should be doing something."

He snapped the can and looked at her sharply. "Maybe you can explain that list on the table."

"Sorry?" She started at the change in the tone of his voice.

"That piece of paper on the table."

She bent forward, peering at the crumpled square of paper, Sophie's large, rounded writing. "What is it? A to-do list." She smiled. "Sophie was queen of the to-do list."

Sophie used to say that without her to-do lists she'd be the most disorganized mother in the world. Jenny never believed this. Sophie had always had a knack for the domestic. Although she was often late—she made being late glamorous rather than just annoying—she always knew where she was going, where she needed to be. She didn't forget stuff. Like smear tests, or her grandmother's birthday. She organized and decorated any environment she was in for more than ten minutes, whether that was a tent—Sophie camped with battery-powered fairy lights—or her room at university, which had boasted nondead orchids, sidelights dangerously draped with Indian silks, black-and-white professionally framed photographs and a dressing

table with little white china-lidded pots for her cotton wool, all of
which had seemed impossibly chic at the time. Jenny had taken her
own makeup off with wet cheap toilet paper and the only decoration
on her walls consisted of her lecture timetables.

Jenny smoothed the paper with the edge of her hand and began
to read.

1. Ollie dentist.
2. Buy fish oils.
3. Thank Suze for playdate thingy
4. Guttering!
5. Cake stall year two next Friday—bake?
6. Smear
7. Car service
8. Lobotomy
9. Speak to Jenny about it ☹

"Speak to Jenny about *it*?" She frowned, puzzled. Why the glum
smiley? "No, no idea, sorry."

He frowned. "The lobotomy. She says lobotomy. Was she so
bloody bored with her life, Jenny?"

"No!"

"She was frustrated. I hate that." He twisted his hands together.
They were hands that she'd seen dance along piano keyboards at
parties involving mojitos and improvised renditions of "Bennie and
the Jets" in happier times. Today, for some reason, they looked
broken.

"Look, Sophie had a good brain on her." She tried to sound calm
and composed and rational but inside she was panicking. She remembered the question in the churchyard, a question, thankfully, he'd
not asked again. But she felt it looming. "She was one of those women
who could have done anything. And she chose her family. That was

what she wanted. You. Freddie. This. Exactly this. She was so happy, really happy. You two had what everyone wants, Ollie. I knew her, Ollie. I knew her better than anyone. And I know she loved you and her life here more than anything."

He leaned against the fridge and letter fridge magnets scattered onto the floor. "I just keep looking for . . . for proof."

"Proof of what?"

"I don't know. Something. Something . . ." he said, his voice drifting off, making the hair lift on Jenny's arms.

She closed the door of number thirty-three with some relief and strode off purposefully toward Muswell Hill Broadway in search of a deli, freshly fallen snow squeaking under her feet. She wondered again what it was that Sophie had wanted to talk to her about. Why the glum smiley? It must have been something bad. Something important, for her to underline it. How incredibly frustrating that now she'd never know.

The Broadway was as it always was, the armada of expensive baby buggies, the glittering shop fronts selling knitted toys and organic beauty creams, the steaming lattes and cinnamon cakes. One second she was finding the familiarity of the street comforting, the next she was winded by loss. She realized there was no one else she could meander along a high street with in the way she did with Sophie. And for this reason only, just one reason among millions of others, she'd miss her forever.

Sophie had loved shopping for its own sake. She'd loved a bargain. In their twenties they'd spent many weekends meandering around Camden Market, Portobello and Brick Lane. She was a collaborative shopper, as happy to find something for Jenny as she was for herself. She adored buying presents, spending money. Her eyes would glow with pleasure as she handed over a wodge of notes or a

credit card, whereas spending made Jenny anxious; she'd been
brought up to think she should save and had been the proud owner
of a post office account that had earned about twopence a year interest since a small child. While browsing with Sophie was always fun,
it sometimes got out of hand. Sophie made her buy things she didn't
often wear. Sparkly things. And there was that time she'd got trapped
in a dress. Sophie, being Sophie, had insisted she try on a vintage
creation—by an acclaimed designer she'd never heard of—with a
strange twisty cut and smocking, in a frighteningly cool shop with
unfeasibly thin shop assistants in Notting Hill. The dress, despite
its age, was completely unaffordable and, in Jenny's uninformed opinion, hugely unflattering. It was also impossible to escape from. It
took two shop assistants and twenty-three minutes to free her from
the dress. Sophie had officially peed herself laughing.

Things changed when Freddie reached school age and Sophie
and Ollie had, bafflingly at the time, left the gritty grooviness of
Kensal Rise and settled in the suburbs, muttering darkly about
schools. How could a good school compensate for not having a Tube
station? She didn't get it. After that it had become harder to meet
up, especially in recent years. Their lunches would no longer spill
into the afternoon with the same abandon. There was always the
school run, playdates, football lessons and a seemingly endless list
of deadlines and responsibilities, none of which involved ingesting
Bloody Marys or getting trapped in dresses. Having given up work
at the small event organizer that demanded such long hours to look
after Freddie, Sophie no longer earned her own money and felt that
she wasn't justified in spending Ollie's money on the utterly frivo-
lous, although of course the odd splurge still went under the radar,
and Sophie was quite happy to throw money at furniture, as well as
endless "finds" on eBay.

Relying on her husband's income had struck Jenny as an uncomfortable dynamic. How she'd hate to have to rely on Sam's. But

Sophie, of course, took it in her breezy stride. She still had funds from her single working years to fall back on, as well as friends with discounts in the fashion industry, and an eye that could whip up showstopping outfits out of the most unlikely sartorial components: Doctor Who scarves bought secondhand from the school Christmas fair, holey jeans exposing a tanned knee, a furry gilet from Topshop and one of Ollie's old The The tour T-shirts from the early nineties. She once accessorized her yellow gingham bikini with a boa made of slimy seaweed on a beach in Cornwall. Needless to say she looked amazing.

Jenny pushed open the heavy glass doors of the deli into a fog of noise and smell and warmth—frothing milk machines, the hushed gossiping of huddled mothers, the sound of babies burping up milk, the smells of cake, coffee and suede boots dampened by the snow— and pushed her way past the buggies to the salad and deli dishes behind the gleaming glass counter. Having glimpsed the interior of Ollie's fridge—beer and milk—she placed a generous order of food with the pretty ginger girl behind the counter.

"Jenny?" said a voice behind her. "It is Jenny, isn't it?"

She turned. A swathe of pink sweater was emerging from the back of the queue. A frizzy halo of brown hair held back in the jaws of two enormous tortoiseshell plastic hairclips.

"Suze?" It was the woman who'd done the speech before her at the funeral. The booming voice. That hair.

"You look totally different out of your funeral outfit!" Suze lunged forward. It was a full-on kiss on the cheek, tea wet and compounded with a hug so that Jenny found herself spluttering into the bobbly cerise sweater. As she did so she came eye to eye with a ginger-haired baby strapped to Suze's back in a sling.

"Here, Lucas!" Suze yanked a fluff-haired blond toddler back by the strap of his denim dungarees. "Stay here or no muffin." The tod- dler looked outraged.

"Wow! How amazing to meet like this," said Jenny, weakly. "How are you?"

Suze rolled her eyes. "Don't ask. You know what it's like with young kids. I feel like I'm losing control of the monkey cage at the zoo."

Monkey? Zoo? What on earth was she talking about? She kept having this problem, not getting stuff. Like everything was happening under water.

"Night feeding problems," explained Suze, reading her lack of comprehension. "The reason I look seventy-five."

Jenny smiled, nodding politely, not wanting to encourage further expounding of Suze's tiredness. She'd noticed this a lot about people with kids: they spent hours talking about tiredness. The Eskimos' dozens of words for snow had nothing on a mother's vocabulary for tiredness.

"Don't look at your mama like that!" Suze smiled and squeezed toddler Lucas's cheek. He muttered something ungracious about the muffin and ramped up the cross look. Suze turned to her. "How old are yours?"

"I don't have any kids myself. I'm just up here seeing Ollie and Freddie," she said quickly, feeling like she should explain herself. After all, what the hell was she doing in Muswell Hill if she *didn't* have kids? She wished the girl behind the counter could be a bit more slapdash and shove the food into the brown cardboard boxes so she could leave now.

"Ah." Suze's eyes narrowed. "Ollie. How *is* Ollie?"

"Well . . ." Jenny hesitated, not wanting to gossip about Ollie behind his back but not wanting to gloss over the situation either. "Could be better, obviously."

"Poor, poor man. Well, at least he's got his mum living with him. Thank God for mothers, eh?"

"She's gone back home, actually. I think he wanted a bit of space."

"Oh, has she?" Suze's face brightened. She lowered her voice conspiratorially. "Between you and me, Jenny, I've tried to help out a few times in the last few weeks and I've always found the mother a bit of a, well, a bit of a brick wall, to be perfectly honest. She doesn't seem to want anyone else getting too close." She shook her head, as if trying to stop herself from saying more. "So how's Ollie coping *alone*?" She drew out the words slowly, as if hinting at the comprehensive length of answer she expected in reply.

"Well . . ."

"As Tash suspected." Suze shook her frizz. "She had a peek through the letter box on Tuesday and said the hall looked like a festival site."

"He's not that domestic at the best of times," she said and then felt disloyal.

"And as soon as he goes back to work . . ."

"Next week. He's going back next week."

"Next week! Blimey," Suze exclaimed, oblivious to the surge of lunchtime diners trying to get past her to the till. She grabbed the sleeve of Jenny's coat urgently. "This is fate, you know, me and you, meeting like this. Fate!"

"Er, fate?" She didn't like the idea of fate anymore. It had pulled some nasty tricks.

"I actually tried to phone you last week, but of course, I'd lost your number." Suze slapped her temple hard with the side of her hand. "I changed handbags and . . . Oh, I won't bore you with the details."

Jenny smiled politely. Alarm bells started to ring.

"It is time, Jenny," Suze announced as her baby regurgitated something onto her left shoulder.

She now had absolutely no idea what Suze was talking about. "Time for what, sorry?"

"Sophie's girls to come together." She rubbed at the milk stain on her shoulder with a wet wipe that she'd plucked from her hand-bag. "I've always said we need a Help Ollie committee and, you know what?" she added determinedly. "We're going to start it!"

Suze obviously didn't realize that of all the people most likely to start a support group with a bunch of women she didn't know, she, Jenny, would be at the bottom of the list. She even found the idea of a book group kind of excruciating, and hen nights only under severe duress. She had never, ever been a girlie pack animal.

"Lucas!" Suze hissed as her son stuck a finger into the golden disc of carrot cake on the counter. "That was your *third* warning. You are now *out* of warnings." She blew her fringe up off her forehead in exaggerated exasperation.

The girl behind the counter finally finished the food boxes.

"Well, I really must be getting back to Ollie's . . ."

Suze grabbed her arm again. It was a viselike grip. Jenny felt a surge of sympathy for the disobedient Lucas. "How are you fixed Wednesday morning next week?"

"Um, working, I'm afraid."

"The afternoon?"

"Working too. Sorry."

"Thursday?"

Jenny shook her head before she even considered whether she was free or not.

"Sorry, I'm hounding you." Suze's face fell, and without her big smile it looked saggy and defeated and Jenny felt sorry for her. "I'll let you get on."

She was hardly running the treasury. She could take off *one* morning if she wanted to. What if it was a genuine help to Ollie? "Actually, you know what, Suze? I'll work it out somehow. I'll come on Thursday."

"Fan-bloody-tastic!" Suze dug into her handbag and pulled out a baby yoga leaflet, scrawled her address on the back of it with a red pen and thrust it into Jenny's hand. "I can't believe I've finally got Jenny Vale, the real-life Jenny Vale, coming to my house."

"You know my surname?" This was all bewildering on some level she didn't quite understand.

Suze winked. "Sophie always spoke so warmly about you, Jenny."

Jenny felt a warm glow inside. "Did she?"

"Although, you were a figure of much intrigue, let me tell you. Her clever copy editor friend with the complicated—" Suze suddenly stopped and flushed from neck to hairline, as if she'd caught herself just in time.

Five

Nothing like dying to give you a sense of perspective. The strange thing is that from up here, a few centimeters below the bathroom ceiling, engulfed in bubble bath steam (I've been watching over Freddie while he has a bath, willing him to wash behind his ears; he hasn't), I've realized that certain universal truths passed unnoticed beneath the radar while I was alive, like, properly alive. I was so busy living I forgot to think about the things I'd miss when I was dead, which is kind of understandable once you think about it. Like that famous Damien Hirst shark in the tank of formaldehyde, *The Physical Impossibility of Death in the Mind of Someone Living*. I always liked that shark. I used to joke that I'd get Ping Pong preserved like that and call it *The Physical Impossibility of Ollie Remembering to Feed the Cat*. Ha!

Anyway, first, the obvious stuff. Family and friends are the most precious things in the world. But you know what? I knew that. (*You know that.* Sorry.) I can honestly say, hand on the place my heart used to be, that I was never someone who took either for granted

while blood was pumping pink around my veins. Every time Freddie
kissed me it gave me a little bloom of pleasure. I'd watch other
women watching Ollie at a party, everyone wanting more of him
than he ever gave—so elliptical, my rock 'n' roll Darcy—knowing
that I was the one going home with him, the one who got to talk to
him for hours late at night, roll around the bed with him, read him
stories from newspapers that made him laugh, the Ted Hughes
poems he loved, placate him with kisses when I'd accidentally deleted
The Wire from Sky Plus and filled up all the recording space with
daytime cooking programs. And I got to see them both asleep—there
but not there, dangling on the edge of dreams—Ollie, the most
handsome man asleep; Freddie, just the most delicious boy who ever
fell to earth. I always used to wonder if I filmed Freddie and speeded
that film up whether you'd actually get to see him growing, like one
of those wildlife films. I guess you would: he's grown five millime-
ters since I died.

I even watched Jenny sleep once, not that I ever told her, because
she'd get embarrassed about it, being Jenny. It was the time I forced
her to come to Bestival by stealthily buying her a ticket and a sleeping bag. (Brief character note here: Jenny is *not* a festival type of
person; she thinks that the "all together now, one love" vibe is dis-
tinctly phony, whereas I've always been a bit of a sucker for it. She'd
much rather visit a stately home garden with sculpted hedges and a
tea garden.) We were sharing a leaking tent, lying side by side in our
new damp sleeping bags, having already lost one phone (hers) and
one brand-new North Face anorak (mine) and, on account of getting
hopelessly lost on the festival site, missed all the acts we had gone to
see, which I assured her was par for the course. Anyway, I'd been
struck by how pretty Jenny looked asleep, not blank pretty like con-
ventionally pretty women, but thoughtful, like someone who had
drifted off over the pages of an engrossing book. She is far prettier
and far smarter than she imagines. I've told her this lots of times—not

enough, I realize now—but she never believed me. Self-doubt. She blames her parents. Personally I blame Sam.

Anyway, to get back to Damien Hirst's fancy shark . . . I made a list this morning while waiting for Ollie to wake up and feed poor old neglected Ping Pong. (Needless to say, the concern isn't mutual. He still hisses every time I pass.) Okay, the list. I do like a list.

A few random things I wish I'd realized before the bus hit

- That, all in all, I would spend twenty-two years of my thirty-five years of life counting calories. That's a lot of unnecessary math.

- That I would only ever wear one-quarter of my wardrobe. That's a lot of unnecessary clothes.

- That I should have had more sex. You can't have sex when you're dead.

- That rare is the friend who inhabits your single life and is still there when your kid starts school. (Step forward, Jenny.) Most disappear into the vortex somewhere between the "we must meet up soon, LOL" email and the Facebook friend confirmation.

- That one-third of the people we invited to our wedding we would not see again in the six years since. (Apart from my funeral, but that doesn't count.)

- That it is okay to imagine marriage will be like New York City and discover that it's more like Brussels. It does not mean that something is wrong, or that you are doomed to divorce. It just means you've hopped on a different plane.

- That turbulence isn't going to bring the plane down. You will live to touch the tarmac again.

- That the guy sitting next to you on the Northern Line, the one with the rucksack and the frenzied, darting eyes, is not a terrorist. He's just been dumped by his girlfriend.

- That every phase passes. The baby stops teething. The tantrums become sulks. The darling baby bootees will no longer fit. He will learn to spell "because." (This said, not sure Ollie will ever remember to put the recycling out on a Wednesday night.)

- That, yes, you can have too many tea lights.

- That I did drink too much. That those glasses were not one unit. They were three. But they didn't kill me in the end.

- That I sunbathed too much. It gave me laughter lines. But it didn't kill me in the end.

- That no life is too short to stuff a mushroom. Stuffing the mushroom is one of the nice bits. It's washing up the baking tray afterward that is to be avoided.

- That no one will notice if you don't bake a cake for the school cake sale unless you apologize profusely.

- Revision: only Suze will notice.

- If you harbor a secret from your friend and you agonize whether to tell them and are *almost* on the eve of telling them when you get knocked down by a bus it means the secret is irretrievable. It's like dropping a laptop in the bath.

Six

No, it was hardly a blood-soaked favela. It was leafy. It was lovely. It was the kind of street where children chalked hopscotch on the pavement and people hung children's dropped gloves on the neighbor's hedging. So why was the 4x4 *Free Zone* sticker on Suze's living room window making her so bloody anxious? Suze's text message yesterday afternoon—"Bake cake guys!"—hadn't helped either. Who were the "guys"? And baking? *Baking!* Jenny hadn't baked since home economics. What did it mean that she was in her midthirties and childless and had never baked so much as a scone? Jesus. It must mean something. Panicked, she'd bought a cake from a posh bakery, a whole wheat apple cake that looked like it would take at least six months to digest, and could in fact double as a bulletproof vest if sewn artfully into a Puffa jacket. In order to take the pretense to the next logical level, she would decant it from its white cardboard box into a cake tin. But she didn't own a cake tin! Of course she didn't. Why the hell *would* she own a cake tin?

She glanced at her watch and groaned. Yes, once again, she'd done her crap shtick of arriving unfashionably early. (She was the only person in London for whom the traffic lights were consistently green and the Tube rarely delayed, as if the great traffic controller in the sky had marked her out for some kind of loser's social experiment.) She waited a few moments, took a deep breath of the pleasant wood-smoke-smelling air and pressed the bell. Three shrunken *Happy Birthday* balloons hanging from string on the door knocker bounced jauntily in the wind.

A heavy plodding, then the cherry red front door was flung wide. Suze beamed at her, a vision in an orange batik blouse with that wedge of hair and, mystifyingly, a round, wet circle on the front of her blouse the size of a twopence piece. "You didn't flake!"

"No." She tried her best not to be offended that Suze had her down as a flaker and tried even harder not to look at the bizarre stain on Suze's blouse, which appeared to actually be spreading like ink on blotting paper.

Suze pulled the stained blouse away from her bosom and flapped it. "Sorry. Feeding baba."

Jenny blushed. Of course! She hovered uncertainly, wiping her sweaty palms on her pressed navy trousers. Apart from the fact she'd lost all social skills since Sophie died, it felt odd meeting Sophie's friends without her, as if she'd turned into one of those traitorous people you introduce to a friend and who then goes on to invite the friend to dinner without you. When she stepped into the yeasty heat, the house reminded her of Sophie's but on a far messier, less cool scale. There was a jumbled row of Wellington boots in tiny sizes pushed up along the hall wall, like the entrance to a classroom. Next to them, children's scooters, five, six, covered in stickers and elastic bands. Toy cars, a one-eyed doll and a bumper pack of recycled loo rolls were heaped at the bottom of the stairs.

The hall walls were painted a cheerful apple green and stamped with children's pictures—collaged topographies made from glued lentils and milk-top foil—and endless family portraits—lots of kids on rainy beaches wrapped in toweling ponchos—blown up too large on canvases so that they'd gone blurry. There was a smell too, yes, unmistakable, a smell of cakes actually baking. And, just as unmistakable, an undernote of urine.

She followed the swinging slab of Suze's bottom down the hall and tried to identify the orange blob stuck to Suze's back jeans pocket—satsuma segment? lone nacho? She heard the crack of female laughter. As she entered the kitchen, a large *Keep Calm and Carry On* poster bossily glared down from the wall. She'd never liked those posters.

"Ladies," said Suze. She stepped aside to reveal her catch. "I bring you the famous Jenny Vale!"

"Lovely to meet you all," she managed, relieved to find only three women sitting round the table. She'd feared an Amazonian tribe in Breton stripes and ballet pumps, heatedly discussing organic baby food and breastfeeding rights.

"Hello!" the voices chimed back. A noisy metal boiling kettle clicked somewhere. It reminded her of a long-forgotten sound from her own childhood. Something in her relaxed a little.

"Take a pew," said Suze, pushing the face-eating frizz away from her face. No wonder. "How do you take your tea, Jenny?"

"Milk. No sugar, thanks." She sat down on the nearest chair, not realizing that there was a gaping hole in the wicker of its seat. She perched on the edge of its hard frame, grateful for her well-upholstered sitbones. "So this is Soph's other life," she said, speaking her own thoughts.

"Yep, welcome to our world." Suze dunked a tea bag in a Union Jack mug of boiling water with her pen-scribbled fingers.

Their world—Sophie's world—certainly looked different from hers. Everything was on a different scale. The kitchen made her and Sam's kitchen seem like a tiny, clinical laboratory. The wooden kitchen island was the size of a small island. Whereas her and Sam's black granite worktops gleamed with lack of use, here the scratched wooden worktops were stained and piled with paper, crayons, glittery pipe cleaners, dirty empty baby bottles, and there was an orange nappy bag, clearly heavily loaded, sitting right next to a fruit bowl. Saucepan handles protruded out of overstuffed drawers. So much kitchen equipment, so industrial. And the fridge! Forget 4x4 carbon emissions; surely this fridge alone was like having a huge cow farting vast quantities of methane round the clock.

"I'm Liz. My daughter is in Freddie's class," said a woman with a smattering of caramel freckles and a cropped pixie haircut, the tips of which were dyed bright red, like they'd been air-dried in ketchup. She was breastfeeding a child that looked too old to be breastfed, ruching up one side of an old T-shirt that said *Talentless but connected* and exposing a blue-veined breast that resembled one of the root vegetables in the cardboard organic delivery box under the table. Although she was wary of anyone who wore slogan T-shirts, let alone someone in a slogan T-shirt with a boob hanging out, there was something genuine in her smile that Jenny immediately warmed to. "I remember Soph mentioning you," she said, only half sure she was right.

The truth was Sophie hadn't told her much about her mum friends or her neighborhood community life. It wasn't until her funeral that Jenny had realized how important it had been to her, or quite how many mumfriends there actually were. Seeing them sitting around this table like this, with the easy, slightly competive edge of sisters, they all seemed so tight. She couldn't help but wonder why she had never been invited into this world before. Had Sophie really thought her socially inflexible?

"Tash," said another woman, in one of those posh, croaky, north London accents that had always made Jenny feel provincial. She leaned across the table and offered a slim, tanned hand bejeweled with large silver rings set with enormous colored stones.

Tash was so beautiful it was hard to look at her directly. She had a swishy curtain of licorice black hair. Feline gray eyes. And full lips—Soph would have called them "blow job lips"—slightly parted, as if she were blowing out air discreetly. (Jenny had read that this was a trick used by Nigella Lawson to look hot in photo shoots and had once tried it herself, only to free a strand of spinach from a canine and shoot it across the room at the photographer at high velocity.)

Tash swished one leg over the other. It was a long, lean leg, shod in a lovely Cuban-heeled boot, the kind of boot with just the right height, a walkable heel that Jenny was always looking for but could never find. A heel height between frumpy flat and foot killer. "My son, Ludo, he's in Freddie's class too. We're the cult of 2Bers, I'm afraid."

Cult? What was 2B? Or was it, to be? 2B or not to be.

"Lydia. Call me Lyds." The woman opposite waved like a little girl, fingers starfished. She was petite and milk-top blonde with delicate pointy features, the kind of fairy-woman Jenny imagined might blow away in the wind unless weighted down by a big expensive handbag.

A pudgy girl peppered in alarming, livid red spots sat, in startling contrast to her mother's fragile beauty, on her knee. "And this is wee Flora."

"Hello, wee Flora." Do not stare at medieval skin condition. Do not mention skin condition.

"I must ask you immediately, Jenny," said Lydia as her daughter jumped off her knee and pegged it out of the kitchen. She stared at the roll of flesh swelling over Jenny's ungenerous waistband. "You're not preggers are you?"

The shock of the question rocked her back into the rattan hole in the seat. "Er, no," she said, extracting herself from the hole and feeling exposed and embarrassed. "Not. Definitely not." She sat up straighter and sucked her tummy in.

"Jenny," said Liz quietly, sweetly coming to her aide, "Flora, Lydia's little girl, she's got chicken pox."

"Oh, *right*!" Perhaps she wasn't so fat that she looked like she should be in a birthing pool. "I've had chicken pox. Really, don't worry about it."

"Swap chairs?" whispered Liz kindly.

"No, I'm fine, thanks." Actually her bum was beginning to ache.

"I thought your speech at the funeral was so lovely," said Liz, placing her baby/teenager down on the floor, where it promptly toddled off toward a kitchen cupboard and started noisily disemboweling it of pans. "Soph would have appreciated it."

"Thanks. Thanks so much," said Jenny gratefully, relaxing a little. Perhaps the meeting wouldn't be so bad after all. They weren't so different. They were all friends of Sophie's. All women!

"It was spot-on." Tash smiled, flashing a broad, perfectly even row of tiny white teeth. Jenny hadn't seen dentistry like that outside Hollywood movies. "You know what? It's so nice to meet someone from Soph's pre-mum life, putting all the bits of the jigsaw together. From what I remember Soph saying, you two go back a long way?"

"Yeah, we shared student digs in the first year of uni." Something tightened in her throat again, remembering the early days. How she'd been mesmerized by Sophie, the loud, garrulous beauty. How honored she'd been to be her friend. "Manchester Uni. We were in the same hall apartment. She made me cheese on toast that first night."

"She was always good on cheese, wasn't she?" Liz smiled, running her hands through her red hair. "Every time I went round to hers for dinner I'd leave with a certain nagging doubt that the lump of supermarket cheddar sweating in my fridge drawer didn't quite cut it."

Jenny remembered the sight of Ollie's pitiful fridge. She doubted it even contained cracked cheddar. She sat up straighter, reminding herself why she was here. This was not about *her*. It was about Ollie and Freddie. She must put her reservations aside and remember this at all times. It was time for her to step up. What was she scared of?

"So did you meet your husband at uni too?" asked Lydia curiously.

"No." Jenny coughed, remembering Suze's comment in the deli about her having a complicated . . . well, love life, surely? They'd obviously muddled her up with someone far more interesting. "We're not married."

Suze looked at the blue stone ring on her finger and winked. "Engaged I see."

"What does he do?" asked Tash, sipping her tea nonchalantly, like this question was a perfectly acceptable first line of inquiry when you'd known someone ten minutes.

Jenny had always disliked the "What does he do?" question. On principle. (Were people their jobs?) But also because . . . "He's a lawyer," she said quietly, trying to wrap the subject quickly.

"Ooh." Tash brightened. "What kind of lawyer, Jenny?"

She braced herself, feeling her shoulders rise toward her ears. "Divorce lawyer."

"A divorce lawyer!" marveled Tash.

"Oh, my God, that's just *so* romantic." Lydia closed her eyes. "Despite everything he knows about the statistics."

"I should take his office number," muttered Tash, digging into the large mouth of her vast handbag. "I could do with a new lawyer. May I?"

She was too awed by Tash's self-assured beauty to say no.

"Ladies, shall we start the meeting proper?" Suze sat down heavily on the chair next to Jenny's, knees cracking. "We'll have tons of time to get to know one another in the next few weeks."

Tons of time? So this wasn't a one-off meeting? Jenny's stomach clenched.

"Okeydokey." Suze busily rummaged for a pen in a pile of school homework. Pen located, she spoke officiously. "Thanks for coming here on this freezing afternoon." She smiled at Jenny and angled her pen toward her. "Especially you, Jenny, taking a day off work."

Tash coughed.

"And you, of course, Tash. And Liz. Sorry, Tash, I'd forgotten you'd gone back to work," said Suze quickly.

"Three days a week," said Tash, examining her nails, which were painted a shade of taupe that Jenny guessed must be fashionable. It would never occur to Jenny in a million years to paint her nails taupe. "Toby's alimony saw to that," Tash muttered.

Liz raised an eyebrow. There was a moment of awkwardness.

"Right," said Suze briskly, pushing the willful wall of hair away from her face. "I don't think anyone will disagree with me when I say that Ollie and Freddie need help right now. And I'm talking proper, controlled, organized help. Don't you think, Jenny?"

They all turned to face her. Feeling spotlit, she felt her right eyelid twitch. What had she got herself into? "Yes, yes, absolutely."

"And we're going to step in. We're going to do what Sophie would have done for us."

"Abso-bloody-lutely!" exclaimed Liz.

"Too right," said Lydia, licking icing off her fingertips. "I mean, have you seen the mess in Ollie's house, Jenny?"

"Nothing that a cleaner couldn't sort out in a couple of hours," she said. What did they expect? Dusted dado rails?

"A cleaner!" Suze scribbled furiously in her notebook. "Ace idea, Jenny. There's that Brazilian who works at number seven who's meant to be great. I wouldn't inflict mine on anyone. Too la-di-da to do toilets. And I'm too bloody liberal to make her."

"But not liberal enough not to care," added Liz wryly.

Suze ignored this. "Now, shall we tell Jenny our concerns?"

"Freddie was sent back from school last week for being too tired. Apparently he fell asleep on a crash mat during PE," Lydia said, her fine-boned face wimpling into a frown. "I don't think he has a proper bedtime anymore."

What was a proper bedtime for a six-year-old boy? She had no idea. "Right," she said, hoping she sounded like she knew what she might be talking about.

"Lola's mum told me he's got lice." Suze winced.

"Oh, God, not again." Lydia groaned, dropping her head into her hands. "My whole life is infested with bloody lice. Flora's head was hopping for weeks last year. I treat it, they come back! I reckon that school has developed some superhybrid of lice, a master race."

"Nazi lice!" said Liz. "Ve 'ave vays of making you itch."

"Leave it to me," said Jenny, feeling her own head itch. She seemed to remember some carcinogenic potion from her own childhood that could nuke an army of locusts.

Suze did a big red tick in her notebook. "Anything else, ladies?"

Liz rested her face in her hands. "Ollie's listening to weird, churchy music, Jenny. All the time. It makes Leonard Cohen sound like the Beach Boys. I worry it's going to make him depressed—well, obviously he's depressed. But *more* depressed. It would make me totally suicidal."

"And dare we mention the beard?" ventured Suze.

"Oh, I do like the beard." Tash smiled dreamily.

"Me too," sighed Lydia. "It's kind of . . . biblical. He looks like Jesus."

"Lydia," groaned Liz.

"Unhygienic," decided Suze. "It's like having pubic hair on your chin. I've never understood beards."

Not as unhygienic as leaving a nappy bag next to the fruit bowl, Jenny wanted to point out. "I don't think we can get involved in every aspect of his life."

Suddenly there was a loud sniff. Jenny turned toward the direction of the sniff and saw that Lydia's eyes were full of tears. She waited for someone to do or say something sympathetic but no one did. Should she say something? Or was it some kind of winter hay fever?

"What about food, Jenny?" said Suze.

"Food?" Jenny said blankly. She had no idea how to run Sophie's domestic life. She, Jenny, didn't have a domestic life. She had Sam and takeaways and meals out and a cleaner. For the first time ever she wondered if Sophie had ever secretly thought her best friend's life a tad tragic.

"Do you think we need to hatch a supper strategy?" Suze reached for a homemade chocolate chip biscuit the size of a saucer, as if just the mention of food had whetted her appetite.

"Er, sorry, what's a supper strategy?"

"It's America's new tactic for smoking out members of al-Qaeda from caves," deadpanned Liz, and Jenny laughed.

Suze rolled her eyes, not amused. "It's a home delivery service of *meals*, Jenny."

"Hey, that's a great idea. I think he'd really appreciate that. I really do."

"Do you?" Suze beamed, delighted to have Jenny's approval. She glanced over at Tash with a look that was not unlike triumph. "Then a supper strategy we shall arrange."

"Lasagna!" Tash slapped the table. She was going to better Suze if it killed her. "Men love lasagna. I make a mean lasagna."

"One of my specialties too actually," said Suze, scribbling *lasagna!!!* in her notes.

There was another loud sniff from Lydia. She dabbed at her small nose with a tissue. "Are you okay?" Jenny asked, unable to ignore it any longer.

"Lydia's *very* emotional, Jenny, heart on her sleeve," Suze explained blithely. "Now, let's talk about—"

"Hopeless." Lydia sniffed, shaking her head. "Hopeless sop,

I am. I could only listen to the first couple of lines of your speech. I was in pieces, *pieces*, wasn't I, Liz?"

"You were, Lydia," Liz reassured her tersely with the minutest flicker of an eye roll.

"How could someone as beautiful as Sophie *die*?" Lydia sobbed more freely now. Liz reached for her hand and gave it a patronizing pat. "Freddie, motherless at six. How can a child ever recover?"

"Deep breath, Lyds. Deep breath. We've all been where you are now," said Suze. "I think we owe it to Ollie and Freddie to be strong now, don't we, Jenny?"

"We do," Jenny said. The others must have hearts of stone to let Lydia sob like this. "But it's okay to cry too. No point in bottling it up." She'd had to run out of Legs, Bums and Tums only yesterday because Destiny's Child's "Survivor" came on and "Survivor" would always remind her of Sophie doing her bootie shake thing in her kitchen. "Or it spurts out sideways."

"You're right, you're so right, Jenny." Lydia smiled at her appreciatively.

"Could we not set up a charity?" Tash wondered, pushing the conversation forward.

"Hmm?" Suze asked Jenny.

"I'm not sure," said Jenny. A charity? For whom?

"We could do the London Marathon!"

"A cake sale?"

"A naked calendar."

A naked calendar! Jesus. "Don't mean to rain on anyone's parade but I don't think it's money that—"

"Jenny's right." Liz frowned. "Oh, it feels awful talking about these things. But he earns quite a lot, doesn't he?"

Jenny nodded. "I guess so. He's one of those producers that you and I may not have heard about but who's very well respected in his field."

"Has he ever worked with Take That?" asked Lydia, brightening.

Jenny shook her head. "Doubt it. It's advertising, film stuff, you know."

"Oh." Lydia's face fell. "I so totally love Take That."

There was an earsplitting yelp from the sitting room, the sound of something heavy and airborne landing. Lydia jumped up and flew out the kitchen. "Flora!"

Liz shrugged, like she'd heard it all before. Another bloodcurdling yell.

"Ludo?" Liz turned to Tash.

"Sounds like it." Tash wearily got up from her seat. "Sorry, ladies, better go and umpire."

"She's not joking either," muttered Suze, the moment Tash left the room. "Ludo's a bloody nightmare. I'd better go and check that he's not swinging baba around by his toenails too."

As soon as they were all safely out of the kitchen, Liz's mouth twitched with a smile. "You don't have to say anything, Jenny."

She laughed, feeling a rush of warmth toward Liz. Yes, she liked Liz best. She liked the fact that she dyed her hair ketchup red. Personally she'd never have the balls. For the hair. Or that T-shirt.

"It's like a little wagon circle, isn't it? I'm afraid we must come across as right little interfering Stepford busybodies."

"Not at all! I had no idea Sophie had this network." That niggling feeling that she'd been shut out from parts of Sophie's life came back to her. "It's brilliant."

"Well, she told us lots about you," said Liz kindly.

What exactly *had* Sophie told them about her? She thought of the list that Ollie had shown her. "Talk to Jenny about *it*." But about what? What "it"? Perhaps these women knew what "it" was. Perhaps if she hung out with them they'd tell her. "I hardly know my neighbors. There's so much neighborly motivation here. It's amazing, really."

"Ah, a lot of local women will become *extremely* motivated where

Ollie is concerned, I suspect." Liz put her mug to her cheek and winked. Jenny noticed how her pea green eyes clashed with the red of her hair, in a good way.

"What do you mean?"

"He's the sexiest dad at the school by a few trillion miles. Everyone's always fancied the pants off him. Dark, devoted and moody." She closed her eyes in a mock swoon. "And a musician."

"You're joking. He's just lost his wife."

"Exactly."

She put her hand over her mouth. "Blimey. It had never occurred to me that . . ."

"He's a wonderful father, handsome, successful, clearly capable of love and commitment and, heartbreakingly, *tantalizingly*, in need of rescue."

"But aren't this lot coupled up?"

Liz glanced at the kitchen door, checking that no one was coming through it. "Loosely," she answered in a hushed voice. "Tash divorced last year, although there's a Polish builder, otherwise known as Marko the Wildebeest. Lydia is married to some City guy whom she never sees. Suze . . . well, Suze's motivation is probably purer. She loves being needed and even the PTA cannot channel all her energies, but then again you never know. And there are many, many others waiting in the sidelines, believe me."

Jenny threw her candor back at her. "And you?"

Something sad and wordless passed across Liz's face. "I loved Soph." She shrugged simply, sweetly. "That's all." And Jenny believed her.

"All good! All good!" Suze burst back into the kitchen, kissing the startled marsupial ginger baby that Jenny remembered meeting in the deli the week before. She was accompanied by a whiff of poo and as she bounced the baby on her knee the smell got stronger. "So our Help Ollie project is full steam ahead, eh?"

"Let's go for it."

"Brill. I'll sort out rotas and stuff from the Muzzy Hill end . . ."

"I wish I could do more . . ." She needed to come clean about her own general uselessness. "I'm a bit in the dark where kids and stuff are concerned, to be honest, Suze. I'm probably the least useful person, much as I want to help."

"Oh, you don't understand, do you?" said Suze. "We *need* you involved in this. We really do. In fact you are crucial to the operation."

"I am?" She hadn't been crucial to anything or anybody for months, maybe never.

"Completely," insisted Suze.

"Why?"

"You know Ollie better than any of us," said Liz, taking a sip of her tea. "We need someone in the group who can speak for him."

"I can't possibly speak for him."

"Look, someone has to," said Liz. "Our job is to organize his domestic life over these coming weeks. Your job is to stay close to him, so that he's got one woman by his side, a woman who is not his mother, or sister-in-law, a woman who doesn't *want* anything from him." She gave Jenny a meaningful look. "A safe place. You know what I'm saying?"

Jenny nodded. The ginger baby reached across for her gold bracelet. His fingers felt silky soft against the skin of her wrist. She studied the top of his scabby cradle-capped head and felt a wave of tenderness for his unphotogenic qualities.

"The fact is," said Suze, trying to hold the wriggling baby still, "you knew Sophie better than anyone, didn't you?"

She nodded, but a little voice in her head had begun to wonder. There were clearly whole parts of Sophie's life that she didn't know at all.

Seven

Curious goings-on in north London, let me tell you.

Three days ago, I nudged my nonatomic self—take that, Stephen Hawking, and suck on it—through the muddy cat flap of Suze's house and gripped onto the tail end of a conversation between Jenny and Liz as it writhed about the room like a barracuda. Something about the local women *fancying* my husband! I'm barely dead, for Pete's sake. I've still got five hundred free mobile minutes left.

But then, people keep surprising me. They are far weirder than I ever realized. Get this.

Two days ago I watched as Jenny sat in her bedroom, bolt upright, absolutely still, like one of those keeno yoga devotees, as the clock ticked and the room fell into darkness. My mother kept ringing on her telephone. Once, twice, three times over the course of a couple of hours. She didn't answer. Sam came back from work and found her in the dark, still sitting upright, tears pouring down her cheeks. He asked her what was for supper. She didn't reply. And yesterday,

I found her making what looked suspiciously like a collage. Jenny crafting! I swear she was actually cutting out bits of paper and sticking them down with the ever useless Pritt Stick—winding the damn thing up, down, trying to pick off the old crust of glue on the top that stops it from being a glue and makes it a smearer of white snotty gloop. No, she's not her usual self at all. I'm *so* relieved that Sam is the Wedding Date Shirker. Jenny needs time to paddle around in her sadness before she makes any big decisions about her future or is let loose anywhere near a bridal department without me.

Meanwhile, in deepest Essex, my sister is channeling all her tears into repeat viewings of *The Bridges of Madison County*. Further south, Dad is spending hours and hours in his shed, constructing the world's most complex hammock frame. He's never wanted a hammock before. Is it something to do with its cradle aspect? Perhaps he needs to be soothed to sleep. Actually suspect he's retreating to the shed to escape Mum, who is still desperately sad. Poor, poor Mum, cloaked in an aura so cold and crunchy it looks like she's been breaded in ice in a dodgy overactive freezer compartment. As for Ollie? My poor love is under siege.

Right now he is staring at the five foil-covered packages that line our kitchen table like crude homemade IEDs. The doorbell rings. He flinches.

"Shall I get it, Dad?" whispers Freddie, running up behind him, Chuppa Chup a lump in his cheek.

Ollie pulls at his beard. He looks like a shipwrecked pirate. "No, it could be . . ."

Freddie pulls a face. "Not more lasagna?"

The doorbell rings again. Ollie raises his finger to his lips. "Shhh. Don't make a sound."

They wait there together in silence, hiding from the enemy. The doorbell rings again. They wait some more. Finally, the sound of receding footsteps on the path outside. Freddie crouches down by the front door and peeks through the letter box. "Daddy, there is something on the step."

"Shit," mutters Ollie, running his hands through his greasy hair. He walks down the hall, stepping over numerous wooden balls—they've been using the hall as a bowling alley—and opens the door, glancing uneasily from side to side as if there might be a hidden sniper lurking on the other side of the cherry tree. He grabs the Pyrex dish and slams the door shut behind him. He puts the dish next to the others and wearily reads the note on the top. "Okay, Freddie, we've got a new one here. And this one is from Tash, Ludo's mummy. That makes it her second in three days. This one is, er, Bolognese sauce." He looks perplexed. "Goes well with the custard pudding, she says. What custard pudding? Oh, right. Here." He peels foil off another package.

Freddie makes a gagging noise and puts his fingers down his throat.

"Got any ideas, Fred?"

"Yes."

"What?"

"Ping Pong."

"Freddie, my son, your mind is dark." He raised his hand into a high five. "You are a genius."

Freddie grins. It's almost a proper beam. Like he used to do all the time. I'm amazed that he can still smile like this, awed at how resilient he is. He opens the back door. "Here, Ping Pong, here, pussy, pussy! Dinnertime."

Later, as the evening falls harder and colder—icicles are hanging like frozen tears from the windowpanes by nine p.m.—I curl into Ollie's old black Converse trainers. They are contained and safe and smell reassuringly of Ollie. I don't want to smell his aftershave, or the washing liquid on his clothes, or his dry-skin shampoo. I want the meaty essence of him, the expelled bodily odors, the flakes of skin, the hot stink of his maleness. I'd actually hang out in his armpit if I could, but I fear this might make him itch.

It's nine thirty now. Ping Pong's paw prints polka across the snow on the deck. There are bald patches on our little scrap of lawn where Freddie and Ollie have scooped up snowballs in cold, red hands and tossed them at each other. In the right-hand corner of the garden, beneath the plum tree that bears the world's tartest, most inedible plums, there is a surprised-looking snowman, a muddy parsnip for a nose, his eyes, withered conkers carefully kept by Freddie the previous autumn. Although the house is a mess, it is warm—a veritable sauna in the trainer actually. Ollie has lit a homey fire in the sitting room fireplace. Making fires is the one domestic thing Ollie's always been good at, having enough of a Bear Grylls bushcraft whiff about it to appeal to him, unlike cleaning the roasting pan. (You never see Bear Grylls washing up his wild fungi cooking pans in the woods, do you? Bet he's got some poor assistant doing that. Bet she's female.)

They are sitting beside the fire now, Freddie curled inside Ollie's knees, resting his head against his chest, listening to the thumpity-thump of his heart, the exact same position I used to snuggle into on winter nights. Freddie's lids are beginning to droop. Ollie strokes his soft curls off his forehead with the plane of his palm. The fire spits and crackles. Its heat gives their faces a healthy glow and hides the puddles of grief beneath Ollie's eyes. They look too beautiful for words. And I wonder why I was ever, ever restless in those last few months of my life? What was I hunkering after exactly, if *not* this? Jenny was right. Isn't she always right? About other people's lives, at least.

Thing is, how the hell was I to know that I'd end up as roadkill on Regent Street? If one's demise could be predicted more accurately—"You're unlikely to last much past Christmas; make it a

good one, Mrs. Brady"—then at least I could have *planned*. Made
an imminent to-do list. A memory box. I would have left Ollie final
instructions—a domestic kick-the-bucket list—with relevant phone
numbers and information. (Remember my mother's birthday. Take
Freddie to the dentist every six months. Do not leave woolens out
because of moths. Feed. The. Cat.) And, more than this, much more
than this, I would have had a chance to appreciate what I had. Take
stock of my lovely life. What's that quote? "I had such a lovely life,
if only I'd realized it sooner." Dorothy Parker? Anyway, I like to
think I would have been able to face my expiration with some grace,
although I realize there's a chance I would have panicked and refused
to accept the fact I was dying, like poor Aunt Linda, and spent all
my money on an alternative medicine clinic in Austria and massage
and vitamin injections.

Did I have an alternative destiny? Was there some small seed of
fate buried within my body that I didn't know about, a lump in the
breast too small for detection? A furring of the left aorta? An
unknown yet lethal genetic predisposition embedded in my helix of
DNA set to activate at age fifty-five like a bomb in the hold of a
plane? I guess we all carry the seeds of our death within us. Then you're
hit by a bus. And those seeds are blown to the wind like a dandelion
clock. It's a fucker, it really is. I realize that nothing else in my life
was a fucker now, even though I thought so at the time. Not the fact
that I couldn't conceive a second child. Not the fact that I didn't
become a film star. Or never found the perfect boot. No, being hit
by a bus is the fucker of all fuckers, end of.

You know the truth? The horrible, grave-chilly truth? I feel
robbed. I feel robbed of my beautiful child, the sock and honey smell
of him, the concavity of his flexible back, his focus as he makes a
Lego spaceship, that pink wet tongue curling out of the corner of
his mouth with absolute concentration. I feel robbed of his laughter
and love, of watching him grow up. And I also feel robbed of the

man I fell in love with, the man I'd watched for three years at university, shy of his looks and his cool-kid reticence, the man who kissed me in a field one cool summer dawn in Somerset and made my heart corkscrew with happiness.

I even feel robbed of my flipping wrinkles! I never ended up looking like my mother, did I? Or my grandmother, a grandmother who lived in near perfect health to the age of ninety-seven, then fell asleep into her cream of mushroom soup one afternoon and didn't wake up again. I will never be able to say, "It was better in my day," or marvel at how no one can remember what an iPhone was. No, I am forever a twenty-first-century thirtysomething, like one of those photographs of women in the forties who died during the war and can only ever be remembered with set curls and red lips. Vintage.

"Was it fun playing at Ludo's earlier?" Ollie asks, interrupting my thoughts before they get gloomier.

"Ludo's dad has gone," Freddie replies, deadpan, cat's-cradling an elastic band between his fingers.

"No, he doesn't live there anymore, Fred," replies Ollie softly. "He lives in another house."

(FYI, with the old au pair, Astrid.)

"But he still sees Ludo," Ollie reassures Freddie.

Freddie ponders this for a moment, his eyes wide, processing. "I think that's better than being in heaven. I wish Mummy just lived in another house."

So do I, my love. So do I.

They sit there watching the flames leap blue and orange. I desperately want to curl up beside them, run my fingers along the coiled ridges of their earlobes. Surely my love must conduct itself to them somehow. Love can't just expire. It's not got a pulse. Therefore it cannot die. Lateral thinking for you.

Freddie looks thoughtful. "If you emailed Mummy on your computer what would happen?"

"Nothing, Fred."

"Have you tried?"

He hesitates. "Yeah. I did once." He looks down, embarrassed. "Didn't get a reply. The account is closed now anyway."

"What about the thingy on the computer when you get the face like it's a telly?"

"Skype?"

Freddie nods. "The one we use to talk to Granny sometimes."

Ollie's eyes are filling. The lump in his throat is rising up his neck. He's trying really hard. "She's not there either, Freddie."

"But she's somewhere!" Freddie shouts. "I *know* she is."

Ollie takes Freddie's face in his hands and holds it. "She is somewhere. And she loves you. She loves you so much. But she is not on the earth, not like you and me."

It's a valiant attempt. How would I explain it?

"Like an angel? A superhero?"

"An angel."

Look, no wings!

Freddie clenches his jaw. "It's still *not* fair."

"It's not fair. It's absolutely not fair."

"Why did the bus driver not die? Why Mummy?"

Ollie's face darkens. "The bus driver dying would not bring Mummy back, would it?"

"No," acknowledges Freddie with heartbreaking forgiveness. I hope he holds on to this gift as he gets older, my sweet soulful boy.

"It was an accident."

Freddie looks unsatisfied. "But . . ."

"Bad things sometimes happen to people. Not very often. But they do."

"Like when Granny lost her purse in the supermarket."

"Worse stuff."

"Like what happened to Mummy?"

"You can be in the wrong place at the wrong time."

"Like Jenny."

Ollie laughs. "What do you mean?"

"Jenny looks like she is in the wrong place sometimes."

Out of the mouths of babes.

"You mean she looks sad?" says Ollie, serious now.

Freddie nods.

"I think she just misses your mummy, Fred."

He spreads his hands in front of the fire and warms them like toast. "Why doesn't someone kiss Jenny better?"

Ha! God, I love this boy.

Ollie smiles softly. "I'm sure Sam kisses her better."

Freddie considers this for a moment, wrinkles his nose in distaste. "I'd rather Sam got run over than Jenny."

Me too! Bring on the No. 23!

"Look, Freddie. It's not an either-or thing. Sam's not about to get run over. Nor is Jenny." He bends down and talks close to his ear. "Jen's here for you."

"Like you?"

"Like me." Ollie strokes Freddie's cheek. "I'm not going anywhere, Freddie."

"Promise?"

He gives a military salute. "Scout's honor."

Freddie still looks worried. "So it's just us two now?"

"Just us two. We'll make Mummy proud."

And *how* proud!

Freddie's forehead knits. There is something bothering him. "I won't get another mummy?"

The room vibrates. I freeze on the mantelpiece.

"Ludo says he now has two mummies," Freddie continues. "One at home. One with his dad. He doesn't like it. I don't think I'd like it either."

"It does sound kind of complicated." A muscle in Ollie's jaw twitches.

He's skirting it! He's not saying there won't be another mummy.

"Anyway, I don't need another mummy. Jenny can take me swimming."

"Fred, no one will ever replace your mummy. I will always love her, and you, more than anyone else in the whole world."

That's better. Almost.

"Universe?" says Freddie.

"Galaxy."

"Cool," says Freddie, leaning his head back on Ollie's shoulder, satisfied at last. Within seconds he is asleep.

Eight

I want a date, Jen," Sam said as he walked into the apartment, shaking glittering blobs of rain off his suit onto the polished hardwood surfaces and clamping shut his black golf umbrella.

"Good idea." Jenny pushed away her manuscript, happy to be disturbed and to finish work for the day. "Wouldn't mind going to that new place in Camden Lock. I'm totally starving and there's no food here, sorry. I've been on the phone to Soph's mum for *hours* . . ."

He dumped his briefcase. "Please turn off that crap."

"What crap?"

"The music."

"It's Lonnie Donegan!"

"Jenny." He pulled off his tie, grinned. "I'm talking about a date for the wedding."

"Wedding?" Jenny froze. Better turn off Lonnie.

"Or have you forgotten that we are engaged?"

"No!" It was just that, compared to the death of Sophie, it, like everything else in the universe, had begun to feel almost insignificant, abstract, a date in the diary that wouldn't happen for a while and could comfortably be ignored in the meantime.

Hurt flickered over his rain-wet face. "Curb your enthusiasm."

She stood up, slipped her arms around his waist. "Oh, Sam, I'm sorry. I'm a little stunned, that's all. We've been engaged for so long and . . ." She kissed him. "After all this time. Why now?"

"Death. It focuses the mind, no?" He stroked her hair off her face. "We've got one life. Let's seize it, babes."

A random, weird thought jumped up in her head: I don't believe him. I don't believe that's why he wants to marry me right now. She pushed the upstart thought away. Yes, they'd been getting on so badly. This must be his way of trying to make things right again.

He put his hand on her jaw, turned her head to face him, to regain her attention. "Life goes on, right, babe?"

She nodded but couldn't help noting that actually it was death that went on and on, and on. Not life.

"Don't cry. I'm not worth it."

She laughed, wiped the rogue tear away. "I don't want you to marry me to *save* me, Sam. I don't need saving. I just need . . ." She hesitated. What did she need? "I think I just need time."

"How much more?" His voice had an edge to it now. "We've been engaged for ages."

Part of her couldn't believe they were having the conversation at all. So many months she'd craved a date, prodded him gently for it, wanted to prove to Sophie, to her parents, that the wedding would happen and she wasn't Waity Jenny. And now? Well, she still felt funereal.

"I'd like to do it as soon as possible."

"As soon as possible?"

"In the summer."

"Next year?"

"This year."

"But . . . but that's not long."

"What's stopping us?"

"Well, nothing, I guess." She dug her nails into her palms.

"You look worried."

"I'm not worried." She was worried. "We're not ready, though. I haven't got a dress. We haven't decided on the venue. . . ."

"Well, you can get a dress easily enough, can't you? And I always assumed we'd just bang up a large tent in my folks' garden."

"Yes, yes, of course." That was logical enough. Her own parents lived in a bungalow built in 1982 with far-reaching views of a chicken farm. His family house was Georgian, enormous, garden like a deer park. What did it matter that she'd failed to enjoy so many Sunday lunches at that house? No, it didn't matter at all.

"I'm reading hesitancy, baby."

"It's just . . . there's so much to do. And I'm really up to my neck in this Help Ollie thing right now. It's taking up a lot of time and . . ."

"Mum will help with all the organizing." Sam's features tightened. "Anyway, you need to get the Muswell Hill ladies to do the donkeywork. It shouldn't fall to you. You're just the . . . the consultant."

"Hardly!" It was now six weeks since that first meeting. They'd had a meeting once a week since, and countless phone calls and emails. Sam already said he wanted her to scale it back. Funnily enough she was discovering that she didn't want to scale it back. That despite her initial doubts she was enjoying being involved. She woke up thinking about what Ollie and Freddie needed, thinking up ways that might make them happier. If nothing else, Help Ollie had given her reason to crawl out from under the duvet in the morning. In a way, and it was hard to accept, given the morbidity of their task, it was kind of fun too, she had to concede that, what with the other women, the collective sense of purpose. And by getting to know Sophie's friends—the life she'd hidden away up there in north

London—Jenny felt she was getting to know another side to Sophie too. And this was important. It meant that in some small way she was still alive. That the story wasn't totally over.

"The wedding will be lovely," he said softly. "It'll make you feel better."

She tried to imagine it. The white dress. The flowers. The confetti. And it made her cry. Oh, God, she was turning into Lydia.

"Don't cry," he said softly. "What is it?"

"A wedding without Sophie."

"Hey, come on." He hugged her.

"She would have been matron of honor and now she won't."

Sam held her by the shoulders. "You can ask someone else."

"No, if she can't do it then no one can. I can't replace her. It would be like pretending I still have a best friend and I don't."

"You might change your mind nearer the time."

"I won't."

"No, you won't, will you?" He sighed, let go of her shoulders and walked over to the fridge to retrieve a beer. "There must be something you can do to get over this." He looked thoughtful, frothed the beer into a glass. "A shrink? Do you think you should see a shrink?"

"Actually I'd like to talk to Ollie." Sam's forehead knitted. She chose her words more carefully. How to explain that without Sophie around to give her blessing she needed Ollie's? "Just let him know, I mean, so he's the first to know. I think that would make a difference."

"For fuck's sake, Jenny." He squeezed the bridge of his nose with his fingers. "This is about *us*. It's got nothing to do with Ollie."

Nine

Something should have stopped them from reaching the altar. That something should have been me. Unfortunately I spent my last meeting with Jenny talking about supermarket loyalty cards. These were not meant to be my last words! They really were not. And now he's gone and set a wedding date.

A few things happened, you see. With Sam. Sam and me. Some were little things. Unsaid things. Others existed only as suspicions and hunches. Others . . . well, there were other things too. I'm not proud of them.

A party, two years ago. It was Wendy Law's thirty-fifth. Tufnell Park, north London. It was a hot, sticky summer's night. Too hot for shoes or long hair. Sweaty and grimy, the streets of London pulsed in the heat. Music poured out of open windows. People fainted on the Tube. Dealers cruised the noisy, hot streets in their convertibles, stereos blaring. It looked like the pavement on Brecknock Road was melting. And in a little walled patio garden off that road we celebrated Wendy's new sapphic epiphany—she'd fallen madly, deliriously in love with a math teacher called Penny. We all had. Penny was totally delicious, supersmart and the dream lesbo lover for any woman. Wendy had never been happier. Their coupling was startling and sexy and satisfyingly ruffled her retard ex who had treated her appallingly. We were all dancing madly outside, old early nineties tunes. Arms in the air. Like you just don't care. That sort of thing. The music whooshed me right back to the time before Freddie was born and I was wild and free and wore red Kickers. I felt sexy for the first time in months. Not like someone who had emptied her boobs of their bounce with excessive lactation or who had a zipper of stitches on her perineum. In short, I felt hot, sexy and twenty-five again.

By two a.m. a hard-core group of inebriated thirtysomethings were dancing wildly. I had the beginnings of what would become a giant blister on the ball of my left foot, the neighbors were complaining and the police had been called. In other words, it was a rockin' party. Even Jenny was dancing with an abandon I hadn't seen before. After months of crap singleton dates with men who were allergic to oral sex—not making this up—she'd settled in with Sam, who was a walking, talking cunnilingus-loving vindication that the crap date purgatory had all been worth it. He was the upbeat end to a women's magazine article. The twist at the end of a comic rom-com. Apart from fancying the pants off him, Jenny saw the idealistic, good man beneath the lawyer's crisp suit, the soft heart beneath the laddish wit. We all did. We thought Sam was great.

We'd done quite a lot of hanging out, me, Ollie, Sam and Jenny. A day trip to Whitstable. Dinners at number thirty-three. A remarkably debauched New Year's Eve involving absinthe and lobster. While Ollie and Sam weren't exactly bosom buddies—Ollie is not the most social animal; he'd happily see no one other than his family and his music studio—they got on pretty well, in the tolerant, buddyish manner of men who are thrust together because of the closeness of their other halves.

I didn't plan to need the loo at the same time as Sam. It just happened that our bladders synchronized. We left Ollie and Jenny dancing to Kylie while we queued outside the endlessly locked bathroom door. I say queuing. Actually we were trying to outdo each other in bad taste seventies rock. Journey! Starship! Kenny Loggins! It was funny, really funny, as things tend to be in the early morning, drunk, after the babysitter has texted to say, "Don't rush back, all fine." I remember snorting with laughter, howling out the lyrics at the top of my voice, thinking I might pee myself. Then suddenly, without warning, it wasn't funny. I hadn't peed myself. No. It wasn't that. It was that his hand was on my bottom. It took a moment to register. Yes, Sam's hand was definitely on my bottom and it wasn't moving. I wiggled it off and made a joke of it, telling him that he was drunk and should go and sober up somewhere and keep his paws to himself. I even tried to think of a seventies rock lyric that would sum it up nicely and make light of the accidental hand but couldn't. Mostly I couldn't because he was looking into my eyes, I mean really looking, like he'd lost something in them. Then he said coolly, "I'm not in the least drunk, Sophie."

"Oh." I laughed, adjusted the waistband of my big white hula-hula skirt. I was still frisky, restless for the dance floor, for dancing motherhood away, just for the night. I hopped from one heel to the other. "Have I got canapé on my tooth or something?"

He was looking really hard now. It felt like I was being sucked into those pale blue eyes, like a little wooden boat pulled toward a giant, hungry whirlpool.

"What?" I said, uncomfortable now, wishing the girl in the loo would get on with it and signal that the wait was almost over by flushing then.

He smiled, a knowing smile. Like he could read what I was feeling, knew how helpless I was to escape. "I know you're the kind of woman who likes to be looked at, Sophie, so I'm looking at you."

"Right," I said, recognizing the weirdness through my drunkenness. We shouldn't be talking like this. Something funny was going down.

"You are so very beautiful, Sophie," he said in a way that was so disarmingly sincere sounding that it froze me to the spot.

"Thanks," I said quietly, glancing around me in case someone was watching or Jenny was coming toward us. There was no one. Yes, I should have said "Fuck off" at this precise point but it's hard when a man is looking at you like that and you've drunk too much and you're not quite sure what's going on. Shamefully, I was a little bit flattered too. For a moment I was not a stay-at-home mother from Muswell Hill. I was Sophie, man magnet. Like I used to be.

"You feel it?" And his eyes flashed filthy.

"Feel what?"

"You know what I mean."

"I don't," I said, knowing exactly what he meant, feeling my body clench with the most appalling arousal. Honestly, up until this point, I'd never felt an attraction to Sam before. It had never occurred to me that he might even be sexy. He was Jenny's boyfriend. That was that. I didn't go there. But now, suddenly, he was someone else too. Someone apart from Jenny, someone who existed in my space, in this private, erotic moment, with me, just me, not me as someone's wife or mother or neighbor, but me as I used to be when I was young and single and could walk out into any street and bring traffic to a screeching halt.

"Sophie . . ." He reached out to me, his hand firm on my waist. I flitted away from him in one move like a dancer. The toilet door opened, a woman came out and I ran in. I shut the door firmly behind me. It was to prove much harder to shut out Sam from my head.

I should have told Jenny, shouldn't I? But I felt horribly guilty and decided to put it down to a blip of high spirits, a drunken conversation late at night in a sexy, charged atmosphere. And Jenny was so happy at that time. She had her hands in the air. She was mouthing the words to "Start Me Up." Was it worth ruining her happiness for a blip? Was it worth telling Ollie, then trying to stop him from socking Sam in the jaw? No. It wasn't. So I told no one and hoped that Jenny and Sam's relationship would run its course sooner rather than later.

I never expected it to last, you see. After that, why would I? The guy had ants in his pants. A cock that wanted walkabout.

The secret was a burden. It was also slightly thrilling. He messed around in my head in that sexy, pureed area between sleep and waking, at the edge of my thoughts, at the edge of my vision. After that I would notice him looking at me over dinner, his eyes always on my mouth. And I'd feel a jolt when his hands brushed against mine, which they seemed to do frequently, and I'd glance up to see if Jenny had noticed. She never appeared to—maybe she chose not to see. And I tried not to flirt, I really did, but it's always come so naturally to me, I'm afraid. It's like breathing. Given the opportunity, why would a woman not want to flex her coquettish muscle? It's fun. Not everything in life is fun. Flirting is.

Then it stopped being fun. It got more intense. In my head. I realized that to stop it all in its tracks I had to reel away from Sam. I started making excuses. Excuses for days out, picnics, foursome suppers. I put it all down to my busy family life, the school, the neighborhood community. And I kept Jenny and Sam as separate as I could from my Muswell Hill social life. Those two worlds had to be kept apart, you see. I didn't want to exclude Jenny, but because Jenny came with Sam, I had no choice.

I comforted myself with the knowledge that it would only be a temporary measure.

I gave their relationship another six months, max. I figured that a guy who'd hit on his girlfriend's best friend was bound to hit on someone else too. It was only a matter of time before he did, and another woman exposed him. But six months passed and nothing happened that ruffled Jenny, nothing that she knew about, at any rate. The relationship was going from strength to strength. When he finally proposed, I must have given the world's most hollow congratulatory whoop. After that point I made a real effort to try to forget what happened at that party. Either that or I had to say something. But what? She was engaged to him. She'd developed this bouncy new walk, like she had little foam wedges in the soles of her shoes, and her eyes shone. The time was never right. And oh, God, maybe there was a teeny part of me that was jealous. I don't feel good about that. I really don't.

Luckily they were engaged for months and months. The wedding never made it to the white stiffie invitation stage. Sam was evasive when it came to setting a date for the wedding and I, along with the rest of Jenny's friends, began to suspect that it might never happen. Nobly, I even encouraged Jenny to demand a wedding date because I knew that this would push Sam away, that he was that type of man. You know the ones: the more you demand, the less committal they are. I thought that if they didn't get married then I wouldn't have to tell her about the party. Or the other things. She would be saved.

I was wrong.

Ten

Hey, Ol." Jenny quickly assessed his mental state. Not looking too good actually. He was wearing grubby tracksuit bottoms, an old Rolling Stones tour T-shirt, and around his shoulders, a pink cashmere scarf. Without thinking, she reached out to hug him. He sank his head against her shoulder and they stood like that for a few moments in silence. It struck her how they never would have done this when Sophie was alive, that somehow the boundaries between what had been a hands-off relationship between a wife's best friend and her husband were blurring slightly.

"First a beard, now cross-dressing," he mumbled, shaking his greasy black hair out of his eyes. "Come in."

She walked into number thirty-three. "I wasn't going to say anything."

"It's Soph's."

"I kind of guessed that."

"Sorry for emotionally blackmailing you round."

"It wasn't emotional blackmail."

"'If you don't come over immediately I might do something silly. Throw myself off the trampoline or something.'"

She laughed.

"I was being a drama queen. Sorry."

"You're allowed to be." The truth was she had been hugely worried about him—he'd sounded so down, monosyllabically depressed—and had grabbed the car keys after that phone conversation and run to the car like a madwoman. She was hugely relieved to see him here, smiling grimly, wearing pink.

"Worse, there's no tea. Sorry." He kissed her on the cheek. "Kettle's blown." She followed him into the kitchen. "Put it on without any water. Went upstairs."

"At least you didn't go out."

"At least I didn't put it on then kill myself. The paintwork would have been completely destroyed. Soph would have been mad."

"She would. Thanks to this kitchen I know the Farrow and Ball paint chart like I used to know the periodic table. Hours she took to get the exact right shade of white—sorry, 'string.'" She checked out the soot mark on the ceiling, unplugged the kettle from its socket and made a mental note to order one from Amazon. There was a mountain of empty beer cans piled in the recycling box. Oh, well, as long as he was eating. She opened the fridge door to assess the food situation. The shelves were crammed with enough foil-covered Pyrex dishes to keep him alive for weeks. It whiffed: not fresh. "Have you not been eating this food, Ollie?"

He fiddled with the fringe on Sophie's scarf. "Kind of lost my appetite."

"Some liquid nourishment here, I see."

"Ah, that's Tash. She restocks the fridge with beer every few days."

"Does she?" Well, that was *not* on the Help Ollie agenda! "Alcohol's a depressant, Ollie," she said, wishing she didn't sound so schoolmarmish and disapproving. "It's not going to help."

Ollie's smile was a flare in the darkness. "Thank you, Mother."
She winced. "Sorry."

"If you could let the ladies know about the lasagna invasion . . .
It's been going on for weeks. Tell them I surrender. I can take no
more. Can it stop now, please?"

"I will report back and request retreat. Ollie . . ." She'd come here
to tell him about the wedding. She'd already put it off on two other
occasions, she wasn't sure why. It never seemed the right time. And
she felt nervous about it. She just couldn't shift the feeling that getting married was a bit like dancing on Sophie's gravestone.

"Thanks, Jen, for dropping everything." He frowned and suddenly looked a hundred years older than he had five minutes before.
Just as handsome, though, funnily enough. "Sometimes, being alone,
especially when Freddie's at school, my head goes to funny places
and I just want to be with someone who knew Sophie like I knew
her. You're the only one. I feel connected to her through you."

Jenny busily cleared a pile of out-of-date newspapers off a kitchen
chair, trying to hide an unexpected flush of pleasure. "You can always
call me. Whatever time of day, you know that." She cleared her
throat, hesitated. "Ollie, I wanted to tell you something." She took
a deep breath. "Sam wants us to get married this summer."

Ollie's face did not change. It was a study in nonplussedness.

"I just wanted to let you know first," she gabbled, feeling silly
now. "Sophie was going to be matron of honor, and I know it will
be, er, difficult for you. But I'd love you to be there. If you can face it."

He smiled, finally. "Of course I will, you doughnut. Jenny Vale
married . . ." He tried the words on for size. "About bloody time."
He hugged her and their faces were suddenly too close. She backed
away, feeling oddly deflated. "Do you think Freddie would like to
be page boy?"

"Ask him." He reached out and touched her arm lightly. "Now
can I ask *you* something?"

"About the wedding?" She knew he'd find it difficult. Poor Ollie.

"No. I was going through Soph's things."

"Oh, right." She blushed.

"Every time I open our wardrobe a tiny, irrational part of me hopes that she'll be in there. That they're not just dresses." His eyes shadowed gyspy black. Had they always been this black?

"I thought I wanted to keep them but now I think that as long as they're there . . . it's like a fucking kick in the face every morning. I can't explain it. Would you sort through them, maybe find them another home?"

"Of course!"

"Just pick out . . . oh, you know. You choose. I've haven't really got the foggiest about fashion, but if you could keep special things for Freddie."

"To be honest, Ollie, I'll probably end up saving Freddie a ton of cheap High Street stuff and throwing away her prized vintage Ossie Clark. I've not been blessed with an innate sense of style, as you can probably tell."

"You scrub up alright, Jenny."

Mortified, wondering if he thought that she was angling for a compliment, or worse, comparing herself to Sophie, she felt the heat rise on her cheeks once more. "And, er, what do you want me to do with the other stuff?"

Ollie's face darkened. She couldn't read it. He looked, as he had done numerous times in the past few weeks, like a totally different man to the one she'd known when Sophie was alive. It was as if Sophie's death had deleted a version of him and someone else was emerging, changing the structure of his face, making it harder and rougher, older. "Oxfam. The mum mafia, I don't know. It makes no difference to me. It's just stuff. Her clothes are not going to bring her back, are they?"

He was wrong. For when Jenny slid back the white wardrobe

doors, there she was, a whole clutch of Nicolas from different years, different parties, shreds of Sophie in the print of leopard spot, in the fluff of a rabbit skin collar, the tilt of a cowboy hat.

There was Sophie's peacock feather dress, the one she used to wear to weddings, when she'd invariably be late, falling through the church doors noisily, turning every head, seeking out Jenny. She remembered how they would stand there wedged together. "Do you reckon it will outlast the wedding registry appliances?" Sophie would joke and they'd both giggle silently until Sophie completely lost it and did the Honk and everyone would turn and glare at them.

Ah, here was the seventies-style caramel silk blouse that she'd worn on their shopping trip a couple of months before she died. This was the time Sophie had bought some yellow heels from Topshop and frog-marched a reluctant Jenny to the tills to buy a navy sequin shift dress—"Not age appropriate!" Jenny had protested, "not age appropriate!"—that now sat unworn in her own wardrobe, like a glamorous relic from a different, sparklier life.

The long cable-knit cream cardie that Sophie used to effortlessly wear to the park with Freddie. (Sophie did knitwear; Jenny wore jumpers.)

Some dresses, unworn, a couple with price tags still attached. There was also a series of more basic dresses and trousers in a Parisian palette of black and gray and navy, the background hum to the times they'd met for coffees in the day, walks in the park, a stolen morning matinee; Sophie's habit of interrupting Jenny's day of editing by luring her for noodles, flour-free lemon cakes at Gail's, or "a quick mosey" around IKEA, "Not to buy. Just to see." They would invariably come home laden with white picture frames, pink plant pots and enough tea light votives to light up north London.

Jenny touched the sleeve of a red vintage dress gingerly, half expecting it to vaporize at her touch like a ghost. This was one of Sophie's favorite dresses, with a sexy slit up the side that showed off her lovely shapely legs. She lifted the sleeve to her nose and sniffed. And there she was again. Sophie's perfume: floral, sexily old-fashioned, the perfume of a 1950s sex bomb. She wondered how many times Ollie had done the same thing, sucked in the sexy essence of her. She quickly let go of the sleeve, feeling voyeuristic.

Two piles. The peacock dress would be kept for Freddie. The jersey dresses would go. The vintage prom dress would be kept. The cashmere sweaters would go. The hats would be kept. So would her wedding dress, obviously, she decided, closing the lid on the white box in which she'd discovered it carefully folded in white tissue paper. The shoes would be redistributed among the mums. Or was that morbid? On she went, tearfully picking apart Sophie's wardrobe, trying her best to discriminate between the clothes that were some-how intrinsically Sophie or valuable and those that weren't. It was hard. Sophie could transform from school-run mum to pop wife to fashion bunny with a swish of a scarf. How on earth would she, Jenny, who hadn't a clue what was Pucci and what Primark unless she studied the label, decide which item was more significant?

She couldn't help but wonder what anyone would make of her wardrobe if she died. Would anyone really get sentimental about her Gap jeans, shift dresses, navy sweaters and rack of white shirts? No, she would leave nothing of note behind. An explosion of T-shirts. A pile of books. Although she did have a very good collection of classic country and western. Perhaps she would be buried with Dol-ly's *Greatest Hits*, like a Pharaoh queen her jewels.

She opened the stiff top drawer of Sophie's dresser. What was this? About a trillion sizes too big. Oh, she realized with sadness, Sophie's old maternity wear. She frowned, puzzled. It didn't make sense. Why had Soph kept it? Sophie had told her repeatedly that the baby thing was all over. That she had tried for a baby with no luck for a couple of years after Freddie was born and had decided to forget about it—she couldn't face the hormonal cyclone of IVF—and end the monthly disappointment. Jenny crushed the clothes to her face. Poor, poor Soph. So she'd never given up hope, after all. Wishing Sophie had confided in her about this, she folded the maternity clothes carefully and respectfully. Clearly you never knew anyone until you'd emptied their chest of drawers.

Soph's knickers. She hesitated. It felt like a violation of privacy. But Ollie had asked her, hadn't he? It would be far worse for him to do this job. Anyway, she could imagine Soph up there in some pillowy heaven laughing her socks off at her friend's prudity. She wouldn't give a toss. When they'd first shared a house at university, a redbrick hunk of crumbling and frequently burgled Victoriana, Soph would pad around in a pair of knickers after a shower, hair wet, conical breasts bobbing, looking for a hairdryer, while Jenny, who'd grown up in a household where long, maroon-colored terry dressing gowns always hid naked flesh—she hadn't seen her own mother in the nude since she was a toddler—did her very best not to appear shocked and bourgeois.

Some of Soph's smalls were reassuringly normal, the fail-safe multipack style from M&S that reminded her of the big yellow ones Soph had worn the night she'd died. But there was also a decidedly slinky contingent, balled neatly to one side of the drawer, obviously *not* designed for practical purposes. Two pairs were actually crotchless! She blushed, trying to push the image of Sophie and Ollie having sex out of her head, knowing that she wouldn't be able to meet Ollie's eyes later if she didn't.

Problem was, Soph and Ollie were one of those couples who it was hard *not* to imagine having sex. They'd had nuclear chemistry. It had been embarrassing to be in the same room as them sometimes. In the early days they'd never stopped touching each other, a hand on a bottom, a hand on a knee, a brush of fingertip against Sophie's lips. Jenny remembered the holiday they'd all gone on together not so long ago: Sophie and Ollie's bedroom had been next door to hers and Sam's and it had been a thin, brickless partition. They'd heard everything. She stuffed the knickers into the bin bag briskly, pushing the memory and its animal acoustics from her mind.

Relieved to have finished the underwear, she started working on the dresser's lower drawers. Parrot green kaftans. A beach sarong. A lilac silk dressing gown in a silk bag. And what was this? Something hard and small wedged at the very back of the drawer, stuffed beneath the polka dot drawer liner. She stuck her hand in and pulled it out. It was a small dark wood box with pretty white shell inlay. Puzzling.

She opened the box carefully, unable to rein in her curiosity. Ooh, letters. A stack of letters, folded neatly. She caught glimpses of handwriting, biro doodles; while others were simply typed. "My beautiful Sophie . . ." Love letters! Oh, God! Startled and guilty to be looking, she snapped shut the box and shoved it back to its hiding place beneath the drawer liner. "Sorry, Soph," she said, looking up at the ceiling. "You dark horse."

Eleven

Absolutely would have paid good money to see Jenny sorting my smalls but I returned to number thirty-three just as she was dropping the black bag into the wheelie bin. "Good-bye, Soph's smalls," I heard her mutter under her breath, making the critical error of releasing the wheelie bin lid before stepping out of the way so that it crashed down upon her head. Sorting a dead friend's knickers is beyond the call of duty, isn't it? Still, I do wish she'd protested more when Ollie suggested giving my things away. Take my smalls! Just not my Acne Pistol boots! I'm not sure I want anyone else to have any of my beloved clothes actually. Well, maybe my sister, Mary, although she hates anything that doesn't come box fresh from Marks and Spencer so she may be slightly grossed out by dead sis's vintage. And I wouldn't mind Jenny taking a few prize pickings, even though she's bound to put the dry-clean on a hot cycle.

Just *not* Tash.

Too late! It's eight p.m. now, three weeks later, Suze's house. It's steamy with the smell of pesto and marinating nappy bags, the windows misted with condensation from London's endless Narnia winter. The Help Ollie squad is sitting in Suze's dark red living room facing off the pile of my clothes on the wooden Indian coffee table, trying not to look scared. Only Tash is eyeing them like a wolf might a small, succulent baby sheep grazing away from its mother. Her fingers twitch at her sides. Her Achilles tendon is stretched, poised to dart forward. The others are less sure, sitting upright on the cat-clawed sofas and drinking wine too quickly. Liz fiddles with her hair. Jenny bites her nails. Suze rises a couple of inches on her seat as she clenches her buttocks to repress wind. Tense times.

"Well *one* of us has to go first, ladies." Tash lurches toward the coffee table, yanks my Jaeger leopard-print skirt out of the pile and flaps it out in front of her. "Come on, let's not stand on ceremony."

Suze takes a deep breath, pulls out a pale blue silk blouse with a pussy bow at the side and holds it away from her body, eyeing it suspiciously, lest it leap up at her and love-bite her neck.

"That'll look great on you," says Tash with a smirk, knowing perfectly well it'll add ten years to Suze.

"You think so?" Suze struggles to push that frizzy foam-wedge of hair through the neck hole. (Suze should sell her locks as mattress filler. Ultimate bounce! No springs necessary!) Tash comes to her aid, yanking it firmly down over her head, releasing an electrical storm of static that makes Suze's hair spark. They're both sweating from the exertion.

"It doesn't seem right, does it?" Liz whispers to Jenny, who is seated next to her on the sofa, sheltering behind a vase full of splayed bare twigs.

"The blouse?"

"No, this." She pulls a long face, glancing over at Suze. "And yeah, the blouse looks a bit rubbish too. How on earth is she going to get out of it?"

"Dunno. I got trapped in a dress once," says Jenny, looking pained. "It was horrible."

Lydia leans toward Jenny on the other side and whispers, "Talking of dresses. I've been wondering, what happened to Sophie's wedding dress?"

Jenny grimaces. "Saved for Freddie."

(Thank you, Jenny. It's now folded like a lily at night. I loved that dress.)

"Oh, God!" Lydia fans herself with a copy of *Homes and Gardens*; a litter of leaflets showers onto the floor. "Don't. It's going to set me off."

Tash and Suze walk over with their new bits. They eye Lydia's emotional magazine fanning warily. Jenny too, I see, has learned to ignore her. Lydia sniffs loudly. I have no idea how such a phlegmatic builder's sniff can come out of such a teeny woman.

"Come on, Lyds," says Suze impatiently, eyeing the fallen leaflets scattered over her stripy rug with irritation. "Let's not get all morbid. Again."

"But it *is* morbid."

"It's what Ollie wanted," said Tash quickly, smoothing down one of my white shirts over her architectural hip bones approvingly. "It really is."

Jenny suddenly slams down her wineglass on the coffee table, leaps to her feet and starts bundling up the clothes in her arms like a madwoman at a jumble sale. "Lydia's right. It's too weird. Shall we just give the rest to Oxfam and be done with it?"

"Good idea," Liz says with a puff of relief, reaching over to fill up her wineglass. "Take all the stuff away, Jenny."

"Oh, but what about these boots?" Tash determinedly pulls on one of my black Acne Pistol ankle boots. Damn. It fits her. "They're too good for Oxfam."

"Ooh. Nice boots." Lydia sits up straight, morbidity forgotten. "What size?"

"My size." Tash knocks her heels together like Dorothy.

I retreat to the corner of the room and crouch down on the dusty edge of Suze's framed Matisse repro print. *My* Acne boots. Mine.

When I wake from my celestial sulk the clothes have been bundled out of sight by Jenny and the tight atmosphere has loosened, like the stitching on the blouse when Suze finally struggled out of it, blinking and sweating like someone emerging after years trapped in a small, dark cave. The wine has wound them all down now too. Good old wine. There's a reflective, dreamy air. Liz is looking sleepy: she was up changing children's urinated bedsheets in the small hours last night. Tash is still admiring the boots. Lydia is lying out on the sofa, hair spilling prettily over frayed turquoise cushions, looking more cheerful. "Ollie and Sophie are forever the perfect couple." She sighs noisily, expelling more air than is strictly necessary to create drama. "They'll never split up now. Isn't that *wonderful*?"

Jeez. Never thought of it like that. Guess there's an upside.

"I read somewhere the other day that couples actually know less about each other the longer they stay together." Suze reaches for a mini pizza. Observational note here. Every time I see Suze she's reaching for food. She's put on at least a stone since I died. It's actually kind of touching: I grieved so much I piled on fourteen pounds! "We assume we know everything so we stop asking," she says thoughtfully. "They're spared that indignity at least."

"Nor will they become one of those couples who sit at a restaurant trying to think of something to say that isn't about the children," Liz adds.

Ha! You think we were never there? Everyone sits at that table at some point in their marriage. It's the one at the back, near the toilets. Bad service.

"Nor will she get to that point when she thinks nothing of fart-

ing loudly while pouring out his Cheerios in the morning," adds
Suze cheerily, mouth full of Parma ham parcel.

Deafening silence.

Lydia's mouth drops open, exposing a hidden brace. "You don't?"

"What?"

"Break wind in front of the hubby like that?"

Suze blushes. It pulsates across her giant pale facescape like the
northern lights. "Well . . ."

She does!

"At least Sophie won't have to face him running off with some
prepubescent," snarls Tash, pushing back her cuticles forcefully with
a cocktail canapé stick. "Not that he would, of course," she quickly
corrects. "Ollie's one of the good ones."

"Let's hope he gets to taste all that with someone else," observes
Liz, as they sit contemplating the farts and other indignities that
Ollie and I have mercifully escaped. "He's only in his thirties."

"Thirty-six." There is a new look on Tash's face, one I've never
seen before. "Too young to be alone forever," she mutters darkly. "Far
too young."

"Too red-blooded," adds Lyds, constructively.

Okay, I'm now rather wishing I hadn't broadcast the fact he was
a needs-it-once-a-day man to them all on numerous drunken occasions while I was alive.

"Interesting, isn't it?" said Tash, eyes flashing. "A thirty-six-year-
old widower is Mr. Eligible, whereas a thirty-six-year-old female
divorcée is secondhand goods."

"You're not secondhand goods!" groans Liz. "Jesus, Tash. You
sound like one of those bitter fat blokes who sit on their bar stools
moaning about women because they haven't got laid since they were
fifteen. The ones with bits of scrambled egg in their hair who don't
fancy Michelle Obama."

"Thanks, Liz!" Tash laughs despite her offense. "Okay, let's put it another way, and be horribly honest: who's hotter, a thirty-six-year-old widower or a thirty-six-year-old widow?"

"Are we talking Angelina Jolie?" asks Lydia thoughtfully, twirling hair around her finger. "Because if we're talking—"

"No, Lydia. We are not talking Angelina Jolie. I'm talking normal. Not loaded either. Because I'm sure I'd have more interest if I *were* loaded, not that I'm talking about myself . . ."

"Absolutely not," says Liz mischievously.

"No, I'm talking about widows." Tash is warming up, getting impassioned now. "I mean, would we be saying that such-and-such widow was too horny to be single for long? I don't *think* so! I think we might find that ick. It's as if women are expected to throw their sexual selves on their husband's funeral pyre in some kind of hara-kiri!"

Good point! I'm with you on this one, Tash.

"*A-hem.*" Jenny is shifting on her seat, uncomfortable at the turn in the conversation. Clearly, she doesn't want to dwell on the sexual habits of widowers. I suspect she'll protect Ollie's chastity for years out of loyalty to me, like a formidable Victorian aunt. "Shall we have a quick rundown on the Help Ollie campaign? It's getting kind of late. I've got to get back."

Everyone agrees, with faintly disguised embarrassment. Parma ham parcels are put back on plates half eaten. Wineglasses are planted back on their bamboo coasters. It's serious again.

"I can report that the supper strategy is working well, Jenny," says Suze, doing one of her officious little councilor coughs.

"Without lasagna?" says Jenny.

"Ottolenghi baked aubergines," says Tash, tapping something onto her iPhone. "With pomegranate."

Oh, jeez. When will they realize that Ollie is a steak and chips and peas man? Put the pomegranate away!

Suze clears her throat. "Let me report back some gaps in his groceries." She consults her pad. "He's out of vacuum cleaner bags,

English breakfast tea and cat food. Who's in charge of placing Ollie's supermarket delivery again?"

Liz put up her hand sheepishly.

"If you could add those to the next order."

"Yes, sir." Liz winks at Jenny.

I like that wink. I like it that Liz and Jenny are becoming friends. I really do.

"Now, have you checked out the Facebook Sophie Brady R.I.P. site yet, Jenny?" Suze asks, tapping her pen on her knee.

Tell you what, *I* have. I have lain on top of the Wi-Fi cloud—feels like sitting on an ant heap, in case you're wondering, itchy with info—and read some of it. Embarrassing and touching is all I'll say. ("Brave?" Reckless more like. "Clever?" Failed my math exam. Twice.) I wanted to correct them, like on Wikipedia, but couldn't.

"There are seventy-five messages in the online book of condolences so far," continues Suze. "I hope we'll triple that number in a week! Make sure you let all your friends know. I'm going to photocopy a note and ask the teacher to put it in year two's book bags."

"Life is *so* fucking unfair!" blurts Lydia suddenly, making everyone jump. "Why didn't someone in a crap marriage die? Why take someone as loved as Sophie? *Why?*"

Oh, Lord, the woman's going to blow. Someone do something.

"Let's take heart from the fact that Ollie could be doing so much worse," says Liz calmly. "Looking on the bright side, well, he's not had a breakdown."

She didn't see him lying naked on the bathroom floor with my pink pashmina over his head last week.

"I can't even begin to imagine how George would cope without me." Lydia sniffs. "Flora would be whipped away by the social services."

"Mine would all have to survive on cat food," observes Liz. "Probably improve their diet considerably."

"And that's why Help Ollie is *so* important," interrupts Suze, clutching her notebook to her pulsating bosom. "It's about the community rallying around and looking after their own. The Big Society! This is *it*, ladies. This is *IT*! We are the rocks against which Ollie can crash! And if he falls we will catch him."

Blimey. Who knew lasagnas could achieve so much?

"Hear, hear!" Tash raises her glass. The room is soupy with feeling.

"We will be there for him until he's feeling better . . ." Suze declares, going into orator mode again. "Or until . . ."

"He can't take any more?" Liz says, exchanging looks with Jenny. The corners of their mouths twitch with repressed laughter.

"*No*, Liz," said Suze crossly. "I mean until . . ."

The room crackles with anticipation. There is a collective intake of breath. I freeze on the wallpaper.

". . . Ollie meets someone else." Suze picks something out of her teeth with the edge of her fingernail. "Don't look like that, Jenny, it can only be a matter of time. Now, anyone for a nice fat green olive?"

Twelve

1. *She*—name tbd—must be kind, clever, selfless and adoring of Ollie and Freddie.
2. She must like cats.
3. She must like six-year-old boys. Lego. Farts caught in cupped hands in the bath. *Toy Story*, 1, 2, 3, on loop every Saturday morning. Football. Jenny. Cleaning sticky yellow wee off the loo seat. Not necessarily in that order.
4. She must not spoil Freddie, only when the moment dictates it, like if he's crying or missing me. She needs to intuitively know when to make the distinction.
5. She must understand I will always be Freddie's mummy and the love of Ollie's life. That's the deal, love.
6. She must be beautiful but not as beautiful as Ollie thought I was.
7. She can't be skinnier than me. Or have better boobs. She can't be the kind of woman who won't eat cake.

8. She must satisfy Ollie in bed, obviously, but not in the way I did. She must be a different kind of lover, so he can't make comparisons, and must not give competitive, forget-the-first-wife blow jobs.

9. She is allowed to have her own children with Ollie but she must treasure Freddie as the firstborn.

10. She must not ever change the living room curtains that I had hand-printed at great expense for a sum so eye watering I never even disclosed it to Ollie. Nor redecorate the sitting room. Ditto.

Editor's note: Does this exclude ninety-nine percent of the women in London? Good!

Thirteen

The letters thumped into her head as if posted through a letter box, making her reverse into the parking space with a loud screech. This is what happened all the time. She'd forget about them. Then, randomly, the letters would be all she could think about and she'd get a tight feeling in her chest, like she couldn't breathe properly. Did Sophie have something to hide from Ollie? A lover? A past that neither Jenny nor Ollie knew about? And why did she, Jenny, care so much? Yes, she hated the fact that Sophie might have kept secrets from her. But she also needed to believe that Jenny and Ollie's marriage had been perfect. Perfection protected the past, kept the boundaries between them all defined, unassailable.

She turned the engine off and rested her forehead on the steering wheel, still so deep in ponder that she did two double takes before registering the woman outside her apartment. Yes, there was a woman standing outside her front door, staring up at the apartment, transfixed. She was wearing a sequined beret that sparkled silver in the sun. Under the beret her long dark hair fanned in the wind, up and out, in an Annie Hall kind of way. There was something about that hair and general demeanor that reminded her of someone. Who? And why was she staring at the house? Sensing she was being scrutinized, the woman glanced over at Jenny but the strands of her long, dark blowy fringe prevented Jenny from getting a proper glimpse of her face. She walked hurriedly away, until, with a flash of sun-hit sequin, the woman turned the corner.

Back inside the apartment, she jumped when she heard a cough. She wasn't expecting Sam back from work so early. "So you're going to Muswell Hill tonight?" He reached for his cigarette box, tapped a fag out and lit it. "Again."

She smiled cheerily—no point trying to talk him round when he was in the mother of all grumps—and made coffee to make the peace. Sam could always drink coffee late in the day. Rarely did anything keep him awake at night: death, divorce, Lavazza, nothing touched the sides. They sat at the breakfast bar in silence, feet dangling from the chrome bar seats. She plunged the cafetiere too quickly. It spurted up over the sides and she felt his fresh irritation at her clumsiness. She mopped up the coffee from the countertop with a tea towel and wished they had paper towels, like a good old Muswell Hill household. But Sam refused to have a kitchen roll in their apartment on account of it being sinisterly suburban and ruining the sleek lines of the Bulthaup kitchen. "Look, I'm sorry, Sam. It's just . . ."

He looked at her with a more forgiving weariness. "I know, I know. Sorry. I suppose I should be pleased you're no longer sobbing under your duvet."

Had she really? The aftermath of Sophie's death had passed in a blur. It was now April. April? She couldn't really remember how she spent her days now, or how she'd got through it. Perhaps things were a little bit better, she realized for the first time. The days somehow had more meaning.

He ground out his cigarette half smoked in the ashtray. "It's just that Ollie's all you talk about, him and Freddie." He gave her a dry half smile. "Oh, sorry, darling. Do I sound like a heartless tosser?"

"No, my love, you sound jealous."

She expected him to laugh—she was joking!—but Sam's blue eyes blazed. "Maybe I am."

She spluttered on her coffee. "Sorry?"

"I feel like you've been stolen from me by Muswell Hill, Jenny. And I flipping well hate Muswell Hill."

"Come on," she laughed, flattered, struck by an image of a leafy avenue swallowing her whole. "What's Muswell Hill got to do with anything?"

"It just winds me up."

She sighed. "Everything winds you up, Sam."

"No. Only certain things. Phony things."

"What's phony about Muswell Hill?"

"It's smug. It's stultifying middle class. It pretends to be in London. But it's in zone one hundred and three or something. It's not even got a Tube."

"Actually you can walk to East Finchley Tube in ten minutes."

"Yeah, if you're Usain Bolt." He stroked the rim of his coffee cup with a finger. He had the cleanest nails she'd ever seen outside a beauty salon.

"Have you ever actually been there, Sam?"

"'Course not. Don't need to visit Baghdad to have an opinion on it, do I?"

"You're being very touchy."

"Well, you've gone to the other side."

"Yes, it's bloody dangerous in the burbs, Sam. Haven't you heard of that new drug, *cake*?"

A smile flickered over his mouth. He was beginning to enjoy

himself. "Those women *plot*, Jenny. From what you've told me you're all plotting."

Jenny laughed, relieved that they were connecting again. "We're not plotting."

"You're like the witches of Eastwick."

"It's the Help Ollie committee, nothing more, nothing less."

"God help the poor bastard." He pondered her for a moment, resting his jaw in philosopher's hand pose. "What exactly are you lot doing?"

"Sorting out Ollie's childcare arrangements, cooking for him, offering practical help," she said, fearing it sounded too woolly. "We've organized a rota of meals to be made and delivered by local mothers, as well as after-school care for Freddie on the days that Ollie can't leave work early. Er, that sort of thing." She hopped down from her bar stool—a high-wire act, never easy, she hated the damn things—and put her arms around Sam's waist, slipping them beneath his shirt to his gym-crunched belly. "Why don't you come? Come to the meeting."

Sam pulled away from her. "Like the reverse psychology, Jenny. No, thanks. I've got the small matter of a wedding to organize. In case you've forgotten, we're getting married in August."

"I know, sorry." Jenny sighed. She should be doing more wedding stuff, and she felt bad that it was falling so heavily onto Sam's shoulders. Leaning against the window frame, she pulled back the heavy beige linen curtains. On the pavement opposite the house, studenty types were engaging in a self-conscious drug deal. A noisy group of young girls, an arm-in-arm mesh of shaggy furs and leopard prints and heels, were tripping past on the way to a night out, their laughs exploding like fireworks in the cold night air, making Jenny miss Sophie afresh with a raw pang, like when something sweet touches a sensitized tooth too close to the root. The raggle of girls turned the corner. Apart from a tramp aimlessly plucking a two-stringed ukulele, the street emptied. She pressed her hands against the cold glass, feeling like she was looking for someone. It took a few moments to realize who that someone was. The woman! That woman, she realized with a nauseous flip of the stomach, who looked uncannily like Sophie.

Fourteen

Secrets, all relationships have them, don't they? The little things we choose not to know about each other, stuffed somewhere we can't see like clothes that we can't bring ourselves to throw away but will never wear again in that zippy nylon bag under the bed.

Sliding between houses, I get little glimpses of all my friends discreetly building little slithers of secrets into the fabric of their day.

Take Lydia, for example. She did not accidentally miss that contraceptive pill. She picked up the blister pack last Tuesday from the bathroom cabinet, stared at it for a few moments, then, without popping one out, put the pack back in the cabinet. Did she mention this to George? Of course not! Did she hump George that night? Of course she did! She ambushed him in a pink teddy nightgown with pom-poms that flicked off her hips.

Take Liz. When she got the Facebook message from Riley, the big love of her life—the screwy, intense, creative one who'd dumped her cruelly before she met her husband, Martin—telling her that he still thought about her every day, how did she respond? Did she write

back telling him that she was happily married with kids and asking
him not to contact her again? No, she did not. She sat staring at the
screen, biting her nails, before finally writing back, "I don't know
what to say," and thus leaving the door wide open for him to respond,
"Say you feel the same." She hasn't responded to that message yet.
But she has gone through her ancient photo album and spent twenty
minutes gazing at an old photograph of her and Riley on a beach in
Ibiza, their eyes sparkling, their bodies baked gold and limbs
entwined. If I'd done the same thing she'd have slapped me. I mean,
how can Martin and motherhood possibly compete? It's like comparing the tummy you had at seventeen with the one that settles
around your middle at forty after two babies and a nightly Sancerre
habit.

While Tash lies to Marko the Wildebeast, her Polish builder, all
the time. I guess the point here is their tryst wouldn't last another
two minutes if either of them told the truth. (That she is bored and
horny and he is well hung, disposable and available.) They have a
little ritual, you see. He knocks three times on her door. The first
question is always, "Anything need doing, baby?" Marko is super
cheesy. He bursts through the front door with thrusting pecto-
rals, Freak Brothers hair flying, pumping with testosterone, like a
soft metal star running onto the stage into a shower of airborne lager
cans. He actually says, "Huh!" Then he shags her hard against the
wall. A few thrusts and he's done, pummeling Tash to the peak.
Afterward he always says, "You love me, baby?" Tash always laughs
and says, "Of course." Bullshit, of course. My dear, she doesn't give
a damn.

And as for Jenny and Sam. Well, things are getting *a lot* stickier
there, let me tell you. The wedding date has piled on the pressure at
a time when Jenny clearly can't cope with it. And it's not just that.
Jenny seems different, like there's something bothering her when
she should be happily anticipating her long-awaited wedding. There

ain't no joy, man. Yes, her best mate's dead. That's probably not lift-ing the mood, granted. But it's more than that. There's a twitchiness about her that she's developed in the last few weeks, a restlessness, some kind of inner struggle. Yes, something has been internalized, sucked in like a breath. For once I haven't the foggiest.

And Sam? Well, he's no stranger to secrets. There I was thinking that maybe, just maybe he wants a date for the wedding because he is finally appreciating what he's got. But what the hell was last night all about then? Who was the woman he was speaking to so intensely at his front door while Jenny was punishing her quads in Legs, Bums and Tums? She didn't look like a Jehovah's Witness to me. They don't do that skirt length. She wasn't selling tea towels either. But she did look like she meant business.

Fifteen

Jenny unclasped her tan satchel and pulled out her creation with fumbling fingers. She so wanted them to like it. It had taken hours. She had a sore thumb from using the crap kitchen scissors. She'd applied the Pritt Stick to her mouth thinking it was lip salve. No, she hadn't got a D in her GCSE art exam for nothing. "Sorry it's taken so long, Freddie. Your mummy fills a lot of pages."

Ollie smiled at her reassuringly and she felt a little less nervous.

Freddie grabbed it. The cover's green holographic cover threw shards of light against his smooth cheek. There was a photograph of him and Sophie on the cover, above which she'd written *The Mummy Memory Book* in her best swirly handwriting in gold pen. He pulled his finger down over it slowly.

"There are boxes, little boxes for you to fill in," she explained, heart in her mouth watching his reaction, willing him to like it.

"So it's like homework?" Freddie looked up apprehensively.

Jenny laughed. "No, not at all," she said, kneeling down to his level. "You just write in it if you want to. Like your favorite holiday with Mummy. Mummy's favorite TV program . . ."

"I like the photos best," said Freddie decisively, pointing to one of Sophie wrapped in a huge yellow towel on the beach, as if trying to absorb the essence of her back through his fingers. He flipped the pages and smiled at the old photographs. Soph's mum had given Jenny a hoard to use: infant Sophie sitting on the beach, all doughy thighs, curly toes, and gripping a sandy red spade; a young Sophie sticking dampers—a flour and water paste—on a stick in front of a bonfire. Jenny had picked through lots of photos of bonfires, actually, the leaping and furious kind that Jenny had never been allowed to build in her own childhood on account of health and safety and the fact that it was a waste of good firewood. She remembered how entranced she'd always been by Sophie's tales of family camping trips to the woods—Jenny's own mother was "allergic to camping" because she swelled up like a whoopee cushion when bitten by midges—and crabbing and sunbathing. It always seemed to be summer in Sophie's childhood.

Jenny's own childhood summers were about fluorescent ice pops from the freezer in the garage, cardigans and picnics on shingle beaches in Sussex aborted because of the rain. They weren't well documented either. Jenny's parents had never come to grips with the "newfangled" camera they'd bought in 1974 and there was a gap of two years, when the camera broke and had not been replaced, when absolutely no milestone of hers was recorded.

As a reaction against her own parents' lack of enthusiasm for posterity, when she went to university she made a real point of photographing as much as she could. This meant that she had a huge mine of memories, so many pictures of Sophie laughing, head thrown back, all her teeth showing, including that funny little chip on her left canine, the result of surfing down the stairs on a teenage boyfriend's skateboard when she was fifteen. No wonder everyone fell in love with her.

At university their photographs, and memories, had become even more collaborative, twisted together like tights spinning in a washing machine. Flashbacks rushed through Jenny's head like a speeded-up silent film: old jokes, fake tan disasters, favorite bands, losing then finding each other at parties, scrawled messages exchanged silently during dull lectures, singing along to Happy Mondays' "Step On" in Soph's crappy old Renault Clio at the top of their voices, holiday scrapes involving too much alcohol and too much sun, bad drugs, bad sex, good sex, one-night stands, shocking home hair dye kits, unrequited love, swapped essay notes, shared lip glosses, pregnancy scares, fertility scares, period pains, the joy of dancing all night and watching the sun come up over a cornfield in the morning and knowing that they'd be friends forever, whatever. Back then absolutely the worst thing that could ever happen was getting dumped by somebody you thought you were in love with. (They'd invariably be fully recovered within three weeks.) Life was about possibilities. Now it just seemed to be about consequences.

She jumped, yanked back from the flashcards of her past. Out of the blue Ollie had put a hand on her lower back, in the gap where her T-shirt had ridden up! It tingled. "Thank you, Jen. The book's amazing."

Her skin fizzed beneath his palm. Horrified by the idea that he'd somehow sense this, she leapt away from his hand as if stung. He looked at her curiously—a look in his eyes she hadn't seen before, registering something—and she blushed fiercely, feeling transparent and caught out.

"Look at that one, Daddy." Freddie laughed and pointed to a picture of Jenny and Sophie as students—*Mummy at College*—before the Halloween ball. Jenny was dressed as a pumpkin, Sophie a far more glamorous wicked witch of the west with black-and-white-striped tights and a billowing black cape.

"Have you seen the one of you and Mummy at the zoo last year?"

She flicked through to one of her favorites, still feeling flustered and midsummer hot. "Ah, there's Mummy and Daddy getting married."

Sophie wore a vintage dress, the skirt bouncing out from her hips fifties-style, a tiara wound from ivy and white flowers on her head, a flower behind her ear. She looked like a naughty rock-and-roll wood nymph.

Ollie pointed to a dumpy-looking figure in a blast of Monsoon cerise in the background. "And there's our Jenny."

She glanced up at him and smiled. Again, there was a funny look in his eye. It felt as if something had passed between them, some silent collective recognition that this was the photographic evidence of how they used to be when things were . . . different.

She was much relieved when he finally left to go back to the studio, leaving her babysitting. The house felt different without him, more reassuringly Sophie's space once more, safer, girlier, less complicated territory. She gave Freddie a bath, admiring his lovely lean boy's body and feeling a fresh twist of sadness that Sophie would not see his shoulders widen, his legs grow long and hairy, his chin develop angles. She tucked him up in bed, next to the uncuddlable beeping Buzz Lightyear toy that he so adored, and read him Dahl's *Twits*. "Just one more page," he begged, until the last page. She stooped down to turn off his side light. "Night, night, sweetheart."

"But . . ."

"It's really late now."

"Tell me about Mummy. Or I won't sleep. Daddy always tells me about Mummy before I go to sleep."

She hesitated. "Does he? Okay. Well, um, Mummy was . . . well, she just wasn't like most people, Fred." She sank back down on his bed again, feeling a maternal buzz of contentment when Freddie nestled his head against her shoulder. Is this how Sophie had felt every night? She'd played it down, but, God, she'd had so much to lose, so much more than Jenny. The injustice that it was Sophie who died, rather than her much more dispensable self, hit her hard again. There was no justice.

"And?"

"Well, Mummy was funnier than most people and cleverer and very beautiful." Freddie didn't look too impressed. He expected better. "She could also be a bit silly, couldn't she?"

Freddie brightened. "I remember her being silly."

"Do you? And do you remember how she loved to laugh? Silly practical jokes. And parties, especially if they involved fancy dress, like in the Mummy book." She wondered if all the stories about Sophie were suitable for Freddie, as so many of the best ones had happened in their twenties and involved copious amounts of cheap white wine. Oh, well, one day he'd be old enough to understand. "Given half the chance I think she would have worn fancy dress every day."

Freddie grinned. "She made me a pirate outfit with a sword holder and everything. I was the best pirate at Josh's party. I won a huge lollipop that cracked my baby tooth."

"That sounds worth cracking a tooth for. I'd like to see that outfit someday." She paused for a moment, remembering. Sophie dancing. Always dancing. Sophie bursting out of dressing rooms in mad red dresses. Sophie playing cards, raising them flirtatiously over her face like a veil. "She was also a very good card player, did you know that?"

Freddie shook his head. "I always used to beat her at Snap."

"That's because you're very clever too. She could thrash Daddy at poker. And she was excellent at chess."

His eyes brightened. "I'm learning to play chess at school."

"She would be very pleased about that."

"I want to learn chess so I can beat Joe. He's in my class. I don't like him."

Who was this Joe? She bit down on her bearlike protective rage, suspecting an outburst would not be helpful. "Why don't you like Joe?"

Freddie shrugged, clammed up. "Dunno."

She remembered how Sophie used to tell her that extracting any information about school from Freddie was like trying to get his Buzz Lightyear to engage in conversation about the Nobel Prize. "If you keep practicing, you will beat Joe at chess. That will feel good."

"Yeah." He pressed his head harder onto her shoulder. "Tell me more things about Mummy."

"Ah, let me see." There was so much stuff about Soph it was almost impossible to pick one thing. "She had a very sweet tooth."

"So her tooth tastes of sweets?"

Jenny laughed. "No, a sweet tooth means you like cakes and sweet things. If we were in a café and I ordered a cake she'd always want the cake I ordered too. A cake monster, Mummy was. Almost as bad as me."

Freddie giggled.

"And you know what, Freddie? You know how Mummy was so good at cooking cakes?"

"Chocolate crispy cakes. We made them with cornflakes. We stirred in melty chocolate. I wasn't allowed to lick the bowl until afterwards."

"Yummy! But do you know the funny thing? Before she had you she couldn't cook *anything*. Well, she could make toast and boiled egg and maybe pasta. But after she had you she learned to cook. She learned so much. And she became one of the best cooks I know."

He smiled. "Because of me?"

"Because of you."

She peered down and saw that Freddie's eyes were beginning to shut. "You made her happier than anything, Freddie."

"I miss her." His voice choked.

"I know, sweetie. She knows too." Atheism be damned. This boy needed to believe. "And she's watching over you."

"Oh, I know *that*," he said, as if she'd stated the bleeding obvious. "She talks to me all the time."

She thought of the conversations that she and Sophie hadn't had and the conversations that they could have had—*should* have had—conversations about Soph's desire for another baby. Those letters.

He twisted Buzz Lightyear's arms upward. "Does she talk to you too?"

"No," she said sadly, as a blast of air shivered Buzz's fabric wings and blew up her nostrils. "She speaks to you because you're special."

Sixteen

This place, whatever it is, this world that runs parallel to yours, is a bit like one of those hard-core Austrian spas where you pay thousands to eat nothing and float around white rooms feeling hungry and helpless. Just without the enemas. It makes me long for simple, sensual things. A crashing Atlantic wave. A warm wind on my face as I cycle. The first lick of an ice cream on a slippery hot day. A cup of sugared tea. God, I'd love a cuppa.

My craving is not helped by the fact that everywhere I turn there are kettles! There are four kettles—four!—on the kitchen counter. Three are gifts from mothers at the school: Lydia, Tash and Posh Brigid with the IVF twins in year four. The nicest kettle is from Jenny, of course. (She knows I'm not the kind of woman who'd ever let a white plastic Russell Hobbs anywhere near my work surface.) Still, no one needs four kettles.

You can't take them with you. I can tell you that for sure. Death is for minimalists.

It's ten a.m., Saturday morning. Ollie is staring at the kettles, rubbing his fingers anxiously through those stiff black hairs exploding from his chin. I know from the exact angle of the arrow between his eyebrows that the kettles are upsetting him. That the kettles are making him feel obligated to the givers of the kettles; i.e., the gift of a kettle will almost certainly require the offer of a cup of tea to the giver of the kettle. It is like the flowers that he had to vase: easier if they didn't arrive in the first place.

No, Ollie is not a sociable beast, nor is he a tea fan. He likes his caffeine, and his social life, condensed into an adrenaliney gulp. The exhaustion of the English breakfast tea bags in the tin is therefore nothing to do with him and everything to do with the endless roll of—mostly female—visitors. That's what we English women do when someone dies. Drink tea. And shop. Incidentally, Lydia's online shopping habit is spiraling out of control. How much smart kitchenware does one household actually need? It won't bring me back, hon.

Ollie drums his fingers on the wooden work surface—rotting, since it is now left to puddle with water—waiting for Freddie. And where is Freddie? Freddie is swimming. Drumroll . . . with Jenny!

A word on this extraordinary event: Jenny hates swimming. More than this, she hates swimming in municipal pools. She hates the changing rooms with their wet verrucular tiles, their lack of privacy. She hates exposing her body to the indignities of a swimsuit. And she hates getting her hair wet. (FYI, chlorine makes her highlights go green.) So imagine my shock when a few minutes ago I spread out through the filter vents into the lukewarm, urinated water of the local pool. There was Jenny standing upside down, her hair whipping around her, her navy swimsuit—Speedo, only Jenny would wear Speedo, as if it were Basingstoke, 1985—gaping at the top, those fantastic bristols dropping toward her chin, only her pale chunky feet stamping above the surface, like a drunk synchronized swimmer. A couple of feet away, swinging on a metal ladder, wearing his red goggles, was Freddie, howling with laughter. And I realized then that Jenny will do anything, absolutely anything, to make Freddie happy, even if it involves standing upside down in a pissy municipal swimming pool on a Saturday morning when she could be in bed with Sam. And I love her completely for that. Feeling reassured and not wanting Freddie to pick up on my distracting wavelength—am wondering if he is in fact sensitive to my presence and has a hard-wired mum-sensor—I shot back through the vent, deep into the labyrinth of heaters and pipes in the pool room; then, passing like a small cloudette of chlorine-scented vapor back over the streets of north London, I came home. And here I am.

As time goes on—can you believe I've been dead for more than four months now?—I'm getting more confident about leaving the house and getting out and about, like a person learning to live with a new disability. My disability is that I don't exist—quite a handi-cap, when you think of it. And I really don't like being invisible. There are no second glances. No whistling builders. I can't help but wonder if this is what old age would have been like.

On the plus side, there are no fares up here. No queues. No stick-ing an Oyster card into a machine and the machine not being able to read it and dozens of people behind you clicking their tongues. (Whenever I see that now I want to swoop down and yell, "One day you'll be *dead*!" in their ears, just to see if it makes them jump the turnstiles. Really, what's the worst the London Transport police can throw at you?)

Sometimes I can get to a place miles away in the time it takes a live human to inhale and exhale their coffee breath: I'm a Japanese high-speed train of a spirit. Other times I cannot move, just cannot; I'm leaves on the line. It's as if I'm falling asleep, or zoning out, or whatever you call sleep when you're in my state—dead to the world?—and when I come to hours later, sometimes days later, I am filled with a terrible fear that something might have happened to

Freddie and Ollie while I wasn't watching over them. But, thank goodness, it never does. It won't strike twice, will it?

Ollie is walking upstairs now, one hand on the banister, the other dug deep into his pocket. He's always got his fisted hands thrust into his pockets these days, giving him the air of a moody teenager. I follow softly behind him, like a whisper of breath against the iron filing black hairs on the back of his neck. With every step, his body releases a tiny whiff and I gorge on it, swilling his essence round and round inside of me, like a sommelier with a fine wine. It is never enough.

He walks into our bedroom, slumps on the blue velvet throw and drops his head into his hands. I curl around his shoulder blades like a feather boa and feel the rise and fall of his bones. He sits like that for some time, head in hands, listening to the sounds outside the window. A car revving. Birds. Someone calling their dog. He flicks through photos on his iPhone. Me in different settings—leafy parks, Cornish beaches, coming down a slide in Kew Gardens with Freddie on my knees, naked in bed eating an almond croissant—and he stops at the naked in bed one, which I think was taken in the summer because I've got strap marks. Then he clicks off his phone, gets up and walks to the dresser. For one awful moment, I wonder if he's going to rummage through my drawers and find the letters. But he doesn't. He opens his sock drawer, that unfathomable cargo hold of mismatched socks. And he pulls out . . .

My knickers! Lordy. The palest pink Agent Provocateur knickers he bought me for Christmas last year, the ones with the little red ribbon ties at the hips. How did they escape Jenny's knicker cull?

Ollie always did love these knickers. They are the kind of knickers that proved their worth by the rapidity with which they were removed. I can barely watch as Ollie takes the knickers and buries his nose in them. He falls onto the bed, knickers still covering his mouth and nose, red ribbon tickling his chin. And then . . . Oh,

God. He unzips his fly, shoves his hand down his jeans, grabs his erection and starts to move his arm.

O-kay. Weird now. I sink back into the wall. He has always had a high sex drive. And sex is life, so I don't know why I'm shocked. Perhaps it's because the sight of Ollie masturbating reminds me of everything I have lost and will never know again: his pumping heart against my breastbone, his soft groan, the salty stickiness dripping down my thigh.

Doorbell! It's like a scream in the softly panting silence. Once, twice. Ollie curses and starts hopping downstairs, one sock on, the other in his hand. Flushed and sleepy—he's a postcoital dozer—he is shoving his shirt into the back of his jeans, lolloping down the stairs two at a time. He trips over Ping Pong, who is regurgitating a Garibaldi biscuit onto the sisal matting.

Tash is standing in the doorway. *Tash!* Wearing red lipstick.

Now, call me paranoid, but I have never seen Tash wear red lipstick. She is not a red lipstick woman. She wears soft pinks and taupes. She is from the Bobbi Brown school of discreet makeup, not a *woo!* M.A.C. girl. Things have changed.

Tash beams. She is holding a heavy white plastic bag that pulls on her palm. "Beer."

"Ah, brilliant." He stands there for a moment, as if trying to remember what social convention dictates he say next. She doesn't budge. She is waiting. "Er, come in," mumbles Ollie.

Tash steps over the threshold and hands him the bag of cold beers.

He smiles. "You don't need to keep doing this, Tash."

Tash waves her hand. "It's the least I can do." She glances around, taking in the details, looking for signs of not coping. "Where's Freddie?"

"Jenny's taken him swimming."

Tash grins. They are alone!

"Would you like a cup of tea? I have a range of water-boiling appliances in which to make it."

Tash puts her hand across her mouth and laughs like a little girl. "I wasn't the only one to buy you a kettle?"

"Nope." He goes into the kitchen, bag of beers in one hand, old sock in the other. "But thanks anyway."

"Looking tidy in here," notes Tash approvingly, sitting down at the kitchen table and resting her bosom on its surface for support, which has the effect of pushing up her cleavage and making it spill out over the top of her blue denim shirt like a rising loaf of bread. As I have settled directly above her, on the smoke alarm, I get an eyeful.

Ollie throws his spare postmasturbatory sock on the work surface then begins to open all the cupboard doors, looking for biscuits. He's clearly had practice at this tea game, knowing that all women would rather have a biscuit with their tea than not, even if they don't realize it until it's winking at them from a saucer.

"Jammy Dodger?"

Tash is not a Jammy Dodger type of woman either. She is a low-carb cracker woman. She takes the Jammy Dodger.

Ollie glances at the clock and sighs. "I guess it is too early to have a beer."

Yes, far too early.

"Never too early." Tash grins. "It's the weekend. I'll join you."

He grabs a beer from the bag, puts the rest in the fridge, sloshes it frothing into two glasses. Then he sits opposite Tash. He stares. No, he cannot help but notice how beautiful she is, can he? No man could. Nor can he help but notice that cleavage. He's always been a boobs man.

"How *are* you?" she asks in that way that suggests he can confide in her, even if he can't with other people.

I'm starting to prickle now. I mean, I *like* Tash. I did like Tash.

We were thrown together at the school gate at reception and her son Ludo gets on well with Freddie, which I'm grateful for as Ludo's one of those slightly thuggish testosteroney boys you don't want to get on the wrong side of. And Tash has been so helpful since I died. *But* . . . she's not the kind of friend I'd have if I didn't have Freddie. She's one of those fun but intense women who always leave you slightly drained. Her conversation is urgent, dramatic, especially if it involves her, which it usually does. And you know the telling thing about her? The screensaver on her phone is not a photo of Ludo. It is a photo of herself, in a white vest, laughing, holding a tennis racket, like something from *Sports Illustrated*! What mother has a photograph of herself rather than her child on her phone screensaver?

Ollie's eyes dart to her cleavage and away. She squeezes her arms together. His eyes are sucked back again. She's waiting for an answer to her question.

"Up and down," says Ollie, trying not to look at her tits.

"Tell me about it." Tash bends down to stroke Ping Pong under the chin. She looks up and fixes him with an eyelash-fluttery stare. "Oh, Ol. Are you not able to find pleasure in *anything*?"

Ollie reddens. He was wanking less than ten minutes ago. "Um . . ."

Tash grins. And it's like she knows. She's sniffed out the fug of sex. I want to shout down at her that it was *my* knickers he was bringing himself on, not her boobs. Put the bazookers away, woman! Save them for Marko the Wildebeest.

"I've been busy. So much stuff to do . . ." He drifts off. He is thinking of court cases and compensation claims and all that other stuff that his brain is so not able to deal with right now. "Thank you for having Freddie after school. It's helped a lot."

"God, anytime!" She rolls her eyes. And it's then that I realize she's wearing false eyelashes. Falsies! At eleven o'clock on a Saturday morning. I'm willing a false lash to drop off and stick on the end of her nose like a giant nostril hair. "Freddie's been a pleasure. A civilizing influence on Ludo. You wouldn't know that—" She stops herself.

Wouldn't you? Something tightens inside of me.

"That's good. I guess that's good." Ollie is studying her face in that quietly intense way he's perfected, his eyes feeling their way across her perfect features like a blind man's fingers on braille.

"Ollie . . ."

There is something about her tone of voice that unnerves me. It is quiet and intimate. It is a voice that I have never heard her use before. It is certainly not a voice that she would ever use to address my husband while I was alive.

"I know it must be hard, so hard on your own. If ever you need . . ." She looks up at him from beneath the falsies. ". . . female company."

Female company! She's been spending far too much time with corny Poles. I am shaking with indignation. The little red light on the smoke alarm starts to beep on and off very quickly. Ollie looks puzzled, then something passes over his face and I know that he knows what Tash is referring to.

"Dinner. A comedy night . . . something that might cheer you up." She stares at her fingers, clearly disappointed that he hasn't jumped.

The more indignant I get, the faster the light on the smoke alarm flickers, as if it's picked up some kind of energy. Or perhaps I really am so incensed I'm actually smoking.

"Thanks." He shifts his feet under the chair, fingers the edge of the newspaper on the table. The air in the room is beginning to vibrate like a plucked guitar string.

"It's just that, you know . . ." She speaks very quietly. "I've been on my own since divorcing Toby. I know what's it like. That's all. I know what it's like."

You have no idea! I want to shout but can't. The light on the smoke alarm blinks even faster.

"Not that I'm equating what I've been through with what you've been through," she corrects quickly. "Not at all."

"Fucking smoke alarm." Ollie suddenly stands up, walks across to Tash's side of the table, stands on a chair and reaches up toward me on the ceiling. His T-shirt lifts up at the front as he stretches, showing a slither of adorably hairy brown belly. He presses the reset button and it stops misbehaving. He steps off the chair but before he has a proper chance to launch himself out of her orbit Tash throws her arms at Ollie's waist, lassoing him like a bison. She rests her blow-dry against his belly as Ollie stands there helplessly. "Oh, Ollie, you poor love," she says.

And it is only then that I see something that hits me harder than the No. 23.

Tash is wearing my Acne Pistol ankle boots.

The smoke alarm starts to wail then. Tash and Ollie leap apart.

Seventeen

Jenny couldn't shake the feeling she was being followed. She'd first noticed the white Fiat, one of those cutesy bubble-shaped ones, near the woods. It had been on her bumper all the way back from Highgate. It was that woman again. The woman who looked like Sophie who was hanging outside of the apartment that evening the previous month. She was sure of it. Again, a stupid, irrational part of her wondered if it really were Soph—admittedly somewhat plastically altered—come to tell her that she'd staged her own death. If only she could stop the car and ask the woman questions that only Sophie would know the answers to. (Q: In what year and where did I end up in A&E because of dry martini poisoning? A: 1996. St. Mary's, Paddington. Q: What was the name of the man with whom I was violently sick while snogging? A: Chris Butterworth, outside Hacienda, Manchester, 1992. Q: What is my favorite sexual position? A: Head in the pillow, bum in the air. Blimey, hadn't done that in a while.) And, yes, she would ask Sophie about the love letters too.

Checking her mirror again, she was relieved to see that the car had gone and she rationalized that there were hundreds of Londoners who might drive from Muswell Hill to Camden at any hour of any day. She was being paranoid.

When she got back home Sam was spread out in the living room with a newspaper, cigarette dangling from his lips. He didn't look up. "How was the lunch with Soph's mum and sister, babes?"

"Sad. Sweet. Kind of funny." She smiled, happy to find him in such a good mood. He'd been unpredictable and irritable in the last few days. And he'd been listening to Radiohead, never a good sign.

He looked doubtful. "Funny?"

"We laughed a lot about things she did. Freddie was writing it all down in his Mummy Memory book. Bless." She smiled and shrugged. "I guess it hit home how much everyone loved her."

"She was indeed much loved." And for a moment he looked soft and vulnerable and almost unbearably pained.

"I wish you'd been there, Sam."

He blew out a smoke ring, puffed away the sadness from his features. "You know I'd just be this eejit in the corner saying the wrong thing."

"No, you wouldn't," she said, feeling sorry for him. He really did struggle to express his emotions. She was sure he'd feel so much better if he let them romp a bit more freely. "Honestly. Ollie would have appreciated some grown-up male company."

"Next time, eh?"

Was Sam avoiding Ollie? It did look like that. Or perhaps he couldn't face up to death full stop. Some people were like that. Her phone started ringing, interrupting her thoughts. She pulled it out of her handbag, glanced at the interface and pinged it to voice mail. "Sorry, Tash again."

He brightened. "Tash Wright?"

"Yes. Er, how do you know her surname?"

He blew out a thick rope of smoke. "Didn't I tell you she phoned me last week?"

"Really?" she said, forgetting for a moment that she'd given Tash Sam's number weeks before. "She wanted advice?"

He rolled his eyes. "Yeah, asked the Questions."

She knew all about the Questions. Since Sam's friends had hit their forties there had been many discreet inquiries about divorce. Tash was probably after a free bit of legal advice in the same way she'd been after a free pair of ankle boots.

"She can talk for England, that one. It's a small world, as it turns out. . . ." He stopped and took a lug on his cigarette, frowning. Something was bothering him.

"What?"

He shook his head. "Just a couple of people we both know. Knows Seb Lewis at Pulson Partners. Small world. Actually she knows his sister."

"Oh, right," she said, not really relishing the coincidence. Sam was one of those people who appeared to be five rather than six degrees separated from everyone else. Especially women. "Sam, it's really weird," she said, changing the subject and sitting down next to him on a scratchy wicker floor cushion. "I had a funny feeling that I was being followed in my car on the way back from lunch." Spoken out loud, it sounded even more monstrously silly.

He looked up, startled. "Followed? By whom?"

"Some woman. On my bumper all the way back from Muswell Hill to Camden." She rubbed her temples, trying to rub some sense into her head. "I don't know. I just noticed her, that's all."

"Woman?" Something unreadable passed across Sam's eyes. He smiled. "Perhaps one of Ollie's new acolytes want you taken out. It's a murky world, the world of the new widower."

"Yeah," she laughed, resting her head against his knee, suddenly grateful that she had him. That she was not on her own. Like Ollie.

After dinner they had sex. Jenny faked an orgasm. It was the first time she'd faked with Sam. As she'd hoped, he promptly rolled over, satisfied, and fell asleep. Needless to say, she couldn't sleep. Her brain was like the bluebottle she could hear banging itself between the double glazing. So when her phone bleeped at two a.m. it was a relief that she was not the only person awake. She turned on her side to read the text.

"U up?"

Her heart quickened. She thumbed back a reply, keeping one eye on the sleeping form of Sam, who was snoring now. "U OK?"

"Blk dogs. Can't sleep."

"Nor me."

She sank back into the bed, sweating now, heart pounding, clasping the phone, willing Ollie to text back. After ten minutes he still hadn't. Her mind started to gallop. Was he in a bad way? What if he did something silly? No, that was stupid. Then again. Anything could happen. He was so up and down. And she wasn't sleeping anyway. And there would be no traffic at this time of night. Sam wouldn't even notice she'd gone, would he?

She drove north in record time. The moon was low and heavy in the sky, full, tarnished silver, and London's empty streets unfolded before her like a computer game. She didn't ring Ollie's doorbell for fear of waking Freddie. Nor did she need to, as Ollie must have seen her shadow through the glass, opening the door immediately. He pulled her toward him, sinking his chin onto her shoulder, where it wedged in the fleshy bit.

He stank of booze.

Even in the half-light she could see he looked terrible, piratical. Then she wondered what she herself must look like, no makeup, bed hair, leggings and Sam's old jumper that she'd thrown on in the blur of the bedroom. "I'll make a cup of tea," she said, sounding uncannily like her mother in times of crisis.

Ollie stumbled into the kitchen in the clattery noisy manner of a drunk man trying to be quiet.

"Stop drinking, Ol," she said, pulling water into the kettle. "You've got to stop it. It's not helping."

He scoffed. "It's helping me."

"No, it's not." She leaned back against the cool brick wall. It broke her heart to see him like this.

"I want her, Jenny. I want her back."

"I know," she replied softly, unearthing two cleanish cups from the cupboard, wishing she hadn't admonished him for drinking. She'd love a stiff drink herself.

"I can't stand *this*," he growled with sudden, startling ferocity. "I can't stand . . . the days . . . the nights. How long do I have to fucking wait?"

"What for, Ol?" she asked softly.

His gypsy eyes flashed. "How long do I have to wait before I have sex again, Jenny?"

Sex! Oh! The question danced provocatively on the delicate boundaries that protect friend from friend's husband. She could feel the heat rise on her cheeks. *"Well . . ."*

"I've embarrassed you, sorry." He shook his head, despairing of himself, then looked up and grinned wolfishly in a way that made something inside clench. "I promise you I haven't lured you round here to have a pop."

"Don't be stupid. I know that." Did she? Yes, yes, she did. Of course she did.

"It's just sometimes my . . . mind boils over."

"I guess it must be very hard." *Hard!* Why had she said "hard"? She blushed furiously again and fumbled in the cupboard for a tea bag. Her clumsiness activated an avalanche of tea bags and takeaway ketchup sachets down on her head.

"I think I might have just had an offer actually."

The boiling water splashed over the sides of the cup all over the work surface. "Really? God. Who?"

He looked at her deadpan, raised an eyebrow. "Tash."

"*Tash!*" Oh, no. She crushed her hand to her mouth in horror. "You didn't . . ."

He looked sheepish. "No. But part of me wanted to."

"Right. Right." She didn't know what to do with herself. She wanted to stick her fingers in her ears. Tra-la-la-la. But then again . . . *Tash!* Outrageous! Tash would never appreciate Ollie. She'd never understand him. She'd . . . she'd use him! And worse . . . how dare she?

He slumped back against the wall. "And now I feel like a piece of shit."

"I'm sure this is all normal stuff," she said briskly, wondering about the box of letters. Had he found it? Was this why he was think-ing about other women? Had something in them given him the green light to seek alternative sexual gratification? No, no, her mind was playing tricks on her.

"You think so?"

"Well, it's a *bit* soon," she managed, her voice high and squeaky. She despised herself at that moment for not giving him her blessing. That was clearly what he wanted. She was the closest he got to Sophie and he was using her as a conduit to get permission to have sex. Damn. Why couldn't she give it? That would be the humane response.

"When is not soon, Jenny?" he growled from behind his long, dark fringe.

"I just don't know, Ollie." The full force of the late hour hit her all at once. She was totally exhausted. She must get home. She wished she'd never come over here so late. What if Sam woke up and found the bed empty? What was she thinking being here in the small hours?

"You think I'm a fucker for even mentioning it, don't you?"

"No!" Yes.

He sank his head to the table in despair then. Appalled, blaming herself for her inappropriate prudity, she stroked his arm, unable to hug him as she normally would have done in case he suspected she was doing a Tash too. He looked up, eyes ink black in the early morning gloom. "I don't want to be alone, Jenny. I want to love and be loved." He dropped his head into his hands. "Oh, fuck, now I sound like a James Blunt lyric."

"For what it's worth I think you're doing brilliantly," she stuttered. He must think her so priggish, so deeply uncool. "You will meet someone else eventually, in time, of course you will."

"I can't fucking stand that idea," he spat out.

"But you just said . . ."

"I know. Both are true."

"Tea."

He pushed the tea away from him as if the sight of it revolted him. "That's the head fuck."

"You've got to think of Freddie, that's all." She put her cup down. "Stating the obvious, sorry." The atmosphere in the kitchen tightened. She really must get back. It was a stupid idea coming here. "Look, it's late. I better go." She did up the buttons on her coat with clumsy fingers. Her head was messy all of a sudden, all whooshes and hisses, a tangle of contradictory thoughts. And then there was that strange, curdly excited feeling in her stomach that she couldn't explain.

He put a hand upon her arm. "I see Sophie in you, Jenny."

Words clumped in her throat. The silence of the house started to pound around them.

"You two were so tight it's almost like a little bit of her has brushed off on you." He hesitated. "Or maybe it's the other way round."

She didn't want to be compared to Sophie. No woman would. "I better get back."

He studied her intensely. "You're spending too much time up here, aren't you? Sam pissed off yet?"

She bit her lower lip hard, fighting tears, suddenly feeling immensely gullible for having driven through the night to be with Ollie, imagining she was so important when all he wanted was permission to shag Tash. It was embarrassing. She was embarrassing. "If I'm crowding you out, I'm sorry."

He stroked featherlight fingers across her cheek. "Jenny, Jenny. You're not crowding me out." She was paralyzed by his touch, the slight rasp of his fingertips. "I'm so pleased you exist; you've no idea how pleased I am that you exist."

The curdly feeling in her stomach became something else, a tugging in her lower body, something so tidal, so powerful, that it stole her breath away. Suddenly it felt like anything might happen.

"Daddy," a little voice whimpered from the landing. They both jumped. "I've wet the bed."

#100 01-24-2018 9:27AM Item(s) checked out to 23410002619074.

TITLE	BARCODE
DUE DATE	
Afterwife	33410012261
279 02-07-18	
Before I go to sleep : a novel	33410011258
870 02-07-18	

Porter County Public Library

Renew: 531-9054, pcpls.org, or PCPLS app

Eighteen

Is it just me or might Jenny be going ever so slightly crackers?

She keeps twitching the curtains of her apartment, staring out at the street like an actress in an TV domestic crime drama. Who is she looking for exactly? And why on earth did she wake up at five a.m. this morning and bellow, *"Don't touch the box!"* scaring the living daylights out of Sam, and me too, quite frankly. Sam had to shake her to make her calm down and bring her back to wakeful sanity. And did I mention that she has still done absolutely nothing, *nothing* about her wedding dress? She has not even bought her wedding shoes! She's only got three months to find the shoes, and it takes her two years to choose a flip-flop. Her roots are three inches long too, slightly green. Dolly Parton would be appalled. Although I do not think that marrying Sam is the best idea in the world—could in fact be the worst—if she is going to do it, she'd better do it properly.

No, she's not herself. Really not. Picture this. Earlier Sam popped out and brought her back a bunch of daffs, which was sweet, give him that. Jenny seemed to barely notice them. She stuffed them into a vase, snapping their stems and making the petals fall off. Inconsequential? I think not! This is a woman who has a photograph of her favorite tree (wild cherry) above her desk, who collected cactuses rather than Barbies as a child and occasionally sings Dolly's "Jolene" to her pet bonsai tree.

It's evening now, eight p.m. And she's still looking a tad deranged. Sam is cooking dinner. She tells Sam she's going to change and disappears off to the bedroom. Is she changing into something slinky? Is she hell! She has put on flannel pajamas and, Jesus wept, knitted *bed socks*. Jenny, have I taught you nothing? The bed socks are purple. Purple! No woman under seventy who is in charge of her own marbles and wardrobe wears purple bed socks.

She emerges without a hint of shame. Sam glares at the bed socks as if they are a personal affront, which of course they are. If socks could talk these would be saying, "You're not getting laid tonight."

She stares dreamily out the window from her parrot perch on the bar stool while Sam stirs prawns and noodles around the gleaming wok and tells her about his client who is fighting his wife for custody of the Aga. She smiles like she's pretending that she's listening. He tells her that his mum has invited them for lunch on Sunday and that she is making beef Wellington and trifle and could Jenny bring the cheese? Nothing too French and stinky. That there's a Tube strike on Monday. That the TV license needs renewing. That Berlin is the hottest city right now and they should go for a weekender, shouldn't they? Jenny nods, not meeting his eye now, suddenly looking stricken. She cannot manage more than a few noodles and does that gulpy thing when you're trying to eat and not cry at the same time. It never works. The throat's not wide enough. You've got to do one or the other. I'm not sure if Sam's noticed or not.

Then he has to notice. As he swerves toward the table, glossy Patisserie Valerie tarte tatin balanced precariously on his palm, she starts to cry. Is it the tarte tatin? Sam asks. Not. Is it Sophie? Sam asks. Jenny says maybe, but she doesn't know. Sam looks irritated. Men hate this kind of answer. They'd rather women wouldn't cry in the first place and if they do cry they like to have the reason hoisted like a flag on a ship so that they can offer a practical solution and move the issue on so it doesn't ruin their supper. He unwisely suggests that she go shopping for her wedding dress tomorrow. This will cheer her up, won't it?

Oh, dear, this will not! Jenny drops her head into her hands and sobs a goddamn river.

Sam puts his arm around her shoulders. She rests her head against his belly and frowns.

I watch the evening slide uneasily around them. Telly noise. Wine. A bubble bath. Jenny's head held too long beneath the froth of bubbles so that she emerges red faced, gasping for breath. They're in bed now. And she's still wearing those damn bed socks. Undeterred, Sam puts a hand on her hip, turns her toward him. He slips his other hand between her legs.

I shouldn't be watching. But it's kind of compelling watching your friend having sex. You know you shouldn't look but you do. I'm a little shocked. I'd have thought Jenny would be a bit more of a live wire actually—she used to be. But her body is very still as he makes love to her.

He's doing the jiggy finger between her legs now, cradles the back of her head in his hand, tells her she's sexy. He enters her with two small ricochet movements. Pummeling faster now, eyes shut. She's looking over his left shoulder. Her lashes are wet, half closed. And it's then that I see it. That look.

That, unless I'm much mistaken, is the look of a woman making love to a man and thinking of someone else.

Nineteen

This is beyond a joke. Tash is back in my boots again. You'd never know that she had twenty-one pairs back at her house in transparent plastic storage boxes and that's not including her multicolored Hunter Wellie collection. She wore my boots when she shagged Marko the Wildebeest against the bathroom wall last week too, leaving a slick of Frizz Ease on the paintwork. And she's had the gall to wear them to the school gate this morning. It's not just me. Other mothers are noticing too, these dead wife's shoes. Those Pistol boots that everyone commented on when I bought them—they were the hot boots of the season, featured in every magazine—and much lusted after.

Posh Brigid is staring, looking puzzled, the collection box for the school playground fund frozen in her hands. Now this is something. Brigid wouldn't notice if she went out of the house with a bra on her head. She wafts through life trailing children—she has five, looks like she's had none—and is so posh that she is a second cousin three times removed to Prince Philip and sometimes in the summer doesn't bother to wear shoes at all. Meanwhile Emily, a key PTA orator, bossily manning the cake stall, is talking to Tash's boots rather than her face and thoughtlessly handing a child cupcakes, not the requested flapjacks. Tash curls the right foot self-consciously behind the left.

I tried to tell her earlier while skimming over the dust-free edges of her wardrobe doors. I really did. But all I could do was ruffle the air molecules. I keep forgetting that I cannot speak, that the words just roll back and forth, cold and hard on my icy tongue like frozen peas. And why was I on her wardrobe doors, you ask? Spying. That's what.

Come on, she's a 34D and two genes short of Katy Perry! Plus, she's looking after Freddie two afternoons a week, which gives her an inside advantage. While there appears to be nothing I can actually do to stop the military march of her seduction other than activate smoke alarms—of all the paranormal powers to have, honestly—I still feel that it is my duty as a dead wife and mother to fully investigate her suitability to the post of shagging my lonely, heartbroken husband. Let alone replacing me, which is, I'm beginning to suspect, her end game.

So that's why I've been on Tash's trail all week, waiting for her to slip up. As *yet* she has not fully incriminated herself. She has not attended an STD clinic or shown any signs of an addiction to cocaine or Calpol Night. There was a wobbly a couple of days ago when a gym-bulked plumber lingered for an unnecessarily long time around her sink's U bend and Tash girlishly twiddled a tendril of dark hair around her finger then sucked it, letting down all of womankind who try their damnedest to speak in gruff, matter-of-fact tones to builders so that they're not overcharged. But the inappropriate divorcée sex didn't actually happen. But then Tash is no fool. She's not about to waste her erotic energies on a plumber. Not when a recently liberated music producer is living a few meters from her house.

I'm not stupid. I can see, objectively speaking, that Tash is hot. If one was to go there—too late for me now—she is one of those women you could almost imagine getting it on with. There's nothing yuck about her. No hairy chin. Nothing that suggests feminine hygiene issues. She's as lickable as a lollipop.

And she has another ace up that draped designer sleeve. Ludo. Ludo, her improbably named son (should be called Battleships or Twister), is notorious as a right pain in the arse. The oldest and tallest in his class, he has become more dominating and difficult since Tash and Toby divorced, someone who has to be invited to parties because of the fear of repercussions in the playground if you don't, like a third-world tyrant invited to a UN convention. But the funny thing is he has been a good friend to Freddie in the last few months. He used to ignore Freddie. He didn't notice him in the same way he wouldn't notice a scab on his knee or a toddler in the path of his football in the park. But now Ludo and Freddie appear to have forged an unlikely bond. They certainly look an odd couple. Ludo, tall, cleft jawed and daft looking: Freddie, the small-for-his-height beauty who looks like he might have dropped off the Sistine Chapel ceiling. In the playground when the other children play "don't step on the bogie" Ludo will even make sure that no one pushes Freddie at the bogie on the playground floor. Maybe it's because they have both lost a parent from the household—one to divorce, the other to death—but he's become Freddie's unlikely protector.

Sometimes I imagine them getting together. Tash and Ollie, not Ludo and Freddie. The two single parents. The two boys. There's a symmetry to it, a ready-made family for Ollie, the child that I couldn't conceive emerging straight from the wrapping, skipping the sleepless nights stage, flat-packed into boyhood.

So what's my problem? This is my problem. Looking over my stone-cold shoulder back to my life I have a new clarity when it comes to friendships. The group of friends that I hung out with on a regular basis are beginning to separate like oil and vinegar in the French dressing jar. They have formed three distinct groups.

1. Proper old friends. Like Jenny. Friends who'd stand upside down in a swimming pool for Freddie while their highlights go green. Friends who know your failings and think they're really amusing. Friends who will never say you look tired even if you haven't slept in years. Friends who genuinely think you look better at thirty-five than when they knew you at eighteen. Those kinds of friends.

2. Circumstantial friends. Like Suze. Or Liz. Really Nice Women who I was grateful to be befriended by at the school gate when Freddie started school. The type of friends who surprise you by *being* your friend. Some of these circumstantial friends were on the path to becoming proper blood sister friends. Like Liz. I think I just needed to live through one more excruciating PTA fundraising disco with her and we would have been friends for life.

3. Friends you don't particularly like. Tash falls into this category. Funnily enough the FYDPL usually starts out by being a God-I-totally-love-this-person when you first get to know them. They're funny and glamorous and have an interesting life story and proper signed art on the walls rather than prints. They make your old friends seem dowdy and irrelevant. It's like a crush. Then gradually you become aware of a sinking feeling when you're scheduled in to see them. You know that you'll emerge from that cappuccino drained. Your hair will feel frizzier. You will feel poorer and fatter. Did I mention that Tash falls into this category? Tash falls into this category.

Anyway, back to my ankle boots. Off they go again! Click clack. They've dropped Ludo off at the classroom, where the moment her back is turned he swings his school bag hard against little Rex's eczema-raw knees. She is back at the school gate now. She is looking around for somebody. Ollie, I suspect. But, unbeknownst to her, Ollie has made a quick getaway and is dashing up the stairs to the school office to deliver the check for Freddie's school lunches, which is four months late. Tash hovers, then gives up and starts click-clacking back to her house, checking her phone repeatedly and texting as she walks.

I'm through the letter box back in her house before she is, watching from the banister as she fiddles in her cavernous black handbag for her door keys. She opens the door and freezes. Suddenly she is looking right at me. She pales. Like she's seen a ghost. (Ha!) For one strange moment I wonder if I've been spotted. Although, being invisible to everyone but Tash would be like some kind of paranormal sick joke. But no, no, she's looking away now, flurrying through to her kitchen to make herself a coffee. The moment's passed.

I settle in to watch.

Only now do I understand why womankind designed net curtains. In the space of five minutes, Tash, beautiful, fragrant Tash, sitting at her oak Conran table on her three-hundred-pounds-a-pop Eames Eiffel chair—her house is full of famous designer chairs—farts loudly, goes for a pee, doesn't wash her hands and takes a bite out of a lump of Parmesan in the fridge. She then sits down, switches on her iPad and spends five minutes updating her status on Facebook and Twitter—"Natasha is having an existential bedlinen crisis"—another ten idling JohnLewis.com's virtual aisles looking at duvet sets, not buying anything. Another eight minutes is idled away in ASOS's accessories section. She puts a gold-plated chain bracelet—seventy-seven pounds—in her basket but doesn't check out. She idly eats some seeds from a jar. One more fart. (Seeds, huh?) She spends the next seventeen minutes of her precious life ordering new socks and pajamas for Ludo from Marks and Spencer's website, but she can't remember her password, cocking up the order. Cursing, she spends another seven minutes on email. She goes there to find the new password sent by Marks and Spencer and gets diverted by a sensational email from Brigid regarding the infamous psycho mother who thinks the no-nut policy is an infringement of her son's human right to have peanut butter sandwiches in his packed lunch and is picketing the school gate with leaflets. Her coffee machine whirs noisily and spits up a coffee, which she throws back into her open pelican throat, chased by a packed lunch fruit bar. She moves a basketful of washing from washing machine to tumble dryer, skim-reads a magazine, then, bloody hell, it's eleven o'clock!

Where does the time go, eh? Well, I tell you what, it goes like that. My ankle boots are tripping up the sisal stair carpeting now. Tash is looking at her watch like she needs to be somewhere soon. She gets changed. Off come the jeans. She fingers a Spanx half-slip and decides against it. (She doesn't need it. This woman does so much Pilates her pelvic floor muscles could shoot golf balls into the next postcode.) On goes a short black skirt and gray tights. She zips up some conker brown knee-high riding boots, tongs her dark hair, squirts some Chanel No. 5 behind her ears and slicks on some pale pink lipstick. Dressed to kill. Or thrill. On a Thursday morning. Where the hell is she going? Interesting.

I don't float home as planned but follow her instead, always a few feet behind like a long summer shadow, down the wet tree-lined streets toward East Finchley Tube. She gets on, crosses her legs, assesses the carriage quickly for loons and settles into her newspaper, flicking past the news straight to the horoscope. The Northern line belches and rattles to Tottenham Court Road. She gets out, smooth-ing her hair with her fingers and swiveling her skirt around on her waist so that it's centered properly again, and checks her watch.

Goodge Street. Backstreets. Roadworks. Small, dark Italian café. She looks nervous sitting at the front of the café, near the window, unable to stay still. She reapplies her lipstick using a little gold hand mirror.

Curiouser and curiouser.

The lipstick is snapped back, shoved into her bag. She is watching someone outside the window now, expression changing.

He's pushing open the glass café door, striding across the café's tiles in his dark suit before I notice him.

Tash leaps up from her seat, napkin falling to the floor. There is a moment of awkwardness while they decide whether to shake hands or kiss each other on the cheek. They kiss each other on the cheek.

Sam sits down, smiles, tugs at his shirt cuffs. "It's good to put the face to the voice at last."

She looks a little embarrassed, to her credit.

"Thanks so much for meeting me like this. I know it must seem a little odd."

"No, not at all. I was in town this lunchtime anyway." She leans forward, resting her face on the cradle of her hands. "So?"

"I'll cut to the chase." He sighs. "Someone's causing me a bit of trouble."

She looks puzzled, her tongue licking her bottom lip. "Sorry. I don't understand."

"Dominique." He drags his fingers down his strained face.

She looks at him blankly. "Dominique? Who's . . ."

"Seb Lewis's sister. You remember Seb, our mutual friend?"

"Oh." She still looks like she doesn't get it. Neither do I. "Dominique. Right." Her expression changes. Something's dawning. "Didn't you two once . . ."

"Look, I know how this looks," he says quickly. "I need to ask you a favor."

"Sorry, but . . ."

His blue eyes flash electric as he smiles his most charming smile. "Natasha, there's no such thing as free legal advice."

Twenty

Three weeks later and Ollie's words were still spinning around Jenny's head like fairground horses: "I'm so pleased you exist; you've no idea how pleased I am that you exist." Every morning she had to shoot those horses down, one by one, reminding herself of her own inherent absurdity, her disloyalty, the sheer vileness of her own brain. What was going on with her feelings toward Ollie? How on earth could she escape them? Damn. She needed distance, quick.

What she needed was a plan.

The next day, she stepped over the huddle of marinating nappy bags in Suze's hall with a new sense of purpose. Yes, it was a bloody good plan, if she said so herself.

"Tea." Suze pressed a cup into her hand as she sat down on a wicker chair, before she had a chance to draw breath. "Sophie's R.I.P. Facebook page now has eight hundred and forty-five condolences, can you believe it?"

"That's a lot of friends she never met."

Liz laughed loudly. "One of them was in her yoga class but had never actually spoken to her. Hey, they stretched hamstrings together."

"Those that stretch together stay together," muttered Tash, picking some icing off a slice of cake and pushing it to the side of her plate as if it might be radioactive.

"Ladies, I have an idea," said Jenny brightly.

"Hit us with it, Jenny," said Suze, looking at her, pouring water out of a bright blue jug.

They all turned to face her.

Jenny took a deep breath. "An au pair." She looked around at the blank, silent faces. There was a terrible silence. Liz coughed and looked down at the table. Er, why weren't they hailing her genius? "Let's hire an au pair for Ollie."

"You are fucking *joking*," hissed Tash, murderous.

Jenny glanced at Liz appealingly. Help! What was going on?

"The thing is . . ." began Liz, face contorting in a way that suggested Jenny had made some steaming faux pas.

"Since when is having some gold-digging freaking eighteen-year-old Ukrainian wearing street market lingerie move into a widower's house a sensible idea?" spat Tash.

What on earth was going on here?

"I can name you two marriages that have been atomized by au pairs," Lydia said quietly, making a funny half nod toward Tash and trying to tell Jenny something with her widening eyes.

"*Three!*" corrected Tash.

"The Sebolds." Suze shook out some chocolate flakes from a silver sprinkler into her palm and licked them off. "Alec had an affair with her for three months while Lily was pregnant. The Wintersons. Actually, that was a manny. Do mannies count?"

"And *me*, Jenny," Tash snarled. "My husband ran off with my au pair!"

Jenny crushed her hands over her mouth. "Oh! I'm so sorry. I had no idea."

"No, of course you didn't," said Liz kindly, putting her hand lightly on Jenny's arm. "Look, an au pair for Ollie is not a bad idea, not at all. Let's look at this with fresh eyes, shall we, ladies? What happened to you, Tash, it's awful but we can't presume all au pairs are the same, can we?"

"I don't see why not," muttered Tash.

"How about we make sure the au pair's got buck teeth and weighs thirteen stone?" asked Jenny brightly. Suze stiffened and slammed the chocolate flake sprinkler hard down on the work surface, sending a puff of chocolate into the air. Did Suze weigh thirteen stone? Oops.

"It makes no difference," said Liz. "Astrid had such bad teeth it looked like she'd eaten a brick."

"Can I just say?" said Lydia, putting up her hand. "What's wrong with Operation Help Ollie, Jenny? *We* can do all the stuff the au pair does."

"Yes, we can," said Jenny carefully. "It's just that Help Ollie can't go on forever."

"Well, I don't see why not," said Lydia, affronted.

"An au pair will give him more autonomy," Jenny said. "And that's a good thing, isn't it?" It would also mean that she could put some distance between herself and number thirty-three and stop these weird . . . feelings.

"Let me digest, let me digest . . ." Suze pulled at the long sleeves of her purple mohair sweater, so that her fingers poked out through the loose stitch like finger puppets, and riffled them back and forth anxiously along her lower lip. "Okay, let's consider the possibility that Jenny is right."

"Don't tell me you're saying our services are no longer needed too?" Tash pushed her cup of tea away and glared at Suze, as if she'd defected traitorously to the other side.

"Come on, Tash, he's probably *sick* of the sight of us," said Liz. "We've become helpful through sheer persistence and he's had enough. We've become the 'helpful friend' that everyone dreads."

Jenny laughed. "It's not that."

"He did end up with four kettles." Liz caught Jenny's eye and they both tried not to laugh. "Three babysitters all turning up on the same Saturday night. A night when the poor guy didn't actually want to go out anyway."

Tash sat up very straight. "Is this all because Lydia let herself into his house last week to do his recycling?" She glared at Lydia.

"You didn't!" Jenny laughed.

"Can I take this opportunity to say, Lydia, that you're welcome to do my recycling anytime," Liz interrupted. "Quite welcome."

"I thought he'd appreciate it." Lydia shrunk back into the floppy roll neck of her gray cashmere sweater sulkily. "Sorry for breathing."

"You wouldn't fuss about like that for your own husband," muttered Tash, crossing her arms over her chest.

Lydia covered her mouth with her hand. "You know, the funny thing is I probably wouldn't. That's food for thought, isn't it?"

They sat in musing silence for a few moments, the sound of children fighting in the background.

"Onwards and upwards!" said Suze, reverting back to her officious meeting voice. She looked around the table. "It's been fun, in a weird way, hasn't it, girls? But maybe it is time to move things on."

Tash bristled.

"Let's vote. Hands up for an au pair."

Liz raised her hand slowly. Suze followed suit. "Sorry," said Jenny to Tash, as she put her hand up too. "Not personal." But she couldn't help but get a little kick out of triumph out of it all the same.

"Okay, three in favor of an au pair. Two not. An au pair it is!" Suze refilled everyone's glasses. "Anyway, I don't know about you but I need to refocus my energies on my own family. Right now I've got a mother-in-law threatening to move into the shed at the bottom of the garden. And a seven-year-old child who can't spell his middle name."

"It is Zebedee," Liz pointed out.

Suze ignored Liz. "I actually sent Chris packing to the pub tonight so that we could have this meeting. He didn't want to go. And you know what? I feel shitty about that now. I keep neglecting my own husband because of Ollie. Not that it's Ollie's fault," Suze added. Following it with the requisite, "Poor Ollie."

"You've done so much, Suze," said Jenny warmly, sensing the downward shift in mood. "I know Ollie really, really appreciates it."

Lydia's eyes were filling with tears. She sniffed and stood up, pulling her handbag over her shoulder. "George didn't really want me to go out tonight either. And maybe I've been pouring all my energies into . . ." Her voice broke and trailed off. "I need to reassess my priorities too."

The oven pinged. Suze leapt up, slid a tray of charred mini pizzas out of her range cooker. Cursing as she burned her fingers, she picked up three of them and threw them into a paper towel, which she handed to Lydia with too much force. "I insist."

Lydia accepted the smoking offering reluctantly. "Keep me posted," she said winsomely.

"Jesus Christ. It's like she's got some irrigation system going on in her tear ducts," Tash muttered as the front door closed behind Lydia. "Is she *ever* going to stop crying?"

"Troubles with George," said Suze knowingly. "That's what that's about."

"They're not happy?" Jenny asked, thinking not of Lydia but Sophie suddenly.

Liz swallowed a mini pizza whole. "Come on, is anyone happy?"

Jenny was taken aback by the question. It was a dangerous

question. No, she wasn't happy. But Sophie had died. How could she be happy?

"Don't all stare at me like that. I mean happy in the way we *thought* we'd be happy when we were young, you know, imagining being married and grown up." Liz stared searchingly into the plate of charred pizza as if it somehow held the answer to her question. "Most mere mortals don't get Soph and Ollie's marriage. That soul mate thing they had. Most of us meet our soul mates in our twenties and the relationship implodes in a bloody combustion of sex and insecurity and clashing levels of timing and commitment." She shrugged. "My experience, anyway."

"Sure as hell didn't imagine I'd be divorced by the age of thirty-five." Tash let out a short, shrill laugh. "What about you, Suze?"

"Happy?" Suze stopped lowering a string of mozzarella cheese into her open mouth like a worm. "I don't really have time to wonder if I'm happy or not, to be honest."

"That answers that question then."

"Actually, Liz, I think I *am* pretty happy," said Suze. "I mean, life's not what I thought it'd be but then, you have no idea what having kids is going to be like before you do it, do you?"

Jenny became aware of Tash staring at her. She could feel the question coming and wished she could duck out of it with a "no comment." She waited. And it came.

"What about you, Jenny? I mean, if I'm Marriage, the Sequel, you're still at the trailer stage, yeah?" Jenny thought there was something about the way she asked the question that made it seem craftily rhetorical. "Glued to your seat. Eating popcorn," added Tash.

Jenny laughed. "Oh, no, I hate people who munch popcorn in cinemas. I discreetly suck lumps of chocolate."

"Sounds like a women's mag question." Liz smiled. "Are you a muncher or a sucker?"

"You have a *filthy* mind, Liz." Suze turned to Jenny with an intent look on her face. "Do you ever wish you'd settled earlier, Jenny? Like Sophie."

"No. I feel like I'm only grown up enough to make the right decision now."

"I'm not sure falling in love has anything to do with being grown up," said Liz with a just barely detectable note of weariness.

Suze patted Jenny on the hand, leaving a smudge of grease on her skin. "Well, I hope you have a marriage like Sophie's."

Jenny smiled ruefully, knowing that she wouldn't have a marriage like Sophie's. No one had a marriage like Sophie's.

"They had the perfect marriage, didn't they? That's the tragedy of it all."

"They had their problems just like everyone else," said Jenny and immediately regretted it. Why had she said that? The letters. It was that damn box of letters again. She wished she could forget them. She wished she'd never found them.

The women swiveled to look at Jenny, the evening newly energized by a shudder of schadenfreude.

"What you do *mean*, Jenny?" Tash asked. "They weren't having problems, were they?"

"No, not really," she said quickly, feeling guilty that she'd betrayed her discretion to Sophie. "Just that they were like any couple in a way—well, a pretty gilded version admittedly."

"I always did wonder why Sophie never had another child," said Tash. She exchanged a knowing glance with Lydia.

Jenny remembered the maternity wear carefully folded in Sophie's drawers. To disclose this would be an even greater betrayal. She kept her mouth closed.

"A shame. It would be easier for Freddie if he had a sibling." Liz looked wistful. "Poor little Freddie."

"He might still get one!" blurted Tash with rather too much enthusiasm for Jenny's liking. "Ollie could have more kids. Why not?"

"Whoa! One step at a time. The guy has not even thought about dating yet, has he, Jenny?" said Liz.

Jenny bit her lip. "No," she lied. She couldn't bring herself to admit even the gist of their conversation the other night. His words would be misinterpreted. She must protect him from himself. From the predators. From Tash.

"Hold your horses!" Suze grabbed Jenny's sleeve. "Has the time come for us to introduce him to other women, do we think?"

"No!" protested Jenny.

"Nothing serious, Jenny," Suze said, eyeing Jenny with obvious amusement. "Just someone to have dinner with?"

Tash sat up very straight and sniffed. "That's not necessary. I'm his dinner partner."

Liz kicked Jenny under the table.

"Well, you know, just the odd dinner." Tash's eyes glittered. She couldn't keep the smile down. "Why is everyone staring at me like that? We're both on our own; it's natural."

Twenty-one

It was a cool, sunny Saturday morning and the scent of white freesias in the window box puffed pleasantly through the café's open window. Coffee. Pastries. Newspaper. Laptop. Bedhead hair. They looked like how they used to look before Soph died, Jenny thought, a happy couple, freshly woken in each other's sleep-sweaty arms, easy in each other's company. It would only be the most acute observer who'd notice how their silences went on a little longer than they used to, the fewer times their hands touched, the way Jenny no longer took a casual bite of Sam's pain au chocolat.

"Hired yet?" Sam looked up from his newspaper, his eyes tracking the pert behind of a pretty, young waitress.

"I may as well have advertised for a nanny for a single Brad Pitt." She'd been worried that every au pair would check the "no father-only households" box but instead she had two dozen replies from women all over the world: Australian, Bulgarian, Irish, Congolese, Thai, Swedish, and, yes, Ukrainian. Seventeen, nineteen, twenty-one years old. Reams of bubbly CVs with thousands of exclamation marks and badly lit photos and declarations of being "hardworking!" and "loving children!" and "no job too small!!!"

Sam gestured to his mouth, meaning she'd got cappuccino froth on her upper lip. "I advise you to just pick the prettiest, Jenny," he said, not looking up from the sports pages. "Seriously, cheer Ollie up a bit." He shook out his paper. "I know what I'd want in an au pair."

"Charming. Actually, Sam, the main priority is Freddie. It's got to be somebody who'll bond with Freddie."

Sam laughed, stole the last remaining bit of croissant off her plate, dunked it in the small pot of jam. "You tell yourself that, Jenny darling."

She rolled her eyes. "Not every man is as Neanderthal as you, Sam."

"Ah, you're so wrong."

Three coffees later, Jenny had a short list. Out had gone the ones who couldn't spell at all—they had to spell better than Freddie, that was the benchmark—and out went the ones with dodgy blanks on their CVs or dodgy jobs—"after college I worked as masseuse"—or unnerving hobbies "dog breeding and rifle shooting" or, rather ominously, no photo. And at Sam's insistence out went the really plain or fat girls. This made Jenny feel mean because she was sure they were perfectly nice, nicer in fact than the prettier girls, and had she been sitting alone in the café—as she should be, if she'd planned the exercise properly—she would have picked a plainer one.

Sam craned to the side, watching over her shoulder. This meant that she had to let a few more beauties through the net that she wouldn't have done otherwise. Only when he went to the toilet did she get a chance to do a quick stealthy mass cull of the sexiest girls.

Finally, a list of five. All nice, bouncy, wholesome girls. Attractive, yes, but none showing cleavage in their headshots.

"Done?" Sam stirred another sugar into his coffee. He always rotated the teaspoon in the cup five times. "Can we reclaim our Saturday now?"

"Yep. I'll email them later." She shut the laptop with relief. Yes, she was closing one chapter of her life and moving on to the next, moving away from number thirty-three. The waitress took away the dirty plates and afterward Sam did that silent bill-scribbling motion with his hands, despite the fact that she was close enough to talk to.

Jenny knew better than to say anything. Sam enjoyed lording it over waitresses. Like he enjoyed being worldlier than her. It was all part of a power dynamic that pleased him in quite a boyishly endearing way. When they'd first got together he'd had to show her how to get the fish off its bone with the back of a knife: she'd previously always got around this by ordering a fillet. He was the kind of man who'd order braised offal whenever the opportunity arose. She'd always preferred a chicken breast done simply, and no, of course she'd never eat the skin. He thought this hilarious.

Sam's phoned beeped. He looked at the message and his expression changed. "Completely forgot to tell you, babes, and I better tell you now in case she mentions it. . . ." He looked a little flustered. "I met Tash for lunch last week."

"What?" Jenny stared at him, puzzled. "Tash? Muzzy Hill Tash?" First a phone call. Now lunch?

He leaned back in his chair, dangled his hand out the open window. "She called again, wanted free advice, and I was just round the corner from her, so, you know, we grabbed a sandwich."

"Why didn't you say anything last week?"

"Sorry. It's crap of me. Been mental."

"But I saw Tash round at Suze's the other night. She didn't say anything either." It didn't really make sense.

"She didn't?"

"No, she didn't."

He smoothed his palm over his shaven head and sighed. "I guess she's embarrassed, poor thing."

An indignant snort noise tunneled out of her nostrils. "She never struck me as the embarrassed type."

"People do find divorce embarrassing, Jenny," he said, putting on his soft, talking-to-the-client voice. "They see it as a personal failure. That's pretty much universal."

"Suppose."

He leaned forward and kissed her lightly on the mouth. "Not us. We'll be one of the happy ones."

Was he right? Yes, of course he was. She smiled. "We will."

"In August you are going to make me berserk with happiness."

She laughed. The sun moved, throwing a shawl of heat against her back. The early June air was drenched with the smell of freesias. And Sam's eyes matched the strip of sky above the Camden rooftops perfectly. In a funny way, she realized, Sam confessing to a meeting with Tash confirmed something fundamental about him to her. Something good. Reassuring. No, Sam wasn't perfect but at least he was honest. She'd take honest and flawed over perfect and shifty every time. Yes, perhaps Sam did have a bit of a wandering eye but at least he didn't do it behind her back. At least she knew whom she was marrying. She'd forgotten how great Sam was. He was great. He was so great! No, she wouldn't have him any other way. She'd been spending too much time with Ollie, and it had confused her. Yes, that was it. She reached over to kiss Sam, harder this time, a proper snog. For the first time ever they clashed noses.

Twenty-two

Her name is Cecille. (Long on the "eeeel.") She is standing outside the front door of number thirty-three, pulling at the straps of the black fabric holdall that is digging into her long Gallic neck, giving her love bites. Twenty apparently, looks no more than sixteen. Her hair is brown and wavy and youth-glossy in the sunshine. She's wearing no makeup, which is reassuring. But she doesn't need it, which is less so. She has olive skin, a full, round moon face that is beautiful from the nose up—eyes like chocolate buttons, improbable eyelashes and very round cheekbones—and plain from the big nose down to the mouth with the chipped front tooth and slightly zitty chin. I'm also pleased to report that there is nothing particularly chic about her. She is wearing the universal uniform of the French square—pressed straight jeans, buttoned-up pink shirt, navy sweater and loafers—which is sweet rather than sexy. A London teen would eat her for breakfast.

Yes, I can see why Jenny plumped for Cecille. She comes from a large provincial family—four siblings, all brothers, all younger than her—from the Poitou-Charentes region in the west of France. Her father is a garage mechanic, her mother a housewife. She also comes with a stack of glowing babysitting references and a place on one of those evening courses to learn finance. What's not to like? Only the fact that she is attractive and French and twenty. Hey ho.

Ollie opens the door and stares at her, surprised, as if he is expecting someone else. Jenny scrutinizes her from behind his shoulder. She nudges him. Ollie smiles, coughs and says, "Can I take your bag?"

Cecille flushes silently. Has she forgotten her English? Perhaps she assumed all British men were a hybrid of Mr. Bean and Prince Philip. "Thank you," she says, recovering herself. Wowzer! That French accent. That's sex appeal without even trying.

"Hello, Cecille!" Jenny says, stepping forward. "How was your flight from La Rochelle?"

"Good, thank you." Cecille smiles nervously, glances at Ollie again.

Jenny guides Cecille through the hall, brushing past Ollie. They both flinch at the touch. Something ripples the air. Have I missed a row between these two or something? Things feel kind of crackly.

"Something to eat, Cecille?" asks Ollie a little brusquely. He's nervous. He always sounds brusque when he's nervous.

"No, thank you, Mr. Brady."

"Ollie, seriously. Call me Ollie."

A wash of color rouges her cheeks, like the brightening of a flower at dawn. She is prettier than the photograph she sent in. Clever girl.

"Freddie!" Ollie bellows up the stairs. "Cecille is here! Come and say hi." They all stare expectantly, smiling fixedly up the stairs, at the reason she's here. No Freddie appears.

"Freddie!" Ollie calls again.

It becomes clear that Freddie has not appeared because Freddie does not want to appear. There is a click of minor embarrassment. Jenny makes a "kids, huh" face and runs upstairs to coax him down.

Forward-wind forty-five minutes and Freddie has forgiven Cecille for arriving on his doorstep and not being me. Cecille is sitting cross-legged on the sitting room floor making a Lego spaceship: it's the way to my boy's heart.

Jenny's phone beeps incessantly. I thread myself through the zipper and into her handbag to check the messages. Suze: "Friend or foe?" Liz: "Report back immediately." Tash: "Hot?" Lydia: "Tash having minor breakdown."

Jenny and Ollie go through to the kitchen. The cleaner has done an extra shift in anticipation of Cecille's arrival. There is the smell of pasta pesto that Ollie's made for lunch. There are yellow tulips on the table. Fresh linen in the spare bedroom.

"She seems lovely. Shall I leave you to it now?" whispers Jenny, looking like she's itching to leave.

He grabs her arm. "Don't go, not yet. What the hell will we talk about?"

"Flaubert. Derrida?"

"Now I'm really scared."

"Ollie, she will be into MTV and Gaga. Talk about that."

Ollie groans. "Oh, God."

Good. The air is loosening a bit between them now. "Just get her cooking. She says she can cook. And she's French. All French people can cook."

"Lasagna?"

Jenny smiles, smiles properly for the first time since she arrived at number thirty-three.

He puts a hand over his mouth. "Oh, no. What have I done?"

"Shhh. Just remember that you will no longer have to rely on Lydia doing your recycling or Suze's bake-offs or Tash's after-school club. You'll be free to go out in the evenings. You've got a babysitter on call," says Jenny.

"I don't want to go out."

She pulls her bag briskly over her shoulder. "Well, you might do one day."

Ollie looks doubtful and fingers his beard.

"Suze is going to invite you to some soirees very soon. Prepare yourself."

"Haven't I suffered enough?"

She laughs, checks her watch. "I better get back."

"Thanks for sorting this out, Jenny."

"It was nothing," she lies. There is a moment's hesitation when she looks like she might be about to kiss him good-bye. But she doesn't.

Twenty-three

A week later, Jenny is dutifully back at number thirty-three, having dropped Freddie back from swimming. I observe her, noting
the tiredness under her eyes, pink from the pool, the twitch in the
center of her pretty, full bottom lip. She looks anxious watching
Ollie and Freddie kicking a ball around the garden, fidgeting,
crossed-legged, tapping her fingers on the deck. I wonder if it's something to do with this Dominique business. Does she know? I suspect
not. Sam can be discreet as a spook when he has to be.

Jenny stands up, brushes down her denim shorts and tells Ollie
she's going to the toilet. But it seems she is not going to the toilet!
No, she is walking past the toilet without so much as a tinkle, eyes
furtive, a woman on a mission. She's creeping along down the landing now. Ah! What's this? She is going into Ollie's bedroom. How
odd. Glancing from side to side as if scared of being disturbed, she
is padding across the sheepskin rug. Crouching now. She's pulling
open the lower drawer of the chest, her fingertips leaving damp
spots on the wood. She's yanking the jumpers out of the drawers,

frantically pulling them out and dropping them on the floor so that
Cecille's ordered neatness is destroyed and they're left sprawling,
arms open, like old skins. Her hands are patting the bottom of the
drawer like a blind woman. She is pulling up the lining paper.

Oh, *no*! Oh, God. I get it now. I shrivel to a black dot.

Jenny sits back on her feet, shakes her head. "Gone?" she says out
loud through the hand crushed against her mouth. "Fuck. Fuck.
Fuck."

Gone? *Where?* And how the hell does Jenny know the letters were
there in the first place? I hear soft, almost silent footsteps, the crush
of the carpet fibers under a bare foot.

"Jenny?" Suddenly Cecille is standing in the doorway, glaring.
"What are you doing?"

Jenny leaps back from the drawers, mortified, mouth opening
and closing. "I . . . I . . ."

Cecille frowns. "Why have you taken out all the clothes?"

Jenny's cheeks are on fire. "I was looking for something." She
looks down at her twisting hands.

"In the drawers?"

"Yes."

"What?"

"Er, something private."

"Private?" Something flashes across Cecille's face. As she is standing and Jenny is crouching she's looking down on Jenny, literally and
in other ways too.

"Sorry, sorry." Jenny starts shoving the clothes back in the drawer
manically.

"I'll do it," Cecille says, squatting down beside her, giving Jenny
a fearsome sidelong glance. "I know how Ollie likes it."

Twenty-four

Light puddled through the trees to the green floor of Highgate Cemetery. It was a lovely day, the sun custard yellow, the sky blue, the kind of day that would have made Sophie grin impishly and declare herself "horny as an old goat." She'd wear one of her glamorous wide-brimmed hats today, Jenny imagined, a Joan Collins–style one with a leopard print sash. And she would smell slightly sweaty, sexy hot skin, rather than anything BOish. She'd be bare legged, of course. Sophie would do a bare leg in any temperature over freezing. Unlike herself, who liked a good opaque. She was wearing opaques today in fact. Navy 60 denier. The tights were making her hot. She could smell her armpits when she raised her arms from her sides. And they didn't smell sexy.

She wedged the round box of pink champagne truffles close to the head of the gravestone. Happy thirty-sixth birthday, Soph, she muttered silently, squeezing her eyes shut and trying to commune, just in case Soph could hear her. I love you so much, Soph. I miss you so much. I wish you were going to get old with me. We never did get to go on a cheesy cruise and sing along to Shirley Bassey impersonators or sit on a beach smoking skunk and getting obese on chocolate torte and growing our pubic hair long and wild like Indian sadhus. You know what? I don't even mind you haunting me—if that is you—and following me in your white Fiat. Although why the Fiat? I think you're more a convertible Mini lady. I just wish you'd show yourself and tell me . . . well, so many things. Not least how to color-block for spring. I'm so bored by navy. You always told me I'd get bored of navy and black. You were right about that. You were right about so many things. Although you *were* wrong about Sam, who has finally set a date for a wedding I'd sell my own mother for you to be at. I haven't got the dress, of course. How can I buy a wedding dress without you to lash me into the dressing room and pull dresses over my head? And by the way, Sophie, the box full of letters wasn't there. I tried to protect you in case you'd done something stupid that you never told me about—tsk, tsk—and find those letters before Ollie did but the box wasn't there. And, yes, okay, maybe I was being a little bit nosy too. Whatever happened to no secrets, Soph? Whatever happened to *us*?

She waited for some kind of answer. But there was nothing but a stirring of the breeze and a small white fluttering butterfly. Feeling a little silly now, she squatted down, waiting for Freddie and Ollie to catch up, relishing her small moment of peace with the silence of Sophie. There were few people around in the cemetery today but it felt fine being alone here, she decided. She'd never had herself down as a grave lover. But she'd fallen in love with this cemetery, a little idyll in London. There were so many graves—over fifty-two thousand, she'd read—and so many effigies—angels, dogs, gods—but it felt magical rather than morbid, stepping out of the noise and grit of north London into another world, a secret ghostly garden. There were many worse places to end up.

The scrabble of small feet. And Freddie was there, panting at her side. He stood a few feet from the grave, uncertainly, gripping his bunch of white posies tightly.

"I've put my chocolates there." Jenny smiled, reading his apprehension, trying to coax him forward.

"Happy birthday, Mummy," he said quietly, putting the flowers on the grave and then leaping back to avoid being grabbed by a ghost. He reached for Jenny's hand. It felt hot, tight and small in hers. She squeezed it, feeling a rare sense of peace and a warm fuzzy feeling that wasn't unlike happiness. Absurd, considering. She was pleased that she'd agreed to come to the cemetery today. She'd made excuses when Ollie first asked, not wanting to intrude, wanting to maintain some distance. But then she thought about it for all of two seconds and knew that if she didn't go and visit with Ollie and Freddie on Sophie's birthday she'd regret it forever. She wasn't sure why. She just knew she had to be here. She'd been at every one of Sophie's birthdays since she was twenty.

It barely seemed like yesterday that she, Sam, Ollie and Soph had celebrated Sophie's thirty-fifth. They'd gone to Odette's in Primrose Hill, got hammered and eaten scallops and then propped up the bar until late, trying not to rubberneck Jude Law sitting at an adjacent table, their discretion failing spectacularly. Sophie had been in a particularly loud, silly mood. She'd put the pink flower from the table vase behind her ear and stabbed herself in the foot with her own stiletto, drawing blood. Ollie gave her a fireman's lift to the taxi, making Jude Law smile.

Ollie appeared, carrying a bunch of yellow roses. She stood back respectfully as he kissed the gravestone. "Happy birthday, darling," he muttered and the love in his voice seemed to vibrate in the warm spring air. He put an arm over Freddie's shoulder and they stood there together in silence, a column of sunshine breaking through the thick canopy, united in missing her. It wasn't like she was part of the family or anything. And yet today, for some odd reason, more than ever before, she felt she was.

"Can I see the grave with the sleeping dog on it now?" Freddie pulled away from them and hurtled down the path.

Ollie stared at the gravestone, his face unreadable, lost in private thoughts. "Gone five months."

"I can't believe it either."

"Sometimes I can't remember what she looks like, Jenny." He turned to her and his eyes were very dark, all pupil. "I have to get out photos. Other times it's like she just popped out to get some milk. And it's like I'm waiting for her to come home. I still get bits of her, Jen. Every day some crappy catalog drops on the mat." He smiled. "It's like the car's braked but all this stuff from the roof box is still flying forward."

She laughed.

"Oh, Sophie," he said, shaking his head again, as if still disbelieving that she could have done anything so stupid as step out in front of a bus on Regent Street.

"Should I give you a minute?"

"No," he said firmly, turning to face her, his face alive and motile again, as if snapping back from the past to the present. "I've hardly seen you since Cecille arrived." His eyes were sharply shadowed by their brows in the sunlight, making them hard to read. "Have I pissed you off in some way?"

"No." Mortified that he should think that. "Not at all."

"What, then?"

"Nothing, Ollie." She shuffled her feet under his long, hot gaze. This wasn't the time. "I'll check in on Freddie." She turned to walk through the shrub-shaded path, sat down on the loyal stone dog, worrying that she'd ballsed the trip up in some indefinable way. "You alright, Freddie?"

He looked solemn, stroked the dog's cold ears. "Don't like it here, Jenny."

"Why don't you like it?"

"Makes Daddy sad. I don't like Daddy sad."

"Oh, Freddie. You are such a sweet, kind boy." She kissed him on his warm forehead. And they sat in silence for a few moments, watching a large glossy black beetle lumber its way over the sticks and bubbles of moss and leaves on the ground. "Daddy won't always be sad, you know."

Freddie said nothing and stared glumly ahead.

"He'll always love Mummy but he won't always be sad."

"Good." He prodded the beetle gently with a stick. "Sad is boring."

"I guess it is." But if sad was so boring, why was she beginning to find this all, in some weird, black way, the most exciting time of her life? In some way she didn't quite understand she suddenly realized that she'd never felt more alive. Not able to compute the contradiction, she closed her eyes, pressed her fingers into the lids hard. God, it was all so fucked up.

"You don't come over so much anymore," said Freddie, staring at her accusingly.

"You've got Cecille now," she said, twisting with guilt. Freddie was the last person in the world she wanted to upset.

"Will you still come and visit us when you get married?"

"You bet!" Jenny pulled him toward her in a hug and glanced up at Ollie, who was sitting now on the grave, arms locked around his knees, staring into the shaded tangle of trees, a silhouette against the gravestone. Would there ever be a time he wouldn't be framed by that gravestone? she wondered.

"I'm worried about the wedding."

"Oh, no! Worried? Why, Fred?"

"Ludo says I'm going to look really silly and that he was a page boy once and had to wear a sailor's suit," he said solemnly.

Jenny laughed. "No sailor's suit, promise. You can wear what you want."

He grinned. "I can wear my Superman T-shirt?"

She hesitated. Oh, to hell with Sam's mother. "Yeah. You can wear what you want."

He slumped against her, leaning into her body. "Will there be dancing? Like *Strictly*?"

"Definitely."

Freddie kicked out his feet in his khaki Crocs. "And will I be allowed to have fun?"

Jenny was puzzled. "You're always allowed to have fun."

"I feel like I'm not allowed to have fun."

"Who said that? Did Cecille say that?" She wasn't sure about Cecille now. Not now that Cecille had something over her. And she would never forget that piercing look she gave her beside the chest of drawers. Yes, she should have gone for Magda, that pale, studious one with the specs.

"No." He shrugged. "It's just that I feel bad when I'm happy because Mummy is dead and that means I shouldn't be happy."

"Oh, Fred. You mustn't feel bad for being happy. Mummy always wanted you to be happy, didn't she?" She pulled him toward her tighter. "She'd be so proud of you being happy."

Freddie was breathily noisily and Jenny could tell that he was trying not to cry.

Jenny pointed at the ground. "Hey, look, that beetle's carrying a leaf now. Ninja beetle."

They watched the beetle with its leafy burden scurry into a hole in the soil. "Daddy doesn't like Sam," he said matter-of-factly, not looking up.

"Sorry?" Jenny couldn't quite believe what he'd said. The hairs on her arms prickled.

"Daddy doesn't like Sam."

"I'm sure he does, Freddie."

"I know that he doesn't." He picked a large white flower and rolled the stem between his fingers.

She glanced up sharply at Ollie, a dark figure in his battered Barbour. Surely Freddie was wrong. But then why had he said it?

As if sensing her gaze, Ollie stood up and walked toward them, brushing flakes of green moss off his trousers. "Pizza?"

Freddie jumped up. "Pizza!"

They retraced their steps through the sun-dappled avenues of tombs in silence. A man in green overalls passed them with a wheelbarrow full of small chunks of broken stone. He stopped. "Ah, you mustn't pick the flowers, lad," he said, looking at the plucked flower in Freddie's hand.

"Sorry." Freddie looked down at his offending hand, bit his lip. He hated being told off by strangers.

"Eh, it's alright." The gardener looked at Jenny and winked. "You just make sure you give it to your pretty mum, eh?"

In her horror she stepped backward, the heel of her shoe catching on the crumbling stonework of Edward Ebenezer Stewart's final resting place. Her ankle turned and she slipped and she dropped her handbag. The tableau froze. Her on the old grave. Tampax and phone and chewing gum rolling out of her handbag. A sharp pain in her ankle. She shut her eyes, wishing that the grave would open up and she could just sink into its dank depths until the awful moment passed. This not being an option, she scrambled back to the ground, noting with renewed mortification that Freddie had picked up the Tampax and was examining it carefully as if it were a rare albino beetle. She snatched it off him and shoved it back into her handbag.

"You alright, love?" asked the gardener, smirking.

"Fine!" She determinedly carried on walking, knees stinging. Freddie ran on ahead of them now. "God, I'm sorry," she said stiffly, mortified, unable to look at Ollie.

Ollie stopped. "Jenny. You don't need to apologize for anything." He put his hands firmly on her shoulders, demanding that she look at him. She looked at him and saw that his lovely dark eyes were creased with repressed laughter. Clearly, he found the idea that she might get mistaken for his wife hilariously funny.

She was a joke.

Twenty-five

'm getting restless. The house is swelling with the unseasonal heat.
I can hear minute cracks spidering inside the bricks, Muswell Hill's
clay soil beneath the house's foundations contracting, hardening,
threatening number thirty-three with subsidence problems. Freddie
is outdoors a lot now, stretching, strengthening those skinny, bendy
limbs, jumping, naked but for his white pants, ya-ya-yahooing,
throwing himself off that trampoline so that he's a flying wild-haired
angel cut out of north London's paddling pool sky.

Cecille is watching Freddie, enjoying him, laughing, her river of
brown hair flicky and sheeny in the sunlight. She is wearing a denim
miniskirt that shows off her slim brown legs. It did not travel over
from France with her and it bears the Topshop label, like so many
of her new purchases. The French square's pressed navy sweater
hasn't made an appearance for a while, I realize. She slings her weight
lazily to one hip, a new feline sexuality about her I've never noticed
before. She yawns, tired because she and Ollie were up last night
until one in the morning drinking beers in the garden, beneath the

warm black sky and the stars sharp as cookie cutters. Yeah, I'm jealous.

So I catch a thermal down the hill, buffeting over the cool air that hangs above the black, still spots of Hampstead ponds, through the nitrate fug of Camden to check in on Jenny. Well, Sam actually. I'm still trying to get to the bottom of this Dominique business that's been rumbling for weeks. Who the hell is she? And what's she got to do with *Tash*, of all bloody people? Jenny's wedding date is rushing toward us all now. I need to find out.

Jenny needs to find out, even if she doesn't know it yet.

I enter through the open balcony window of Sam and Jenny's apartment. Bingo! Jenny isn't at home. Sam is. But who is this powdering her nose in the marble bathroom? Oh, damn, his mother, Penelope, the battle-axe from Sussex with the overactive salivary glands. She spits when she talks and little strings of saliva link her upper and lower teeth like a brace when she smiles. She creates a dust bowl of perfume wherever she goes too. The perfume is so strong and pervasive, as if it's made of those nanoparticles that are so small they can pierce the epidermis. She should only be allowed in well-ventilated areas.

"Her phone's still on answer?" Penelope says tersely, applying a layer of powder to her face thick as pollen. "Surely she knows I'm here to discuss the floral arrangements."

Sam pushes up his shirtsleeve and glances at his Rolex. "Give her a minute, Mum. She's probably just caught in traffic."

"I'm not even going to ask where she is, Sam," Penelope sniffs. Which is her way of asking.

"She's not in Muswell Hill, actually. She's having her roots done."

"Thank goodness." She laughs shrilly. "Not like her."

What a cow! I think we can safely declare Penelope to be the mother-in-law from hell.

"We're going to a party tonight."

Penelope sits down at the kitchen table, spreading her hands on the surface so that the veins pop out like pipes. She examines her manicure in loaded silence. "That's nice."

"What?" says Sam.

"Nothing."

"Come on, Mum. I know that face."

"I'm concerned about Jenny. Very concerned, Sammy." She spits a fine coat of drizzle on her son's hand. "She's not playing ball on the wedding. Everyone's waiting for her to get back to them. It's not like she's not had many offers of help. Did I tell you that Clarissa Ridge-mont's daughter has offered to give her a free makeup session? She's waiting for a yea or a nay too." She shakes her head. "It just looks like bad manners, I'm afraid."

"I'll talk to her," Sam says wearily.

Penelope gives him one of those scrutinizing looks that only mothers give. "Is everything okay between you, darling?"

"Yes, yes, of course." He is a man who could lie to anyone, including his mother.

"It's just . . ." Penelope looks down at her hands.

"What?" He slams down his coffee cup. "What, Mum?" He turns the tables nimbly, so that his disloyalty is now hers.

"I feel you should both be more excited, that's all," she says, pick-ing her words carefully, like the flowers in her front garden. "I remem-ber when your father and I got married, gosh, I was hopelessly beside myself, I really was!" She swivels her gold wedding band around her fat pink finger. She's going to get buried with that ring. "And your sister. Pip was like one of those gypsy brides, wasn't she? You know, the ones on telly."

"Jenny's best friend has just died, Mum."

"It was some time ago now."

"Try telling her that."

They sit in silence for a few moments. The traffic hoots outside.

There is the rhythmic drum of a police chopper, flying above the houses. "I thought the point of having the wedding this summer was to start a new chapter." She won't let this go.

"It is." He looks down at the table, like he can't look his mother in the eye either.

"The funny thing is, Sam, Jenny doesn't look like a woman about to get married. She looks . . ." Penelope hesitates. "I don't know, fevered."

Sam throws his shaven head back and laughs. *"Fevered?"* He drops his head in his hands and lets out a mock groan. "Mum, please. This is not a period drama."

"Skittish, not happy, not sad, not bereaved even! Not like I was when poor Mark got tongue cancer! I couldn't get out of bed for two weeks. I lost sixteen pounds. That was the only upside," she reflects, sipping tea.

"Mum, will you please just leave it?" There's a growl to his voice now that shakes the air particles in the room like a maraca. He gets up, walks to the window and looks down the street. His eyes flicker and focus in recognition of someone or something.

I swoop over to the curtain rail.

Ah, Jenny's back! Getting out of the car, glancing around. Up the street. Down the street, like she's seeking someone. Looking, yes, *fevered*! Oh, dear. I want to sound out a warning. Mother-in-law's here! Stop the divving around. Approach with caution. But all I can do is madly wave my nonatomic arms in frustration. I am the world's most useless guardian angel.

What the hell is the point of *me*?

Twenty-six

Jenny glanced behind her one last time. No, no sign of Sophie's hubcabbed celestial chariot, or whatever it was. Was she imagining stuff? Had she lost it, like Sam said? The thing was she'd come out of the hairdresser, jittery on coffee and *Hello!* magazine ingestion, and was walking down the street to her car, sharply aware of the pins in her ill-advised wedding rehearsal Sarah Palin updo—the overbearing stylist had insisted—pulling at her scalp, when something caught her eye. She'd turned. It was a woman walking quickly away, her beige trench coat flapping open in the wind like a tent, a mass of glossy brown hair piled up on her hair, tendrils loose around her neck. A gash of red scarf. She got into her car—and yes, it *was* a white Fiat—slammed the door and revved off, starving Jenny of proper scrutiny of her face. But she was pretty damn sure it was the same woman. The same woman who'd turned up at her apartment all that time ago, the one who looked like Sophie. How could she forget her?

More important, how the hell could she forget that Penelope was

coming over? And now she was late, for once. Standing on the doorstep of her apartment, she checked her iPhone, which had turned
itself on to silent as it so often did in her handbag, and saw she'd had
four missed calls from Sam. Anxiety bubbled in her tummy like gas.
She knew she was in for another earful from Sam. And some silences
that could kill from Penelope.

She would fail as a potential daughter-in-law before she even
opened her mouth. What with her bad Sarah Palin hair. Her pimply
chin. The insomnia and bad dreams bagging around her eyes, the bad
dreams that had bugged her ever since visiting the grave on Sophie's
birthday. The same ones over and over, like an endlessly repeated
miniseries. The most popular was the one when she spilled red wine
on her bridal dress then on closer inspection realized that it wasn't
wine but blood and that she'd got her period early and Sophie had
to run off to find Tampax but couldn't because all the shops were
shut because they were in the country and shops were never open in
the country and so the vicar had to ask the congregation, "Is there
a Tampax in the house?" And the day and the dress were ruined.
After that dream the following day would always pass in a blur. Like
she was wearing a pair of glasses that weren't the right prescription.

The wedding was beginning to feel like a reptile bought from a
pet shop that had grown bigger and fiercer than its owners could
cope with, and unmanageably hungry. She'd said that she'd prefer a
simple, small ceremony but kept getting shouted down by Sam's
family, who had forked out a small fortune. Now her own parents,
who could ill afford it but didn't like to feel they weren't stepping up
to the high-water mark set by Penelope, had felt compelled to donate
seven thousand pounds of their savings. It left her feeling guilty
and beholden and anxious. And, no, she still hadn't bought the dress.

Penelope would be bound to ask about the dress today. It would
be top of her bullet point list. And to prove to Penelope that she had
actually *tried* to find a dress and wasn't a complete timewaster, she'd

have to relive the shopping trip with her mother the week before, which had ended with a tense coffee and a stale Eccles cake in John Lewis's fourth-floor café and her mother saying she was "the world's fussiest bride."

Everyone said when you saw the right dress you knew it was the One. But she didn't know. They all just looked like shockingly overpriced bits of fabric to her. She had yet to find the dress. And the dress had yet to find her.

As she fumbled for her keys it started to rain lightly. She stopped for a moment, resting her hands on her knees, thankful that she wasn't being watched and that she could snatch this one moment to realign herself, catch her breath before Penelope, before the party.

Something caught her eye. She looked up through the bead curtain of rain. Oh! There was someone at the window of her apartment, waving. It was Sophie! Clear as day. Sophie standing there in the frame of her sitting room window, her dark hair tumbling over her shoulders, waving manically! She stumbled backward, wobbly with joy. But then, slowly, heartbreakingly, the arm disappeared and all she could see was Penelope's stern, frowning face looking over the mountain range of her bosom. Get a grip, she told herself. Dead people do not wave from windows. Nor do they drive Fiats. Get a grip.

Twenty-seven

Forget knock, knock, knocking on heaven's door, I would just like to know if I am on the waiting list, thanks all the same. I can pinpoint the moment when it all began—collision between big bus and big pants—but I have no idea when it will end. And don't all things end, eventually? Blair. Bootleg jeans. Teething. Youth. Isn't that the lesson we don't want to learn?

Don't get me wrong, I'm in no hurry to leave. Not when Freddie and Ollie are still here. It's just that it's exhausting and frustrating not being able to make my presence known to anyone but terrified household pets. Ah, the restless ghost of Sophie Brady. Wooo!

It's so frustrating not being able to alter the course of events, only to see them. Like Jenny's wedding. She's about to marry a toad and I can do damn all to stop it. I can't even sleuth down Sam's secrets. I can't do anything.

People have existential crises about the point of life. (Is this it? Well, no, actually, it ain't.) But I guess I'm in crisis about the point of being dead. It's not like I've got wiser and more spiritual. In fact, worryingly, the opposite appears to be happening. I'm getting pettier, more irritable. Yes, more like a live human in fact! Let me list the ways.

- Cecille rolls Ollie's socks into balls and lines them all up in his drawer like a plot of small cabbages, or rather, *petit choux*. I used to just put them in a pile on the dresser. This really irritates me.

- Cecille irons his underpants. Not even I ironed the grunderpants. Beyond call of duty. More than pisses me off, obviously. She has even ironed him underpants for Suze's party. Does she think he's going to pole dance or something? Widower-gram! Yay.

- Worse—could there be worse? Yes, there can!—Cecille also irons her own knickers. No woman of twenty irons her knickers. And it's *not* career appropriate to iron your frilly smalls— not for Cecille, M&S multipacks—while your boss and his son are sitting a few feet away on the sofa watching the footie on telly.

- The new butterfly tattoo on Cecille's left buttock. Couldn't help but be rather pleased when it got infected. See how lacking in Buddha-like compassion I am?

- The way she pretends to *"adore"* Ollie's favorite nettle ale—come on, you're French, fooling no one, love—and sits on the back step sipping it, sunlight threaded in her hair, gazing at Ollie through those long lashes.

- The question of my secret letter stash is eating away at me. I still have no idea where they are, which is very worrying. Cecille, mistress of the drawers, is chief suspect. If she does have them, does she have any idea that she is custodian of a bomb that threatens to shatter lives like windows?

Twenty-eight

Jenny maneuvered her Sarah Palin updo out of the orbit of a particularly unflattering downlighter and surveyed Suze's party, still disbelieving that she'd actually dragged Sam up here, despite the showdown with his mother earlier that day. There were twenty, thirty people in the living room, she guessed, clutching large wineglasses or small bottles of beer, laughing, shouting over each other, their tongues working within their cheeks to extricate bits of Suze's sticky cocktail sausages from between their teeth. They seemed to meld into a certain type that she'd become familiar with on her visits to the neighborhood: women in their thirties and forties, nicely dressed, media-ish, tired looking, a few pregnant; fortysomething men with superfluous body hair. Yes, she definitely recognized some of the individual faces. The man in the suit and the trilby, the self-conscious twiddle of mustache. The lady with the white-blonde Gaga do. It took a moment for her to realize that she recognized them from Sophie's funeral all those months ago.

Snatches of conversation slid about the room. "How is your new nanny working out?" "No, honestly, thanks, I'm on the wagon. Total torture." "I know I shouldn't say this but she looks fabulous on the chemo. She's lost a ton of weight, hasn't she?" "She only gives you the time of day if she thinks you might be able to offer her eldest a work placement; I wouldn't worry about it." "I hear you've got gay guinea pigs too! Let's throw a gay guinea pig disco!"

"No Ollie, then?" whispered Sam into her ear. "If he's a no-show I predict a riot."

Jenny swallowed hard. Ollie was late. He wouldn't come. No, he wouldn't. It was probably better like that. What with Sam being so chippy about him.

"Ow. What the . . ." He stepped away from a large urn of twigs, one of which was poking him in the backside.

"It's a twig, Sam. They're ornamental. You can't be angry with a twig."

"Jenny!" Suze's hair suddenly engulfed her, teased into an even greater fro for the occasion, a candyfloss fire risk. "It's good to have you back in the 'hood, lady!"

Jenny kissed her warmly on both cheeks. It was surprisingly good to see her again too. She realized she'd missed them all. "Suze, this is Sam." She glanced at Sam nervously, daring him to behave. "Sam, Suze."

"Ooh, the divorce lawyer!" Suze giggled, poking Sam in the ribs. "I'd better keep you away from my husband. Don't want him getting any tips, eh."

Sam shot Jenny a hard WTF look over his wineglass. Oh, dear.

Suze swayed on her high, wooden-heeled clogs. "Oh, I'm sorry," she hiccuped. "It must be like being a doctor and having people ask you questions about their gallbladder all night."

"Ha!" Sam said with a gritted smile.

"Jenny's been a real star these last few months," Suze continued obliviously. She put a hand on the sleeve of Sam's crisp blue shirt, dusting it with canapé crumbs. "We wouldn't have been able to run the Help Ollie committee without her."

"Oh, rubbish," said Jenny quickly. "You're the one who put in all the donkeywork, Suze."

Suze looked satisfied at this, not being sober enough to feign modesty.

Sam brushed the crumbs off the sleeve of his jacket with a subtle flick of his hand. "So Ollie's survived. The operation's over?"

"*Well*, the last few weeks have certainly been a bit quieter because of"—Suze hesitated as if she couldn't quite bear to say her name—"Cecille."

"The precocious French girl?" Sam brightened, looking around the room. "Is she here?"

Suze laughed. "No, Sam. Hopefully, she'll be babysitting tonight." She leaned toward Jenny. "Now, hon, have you heard the latest on Cecille?"

Jenny shook her head. Something knotted in her stomach. Thinking about Cecille gave her a feeling much like bad indigestion.

"Our little *fille* has changed," said Suze cryptically. "Let me tell you."

"Like how?" asked Jenny, fearing she was going to like this conversation less and less as it went on.

Sam raised an eyebrow. "Go on."

"Remember those sweet little sweaters and loafers she used to wear?" Suze paused for effect. "Gone! She now wears miniskirts. Little T-shirts." She pulled her silk blouse tight across her breasts to illustrate the point. Sam spluttered into his drink. "There are even reports of a *tattoo*!"

"A tattoo!" Oh, God. She had a vision of a terrifying *maman* appearing at her door, armed with a pastry rolling pin, to fish out her darling *fille*.

"There are also rumors of her going out and coming back rat arsed."

"Aren't French girls meant to sip half a glass of wine over a three-hour meal?" said Sam archly. "I do like the sound of this Cecille, Jenny. Sounds like you picked the right one after all."

Jenny ignored him.

Suddenly Lydia popped out of the crush of partygoers like a cork. "Hi! I'm Lydia." She stuck her small, diamond-encrusted hand out at Sam.

"Delighted," said Sam, shaking her hand. "Another Help Ollie foot soldier?"

"Absolutely." Lydia beamed. Jenny noticed how her neat breasts were contoured candidly by her pale pink pussy-bow blouse. She noticed Sam noticing them too. It hit her that she, Jenny, would never wear pale pink. Only women who thought they were pretty wore pale pink.

"Jenny!" Liz was striding over now, legs kicking out of a green silk dress that contrasted with the punkish red tips of her hair. She reminded Jenny of a firework. Jenny hugged her warmly. "Love the green dress."

"Love the hair!"

Jenny patted the Sarah Palin updo. "Can we not mention it, Liz? Misunderstanding in the salon."

"Ah, one of those. I like it, though." Liz laughed, and turned to Sam. "And you must be Sam. So we get you up to Muzzy Hill at last. We were all beginning to wonder if you existed at all."

Sam eyed Liz with obvious wariness, circumspect of any woman who dyed her hair a color that wasn't pretending to be natural for the obvious benefit of the male gaze. "Great minds, Liz. For all I knew, the whole Help Ollie could have been one huge conceit cooked up by Jenny and she was up here having rendezvous with a mysterious lover," he deadpanned.

Jenny tensed. Was that what he really thought? There was

something hard in those blue eyes that suggested he wasn't entirely joking.

"So now you see," said Liz, unruffled. "It's quite the den of iniquity. Have you found the lover?"

"Oh, I will." He smiled, giving Jenny a mock steely glance that made the hairs on her arms stand to attention.

Liz glanced quickly at Jenny as if to check her reaction, as if sensing the tension. "You never know, Sam, you may end up moving up here yet."

Thank goodness Liz was more than a match for Sam at his most laconic. She wanted Sam to understand that he couldn't just write these mothers off as bovine suburbanites. That he'd got them all wrong. They were great!

"Oh, God, it'd be totally wonderful to have Jenny up here," gushed Suze, slouching forward toward Sam drunkenly. "Do you really think you might—"

"Hate to disappoint you, ladies," Sam corrected, shooting the idea dead in its tracks and edging back from Suze's fro. "More chance of us moving to Kabul."

"That's what they all say," said Liz, eyeing him somewhat combatively from behind her wineglass. She nudged Jenny gently in the ribs. "Then you have kids."

Sam looked away into the party. "Guys, you're really selling it to me."

Jenny felt a wave of indignation. Why couldn't he just play along? Why did he have to be so . . . so bloody *superior*, all the time? She'd had to socialize with some of the dullest human beings on the planet at some of his friends' parties. She never complained. She smiled, she laughed, she did what partners are *supposed* to do.

"Oh. My. God. Congratulations!" squeaked Lydia, seizing the mention of kids as the logical entrée to the next step of conversation.

"How are the wedding plans? Tell us everything. I am a wedding fiend. Love it, love it, love it!"

Jenny studied the floor, remembering the awful, brittle conversation they'd had with Penelope this afternoon about her wedding dress, or lack of one.

"Coming along, coming along nicely," said Sam, lifting himself off his toes for a moment in the manner of a TV policeman. "Yeah, cool."

Jenny felt relieved. She didn't want to wash their dirty linen in public either. "Fine" was all she added.

Lydia grabbed Jenny's hand. "The dress!" She lowered her voice to a stagey whisper. "Have you found *the* dress? Close your ears, Sam! Close your ears."

Oh, God. She would have to bring it up. "Yeah, well, almost."

Sam shot her a dark look.

"Well, I want to be the first to know when you do." She let out a loud, wine-fumed sigh. "This is all *so* romantic, Sam. None of us can quite get over it." Her eyes started watering ominously.

Oh, no, thought Jenny, looking helplessly at Liz. They both knew what the other was thinking. She's going to cry. Make her stop!

"Right," said Sam, his eyes wandering around the room over Lydia's shoulder while somehow still keeping her as the focus of his attention. It was a look he'd perfected at industry dos, he'd once explained to Jenny, where over-shoulder scanning was necessary if one wasn't to expire of boredom before ten p.m. She wished he'd bloody well stop it.

"But a wedding between a divorce lawyer and a copy editor." Suze grinned, pushing the fro off her face with her wineglass. "I'll be looking out for the spelling mistakes in the order of service. And speeches lifted from the Net that might infringe copyright law."

Sam laughed, properly now, the beer having finally loosened him.

Jenny noticed his eyes alight on someone or something in the crowd. He shuffled his body, widened his chest, moved his legs further apart like compass points. Following his sight line over Lydia's shoulder, Jenny saw Tash trailing through the crowds in a long, gauzy leopard print dress with a neckline cut so far south it should come with its own passport, licorice hair swooshing around her shoulders, tanned legs appearing in tantalizing slithers through the slit in her dress. To Jenny, used to the little black high street dress and smudged-mascara-behind-specs look of her nice little publishing parties, Tash's glamour was alien and dazzlingly retro, Ferrero Rocher to her own comforting Dairy Milk.

"Hey, Jenny," said Tash, almost bashful as she glanced at Jenny, as if unable to decide on how much to give away by her greeting. Yes, thought Jenny, actually I *do* know you had lunch with my fiancé. You should have mentioned it.

"Hello." Sam became aware of the others studying him, waiting for an explanation of why an introduction wasn't necessary. "We've met," he said matter-of-factly.

"Really?" exclaimed Suze, frowning, trying to work out how this extraordinary detail had escaped her. "You've met? You and Tash?"

"We've met," Tash confirmed breezily, kissing Sam on the cheek. Jenny stiffened.

"So how's it all going, Natasha?" Sam asked in a businesslike manner, designed to quell the palpable waves of intrigue radiating from Suze, Lydia and Liz.

It didn't quell anything. He'd called her Natasha now. Most interesting.

"Can I thank you for lending me your clever legal head fiancé, Jenny?" said Tash, resting her hand lightly on her arm.

"Anytime," said Jenny, not intending to sound so clipped. She suddenly wished she'd worn something racier, rather than the navy shift. Sophie would have got her to wear the sequin dress. Or something with a slit. Yes, she would buy a dress with a slit.

Tash surveyed the room and frowned. "No Ollie, then?"

"Not yet, no," said Liz. "Sadly."

"Told you he wouldn't come."

"Give him time, give him time," slurred Suze.

"Cecille's probably grounded him," quipped Liz.

"Ladies, ladies." A man appeared dressed in high-waisted jeans and a black blazer. He put his arms around Lydia's waist. "This is my husband, George," said Lydia wearyingly, as if referring to a pesky child who should be in bed. "George, this is the wonderful Jenny. Soph's best mate. And Sam, her fiancé."

George nodded, displaying a shopfront of bad dentistry. "Good to put faces to the names at last." He turned to Suze. "Trust you're not getting Lydia waywardly drunk again? You must bust your annual alcohol units each time you meet to debate who's going to feed Ollie's cat."

"George!" hissed Lydia, giving him a sharp look. "Sorry, ladies."

"Evidently you lot need to find yourself a new widower and fast," quipped Sam. George roared with laughter, making his belly wobble above his brown leather belt.

"So cynical, Sam," purred Tash, looking at him indulgently. "Even for a lawyer."

George turned to Sam. "You realize, don't you . . ." There was a moment of awkwardness when it became clear that George had forgotten his name already.

"Sam," Sam said, picking up on it. "Jenny's sidekick."

"That we have no hope of competing with a young, handsome widower, Sam."

Sam grinned, clearly warming to the bumptious George. "I do realize this, George, yes."

Jenny frowned. She hoped Sam wasn't going to run with this one—he enjoyed running with anything with the whiff of bad taste. He could be a liability at a party.

"How can you two joke so lightly about something so *tragic*?" blurted Lydia, all her anger directed at her husband.

There was a moment's uncomfortable silence in which everyone cleared their throats. "Well, you gotta laugh or cry, eh?" George said, putting an arm over Lydia's shoulder. "I know what Sophie would have preferred."

Lydia shrugged the arm off, picked a half-full bottle of wine off the sideboard and sloppily poured herself a glass so that it spilled over the sides of the glass onto the wooden floor.

"Easy, sweetheart," George muttered under his breath.

"It's a fucking party," Lydia replied through teeth so close she looked like a ventriloquist. "Piss off."

George switched his attention from his wife to Sam. "I haven't seen you around, mate. Are you a member of the 2B mafia? Do you have kids at the school too?"

"No, no kids," said Sam with a tight smile.

Jenny looked away. Why was she finding it harder and harder trying to imagine them with kids? Sam bottle-feeding the baby, changing its nappy, the muddy Wellie boots and scooters in their pristine hall. No, impossible to visualize.

"But they're getting married this summer," said Suze, as if to explain the improbable scenario of her guests being childless. "The patter of tiny feet can't be far off."

"I fully recommend just the one," George said.

Lydia shot him a gladiatorial glare. Clearly she didn't see the joke.

"No more?" Suze smiled, not picking up on the hissing signals of impending marital implosion. "Go on, just one more, Lydia."

"I would," Lydia said murderously in a voice so low it was barely audible. "George isn't so keen."

"I'm too old for this game. We've been tired since 2004, haven't we, Lyds?" said George affectionately.

"God, that's nothing. I've been tired since 2003," said Liz cheerfully, gulping back her wine. "You get used to it after a while. It becomes the norm. In fact I think I'd feel weird if I wasn't tired."

"True, true. It's a question of surrender. You know what? I realized the other day that I haven't actually bought a CD since I had my first," marveled Suze, as if this was something to be proud. "I've never downloaded anything from iTunes. And, excuse me, but what the hell is an *app*? Is it a new erogenous zone?" She howled with laughter. "Check out the app on me."

Jenny could sense Sam stiffening. Poor Sam. The evening was all turning out exactly as he'd feared. She felt a wave of affection and sympathy for him. A fish out of water, what on earth was she thinking dragging him up here?

Tash glanced at her watch. "I wonder if I should call Ollie?"

"No need! Look!" Suze let out a joyful yelp, grabbed Jenny's arm and pointed to a shadow behind the bay window. "I told you he wouldn't flake it!"

Twenty-nine

I escort Ollie to Suze's front door, what remains of me wound tight around his left wrist like a watch strap, as needy and nervous as a mother taking her son to a first playdate. This is the first party he's been to since I died. Dead proud, I am.

If I'd been widowed I'd have a face like Keith Richards sucking a hornet, but Ollie's just slimmer and hairier and grayer. Nothing diminishes his cuteness. Tonight he's wearing the shoes I bought him for his birthday last year, chunky brogue boots hiding an endearing odd match of socks. His white (ironed) boxers peek over the top of his belted jeans when he bends over to tie a loose lace. He's still the got the world's sexist ass.

The door blasts open. It is Posh Brigid, barefoot in a fluoro lime green dress. She is squealing. "Ollie!" She thrusts his head down on her glitter-dusted décolletage. Then, gripping his hand as if he were a little boy that might just run off in the other direction if she didn't, which he might well do, she parades Ollie into the thrum of the party.

Inside the house we hit a bank of alcohol fumes and noise—voices, glasses, music. Then Ollie is spotted. There's an immediate deathly hush.

Panic streaks across Ollie's dark, beautiful eyes. Spotting Jenny and Suze, he staggers through the crowd toward them, leaving a disappointed, openmouthed Brigid in his wake. As he moves through the party the crowd parts. A laying on of hands. Men reach out to touch his arm lightly in a brotherly, supportive way, while women go straight for the exposed flesh: fingers or cheek. Ollie finally arrives at his destination. Sam claps him on the back. He does it with too much force. Sam gabbles a sheepish apology for not visiting and Ollie tells him not to worry about it. Apology and forgiveness out of the way, Sam hands Ollie a beer. Ollie drinks. He finishes the beer in minutes, doing his best to appear cheerful, as if cheerfulness itself is a defense against the grief pickers, the people who will ask any question just to sample the pitch of grief's rawest notes.

I use the opportunity of being this close to Sam to try to read him. I buzz around his smooth-shaven head. I peek down into the glacial blue eyes but see nothing but a small white ring of what could be a cholesterol deposit. He is looking at Sam. He is looking at Tash. He is not looking at Jenny. Has he not actually noticed how hot-damn gorgeous Jenny looks tonight?

Her hair is lovely. I like it piled retro like that. Those green cone heels rock. The navy dress is, well, navy—should have worn the sequin one—but she looks so very pretty, even if there is a microscopic muscle on her left eyelid flickering in spasm.

I shift my attentions to my beloved. He's on white wine now, always a bad idea. And he gets more moody looking with every refill. Is he really ready for his first party? Suddenly not sure now, not sure at all. I'm worried.

Someone else is drinking too much as well, I see. Lydia. Swaying beneath a potted palm like a woman on an inflatable boat. And she is staring at Ollie so intensely that even Ollie has noticed. Just as well that George is in the kitchen debating whether Woody Allen has lost his sense of humor with a drunk Danish man wearing a trilby.

Oh, no, here comes dear old George, looking for the wife. His belly arrives ahead of him, obliviously bumping into people like someone carrying a rucksack on a crowded Tube.

"You okay?" He slides his hand around Lydia's slim waist.

She steps aside and the hand slips down to the small of her back, then off.

"What the matter?"

Lydia sways on her heels. "Nuffink."

"You must be dead tired from Flora waking up last night." He strokes her cheek. "Darling, she's got to learn to take herself to the toilet. You can't be getting up night after night."

"It's not that." Her bleary eyes are still focused on one person and one person only and it's not her husband. George follows her gaze.

"Why are you staring like that?" Insecurity makes George's voice higher than normal. A muscle clenches in his jaw.

Lydia continues staring with what can only be described as longing at Ollie, who is chatting to Tash and Jenny now and refusing the figs wrapped in Parma ham. He's never going to be a canapé kind of man.

"You're drunk, Lyds."

"Oh, God, like, who cares?"

"And you're being kind of embarrassing."

"Yeah? And you're being ridiculous."

Wonder if in fact he is being ridiculous. Wonder if Lydia is at least thinking of elbowing her way onto Ollie's new wife list, ignoring the minor impediment of herself being married already.

"Lydia, stop fucking staring at Ollie!" George is cuckold red now.

Lydia shrugs, as if she doesn't give a shit. And she doesn't. Yes, she's really drunk.

Fear this cannot end prettily.

"What's this about?"

"God, you're boring, George. Please stop going on."

"Or is it so obvious that I've refused to see it?"

She turns round fiercely. "What's so flipping obvious, George? That Ollie has made me *think*, think hard about things that matter?" Her pale pink pussy-bow blouse trembles on her breasts.

"Now you sound totally adolescent."

"We have one life, George. *One!*"

He snorts. "It's taken you this long to work it out?"

"Our relationship. It could be the only one we'll ever know! It could be . . . be . . . this, then *death*! I thought my life would be"— she wrings her hands together—"bigger somehow."

George sighs wearily. "Do you think you'll ever reach your limit for drama and self-obsession, Lydia?"

Lydia's bottom lip wobbles—what's taken it so long?—and I feel sorry for both of them. I think of all the times that I've seen Lydia and George at parties or PTA meetings and outside the school gates and how I've always thought they were an odd couple but a happy one and that it is nice when two different people come together to prove to the world that you don't have to be samey—me and Ollie are a bit samey—to have a good marriage. Has me dying not only smashed a hole in my own family, but punched small holes in the glasshouses of other people's marriages too?

With a loud sniff Lydia turns on her gold heel and storms toward the toilet, leaving a bewildered George standing with his hands fisted at his sides in impotent fury, trying to look like nothing has happened.

Everyone at the party knows that something has happened, of course. Tash's and Liz's eyebrows are question marks. Ribs are elbowed.

When Lydia emerges from the toilet she is tear-streak free, pink lippy on. The pussy bow has been smartly rearranged. She smiles at George, a cold, hard smile that doesn't crease her eyes, but refuses to talk to him and the party continues apace. When George takes a call on his mobile then announces that Flora has been sick and he's going to go back to take over from the babysitter a cross-stitch of knowing looks threads across the party. The main show over, I settle onto Suze's mantelpiece, sliding between the wedding pictures and children's piano certificates, thoroughly exhausted. I am no longer the life and soul of the party.

Ever gone to a party and not drunk while those around you get plastered? Being dead is a bit like that. Being dead at a party is even more like that. I try not to dwell on the aching sadness that *I* am not on Ollie's arm or fall into the memory trap of Parties Past. Like the warehouse party in Hoxton in 1995 when we actually got stuck in the building's industrial lift for two hours and when the thing finally juddered to the top floor and we were caught on the job by a whooping huddle of partygoers. Or the dinner parties we threw when we lived in Peckham when the words "dinner party" seemed so ironic and hilarious and everyone put on their most glam seventies Halston-style dresses from Oxfam and the only thing I knew how to make was chicken curry with Patak's paste. Or indeed our wedding party, where I shook and whirled my dress to our very own hired Elvis while my girlfriends clapped me in a circle and I felt like the luckiest woman alive. Anyway, that stuff.

The party crackle rises and falls around me. The alcohol fumes get stronger and stronger, the body heat turns the air pink and there is a smell of BO that can no longer be masked by Suze's scented candles. So I take a minibreak around the house to get some air. After gliding upstairs on a thermal of body heat, I gaze longingly at Suze's children asleep angelically in their beds. They make me pine for Freddie. Quibble the hamster freezes with fear as I pass. He is so still I worry that I've brought on cardiac arrest, then, thankfully, he scuttles back into his hay nest. I have a good nose around Suze's bedroom. (A vibrator in Suze's sock drawer! Suze, who knew?) I am touched by the fact that she and Chris sleep on two pillows embroidered, albeit slightly cheesily, with the word "LOVE" and their names. And it makes me realize how the unsexiest couples can be the ones most happily humping away. There is a certain majesty in a solid middle-aged marriage, no? We value youth and passion but perhaps it's here, among the gray pubes and middle-aged spread and loose pelvic floors, that the real romance exists, having been tested to the point of exhaustion.

Moving on. Into the bathroom. Posh Brigid is texting somebody while sitting on the loo. Even though there is a sign saying *Only loo paper, please!* she flushes her Tampax down the toilet. The woman after her—Sara, the upholster to the stars, once did three chairs for Kate Moss—rifles through Suze's bathroom cabinet and borrows Suze's mascara. (Brave. Suze's family is blighted by recurrent conjunctivitis.) Another woman borrows her deodorant. (Rather her than me.) While Adam Cross from number thirty-five is sick in the toilet, leaving the tap running to hide the noise of the retching while another woman waits impatiently outside, crossing her legs tightly.

Out through the fan in the bathroom window, slitting between its blades like someone in a revolving door. Outside the fresh air is cool, luxurious, like a waterfall tumbling down a rock. There is the peaty smell of barbecues. The social smokers puff away, united by a feeling of contraband naughtiness. When they come back into the party they carry the tang of tobacco in their hair. As everyone gets drunker, the sensible school gossip burns away and is replaced by the hot fumes of bawdiness, bad jokes, drunken confessions of how they voted Tory for the first time in the last election and crushes on tennis coaches and other parents. And, of course, outrageous flirtation.

Suze has unbuttoned her blouse so that her Grand Canyon cleavage is on show. Every time she laughs it undulates. (Middle-aged romance or not, kind of wishing I didn't know about the vibrator now, actually. Not sure I will see her in the same light ever again.) Pete from four doors down has a hand on the romper-suit-clad bottom of the hot New Zealand single mum, Zara. Someone has found the courage to skin up a spliff in the kitchen. Tash is zigzagging round the party making An Impression: she is one of those women for whom a good time means feeling like the hottest female at the party. Fear I might once have been a *little* like this.

Jenny and Ollie are locked in deep serious conversation, which is hard to make out over the rolling noise of the party. She is wearing her intense listening face, head cocked at an angle, saying very little. She's one of the few people that genuinely want to hear what you say, as opposed to those people who are merely looking for an opportunity to slide their views into the gaps in the conversation.

Oh, what's happening? Jenny is looking down at the floor. She is shifting from foot to foot. She looks sad all of a sudden. Ollie is putting down his drink on the fireplace, picking his jacket up to leave.

Suze spots the dissent immediately and strides over so purposefully her cheeks wobble like jellies. "You're not going?"

"Yeah, going to call it a night, Suze," he says, flipping his hair off his face.

"Very wise. I'd make your escape now before she pins you to the sofa with a cocktail stick," says Liz.

Ollie slips on his jacket. "Thanks. It's been great."

"Has it, *really*?" Suze wants more. She wants more juice, more reaffirmation of her own social skills to lift the grief-struck widower from the tear-sodden depths of his misery.

Ollie just wants out. Even at the best of times, he's the kind of person who would always rather just slip away without saying good-bye.

There is movement in the hall. Suze swivels, eyes widening. "You're not going too, are you, Lydia?"

Lydia is in her white fake fur bolero, still swaying. "George has gone already. I'll walk back with Ollie."

"He'll have to carry you, at this rate," says Jenny, looking none too pleased at this idea.

Lydia hiccups. Then, suddenly, out of nowhere, Tash is galloping toward them, a fluttering vision in silk leopard print, breathing heavily through her nose like a horse. "But I thought *we* were walking back together later, Lydia."

"Oh, sorry, Tash," Lydia says, not sounding that sorry at all. She hiccups again. "I need to check on Flora."

"Well, maybe I should call it a night too."

Suze grabs Tash around the waist. "You are not going anywhere, lady! It's only eleven thirty. It's socially unacceptable to leave a party before midnight."

"But . . ."

"And, missy, I know that Ludo is at his dad's, so you haven't got the babysitter excuse either."

Checkmate. Tash is stuck. She doesn't look happy about it.

Outside, a soupy summer fog is licking the pavements clean. Lydia slips her arm through Ollie's and leans against him. Seeing them walking together like that, two dark figures in the romance of summer mist, I splutter helplessly. They look pretty together, no denying it, Lydia all fluffy and bundled up, a babe in the woods in that bolero. Ollie's hair long and damp with fog, his walk drunken and laid-back, his boots dragging on the slippery pavement like a cowboy's.

I must stop.

This is Lydia we're talking about, sweet little Lydia. Lydia, who learned how to make lasagna especially for Ollie. Lydia, who sobbed throughout my funeral and still cries herself to sleep about me. Lydia, who has spent three hundred pounds on bereavement kitchenware. I cannot blame her when she leans her body more and more to the left. When she rests her blonde head against Ollie's shoulder. When she tells him he is "a total inspiration." Can I?

We get to the door of number thirty-three. Lydia lives about two hundred yards away. They hesitate. Ollie says to Lydia, "I'll walk you to your door."

"Can't I come in?"

"Come in?"

"Yes. I'd kill for a quick cup of tea. If I go home I'll wake up George."

"Oh, right."

Right!

They walk down the paved path, and as they walk, Lydia moves closer and closer to him, as if she wants to dive into him like a sleeping bag. By the time his key is in the lock the toe of her boot is scuffing against the heel of his, her hand on his back. He turns the key, knocks the door fully open with his knee. They are in the hall. They don't get any farther.

Lydia starts to sob.

"Lydia?" he says, aghast.

"I'm so sorry, Ollie, crying like this."

"What is it, Lydia?" The tenderness of his voice fills me with longing. He always was the world's best shoulder to cry on.

"George."

Ollie frowns. His face is full of shadow. His unease taps out a rhythm through his foot.

"It's gone wrong, Ollie. Wrong between me and George."

"What's happened?"

"It sounds weird. . . ."

"Go on."

She takes a deep, shaky breath. "He doesn't love me like how you loved Sophie. And now I've realized it, I can't unrealize it and it's completely doing my head in."

There is a whirring silence. A smile twitches at the corner of Ollie's mouth, like he's trying not to laugh. "Hey, you just need to sleep it off. Let's get you home, honey, come on."

"No. I'm going to pull myself together and we're going to have that cup of tea," Lydia says firmly. She lets go of his arm and staggers into the kitchen, tripping over Freddie's football boots that he's left in the middle of the hall. When they are both in the kitchen she closes the door behind her, leans against it and giggles coquettishly. "Don't want to wake Freddie."

It takes Ollie four minutes to find the tea bag. Yes, he is definitely inebriated too.

"Sit next to me." She pats the chair next to hers.

Ollie sits obediently. The tea is forgotten.

For a moment Lydia appears relatively normal and sober. "I can't bear this any longer." She starts to cry.

"Oh, Lydia, don't cry."

"I could leave him." Her head falls against his shoulder.

"All marriages are hilly."

"Yours wasn't."

Ollie pulls at his beard. For the first time, I really don't know what he's thinking. He looks gaunt and a little bit like Jesus.

"Men like you know how to love a woman properly."

Ollie laughs then, really laughs, like this is the funniest thing he's heard in years. He doesn't look like Jesus now.

Lydia abruptly stops laughing. The lids of her eyes lower. "I'd leave George for you, Ollie."

Ollie starts away from her. There's a terrible silence. The little red light on the smoke alarm is beginning to flash. "You've had a lot to drink. Come on, sweetheart, I'll take you home."

Lydia wipes the tears away from her eyes. "I wouldn't expect to take Sophie's place, I really wouldn't. . . ."

Ollie's eyes are filling with tears now. And I don't know whether this is because he fancies Lydia or because he misses me or because he hasn't held a woman in his arms for so long. He puts one finger very softly on Lydia's mouth. "Shush."

I didn't expect this. The finger-on-the-lips thing. I didn't expect it at all.

Oh, fuck. It is going to happen. It's going to happen. Lydia tilts her face toward him and closes those lovely green eyes. The smoke alarm is flashing wildly now.

Then I hear footsteps. The shiny orb of kitchen door handle is slowly rotating in the gloom.

"Ollie?" The kitchen door flings open. Cecille stands there in her short satin nightgown, hands on her hips. "Iz everything okay?"

Thirty

Unsettled by the near-miss kiss, I helicopter off, moving directly up and out, and spend the night in the wonderful peaty wetness of Queen's Wood, only coming back home as the streets are beginning to smell of cooking bacon and lumps of Sunday newspapers thump onto doormats. And who do I see? I see Jenny, hiking up the road, slipping backward in her sandals up the hill, carrying her swim bag. She hesitates outside Ollie's door and takes a deep breath, as if summoning courage for something that is not just municipal swimming.

"Jenny!" Freddie barrels into her arms. He is already wearing his red swimming goggles. "You going to walk upside down today?"

"No chance!" She kneels down and peers directly into his goggles, as if looking through a telescope. "I've had my hair tinted. I don't want to look like Shrek again."

"Smoky bacon?" The highlight of any swimming trip for Freddie has always been putting coins in the vending machine, watching the

spirals rotate and that shiny packet of crisps falling magically into
the black tray.

"If you swim a length."

Ollie steps out of the kitchen into the hall, stifling a yawn. His
face lights up when he sees her. "You look criminally well after the
party last night."

"Croissants and painkillers."

Ollie tussles his floppy dark hair, runs his finger through his
bison beard. He looks like he hasn't slept. "Come on. Coffee." He
pulls her by the hand toward the kitchen.

"*Allô,*" interrupts Cecille.

How long has Cecille been standing on the stairs? She wears a
navy silk dressing gown that gapes open over her pert décolletage.
The same one she wore last night. The one that foiled the near-miss
kiss. I owe this dressing gown.

"Morning, Cecille," says Jenny, trying and failing not to stare at
the décolletage. "How are you?"

"Very, very well." Cecille flicks her eyes coquettishly at Ollie,
head poised, one hand on the banister in a cinematic manner.

Freddie is pulling on Jenny's hand. "Come on, Jenny, let's go.
Let's go swimming."

"Okay."

"What about coffee?" Ollie looks disappointed.

"Best to beat the crowds," Jenny says quickly.

"Oh." Ollie rubs his eyes. "I'm going back to bed then."

"I cook fry-up first," purrs Cecille, pulling the belt tight on her
dressing gown, showing off her slim waist.

He grins. "Cecille, you're an angel."

Whoa! Who's the angel here?

"Have a good breakfast," Jenny says tightly, as she rushes out of
the house with Freddie, a great spume of emotion trailing behind

her, thick and white as an airplane trail. I get caught up in its tail-wind, spun in its vortex as we hurtle toward the door and I am sucked in, in, inward into Jenny. Suddenly I'm somewhere very red, pulsating. It's like being inside a small red tent at dawn. Ba-boom, ba-boom. It's a heart, alright. And, I tell you what, Sam isn't in it.

Thirty-one

The rap on the car window made her jump.

Jenny squinted into the dirty Camden sunshine. The first thing she saw was the hand. A tiny dolphin tattoo on the wrist. Her eyes zipped from hand to face, a beautiful face wearing large white sunglasses. She froze. It was the woman from the white Fiat, the one who looked like Sophie but seen up close was patently *not* Sophie. She had the same thick dark hair. The same oval-shaped face. But she was most definitely not Sophie. Well, of course she wasn't.

"Sorry, I didn't mean to startle you," the woman's mouth was saying. She had a soft lilting voice, well spoken. Nice even teeth.

Jenny opened the car door, warily, heart starting to pound. "Can I help you?"

The woman's eyes glittered. "I hope so," she said, sounding just a little bit crazed. "I do hope so."

Oh, God, a nut. Camden was full of them. She'd got a nut on her tail. A nut who looked a bit like Sophie. The hairs prickled on her arms. Wanting to get away, she got out of the car and locked the door, in case the nut was hoping to nick the car. She conceded that the woman was a surprisingly well-turned-out nut. Maybe it was someone normal who had had a breakdown. Someone who'd bought lots of nice clothes before she lost the plot. "Excuse me," she said in her polite nut-avoidant voice, stepping past her to the sunny pavement and edging closer to the safety of her apartment.

"I just need to talk to you, if you don't mind." The woman started walking next to her.

Jenny felt properly uncomfortable now. What did this woman want from her?

She put a hand on Jenny's arm. "Please, Sophie."

The blood drained from her head. It took a few moments to collect herself. "What? What did you just call me?"

"Your name is Sophie, isn't it?" The woman squinted in the sunlight, more unsure now.

"No, no, it isn't."

The woman looked puzzled. "Really? Sorry. I . . . I . . ."

"Why did you think I was called Sophie?"

The woman looked down at the ground. "I got confused." She stopped, looked up, her brown eyes panicky. "It's just Sam," she blurted out. "I know Sam. There was something . . ."

Jenny's stomach knotted. "Sam?" She was beginning to get a really, really bad feeling about this.

She narrowed her eyes. "You're his girlfriend?"

Jenny didn't answer immediately, not taking her eyes off the woman's face. "Fiancée."

"Fiancée?" The woman's face fell. She started walking backward. "Right, right."

"Wait! Why do you want to know? Hang on a minute," Jenny called out as the woman turned on her blue heel and started to walk smartly away down the street, glossy dark hair swinging behind her.

Thirty-two

S he looks like Sophie?" Sam exhaled tusks of smoke from his nostrils. It scarved up toward the speaker in the ceiling, trembled by the bass of the Kaiser Chiefs.

"A dead ringer." Jenny sat on the cold black granite worktop. For a moment she felt like she was perching on the edge of a building, ready to jump off.

"Don't be weird, babes. Sounds like a Camden nut job to me." He flicked his ash into his favorite fifties-style pink glass ashtray.

"Sam, she thought my name was *Sophie*. How freaky is that?" She leapt off the worktop. It was giving her vertigo. "She said she knew you!"

She noticed that he'd paled a little beneath his weekend stubble. Aware of her scrutinizing him, he turned and started fiddling with a foil packet of coffee, letting his cigarette burn down. "I told you, babes, you need to chill out."

"I don't! I am chilled out!" she shrieked, spitting in an unladylike fashion across the kitchen. "Sam, she asked if my name was Sophie. Why would she ask that?"

He picked up his fag, shifted behind a veil of smoke, glancing up at her sideways. "A white Fiat, you say?"

"A white Fiat. One of those ones shaped like soapsuds. And she had a tattoo!" she said, suddenly remembering. "A little dolphin on her wrist, poking out from under her watch strap." He closed his eyes and pinched the skin at the top of his nose very tightly so it went white. "You know who it is, don't you? You do. Tell me."

"Dominique."

"And who the hell is *Dominique*?"

Sam drew his hands across his jaw, as if even the memory of her exhausted him. "She always was a bit Looney Tunes."

"You've never mentioned her before!"

Sam crossed his arms. "Haven't I? Well, I guess I wouldn't. It was no big deal."

Okay, she had never been one of those women who demanded a detailed biography and score out of ten on the attractiveness charts for every ex. But still. Who the hell was Dominique? And what would he give her out of ten?

"It was before you. Obviously."

"When?"

"I can't give you the precise calendar dates, I'm afraid."

"When, Sam?" She was shaking now.

He reached for her hand. "Look, Jenny, there were quite a few women before you. I've never pretended there weren't."

"So she was a fling, just a fling?"

He nodded. "A fling."

She looked away from him, eyes blurring with tears. "I suspect you meant more to her."

"Come on, darling. We're getting married in a few weeks. Let's forget about the past." He touched her jaw lightly, drawing her toward him. "I love you. You have no reason to worry about other women." He picked up her hand and kissed it. "Don't get in such a flap about everything."

"But *why* did she think I was called Sophie?" She couldn't let this one go, she just couldn't.

"Maybe she just got confused." Giving up on the bodily contact approach, he spooned some coffee beans into the grinder and flicked the switch. "Sophie is a common enough name."

She leaned back against the wall, spent. She was no longer sure of anything. The grinder sounded like her own brain, reducing all certainties to pulp. They were silent for a few moments while he made coffee. She watched him and wondered.

"Hey, what do you reckon about Mum's idea of having the local brass band welcome people into the marquee from church?" he said, pouring the coffee into two little cups.

"What?" She could still see Dominique, those intense brown eyes peering in through her car window, searching for answers in her own face.

"A brass band."

"God, I don't know."

"I like a brass band."

"I hate brass bands."

"You'd make Mum very happy if you said yes. Here you go. Coffee."

"I don't want coffee."

"Okay, I get the mood you're in. I won't mention traditional Mum's Morris dancing suggestion."

"Please don't."

He took a sip, winced slightly. "Mum was also asking about the wedding dress."

"Sam, she gave me a hard time about it last month," she said, remembering the dreadful meeting the day of Suze's party. "I don't need it again. I will get the wedding dress. I'm not going to walk down the aisle naked."

"Shame." He smiled. "Actually, sweetheart, she's asked me to ask you whether you want her to go shopping with you. For the dress."

"No!" She caught herself, took a deep breath. "Sorry, that's very kind of her, but no."

"I'm trying to be understanding here." He put his coffee down, eyes flashing dangerously blue. "But are you waiting for Sophie to reappear and go shopping with you or something?"

Maybe she was. Maybe that was what it was.

"Babes, it ain't going to happen."

"I'll get it soon," she said tightly.

"I think everyone would feel better if you did." He pulled a strand of hair off her face and tucked it behind her ear. His fingers smelled of Marlboro Lights. She didn't like it. "By the way, Mum and Dad are coming over for brunch on Sunday. Perhaps you could think what kind of food we need to get in. Mackerel? I rather like a bit of mackerel of a morning."

"I take Freddie swimming on Sunday mornings." She hated mackerel. She struggled with oily fish. They were oily.

Sam stirred more sugar into his coffee with an angry vigor. "Maybe Ollie could take his own kid swimming now."

"It's our thing."

He looked up. "Is that wise?"

"What do you mean, *wise*?"

"Freddie's getting attached to you, Jenny." His voice became soft and remedial. "Look, I know you've pulled back from Ollie a bit since Cecille arrived." He threw back his head and drained his cup. "But not really from Freddie."

"Of course I haven't bloody well pulled back from Freddie!"

"You're not going to be able to continue being as hands-on as you have been, are you? Not when we're married."

"I don't see what difference me being married makes! I'm there for as long as he needs me, Sam."

Something hardened in his eyes. "Then it's a life sentence."

She stared at Sam in disbelief. "I *love* Freddie, Sam. Don't you get it? I love him because he's lovable but also because he's Sophie's boy. I will always be there for him. And I don't care if that's a life sentence. I bloody well hope it will be."

Sam broke off a corner of a bagel left over from breakfast and took a bite, then chucked the rest of it to the side, never taking his eyes off her face. It was funny the way he was looking at her. "You'll feel different when you have your own kids, that's what Mum says."

"I don't see it's any of her business."

He didn't speak for a very long time. "This is about Ollie, isn't it?"

"No!" How to explain that whenever Ollie was in the room, the room seemed brighter? That was all it was.

"The Hugh Hefner of N10."

"Don't be ridiculous."

A vein pulsed on his temple. "Did you ever think about how it made me look at that terrible party you cattle-prodded me into going to, when you were locked into deep whispery conversation with Ollie and I'm standing there, like a bloody eejit . . ."

She spoke carefully. "I was just aware that it was his first party without Soph. I wanted to make sure he was okay."

He turned to face her, and she felt pinned by his gaze, like it had skewered her there in this life, this moment. "Is there something you want to tell me?"

She closed her eyes. If she kept them shut maybe this would all go away. But Sam was still there when she opened them. Yes, yes, she knew that beneath the bluster, Sam was hurting, jealous even, and that she should be doing more to placate him, convince him that

Ollie meant nothing and that she was all Sam's, heart, soul, body, forever and ever. Why wasn't she? Couldn't she?

She squeezed her eyes shut and saw a flicker book of images on the blood black of her lids: Sophie's gummy smile; Sophie throwing her head back doing the Honk; her crooked body lying in the road; her yellow knickers; Dominique's dolphin tattoo; Sam tearing off a bit of bagel, looking at her in a way he had never looked at her before. She couldn't process any of it. It was all part of a strange algorithm she didn't understand. "I'm taking a shower."

She stripped off her clothes and gazed at her naked body in the mirror—in the unflattering bathroom lighting she looked pale, soggy and fleshy, rather like a huge scallop—then got into the shower, turning it on at its hottest so that it was on the very threshold of burning her skin. She stood there for an hour, the hot water pouring down her head, over her eyes, into her ears, trying to wash it all away.

When she reemerged, Sam had gone out. Thank goodness. She peered out the window and took three deep yogic breaths, which made her feel slightly dizzy. Jolted by a hoot from the street below, she opened her eyes to see some schoolchildren pointing up at her and laughing. She was still wrapped in a bath towel! She fled to the sofa and stared blankly into the spotless, expensively furnished sitting room, Sam's coffee cup still on the side, his cigarette stub in the ashtray. Her skin was cool now, hair frizzing at the ends as it dried. Traffic rumbled outside, the kitchen tap dripped and for a powerful, lucid moment she felt like her life was unraveling, there and then, unspooling like loo paper rolling across the walnut floor. Soon it would be everywhere, sheets and sheets of it, blown about by the wind. And as it was impossible to roll loo paper back neatly onto its cardboard tube, it would be impossible to put her life back as it was too.

If she went on like this Sam would dump her. After being engaged for so long, to lose him now would be like queuing all night on the pavement to buy a ticket to Wimbledon's Center Court only to turn around and go home the moment her name was called. Yes, he'd dump her. Or, just as bad—no, worse—he'd nuke her friendship with Ollie, impose some kind of Ollie purdah. Then she wouldn't see Freddie either. Oh, God. Unimaginable. She needed to do something, something persuasive, placating and symbolic.

And fast.

Thirty-three

Four days later, Jenny stood anxiously shifting from the sweaty insole of one tan gladiator sandal to the other on Tottenham Court Road, rather doubting her flash of genius. Could this really be the solution to the Ollie-versus-Sam problem? The bridge across the boiling waters? Well, she hadn't had any better ideas. And she needed to move on. She needed to stop thinking about the letters she'd discovered in Sophie's drawer. Stop thinking about Dominique. Ollie. The entire bad thought disco in her head. Sam was right. She needed to chill right out. Grief had knocked her off course. It was time to get back on track again. This was a start.

Twelve thirty. Jenny checked her phone in case he'd sent a message. Nothing. Maybe he'd blown her off. She'd pretty much forced him into it, after all, flexed the power of bridal entitlement like a biceps. She would give him five more minutes. Two more. One more, just in case. Until the lights changed. The pavement began to swell with office workers on their lunch break. Although it was blustery, it was hot, making her grateful that she'd slathered on the deodorant as well as having got herself fully waxed and plucked. Today, special reinforcements would be necessary. One more light change.

Just as she turned to go, defeated, there he was, waving, walking up the street in a slim-cut black suit, white trainers, his floppy dark hair alive in the wind, more vivid than anyone else, like he was in high-def color and everyone else was in black-and-white. I'm always going to remember this moment, him walking up the street like that in his black suit. I'm going to remember it forever, she thought.

She kept her thoughts to herself.

"Am I late?"

"I was just early," she said, even though he was late.

As they started to walk down Oxford Street Jenny became very aware of the wind, of the way it was blowing her blue dress flat against her body, showing everything: bust, belly, swell of pubic bone.

"Pretty dress," Ollie said, giving her a sidelong glance.

She swung her big handbag over her torso shyly. "Thanks."

"I've brought supplies." He rummaged in his trouser pocket and pulled out a packet of Haribo. "I'd have brought harder drugs but I fear your disapproval."

Jenny laughed. "I can't believe I'm making you do this."

"Nor can I."

She'd already told him why she'd asked. It was quite simple. Easy to explain. He was here because Sophie wasn't. That was the reason. He understood that. She understood that. By taking Ollie wedding dress shopping she was firmly placing him in the role of Gay Best Friend. This would clarify the relationship for all of them and stop her life from unspooling. He could be gay! He could. He could be gay and musical and sexy, like Rufus Wainwright. They must all completely forget that he was heterosexual.

Selfridges. Ollie pushed open the heavy glass doors, then stood aside to let her through into the hungry scrum of the handbag department—who were all these women feeling so rich in the middle of a recession?—before they jostled their way toward the huge escalators that cut through the fabric of the building like a giant zipper. Jenny held on tightly to the rubber handrail. She hadn't been to a big department store since Soph died. The glass, the chrome, the lights and noise were overwhelming. As if sensing her discomfort, Ollie put his hand on the small of her back. It burned a palm shape through the thin cotton of her blue dress.

He leaned over her from the step below, resting his chin on her shoulder. "Now, so I know, Jen, are we going white or off white or something more radical?"

"Off white. A lady at John Lewis said it was 'softer on the mature bride's complexion.'" His mouth was centimeters from hers. He was too close. She stepped up on the escalator.

"She actually said that? Jesus. I'm scared now." He smiled at her, almost shyly now. "But do *you* want off white?"

"I don't know what I want. And I should warn you now that I have to battle my inner Dolly Parton, Ollie. I'm always drawn to the most hideous dress in the shop. Your job is to stop me from buying something that should not be seen outside Nashville."

"I may not." His breath was on the back of her neck. For a moment she thought she smelled everything she loved in it—coffee, fresh air, sleep, sex—then she caught herself and mentally shut her nostrils. "I may let you go rhinestone yet."

They burst into the bridal suite, the eyes of the groomed staff peering at them curiously, discreetly. Perhaps they were wondering about the handsome man with her, who he was, why he was there. If he was gay. She caught sight of Ollie's face in the ornate white mirror on the wall opposite and started at the familiarity of it, almost as if she'd inadvertently caught a glimpse of her own reflection.

"How can I help you?" A headmistressy shop assistant with a name badge—*Penny*—approached them, beaming. Her teeth were so white they looked almost blue, like teeth under UV light at a disco in the eighties.

"I'm looking for a dress." State the bleeding obvious. "A wedding dress." Even worse. She could feel Ollie smiling next to her, shifting from trainer to trainer at the inherent weirdness of the occasion.

"Well, you have come to the right place." Penny waited for Ollie and Jenny to laugh. They laughed. "What sort of gown are you looking for?"

Something about the word "gown." It made her feel old and musty, or like someone about to be admitted into surgery in a hospital ward.

The shop assistant raised a questioning eyebrow.

"Modern?" Ollie offered.

Jenny nodded gratefully. "Yes, yes, modern!"

"Modern gowns for the modern bride," repeated Penny with rehearsed enthusiasm. "If you'd like to follow me." Feeling like schoolchildren in a lingerie department, she led them giggling to a rack of serious dresses, all lined up on a rail like different mismatching sections of one long billowing curtain. She could feel her heart start to slam. Just the sight of the dresses made her anxious. They were all so forbiddingly romantic. And she was so . . . so . . . prosaic somehow. Sophie used to be able to wear frills and flounces and look like Kate Bush. Whereas if Jenny so much as went near a lace hem she looked like one of those madwomen who wander around Portobello Market mumbling about the summer of 1974 and how better the area was before the bankers moved in.

"Like?" said Ollie, picking a cream column off the rail. "Not like?"

"Like." Jenny nodded, trying to work out if like was love. No, not love.

"Do let me know if you'd like me to put any of them in the dressing room," exuded Penny, block heels wedged in the deep pile carpet. She smelled a sale and clearly wasn't going anywhere.

"This is cute," Jenny muttered, fingering some intricate pearl beadwork around the neckline of a dress.

Penny was there in a flash. "Stunning! I'll put it in the dressing room. What is your size?"

She felt embarrassed to be revealing such information in front of Ollie. "A size twelve?" She immediately regretted presenting as a question.

Penny gave her a quick once-over. "I'll put a couple of fourteens in there too, shall I? The sizing varies so much from dress to dress."

Jenny blushed again, hating the thought that Ollie would think she was trying to pretend she was slimmer than she was. Which, of course, she had been.

"I'll let you know if we need any more help, thanks."

Penny stepped backward with comic servility just as a twenty-something blonde and her equally blonde mother giggled into the bridal suite. Something about their excitability gave Jenny a pang of longing for a feeling she didn't yet feel. She would soon. Yes, she would. As soon as she had her dress. Obviously, the dress was key. You couldn't be a bridezilla without a bridal *gown*.

"This rocks." Ollie held up a long oyster-colored dress with a pale blue sash around the waist.

She fingered the frilly sleeves. "A bit trannie?"

"You've ruined it for me now." He flicked it away on its hanger, making a metallic whoosh sound on the tracks. "This one?" He held up a long white dress with barely any embellishment.

She cocked her head on its side. "Gorgeous. And yet. No sparkle."

"You're right. The girl must have sparkle."

He was silent for a few moments and when she next looked up at him she could see that something had changed. He looked quite different from how he'd looked a moment before. He was frowning into the rack of dresses with a strange, distant look in his eyes. Oh, God. He was staring at a fifties-style dress, a dress just like Sophie's wedding dress.

Sophie's had been a vintage dress, cinched in tight at the waist, the skirt flouncing out as if hooped, filled with layer upon layer of petticoat, so that she looked like a Degas ballerina when she leaned forward. Most keenly Jenny remembered the morning of the wedding, its intimacy, the excitement. It was just her, Sophie and a makeup artist with pea green eyes called Lottie in a little boutique hotel with lilac upholstery. Jenny could still hear the hiss of the glasses of champagne and smell the basket full of untouched toast and croissants, a freshly showered Sophie sitting on a stool in her white hotel dressing gown, nervous and happy, a river of dark, freshly washed hair falling down her back.

She had watched, awestruck, as Sophie had got more beautiful with each stage of the prep process: hair dried and curled, makeup applied, diamonds clipped to her ears, blue lace garter snapped to her thigh, flower behind the ear. Sophie had worn a red flower behind her ear that day. Jenny had helped Lottie wire it and pin it on, holding the spare pins between her front teeth. She remembered wondering what it must feel like to be so blessed. Never in her wildest dreams would it have occurred to her that Sophie would be dead a few years later. Or that she'd be here choosing a wedding dress with Sophie's groom.

She felt a shudder of guilt. In her haste and selfishness to convince Sam of the platonic nature of her relationship with Ollie she'd not considered Ollie's feelings. She put the dress she was holding back on the hanger. "Let's go, Ol."

"But we haven't found your dress."

"I can get my dress another time."

"This is the time." He slipped his arm around her waist. She felt the cuff of his suit against her skin. "I want to help you, Jenny. I really do."

She blinked back unexpected tears. There was a part of her longing for him not to facilitate any of it. For him to stop the wedding, to tell her it was too much too soon. To tell her to stop being such a bloody idiot, and to lead her away someplace dark and quiet until the feelings that were mashing up her head abated. "You're sure?"

"Sure. You need to try this shit on."

Penny appeared by their side. Jenny tried to ignore her.

"I hate trying stuff on."

She could hear Penny tutting beneath her breath.

"How many weeks until the wedding?"

"Four."

Penny gasped before whipping their choice of dresses away to the dressing room with a stagey kick of the heels.

It didn't take long for the changing room to whiff of sweat as she struggled into dresses, out of dresses. And yes, annoyingly, the shop assistant was right. In two dresses out of three she was a fourteen. She couldn't help but dislike like those dresses. She yanked on the size twelve off-white column number, plain apart from a sash bow studded with crystal—just the right amount of twinkle?—and emerged self-consciously from the changing room, not knowing how to dangle her arms, aware of her corset-fortressed bosom spilling over the neckline. "This one?"

At first Ollie didn't say anything. He just stared.

"You don't like it?" She shyly pulled up the dress to hide her cleavage.

"You look beautiful."

Jenny blushed, fiddled with a bit of handmade lace. Had she found the One?

"But . . ."

There was a but! She deflated.

"It doesn't show off your shoulders."

"My shoulders?" Jenny had never noticed her shoulders. No one had ever noticed her shoulders. It was like noticing her elbows. Her shoulders were entirely unremarkable.

"Try on the one with the cutaway sleeves."

"You're not meant to do cutaway sleeves over the age of thirty-five."

"Says who?"

"I don't know, the fashionistas. Women who know about these things."

"I think we know what Sophie would say."

"Bollocks to that." She leapt back into the dressing room and eyed the sleeveless dress combatively. It looked heavy and overly worked, the kind of dress that would look stunning, as Penny might say, on the sylphlike twentysomething with the waist-length blonde hair in the next-door cubicle. Plus it was size fourteen.

It was harder to get into than the others. Penny had to lower it down over her face like a piece of armor. A sharp tug on the inner corset lost her a lungful of breath. Then there were dozens of pearl buttons that ran up the spine, each one requiring the fingers of an elf to fasten.

"Almost there!" Jenny called out to Ollie through the curtains, as Penny fastened the last button. "Don't run off to the pub just yet."

"Stunning," sighed Penny, standing back, hand at her throat.

Jenny stole a glance at herself in the changing room mirror. The dress made her look different in some way she didn't quite understand. It was genuinely hard to tell if she looked lovely or totally awful.

"Come on," Ollie called from the other side of the curtain.

She yanked back the edge of the curtain. Penny gave her a little push on her flank, as if nudging a horse from its box, and she nearly fell out of the dressing room. Under his gaze she could feel herself sweating. "Awful?"

"Look at yourself in the mirror." Ollie held her by the shoulders and swiveled her round to face the long gilt mirror. "Do you realize how beautiful you look, Jenny?"

She caught her breath. It felt like the corset had just been yanked two inches tighter.

"I think you should wear dresses like this every day." He walked over to her and kissed her on the cheek. "Sam's going to want to rip the fucking thing off."

"Truly stunning," said Penny, hand at her throat.

"It's the one, Jen."

She looked at her reflection again. Now that Ollie had given the dress his seal of approval she loved it too. It was the dress! It was an amazing dress!

"Sold?"

Jenny swallowed hard. "Sold."

So why did her hand shake so badly as she handed over her credit card at the till? Penny grabbed one end of the credit card to take it. Jenny didn't let it go. Penny pulled. Jenny didn't let go. Her mind had started to whir with one word. D-d-d-d-d. Dominique. Dominique. Dominique. Why was it repeating on her now? She'd done her best to put it behind her and believe Sam's explanation. She thought she'd put it to bed.

"May I?" Penny said tersely, strengthening her grip on the card.

"You alright, Jenny?" whispered Ollie, giving her a funny look.

"It's so much money. I'll only wear it once." *Dominique. Dominque. Dominque.*

Penny gave her a tight, mirthless smile, releasing her fingers from the credit card. "Perhaps you'd like to sit down and take a moment."

"Jenny, you, more than anyone, deserve a beautiful dress." Ollie put an arm around her shoulder. "Don't worry about the money. Don't you love it?"

She could taste the salt of tears in the back of her throat. "Yes, but . . ."

"If you wouldn't mind moving aside a little," said Penny, irritated now, "I will serve the next customer while you . . . make up your mind. Thank you."

The mother and daughter pair stood behind them, the mother clutching a flamboyant white feather headdress. They were still giggling.

"Stop," said Ollie suddenly. Everyone turned to look at him. He dug into his back pocket. "I will pay for the dress."

"No! Don't be ridiculous. You absolutely can't pay for the dress!" protested Jenny, mortified at the turn of events.

"I want to."

"It's not the money . . ." she began, suddenly not quite knowing what it was.

"Shh. My call."

Penny's hand shot up like a piston to grab Ollie's credit card. As she determinedly shoved it into the card machine, she looked up at Jenny and winked. "It's your lucky day."

Thirty-four

O llie *bought* the wedding dress?" Sam is saying, hands gripping the steering wheel so hard his knuckles are white. He doesn't look happy, not at all. From up here, somewhere near the car's padded ceiling, I can see a vein pulsate on the top of his shaved head. Feel sorry for Jenny now.

"Yeah." Jenny squeezes her lower lip with her fingers. She has Heathrow's lost luggage depot around her eyes. She doesn't look happy either. And she should do because the dress that Ollie bought her really is beautiful. When Jenny unzipped it from its cover last night I settled on its folds like a moth, absolutely still on its silk. She spent the good part of an hour just staring at that dress, walking around it, viewing it from different angles, like someone in a gallery puzzling over a painting.

"Is there anything the guy *can't* do? No wonder half the women in north London are wanking off about him." He gives her a side-long, confused glance as he says this. Like he can't quite work out what's going on. He senses change in her, I think, sniffs it like a wolf in a changing wind, but he can't identify it. To be perfectly honest, nor can I. What's going on with my Jenny?

"He's just gay enough!" Jenny says brightly, sounding slightly rehearsed.

Sam doesn't smile. He slams the horn at a van driver. "Yeah, yeah. Sophie probably cut his balls off."

Jenny rolls her eyes and looks despondently out the window. Senses this conversation is not going perfectly to plan.

"That's the problem with good-looking women." He spits out the word "women." "I see them in my office all the time. They castrate their husbands, thinking it's what they want, but the moment he submits to her she runs off with her personal trainer."

Jenny is gazing out the window, not listening, her wide blue eyes somewhere else. "It's beautiful, Sam."

"Sounds it. You two, out shopping."

She turns to him and grins. "I'm talking about the dress."

Natch.

Sam pulls up outside Tash's house, today's meeting venue. "That'll be twenty quid, Miss Vale."

"Will a kiss do?" She bends over to kiss him.

"A snog, thank you." He holds Jenny's pretty, round face in his hands, thrusts his tongue into her mouth. It's a short, sharp snog.

"Gosh," laughs Jenny, hopping out of the car and away from that long, hot tongue pretty bloody quickly. "I shouldn't be too long. It's just a catch-up meeting with the girls, really. Hey, you shooting straight home?"

"Where else do you think I'd be going?" he says, suddenly defensive, face slamming shut like the car door.

Temper, Sam. *Temper.*

* * *

n a small monochrome apartment not far from St. Albans a woman is preparing for Sam's arrival. She is zipping up a black dress. Beneath the dress is lingerie, black with pink velvet trim. It matches. She is lighting a scented candle—Invigorating Gingerlily—which illuminates the heart-shaped contours of her face. She sinks into her rose pink sofa, waggles one heel-shod foot back and forth, back and forth, slapping the sole against her skin, and waits. She doesn't know that she has a fleck of red lipstick on her front tooth. There is something terribly vulnerable about this fleck on the tooth, the flaw in her makeup.

The distance between her and Sam narrows and narrows until there are just a few clouds between them, five miles, a street, a paved drive. He pulls up, squeezes the skin between his eyes, steps out of the car, shoves his blue shirt into the back of his jeans where it's ruched up. He has a panel of sweat on the back of his shirt in the shape of a crucifix. He knocks three times, not softly.

She opens the door wide, face full of hope and lipstick. "Hey."

"What the fuck do you think you're doing?"

Thirty-five

"Crisis!" Suze declared with rather too much relish for Jenny's liking. She'd been hoping for a good nose around Tash's apartment and a gossipy catch-up and instead it seemed like she'd walked into one of the government's emergency Cobra security meetings. "Will someone tell me what's going on?"

"There are rumors, Jenny. Rumors."

For one dreadful moment she thought they might be inferring something about the wedding dress. She hadn't thought how it might look. "What? What is it?"

"On Saturday night a friend of a friend of a friend saw Ollie out drinking with one of his mates at the Royal Oak." Suze waited for her words to sink in.

Jenny felt a big sense of relief. It had nothing to do with her. "This is bad?"

"There was *a lot* of drinking," added Lydia, pausing for effect. "And laughing."

"It must be stopped," Liz said in a German accent. "Immediately."

Jenny laughed.

"Liz!" said Tash crossly. "This is serious."

Jenny straightened her smile. "Was the drinking out of control?" She remembered Sam's comment about them all being addicted to Ollie's grief and felt a little uneasy.

"Well, they ended up in Chicken Cottage. You don't end up in Chicken Cottage unless you're trollied," said Liz.

"Sorry, I'm not with you. What's the big deal?"

"You tell her," mouthed Tash to Suze. Tash's eyes flashed dangerously.

"Jenny, I'll cut to the chase. There was talk of a woman . . ." began Suze, wincing slightly as she said the word "woman."

Jenny felt the hairs prickle on her arms. "A woman?"

"This friend of a friend . . ."

". . . of a friend," added Liz waspishly.

". . . heard Ollie talking about how he had . . . feelings for this woman." Suze stopped. "Well, sexual comments were made."

So it had happened! He'd moved on. Jenny clamped her hand over her mouth. "Fuck."

"Yes, that word was mentioned," said Liz with a glint in her eye.

"It's too soon," said Lydia, her eyes filling with the inevitable tears. "He's far, far too vulnerable."

Jenny felt a wave of nausea whoosh over her. She was struggling to hold it together now and wanted so badly to dart out of that door and run down the hill, back into the crowded, anonymous fug of the city.

"What the hell shall we do?" asked Tash.

Breathe. That's what she must do. Breathe. Jenny took a deep breath and gagged on her sip of wine. "I guess it was going to happen," she managed.

Suze touched Jenny's hand with her soft, pudgy fingers. "It's more complicated than that. We think we know who the woman is."

Her heart started to thump in her chest. "Who?"

"Cecille." Suze spoke as if the answer pained her. "Cecille."

"Cecille!" Jenny sat bolt upright on the chair. "Cecille!"

"Now do you see why we're concerned, Jenny?" said Lydia quietly, eyeing her with renewed curiosity, as if her reaction had given something away.

"He'll get hurt," said Liz knowingly, nibbling her way around a kettle chip. "Or Freddie will. Let's face it, it's unlikely to end prettily."

"We think someone needs to speak to Cecille," said Tash firmly. "You—"

"Ollie would go nuts if we interfered," said Jenny quickly, remembering Cecille's face that time when she was caught looking for the letters. Oh, the superiority of youth.

"I told you. We can't just wade in there, Tashie," Liz agreed. "It's none of our business."

Tash flicked her licorice hair crossly. "Makes me want to flipping hurl," she said, summing up the general feeling in Jenny's own digestive tract.

"We've put so much effort into helping him through this. To see all our hard work fall away because of some little French *minx!*" Lydia's eyes watered again. "It's too much to bear."

"I'm afraid I can't say anything to Cecille," said Jenny. "She'll only tell Ollie anyway."

"Can you at least find out if it's true, Jenny?" Tash said through a mouthful of chewed fingernails. "From Ollie, then?"

"It may be a way of stopping the gossip," added Suze.

"Gossip?" Jenny's sinking feeling sank some more. "Who else knows?"

Liz laughed. "The school gate is a-*blaze*, Jenny. Clinton and Lewinsky had nothing on this story."

"Look, I think we at least need to let him know what the other parents are saying, before things . . . blow up," Suze persisted. "*I'd* want to know. Wouldn't you, Jenny?"

"I could tell him," began Lydia.

"I think it would be best coming from Jenny," interrupted Liz. "Jenny's closest. Plus she's got a sane, rational head on her shoulders. She'll be able to keep the conversation as unemotive as possible."

"Thanks! And I wouldn't?" said Lydia.

"*No,*" said Liz, Tash and Suze in unison. "You wouldn't!"

Jenny pushed her nails into her palms. Get a grip, she told herself. Ollie is not yours. He is not Sophie's. Sophie is dead. You are about to get married. Ollie is free! He can do what the hell he likes. He can marry an au pair if he pleases.

"Jenny?" Suze asked, looking at her strangely over the neck of the wine bottle. "Are you okay?"

"Oh, Jenny." Liz put an arm around her shoulder, just as horrifying unstoppable tears started to bubble up through her tear ducts. "Oh, Jenny, you're really not okay, are you?"

Thirty-six

I watch her pad slowly out of my bedroom, naked but for Ollie's big blue shirt. The dimple on her left buttock smiles at me. She has long tanned legs. Her lips are bee stung from kissing. Her skin is rashy on her neck, where his beard has been. So are her upper thighs. She walks past Freddie's room, where Freddie, my poor darling Freddie, stirs in his bed. I hover a few feet from the carpet outside the bedroom door. I dance round her. She is oblivious.

I did not see it happen. I chose not to. But I did see the warning signs, her twirling hair around her index finger while leaning across the table, the way she rearranged her top so it showed more cleavage. I saw how after every glass of wine—four and counting—she moved closer to him, found ways to casually touch him, a knock of knee against knee, feather fingertips on his arm. I witnessed the small wrap of white powder and the two thin lines racked out on her Chanel compact mirror.

The kiss was hungry and urgent. Panting, grabbing at each other, they bundled up the stairs, heading for the privacy of the bedroom.

Ollie had the presence of mind to wedge a chair against the door, presumably to stop Freddie from joining them. Cecille is out. That was the last thing I saw, that chair. I sucked myself through that keyhole pretty damn fast. And I waited, guarding Freddie's room while they did it, wondering where he was touching her, if she felt different from me. Wondering if he was thinking of me at all, even a little bit, or if, as is more likely, he was lost in the sensual tangle of limbs and skin and that luscious glade of hair.

I twist round the corner to peek into the bedroom. Ollie is lying there, spread-eagled on the white sheet, panting and naked, spent. There is something glistening on his cheek. He turns over and buries his head into the pillow. His tears make me feel better.

"Ollie?" She is pushing open the bedroom door with her hand. "Are you alright?"

He says nothing, head embedded in the pillow.

She starts to look vulnerable and hurt. I feel for her now. "Shall I go?"

He sits up, squints at her standing there in the puddle of hall light. "Sorry, I'm so sorry."

She reaches for her top, pulls it down over her head. "Forget about it."

"You are lovely. It's just that I can't . . . Sorry."

"Stop apologizing. I understand." She doesn't look like she understands. She looks rejected. Dressed, she hovers for a moment, waits for him to tell her to stay, and when he doesn't she slings her slouchy beige handbag over her shoulder. "See you."

"I'm truly sorry."

Thirty-seven

The sky was milky blue, the air swaying with midges and barbecue smoke. Through the gap in the fence at the bottom of the garden Jenny could see a slice of London in its filmy bowl, the Gherkin, the wheel, the buildings that somehow reminded her she was in London but, up here in Muswell Hill, elementally separate from it too. Her body had that pleasant sagging postswim feeling, which meant getting out of her deck chair anytime soon was inconceivable. Ollie was laid out on a towel on the grass beside her, skin darkening piratically in the sun beneath his beard, an old spliff stub in an ashtray next to him, a big bag of kettle chips open at his elbow. He had his eyes closed, which should have made things easier, but didn't. Yes, she was failing spectacularly in her appointed role of romantic interrogator. How could she possibly ask him about Cecille when the ingénue was roaming the house in a denim miniskirt and slogan T-shirt reading *The Answer's Yes!*

Ollie opened one eye, looking at her dozily. "Still in love with the wedding dress?"

"Yes, of course." She picked up a peppery blade of grass and chewed it, omitting to tell him that every time she looked at the dress she burst into tears. It wasn't the dress's fault. It had done nothing but hang there and look beautiful.

"Can I see you in it?" Freddie slung his wiry arms around her neck from behind, pinning her into her deck chair. She could smell the chlorine of swimming pool on his skin.

"No one can see it."

Freddie's arms loosened. "But Daddy saw it."

"Ah, but he came shopping with me." And he's my gay best friend, she informed herself privately.

Freddie let go of her neck, picked up a small plastic bat and started hitting the orange swing ball hard around its pole. "Mummy used to take me shopping. She said I was the best shopper." He whacked the ball really hard. "I don't see why I can't see the dress."

"It's bad luck to show people your wedding dress before you get married, Freddie, that's all," said Ollie, yawning. The sun caught a shade of amber in his otherwise black beard. He really was absolutely gorgeous. Catching herself staring, she looked away quickly.

Freddie threw the bat down on the grass. "Bad luck?"

"Yeah, bad luck."

"Don't show me the dress then!" Freddie looked panicked. "I don't want you to have bad luck too."

"Oh, Freddie . . ."

Ollie pulled him onto his knee, rested his chin on his shoulder. "Hey, hey. It's not really bad luck, Fred, just an old wives' tale."

"What's an old wives' tale?" he asked quietly.

"Like a fairy story."

"Oh." Freddie frowned, looking from Jenny to Ollie and back again, uncertain. "And fairy stories don't happen, do they?"

"No, fairy stories don't happen, Freddie," said Ollie quietly, pushing his nose into Freddie's neck.

Jenny's phone started to ring. Sam. She rummaged in her stripy blue "summer" bag—Soph would surely be impressed at this seasonal rotation—and flicked it to answer. "Guys, I've got to get back. Great swim, Freddie. I reckon you'll be doing a whole length next week." She'd ask him another time. Or not.

"Thanks, Jen. Look, I'll drive you back." Ollie stood up and brushed grass seeds off his baggy cargo shorts, shoved his feet into pink Havaianas flip-flops. "Cecille's here, somewhere."

She froze at the mention of Cecille's name. Looking back at the house she caught a glimpse of her behind the glass French doors, a swish of hair over a bare shoulder.

"Freddie, you want to watch *Deadly 60* with Cecille while I drive Jenny back?"

Freddie's bottom lip pouted. "I want to watch *Deadly 60* with Jenny."

"Really, Ollie, you don't need to drive me back."

"I want to drive you home." He flicked his aviator shades down over his eyes, making him look instantly rock star. "I want to talk to you."

O llie leaned forward over the steering wheel, resting on it, as they sat stationary in the street. "Are you going to tell me why you're acting so weird?"

Jenny stared determinedly out the window at the splashes of sun on the vivid green trees that lined the avenue. "I'm not acting weird."

"You won't look at me."

Jenny turned to make a point of looking at him. "I'm just tired from the swimming." She smiled. "And I'm looking at you now."

He raised a black, devilish eyebrow. "You forget that I actually know you quite well now. It's been the surprise ace of being widowed."

"Okay." She felt the heat rise on her cheeks. She was going to have to do this. Deep breath. "Ollie . . ."

His eyes danced with amusement. "Yes, my darling Jenny."

"I feel so embarrassed saying this and I'm not sure I even should be saying it so please don't be cross with me. . . ."

He frowned, took his sunglasses off. "Ominous."

"There's been, er, gossip." God, this was awful. Why the hell had they appointed her to be the one to interrogate him? Lydia should have done it.

He laughed. "Gossip?"

"At the school gates. About you and . . ."

"Fuck." He turned the key in the ignition, stepped too hard on the gas. He wasn't laughing now. For a moment no one spoke. "Tash is the soul of discretion then."

"I don't think it was her that said anything."

"So who else is going to spill the beans?" He slammed the horn hard at a white van. "As far as I was aware it was only me and Tash in the bedroom, or has Suze got a lens trained on the house?"

Tash? *Tash?* In his bedroom! Had she misheard him? Was Tash the woman Ollie had been talking about in the pub? Not Cecille. Tash! Oh, God. She covered her mouth with her hand, feeling like she was about to hurl out the window.

They drove along in awkward silence. This was it, she decided. This was the end of their long, unexpected dark journey that had started when Sophie died. Yes, she'd been a channel for his grief. A conduit to Sophie, to the past. Now he didn't need her. And this was good. Her work was done. He pulled up on her Camden street. She put her hand on the car door handle, unable to look at him as her eyes were prickling with tears. "So is it serious?"

"What do you think?"

"No idea." She suddenly wished she had long dark hair like Tash.

Or Sophie. Or Dominique. That she wasn't mousy with green high-lights. That she didn't have thighs that rubbed together. That she wasn't a woman whose signature color was navy.

"I know what you're thinking, Jenny."

Thank God he didn't.

"But it just happened. Cecille was staying at a friend's. Tash turned up with a bit of coke."

She snorted. "Helpful."

"In a funny way it was, Jenny. Just getting off my head." He stopped, frowning, his dark eyes melting into that faraway blackness that lately was making her heart flip in her chest like a fish on a deck. "I'm dreading seeing her at the school gates. Shit, Jenny. Does every-one know?"

"I don't think anyone knows about Tash."

"What do you mean?"

The conversation was beginning to take on a surreal edge. "The rumors were about Cecille, actually."

Ollie slapped his forehead with the back of his palm and laughed. "Do you mean that you didn't know about Tash?"

"No, I didn't."

"Can you keep a secret?" He put a hand on her knee, looked up at her boyishly, appealingly. She wanted to slap the grin off his face. "Please?"

"Of course. Look, I've got to go, Ollie."

"Do you hate me now?"

"A little bit."

His eyes darkened. "I haven't forgotten Sophie, Jenny."

Jenny bit down on her lip very hard to stop herself from crying. She couldn't look at him. She hated him. How could he? How?

"It wasn't perfect. You seem to think me and Soph were com-pletely perfect. Everyone thinks that. It doesn't help." He pulled at his beard, his features strained to the point of contortion. "Maybe this is my way of reminding myself that we weren't. Then I don't have to feel like I've lost absolutely everything that will ever be good in my life."

"Oh, Ol." He was breaking her heart now. "I understand that. But you don't need to do *this*."

"She was bored, Jenny. Sophie was bored."

Jenny looked down. She thought of the hidden stash of letters and once again wondered what they were and where they were. If they held the key to this.

"She wanted another baby," he said quietly, his voice breaking.

"Yeah, I know. I found her maternity stuff in the chest of drawers."

"I think maybe she blamed me for that. You know, on a subconscious level."

"She didn't. She really didn't."

"You know the worst thing, Jenny?" It felt like the world had shrunk down to just them, just them sitting in the car. "That it felt good. The coke. The sex. It made me feel alive."

Jenny closed her eyes. She didn't want to hear this. Yet she needed to hear this. She needed to come to her senses and cement the dissolving boundaries.

"And I don't know how it can be possible to miss someone so much, ache for them every minute of every fucking day, and yet still find pleasure in someone else. My brain can't compute it."

"Where was Cecille when . . . this happened?"

"Out."

"Right." It was then she realized she had her hands over her ears like a child.

"You're judging me."

"I'm not judging you."

"It's just sex, Jenny."

"You don't have to justify yourself to me, Ollie. You really don't."

"I feel like I do."

"Well, you don't." She put one foot on the pavement and stepped up and into the bright sunlight, which no longer felt warm and bucolic but dehydrating and dirty.

"It was soul-searchingly shit afterwards. For the record."

"I don't keep a record."

"Jenny . . ." He wouldn't let her go. He wanted something. She couldn't give it. He reached out to her. His skin sizzled on hers. "You okay? I'm concerned about you."

"Me?"

"Yeah, you."

"Tired, you know."

"Wedding stuff?"

"Think so," she replied tersely.

"Jenny, it'll be fine. Totally fine. Everyone is gunning for you two." She kissed and inhaled him. "Stay out of trouble."

It was only as she stood on the sunny pavement, watching the silver bullet of his car recede into the distance, that she realized that Ollie hadn't actually denied any involvement with Cecille.

Thirty-eight

Whoa! Is there something I don't know here? If I thought Jenny was looking doolally before, she is looking positively *deranged* today, wild-eyed, foot pressed hard on the gas, shooting north like a boy racer. She spins down Fortis Green, then does a loud screechy turn into one of the avenues, making me bounce like a ball in the back. I expect her to stop outside number thirty-three—what has Ollie done?—but, no, she's turning right! She's screeching to a halt outside Tash's house. Ooh, this could be interesting.

"Hey, this is a lovely surprise," says Tash, answering the door, looking puzzled. She smells of roses—Jo Malone perfume—and is naked beneath a long, gray cashmere dressing gown that has no visible moth holes. There is not one pube on her entire body. She is as smooth as an egg. I wonder if he liked that.

Jenny storms right past her. Half Jenny, half juggernaut, she's heavy-load vehicle intent on destruction. I'm scared, and I'm the ghost.

"Excuse me," says Tash, half joking, stepping back.

"I know about Ollie, Tash," Jenny hisses, releasing the demolition ball. "I *know*."

It's like she's speaking for me here. Hey, this is great.

"Look, Jenny," stutters Tash, cheeks flaming. "It's . . . it was just one night. I don't know how it happened."

"Bollocks!" Jenny grips the back of a chair, like she is about to pick it up and throw it across the room. Tash looks worried. It's a Hans Wegner.

Tash's exposed tanned décolletage rises and falls more quickly now. You can almost hear her brain whirring, trying to think of a way out. But there's no way to turn. Jenny has her by the vajazzles. "Cocaine! What the fuck were you *thinking*?"

"You're not going to tell the others, are you?"

Jenny is not moved. She turns away from Tash, like she can't bear to look at her anymore, stares out the window at next door's mossy green drainpipe, hot air tusking from her nostrils. "I might do."

"Please, Jenny."

"Fuck off."

Woo! Go, Jenny!

"Don't be such a bitch!"

"*Bitch?*" says Jenny, turning away from the drainpipe to face her slowly. "Bitch? You are the bitch, Tash."

Tash's face hardens now.

Even I wonder if Jenny might have overstepped the mark a tad.

"What's your fucking problem, Jenny?"

"That you've been pushing cocaine and sex on Sophie's husband!" Jenny is shouting properly now. I haven't heard her shout properly for years. She's got some lungs on her.

"He's not her husband. Sophie's *dead*."

"Hardly!"

Tash narrows her eyes. "You know what, Jenny? You sound jealous."

Jenny starts. "Don't be ridiculous."

"Is this what it's all been about?" Tash can see she's hit a soft spot and goes in for the kill. "Jenny the ringmaster. Jenny, Ollie's confidante. Have you ever reflected on your own motivations, Jenny?"

"I am about to get married," Jenny utters in pale-faced defense. Tash rolls her eyes. "As if that has any bearing on it."

"Fuck you, Tash."

Tash's eyes narrow to dark glossy slits. "You think you're so perfect, don't you, Jenny?"

She's getting nasty now. Not sure I like the turn in this conversation.

"Look, I was Sophie's best friend. That's all. I don't pretend to be anything else. I didn't apply for any post. Suze just asked me to help—you all did."

"Best friend?" Tash smiles. It is not a nice smile. "I'm not sure I'd count Sophie as my best friend if I were you."

Jenny's hands fist at her sides. A sinewy muscle on her neck twitches. "What are you talking about?"

Tash looks a bit lost for words, like she's unsure how to follow up. Then she smirks. She is suddenly no longer beautiful. "You've got no idea, have you?"

There is a rumble like thunder in the distance. I'm not sure if it's a train or something far worse hurtling toward us on the tracks.

"About what?"

"Nothing," she says quietly, pulling her dressing gown tight over her slim, tanned body. "Nothing."

"Tell me."

"Look, Sophie told me about Sam's roving eye." She wrinkles her nose in faux empathy. "Hardly a best friend's discretion," she scoffs.

Shit! It's something far worse.

"Roving eye?" Jenny's hands are shaking. She pales. "She said that to you?"

Oh, God. It was just school-mum drinks chat ("A friend of mine . . ."). I told them, I think it was at Suze's one night, that I had a best mate who was waiting to get married to someone with a wandering eye and wondering what I should say or if I should say anything. We ummed and ahhed and drank and debated the ethics of interfering in friends' relationships. What you should say, what you shouldn't, how it's best to stay out of it and let matters run their course. Drunken, silly stuff. That was the end of it. Or so I thought. I didn't imagine anyone would remember the conversation. Or they'd ever get to know Jenny.

"You're full of bullshit." Jenny shakes her head, refusing to believe it. "You're unbelievable."

"What about Dominique, then?"

Jenny gets one shade paler. "Dominique?" Her voice is very quiet, little more than a whisper.

Tash presses her fingers into the lids of her closed eyes and winces. "Look, Jenny, I don't know how we got here. I like you. I really do. This is all a bad look. I'm really sorry. Can we make peace?"

Jenny slumps against the table, the rage from earlier evaporated. "You can't say that and just expect me to forget you said it."

"It's no big deal. It's in the past, Jenny. I'm sorry I ever mentioned it. I really am."

"How do you know Dominique?" Jenny whispers hoarsely.

"Oh, from years ago. She's a sister of someone I used to work with."

Something shifts in Jenny's face. She's made the connection. "The guy you and Sam both know?"

Tash studies the floor. "From my marketing days, yeah."

Jenny stands up straight, urgent. "You have a number?"

"A number?" Tash looks flustered. "Er, no."

"Please, Tash. This is important."

Tash hesitates. "I'll have a pop at tracking down her number if you agree not to tell the others about me and Ollie."

Thirty-nine

t is eight thirty p.m. Freddie's light is off, but the burnished evening sunlight is seeping from the sides of his blackout blinds and he is sitting up in bed, twisting the limbs of Buzz Lightyear. He lifts Buzz in front of him and addresses him sternly. "Mum, do you remember that Joe kid in my class?"

Whoa! I am Buzz now. I am a Space Ranger. Excited by my transformation and the possibility that we may finally be able to communicate via the third party of a clairvoyant toy, I try to make Buzz do something, for the laser to flash on his arm. Needless to say, it doesn't. "Yes, of course I remember, darling," I say. Buzz's mouth doesn't open. Freddie doesn't seem to care.

"Joe jacked my Ben Ten ruler that Granny gave me."

"Have you told the teacher?"

Freddie purses his lips thoughtfully. Is he receiving me? He is silent for a moment, head cocked to one side like he is listening.

"Okay, I'll speak to the teacher," he says.

Explode with joy! How mad is that? I am communicating beyond the grave! Or is it just that he is *my* boy still? That the glorious six years we spent together was enough to cement me—and my love—in his bone marrow. He knows what I would say to him because he still knows his mother.

"To infinity and beyond," whispers Freddie, flying Buzz up into the air and whirling him around his bed, his wings clipping the blobs of Blu Tack on the walls.

You see, while everything else is going grayer as the weeks pass, Freddie's resilience gets ever brighter. He is sad and he misses me and he talks to me and he opens the memory book that Jenny made and brushes photographs of me with his little fingers. And sometimes he sleeps with my old nightie pressed into his nose. But this is okay. I believe he will be okay. I really do. While I know that problems may manifest themselves later after my death, probably in his teenage years when he hates me for deserting him and being so stupid as to step out into the road drunk, right now he is my little warrior. He still smiles and laughs and plays. He has a solid hidden ore of happiness buried deep inside.

I watch over him until morning. I watch over him as he sings a song in the year two assembly about rain forests. I bob against the ceiling like a balloon, buoyant with pride, anxious he'll screw up. But he sings his heart out, gazing fearlessly at the audience, some of whom, feeling the poignancy of my absence, wipe away tears with their sleeves while holding up their camera phones. His voice, the wonderful voice he gets from Ollie, is clear and pure, life itself. He finishes the song. Applause erupts. I am a shower of sparks, a berserk Catherine wheel that has come loose from the monkey bars on the gym wall. Ollie and Jenny are watching too, sitting four rows from the back, clapping wildly. And we are all united in one thing. Our love for Freddie.

After the assembly Joe returns the stolen ruler.

Leaving Freddie to bask in the triumphant return of the ruler, I leave with the huddle of proud parents out of the sweaty, echoey hall.

Ollie shoots off to the studio. Liz and Jenny break ranks with the other 2Bers—how they manage to escape Suze's clutches I have no idea—and slip off for coffee. It's incongruous seeing Jenny in my old haunts, on the coffee mum circuit. She looks far more comfortable than I'd ever have given her credit for. I feel a wave of guilt for having compartmentalized my life so brutally.

The cafés on the broadway are cluttered with children and huddles of Fortismere School pupils with their dog-eared Penguin paperbacks and iPods, the girls in thigh-skimming floral tea dresses, the boys flicking their long lanky hair out of their eyes. Liz and Jenny squeeze onto a little round table near the open window of a café and order brownies. Liz is wearing a billowy orange dress that clashes brilliantly with the scarlet tips in her hair poking out beneath her seventies-style fedora. Jenny is wearing navy.

"Hey, it's good to catch up after all this time," says Liz cheerfully, her cheeks chipmunked with brownie. "Sure I can't tempt you with a glass of vino?" She raises an impish eyebrow.

"Sadly, can't edit with wine goggles on," says Jenny. "One glass of wine and I think every manuscript is a masterpiece."

Liz gasps with mock drama. "You mean they're not?"

Jenny laughs and sips her Diet Coke.

Liz shoves the plate of brownies toward her. "Please finish them off. I'm a stone heavier than I was last year. If I carry on like this they'll have to winch me out of my bedroom through the ceiling using a crane."

Jenny obliges. Glad to see she's not gone off puddings. There is a lull in the conversation. They people watch. A teenager bounces by on chunky neon trainers. A elderly lady totters past licking a Fab ice lolly with a lap dog under her arm. There's a flotilla of prams as a baby massage group spills out of their session.

"I feel quite the fugitive," laughs Liz. "Breaking ranks." She leans back in her chair, lifts her face to the sunshine and closes her eyes.

Jenny rests her chin in her hand and gazes at the pavement, her face clouded by thoughts.

Liz opens one eye and peeks at her. "So you're geared up for the wedding?"

"Yeah, yeah." Jenny's face shadows. I don't like it when Jenny's face shadows. I'm finding it harder and harder to read. Something funny happens to her face when she talks about the wedding.

"Do you need a hand with anything?"

"That's very sweet of you, but no. Future mother-in-law is very much on the case."

"Ah, I see." Liz smiles, eyeing her more watchfully. "Nervous?"

Jenny stiffens, puts her cake fork down. "Yeah, guess that's what it must be."

Liz smiles kindly. "It's normal to have wobbles, Jenny."

Hmmm.

"I had *huge* wobbles." Liz ruffles her hair, depositing a brownie crumb in its rosy thatch. "But it was a dream on the day, a total dream. And we had the best bonk afterwards!"

Jenny laughs and blushes, then she looks pensive.

Liz sees it too. "You're not having second thoughts, are you?"

Jenny bites down hard on her lower lip. How I wish she would talk! Liz is a sane woman. She'd understand! Tell her!

"Jenny?" Liz looks more concerned now. She's on the scent. "There's no one else muddying the waters here, is there?"

"No!" Jenny practically ejects herself from her rattan café seat. "It's just that marriage is such a big step. Bigger than I thought. I know that sounds deeply immature."

"It doesn't, not at all." Liz hesitates, unsure how to push the conversation forward. "It must be hard, you know, losing Sophie and . . . well, spending so much time with Ollie."

"Ollie hasn't got anything to do with this," Jenny retorts quickly.

Liz twiddles a spike of scarlet hair, not taking her eyes off Jenny's strained face. "Sometimes feelings can be confusing, that's all." She looks away wistfully. And I wonder if she's thinking of her ex, Riley. The one she finally defriended on Facebook this morning and by doing so deleted all the past-mooning and embraced her lovely present. "There's not one woman alive who hasn't been confused about who she loves at some point in her life."

"I don't know what you're talking about, Liz, sorry." (I'm not sure quite where she's going with this either.) She bends down and picks up her handbag. "Sadly, I've really got to get back to work."

"Me too." Liz scoops up the last bit of brownie with her fork. She looks up and smiles cheerfully. "But you know what, Jenny? It's not over till the fat lady sings. Remember that."

Forty

Jenny's heart leapt when the phone rang. Could it be Tash with Dominique's details, finally? It had been two weeks since the showdown in Tash's house and she still hadn't given anything to her. It was almost impossible not to say anything to Sam, to go on as normal. But she didn't want to say anything until she had the facts, if there were facts, if Tash wasn't making the whole thing up, which was the most likely scenario. She wasn't going to hand-grenade her relationship for nothing. She picked up the phone. "Hello?"

"Jennifer." Her mother was the only person in the world who called her Jennifer.

"Oh, Mum. Hi. Yes, yes, I'm really well, things are great. I'm at work right now, though. Yes, I know it's the weekend." She'd taken on extra work so she didn't have to think too much, or spend too much time with Sam. "I know, I know, it's just that I've got this massive manuscript." Explanations were fruitless. For as long as she worked at home her mother would not believe that she was actually working. Work was something you went to. It was something that required a smart pencil skirt and a commute and a cookie at eleven a.m. "How are things, Mum?"

Her mother paused, cleared her throat, the throat clearance giving Jenny a taster of the answer. "I'm worried, Jennifer."

Not this. Not again. "The wedding is all under control. Promise," she said in what she hoped was the reassuring voice of a calm, organized bride rather than one who was trying to sleuth into the past life of her fiancé and went to bed every night and had weird dreams about her dead best friend's husband.

"Your father's concerned."

"Look, Mum, the marquee is going up in ten days' time." As she spoke it was like listening to badly dubbed telly, as if there was a time lag and it wasn't her speaking. "I have shoes! Lovely white shoes. I have a wedding dress! I will have my hair colored at the weekend. I will not look like Shrek, okay? Everything, I promise, has been crossed off the list. Do not fret," she said, wondering how long she could keep up the wedding prattle before her brain seized up. It was as if the whole subject was too big and complicated for her to process, the nuptial equivalent of quantum physics.

Her mother did one of her tight little coughs. "I have no doubt that Penelope will have organized everything expertly down to the last napkin ring."

Jenny felt a wave of sympathy for her mother, who understandably felt usurped.

"Don't you want more of a say, love?"

"I've had my say, Mum." Yes, she'd let the details ride over her. And Penelope had such fixed ideas. She really did care about whether the guests should have little net pockets filled with pink almonds.

Her mother sniffed. "I just think the Vales should be more involved, that's all."

"How about I ask Penelope today if there's anything you can sink your teeth into? She's coming over for dinner tonight."

"But don't say anything, Jennifer. I don't want to cause an atmosphere." There was nothing her mother hated more than atmosphere.

"I'll have a run through Sam's spreadsheet later and phone you tomorrow with an update." The word "update" always sounded impressive and efficient. "Right, let's speak soon . . ."

"Don't 'update' me, Jennifer."

"Sorry."

"Darling, you sound down, very down."

"I'm not down. Just a bit tired."

"Why are you tired?"

"I don't know. Work, I guess."

"You need to stop working. Working doesn't suit brides."

"I'm committed right until the wedding. I need to get it all done before the honeymoon."

"Ooh, any idea where . . ."

She glanced up at Sam, who was engrossed in tapping something into his iPhone. "No. Sam is proving very good at keeping secrets."

The moment she hung up, her mobile started vibrating on the kitchen table.

"Like living in a bloody call center," said Sam, lighting a cigarette and blowing smoke out the open window grumpily.

Once that phone call was finished she sat down next to Sam, wondering how to break it to him. "That was Ollie in New York."

"I know that. You were using your girlie talk-to-Ollie voice."

She'd ignore this. "Freddie's got chicken pox."

"Tell him not to pick."

"Actually he's really sick, Sam." She hesitated, unsure how to sell this one. "He's been calling for me."

Sam flexed his bare right biceps, prodded it, checking its muscle tone. "And?"

"I've got to go to Muswell Hill."

He fingered the bulge of his biceps with his left hand. "Not tonight?"

"Ollie wouldn't ask unless he was worried, Sam."

"My parents are coming to dinner any minute to run through the wedding. The chicken is in the oven. And you want to run off?"

Trying to placate him, she stroked his shoulders, smoothing over the little black dots where the hair was growing back after his shoulder wax. "We saw your parents last week." Every bloody week! "And Freddie really is sick. I kind of have to do this."

"He's got chicken pox, not cholera, babes. You do not *have* to do this. Anyway, what's going on with the French bird? Where's she?"

She started a little at the mention of Cecille. She'd been trying to make herself forget about Cecille. It was best just to deny her existence. "She's struggling a bit apparently. I may have to stay the night, I'm afraid."

A low growl came out of the back of his throat, which may or may not have had something to do with the cigarette.

"It'll only be one night." She resumed her shoulder stroking. "Ollie's back tomorrow."

Sam stood up, flicking her hand away. "This is about you, not Freddie. Can we at least be honest about that?"

"Honesty?" The word "Dominique" hissed on the tip of her tongue. "I'll tell you what, Sam," she began, only to be interrupted by the doorbell and Penelope's shrill voice rising from the street through the open window.

Forty-one

Cecille appeared at the door of number thirty-three looking disheveled, her normally smooth dark hair frizzed, a large white shirt sloppily half tucked into her brown leather belt. She looked like a teen on a bender, and for once, genuinely pleased to see Jenny. "Nightmare," she said breathlessly. "Thanks for coming."

"Has Freddie still got a temperature?" She had phoned her mother back again for advice—much to her mother's delight—which amounted to a bottle of Calpol and a bottle of pink calamine lotion.

She bustled into the hall with her medical supplies, a little part of her hoping that in some small way her stepping into the crisis like this, taking control, well, it might right the humiliation of being discovered poking around Ollie's chest of drawers for those letters. It might make things less embarrassing for everyone.

"You go and have a cup of tea or something, Cecille. I'll take over," she called over her shoulder, dropping her overnight bag in the hall and leaping up the stairs.

Freddie was a pathetic, spotty mess dozing on his bed. She put her hand on his forehead. Hot. Where was the thermometer? Was this the thermometer? She picked up a plastic probe from the bedside table. It took a moment or two for her to work out which orifice it was designed for. She chanced sticking it in his ear. One hundred and two Fahrenheit. She scrambled into her handbag and Googled kids' temperatures on her iPhone. Okay, yes, hot. She must definitely wake him up and give him medicine.

"Freddie, Freddie, sweetie," she said, wobbling his shoulder gently.

He groaned and turned over in the bed.

"Freddie."

"Mummy."

"Freddie, it's me, Jenny."

"Want Mummy," he muttered, eyes still shut.

"It's Jenny. It's okay."

He opened one eye very slowly. "Jenny?" He looked puzzled, taking a moment to get his bearings. "Are you going to stay with me?"

"I'm here now."

"Promise?" he said, blinking back the tears and trying to be brave.

"I'll stay until Daddy gets home. Now I'm going to give you some medicine." She poured a spoonful out, spilling pink sticky liquid all over his Spider-Man duvet cover as she did so. Using a bit of loo roll, she carefully dabbed the calamine lotion over his raw skin so that he looked like he'd been dunked in strawberry ice cream. She cupped his little hand in hers when he tried to scratch. "Try not to."

Freddie began to cry quietly. "It hurts."

"It won't hurt soon. The medicine will kick in. Medicine is great stuff." Jenny slipped off her shoes and lay down next to him. "Shall I read you a story? Then we can think about stories, not itching."

He shook his head.

"Not even pirates?" Surely pirates would work.

He shook his head again.

"Tintin?"

"Tell me things about Mummy." He dropped his head on her chest. It was a comforting weight, griddle hot where his skin touched hers. "Did Mummy get sick too?"

"Now that's a good question. Because you know what? Mummy was the least ill person I knew."

Freddie smiled.

"She got sick like you when she was a little girl. She had mumps and chicken pox and stuff. Everyone does, I'm afraid. But when she was grown up, she was ridiculously healthy. I don't ever remember her with a cold. She must have had colds, I guess, but nothing ever stopped her. She didn't moan about anything like that. Not even when she was pregnant. You know, Freddie, the night before you were born she was dancing!"

He smiled sleepily. "Dancing?"

"There was a big thirtieth birthday party, an old friend of ours from university. Most pregnant women about to give birth don't go to parties, Freddie. They sit there with their feet up in front of the telly, moaning. But Mummy insisted on going. She hated missing a party. And she was convinced that you were going to arrive late anyway."

He looked puzzled. "Arrive late for what?"

"The date the doctors said you'd come out of Mummy's tummy. It's called a due date." She smiled, remembering it all, Sophie's fecund magnificence. "I'll never forget her dancing that night. She was *enormous*. And she was wearing this red dress and dancing with bare feet because her feet had swollen up and she couldn't fit into any shoes."

"So she danced me out of her tummy?"

Jenny laughed. "Yes, I guess she did."

He lowered his lids dreamily. "I loved it when Mummy danced."

"Everyone loved it when your mummy danced. She always looked so happy dancing, and that made other people feel happy too."

"So did I pop out on the dance floor then? Like I was on *Strictly*?"

"Nearly! She made it to the hospital in time. Just. You came out about six hours later."

"And then what did she do?" He scratched his leg. Again Jenny cupped his hand, held it firm to stop the scratching until the itch subsided.

"Daddy wrapped you in a blanket and Mummy cuddled and fed you."

"Were you there, Jenny?"

"I was fetching your mummy a cup of tea from the hospital café at the moment you were born. I saw you when you were about ten minutes old, though."

Freddie smiled. "You were almost there, then?"

"Almost." This seemed to please him. Jenny ran her fingers through his sweaty fringe, remembering seeing Freddie for the first time, how shocked she'd been at his red raw tininess, his rabbit weight. She'd fallen in love with him immediately, completely.

Freddie yawned. "What was I like?"

"Very tiny, very beautiful. And you looked just like Mummy when you were born. Dark hair, little pin curls. Mummy's nose."

He frowned. "I wasn't dancing?"

"You were a bit young to dance. You just wobbled your head."

"I'd like to see you dance, Jenny."

"Me? Dance?" She shook her head and smiled at the thought. "I am, sadly, a truly terrible dancer. Two left feet."

"If you had two left feet one would be a right foot."

She curled a bit of hair behind his ear as his eyes shut. "Clever socks."

Cecille snapped open a can of Coke and sat down at the dining table with a sigh. "I so worried."

"He's asleep. Temperature's down. Please don't worry anymore." Jenny sat down opposite her at the kitchen table, admiring the way

Cecille's fine boned hands circled the Coke can. Was it Cecille's tiredness that was bestowing such a louche Gallic sexiness this evening? Or maybe it was something to do with the insouciantly unbuttoned man's shirt. Yes, a man's shirt. Jesus. Was it Ollie's?

Cecille folded back one of the cuffs that was falling down over one of her hands, as if sensing Jenny's gaze.

"So you think Ollie will get back tonight?" She dragged her eyes away from the shirt.

"Very late." Cecille said, glancing up at the clock. "If plane's on time." She tipped back her head, sipped her Coke.

Jenny calculated that there was about an hour to kill before she could reasonably go to bed without appearing rude. She didn't relish the idea of hanging out with Cecille, obviously, and cursed herself for having forgotten her book in her hurried packing. Perhaps she would phone Sam; yes, that's what she would do. He would still be eating the roast chicken and probably wouldn't pick up but it was an opportunity to leave a contrite message without getting sucked into further conflict. "I'll go and dump my bag and make a call." She hesitated. "Er, where should I sleep, Cecille?"

"I put you in room next to Freddie's," she said authoritatively, the mistress of the house. "You will have bad night, Jenny, I'm afraid. Freddie wake up a lot last night. Five, six times."

"Oh, poor thing."

"Yes, I know. Very hard." Cecille yawned, exposing pink tonsils. "I'm not used to it."

Jenny still couldn't take her eyes off the shirt. She definitely recognized the blue-striped lining inside the upturned cuffs. Had Cecille just found the shirt in the washing basket and mistakenly thrown it on?

"First I will make something to eat. What you like?"

"Don't go to any bother, really. Toast. Cereal is fine."

Cecille wrinkled her nose at the idea of toast or cereal for supper. "I make steak."

Jenny's heart sank at the thought of sharing a proper sit-down meal with Cecille. Cecille wearing Ollie's shirt. "Please don't cook on my account."

No matter, she returned to the kitchen after phoning Sam to find Cecille chucking a fist of butter into the frying pan. She fried two steaks for an alarmingly brief moment, before sliding them onto the white plates in a pool of blood, alongside some buttered French beans. Yikes. The steak was practically mooing.

"Hope you like," Cecille said cheerily.

"Wow. This looks . . . amazing," she attempted. "At your age I couldn't cook at all."

Cecille giggled, chuffed. "Beer? Wine?"

"A small glass of white would be lovely, thanks."

"May I have some wine?" Cecille asked, suddenly bashful.

"You don't have to ask me, Cecille." She felt herself warming to Cecille, wanting to connect with her. An ill child stirred up a lot of emotion. And, yes, it was sweet, and responsible, of her to ask if she could have a drink. There was no sign of the catty superiority she'd seen that time with the letters. The rumors about Cecille were clearly absolute tosh. The gossip mill gone into overdrive. "You're off duty now. I'm here. Have a glass of wine."

Cecille poured out two glasses of wine, disappointingly small as politely requested.

"Cheers," Cecille said, lifting her glass.

"Cheers," said Jenny, digging into the bleeding meat. How ridiculous that it had taken Freddie getting chicken pox for her to have a proper conversation with Cecille after all this time, she told herself. "You are doing an excellent job, Cecille, by all accounts."

Cecille frowned and stopped chewing. "What accounts?"

"Ollie. The mothers I know at school. Me." She smiled. "For what it's worth."

Cecille shook her head and looked glum. "Not the other mothers, Jenny. The mothers don't like me."

"Oh. Why do you say that?" She shifted on her chair, feeling uncomfortably two-faced now.

"They look at me"—she narrowed and hardened her eyes—"like *zat*."

"Oh, no. Really?" Then she remembered the slate-hard stare Tash had given her not so long ago.

"They jealous," Cecille declared matter-of-factly, slicing a neat cube out of her steak.

Jenny spluttered into her wine. "Jealous?"

"About Ollie."

Something tightened in Jenny's chest. Damn it, Cecille was probably right.

"They want him, you know."

Jenny smiled at the sweet adolescence of the word "want." "Like who?"

"Lydia."

"*Lydia?*" She dropped her knife and it clattered to the table.

Cecille glanced behind her as if to check that no one was listening. "Lydia tried to kiss Ollie, Jenny."

"I think you might have muddled up—"

"It was late, Jenny," Cecille interrupted. She dropped her voice to a whisper, as if telling a ghost story. "It is weekend. After party. Suze's party. You remember?"

She nodded. Suze's party. The night Lydia and George had that terrible row. She leaned forward, not wanting to miss a word. "I remember."

"They think I asleep. But I not! I not asleep! I come downstairs, and I see Lydia like this . . ." She pursed her lips, closed her eyes. "They only stop because I come downstairs."

She covered her mouth with her hand. Not another one. "No!"

"*Yes!* And not just Lydia. Tash! Tash left bra, here, here in house!"

In her mind's eye Jenny suddenly saw lots of bras, dozens, hundreds, different shapes and sizes, all belonging to different women, floating through the house like an army of zeppelins, through the hall, across the landing, into Ollie's bedroom.

"You see now?" appealed Cecille, desperate that her point was not being lost in translation. "They are all jealous of me. Me, living here with Ollie. That is why they are so . . . cold."

"I guess everyone is very protective of Ollie," she attempted, still reeling from the revelation about Lydia. Lydia! "They were good friends of Sophie's."

"Sophie. Sophie. Everything always about Sophie," sighed Cecille, resting her chin on her hands like a cherub. "So . . . so *frustrating!*" She gave Jenny a sidelong look, as if trying to work out whether to trust her. "I just want Ollie to be happy," she added quietly. "He can't be happy when he live in past, Jenny."

"He needs time."

"That is what I tell myself. Just wait, wait, Cecille, I say." She wrapped her perfect small hands tightly around the stem of the wineglass with a heave of sadness. "But very, very hard."

Jenny stared at her silently for a moment, slowly becoming aware of a disturbing undertow to the conversation. It could have just been a turn of phrase . . . but it did appear that Cecille was attached to Ollie in a way that was not strictly within the terms of her au pair contract. "Cecille," she ventured gently, "Ollie is on his own. He's very handsome. Well, um, I hope I'm not speaking out of turn but I could imagine it might be easy to develop . . ." She felt the heat rise on her own cheeks as she spoke and tried to cover them with her palms.

"He is amazing man, Jenny. He makes me laugh." Cecille's eyes glazed over dreamily. "And I love the way he plays guitar. He is like . . . like poet."

"Cecille . . ."

She looked up defiantly. "I *love* him, Jenny!"

Oh, God. Jenny squeezed shut her eyes. "Don't say that. Please don't say that."

"He is first man I love." She put a hand against her heart, her face glowing. "But this love, this love hurts a lot. I didn't know love hurt so much."

"Oh, Cecille. You need someone your own age. Ollie is grieving. He is just not . . . not available."

"Oh, no, Jenny, he loves me too," she said matter-of-factly.

She heard a loud rushing in her ears. Then the long extended screech of bus brakes. The room started to sink away from her. She slumped her head into her hands. Why wouldn't he fall in love with Cecille? She was lovely. And beautiful, if you ignored the zits on her chin. It all made a sickening kind of sense. He'd rebounded into the golden open arms of youth, someone with whom he had no past, no baggage, someone who didn't look at him and see the missing black shape where Sophie should be, like a figure scratched out of a photograph.

"You are only one who understand, who knows him well like I do. Tell me what to do, Jenny. Please tell me what to do," Cecille begged. "I try everything to understand him. Everything! I try to understand Sophie too. Every little thing about her. What he loved about her. What he . . ."

She got it then. "Cecille," Jenny said, suddenly seizing the moment by the scruff of the neck, "I do understand, I really do."

"You do?" Cecille's shoulders dropped, unburdened.

"I do," she said in a soft maternal voice. "And I also understand now why you took Sophie's letters from the bottom drawer of Ollie's chest of drawers." Cecille flushed and stared down at the table. "You did take them, didn't you, Cecille?"

Forty-two

In the shadowy gloom of the guest bedroom Jenny held the letter with trembling hands. She had folded the other love letters, placed them carefully back in the box, the ones from starstruck admirers going back years: Sophie had been a hoarder of the brokenhearted and besotted. But not this crumpled tormentor. Flicking on the sidelight, she pulled it out of its envelope and smoothed it over her bent knee, making herself go through the horrors all over again, and again, until it finally sank in. No matter that it made her feel faint, that reading it was like giving blood.

Sophie,

I am writing to apologize for my brashness both at the party, and since. You were right to reject me, then and now. But it seems to me that what is right and what feels right are two different things. I suspect that is why you came to meet me late last week, wearing that sexy red dress which is now imprinted in my mind forever. (Did anyone ever

*tell you you have dancer's legs?) It's hard to believe that you met me
just to rebuke me so seductively. My lawyer's brain cannot help but
wonder if you came because you couldn't not. And did you really need
to meet me for a long walk in the park to tell me—again!—to back
off, or suggest that "let's be friends" lunch by the river? I think not.*

    *Sophie, ultimately I do not want to feel this way any more than
you do—life is complicated enough—but I cannot help it. The question is, can you? Your court, babes.*

                                                Sam

The postmark? Almost two years old. At that point she and Sam
would have been madly in love, freshly in love. Wouldn't they? Oh,
God. What party? There had been so many parties in the early days.
Had he made a pass at Sophie? He must have. But why hadn't Sophie
told her? *Why?* The betrayal winded her again. It made Tash's revelations about Dominique pale into insignificance. She was strong.
She could take anything, even her best friend dying. But she wasn't
sure she could take this.

Rage boiled up against Sophie. Wasn't Ollie enough? And why
had she kept the letter? Was she planning to show her one day? If
so, she'd left it pretty damn late. Too many questions. She started
to weep. Even in the best-case scenario—Sophie had repeatedly told
Sam to fuck off—there had been secrets where she would have once
sworn on her life that there was nothing but confidences. And why
the hell did she wear a red dress to meet Sam? She knew the dress.
The vintage one. With the slit up the side. It was Sophie's favorite.
And walks? Lunch by the river?

But the worst bit, worse by far, was that Sam had wanted
Sophie, not her. How stupid to believe that Sam had picked her out
from the ark of gorgeous women and said, "You. You're the one,
Jenny. The others don't do anything for me." It was all flooding back

now. The things she'd ignored. The way Sam used to stare at Sophie. The way they sometimes held each other's glances a little too long and she'd been surprised at the intimacy of their conversational short-hand. The way he always seemed angry with Sophie for no apparent reason. Was it the anger of a man who couldn't have her? Or had he? Oh, God. She spun further into the vortex. There was no way out of it.

Curling onto her side in a fetal position, she wiped the tears and snot away with the back of her hand and shoved the letter under her pillow. She must hide it, she realized. Ollie must not see it. Clearly he had never read it, of that she was sure. He would have pulped Sam if he had; all hell would have broken loose. No, Ollie had been in the dark. Just like her. And now he couldn't know. Not after everything he'd been through.

A bang from downstairs. The front door? She flicked off the sidelight quickly, as the sound of something heavy dropped to the ground. A bag? Coughing. She knew that cough! Ollie was home. She tensed, coiled, a buzz of excitement overtaking her misery. Do not say anything about the letter, she told herself firmly. Say nothing. Scared she wouldn't be able to keep her mouth shut, she decided feigning sleep was the best policy.

Eyes squeezed tight, she listened to the soft scuff of his feet on the stairs, the wooden floorboards, the creak of Freddie's door opening. There was silence for a few moments, then footsteps again, the creaky closing of Freddie's door, the heartstopping opening of hers. Through the filigree of her wet lashes, she could see his floppy-haired figure silhouetted in the doorway. The mattress depressed as he sat down on the edge of the bed. She wished she'd not decided to pretend to be asleep now. She wanted to sit up and lick his face like a puppy. He was a survivor like her. He was . . . he was everything, the only light in the grayness.

"Jenny," he whispered, placing a hand gently on her shoulder. She caught the dry air smell of airplane on clothes. "Are you awake?"

She lay there rigid.

"Jenny?"

Her eyes pinged open. The sight of him sitting there was still a shock. She'd been anticipating him in her head all night and here he was. Warm, human, smelling of airplane air and chewing gum. "Ollie."

"Sorry, did I wake you?" In the gloom she could just see his eyes were amused like he knew she'd been faking sleep. A strand of dark hair curled over one of his eyes and she longed to nudge it gently aside with her fingers so she could drink in the whole of his face at once. In his presence the terrors of the night—the past, the betrayal—began to fade and take on a surreal, blurred edge like something that had happened long, long ago. There was no one else she wanted sitting on her bed, she realized. Not even Sophie.

"You are a star, Jen. Thank you so much for coming over." Ollie's breathing was a soft, animate thing in the darkness.

"No problem."

"Have you got a cold?"

"Yeah." She sniffed.

The bedsheets crumpled in the darkness as he moved closer, the curve of his back sinking into the curl of her stomach. They fitted together perfectly. Like he'd been ergonomically designed. They lay like this in the darkness for a moment, their breathing synchronizing slowly. "I don't know what I'd do without you, Jen."

"I'd do anything." The words twanged in the darkness. She wished they sounded less sexual. She was very grateful for the dark. "To help, you know."

"I know." He had a smile in his voice now. "Cecille okay?"

Cecille. Her name spoken out loud spiked the intimacy.

"Yeah, she's been sweet."

"Good, good."

"But she's in love with you." It just shot out before she could help herself.

He paused for an eternity. "I know."

"She's too young, Ollie."

"She's twenty."

She bit hard on her lower lip. There was nowhere else in the universe she'd rather not be now. Anyone else other than Ollie she'd want sitting on the side of her bed.

"You're angry."

"Imagine how you'd feel if you sent your daughter to a foreign country to work for a family . . ." She turned onto her side away from him and stared at the black wall, convincing no one. "Oh, what do I know? Do what you bloody well want."

He surprised her by tucking a strand of her hair behind her ear.

"Nothing happened, Jen." His breath was warm on her bare shoulder. "But, tell me, how long am I meant to live like a monk?"

"I don't know." All she knew was that her life was plummeting downward. And she was going to smash into the ground. Everyone in the world was in love with Sophie. Even her own fiancé. Sophie had eclipsed her, even in death.

"I played by the rules. But when did life ever play by the rules?"

"So I guess that's why you fucked Tash then. What about Lydia? Are you going to do her too?" She was still talking to the wall and hated the way she sounded so stiff and bitter.

"I just want to be free," he said, so softly she could barely hear him. "Free."

"You are flipping free!"

He was silent for a long time. "I am not."

She was the person strapping him to his past. She was the ballast who must be shed. She must get up tomorrow morning and walk away and not come back and let him get on with his life. He must be free of the past. Of Sophie. Of her. And she must be free of the whole damn lot of Sophie-in-her-red-dress worshippers. She needed her own church.

"Jen." He slipped one hand on her waist, making her take a sharp intake of breath, pulled her over so she could face him. His eyes were luminous. "I couldn't bear it if you despised me, you of all people."

She sniffed tearfully then, unable to hold back the tears.

"Hey, baby, what's the matter?" His voice was full of such tenderness it made her cry harder. And he'd called her baby. She hated it when Sam called her baby. She loved it that Ollie had just called her baby. "What's the matter?"

"I . . . I . . . I don't know. I guess I've been getting too close to you, to Freddie, to everything up here." She wiped away the tears crossly on the back of her hand, arching her body away from his confusing touch. There was an intimacy in the darkness and blear of the hour that filled the room with too much possibility. Even the letter under the pillow. Despite the horrors it contained it was oddly liberating. There was nothing that life could throw at her now. "I was Sophie's best friend. Not yours. Sometimes I forget that."

He stared at her intently. "But things have changed, haven't they?"

She heard her heart pounding in her ears and slowly became aware of something in the room, something thrilling and unutterable.

"I didn't know you before, not how I know you now. You and I, we're not who we were, Jenny."

The city rumbled distantly outside the window, yet it felt as though she and Ollie were the only still point, at the very center of the city, the most vital bit of it, and everything rippled out from them.

"You and Sophie were an impenetrable little world when you were together." His voice broke now. "I would not have been surprised had you backed off after she died. Lots of her friends have, you know—sunk away like I never knew them. They look at me like I'm a bad omen."

"People just don't know how to react."

"No, it's not that. It was Sophie who drew them into our orbit, her dazzle, her drama . . ." He stopped and frowned. "But you, *you*," he said more urgently. "Since she's gone you have got bigger and bigger, brighter and brighter. It's like you've come into focus. Sorry, I can't explain it." He sank his head down, resting his forehead on her shoulder. "I'm not making any fucking sense."

But he was making perfect sense. And the darkness of the bedroom was suddenly buzzing and alive like the darkness around a bonfire on a summer night.

"I feel like I've gotten to know you for the first time. I feel"—he hesitated, his voice lumpen—"that if you weren't in my life, in Freddie's life, it would be a terrible, terrible thing. That's all."

She sobbed unprettily. He hugged her tighter. Instinctively, she reached for his head, threading her fingers through his forest of black hair, losing them there, realizing as she did how she'd longed to do this. He took her other hand and kissed the tips of her fingers, one, then the other, another, and with each kiss she felt a liquid tug toward him.

"I know what I want to do and I know I shouldn't."

"Don't," croaked Jenny hoarsely, wishing he would.

He ran his fingers along her jawline. "You are so beautiful."

Beautiful! Beautiful? His words fluttered around her head like butterflies. And at that moment, for the first time in many months—years—she actually felt beautiful. A long, soft sigh came from deep within her as if she were exhaling a breath she was unaware she'd been holding.

"I've come to see you as mine, just a little bit. I so rarely see you with Sam, it's quite easy for me to delude myself. I can't get my head around the fact that you're about to get married."

Married. *That* no longer made sense.

He wiped a tear off her cheek with the pad of his thumb. "In another life we could . . ."

"Please don't, Ollie." Sophie had been dead not quite eight months. Eight!

"I'm sorry. I'm so sorry." He closed his eyes and a tear glistened in the corner of his eye. "I'm lost, Jen. I'm a fucking mess."

His mouth was inevitable then. He tasted like cigarettes and old coffee and tears. His beard rasped deliciously against her cheek. His lush soft lips moved down her face, buried into her neck, and the scent and feel of him filled her world completely.

"No. We can't, Ollie," she finally managed, gasping for breath.

His lips reluctantly moved away from hers. "You're right. We can't." He fell back on the pillow, stared up at the ceiling, breathing heavily. She didn't speak. He didn't speak. There was nothing left to say. The rightness and the wrongness were irresolvable. Slowly his lids began to close and his breath found the long, drawn-out rhythm of the jetlagged. She lay there, awake, heart slamming—the letter beneath her, Ollie beside her—fevered with longing and self-disgust. Soon, there was a pink glow at the crack in the curtains. Dawn was breaking. And with it, a terrifying new day.

Forty-three

What the hell's been going on? I take a minibreak and everything goes tits up at number thirty-three! Obviously I had no idea that poor little Freddie had chicken pox or I wouldn't have gone on my weekender. I feel horribly negligent. I only went because after my recent solitary in Ollie's trainer I was yearning for fresh air. I caught a keen southeasterly from the street's highest chimney—number fifteen's wonky one—and hung on to it as it picked up speed, bouncing over rooftops and electricity pylons, until I clipped the canopy of Highgate Woods. What can I say? Joyous. I was more air than anything else, a shape only, a balloon without its rubber skin. I could freefall with no fear, spin round and round the uppermost branches of the trees, elastic as a teenage Russian gymnast, then rest for a while in a blackbirds' nest alongside twigs, feathers and a scrap of Snickers wrapper. I need to rest more and more now. Getting old.

It's not just London's air pollution levels—soaring now in this sticky summer—I am definitely getting fainter, a fading footprint on the beach. In the heady early days of my afterlife I was able to slice through the days like a hot knife through butter. But now it feels as if the air is thick and viscous. I seem to get stuck in it like one of those crumbs that are impossible to remove from the Golden Syrup tin.

Anyway, I'm back from my treetop weekender now. And something has clearly happened in my absence. Freddie is spotty, obviously, but over the worst. It's Ollie I'm worried about. He is subdued and has been staring out the window for hours. The house itself feels altered too, in some way that I can't put my finger on, like it might have subsided a millimeter or two into the ground or is leaning a teeny bit sideways. I don't know. It just doesn't feel like it did. Not like the number thirty-three of old.

I check in on Jenny too, and discover she is in an even worse state. There's a dissonance in that horrible sterile Camden apartment, crackling, hissing, like a melting nuclear reactor. The atmosphere is so poisonous I have to limit my exposure. It's just as well Sam has stropped off to the country with his parents. Imagine he'd be freaked to see Jenny like this too, crying like a baby in the bath. Worried about her, really worried about her now, I stay close, dangling from a leather tassel on her bag, wondering where we are marching to and with such demented purpose. Which is how I find myself here, in Starbucks, Great Portland Street, stuck to the air vent above the coffee machine like a bit of chewing gum.

Not crying now, Jenny has got a face as long as Lyle Lovett's. Her eyes are still pink. Her hands are shaking. She's checking her watch. Nibbling a finger. Checking that watch again. Has she been stood up? She takes the last swig of her coffee. She picks up her handbag off the floor.

She's been stood up.

Then the glass doors swish open. A rash crawls up Jenny's collarbone.

A woman walks in—the woman I once saw Sam secretly meet?

Yes, I think so. She looks around. She sees Jenny and starts. The woman's hair is pulled back into a ponytail, like I wore mine on bad hair days. She is dressed in a nude jersey dress, bright yellow ballet flats. "Jenny?"

"Dominique?"

Oh, my God. Dominique. I'm settling into my front-row seat here.

"I'm sorry I'm so late." Dominique smiles nervously, scrapes the chair across the floor.

"I hope you didn't mind me emailing. Tash said . . ." Jenny falters, as if unsure whether she's allowed to declare her source. She can't take her eyes off Dominique's face. "Can I get you a coffee?"

"No, thanks, I've got to be somewhere pretty soon." There is tension around Dominique's mouth that purses, like it's got a drawstring inside.

"I needed to meet you properly," says Jenny finally, twisting her fingers together in her lap angularly like crab claws. "There's been a lot of stuff . . ." She blows out air, collects herself. "Between me and Sam. So many unanswered questions. I need to know what's going on, that's all. I'm not looking to blame anyone."

Dominique shifts on her chair. She's already regretting coming. "Look, to be perfectly frank, Jenny, I always thought that one day Sam and I would get back together."

"Back together?"

"I wondered if he was with anyone, what his situation was, so I tracked him down." She looks down at the table. "I realize this all must sound a bit bunny boiler. I didn't mean to freak you out. Sorry."

"You must have liked him a lot."

Dominique glances up from her hands. "I thought we'd marry actually."

Jenny closes her eyes, bracing herself. It's bigger. It's bigger than she thought. "When were you two together?"

"Summer, two years ago," Dominique says in the definite manner of a woman who's been counting the hours ever since.

"Two years ago?" Jenny repeats in a whisper, her hand crushed over her mouth, paling.

Two years ago! Then we're talking about around the time he made a pass at me too. The little turd.

"We overlapped?" Dominique looks down guiltily as she speaks, like she may not have been entirely ignorant of the fact.

"We did." Jenny shakes her head in disbelief. "Jesus."

Yes, we *all* did.

The two women stare at each other across the round dark wooden table, me from the air-conditioning vent. An irritated Starbucks person sweeps Jenny's empty cup off the table.

"I better go." Dominique, clutching her large red tote, stands up to leave.

"One more question." The clatter in the café seems to quieten for Jenny's inevitable question. "Why did you think I was called Sophie?"

Dominique hesitates, wondering what the right thing is to say. The mouth purses again. She holds her handbag tighter.

I wait. Jenny waits. Her left knee jumps up and down inside her trouser leg.

"Did you know there was someone else?"

"Look," Dominique says, defensive now, "all I knew was that he'd got this . . . this *thing*, some stupid schoolboy crush, unreciprocated, on some woman. Sophie, her name was Sophie."

"Unreciprocated?" Jenny asks in a scared whisper. "You're sure?"

"Yes, unreciprocated, definitely," she answers firmly. "That was what was so totally frustrating about the whole situation." Dominique speaks faster, harder, like aggrieved exes do. "He said I reminded him of her. That I was like her, but . . . but better." She shakes her head and laughs hollowly. "I thought if I hung in there . . . I can't believe how stupid this is making me sound. I'm not that woman, not the woman you must think I am, Jenny. He was just one of those men, you know, who turn you into someone you're not. Do you know what I mean?"

Jenny nods. She knows exactly what she means. And so do I.

Dominique leaves quickly, with a worried backward glance, wondering what she's done. I flatten against the ceiling, desperate to be human again and wrap my arms around Jenny and hug her and kiss her and tell her it is going to be alright and that he had a silly, stupid crush on me but she was always the woman he really loved, that it was just my vanity he flattered, that it never went anywhere because I would *never* do that. I didn't act faultlessly. I'm a flirt, a tease, an erotic fantasist, but I'm not a traitorous friend. Instead I have to watch helplessly as my dear friend finally breaks, there and then, in the middle of Starbucks, oblivious to the people staring. She sobs noisily until a barista brings her a tissue then steers her firmly by the elbow out the door to the crowded street.

Forty-four

Have you lost your fucking *mind*?" Sam shouted, kicking his weekend bag along the floor. "I've just got back from a marquee meeting onsite. We can't possibly cancel the wedding."

Jenny held on to a steel ridge of chair for support. If only she could think straight. But she'd been crying for so long her brain had gone smeary. She could not think. She could not breathe. All she knew was that if she put on that wedding dress she'd evaporate in a shower of green sparks like the Wicked Witch of the West. It would be the most dishonest thing she'd ever done. "I'm sorry, Sam."

His expression sagged. He finally realized she meant it. "Jenny, please." He lowered his voice so that it sounded almost like a threat. "I am trying to protect you from yourself. You are angry. You are hurt. Understood. I apologize. I will apologize until the day I die. I am in your debt, okay? Whatever it fucking takes. I'll do whatever it takes, Jenny, to make you realize that it was nothing, absolutely *nothing*." He angrily swiped the letter off the table. "I don't know why the silly bitch kept it!"

"Maybe she was going to show me." All night she'd been think-ing of the times that Sophie had tried to talk to her about something: the *it* in that to-do list Ollie had found months earlier.

"Come on. She probably kept it because she enjoyed it. I bet she kept all her love letters, didn't she?"

"Sam . . ." This was a way out. It was her way out and she was going to grab the bucking bronco by the horns and hold on tight.

"She was never happy unless every last man in the room was drool-ing after her. She fucking loved it." His face paled with repressed anger. "Do you remember her at parties, dancing? Dancing in those stupid sequiny dresses. Look at me! Look at me! She may as well have written that across her forehead in red lipstick," he spat. "A tart."

Her instinct was to leap to Sophie's defense. Not this time. "It doesn't change anything." There was a calmness and conviction to her voice that surprised her. "It's too late, Sam."

"I'd say *this* was a bit fucking late actually, Jenny. Would you just snap out of it?" He tried and failed to smile. "Please, Jenny?" he asked, more desperate now. "You want to throw this away? All this?" he said, gesturing around him, as if the apartment itself was some-thing she couldn't possibly give up.

I hate this apartment, she thought. I hate its high-tech hardness. When I have my own place I'm going to have knitted patchwork cushions and an old wooden work surface stained with tea and a radio with a big fat dial that I can turn. "You fucked around with Dominique too." She blinked back tears. "And I was so in love with you."

He groaned. "I really, really tried to get her to back off, stop stir-ring things up. I even asked Tash to have a word with Dominique, Jenny. I did everything I could to protect you. You've got to believe that."

She turned away from him, still hurt that he'd crept into her Muswell Hill world and taken the confidence of one of her new friends, used it to his advantage. He used everyone to his advantage. "It makes it worse."

He dropped his head into his hands. "I don't understand."

"Why did you want to set a date, Sam? After all those months. After all that foot dragging. That's what I don't understand."

He looked up at her with red, hurt eyes. "Because I loved you. Because . . ."

"Why?"

"Sophie's death. It made me focus. I'd lost her. . . ." He stumbled on his words before he realized what he'd said.

Something twisted in her stomach. "You mean it was all over and there was nothing left to play for?"

"No, it made me feel I'd been given a second chance. When she was alive I lived in fear of her saying something to you, fucking up everything. It hung over me, my own stupidity. When she died . . ." He shook his head.

"You thought you'd got away with it?"

He was silent for a moment. "I'm sorry." He shook his head. "I couldn't help the way I felt about the others. I love you."

Others! How many were there? She couldn't listen to this. "None of this makes sense to me anymore either. Don't you see?" she shouted. "It just doesn't make sense to me."

"If it made sense before, it can make sense again," he pleaded. "We have a connection. We always have done. The good times, think of the good times, babes. Me, you, Soph and Ollie, the picnics, the parties, that lovely weekend on the narrow boat in Oxford, do you remember?"

That hot summer weekend. The gentle sway of the boat. She clearly remembered Ollie and Sophie sitting on the roof, Ollie licking a bit of ice cream off the tip of Sophie's nose, while Jenny watched from the deck, thinking that if she had ice cream on her nose Sam would make a hand gesture for her to remove it or pass her a tissue.

She remembered thinking on that boat that only beautiful people like Sophie got loved like Sophie was loved. That plainer women like herself shouldn't expect so much. She now also realized that it was likely that Sam had spent the whole weekend ogling Sophie in her bikini. "Sam, it's over."

He was angry again. His hands fisted at his sides and for one terrible moment Jenny thought he might hit her. "I smell a rat here. This is all too convenient, isn't it? Isn't it?" he hissed. "If you really loved me, you'd believe me."

Jenny shut her eyes. He was right. She knew he was right. Ollie's kiss had changed everything. It would have changed everything even if Dominique and the letter had never come to light. It had set her on fire in a way she never thought possible. However sickening and shameful her feelings, there was no going back. She'd rather be single forever than marry someone she didn't feel that with. It was the *grrr*. The *grrr* that Sophie used to talk about. It had happened to her.

"Listen, Jenny, you have two choices. You stand here right now and tell me like a grown-up what the problem really is and we might, we just might, be able to avert total fucking disaster. Or you watch your world implode from within very, very shortly."

"I don't think I love you anymore." A final cut. Let it implode.

"You bitch! You stupid bitch."

"I'm sorry," she said, beginning to sob, the certainty of a few moments earlier beginning to fray at the edges with guilt.

"This is about Ollie, isn't it? You think I was the one with the game plan. When all along it was you, waiting to step in there." Sam laughed hollowly. "Jenny, do you honestly think that Ollie would want *you*?"

Jenny took a sharp breath.

"You poor, poor deluded woman."

Legs shaking, she fled the kitchen, ran to the bedroom and started stuffing her clothes into a holdall. Sam didn't try to stop her.

Her life packed up surprisingly small. A capsule life packed into a capsule bag. She walked back into the kitchen to say good-bye. He was sitting at the kitchen table, face flattened against the glass, crying. It was the first time Jenny had ever seen him cry.

"Sam. I'm so sorry."

"Fuck you."

She hesitated for one moment at the front door, then, closing it behind her for the last time, she stepped into the grimy Camden sunshine.

Forty-five

When the carriage clock on her parents' mantelpiece hit eleven a.m., the exact time she would have been getting married three weeks before, Jenny still got goose bumps. And so the calendar marched on, every date an echo of another life that was almost hers, the stuff scribbled out in her diary. They would be back from their honeymoon now. Would she have stopped taking the Pill? Might she even be pregnant?

No, she didn't want that. But she didn't want this either. Living with her parents. The smell of the chicken farm in her nostrils. Aged thirty-six. With shingles.

The shingles were her hair shirt. Sam's friends and family certainly thought she was the devil incarnate. Her own friends and family had decided that she'd lost the plot. Only Liz had emailed repeatedly to wish her love and luck and "whatever else you need right now," reassuring her that any decision she made was the right decision because she'd made it. Jenny was immeasurably grateful for Liz's lone, sane voice.

Yes, it *was* her decision, therefore it had to be the right one, she reminded herself during the most wretched moments—in plentiful supply in the small hours—or on days like today, when she'd finished a manuscript too soon and the empty hours she needed to fill rolled away in front of her like the pen on her parents' maddeningly slanted desk. Even her hair was wretched, a mass of tinder-dry frizz. She couldn't control her life. She couldn't control her hair.

"Shouldn't you think about getting dressed?" Her mother burst into her bedroom. She never knocked. "You'd feel better if you got dressed, Jennifer. Here, love, nice cup of tea."

"Thanks, Mum." Jenny scratched the base of her shingled back, realizing now how much torment poor Freddie had gone through with his chicken pox.

"Don't scratch. You don't want scars on top of everything else."

It was an uncomfortable paradox that the more she was in need of her mother—and what would she have done without her dear mother in the past few weeks?—the more her mother irritated. Sometimes, quite irrationally, she thought she might actually detest her mother. Then she'd catch herself and realize that the only person she actually detested was herself, and she was merely projecting onto her mother in the manner of a selfish, angsty teenager and she'd feel a wave of shame for her own ingratitude, followed by an urge to bury herself in her mother's bosom like a sobbing toddler. She picked up her tea, followed her mother's beanbag figure into the sitting room and sat down heavily in the foamy scatter cushions, next to the stale potpourri that would forevermore be the Proustian perfume of this whole disastrous episode.

"Try and put your best foot forward and cheer up a little bit, love," said her mother kindly, perching a little awkwardly on the corner of an armchair, not sure where to position herself around her daughter's aimless grief. "I know it's hard. But we all have to take responsibility for our decisions. Not let them eat us up."

Jenny suspected that her mother really thought that most women in their latish thirties might have chosen to believe their fiancé's protest of innocence, whatever the damning evidence to the contrary. Sometimes she was almost tempted to confide in her about Ollie, to help her mum understand. But she always bottled it. How could she explain she'd fallen in love with her dead friend's husband?

Hers was a betrayal so deep, so corrosive, that she could not bear to look at her own face in the mirror, let alone share it with anyone. Yes, she could live with herself for jilting Sam so close to the altar. He would, she was absolutely sure, meet someone else fully deserving of him and be completely fine. But falling in love with Ollie? It didn't matter what Sophie had hidden from her, what she had felt or done, falling in love with Ollie was still unforgivable. Sophie was the girl who had shared her cheese with her the first night at university, the only "it" girl who ever thought she was worth bothering with and who made her laugh and laugh.

Sophie's betrayal was quietly buried beneath the soil in Highgate Cemetery. Her own betrayal was still alive. The hunger of that kiss haunted her. Sometimes she'd wake in a panic in the night, sitting bolt upright on the pillows of her old childhood bedroom, sweating, panting, convinced that Sophie had witnessed the kiss too. That she wasn't dead after all. For once the thought of Sophie alive was no longer comforting.

During the day, it was easier to train her mind. She would tell herself that the kiss—the peculiar *rightness* of the kiss—between her and Ollie had been nothing but a symptom of grief, a clumsy grope for human comfort. But then the yearning for him would spring from her body like a trap and there was nothing she could do about it. He was there when she woke every morning, his hand in her hair, those dark, heartbroken eyes searching hers. And that tug, tug between her thighs.

He had phoned a few times since she'd fled for Kent. She hadn't

answered the calls, dreading that he would assume that the kiss had
had something to do with the whole runaway bride episode, which,
of course, it had. So she responded with perfunctory texts and emails,
and made occasional journeys to London to see Freddie, who was
busier now, more sucked up in school, playdates, football, moving
away from the black smoking crater of the previous January. She
liaised with Cecille, who would frequently come and collect Freddie
from a place in town so that she, Jenny, could ostensibly get straight
back on the train, but really to avoid Ollie. She never dared ask
Cecille how Ollie was.

Avoidance was the name of the game.

Helpfully, the wedding guest list itself provided a concise record
of everyone she must avoid at all costs. Buyers of wedding presents.
Witnesses to the shame of the rom-com gone wrong. While many
of them—the ones who would be seated on the left-hand side of the
church, Sam's side—had communicated their judgment with a thunderous silence, those on her side were still foraging for explanations.
But she did not want to have to explain herself. She could not.

"Are there any practical things I could give you a hand with,
love?" asked her mother, disturbing her thoughts. "Did I tell you that
all the wedding gifts have gone back now? Dad's sorted it."

"That's great. Thanks so much."

"What about the wedding dress, love?"

"Sam's probably burned it and scattered the ashes in the toilet."

"Oh, don't say that. I was hoping Ollie might get a refund. Have
you asked him what he wants to—"

"No."

Her mother gave her a sharp look. "Well, I think you should,
Jennifer. It was so generous of him. Everyone's lost out here, you
know."

"I know, sorry." Of course no one had ever got round to booking
wedding insurance, and the bills for the marquee, the caterers, the

brass band had all rolled in. "I'll pay you all back eventually, Mum. I promise."

"I know you will." Her mother's voice softened. The tip of her nose pinked as it always did when crying or sneezing was imminent. "I just want to see you happy again, that's all."

Jenny pulled her mouth into a smile shape.

Her mother wasn't convinced. "I really think you should go and see a friend, Jennifer. I know you feel humiliated and want to lick your wounds, but a girlfriend is the world's best tonic. Marj has pulled me through some really tough times. And Dawn. Dawn was a saint when me and your dad were rocky."

"I've got you and Dad and Bobster."

Hearing his name, the dog jumped up, wagging his stinky tail against her face. "Why don't you take Bobster for a walk, Jennifer? It's a lovely day out there. It would get you out of the house and it would make one old canine very happy."

"Okay." Anything to bring the conversation to a close. She drained her tea, stood up.

"And Jennifer?"

"Yes, Mum."

"You do know that you can stay here as long as you like, don't you? There's no rush."

"Thank you, Mum. But I'll only be here until the end of the month, latest. Come on, Bobster. Walkies."

Almost four months later she was still there, gazing out the window at the strings of colored Christmas lights draped over the post office in the distance, the smell of chicken shit in her nostrils. She was relieved that her parents had gone out to do the nativity churchy thing on their own. This gave her time to think and check and double-check the details of her forthcoming escape. She had a one-way ticket to New York. She would leave on January the sixth. The anniversary of Sophie's death. That seemed fitting somehow. Sophie had gone over to the other side on that day. Jenny would cross the Atlantic.

Some people might have dropped to their knees in a church and asked God what to do. She'd dropped to her knees in the vegetable patch and asked Dolly Parton. Dolly, the guru of heartbreak and mistakes in love, the mistress of picking yourself up and dusting yourself down. She asked. And she was answered, in a Tennessee drawl. *Move somewhere else, honey. Start over. And don't get mud under your fingernails.*

She'd spent weeks Googling New York apartment share ads on Craigslist and visualizing herself sitting in diners tapping at her laptop, drinking macchiatos. In New York City she wouldn't be looked upon as a freak for being thirty-six and single. No, there in the city of reinvention, anything was possible. She might even wear yellow. She could Skype Freddie regularly. He could come and stay when he was older. She could be eccentric, the New York spinster that took him to see weird movies and art shows and filled him with memories of the Staten Island Ferry and Coney Island and the roller disco in Central Park. Maybe she'd live at the Chelsea Hotel.

She gazed across the frozen field—its frosting was slowly beginning to melt in the winter sunshine—and wondered if Sophie would follow her.

Shortly after she'd died she had worried that she could no longer quite remember what Sophie looked like. But now the opposite was true. Sophie was sticking close now, too close. That honk of laughter would ring in her head as she walked Bobster along the quiet country lanes. Sometimes she swore she could feel Sophie's warm Wrigley's breath on her hand. Or she'd look out across a field and for a moment she'd see Sophie dancing, sylphlike, barefoot, her thick, dark hair fanning out around her, her hands weaving the air, exuberant and beautiful. And she'd forgive her anything then, anything at all.

Something was rubbing against her ankle. She looked down, grinned. Bobster was doing what he always did so expertly, dragging her back from the past into the present with stinky licks that smelled of canned venison.

She ruffled him behind the ears. "Come on. Yes, yes, I know. Time for your walk." Pulling on her anorak—all she ever wore was anorak, jeans, fleece and Wellies now; it made getting dressed in the morning so much easier—she peered out the window to check for rain. The sun was hidden behind a gray cloud shaped like a giant boulder, and the sky below it had gone rice pudding yellow. Christmas trees twinkled in the leaded windows of the huddle of new-build houses.

The front door clicked shut behind her. Bobster yelped. Seeing that he'd got caught up in his lead, she bent down to untangle his foot, instantly feeling the cold damp of the ground seep through the knee of her jeans. "There, Houdini."

A loud growl of motor startled them both. She looked up to see a VW van reversing into her parents' small gravel drive. The van braked noisily.

"Excuse me," she began, about to start the "this is not actually a public carpark" speech, before tumbling backward in shock.

Forty-six

S mell that air!" Suze pushed her briar of hair out through the car window and sniffed. "Bloody lovely."

There was a scuffle in the back of the van, a series of shouts, small sticky palms pressed against the windows. The vehicle juddered on its wheels.

"Flora, stop hitting Ludo!"

"He's stolen my raisins. Evil raisin stealer. I so hate you."

"Now look what you've done!"

"Ludo! I'm at my wits' end."

"Get out. Ow. That's my foot."

Jenny watched, speechless, as Liz appeared, trailing a child. Then Tash's leg, one, then the other. She smiled shyly, as if unsure of her reception, and looked relieved when Jenny smiled back. Then Lydia, bundled in meters of cashmere and a cutesy white bobble hat. More children. More noise. She blinked, unable to take in the surreal sight.

"Found you at last." Suze put an arm around her shoulder and squeezed.

Jenny was speechless. She no longer had the social skills. Still, no one seemed to mind, all leaping up and kissing her at once. It was delightful and horrifying in its unexpectedness.

Liz reached for her hand and held it tight. "Bloody good to see you, Jenny."

"God, you too!" She only realized quite how much she'd missed Liz now that she was here. "But . . ." She shook her head in amazement, laughing. "How on earth did you know where I was?" They all began to talk at once.

"Ollie dug your folks' address out of Sophie's address book, duh."

"If you won't come to Muswell Hill, Muswell Hill will come to you."

"We're the persistent friend equivalent of Japanese knotweed."

"Does all countryside smell of poo, Mummy?"

"Aren't you going to ask us in for tea? I'd kill for tea."

"Hurry up, I'm bursting to pee," said Lydia, hopping from one leg to the other.

It was then that Jenny noticed Lydia's tummy, its perfect convexity swelling like a giant egg from between the folds of beige cashmere.

Lydia grinned and patted it. "A happy accident."

"Bloody hell! Congratulations," said Jenny. It had been decades since she last saw them! "Come in, come in."

Inside her parents' not-big-enough house, she distracted the children with a scratchy *Star Wars* VHS tape and the seasonal tin of chocolates. It was harder to know what to do with their mothers. "Drink?" Feeling a little gauche and unused to company, she rummaged through the drinks cabinet. It consisted of a sticky and unfashionable mix of supermarket whiskeys and yellow liquors.

"Sorry, no wine. Anyone stomach sherry? It's that or strawberry liquor from duty free."

"Sherry, lovely!" they all chimed, then winced as they took their first sip.

Suze raised her glass. "Happy Christmas, Jenny!"

"Happy Christmas. Now will someone tell me what the hell you're all doing here?"

"We could ask you the same question," said Liz, peering out the window.

"You might as well have emigrated to Alaska," said Tash, also looking out the window and surveying the scrub of field with an undisguised look of horror.

Jenny smiled, pleased that she felt no animosity toward Tash, that the scene in Tash's kitchen felt like it happened three thousand years ago. And Tash smiled back, knowing she was forgiven. "Probably would have been more going on," Jenny said.

"God, you *are* brave," sighed Lydia. "Having the guts to run for freedom days before your wedding. I think there's something kind of *Thelma and Louise*–ish about it."

Oh, how Jenny wished that was the case, rather than the sad, shameful mess it had begun to feel like. She looked down at the floor. "Hardly."

"What on earth *happened*?" demanded Suze, leaning forward over the dining table, so that her breasts swelled across the polished dark wood.

"Suze, I'm sure Jenny will tell us, if and when she's ready," Liz said protectively. "You don't have to say anything, Jenny. We're just all horribly nosy, as you know."

"The honest answer is . . . well . . ." No, it wouldn't come. Honesty failed her.

"No matter," said Liz, helping her out of the tight spot. "Tell us when you're ready, Jenny."

She smiled gratefully at Liz. "Seriously, have you just come to say hi? I am very, very touched. I don't deserve it at all."

"Actually there is another agenda." Suze sat up straight, switching right into meeting mode. For a moment it was like being back in Suze's kitchen.

"Oh. Things are okay?" she asked.

"Well, Help Ollie more or less disbanded after you left. Cecille was, I suppose, doing a good enough job," Suze said reluctantly.

"Great." She was relieved to hear that. All was okay.

"*But* I fear we are needed again," declared Suze solemnly.

Jenny felt the blood drain from her head. "Oh, no. Is Freddie okay?"

Liz put a hand on hers. "Freddie's fine."

"Ollie?"

"Ollie is less good," said Suze cryptically, exchanging glances with Liz. "Despite all our best efforts."

"We've done what we can, Jenny," said Lydia, her eyes beginning to well dangerously. "We ordered his Christmas tree, helped decorate it, gave him a list of the hot toys in year two, put in the Christmas supermarket delivery order . . ."

"He was baked about three million mince pies by the local ladies," laughed Liz. "As you can imagine."

Jenny smiled. She could imagine.

"He's had *so* many offers for Christmas," sighed Suze, reaching for another chocolate. "I'd say pretty much everyone on the street has invited him for lunch or tea or something Christmassy since school broke up. I even bought them both stockings, just in case."

"Oh, no. Don't tell me he's on his own for Christmas. Where's Cecille?"

"Gone home to France." She raised an eyebrow. "And not coming back. She's got a new Italian boyfriend and is following him to Milan like a lovesick puppy."

Jenny felt a shot of relief. "But his mum . . ."

"He muttered something to Brigid about going up to his folks' house in the lakes," said Suze. "That was last week. But there's no sign of any movement. He's still at number thirty-three as we speak. I've had a few peeks at the house—"

"In other words, she's been stalking him," said Liz matter-of-factly, peeling the colorful wrapper from another chocolate.

Suze ignored her. "And I see no sign of imminent departure, Jenny. No sign at all! None of us can bear to see him so miserable. And no one, no one, least of all poor Ollie and Freddie, should be alone for Christmas."

"Tell her about the incident," said Lydia, sniffing hard now. "Sorry, ladies." She waved her hands in front of her face. "Hormones."

"What incident?" She feared the worst. Ollie felt very close all of a sudden. She'd pushed him as far back in her mind as she could and now he was back again. She could feel him, smell him, peel the memory of him back like a clementine.

Suze cleared her throat. "He did agree to one drink, last week. And he got very, very drunk."

"So drunk he ended up in Chicken Cottage," added Tash. "With Posh Brigid."

Posh Brigid! Oh, God. Another. She didn't want to hear. She knew it was just a matter of time before Ollie met a woman and she didn't want to hear it from someone else. She didn't want the indignity of failing to look happy for him.

Liz, as if reading her mind, put an arm on her hand. "Nothing like that, Jenny. No funny business. Brigid is a mum at the school, very happily married."

"He got very, very drunk. And he started crying."

"Oh, no." Jenny started to bite her fingernails, thrown back into her chair with the horror of it all. "Christmas without Soph was always going to be very hard. Poor Ollie."

"It's not just Sophie he is missing," said Liz gently.

There was a crashing silence, broken only by the plaintive cry of Obi-Wan Kenobi. She felt all their eyes burning into her.

"He misses *you*, Jenny," said Tash with an openness that Jenny had never witnessed before. "He told Brigid. He misses you desperately, darling."

Jenny's throat contracted and closed. She couldn't breathe.

"I think you disappearing like this . . ." Suze tried to choose her words carefully. "Not to lay on the guilt, but he's been really struggling these last few months." She hesitated. "Did you not think . . ."

Jenny bit down on her lip. She could not possibly explain. Never. Her feelings for Ollie were her own dark dirty secret.

"We know you've been going through your own shit," Liz said kindly. "And it must be horrible for you, it must feel like your world has fallen apart."

"I'm fine."

"You don't look fine," said Lydia quickly.

The tears came then. There was no stopping them. Suze immediately pressed her into the fleshy mound of her bosom. A small child's fingers pressed the last Caramel Keg into her hand. Another small hand dabbed her cheek with tissues.

"Let it all out, Jen," said Suze, slapping her hard on the back, as if she were trying to burp her. "Let it all out."

"Oh, God, you've set me off now too," wailed Lydia.

"Oh, no, Lydia's started," howled Liz. "Hit the flood sirens!"

Jenny snorted with laughter through her tears. As she emerged gasping for breath from the group hug—friends who may never be as dear as Sophie but had become real friends all the same—she felt different. Like a heavy bag had been picked off her back. Girlfriends were a tonic. Her mother, for once, was right.

"It's snowing!" yelled Ludo. All the children jumped up from the floor and pressed their noses against the cold window, entranced as snow whirled in eddies over the field. "Wow."

Jenny was not sure whether it was something to do with the snow or something to do with the hug or the fact that Ludo reminded her so unbearably of Freddie at that moment, but forty minutes later, against her better judgment, she found herself scrawling a note on her parents' telephone pad and picking her car keys off the duck hook on the wall.

Forty-seven

've been dead for almost a year. In that time Freddie has lost two baby teeth, jumped from a size ten foot to a twelve and grown two inches. He has six chicken pox scars on his stomach where he scratched. He is, like, totally over Beyblades and into the canoeing game on the Wii. He has a crush on Ani, a Sri Lankan beauty in year four. He has learned six handy new swearwords to toss about in the playground when necessary and wants to watch *X Factor* instead of *Deadly 60* or *Strictly*.

Ollie meanwhile has gone gray, gained and lost a beard, shed fourteen pounds, worked his way through the entire *Mad Men* box set twice and no longer listens to Tibetan monks chanting for light background music. He doesn't wank over my knickers either. The boiler is up for its yearly service, which he'll undoubtedly forget. The smoke alarm batteries are almost dead, and he'll forget to replace them too. Against all the odds Ping Pong and my potted palm appear to have survived.

My grave is covered in a crisp crust of snow today, the first

Christmas snow we've had in decades, ruining all the bookies' cof-
fers. There is a Gothic shoot of vivid green ivy fingering my gravestone. Over the last year there have been bluebells growing beside
it, daisies, dandelions, layers of mulching autumn leaves alive
with beetles and bugs and, on more than one occasion, a pregnant
badger. The mound of earth that duvets my coffin no longer has that
morbid freshly dug-up vegetable patch look either. See. I've almost
settled in.

And yet.

I'm still here, aren't I? Not in a dank patch of cemetery but curled
beside the rows of Christmas cards on the mantelpiece above the
hissing log fire like Ping Pong's elderly, dozy grandma. No, I'm certainly not what I was. I am smaller, weaker, gray as a cup of old tea.
As in life, as in death, it seems: we're all only going one way and
there's fuck-all anyone can do about it. On the other hand, I do
sometimes wonder if I am fading because I am fading from the lives
of those I love. There are very few obvious traces of me left now. No
scent of my perfume, none of my pubes rolling on the bathroom
floor. My voice has been deleted from the answer machine. The
clothing catalogs have stopped falling through the door. My email
account no longer exists. There has been a settlement with the bus
company stored away for when Freddie's older. (I want him to spend
it sensibly on lost weekends at music festivals, Italian leather shoes
and whisking beautiful girls to Paris. I want him to feast on life
itself.) I am fragments of memory now, photographs on the wall,
footage on the video camera, an echo in Freddie's beautiful features,
his sweet tooth, his bubbly laugh, the glistening ore of love in his
heart. And this is okay. I tell myself this is okay. This is enough.

What is far less okay is the fact that I have not been able to alter
the fates of those I leave behind! My pitiful lack of supernatural
powers has rendered me totally hopeless as either matchmaker or

kibosher of weddings: I'm afraid I can claim none of the credit for Sam and Jenny's torching. It makes me sad that Ollie and Freddie will spend their first Christmas alone. And probably their next too.

The lack of woman at number thirty-three is obvious. This is a house craving estrogen, or at the very least someone who cares about the removal of the sticky Lucozade-like substance in the hinge of the loo seat. It's very much a male domain now, more den than home. There are no beauty products or periodphernalia in the bathroom cabinet, no stashes of toffee ice cream, a scarcity of puddings full stop. I fear that the Christmas pud will never make a reappearance in this house again, the pud being a girl's pud, Ollie and Freddie much preferring chocolate biscuit cake. The Christmas tree is up, though, next to the mountain bikes scuffing the pale wall in the sitting room with their rubber handlebars. The tree is smaller than last year's—I always was a sucker for a big Disney tree—and has been decorated by Freddie and Suze's kids, a gaudy riot of multicolored tinsel and plastic balls. (My tasteful wooden angels and pine cones are collecting dust in a box in the loft.) Paper chains made at school by Freddie dangle perilously over the fire. A tin of uneaten mince pies languishes in the cereal cupboard. The fridge is full of beer and Parma ham and sausages and cracked hard cheddar. Needless to say, upstairs there is a *vast* amount of empty closet space.

With some effort I extricate myself from my warm nest beside the Christmas cards on the mantelpiece and wheezily thread myself through the banister to check on Freddie. My beautiful boy is on the computer in the study playing "Dom from Canberra" and "Brad7 from Milwaukee" on a Mathletics game, yelping with delight when he wins, his pupils dilating with pleasure. I leave him absorbed in his game and slide back down the banister to be close to Ollie, who is dozing on the sofa, cashew nut dust powdering his old sweater. (Who will buy him a new cashmere sweater for Christmas? I always bought him a cashmere sweater for Christmas.) His lips part a bit, his eyes move rapidly beneath their lids like he's dreaming. The news is rolling on the telly but it is on mute. On the coffee table a bottle of nettle ale is half drunk, warming, alongside a pile of studio CDs, out-of-date newspapers and one of Freddie's socks. I settle beside him, warming myself on the edge of his thigh, my husband the host. And it is only then that I sense somebody outside the house: the slip of snow under a sole; a melting of a snowflake on a hot cheek.

The doorbell rings. There is a power surge in the house.

Ollie keeps on dozing. Wake up! Wake up, darling! I wham against his side, making as much impression as a baby duck's feather tickling the steel hull of a ship. He sleeps on, still as a moth. The doorbell rings again. The shadow is moving from one foot to the next. The shadow is a familiar shape. And it is walking backward, receding.

No, the shadow has stopped. It is turning. It is walking back up the path, faster this time. One more a quick, sharp ring. Ollie opens a bloodshot eye. He scratches his balls. His brain catches up with his ears and he staggers down the hall toward the door, shedding cashew crumbs. He opens the front door. His face lights up, like all his Christmases have come at once.

"Hi," Jenny says. There is snow on the tips of her dark lashes, like tiny white pom-poms.

He just stares at her in silence, grinning like a loon.

She smiles shyly. "Er, can I come in?"

They are in the hallway now and the air between them is sparking, ticking, as if we're in a forest of electricity pylons. She flicks snow off her hair. A flake lands on his neck, melting instantly.

"You look different."

He rubs his hand over his jaw. "I shaved the biblical beard."

"Ah," she laughs, blushes.

They are in the middle of the sitting room now, lit by the firefly glow of the fairy lights. Jenny doesn't realize that she has a long tail of green tinsel stuck to the bottom of her snowy boot.

"You disappeared," said Ollie, still staring at her weirdly. He is pulsing with a strange, pent-up energy that is familiar to me yet hard to identify.

She looks down at the floor. "Sorry."

His eyes don't leave her face. Like he's scared it might go somewhere if he looks away for even a second. "I missed you, Jen."

A bittersweet possibility begins to dawn. Could they? *Would* they? Have I been . . . Oh, my God, have I ignored what was under my nose all this time? I consider the match for all of two milliseconds and I'm flooded, for the first time since I died, with a delirious cascading rush of hope.

Jenny smiles twitchily, like she could just as easily cry. "I'm sorry for being such a crap friend." I can see her backing away. "I really am, Ol."

I want to fill her heart and tell her it's okay. There is no other woman on planet earth I'd rather replaced me at number thirty-three. You even helped me choose the living room wallpaper! You have legacy here. Oh, Jenny. Look after my boys. Take them, hold them close; and make them eat some broccoli.

"I'm going to New York in the New Year," she says, unable to meet his eye. "I didn't want to go and leave without saying good-bye properly."

Ollie looks stricken. "New York?"

"I need to start again."

Oh, Jenny, darling Jenny. Please don't screw up, not this time. Everything is at stake. *Everything*.

"New York is so far away."

"That's kind of the point."

"You can start anywhere, Jen." He takes her hands in his. "Stay with me."

She stares at their entwined hands. "I can't," she says in a whisper. She's beginning to shake like a leaf. "You are . . . you are Sophie's husband."

Jenny, Jenny, I am dead as a dead parrot! Ceased to be! I must do something. I must. Using all my last reserves of flagging energy I whirl dementedly round and round her head like a dancer in a Gaga video, trying to make her see me or sense me or whatever it takes to make her realize that here is her chance. This is it.

In my usual grand paranormal style, nothing happens.

"Please listen to me." I see it in his eyes then, his love for her. He is no longer mine. Our love has been recycled.

She pulls away from him. "Don't, Ol."

I whirl again, frenzied now, desperate. The future is slipping away, the last grain of sand through my clay-cold fingers.

Jenny steps backward, touches her forehead. "Oh."

"You alright?"

Jenny looks puzzled. "Yes . . . yes, I think so."

Freaky. Did I just do that? I do it again, harder this time. Her eyes squeeze shut tighter. "Oh," she says, touching her forehead again.

I did it! I only bloody well did it! I can commune with more than hamsters and smoke alarms.

"Here, sit down." Concerned, he reaches for her, steadies her with his hands. She perches on the sofa arm.

"Give me one minute, then you can go again, okay? You can go to New York. Go where you damn well want. Just hear me out, please?"

Jenny nods. There's still a chance. Relief tunnels out of me, long and light, like a last breath.

Ollie's brows knit together and he speaks slowly and carefully like a man desperate not to screw up. "I love Sophie from the bottom of my heart, Jenny. I miss her every day."

"Me too," croaks Jenny. She puts her hand down on the sofa to steady herself and accidentally presses the remote control lying on a cushion. Music starts to pour out of the speakers, filling the room with something twangy, bluegrass.

"But she has gone, Jen. And losing you for all these months felt like another huge loss and I've missed you, missed you so much." His eyes darken. "Freddie keeps asking after you."

She gulps. "I'm sorry."

The music rises and falls around them. Harmonica. Guitar.

"I know that I'm a fucking car crash." He smiles at her so tenderly then, it makes me want to weep. "And I know that any sane woman would run for the hills, but I *love* you, Jenny. I love you not only because Sophie loved you and she would want me to love you too but because when you are with me it feels like the world is not so crap and you take me to a different place from the one I am in. Does that make sense?"

She bites her lip, shakes her head. "You fucked Tash."

"I wished it was you."

Jenny drops her head into her hands.

"Sophie would want us to be together, I know she would. Of all her friends, she adored you, Jenny. She completely adored you. You were like a sister to her."

"Even weirder."

"Sophie liked weird. When did she ever play by the rules?"

Jenny smiles and swallows hard. She is trying not to cry.

He is solemn now. "We loved each other totally but it wasn't perfect, Jenny. And it did not need to be perfect, nothing needs to be perfect . . . just enough."

She looks at him with such longing then, I wonder if she's about to lurch forward and take a bite out of his arm.

"You must not see us, me and Sophie, as something that is, was, unattainable, unrepeatable. God, it's so hard to explain." He shuts his wonderful gypsy eyes, presses his fingers against them. "It's just that . . . I think you're totally wonderful. That's all. Please say something, Jenny."

Jenny doesn't say anything. Instead she looks up and she starts to smile, a big wide sunshine smile.

"Come here, you." He stands up, pulling her with him, slides his arms around her waist and rests his chin on her shoulder and slowly, falteringly, like teenagers at their first school disco, they start to sway to the music. Jenny is stiff and shy at first but as the song progresses she relaxes, lets her body be led by his. And there they are, dancing in the living room lit by fairy lights, stepping on each other's toes, the green string of tinsel still stuck to the sole of her shoe.

The track finishes.

Snow is swirling in thick whirlpool flurries outside the window now. It's a strange backdrop, like it's just the two of them in one of those toy snow-shaker domes. They are looking at each other in astonishment, as if they can't quite believe the feelings whooshing up inside them.

Then it happens.

The power of the kiss flings me hard against the ceiling. My husband's sad blue body turns pink as she breathes life into his lungs, softly sucking the last bit of it out of me, like a sweet passed between the mouths of lovers. They are kissing and kissing. The music starts up again. He laughs, and a new song begins.

THE
CHÂTEAU

ALSO BY PAUL GOLDBERG

FICTION

The Yid

NONFICTION

How We Do Harm (coauthored with Otis Webb Brawley M.D.)
The Thaw Generation (coauthored with Ludmilla Alexeyeva)
The Final Act

TRANSLATION

To Live Like Everyone by Anatoly Marchenko

THE CHÂTEAU

PAUL GOLDBERG

PICADOR

NEW YORK

THE CHÂTEAU. Copyright © 2018 by Paul Goldberg. All rights reserved. Printed in the United States of America. For information, address Picador, 175 Fifth Avenue, New York, N.Y. 10010.

picadorusa.com • picadorbookroom.tumblr.com
twitter.com/picadorusa • facebook.com/picadorusa

Picador® is a U.S. registered trademark and is used by Macmillan Publishing Group, LLC, under license from Pan Books Limited.

For book club information, please visit facebook.com/picadorbookclub or email marketing@picadorusa.com.

Title page illustration of man by David Curtis Studio

Designed by Steven Seighman

Library of Congress Cataloging-in-Publication Data

Names: Goldberg, Paul, 1959– author.
Title: The Château : a novel / Paul Goldberg.
Description: First edition. | New York : Picador, [2018]
Identifiers: LCCN 2017028305 (print) | LCCN 2017030203 (ebook) | ISBN 9781250116109 (ebook) | ISBN 9781250116093 (hardcover)
Subjects: LCSH: Reporters and reporting—Fiction. | Fathers and sons—Fiction. | GSAFD: Black humor (Literature) | Mystery fiction.
Classification: LCC PS3607.O4434 (ebook) | LCC PS3607.O4434 C48 2018 (print) | DDC 813/.6—dc23
LC record available at https://lccn.loc.gov/2017028305

Our books may be purchased in bulk for promotional, educational, or business use. Please contact your local bookseller or the Macmillan Corporate and Premium Sales Department at 1-800-221-7945, extension 5442, or by e-mail at MacmillanSpecialMarkets@macmillan.com.

First published by Picador.

First Edition: February 2018

10 9 8 7 6 5 4 3 2 1

For Susan Keselenko Coll

Мы живем, под собою не чуя страны . . .
—Осип Мандельштам

We live not feeling the country beneath us . . .
—Osip Mandelstam

PART I

||||||||||||||||||||||||||||||||||||||||||||||||||||||||||||||||||||||||||||||||||||||||||||||||||||||

I like to think big. I always have. To me it's very simple: if you are going to be thinking anyway, you might as well think big.

——DONALD TRUMP
The Art of the Deal

||||||||||||||||||||||||||||||||||||||||||||||||||||||||||||||||||||||||||||||||||||||||||||||||||||||

1

THE BUTT GOD

Let us not focus on the events that sent Zbignew Wronski over the railing of a forty-third-story balcony of the Grand Dux Hotel on South Ocean Drive in Hollywood, Florida, on January 5, 2017. Salacious rumors are usually true, but it's unlikely that everything said about the man known as the Butt God of Miami Beach could be.

It is plausible that immediately prior to the plunge, Zbig was with two women, only one of whom was his wife. The sometimes-Pygmalionic sometimes-Oedipal ethics of cosmetic surgery being what they are, it is plausible that the other woman—if she existed—was a "patient." "Client" would be a better word. To qualify for the moniker "patient," one should be ill, which no one in Dr. Wronski's care was. He was an exterior designer. A posterior designer.

Consuela Ramirez-Wronska unquestionably was a client. Her taut buttocks, tanned, set like jewels in a black thong, continued to grace the Web site of Zbig's practice for many days after their maker's fatal plunge. A "before" picture was not provided.

Big Zbig collaborated with a specialist in vaginal tightening. This partner didn't seek to be known as either the Vagina God or the Vagina Caesar. A little man who liked money, he would have been fine with Vagina Elf.

For years, rumors circulated that Zbig's clients tested their rejuvenated nether regions with their tall, handsome, broad-shouldered Slavic surgeon.

Had the ancient, some say outmoded, Hippocratic rules of medical ethics been applied, that test would have been regarded as problematic. Some might suggest that it would have been more appropriate to utilize a simple device that faithfully mimics the human organ. But even if these rumors were grounded in fact, it was clearly agreeable, even upon reflection, to all parties in- volved. Zbig's disciplinary file at the Florida Board of Medicine in Tallahassee was pristine.

An artist must either love or hate his or her medium in order to reimagine and reshape it. Men's butts left Zbig indifferent. He didn't do men; this might as well be established early.

Before drilling deeper into Zbig's life and his death in a search for clues about his final flight, we will consider the flight itself:

You are over the edge, you versus gravity, uninsulated, un- parachuted, with nothing to forestall the shattering of the atri- um's nine-foot glass panes, a gentle bounce off a steel girder, the breaking of the pipes of the sprinkler system, the final fifty feet of flight in the halo of glass shards and streams of water, toward the indoor palm trees and bar stools. Do your thoughts focus on the circumstances that caused your flight? Does it matter whether the genesis of flight is voluntary, accidental, premedi- tated, impulsive, or the consequence of foul play? Do you experience fear, a fleeting mourning for your life, or do you swallow the swill of salty air, morning mist, cloud and fog, stretching the boundaries of ecstasy, surrendering to rapture, convincing yourself of your power to deploy your exaltation as a mystical tool for changing the inflection of your gravitational doom?

Decades earlier, when Zbig was a student at Duke, his roommate—a fellow Slav—was obsessed with the raspy-voiced, screaming Muscovite poet Volodya Vysotsky, the kind of bard who uses exclamation marks more than any other form of punctuation:

Я коней напою,
Я куплет допою,-
Хоть мгновенье еще постою на краю!

I'll water the stallions,
I'll finish the song,
I'll stand on the edge for a moment more!

The roommate's name was William M. Katzenelenbogen.

The dateline changes to WASHINGTON.

We are at Martin's Tavern, a storied Georgetown bar, where we find William M. Katzenelenbogen.

Martin's is not an imitation pub, not faux English, not a dive. Washingtonians have come to Martin's for generations, sometimes several times a week. It is said that JFK proposed to Jackie at a Martin's booth (Booth No. 3), that—presumably on a different night—Dick Nixon poured ketchup over everything, and that J. Edgar Hoover was seen playing footsie with

Boyfriend Clyde or perhaps trawling the place for cute, clean-cut boys. Martin's is what a pub should be: you can bring the family if you've got one, or you can sit at the bar and be as withdrawn as you wish. Martin's treats gin with respect.

Bill's appearance evokes the image of an outsized terrier. He is six feet tall on the dot. Lean, with no trace of a middle-age paunch, he sports a closely trimmed beard and an identically cropped head of coarse hair. His hair color was never static. It turned from straight and blond to curly and light brown some-time before college. Now, fifteen minutes past middle age, it looks like a fragment of the coat of an elderly Airedale. Not the back of an elderly Airedale, which is salt-and-pepper, but a front paw—an arm—which turns salt-and-cumin, or some such.

Bill has ordered Tito's and regular Bombay (not Bombay Sapphire), a vodka and a gin, mixed 1:1, shaken, with not a thought of vermouth. Rinse out the shaker. He fucking hates vermouth.

It's January 6, 2017, 6 P.M.—two full weeks to go before inauguration, installation, ascension, coronation, sanctifica-tion, consummation, or putsch—whatever is the right name for this thing that history has dragged in.

The image of the president-elect is on two of the television screens above the bar, a silent montage of his puppet hands, his pouting lips, his aggressively orange face topped with the mop of misshapen yellow hair.

The third screen serves up grainy images of the massacre du jour, this time at the Fort Lauderdale–Hollywood International Airport. A crowd on the tarmac waits, panicking in place. A high school yearbook mug shot of the shooter flashes on the screen. Not ISIS this time—just a baby-faced psychotic, being a good boy, obeying commands from the voices that whisper in his skull.

On second thought, it's possible that inner voices do not whisper. They may toll, like bells, for thee, and thee—and thee. Possibly, some of these voices are more legitimate than others. Some may be healthful, even beneficial; how is one to know? As a science writer—make that a former science writer—Bill doesn't have a blessed clue. No one to ask, no place to look for answers, no reason to.

A Twitter icon pops up on one of the Trump screens. It's about Putin ordering the hacking of the election and celebrating—dancing like a Cossack, presumably—when his boy prevailed.

Fuck it, all of it, Bill declares, looking away, turning his attention to the wood grain of the bar, his eyes contemplating the complexity of its gentle waves, seeking solace, escape even. Of course, Bill is mistaking these asymmetrical shapes for nature's assurance that this episode of search for simplicity shall pass, as it has at various times in Italy, Germany, Spain, the USSR, for nature itself gravitates toward democracy and social justice, self-correcting, inevitably, conveniently.

The act of reading reassuring, determinist messages in the wood grain is yet another indicator of being intensely in need of a drink, and, fortuitously, a drink is precisely what is about to happen in Bill's life.

The bartender is new and needs to be instructed.

"Tito's and Bombay—is there a name for this?" he asks, filling the martini glass with the liquid he has expertly clouded via intensive interaction with ice in the shaker.

"TB," Bill improvises.

"Would a twist make it better for you?"

"Worse."

It would take more than a twist or even an olive to make things better for William M. Katzenelenbogen.

Bill is a science writer and an investigative reporter: an investigative science writer, one of the best of his generation, a serial finalist for the Pulitzer Prize and the Loeb Award for Excellence in Financial Journalism as well as a laureate of a boxful of lesser prizes, most of them dispensed by the Association of Health Care Journalists and something called the Washington Professional Chapter of the American Society of Professional Journalists.

A top-flight journalist in his thirties and forties, he flew into turbulence after crossing into his fifties.

Two hours ago, he was discharged, unceremoniously—for cause—presumably to be replaced on *The Washington Post* payroll by three low-paid, tech-savvy youths.

He marched out of the newsroom brandishing a broomstick, which, witnesses said, he held with pride and devotion, like a cross at an Easter procession. A two-man Easter procession this was: a rent-a-cop followed. All of Bill's friends had taken buyouts or been fired years earlier. He was the last of the generation. There should have been music. Incense should have been burnt.

Why the broomstick? you might ask.

Reporters of Bill's ilk get lectured about the need to stop using the word "nail" as a verb in discussing targets of inquiry. At thirty, shortly after joining the *Post*, he stopped making references to castrations with dull, rusted blades. By forty, he mellowed a bit more and stopped likening the art of writing stories to the act of shoving broomsticks—indeed, entire brooms—up the recti of people who had betrayed the public trust: corrupt government officials, avaricious CEOs, data-cooking scientists.

At one point, Bill proposed developing a scale for measuring impact in inches shoved, and in 1998, a group of interns presented him with just the broomstick he proposed. It was a fond gift for what amounted to contributing to delinquency of newsroom minors.

This broomstick was to be aimed at *proverbial*, as opposed to corporeal, assholes. In the newsroom parlance of the post-Watergate era, a broomstick salute seemed to be a fitting punishment. A good investigative story is a weapon, the enemy is the enemy, and denying humanity of the enemy is a requirement in all combat, including the combat that is journalism.

For nearly two decades Bill kept the broomstick hidden behind a filing cabinet near his desk, a time-capsule-preserved artifact from the days he thought such things were funny. He moved and rehid the broomstick when the *Post* relocated to its techy new quarters.

The first inch shoved was marked "Denial of all Allegations"; two inches—a "Letter from Lawyers"; three—"Acknowledgment of Minor Clerical Errors"; six—"Tearful Apology"; eight—"Resignation"; eleven—"Restitution"; fourteen—"Conviction"; eighteen—"Meaningful Change." Arrows near the tip of the broomstick pointed in the direction of "Revolution," indicating that an additional broomstick will be required.

Bill was not about to leave this time-honored journalistic artifact, this totem, in enemy hands. The other aged memento he took was his Rolodex, which he dropped into the bike messenger's bag that served as his briefcase. He hadn't updated any of the yellowed cards in two decades, but the Rolodex was in perfect working order: it spun.

Being jettisoned by your profession—for insubordination, let the record show—was the biggest betrayal in a life rife with them.

The firing was simple: an officious, heavyset, middle-aged woman with long fingernails (from Personnel, presumably) read the verdict. There was no editor in the room. They were busy chasing details on the Fort Lauderdale airport shooter.

There was a paper they wanted Bill to sign and an envelope containing a check he would earn by agreeing to various crap the *Post* wanted him to do and not do, but Bill said "Fuck You." He didn't sign shit. He had neither grounds nor plans to sue; the Fuck You was a matter of principle.

It's difficult to be fired for cause at the *Post*. It means somebody up high has generated paperwork and the Newspaper Guild was asleep. Being fired for cause means no severance package. (The check dangled in front of him was a pittance, he presumes.) His upcoming paycheck will be his last. And "insubordination" is just another word for being moved to a stultifying beat and being forced to write stories that need not be written and demoralizing you enough to force you to phone it in for a few years and finally quit. What do you expect when you dispatch someone like Bill to Fairfax County, the place he doesn't know how to find or what to do with once he is there?

After the Easter procession, Bill heads to Martin's, and here he is, on his beloved bar stool, in the southwestern corner, his broomstick leaning like a personal flying device against the bar. He is receiving an ice-cold TB.

If wine at a communion symbolizes the blood of Christ, a TB at Martin's symbolizes Christ's spinal fluid.

"I'll have what he's having," says a young woman, sitting down, and in the same motion, Yogically, lifting the broomstick. She handles it with care, reverence even, like a fragile artifact from the distant past.

"Another TB coming up," says the bartender.

"TB?"

"TB."

There is no hug, no handshake, not even a tap on the shoulder, just the raising of the broomstick. She lifts it, turns it over, admires the scale. There is a boundary between them, perhaps professional, perhaps personal.

"Gwen, a pleasant surprise," says Bill, staring at the nadir of the cone of his martini glass. She is in her midthirties, a redhead, freckles. She settles in, crosses her legs.

Gwen was once a gonzo take-no-prisoners reporter. A star straight out of Harvard, she went from intern to Style at twenty-two. She was the princess of Style, pounding booze, banging out Salingeresque copy by the yard, covering social Washington—reporting from parties—producing dross about misbehaviors of people convinced of their larger-than-lifeness. No one since Sally Quinn had a better ear for quotes or eye for mischief. Bill thought she wrote like a dog eats—fast, gasping, grunting, hiccupping, with emanations of saliva—but it was young, energetic prose. And she was a hoot to drink with. His thoughts about her were mostly chaste. They'd slept together only once.

"I heard," she says, awkwardly placing her hand on the back of his neck and leaving it there. "I thought I'd find you here."

Bill takes the first sip of TB, its coldness deadening the nerve endings as it seeps toward the absolute darkness of his aching Russian soul.

"I almost forgot: it takes eighteen inches to get 'Meaningful Change,'" she says, running the broomstick through her loosely clenched fist.

"This seemed hilarious at the time," she adds upon reflection. "It's deeply offensive, actually."

She should know. She was the lead author of the scale, one of the interns who produced this object.

"Gwen, our president-elect would dismiss your reaction as political correctness."

"An argument for political correctness, in my book."

"Was this a flavor of 'locker room talk' then—'newsroom talk'?"

As Bill considers her legs through the prism of the martini glass, his peripheral vision registers the amused look on the face of the bartender. They are nice legs, draped in black tights, with lots of distance between the knee and the herringbone tweed hem. He reflects on the freckles that live beneath those tights.

In 2008, Gwen was dismissed, publicly, humiliatingly, for fabricating a story. Then it turned out that many stories over many years were tainted. As of today—January 6, 2017—they have something in common—discarded by the *Post*; she for fabrication, he for insubordination. Both guilty as charged.

Bill takes another sip.

"Remember what you told me when I was shit-canned?" she asks.

"No."

"You said, 'Write a fucking memoir. Take responsibility for things you did and things you didn't do: going down on French poodles, smuggling baby pandas to private zoos. Apologize for slavery, apologize for the Holocaust, apologize for the loss of habitat of gorillas and the clubbing of white baby seals. Accept all responsibility, falsify backward if you must. You are no longer a reporter; it doesn't matter anymore—the worse the better.

Nobody has ever gone wrong by taking too much responsibility. Own your guilt, own your unmooring, reach for more, more, more.'"

"Sounds like my voice."

"It was quite an oration—and good advice. It saved my life."

"How would you have done it?"

"The big *it*? I lived in a high-rise across the river—thirteenth floor."

"High enough."

"Your advice, it was amoral: survive, lie backward, emerge on the other end, come out on top."

"I am an immigrant. A refugee even."

He drains his martini glass and motions to the bartender to refill it.

"What does that have to do with anything?"

"We scrape."

"You told me that if I play it right, I would own something big: remorse. Your words exactly: 'You can't overdo remorse. It's infinite.' And another thing you said: 'When you stake out your claim on remorse, name your Porsche after me.'"

"Did you?"

"A Porsche named Katzenelenbogen? No. I named it Remorse. Same as the memoir. Have you read it?"

"No. What color?"

"The Porsche or the memoir?"

"Porsche."

"Yellow. You should've kept in touch. I fell from grace, sure, but I didn't die. I kept thinking about you all afternoon, since I heard about the firing: 'If Bill were a disease, which disease would he be?'"

"Is a 'fuckup' a diagnosis recognized by the American Psychiatric Association?"

"I was in the realm of the American *Medical* Association. You are diabetes, Mr. Katzenelenbogen."

"Me? Diabetes?"

"Your wounds don't heal."

"You associate me with open sores? Amputations?"

"I guess it might explain why I want to touch your hand and tell you it's okay."

They look away from each other. She was once forbidden, first as an intern, then a disgraced reporter, a falsifier of fact, a betrayer of public trust, a threat to the safety of journalistic boundaries.

He reached out to her when she was found out, when she was unmasked. He listened. He offered advice, good advice at that, it turns out. But at the time that was all he could be, an off-the-record friend, a secret well-wisher. She was radioactive, and he had no death wish.

"It's great to see you, Gwen, don't get me wrong, but why are you here?"

"To watch you drink, take you to your apartment, and tuck you in."

"To make sure I don't blow my brains out?"

"Returning the favor."

She pinches his cheek in the boundary-transgressing manner of old Jewish ladies; where did she learn that skill?

They down three rounds of TBs, soak the toxins with liver and onions, a Martin's specialty, then get a second wind.

The walk up Wisconsin Avenue to Bill's apartment takes about half an hour.

"Why did we get into the racket?" he asks as they pass the gray marble hulk of the Russian embassy.

This little strip of the USSR just happens to sit on the highest point in Washington. If the president-elect is planning on draining the swamp, this joint is as far from a swamp as you can get.

"Journalism? It was very personal, I guess. I was tired of being told that things were not as they appear," Gwen answers.

"Such as?"

"That the smell on my father's breath wasn't alcohol. That my mother wasn't kissing the next-door neighbor. That Mom and Dad weren't really fighting last night. That they love each other. That Grandma's death didn't matter because life is for the living. That my dislike of spinach was illusory. That I could discuss anything with my parents, that they accept me the way I am."

"Gwen, that's dysfunction, alcoholism. What does it have to do with career choices, the mission in life?"

"I thought that as a reporter I would be able to tell the truth as I saw it, with the emphasis on *as I saw it*. No second-guessing, no denials."

"Yes, Gwen, the world is knowable, or so we journalists want to think. We are wrong."

"It seemed knowable at first, until lies took over, yet—paradoxically—I am no worse for it. What about you?"

"I had no choice. My mother was murdered by a quack. My father is a felon."

"Convicted?"

"Which? The quack or the felon?"

"Both."

"It gets complicated—but both are guilty as fuck."

"Your father—tell me about him."

"If you cross American fraud with Russian literature, you get what?"

"I give up."

"You get Melsor Yakovlevich Katzenelenbogen, an expert in both—my beloved father."

"I can see the two of you are close. Are you even in touch?"

"We haven't talked in a while."

"A few months?"

"A few years."

"Two?"

"Ten, maybe twelve. Let me guess, you come from a line of wing nuts?"

"Not at all. Progressive as can be. Professors at the University of Michigan. Dad is in the English department, Mom is an ethicist. Why would you ask?"

"Being a reporter."

"You were judging, actually. You can't find a smidgeon of charity in your cold heart to forgive your poor old father, an asshole though he could be. Judging, judging, judging."

"That's what we do. We are judges of the benchless sort. That thing about crime, punishment, betrayal, it runs right through the gut."

"It can't be helped, I suppose."

Bill's palm brushes against her back as they walk up the stairs and enter his apartment. Her overcoat is soft, blue, cashmere, maybe camel hair.

He lives in a one-bedroom, above a restaurant on the corner of Wisconsin and Macomb.

"This place hasn't changed in a decade. Eight years, forgive me. Danish modern, Swedish functionalism, industrial this-and-that. I would never have believed that a guy like you would gravitate to this."

"I look like a Salvation Army sort?"

"Sort of. And this place is like something out of *Dwell*."

"Cognac, anyone?"

"No, I am good. I am open to one kiss—just one, half on the lips, a little longer than casual, but not by much—hear me?—and then I will go home and sleep in my bed, alone."

"Of course, it wouldn't be contextually inappropriate for you to spend the night, if you can pardon the multiple negatives."

"I disagree. You'll fuck me for the license to talk all night about the boundary between fact and fiction and right and wrong."

"Maybe."

Gwen kisses him on the cheeks and quickly pulls away.

"Spare me, Bill . . . They are porous. No hard walls—it's a continuum. Playing with them is like scratching a scab—don't, Mr. Diabetes. With that, I bid adieu, with full expectation that you will call me when you are ready to ask me out on a proper date, which you didn't do last time I was here—asshole."

2

REMORSE

If you are a reporter and you are good at it, it's not an avocation you are pursuing. It's your mission, your you.

Journalism, as Bill has always seen it, is the solid core of the universe surrounded by nebulae; feathery, cold, unexplored, a soft, vertical wilderness. As these images start to spin around him, he is coming to terms with being ejected into that realm of disconnected irrelevance, the vast kingdom of uselessness. It's a good thing Bill isn't prone to crying—he considers displays of emotion unmanly. Had this not been the case, he might have started to cry and never stopped.

Things sucked for Bill from the outset of his career, or his mission, or whatever it is, or was. His curse: when he was in his prime, Americans could accept an immigrant in almost any role—a doctor, especially in an obscure abbadaba subspecialty, an engineer, even a Web security consultant—but not as an investigative journalist. Bill could reach the top tiers, never achieving the pinnacle. Something about the ever-so-subtle remnants of his Russian tonality and his so-unpronounceable and so-unspellable name—a name he sometimes, for the sake of user-friendliness, abbreviates as KZB and WKZB—made the doorkeepers bar the entrance to the club.

Two caveats:

- That's what Bill believes, and
- The world may have changed.

It's his misfortune to be a man of acronyms. It's even less fortunate that the shorter of these acronyms—KZB—sounds as sinister as a secret police organization and the longer— WKZB—like a radio station: "You are listening to WKZB! Radio Moscow! All bullshit all the time."

The thought of waking up post-career terrifies.

"Will the sun rise?" is the first in a series of questions asked by all journalists as they imagine this separation.

"Will I have a place under it?" is the second.

It's January 7, between 4:32 and 6:07 A.M. Bill denies being awake. He is purifying his consciousness, purging thoughts as they emerge, snipping off their snake heads. It's an intracranial dialogue, Socratic masturbation:

Was I really fired?

Zap it . . .

Is this a dream?

Purge . . .

I need to get to my desk ASAP, tons of calls to make.

Away, consciousness, away, take yesterday with you, surround it in a cloud of infamy, lift it, take it to the middle of the sea, piss it out. And, please God, please, let yesterday be struck from the record, let me return. Have I not been through this separation in a dream, time and again, and yet I went on? Let this be that.

He thinks he sees his mother's face. He sees her as she would have been on her final day. He wasn't there, was precluded from getting there. Does she understand that FDA-sanctified drugs, legally administered in gonzo doses by a state-anointed physician who is sort of prominent in his field, are about to push her off the ledge, that in her case the line between therapy and execution has been erased, that her death is not from disease, but from treatment thereof, that scientific nonsense on the dawn of the twenty-first century is more lethal than the most lethal of diseases—hers?

Does any of this matter, or is meaning contained entirely in the fall?

Beset by visitations, Bill doesn't want the sun to rise. Prostrate, his shoulders plastered against the mattress, he wrestles against the sunrise, bargaining hopelessly with the God whose existence he denies.

At 6:07 A.M., a text from Gwen.

It's a link to a story: PLASTIC SURGEON PLUNGES TO HIS DEATH.

Gwen's message: "If u r reading this, ur brains r still in cranium. If not, fuck u."

Readers who have had three or more years of therapy or earned a master's of fine arts degree in creative writing will ask: How did Bill *FEEL immediately* upon learning about his friend's death? They should be encouraged to wait for this story to develop in accordance with its own rhythms or proceed to generate their own material reflecting the manner in which they were treated and/or trained.

Feelings can be emanations of our inner lives, but not always. A plot point this is not. That would be too easy.

"Fuck," Bill texts back. "He was my college roommate. Great guy. Friend."

This is what shock and grief look like in January 2017. An expletive via text. Is there time to experience the suddenness, unexpectedness of news, to dwell on the feeling of loss? Does it set in? Can it, after the original moment, the moment of discovery, slips out of reach?

"Shit," you say, adding "Fuck" for good measure, if the loss is unfathomable.

Why did she send it?

Surely she remembered Bill's appreciation for a bizarre story. He collected them once, creating a repository, a database, of four-paragraph beauties. Much of this repository involves utilization of hand tools and stuffing whole bodies or body parts into fifty-five-gallon drums. Life in four paragraphs with a perfectly chiseled AP lead is a haiku. A searchable database it is: try "fifty-five."

How could she have known that Bill and Zbig were roommates at Duke, that the two had fond nicknames for each other. Zbig's was Ye Olde Olde Sheep-Plugger of Warsaw. Bill's were less imaginative: KZB, WKZB, Mad Russian, and, for some reason, Igor. How was anyone to know that they remained close for the first two decades after graduation, that it was as unthinkable for Zbig to come to D.C. and not call Bill as it was for Bill to come to South Florida and not call Zbig?

Had they come to each other's realms more often, they would have surely remained closer friends instead of allowing their friendship to dissolve into Facebook displays of communication of useless fact that extends the genre of braggy, soulless Christmas letter into a year-long affair.

Bill follows this with another text: "I still have my wits (or at least brains) within me."

"Seriously? You know this guy?" she texts back.

"Did."

"Your next gig: write a book. Death of the Butt God."

"U r crazy."

No. Bill is not having feelings—not yet. He is texting the pesky buggers away. What about the book? Is it possible that Gwen is right? Symmetry is hard to miss. Bill had pointed Gwen toward ownership of Remorse, which she now does, in fact, own, and which generates rents that enabled the acquisition and maintenance of one yellow Porsche.

Gwen promoted her memoir exceedingly well, wisely declining to do a *Playboy* photo shoot, but letting it be widely known that one was proposed. She did undo her blouse for *GQ* and she did write a narcissistic whatnot for *Cosmopolitan*.

Remorse did well, spectacularly so. Movie rights were sold, a film was actually produced, and Gwen established Remorse Ltd., a crisis management consultancy specializing in contrition. You need Gwen when the broomstick is in, more attractive options are used up, splinters are a viable threat, and sitting a challenge.

Now Gwen is pointing him toward ownership of Grief, or the Edge, or the Fall. He might even stand poised to recapture *Vertigo* from Alfred Hitchcock. Imagine the rents on that.

Later that day, Bill clicks around on the Web, finding that a British tabloid took a less than decorous stab at the Zbig story: BUTT MAN'S SPLAT. It takes a Brit's pervy mind to speculate about Zbig having been with two women "only one of whom was his wife."

The story cites "an individual with direct knowledge of the police investigation," shorthand for a badge-carrying drunk, a cop who talks too much at bars. According to this report, the dead man wore Brunello Cucinelli, a light-colored suit. Bill looks it up: a mod jacket that's a bit short, high-water pants; probably goes with long, narrow shoes or Converse sneakers. In his final moments, Zbig was seeking—commanding—attention.

Bill can't imagine spending five thousand dollars on any suit, let alone a suit that looks like that. And why the two girls, if that was indeed the case?

The stiff is a friend. Make that "was" a friend. A stiff is was—always. Also, make that "a close friend."

You can learn a lot about a guy by analyzing his doodles. Some doodle circles, others phalluses. Bill's are rectangles, intricate amalgamations of rectangles. Call them boxes, call them grates, call them prison windows. Maybe he seeks to place things in boxes, a classifier of everything, holder of nothing.

Or maybe the boxes he is doodling are memorials to his late friend Big Zbig, a valiant rogue who fell in the midst of gallant pursuit of beauty, who had been photographed, body-bagged, and boxed. The man was a hoot, the man was larger than life, the man was an operator, the man was a magician. This was not the death—or the life—either he or Zbig ever imagined, but one doesn't get to pick.

Investigators don't require time to generate hypotheses. The process is preverbal: hypotheses flash before words form. Alas, in the case of Bill's version of his college roommate's final flight, no explanation appears at his cranium's door. A feeling forms in its stead. It's oblique, something from the nether reaches of the soul: it's a sense of flight devoid of a graphic component.

That raspy, screaming Muscovite Volodya Vysotsky, the

Russian Rimbaud, captured that feeling before his demise from booze and opiates. Vysotsky owned the genre of death that Big Zbig entered in the early morning of January 5, 2017, the sort that has you soar with the birds as the rest of us sink in the muck. "I'll water the stallions, I'll finish the song, I'll stand on the edge for a moment more!"

Before there can be grief, before emotions blow in, Bill remains suspended in the undifferentiated feeling of flight. What is this? Could be a spiritual remnant of Zbig, a lingering, transmitted final wish. I wish I could fly. I wish I could land splatlessly. What-ifs are corrosive. How different things could be if Pushkin wore body armor, if Trotsky had a Kevlar helmet, if your grandmother had wheels. The wheels bit is the sanitized American translation from the Yiddish original: What if my grandmother had balls?

The answers:

- In the Anglicized/sanitized version, she would have been a streetcar;
- In the authentic Yiddish version, she would have been my grandfather.

Vysotsky's song rings in his head, like the ISIS-sympathizing intracranial voices that ordered yesterday's shooting in Fort Lauderdale:

Чуть помедленнее, кони, чуть помедленнее!
Вы тугую не слушайте плеть!
Но что-то кони мне попались привередливые,
И дожить не успел, мне допеть не успеть!

Slow down, my stallions—slow!
Do not gallop, do not heed the whip!
But the stallions they gave me do as they wish,
If my life is cut short, then perhaps not my song!

Back in the 1980s, in a Cold War film drama called *White Nights,* Mikhail Baryshnikov performed a dance interpretation of that song.

To hold off feelings a bit longer, Bill looks it up on YouTube. He keys in three search terms—Baryshnikov, White Nights, Vysotsky—and up it pops.

Next, Bill turns to the Web to check whether Tesla makes hearses. It doesn't, which is just as well, because Zbig would have wanted the thing driven in "ludicrous mode," crazy fucking fast. Is there a finer tool for spreading ashes?

Bill's grief receptors are taking their time. He loathes the chills that signal their arrival. He focuses on the feeling of flight. He experiences height in the same way as sharpness, as in sharpness of a blade—it's a feeling of coldness. He fixates on flight in its least impeded, purest form. Not airplanes, not even gliders.

He begins by looking up BASE jumping on the Web, finding videos of bird-suited men and, occasionally, women, flying close to rock ledges, jumping out of helicopters, performing somersaults off diving boards positioned over fjords, opening the doors of ski resort gondolas, and—yes—flying off tall buildings.

This pastime overshadows grief. This is a good thing.

Bill cannot rattle off the list of events that preceded Big Zbig's final flight, but he is an expert in obtaining information and has a box of dusty plaques to show for it. We have mentioned that at another point in his career, he was a serial finalist for the biggest awards in American journalism. They can take away your job, but not the skills and passion you bring to it.

Journalism has few rules, no entrance exams, no license, no shingle, no possibility of expulsion from the ranks, if you don't count firing and being unable to land on your feet. There are a few rules of thumb, however, including not ending sentences with ", however," unless absolutely necessary.

Another rule: if you must mix your life with your craft, you can, sort of, but watch your step.

If you are—or were—with the press, you know how to obtain recordings of 911 calls. Of course, you don't need to be with the press. You can get these if you are an ordinary warped human being.

DISPATCHER: 911—Can I help you?

CALLER *(speaking rapidly with a Spanish accent)*: Somebody fell down from—I don't know what floor. He fell from—through the glass, there's glass all around—I think he is dead . . .

DISPATCHER: Uhm . . . Excuse me?

CALLER: Someone fell through the atrium, and I don't think he is okay, I think he is dead, yes. He is near the bar.

DISPATCHER: Is he breathing?

CALLER: I don't know.

DISPATCHER: Sir! Is he breathing?! Could you check?! It's very important!

CALLER: Okay.

DISPATCHER: Please . . . this is very important!

CALLER: Hold on . . . I can't tell . . . He broke a bar stool. Just stepped in some foam. Sorry.

DISPATCHER: Please . . .

CALLER: No . . . He is definitely not okay.

DISPATCHER: Sir! Is . . . He . . . Breathing?!

CALLER: No. Not. He is dead.

DISPATCHER: Thank you. We'll send a unit . . .

Bill texts the recording to Gwen.

"What an opening! Get to work," she texts back immediately, adding the emoticon of an airplane.

"Not sure I am up to this. This is my friend's skull that cracked open."

"How do u know re: skull?"

"The 'foam' in the 911 call is not foam."

"Brains?"

"Brains."

Gwen texts back immediately: "Lean into it! I'll drive u to National. xo."

"I guess I'd fly to Miami International."

"Fort Lauderdale has reopened—just checked."

"Mopped up the blood and spackled the bullet holes . . ."

"The American spirit, Bill. We press on."

Gwen is right. This is starting to look like at least a story, maybe even a book.

Bill devotes January 8 to reading newspapers—every newspaper he can find—and brooding.

After dispensing with his usual two, Bill stumbles out to CVS and gets two more. By 2 P.M., he has read *The Washington Post*, *The New York Times*, *The Wall Street Journal*, and *The Financial Times*. Next, he turns to the pile of old *New Yorker*s, *Atlantic*s, and *New York Review of Books* on his coffee table.

That pile sucks him deep into its vortex, prompting him to desecrate the margins of these esteemed publications with little drawings of Donald Trump and scribbles declaring that "we are so fucked."

No question about it: Bill is seeing a convergence between East and West. Authoritarian strongmen are succeeding where proletarians had failed. They didn't unite, those proletarians of the world. The United Front against Franco and fascism was not a success. The prewar clusterfuck of Stalin, Hitler, Mussolini, Hirohito, and Franco was a more formidable, more pragmatic life form. It took an incompetent like Hitler to overreach and, in a fit of narcissism, blow it all. America had the opportunity to join that alliance, but didn't. Bill predicts that in exactly ten days, after the coronation, after January 20, 2017, we will become a part of something similar, a new kind of an international criminal conspiracy.

Bill would have benefited from a drink and would surely have poured himself one had he not forgotten to do so. Such are the perils of living alone. He continues to brood through January 9 and 10, allowing his thoughts to roam as they please.

There are three Russian Baltika beers in the refrigerator; he has no idea where they came from or how long ago. Indian dinners in the freezer are of uncertain age and provenance as well. There is no vodka, no gin, no whiskey of any sort. Fortuitously, there is a half-gallon bottle of gold-colored Appleton rum. Again, no way to know how it got there and when it got there. Bill doesn't like rum—Appleton tastes like perfume—but it's here, it has been through a still, and it suffices.

His thoughts during those three days of near-seclusion invariably return to the *Post*. His dismissal is different from those of his colleagues a few years ago. At that time, the paper was heading in the direction of the graveyard. Now, dripping with Amazon money, it's expanding, hiring. And the offices are new, Google-like.

They didn't fire William M. Katzenelenbogen because they had to. They fired William M. Katzenelenbogen because they wanted to. It sucks—all of it—but Bill feels little anger toward the *Post*. Granted, had he been given the courtesy of selecting the true cause for his termination, he would not have chosen "insubordination."

Using hard, objective metrics, his performance was never anything but fine:

- Attendance—exemplary.
- Ability to grasp complicated policy concepts—observed.
- All reporting calls—made.
- Punctuation—in place, as required.
- Deadlines—met, always.

His sin, his fatal flaw, was his inability to conceal that he hadn't given a shit about anything he had written in six years. Longer, actually. The precise moment of the onset of not-a-shit-giving is rarely visible to the sufferer. The evaluee's ability to bang out a yeomanly story may be unaffected by this condition, but when you feel nothing, there is nothing. Bill had become a news-room zombie, one of the typing dead.

The only thing the *Post* had on him had nothing to do with anything.

The bozos from WRC-TV Channel 4 showed him taking a deep nap at the Fairfax County Government Center while covering a hearing of the Board of Supervisors.

This wasn't an act of hostility on the part of the WRC crew—they had the camera sweep across the room, and there he was, head tilted back, mouth open, possibly snoring. They couldn't help letting the camera linger a bit, even look into his mouth for a moment. There was some light joshing back and forth by the news team that night; the bozos never figured out that he was from the *Post,* their colleague, or they wouldn't have done this to him. Journalists have professional courtesy; it's a fact.

Bill's sleeping patterns were erratic during his marriage (more on that later), but they were normalizing after separation (more on that later as well). He has no recollection of sleeping at that meeting, but he can demonstrate that dozing off didn't de-tract from the quality of his coverage of that or any other story.

Mostly, he is still hoping someone will tell him how, under which laws or which country, sleeping at a boring-as-fuck hearing constitutes insubordination. Punching an editor is insubordination. Napping at the Fairfax County Government Center is innocent, healthful even.

It's Bill's fault that it's now up to untested recruits to cover the gangs of suit-clad honest crooks and alt-right ideologues of the nascent administration. They will be on their own, kindergarteners in the minefield. You need decades of experience to cover conflicts of interest—there are no shortcuts. Even assuming the confluence of good work ethic and good fortune that produces great journalism, hasn't the rise of the soon-to-be President Donald exposed the limitations of significance of truth-telling?

It hasn't been traditional to ice reporters in America, but Bill sees no reason for this tradition to endure, just like there is no reason for anyone to believe that the people will notice when these little guardians of the public trust and social justice get shot out of the Washington sky. Their demise will be taken in stride. Reporter. Shot. Execution style. In the back of the head, face turned into a crater. To be expected. Happens all the time in Putin's Russia. We are catching up.

Not being employed at fifty-two, Bill accepts the overwhelming probability of spending the rest of his life trying to land low-paying gigs.

Perhaps there is a story in Zbig. Perhaps Bill is the right man for telling Zbig's story, assuming he can still write. It would be perfect for *The New Yorker*, but he doesn't know anyone there, and they rarely take stories from outsiders, and Bill is now most definitely an outsider.

He needs a bolus of money—now. A book advance is the answer—same as it was for Gwen. It's hard to imagine that any editor would be crazy enough to turn down a book about the spectacular demise of a South Florida plastic surgeon known as the Butt God of Miami Beach, but it's possible.

This would be a sympathetic portrait, of course, insidery, done with the right mixture of responsibility, respect, and, if appropriate, restraint. Humor, if any, would be dark, dry.

Bill's previous book idea crashed and burned. It involved the role of political philosophy in the design of clinical trials of cancer drugs. The idea was brilliant, argumentation airtight, but no editor had the cojones or vision to make the acquisition. Soon after that project crashed, Bill's agent said he would no longer take nonfiction projects on drug development. Fuck him!

With this Zbig thing, there could be multiple takers, a bidding war. He'd need to find another agent quickly, but that shouldn't be difficult. This thing has the makings of a book, a play, a movie, a musical, an opera even. DEATH OF THE BUTT GOD. It would be an investment in Bill's future, and certainly an investment in his past—the safest investment of all. This is magical thinking, perhaps, but it's either that or driving an Uber.

Actually, Uber is not an option. Bill doesn't own a vehicle and his driver's license has expired.

Gwen is expecting a call, no doubt, but a smattering of texts is all he has in him.

In Bill's past life, the *Post* would have picked up his travel expenses.

Post-*Post*, Bill needs to shell out his own cash. There will be no expense account on this trip. Bill will be playing for keeps.

He uses his own $398 to buy the ticket to Fort Lauderdale. But where can he stay? The Diplomat? The Grand Dux? The Fontainebleau? He is already past the point of no return on meeting his rent for February.

Bill—swallowing whatever pride he may still possess—takes the first step toward détente with his father. At 4:37 P.M., January 10, he makes a phone call, and Melsor's current wife, whom he has yet to meet, graciously invites him for a visit. Done.

Bill grasps the rough contours of his next project.

He knows about Zbig's getup—a Brunello Cucinelli suit made of something called Wales wool; $5,000ish. (A Brioni—$8,000 or thereabouts—would be better for the book proposal, but the truth is the truth.) Bill knows that Zbig's brains had spilled. He knows roughly where it happened. Having once been a police beat reporter, Bill has seen spilled brains on several occasions. They are spongy, light colored, bloodless, slimy like the soft underside of a bolete mushroom on a misty day.

Will he be able to pinpoint the cause of the fall? Will he be able to find the exact point of impact? The glass panels of the atrium ceiling were surely replaced within days. Will he be able to stand being there? That last one is an emotional question, and in Bill's life emotions have learned to wait.

Why is he investing his bottom dollar in a story about which he has no better clue than a casual passerby? The two men weren't particularly close in their middle age. Bill and Zbig hadn't seen each other in five years.

In his quest for insight, Bill obsessively listens to the audio file of the 911 call, clicking "Play" immediately after the recording stops running.

———

January 11 is cold enough to feel better about the future of the planet. Perhaps the polar caps aren't melting. Perhaps oceans will not rise. Perhaps we will not drown. Perhaps this Trump will not be so bad. Perhaps the bullet intended for you will fly by and hit someone else.

Bill squeezes his luggage—a scratched-up ancient Halliburton bag and an electric-blue bike messenger's bag—in the back of the Porsche and sits down.

"You look *so* uncomfortable, dear," says Gwen, and revs the engine.

Dear?

The Carrera Cabriolet looks more like Mockery than Remorse.

The roar of the engine makes conversation difficult, the speed makes it unnecessary.

"Are we dating, Gwen?"

"You are off to South Florida last time I checked. You don't need a romantic entanglement, not that this is the right time and place to consummate one. Reconsummate, I should say."

He is silent.

"Say something, Bill. What's on your mind?" she shouts over the engine.

"Marx!"

"Karl?!"

"Karl! The theory of alienation! Manuscripts of 1844! Economic and Philosophic!"

"Seems random!"

"Completely nonrandom! In early Marx, division of labor alienates the worker from the product of his work, from society, some other shit, and—finally—himself!"

"What does it have to do with us?!"

"It has to do with me, pardon my navel-gazing—and us by

34

extension, probably! I am realizing that the past few years at the *Post* left me alienated from something that used to be at the core of what I was! Storytelling!"

"Storytelling?! They had you doing shit work! You were programmed for alienation!"

"And it worked! I am not sure I can do this anymore! And if I can't, what am I?"

"*This* is a story, Bill! Tell it, dammit!"

At National, she stops the car, faces him with a smile, and takes off her glasses as an invitation for him to go in for a kiss, which he does.

"You saved my life, you know," she says, pulling back for a moment.

"And you mine, maybe."

"Has anyone told you you have a scratchy beard?"

"Never."

"And, you should know, I am scheduled to pop in for a one-day conference. NFL team owners . . . very hush-hush, about players beating their wives, so you don't know."

They kiss again.

"Did I say very hush-hush . . . Middle of the week . . . But I will have to get back same night, preexisting meeting I can't change."

"But would if you could?"

"I surely would . . . So, just time for dinner . . . In Florida . . ."

"Alas . . ."

"Alas . . . Where are you staying, by the way?"

"At my father's."

"The fraudster poet? Oh my . . ."

Bill opens the door, gets out, and grabs his bags.

"Keep me in the loop!" she shouts, and in a burst of unbridled speed leaves him on the departures curb.

3

INSPECTOR LUFTMENSCH

On the morning of January 11, as the Fort Lauderdale–bound plane taxies toward takeoff, Bill has no trouble tuning out the college students who seem to form a tight ring around him.

He wears a scratchy gray herringbone sport coat (Bill Blass), a pair of thoroughly weathered Carhartt jeans purchased in New England a decade earlier, and a pair of sock-free ancient Sperry Top-Siders.

The Top-Siders look like they might emit the sweet scent of the rotting flesh of a water buffalo slaughtered on a hot day, but thanks to systematic treatments with baking soda they are utterly odor-free. His Halliburton bag subtly pushes the limits of the definition of a carry-on. His bike messenger's bag is a monument to resourcefulness. It's made by a Swiss company called Freitag out of a tarp used on a European truck. You can find one of these bags at the Museum of Modern Art in New York.

Bill looks like the sort of professor you would want to smoke pot with, the sort who knows his shit, takes pride, and grades tough.

Bill pulls out his reporter's notebook and starts to summarize his theory of the case.

"Meaning" is the first word he commits to paper.

This word is given the place of honor atop a thin, narrow page.

What is said meaning?

He can only brainstorm, free-associate, philosophize.

Meticulously, down the length of the page, Bill draws a large question mark. It's cartoony to begin with, and it becomes more so as it grows thicker. Curly doodles make a home inside it.

Bill proceeds to sketch the outlines of the Dux. It's a twin-tower affair, South and North, a lot like the nearby Diplomat, but bigger, taller.

He draws a birdlike creature beneath the top of one of the towers: a soaring BASE jumper in a flying suit. The soaring BASE jumper needs birds to keep him company, and Bill draws the birds. Why is he—William M. Katzenelenbogen—flying south? What beckons him? Where is said "meaning"? Where is its hiding place?

Consuela Ramirez-Wronska, the latest Mrs. Zbig, didn't return Bill's calls. Presumably this means that she wouldn't cooperate with his investigation, if that is what it is.

Does Bill think it possible to investigate an occurrence that left him without a clue, to launch an open-ended, directionless, hypothesis-free, Bayesian search for the hidden? When you have no beginning, you aren't entitled to an end.

Suddenly, an idea flashes in Bill's skull. It is as cartoonish as the question mark—and Bill dutifully commits it to paper:

EXISTENTIALIST INVESTIGATIONS L.L.C.
William M. Katzenelenbogen, Inspector Luftmensch

Devoid of evidence, with no mandate, lacking credentials, un-burdened by clients, without even a tinge of funding, this is to be an investigation by instinct, experience, spirit. You would go from place to place to place and *feel*.

You, Sir William, have become a sleuth of air, a marathoner of the clouds, Inspector Luftmensch.

Only one person can bring you down, Sir William, and surely you know that you are heading directly into his domain.

Even if you would rather be any place but South Florida, you may not be immune to the feeling of infinite possibility manifest in the first exposure to sunlight that pierces the cab's windshield the instant you emerge from the shadow of structured parking at Fort Lauderdale–Hollywood International Airport. Even if you would rather be any-place-other-than, how can you not take note that this flash so completely captures the absence of cultural constipation? Has any place, any culture, so fully embraced the pursuit of pleasure with such small-*d* democratic small-*c* cate-chism? If you are an asshole, be an asshole. If you want a machine gun, get a machine gun. If you want to snort coke, snort coke. If you want to defraud your neighbor, defraud your neighbor. If you want to fuck a giraffe, arrangements can be made to enable you to fuck a giraffe. If you want to vote for him whose name is too painful to utter as coronation nears, vote for him whose name is too painful to utter as coronation nears. If you want to be a machine-gun-toting, coke-snorting, giraffe-fucking, neighbor-defrauding, Trump-supporting fascist ass-hole, *be* a machine-gun-toting, coke-snorting, giraffe-fucking, neighbor-defrauding, Trump-supporting fascist asshole.

Squinting, Bill reaches into his messenger's bag and puts on a well-worn black baseball cap with a big red *W* above the visor. He acquired it for those occasions when he has to blend in. If *The Post* didn't pay for it, it should have. Next, he puts on a pair of counterfeit Ray-Ban Wayfarers. Having thus prepared himself for the scorching sun, he thinks of the cold darkness of Moscow of his childhood. If absolute opposites attracted absolutely, Florida is where he is fated to end up.

Bill is in a black Lincoln driven by an elderly Cuban gentleman. As they wait for the drawbridge on Hallandale to come down, the driver complains about being unable to make a living. The Cielo Limo Service black cars are meant to be shared, he says, but the assholes at the curb gave him just one passenger and, after arguing explosively in Spanish, ordered him to move on. Translation: he is driving Bill all the way to Hollywood for the miserable sum of eleven dollars. The tip better be good.

Bill feels intense kinship with taxi drivers. Immigrants fall into four categories: those who drive taxis; those who once drove taxis; those who aspire to drive taxis; and those who fear that one day circumstances will force them to drive taxis. Of course, there are overlaps. Bill is an unambiguous Category Four immigrant. He is so empathetic that his Uber rating—awarded by drivers—is 5, the perfect score.

Years earlier, in Boston, Bill took a cab driven by a gentleman who identified himself as a former editor at Random House. He wasn't even an immigrant.

If the book thing crashes and burns, he will need to renew

his driver's license. Uber drivers told him that the company makes it easy to acquire a car, even if your credit is for shit.

It's possible that in the architect's initial sketches the twin towers of the Grand Dux billowed like sails. Alas, implementation created challenges.

Unless you are very, very good, concrete doesn't billow; neither does glass. The towers ended up acquiring the look of tall round-top structures, twin phalluses, the Twin Dicks of Hollywood, one pointing north, toward Fort Lauderdale, the other south, toward Sunny Isles.

Who would have thought that by enslaving light and space you build a dungeon? Usurping space and gulping air and sucking light, the atrium protects from storms that uproot palm trees, making a sport for those inside to watch seabirds crash into the glass. Do birds' eyes register surprise as their necks snap?

Bill looks up immediately, hoping to spot the glass panes shattered by his friend's body, staring foolishly into the midday sun. This effort to spot a pair of panes that aren't like the others produces darkness.

"Idiot," he says to himself. To see the point of impact, he will need to go up and look down.

Stretching from South Ocean Drive to the Atlantic, the atrium of the Grand Dux is so massive that no one notices anyone; no one can.

Even the indoor pool is entirely within view, displayed through the glass behind the registration desk.

A generation earlier, Morris Lapidus, the father of Miami modernism, designed a staircase to nowhere in the lobby of the Fontainebleau Hotel, a few miles south from the spot where Bill now stands. The purpose of that staircase was to allow ladies to display the magnificence of their dresses.

It isn't a travesty but a sign of the times that at the Grand Dux the display accentuates the undress. There are columns, but no walls. The place screams of sex; not godly twosomes, but threesomes, foursomes even, which means it is first and foremost about lonesome onesomes dimly illuminated by free PornHub vignettes playing softly on the iPad. It is about money, mostly, the sort that flows without regard for either sense or the Arabic number behind the dollar sign and, Bill presumes, brings no happiness. Perhaps people live like this in their dreams or for a few days a year.

This place is not an edgy performance art project funded by the now-endangered National Endowment for the Arts. It's glass, steel, concrete, self-sustaining, corporate. It's where the mainstream culture dwells.

The elevators—glass tubes with clear, domelike ceilings—hang on the ocean side of each tower.

Other passengers—a young woman and her two children—lean against the glass, exuding a sense of invincibility as the cabin speeds past the roof of the atrium. The woman, who is probably Gwen's age, looks away. She wears a gauzy coverall over an orange bikini and gold-colored flip-flops. She is occupying the very spot where Bill needs to be if he is to spot the panels Zbig's body broke on the way down.

In his ensemble of a threadbare but still scratchy jacket and other staples of the journalistic wardrobe, Bill might as well be a space traveler. Each party pretends that the other is invisible. It's 3 P.M.; the sun has long ago incinerated the swill of mist and salty air that makes men drunk, replacing it with the burning clarity of the day.

The phone goes off. A text from Gwen:

"Respiring? Ambulating?"

Bill ignores it for now; he will respond later.

He leans in the opposite direction, gravitating toward the elevator's steel door. It's solid. This is instinctive. Being in Florida—which for Bill has always presumed business—for more than three days gave him suicidal thoughts even before his life began to suck. There is death by water, death by fire, death by wild beasts, but the flavor of death he associates with Florida involves plunging from great heights. Perhaps this primal fear is fueling his fascination with Big Zbig's death. Didn't Zbig always do the things Bill feared?

Bill doesn't know how those death thoughts, those impulses, crawled into his skull when he first experienced that feeling a quarter century earlier. Is it technically a suicidal thought? Can such things be dismissed? Should Bill seek treatment? (The answer is probably yes, but how is Bill to know this?) Is it a warning? A premonition? Is it, God forbid, fate? Bill has no such thoughts anywhere else on the globe, not even in New York, where buildings are taller and where observation platforms abound.

The young woman steps off the elevator on the thirty-seventh floor.

Bill takes a pair of shaky steps toward the elevator's glass wall. He wants to see the point of impact—two panels that don't look like the others. He spots them immediately, and a minute later he is back in the lobby, staring at the exact place where Zbig's cranium released its spongy stuffing.

The point of impact is about fifty meters from the South Tower. The North Tower is one hundred meters away. This is the heart of the atrium, the area near the bar, near the oasis of potted palm trees. Was Zbig aiming for those? Was he aiming? Was he aimed?

Back in the atrium, he sets down his bags and touches the square of white terrazzo. Has anyone not seen crosses by the roadside, presumably at the spots where someone's loved one had been killed?

Some of these are adorned with plastic flowers, teddy bears, and other Grim Reaper bric-a-brac. Perhaps the dead come out and play with children's toys. We don't stop and bow at those shrines. We drive past. Should this be different? Perhaps Bill should make a shrine of it. Turn it into a monument to gravity, put down a votive candle, get incense going, incinerate photos of Marley and Vysotsky, invite Baryshnikov to improvise a solo on the subject of the boundary separating freedom from death.

Bill rests his palm lightly on the square, hoping for a flash of insight, a message from the netherworld or the world above, some remnant of the swill of salty air, morning mist, cloud and fog, surrender to rapture, the power to deploy exaltation as a mystical tool for changing the inflection of doom. It's a prayer of sorts.

"Gimme something, asshole," Bill says to his dead friend at the exact spot of the splintering of his cranium.

Nothing . . .

"Well, fuck you, dude. I'll fucking find out, like it or not. Motherfucker."

Bill picks up his bags and heads toward the revolving door just as a security guard begins to approach.

4

SVOLOCH'

Usually, family members have good reasons for missing a dozen years of each other's lives, and Bill's reasons for avoiding his father warrant respect.

Since neither Bill nor his father—Melsor Yakovlevich Katzenelenbogen—has missed contact with the other over such a long time, it would have been feasible for them to put off the reunion for another dozen years. This would constitute the path of least resistance.

Melsor lives less than a mile away from the Grand Dux. Had this been Boston, New York, or even Washington in August, Bill would have grabbed his bags and walked. But South Florida is a different kind of hot, and a scratchy Bill Blass jacket is not the thing you wear.

As he gets into the cab, the phone rings. Gwen again; he'll call her back in a bit. It seems she gives a shit, but why? Repaying the debt?

Gwen's falsehoods didn't start a war. She didn't reveal the

names of CIA operatives. But she did jot down a series of conversations that sounded like something out of *Franny and Zooey*. This resemblance tracked word for word through a long conversation. She claimed to have recorded this conversation at a meat market of a pool party for young professionals. Upon investigation by the *Post*'s ombudsman, another story included a passage that closely tracked *The Bonfire of the Vanities*.

After the first indications of the scandal went public, a prominent Republican lobbyist whose fly Gwen once famously reported to have seen wide open at the conclusion of a black-tie affair walked into the *Post* ombudsman's office, accompanied by an attorney and a paramour. The latter swore that she had, in fact, unzipped the fly in question for the purposes of performing a sexual act at a much later time that evening. It's difficult to prove the negative, but this was as close as one can get to establishing that during the black-tie event in question the fly that Gwen had described as undone was, in fact, not.

Remorse—the book's title was Bill's idea as well—was exactly what Bill envisioned, though it was produced without his participation and he is yet to get around to reading it.

Another text: "R u at ur father's yet"

"No"

"Prodigal son. Ha!"

"Yeah . . . Ha . . ."

"Courage . . ."

Two garbage containers positioned at odd angles block the ramp leading to the entrance of the building.

Brass letters on a white wall identify the place as "Château Sedan Neuve." The positioning of containers suggests that they are being used as a barricade in the Paris Commune sense of the word rather than as receptacles for construction rubbish.

This château is well fortified. There are the aforementioned barricades, there is a tall temporary construction fence, and there is a nearly identical permanent chain-link fence that seems to be protecting the building's structured parking.

Bill hands the driver ten dollars, grabs his Halliburton and bike messenger's bags, and asks to be dropped off in the midst of traffic on South Ocean Drive.

There is screeching of brakes behind the taxi, and the driver, a tough Nigerian, deals with this outpouring of rage by opening the window and slowly displaying the middle finger of his left hand. He stays in place even after Bill gets out of the car, prompting the asshole driver behind them to continue to blow the horn, evidently choosing surrender to road rage over changing lanes.

Bill, too, considers displaying his middle finger or fingers, but reconsiders after realizing that he is staring at a white Bentley convertible piloted by a scruffy-looking young man. It's possible that the driver is the youngest senior partner in the history of Cravath, Swaine & Moore LLP, and thus was able to purchase said $225,000 vehicle with legitimately earned money. More likely, the young man used funds obtained by means more traditional for South Florida, which would also increase the likelihood of his packing heat, possibly even silencer-modified heat. The convertible would afford the young man a clear shot. Seeing no measurable upside, Bill decides that it would be prudent to refrain from expressing his contempt to the honking asshole.

The barricade situation is frustrating. The building is unmistakably present, wedged between South Ocean Drive and the ocean. It has to be around twenty stories high, its shape vaguely reminiscent of a wave. But how is he to get there?

Bill had visited South Florida several times over the previous twelve years, always avoiding visiting his father. This bypassed the mitzvah of vodka drinking and the necessity of wooden conversation at dinner. Bill is perfectly capable of shooting vodka; around his father, it's safer to sip. And, of course, he sees no need for silent reliving of old resentments.

Bill has never seen this place before. Avoiding a visit to what passes for the ancestral home and meeting the lady who is technically his current stepmother are the biggest benefits of all.

Bill walks toward the twin containers, stops for a moment, and after ascertaining that no one is watching, out of habit, climbs up the container's built-in ladder and looks in. Even when things were good, even when they were very good, Bill amused himself by Dumpster-diving for modern classic furniture. Some of his best finds came from containers, and in Florida you have to be prepared for crazy shit.

These containers are empty. Since there is no active construction in sight, they are indeed being used as roadblocks, barricades.

The ramp to the building's lobby is clearly verboten.

As Bill ascends the forbidden ramp—the grand entrance—he has no difficulty imagining the place in the 1970s, as wealthy Floridians nonchalantly dropped the keys of their coral-colored Coupes De Ville into the waiting hands of valets. Both the bearers and the receivers of the keys were immigrants—the more- and less-fortunate brothers. What is valet parking but an exercise in humiliation? It has nothing to do with the parking of a car. Servitude is the principal commodity being served. Is there a better way for an immigrant to measure his station in life than by having a fellow immigrant slavishly bow?

As he walks up the ramp, Bill becomes painfully aware of the fact that Florida is bathing the street with entirely too much light. His *W* cap isn't useful. His inner eye seeks darkness, finding it in the dozen shiny black spots by the curb. On second look, Bill realizes that the black spots are actually garbage bags lined up one by one, next to a three-legged table with a green Formica top and wooden chairs, probably hundred-year-old Thonet, painted jolly canary yellow.

He walks up to one of the bags. A gaping rip in its side exposes its contents. Bill moves it lightly with his Top-Sider. A couple of shards of porcelain fall out on the pavement.

Picking up the larger of the shards, Bill sees that it's a fragment of a saucer—about a third of one. The stamp on the bottom reads "Made in Czechoslovakia." The saucer is bright orange, with white polka dots. Probably from the interwar years, a happy, goofy design, either unsuspecting of the shit to come or denying its inevitability. Bill can sympathize with refusing to acknowledge the inevitable. This is in part due to the fact that today is January 11, and the passing of the scepter is nine days away.

Knowledge has a way of dancing into Bill's arms and staying forever trapped. He doesn't know why. You can't think about all your troubles all of the time, and one way to mitigate toxicity is to look at the stuff in front of you, grazing on words, shapes, concepts, chewing the brain cud.

What harm is there in knowing a lot about dogs, cars, horses, economic policy, and real estate? Bill knows many things entirely too well and is enthusiastic about most of them. Design is one of those things. He knows chairs especially well. Unable to walk past a construction Dumpster without peeking in, he has gathered many a roomful of remarkable furniture.

Bill's apartment—the modest place which he will be unable to afford past February 1—is indeed, as Gwen noted, worthy of a profile in *Dwell*. Running past a Dumpster a few years earlier, he spotted the lower part of what was surely a Harry Bertoia Diamond Chair, and indeed it was. The chair was wearing a pristine Knoll white cover.

On another occasion, he noticed the back of a George Nelson daybed sending an SOS from a pile of rubble. Bill came to its rescue. Then, in the alley behind his apartment, someone left a Saarinen Womb Chair, perfectly orange and in need of nothing more than cleaning. A few weeks later, an Alvar Aalto Chair 44 showed up on a curb in Cleveland Park. A Danish dining table—designed by Hans Wegner, made by Getama—was cluelessly priced at a yard sale, and a half-dozen stackable Eames fiberglass side-shell chairs in vibrant pastels awaited him in a massive garbage pile behind Duke Ellington High School of the Arts, in Georgetown. The same pile yielded three large steel bookcases and a battleship-gray steel desk.

The apartment is nice—it will hurt to lose it. What would he do with his stuff if he were to decamp for he-knows-not-where?

Last time he looked, his checking account balance was $1,219.37. His savings account was at $7.49, and when he left Washington he had exactly $200 in his pocket. (Now it's $177.) He has no credit card—just a debit card, for the ATMs, not for borrowing. His *Post* expenses went on his *Post* card. He has it still, but, well . . .

His rent, which will come due in less than a month, is $1,750. This project—the book—is his only plan.

You might ask why Bill finds himself flat-ass broke at the end of an illustrious career with one of the nation's premier newspapers. The answer is: refine the question. He is not *flat* broke. He still has $1,403.86 when you sum up his checking and savings accounts and cash on hand. It's not $14,038.60, and it's not $140,386.00, because of an episode of marital unpleasantness.

He was married once, and is technically married still, to a woman he first met at the Hillel Jewish student organization at Duke.

She was from Chicago, he from Moscow by way of Washington suburbs. In those days, Friday night services at the Duke Hillel concluded with dancing. The Jews of the New York/ Miami vortex turned on the Hillel community–owned boom box and discoed into the night. Some surrendered their worldly names, becoming Disco Dave, Disco Rick, Disco Kevin, Disco Nina, Disco Deb, Disco Davia, etc.

Lena didn't disco. Bill didn't disco. She had an acerbic sense of humor, which Bill found attractive. She had a Russian name, but was American through and through—the best of both worlds. She could talk about shit that mattered, and who could possibly object to the notion that the ability to discuss shit that matters is an important element in any relationship, especially any relationship that involves Bill?

After three years at Duke, he was starved for conversation. It was fated, *bashert*—call the caterer, you might say. Yet, Bill was surprised by the what-have-I-done feeling the first time she spent the night in his room. Zbig slept in a women's dorm on the West Campus that night and on many other nights.

The lovers broke up with what sounded like a sigh of relief. After graduation, Lena went off to law school at UChicago, and Bill took a bus to Washington, to become a writer, or a fighter for justice, or something in between.

They met again a decade later, starting an on-and-off relationship, which was unambiguously in the off phase when he drunkenly fell into bed with Gwen. It flipped back to on, then—almost immediately after a low-key in-the-rabbi's-office marriage ceremony—it flipped back to off.

Their incompatibility could be explained in a geometric manner, by their relationship to the concept of injustice. Awake, Bill had just one stance: warrior. To him, many things were akin to fascism. Bring it on, the bigger the better! Onward, Comrades, fight to the last drop of blood, victory will be ours!

Lena, by contrast, collected injustices, wallowed in them, bouncing out of a law firm, relegated to a life of underpaid unhappiness in the government, which resulted in an Equal Employment Opportunity action against her former employer, the Equal Employment Opportunity Commission. After much unfairness at EEOC, Lena was driven to a nonprofit, where money was tight and battles for a place at the trough especially vicious.

A one-bedroom apartment affords few hiding places, and Lena's nightly accounts of the humiliations she had experienced at work made for mediocre foreplay. The disappearance of sex brought on many accusations, all of them leveled against Bill. "Yes, Lena," Bill wanted to say a few months into the marriage, "you are right: I don't appreciate you. I don't remember whether I ever did or why," but, being a good boy, he said nothing of the sort.

Instead, he made a wholehearted effort to get in touch with his softer side, to find it within his psyche, along with that thing called empathy. This was a quixotic quest, which required much assistance from trained professionals. During this time, Bill's savings were depleted, mostly to pay for shrinks—his and hers—and lawyers in her long-pending and ultimately unsuccessful EEO complaint against EEOC.

To divorce, he borrowed against his modest 401(k) account, paying substantial penalties, but what the fuck? You do what you have to. They did get as far as an excellently worded separation agreement. The final divorce has been pending for a year now; it was just a matter of scheduling a hearing and shelling out the final installment of a few grand.

Why is Bill here, in Florida, poking black garbage bags by the curb, grazing on another person's misfortune? Surely he understands that this is not a trash pickup. Idiot, couldn't he recognize an eviction? Has he not seen evictions before, the "packing," which involves throwing everything in trash bags, breaking whatever breaks, the removal of belongings to the curb, the slowing down of traffic as passersby seek to vulture on another's misfortune? The stopping cars, the vanishing chairs, sofa stuffing wet from rain. Does Bill not recognize that his turn will soon come? Maybe he does. Perhaps this is why he lingers over the black bags.

Were it not for the intense pain of impact on his back, thoughts of this sort would have continued racing through Bill's mind.

Bill looks over his left shoulder to see what could have hit him.

He looks up just in time to step out of the way of a tiny woman—shorter than five feet, stooped, emaciated, cachexic perhaps, wearing a white nightshirt, a pink bathrobe, and fuzzy Carolina blue slippers—aiming to whack him one more time across the back with a curved aluminum cane.

She got him once as he stood pondering the deeper meaning of her black plastic bags. *"Fashist!"* she screams as her cane lands on the black plastic bag instead of squarely across Bill's back.

The impact crushes more pieces of porcelain.

"Svoloch'!" the woman shouts even louder as the porcelain, her family's onetime treasure, absorbs the force of the blow.

She lifts the cane and hits the bag again, repeating the words in succession, reminiscent of the rhythm of a beating heart.

Fashisty, svolochi, svolochi, fashisty, fashisty, svolochi, svolochi, fashisty . . .

Now oblivious to Bill, she hits the bag, and hits, and hits it again as contents shatter and crumble.

Jesus, that word: *Svoloch'.*

At this point, dear reader, please consider yourself beseeched to learn the word *svoloch',* which roughly, very roughly, translates as vermin, or lowlife, or scum, or maybe swine, or maybe, with stretching, a whore. A dozen years have passed since the last time Bill heard that word.

It comes from the Russian word *volok,* the making of felt, fibers condensing, pressing together, haphazard like hair that mats beneath a dog's ear, uncombed, uncombable.

Svoloch' is what we become when our lives are deprived of what makes us strand-like, individual, noble, like the pursuit of truth, beauty, justice. *Svoloch'* is the making of life into felt, the turning of individual strands into filthy uniform matter.

What can Bill do but turn around and walk away at a brisk pace, leaving the old woman alone, crushing the *svoloch*ness and fascism in her bags by the curb?

5

REFUSENIK

Retreating rapidly to South Ocean Drive, Bill follows the construction fence to its northernmost corner.

He turns right, and, indeed, encounters a gate. It looks more
like a checkpoint at the gates of Fort Meade, the federal government's cyber-spying outpost in rural Maryland, than an entrance
to a civilian facility. Two men sit in a booth next to the gate. One
appears to be Hispanic, the other Slavic.

Bill raises two fingers of his right hand to his temple. This is
a quasi-military salute he seems to have more or less spontaneously developed, a gesture he uses too often. He doesn't like
giving out his name; instead, he keeps moving, daring the rent-
a-cops to stop him, which they do not. He passes through the
gate at 5:37 P.M.

"Arbeit Macht Frei," he says out loud as the gate opens. Work
will set you free. Those clever Nazis put this saying on the gates
of death camps. It's a private joke between Bill and himself. He

says it at many gates. When you live alone you learn to amuse yourself.

Bill turns right, stepping into the structured parking lot, where he wastes a few minutes analyzing the car population.

Using his reporter's notepad—a thin pad that fits nicely into a back pocket—he sets up a table to organize the data, entering the number of Lexuses (17), BMWs (12), Mercedes (9), Audis (1), Cadillacs (1), Porsches (0), Jaguars (1), and Range Rovers (2). Even without Porsches, the place looks like the microcosm of the parking lot of the Washington Hebrew Congregation.

Of the forty-four vehicles Bill catalogues, twenty-nine display bumper stickers declaring: "TRUMP: Make America Great Again!"

These stickers had been on the bumpers for months—perhaps for a year or more. They had to be attached at the time when the long-shot Republican presidential contender slandered Mexicans, pledged to bar the doors for Muslim immigrants, and, with great creativity and determination, searched for new ways to piss off women, people of every color, the media, veterans of foreign wars, the handicapped, the Jews.

It stands to reason, subtly, weirdly, that a high-rise almost certainly dominated by immigrants would be a bastion of Trump's brand of xenophobia. Where is it written that people must love their own kind?

It's equally noteworthy that these fine vehicles are parked next to columns that tell stories of neglect and water damage. The garage ceiling is chipping as well, exposing rusted steel armature. With concrete crumbling away from rusting rebar, this château has the look of a Soviet-style perpetual construction project, a kind of place where nothing will be completed and nothing can be. In settings like this one you smell the incineration of millions of dollars.

Who are the inhabitants of the Château? Are these Russians, people of his parents' generation?

Let's say you come to America in your midforties and retire in your midseventies. For the first few years, you scrape, and then, if you are lucky, the stream of money normalizes, but what does it take to make it gush like a busted fire hydrant?

Fraud is always the answer, and Medicare the target of choice. Medicaid, too, can be lucrative. Being litigious works. Medical malpractice and employment discrimination suits are fine. To arrive at Château Sedan Neuve by age seventy-five, you need a good angle, one that may entail consumption of large volumes of blood. These folks might have earned incomes that placed them in the top second or third percentile for all Americans, but for us immigrants they are in the 99.9999th. With February rent due, Bill is on the opposite end of this distribution: the 0.0001st—the edge.

After concluding the car survey, Bill steps into what appears to be the entrance to the building. Again, he isn't challenged. The door stands wide open. Next to the elevator, he spots a lime green chair, very '70s funk. Not exactly his sort of thing, but he likes it enough to flip it over and consider the label. No surprise: designed by Milo Baughman, working for Thayer Coggin—nice. He sets it back down by the elevator door.

Not quite ready to face the inevitability of seeing his father, Bill delays pushing the eighteenth-floor button and instead pushes "L."

His back is starting to stiffen—the old woman got him

squarely across the spine. More than that, the crook of the cane landed on his shoulder blade. Three Advils would be indicated, but Bill's curiosity triumphs over pain. He wants to see more of the Château, perhaps even figure out who designed it forty or so years ago.

Two sawhorses, police tape, a "Do Not Enter" sign in English, and a "*Vkhod Strogo Vospreshchen*" (Entrance Strictly Forbidden) sign in Russian greet him in the lobby. Bill isn't deterred.

The lobby floor is marble, three or four tones of stunning taupe-to-brown stone, as elaborate as the Moscow Metro of his memory, except the dominant design here is not hammers, sickles, and heroic workers, peasants, and soldiers, but rather oversized paisleys, six-foot paisleys in shades that cascade upward, from lighter to darker. These waves of marble are intended to be reflected in the mirrored walls.

Roughly half of the mirrors are still here. Others grew destabilized by moisture and fell to the floor. Shards of thick glass are left in place.

In the center of what had once been the suspended ceiling, a smoky-glass chandelier remains pristine despite the many streams of water that passed through it. Its arms are oblong, ominous, biomorphic, like formerly vital organs of a frozen cadaver. "Venetian glass," Bill diagnoses.

Bill wanders deeper into the belly of the Château, realizing to his surprise that he is now walking through a puddle of clear water that reaches to his ankles. It appears that water pouring into this lobby is not an anomalous event, but a fact of life. The panels of suspended ceiling are gone, as are many of the interior walls.

Subtractions add to the magnificence of this set.

Behind a partition, Bill stumbles across a stack of water-stained sections of a sofa. The sections have that certain 1970s playfulness, which is to say they are just the right kind of porny, the enduring form of porny; it's Thayer Coggin.

Milo Baughman was the inventor of the sectional sofa, and Thayer Coggin produced it. No need to flip over the pieces. There is never just one Thayer Coggin in the interior, there has to be a flock, and stirring up mold is never a good thing.

Bill snaps a few pictures with his phone and shoots three of them to Gwen.

Behind another partition, he finds stacks of chrome Thayer Coggin chairs with the same green vinyl he had seen on the chair by the elevator. There are at least eight stacks, twenty chairs each. In New York, this would have the street value of $36,000; in tight-assed Washington, maybe $18,000.

Here in Hollywood, Florida, these chairs will end up in trash containers, assuming someone gets around to clearing the rubble. Bill toys with the idea of salvaging the pieces, but (a) doesn't have the cash to ship them home, (b) has no way to sell them for what they are worth, and (c) a businessman he is not. His interest in design is pure—for its own sake—which oddly makes this find both less and more useful.

Eight square Thayer Coggin tables suffering from various levels of delamination are strewn about in no particular pattern. The ones lacking legs are either leaning at perfect forty-five-degree angles or are flipped upside down in the puddle beneath.

In a corner, Bill spots at least a dozen objects that are vaguely reminiscent of birdcages. Recognition is immediate: Warren

Platner chairs in Knoll orange fabric, white with mold. The Platner tables are in a different pile. For a serious, knowledge-able collector of modern furniture, this is the equivalent of the lost ark.

He is a witness to an epic disaster. A waterlogged, crumbling building on this stretch of the Gold Coast is as incongruous as an automobile graveyard in Midtown Manhattan. And another thing: this crumbling château is clearly a landmark of Miami Modern architecture.

"Holy shit; is there a war out there?" Gwen texts back.

"No, but this place is probably designed by Morris Lapidus."

There is silence on the other end—long enough to enable Gwen to Google Lapidus.

"THE Morris Lapidus?"

"There's but 1."

Either that or it was someone who was riffing on Lapidus so shamelessly that he might as well be Lapidus. Lapidus dilapi-dated. Lapidus dilapidized. Lapidus with a stick up his assidus. Realizing that he is becoming punchy—badly in need of a glass of vodka—is all Bill needs to know he's finally ready to ring his father's doorbell.

He wades back to the elevator, breathes in, and presses the eighteenth-floor button.

Château Sedan Neuve is not so much French as it is Frenchie. Bill has never been to France, never got around to going, didn't have the time or money, even at the apex of his career, but of course he knows that nothing in France looks anything like this.

In the elevator, Bill notices a leaflet attached with thick packing tape to the Formica wall.

No, "leaflet" is not the right word.

French is a better language to use in the setting of this building and this elevator, making the word *pasquille* particularly apt.

Paskvil', the Russian derivative of the French *pasquille*, is better still.

Make Château Great Again!
We need New Board Lidership!

On December 31 your purse and wallet becomed $28,000 liter to pay for "misselenius" projects!

Triumverat of <u>Mental Lilliputs</u> on Condo Board, which take command from notorious Evil Dwarf put millions of YOUR DOLLARS in THEIR pockets!

Evil Dwarf has two Members in his pocket!

As YOUR property become unsailable, THEY get Lexuses!

- *Don't behave yourselfs like Sheeps!*
- *Don't behave yourselfs like Blinds!*
- *Don't behave yourselfs like Backless Slaves!*
- *Sign Petishn!*
- *WRITE FLORIDA GOVERNOR RIK SKOT!*

Don't vote for Old Board!

Three of five Members—collect SPECIAL ASESMENTS for "misselenius" reconstruction and not doing reconstruction and instead accelerate temp of **DeSTRUCTION!**

Triumverat's Next Dimolition: North Pool Deck and balkonys, which was inspected 7 years ago and those that need be repeired were. *(All statements made above can be proved by documents.)*

You will find pletora of open contracts made by Board where works are not define—and not deadline! Big (multimillion!) constructions (destructions) begin as "changeoforders." They have no permits and are now on changeoforder 27rd to **DESTROY** your balkonys.

STOP THEM DESTROYING OUR PROPERTYS AND OUR LIVES!

Sencirily,

Concerned Property Owners of Château Sedan Neuve

Open Your Eyes!

Bill rolls his eyes at the grand choice of words in the *paskvil'*. *Triumverat* . . . Evil Dwarf . . . Mental Lilliputs . . .

The *paskvil'* is so ripe with venom, it dares you to place a glass bowl beneath it. The toxin can be rushed to a laboratory, compounded, tried in rats, and, finally, tested in the clinic. It can be stood on its head, turned therapeutic—and, at a price of $16,000 a dose, make someone rich, perhaps even Bill, albeit not soon enough.

Bill feels blessed not to know the facts that would have made the *paskvil'* acquire context, and, through the act of bloodsucking, come to life, lose poetry, become prosaic. That's the thing about a proper *paskvil'*: it's always better without context, as an abstraction; if you want an axiom in life, this is it.

As the elevator struggles on its heavenward climb, Bill stares at the *paskvil'*, rapidly losing hope that the cables pulling the flying jalopy would pop, trapping him in the shaft for days or weeks, thus liberating him from reaching the destination, the eighteenth floor, the penthouse apartment of his father, Melsor Yakovlevich Katzenelenbogen.

Proximity to his father is making Bill remember that America was and perhaps still is the land of opportunity.

A little more consumer math: before he paid for the tickets and left Washington, Bill had $1,420 in his checking account and in cash, a figure representing his net worth.

Imagine a scenario where Bill dies. Assuming selection of the Costco "In God's Care" casket, which costs $1,299.99, how much money can Bill spend between the time of his departure from Washington and his departure for life everlasting without his net worth going into the red? (Assume that burial plots are free and body handling and transportation expenses are zero.) The answer is brutal: less than his February rent.

This is a slow elevator.

The Château's eighteenth floor is actually its seventeenth. In a numerology win-win worthy of Henry Kissinger, the thirteenth floor is skipped, and the eighteenth—symbolic of the Hebrew letter *hay*, the thing that looks like a dog with a severed front paw looking for the left margin of the page, and which stands for life—added. This observation confirms his suspicion that, notwithstanding all the Frogginess in the world, things Hebrew matter at the Château. And missing thirteen is a bow to Christians, if any.

Bill is hoping that the hallway will last forever. He notes the horizontal, six-foot-long, paisley-shaped ornaments inserted between apartment doors. The hallway is done in vomit-inducing peach. Bill is certain that the original color of these body-bag-sized paisleys had to be purple, and that the walls on which they were mounted had to be muted green, the color you get when you cross turquoise with avocado, if such hybrids are possible.

He pulls a quarter out of his pocket, inserts its edge into a crack in the peach paint, and presses. The piece of paint that chips off is larger and more noticeable than Bill hoped for, but it does reveal that in its glory days the paisley had indeed been purple and the walls green, or something like it. Morris Lapidus, the guy Bill now believes to have been the Château's architect, was paying homage to the colors that made South Florida great.

Bill congratulates himself with a modified version of a touchdown victory, a little dance, and would anyone who had been in a situation such as his—seeing the father you haven't seen since the trial twelve years earlier and for the first time actually meeting your father's wife of eight years whom you have seen only on Facebook—feel so smug as to condemn Bill for procrastinating? Of course, he needs a drink, of course, he needs three Advils, but he also realizes that getting these someplace else—anyplace else—would be a safer, more rational thing to do.

Finally, Bill reaches the castle in the sky and knocks on the door inscribed with his family name.

6

WILLIAM

"Zakhodi Ilyusha, dobro pozhalovat',*"* says Nella, opening the door. [Come in, Ilyusha, welcome.]

William M. Katzenelenbogen, a reporter whose byline had graced *The Washington Post* for many years and was not unfamiliar to journalism prize juries, is actually neither William nor Bill.

William is his second first name. His first first—given to him in Moscow by his parents in 1965—was Ilya. He added *W* in the front and *M* in the back after coming to the U.S. in 1975, as in W-Ilya-M, in an effort to become more American.

Deferring to Bill's preferences, we will continue to call him Bill, using variations of his first first name, Ilya or Ilyusha, only in situations where these variations are invoked by others.

If Facebook is to be believed, Nella is seventy-three, a decade younger than Bill's father. In the flesh, she is even more slight than Bill imagined, her facial features angular, her hair solid black. She wears a light blue tunic and sandals. It's a look that could be classified as beach bohemian.

Nella is the second stepmother on Bill's life journey. There was no occasion for them to have met. His mother died, and his first stepmother was a neighbor who simply moved in and moved out—eight months, presumably with nothing. What was her name? Bill knows nothing about Nella, either. The only tidbit: she and Melsor stepped off a cruise ship in the Florida Keys and signed papers at a tropical courthouse. For all Bill knows, the lovers met on the same cruise.

How is Bill to greet her? A hug? An air kiss? A handshake? Bill opts for nothing.

She glances at the Halliburton and the bike messenger's bags he sets down in the corner. She assesses his luggage in the same surreptitious sort of way in which one glances at someone else's bank statement.

Clearly, his luggage fails to meet with her approval.

"*Spasibo,*" he stammers woodenly. [Thank you.]

"*Nezachto,*" Nella responds in kind. [You are welcome.]

"You wouldn't happen to have Advil or something like it?"

"Two?"

"Three."

"Big dose. Someone hitted you?"

"I saw an eviction. An old woman, presumably with dementia, hit me across the back with her cane."

"You are guilty yourself. In Florida, you should watch out, look over your shoulders."

"What was her name?"

"Roza Kisel'. She was from Nevada."

"Did she run out of money?"

"She is too crazy to know to pay special assessments. They foreclosured her, so to say."

"What happens to her next?"

"*Dzhuyka* sends person from mental health. They come to take them away for a few days. Then they let them go almost every time."

Bill remembers the word *Dzhuyka*. It's Russian-English for Jewish organizations that provide all manner of social services. These can include the Jewish Council for the Elderly, Jewish Family Services, Jewish Community This & That. The word *Dzhuyka* comes from the word *Dzhu*. Makes sense: *Dzhuz* go to *Dzhuyki* to get help.

"Sad."

"What do you expect? This is *luxury* apartment. Only one high-rise in Hollywood is closer to beach—have you seen Aquarius? It's practically *in* water."

"She may still have money to keep living there; right?"

"Maybe. But too late, so to say. *Dzhuyka* will try to put her in crazy house. They have special wan."

"Special wan?"

"Yes, wan—microbus, with driver, like ambulette."

Will *Dzhuyka* send wan with driver for Bill, a quasi-*Dzhu*, a proto-*Dzhu*, with the blood of Armenians and Russians mixed into the cauldron, when the time comes for him to wander away from his garbage bags?

Melsor had once been a poet. Perhaps he is still. He was a refusenik, too. His photo—wearing a pair of too-large Sophia Loren glasses and a Peruvian alpaca sweater given to him by visiting Americans—was blown up to poster size and displayed at vigils across Sixteenth Street NW from the Soviet embassy in Washington. It's an icon of the Soviet Jewry movement.

If you happen to know anyone who had been involved in the Union of Councils for Soviet Jews or Student Struggle for Soviet

Jewry, ask them whether they remember Melsor Katzenelen-bogen.

Some people thought there were two of them, Melsor-pre-emigration and Melsor-the-American.

The Moscow Melsor was an expert in the silver age of Russian poetry: Akhmatova, Tsvetaeva, Mandelstam, Blok, Gumilyov. He wrote poetry, too. It was derivative, but it seemed daring at the time.

For five years, as Melsor sat in refusal in Moscow, his songs of freedom were being translated into English by comparative lit majors at some of America's finest colleges. Set to music, they were performed at youth group meetings in synagogue base-ments. What's better than a song for covering up an awkward rhyme?

In those days, young American Jews had long hair, cared pas-sionately about Father and Son Guthrie, and guitars were used.

In 1978, at age forty-four, Melsor busted out of the tyranni-cal state of his birth. His blond, Slavic-looking wife and equally blond son came with him.

Melsor-the-American first became a poet laureate of the Jew-ish emigration movement. He was sent on a victory tour of Jew-ish community centers—the *Dzhuyka* Tour—where he recited the cycle of poems he wrote in Moscow. The cycle was titled *Songs About Freedom*. Not *Songs* of *Freedom*, but *Songs* About *Freedom*. The idea was to imagine freedom prior to attaining it.

America greeted Melsor with betrayal and woe.

He thought he had a government job lined up, but he didn't interview well and the bureaucrats at the Voice of America, Radio Liberty, and *America Illustrated* magazine—the three best troughs for literary immigrants—apparently recognized in him a perpetual troublemaker, an employment discrimination lawsuit waiting to happen. All three were government agencies, so the pay and benefits were superb.

The Voice wouldn't give Melsor an interview. His Moscow acquaintance, Boris Goldfarb, a poet, was ensconced at the Voice, working as a journalist. Clearly, Goldfarb was in a position to make key introductions, but he was doing nothing of the sort. Infuriated, Melsor handwrote an open letter in which he called Goldfarb a *poeticheskoye nichtozhestvo,* a poetic non-entity.

The open letter had a title: "*Prisposoblenchestvo,*" which translates literally as adaptation to surroundings, but means sucking up to Americans. "*Prisposoblenchestvo*" was submitted to a New York–based Russian-language newspaper, *Novoye Russkoye Slovo,* which failed to publish it. Bill was strong-armed into preparing the English-language version for submission to *The Washington Post* and *The New York Times,* but these news outlets were deprived of the opportunity to consider the piece, because Bill deposited the envelopes into a garbage can instead of a U.S. Postal Service box.

As an adult, Bill met Goldfarb a few times in Washington and—just as he suspected—found him to be the sort of old guy you can drink vodka with. Mostly, Bill appreciated the depth of compassion with which Goldfarb asked, "How is your father?"

Melsor lived hand to mouth, editing, writing, adjuncting, teaching courses and workshops until there was no one left to teach. Bill escaped to college and went on to become a reporter, and his parents moved from the Washington suburbs to New York. Then a catastrophe struck: Melsor's wife, Bill's mother, Rita, was diagnosed with breast cancer. Not a small lesion you zap out and go, but an aggressive disease that needed an aggressive doctor. Melsor challenged the disease as though it was Bolshevism. Rita was fatalistic. Melsor waged war. Bill, by then living elsewhere, was unable to do more than provide information and mutter "Oh shit" when it was ignored.

Some men lose their bearings in the face of death. Not Melsor. Loss made him soar. He got into business, providing transportation for the sick, predominantly Russian-speaking Brooklynites. In a matter of months after Rita's death, he emerged as an owner of a fleet of "ambulettes," vans defined as "invalid carriages" in New York Medicaid regs. The business required maintaining ties with doctors, whom Melsor either knew or found ways to court. It was about connections, an exercise of communication skills, making reality conform to his will.

Last time Bill and Melsor saw each other, the elder Katzenelenbogen stood trial at Kings County Supreme Court, accused of Medicaid fraud.

After their falling-out, Bill didn't give his father much thought. The two men ended up on opposite sides of the law, and—perhaps more importantly—on opposite sides of the boundary between the world of real things and the territory the elder Katzenelenbogen called home. Since no words were spoken between them during that dozen years, Bill has no preconceptions of what turn their South Florida reunion might take. Perhaps his father will give him the cold shoulder, a reasonable possibility since he isn't known to possess a warm one.

Perhaps he will, again, accuse him of betrayal. Is it not to be expected that sons hold on to the suitcases their fathers stuff with fraudulently obtained cash? Is it not to be expected that sons commit obstruction of justice and money laundering to honor family ties?

Bill hears crackling sounds emanating from the apartment's hallway.

Of course, Melsor would need to complete watching a Fox News segment or something equally important before opening the door and greeting the son who made a reluctant first overture toward an uneasy truce.

"Kak on?" asks Bill in Russian. [How is he?]

"Krutit dela, krutit," Nella responds with a classic Russian-woman sigh. [He is cranking business, cranking.]

Bill knows enough to fear this prospect. With the elder Katzenelenbogen focused on business, someone is sure to get fleeced, someone is sure to get indicted. The latter someone may very well be Mr. Katzenelenbogen himself.

While he knows of no deaths, given the sinister nature of the windmills his father has selected for tilting at, one of those could easily occur.

"A kak zdorov'ye?" [How is his health?]

"Kak-kak, kak u byka. Kazhdoye utro po pyat'desyat raz otzhimay-etsya." [Like a bull. Does fifty push-ups every morning.]

"A zdes' on?" asks Bill. [Is he here?]

"Zdes', zdes', ratsiyu slushayet. Seychas doslushayet i vyydet." [Yes, he is here, listening to a radio. He'll finish it and come out.]

Her choice of the word *"ratsiya"* strikes Bill as curious. A *ratsiya* is a two-way radio, a delicate piece of technology, the sort used by Cold War spies.

Bill follows Nella to the kitchen, then wanders out to the great room.

The view is breathtaking—he can see the contours of the South Florida coast all the way to South Beach. The brightness he takes for granted outdoors is stunning indoors. His gaze follows six pelicans flying within a few feet of the balcony.

Clearly, Melsor Yakovlevich Katzenelenbogen has found someone to hold on to the cash-filled suitcase or suitcases. He landed on his feet, and this may be something to be proud of.

"*Letat' zdes' khochetsya; pravda?*" says Nella. [One wants to fly here; yes?]

"*Da,*" Bill responds. [Indeed.]

After contemplating the view, Bill notices a moving scaffolding cradle suspended on thick steel wire ropes next to the balcony. It's the sort of gizmo you see dangling from steel beams mounted from the roof.

"What is this about?" he asks Nella.

"They try to frighten him."

"Who is? With what? Over what?"

"BOD, who else?"

"What's BOD?"

"Board of directors, condo board. They hang *lyul'ka* to send him message: shut up or we knock down your balcony. He gets them angry."

"*Lyul'ka*" is the Russian word for a cradle, a scaffolding cradle.

"Is that legal?"

It is not lost on Bill that he has seemingly stumbled into a vaudevillian act. The speech pattern: one character naïvely asks questions; the other responds with worldly wisdom, pointing out the obvious.

"What's not legal?"

"What they are doing."

"Listen yourself to what you say. We live in Florida. Understand? Flo-ri-da."

"Was that his leaflet in the elevator? The one with the Evil Dwarf and two members in the pocket?"

"What you think?"

As his familiarity with the patterns of Russian English—call it Runglish, Englussian, or Englishish—returns, Bill takes this as a yes. He doesn't envy that condo board. He doesn't envy anyone who has at any point tangled with his father.

Nella sits down in an uncomfortable-looking, translucent chair in front of the window.

"Look at how she jumps," she says in English, pointing at the expanse of blue and a moving white stripe in its center. "How beautiful . . ."

Who is this "she"? Why is she "jumping"? What is she referring to?

Bill looks out the window. The "she" in question could be that speedboat, a massive, roaring one at that, leaping from one cresting wave to another.

"You are talking about that boat?" he asks, also in English, just to be sure. "No one else is jumping?"

Nella is absorbed in following the speedboat and its white wake. She nods.

To be sure, Bill is at the top of the list of people he doesn't envy. Were this list not limited to the living, his mother would merit the topmost position.

Bill continues to look around. A funky 1970s Sputnik lamp, like a UFO transporting little green space travelers, hangs in the foyer, looking like a lost shard of the magnificent light fixture on the ceiling of Eisenhower Theater at the Kennedy Center. The thing is so perfect for the space that it has to have been hand-picked by the architect.

The furniture, however, would have made Lapidus vomit.

Milo Baughman would slit his wrists. Warren Plattner would self-immolate. It's white and leathery—a big, shiny sectional so squeaky that you can hear it from across the room. This is not Herman Miller. This is not Knoll, definitely not the sort of thing Bill rescued from garbage containers and is now set to lose. Perhaps he should have moved the stuff to a storage locker before leaving for Florida. Maybe he still could, on return to D.C.

The sectional and other stuff in the apartment are a mixture of things emanating from China, Turkey, and, to a lesser extent, Israel, claiming to be based on European design, and catering to Russian immigrants.

The art around him seems incongruent with either the noble traces of the Lapidus design or the shiny white sectional. The walls are covered with big canvases in big frames with faux gold coating decidedly non-modernist curlicues.

He counts six seascapes and a particularly disturbing painting in which his father and Nella are superimposed on a copy of a landscape by the Russian artist Isaac Levitan, *Golden Autumn*. Melsor and Nella at the river bend in Russian countryside, marring a copy of a path-breaking early-twentieth-century painting. There are more travesties in that painting than Bill is able to count, so he stops at the first six. What's next? Will rich Russians have their portraits painted among the bears in Shishkin's *Morning in a Pine Forest*?

"*Krasivo, da?*" says Nella proudly. [Pretty; yes?]

"*Da. Krasivo. Ochen'.*" [Yes. Pretty. Very.]

It's possible that Bill would have been better off staying away from the investigative track in journalism. His sense of outrage and his obsession with science and all flavors of betrayal of the public trust made him as much a dinosaur as these pterodactyl-like creatures flying in formation outside the window.

Perhaps he should have covered design, but that, too, would have been a betrayal. His obsession with design is a personal obsession. His career was—had been—driven by pursuit of professional obsessions, his private war against those who lie, cheat, and steal. By exposing villains, Bill distinguished himself from his father.

Bill continues to stare out the window, past the cluster of high-rises that people more familiar with South Florida municipalities recognize as Sunny Isles.

As darkness sets in, the contours of South Beach are no longer visible in the hazy distance.

The door of the *kabinet* opens, and Melsor bursts into the room.

It's impossible to establish beyond the shadow of a doubt what a Jew looks like. People have tried, God knows, but this was tough even before immigration and assimilation eroded the centuries-old boundaries that separated small Jewish towns from the rest of the universe.

A literary agent, the asshole who dumped Bill over the drug approval book, once told him that Jews come in two varieties—carrots and potatoes. Carrots are narrow in the shoulders, pointy-headed. Potatoes are broad-shouldered, square-jawed. This has nothing to do with height. You can be a short carrot or a tall potato—or the other way around. A carrot can beget a potato or vice versa. A carrot can be a potato's sibling, too.

All of this is a precursor to saying something that feels uncomfortable, but must be dealt with: if you have a sense of what a Jew looks like, you may be able to detect that Melsor Yakovlevich Katzenelenbogen doesn't look *entirely* Jewish.

You might suggest that Melsor's semi-Armenianness could

be rendered visible if you spend some time staring at Arshile Gorky's portraits and then, without an interruption, cast a glance at the living, breathing Melsor Yakovlevich Katzenelen- bogen. The name "Katzenelenbogen" was passed on matrilin- eally. His father's last name was Matevossian. The couple didn't last past his birth.

Bill's quarter Armenianness is entirely invisible, drowned out by his mother's half Russianness. Melsor is a potato; Bill a carrot. Quarter Russian, quarter Armenian, and two-quarters Jewish on two sides, Bill looks like none of the above, a human terrier, a Katzenelenbogen Pinscher.

Now, in January 2017, Melsor seems shorter, more broad- shouldered, lower to the ground, heavier on the heels. His head is shaven, but, years notwithstanding, he seems strong. He must have started working out after the trial.

Also, there is gold. Around his neck, Melsor wears a massive gold chain with a proportionally sized star of David. There is a bracelet and a pinky ring. This jewelry is not intended for self- beautification. At the top of their lungs, these tokens shout: "I am dangerous! Don't fuck with me!"

"This is the guy who taught courses on the Silver Age of Rus- sian poetry," Bill says to himself. "Did Gumilyov wear gold chains? Did Mandelstam have a Mogen David? Did Blok sport a pinky ring?"

In their lives, lead was a metal of greater significance than gold.

Melsor was just past seventy the last time Bill saw him. It was in the Kings County courtroom. He slumped in the biggest wheelchair his lawyer could find. Clear fluid was dripping into his veins, something gaseous was being pumped from a torpedo- sized tank through a mask that fully covered his mouth. The jury found him not guilty and the judge noted his heroic past and praised him for cooperating with the Department of Justice ji-had to stamp out Medicaid fraud.

The flavor of fraud of which the elder Katzenelenbogen was not guilty, but from which he was apparently able to stash away considerable proceeds, is called the "ambulette" fraud. Its details will be revealed in due course.

A dozen years after the trial, Melsor seems to be feeling better. He paces madly, blurting out obscenities, and barely nodding to the son he hasn't seen in quite some time. Should they embrace? Would a simple handshake suffice? Would it be better to wait a bit and do nothing until the need for greeting passes?

"Ilyusha, rasskazhi podrobno, kto byl v budke kogda ty syuda zashel. Eto ochen' vazhno."

Mercifully, the elder Katzenelenbogen is addressing his son from across the room, standing beneath a gold-framed painting of a ship, commanding it like a corsair, a Judeo-Armenian Captain Blood.

[Ilyusha, tell me in detail, who was in the guard booth when you walked in. This is very important.]

The pirate ship on the painting is a two-mast affair. It's listing, about to dip gently to its side and go to sleep. The sharks are circling beneath the surface, readying for a feast.

Melsor is costumed for the part of the ship's captain. He is tall, broad, boxy. Blue shorts that come down to his knees, and his blue-and-white horizontally striped T-shirt are classic maritime stuff. In Russian, a version of this shirt is called *tel'nyazhka*. It's obvious that on a hypothetical formal occasion, Melsor would wear a navy blue double-breasted jacket, preferably with the insignia of a fictional yacht club, the bigger the better, Commodore Bloodsucker.

Melsor is clearly a man of many questions, and every one of them is urgent.

"*Ty po-russki ni s kem ne govoril posle togo kak voshel?*" [Did you speak Russian to anyone after you walked in?]

"*Net, ni slova.*" [No, not a word.]

"*Eto yest' ochen', ochen' khorosho. Okh kak povezlo! Dazhe ne predstovlyal sebe takoy rasskladki.*" [Very, very good! Very lucky! Didn't even imagine this sequence of events.]

Melsor sounds like he has won the lottery, but Bill knows better. The winning ticket has something to do with him. He bought it, or—worse—he *is* it.

"*Nu khot' ryumku rebyonku naley. Ved' skol'ko let ne videlis'.*" [At least pour the boy a shot glass. You haven't seen each other in years.]

"*Nakryvay, nakryvay na stol. Delo yest'.*" [Set the table, set the table. We have business.]

Nella emerges with a chilled bottle of Grey Goose on a tray full of familiar salty things that Bill loves and has missed.

The bottle is full, but not sealed. Bill has the capacity to interpret this: Grey Goose, a French vodka, bespeaks prosperity and generosity. That's a good thing. Its cost is a bad thing. The solution: procure a bottle of Grey Goose, consume its contents, then keep the bottle in perpetuity and continue to fill it with something more in line with what you wish to spend.

Even among his countrymen, Bill has encountered the notion that all vodkas are created equal, that you cannot distinguish French-made Grey Goose from a vicious rotgut.

In reality, it takes little expertise to distinguish Grey Goose from an impostor. Here is how you do it:

- Chill both bottles.
- When they reach the same temperature, sniff, then take a sip.
- If the vodka gives off no odor and tastes lighter than air, if it makes you feel like you could have drunk all night and still have asked for more, you have sipped a decent vodka.
- If the vodka gives off the odor of turpentine and tastes harsh and dry, like rubbing alcohol, yet still exhibits the sweet, cloying undertones of ethylene glycol, if one sip makes you feel like you may not be there to watch the sun rise over the ocean, you are drinking a rotgut. Halt the test. You will not be able to appreciate a decent vodka for at least six hours.

Alas, Grey Goose is a canard. After it's poured and consumed without a toast, Melsor brings up a half-forgotten scandal: "There was old Jewish man who told his lover—in bed—not to sleep with black people."

This sends Bill into mental fact-checking: Donald Sterling is the gentleman's name. He happened to own an NBA franchise. And he didn't say, "Don't sleep with them." He said, "Sleep with them if you want to, just don't be seen with them at my basketball games," or something like that.

This disgrace occurred in the spring of 2014. How could it possibly be so important in January 2017 that you would bring it up as Topic One in conversation with the son you haven't seen in twelve years?

Melsor has more to say: "Everyone shouted, racist, racist. But he was, so to say, in his own bed, with his own mistress—and she taped him!"

Grey Ruse—or is it Grey Russe—is vile, but at least it's cold. The conversation is turning vile, too, but it's better than anything that actually matters. As for Grey Russe, Bill decides that the moniker is unacceptably cute. He feels ashamed for having thought of it. Grey Ruse, on the other hand, is solid, accurate, appropriate. It will stay.

Bill knows what will come next: Melsor will develop the First Amendment argument, which holds that you have the inalienable right to say whatever you want as long as the band of your Jockey shorts is below your knees and you are cooling your heels, waiting for Viagra to kick in.

Bill knows that it's best to say nothing, and he makes a valiant effort to keep his mouth shut.

"Where is freedom of press when Jewish man can't say what he wants In! His! Bed! With! His! Lover! Where is, so to say, First Amendment to Constitution?"

Melsor is energized. He is the same he had been when he railed against the Soviets. Getting into a political argument with the father you have been avoiding for twelve years is never a good thing, but Bill is in it now.

"The First Amendment is where it's always been. It gives you a broad range of protections, which fully—yes, fully—extend to the right to be a racist asshole pig. Sterling's speech is fully protected," Bill interjects, still hoping that this will be a limited involvement.

This doesn't come out right. Too much confrontation too early. He will try to complete the argument and make the whole thing drop. He is trying to stick to the facts.

"Sterling controlled a government-regulated franchise, and

his contractual obligations included clauses that precluded expression of racist views. This was a licensure issue, a franchise issue, not a First Amendment issue. You can still tell your mistress whom to sleep and whom not to sleep with."

This is not great, either. Bill looks askance at Nella, who seems unperturbed. He likes this woman, sort of. She is unflappable. Perhaps Bill will be able to complete his argument, or his point of information, and the whole thing will go away.

"The same applies to your wife, or your boyfriend, or all of the above, as long as your bed is large enough and you don't own a basketball team."

"Donal'd Tramp was only candidate talking about this."

Melsor has difficulty with the name of the president-elect. Russian speakers run into brick walls when they encounter soft English Ts and rolling English Rs.

For some nuance-drenched reason, on the way out of Melsor's mouth, the T and R in "Trump" form a Harley-Davidson–like T-R-R, making the U slip off the saddle, becoming A-like—TR-R-A-MP.

The Russian mouth has less trouble with "Donald." But once you have a thing like Tramp, why stop, you might as well stick a soft sign behind the L. Make it a soft, rolling L. Make it "Donal'd."

"Your Donal'd Tramp paints with a broad brush," Bill replies. "That's just one of the things that's so scary about him."

At this instant, the reader should be reminded that by unpacking this exchange further, we do not endorse Bill's interpretations of events that unfold around him—and especially not his actions. Our role is to convey these events as they occur.

Bill possesses the insight to recognize the soft sign in "Donal'd" for something much greater than a term of endearment, an effort to make Tramp your own, to embrace, to adopt. To grasp this distinction fully, we might consider Nikolai Berdyaev, a Russian mystical philosopher. Being a mystic means caring greatly about small things for their potential to hide (and reveal) big things. His wackiness notwithstanding, Berdyaev explained the Russian revolution so much better than any earthbound colleague ever could.

Per Berdyaev, a Westerner is a creature of reason, a Russian a creature of faith. A Westerner rationally accepts contradictions. A Russian lets his soul do what it craves: worship. A Westerner studies Marx, critiques him. A Russian genuflects.

That soft sign after the *L* in "Donal'd" is a big thing, and Bill knows it. It channels the hugeness of Tramp. It is the Tramp Shekinah, the part of God that—sometimes, rarely—is rendered visible, embraceable even. Some mystics contended that Shekinah was the fuckable part of God, corporeally, literally—laugh not, or do. They say Moses did it.

In any case, now you have the man of the hour: ladies and gentlemen, give it up for Donal'd—with a soft sign—Tramp. Donal'd Tramp, Russified, made more dangerous through this metamorphosis of Russification.

When Bill was a child, in kindergarten in the USSR he learned songs about "Grandfather Lenin." He failed to let that little murderer of millions into his soul. Now, circa the summit of middle age, here in Florida, Donal'd Tramp is knocking on the same door.

As the words "Donal'd Tramp" roll off his tongue, the sound is so smooth, so organic, that even Bill craves a gulp of Grey Ruse straight from the bottle.

If you name a thing, you own it. If you un-name it, you unload it like a toxic asset, trample it, Donal'd Trample it. And for this reason, Donal'd Tramp trumps Donald Trump.

"I advise you get used to Donal'd Tramp, so to say."

Bill is in a fight now, dragged in, pissed at himself, unable to turn back: he is in no mood to be disarmed, won over, convinced—certainly not on this subject. He wants out of this conversation, out of this apartment, out of fucking Florida.

To gain control, Bill tries to do what all reporters do.

He asks a question: "I've been hearing a lot about 'political correctness' lately. I have no idea what it means."

"Not believing propaganda. Instead of saying that we are brothers, recognizing that some of us work and others, so to say, lazy."

"So, you want to crank up oppression, discrimination based on race, sex, religion, country of origin, sexual orientation—that sort of thing? Is this what you mean by rejection of political correctness?"

"And what do you, liberals, so to say, propose?"

"I find this bewildering, especially with your Donal'd Tramp, especially now, ten days before coronation. I live in an international city. It's diverse—please don't try to dismiss this as political correctness. It really *is* diverse. I notice that people differ from me, but I don't give it any thought. Ever. I don't know any other way to be."

"It's gone too far. It's not only black lives which matter. All lives matter, Ilya."

Bill tries to ignore the needling use of his birth name.

"I agree. All lives matter. I covered cops for years and loved it. But what you are referring to is actually complex, and the things you try to dismiss as political correctness are fundamental, things that were firmly in place before you and I set foot in this country. With Donal'd Tramp, I see the smoke screens that existed in Germany: the murder of Horst Wessel and the

Reichstag fire. I can see why your Putin would support your Tramp, but how can you, an immigrant—a Jew? That man is, plainly, a fascist."

"Not against us. Against Muslims, Mexicans. We don't even know how many refugees that Muslim let in."

This time, Bill stops himself. He doesn't ask: "Do you remember fleeing oppression? Do you remember being welcomed by America, not just the government, but the Maryland *Dzhuyka* that paid our rent and gave us subsistence money?" He takes another drink.

"Do you remember having once been a refugee?"

Bill looks up at Nella. Is she, too, to adapt the local lingo, a "Trampist"?

As their eyes meet, Nella takes another gulp of Grey Ruse and pronounces, more or less vacantly, as though repeating an axiom:

"Americans voted for Muslim foreigner. Twice!" she chimes in. "You not only break law—you break Constitution! Where else such things possible? Only in America!"

A Jew-Nazi—definitely. Bill is surrounded. He will have to learn not to respond to provocations.

"Finally, they elect normal white person," Nella agrees. "Obama didn't want to fight Muslims. Tramp will."

Ignoring this comment, as he must, Bill glances at two books on the coffee table. Pictures of Tramp as a much younger man stare at Bill from the book jackets. One is titled *Iskusstvo Sdelki*. The other is the English-language original, *The Art of the Deal*. These are, as far as Bill can tell, the only books in the house.

"Ya chitayu perevod beglo, a v nekotorykh momentakh smotryu v original," says Melsor after noticing that Bill has been looking at

the books. [I go through the translation rapidly, and then, in some cases, I look at the original.]

Melsor gulps down another shot of Grey Ruse and addresses Nella: *"Idi, vklyuchi."* [Go turn it on.]

Nella emits a deep sigh, downs her Grey Ruse, gets up, and leaves the dining room.

"Turn on what?" asks Bill.

"That thing," says Melsor, pointing at the scaffolding cradle outside the balcony. "There is machine on roof—generator."

"What generator?"

"For electricity. She knows what she does."

"What does a generator have to do with us?"

"It's already dark. We go for ride."

They stand on the balcony, looking south, at the lights of the high-rises, past the lights of the Diplomat, past the Grand Dux.

The balcony is narrow, three feet or so, not deep enough to put in a chaise *and* get past it. It's exposed, and tiles make it slippery. With his Florida phobia, Bill feels the need to touch the building's wall at all times.

Most of the balcony's length—twenty feet or so—faces east, overlooking the ocean dead-on, but a short dogleg—ten feet—winds around the building, facing south. It takes courage to get out there when the wind howls.

Of course, the moving scaffold could have been lowered to the balcony in order to scare Melsor.

Bill can see how someone would wish to attempt such a thing. Given what the two had been through—even during their protracted periods of no contact—he is able to sympathize with people who seek to oppress Melsor Yakovlevich Katzenelenbogen.

There is, of course, another plausible reason for the cradle to be where it is. The balcony on which Bill now stands could need work, defensibly, genuinely, structurally, perhaps even urgently. Why would it not need a little help after four decades of getting battered by salt and water?

Steel rods that support balconies—rebar—need to be treated with Teflon. If they aren't, they rust, become unstable, collapse. This process can take a long time or a short time, depending on the quality of rebar, the quality of concrete, and the levels of exposure. Bill had once or twice covered building collapses, and he knows that in the 1970s, when the Château was built, Teflon wasn't widely used to coat rebar. The crumbling, bulging layer of concrete is a symptom of rust that spreads beneath. In the worst-case scenario, a balcony can fold like origami beneath your weight. In a disintegrating building full of Bill's compatriots, this would be regarded as the natural order of things.

Bill believes momentarily that he feels the balcony move, but quickly realizes that it's the cradle, not the balcony, that's shifting in the wind. While Bill is leaning toward the building, his father stands in the middle of the balcony, not holding on to anything but his glass of Grey Ruse, like a Soviet sailor on deck. There is choppiness, sure, but he has seen worse. While Bill takes wide steps, his father takes almost no steps at all.

Looking down toward the ocean, with blasting wind and the moving scaffold cradle next to it, the balcony feels even more precarious than it looks.

A sound of what can be described as something similar to a motorcycle engine comes down from the roof.

"*Poyekhali,*" says Melsor. [Let's go.]

Where? Why? Bill sees no point in asking.

"*Poyekhali*" is never a neutral word.

This was, in fact, Yuri Gagarin's last word before he became the first man to be shot into space. Sure, it's a verb of motion, but the expression "fuck it" can be within the range of meaning of its translation. It follows "*poyekhali*" like spent rocket fuel.

Melsor downs his vodka, throws the plastic cup into the cradle, and, grabbing onto the railing, steps on a plastic chair, the sort that costs seven dollars at Costco. The chair's legs strain, bowlike. Melsor throws his right leg over the balcony, aiming to jump straight into the cradle.

The cradle moves outward, half a foot into the abyss, and with his left leg still anchored on the bowing plastic chair Melsor grabs onto the cradle's side, bringing it closer to the balcony. That done, he slides over the edge and smoothly shifts his feet to the bottom of the cradle.

"*Khorosha lyul'ka,*" he says. [A fine cradle.]

Bill's assigned function in this family, when he was in this family, when there was a family, was to accept reality no matter what it dragged in. And now here he is, clinging to the side of a building as his eighty-three-year-old father dangles in a cradle suspended from the roof by nothing but two crane-like gizmos and two taut cables.

"*Davay,*" says Melsor. The word is usually translated as "go."

Melsor's cradle slides outward, toward the stars, but he pushes on it, like an acrobat on a Russian swing, and the thing returns, slamming hard against the building, and loosening an undeterminable amount of material—concrete and aggregate—that falls to the ground seventeen floors below.

"*Yob tvoyu mat',*" says Melsor with what seems like just the right mixture of wonder and confidence. [Fuck your mother.] Melsor grabs the edge of the balcony and the edge of the cradle, uniting them in a vise grip.

"Davay," he repeats, and, cursing fate, Bill heeds the parental command. *"Poyekhali!"*

Suddenly, Nella appears on the balcony. In her hand, she holds a twelve-inch steel ruler, which she hands to Bill.

"For slice door," she says.

This makes sense on a preverbal, preintellectual level: if they hand you an item, you take it.

"Slice door . . . ," Bill repeats, accepting the ruler. "What *is* a slice door?"

"What is that?" Nella seems genuinely surprised by his ignorance. "Slice door? *Durak ty?*" [Are you a fool?]

She speaks with the sort of familiarity that his people acquire post-alcohol. Then she points to the sliding door of the balcony.

"This is slice door!" she announces. "It doesn't open inside or out. Understand?"

With that, she slides the door to the closed position.

"If they lock it, this will open it. You put steel ruler in where lock is and it open."

Why is Bill doing this? Does he not have a life of his own? Why does he follow this refusenik fraudster poet on what will surely be an illegal, idiotic venture that, assuming they return alive, could land both of them facing trespassing, reckless endangerment, breaking and entering, and God knows what other felony charges?

Melsor could certainly afford a lawyer, but presumably doesn't have one.

Bill already has a lawyer he can't afford.

Why do all the other geezers become normal geezers, slumping properly into their wheelchairs, slobbering, emitting random exclamations, when this, *his* geezer, is suspended in a cradle—make it a *lyul'ka,* because Russian words have a way of being better—swinging outward, toward the stars, grabbing onto the edge and beckoning—ordering—Bill to step off?

Fuck you, you corsair asshole bloodsucking prick, thinks Bill, but does as he is told, for he is, in his miserable Russian soul, a good boy.

The cradle shifts underfoot, Bill's body adjusts, and he grabs onto the sides. This is the only way to stay upright. Cradles are designed to allow a workman to reach through the sides. Being something other than balcony railings, they are almost completely open. And, yes, they shift in the wind. And let's suppose for a moment that you stumble in a *lyul'ka*. Nothing will keep you from falling through its side.

From the instant Bill sets his uncertain foot in the cradle, he feels only three things: nausea, fear, contempt. Make it four: bewilderment.

In an obscure short story, the great Mikhail Bulgakov used the designation *"krovavaya lepyoshka,"* literally, a bloody flatbread, to describe the hapless souls who fall from great heights. After more than five decades, would Bill now be reduced to a bloody flatbread? Would he join Zbig?

Bill knows that cradles spin out of control, and turn over, and fall, which means that anyone who rides in one without a climber's harness clipped on to an independent rope is, by definition, insane.

Bill stands in the cradle's dead center, trying to trick himself out of nausea, suppressing vomit, grabbing the *lyul'ka*'s sides with both hands. Melsor moves around freely, cursing, bending down, opening the door of what looks like a breaker box, presumably trying to find buttons that can be pushed, recklessly, Russianly, to test things out.

Obviously confused, he shouts to Nella, who has returned inside.

"It's on thick orange cable," she says in English. "Push button and it will go. You still not understand? *Tozhe mne . . .*"

It's a dismissive expression describing someone who may think he is a big deal, but is, in reality, a nothing. Clearly, Nella knows many things Melsor doesn't have a clue about.

Melsor pushes a button and the cradle jolts downward.

"Poyekhali nakonetz!" [Let's go at last!]

"Where are we going?" Bill shouts over the blasting wind.

"You will see. Don't shout. I hear."

The cradle is now under the balcony, which allows Bill to glance at its underside. It seems fine, except for the small, freshly knocked down doughnut-sized chunk of the balcony's edge, where the Melsor-bearing *lyul'ka* made impact a few minutes earlier.

"Why couldn't we just take an elevator?"

"They will see us in elevator."

"Wouldn't they see us, the people inside these apartments?"

"No. Person here is in Canada. He will not come back."

"What about under him?"

"Under him—dead, both. For sale. It will never sell."

"And beneath the dead?"

"Also for sale. Speculant. Lost shirt, so to say. In deep *zhopa*. Didn't know he stepped on shit. Under that we have good man, so to say, *nash chelovek*."

A *zhopa* is an ass. *Nash chelovek* is one of us. As their *lyul'ka* jerks downward past the bottom of the seventeenth-floor balcony, the father and son switch back to Russian.

"Russkiy?"

"Amerikanetz, no s nami idet." [An American, but marches with us.]

"A my kuda?" [Where are we going?]

"Etazhom nizhe Amerikantsa." [One floor below the American.]

"Trinadtsatyy?" [Thirteenth?]

"U nas net trinadtsatogo." [We don't have the thirteenth.]

Of course, how could there possibly be a thirteenth at the Château? At a lesser place, they have thirteenth. Here you speed directly from twelfth to fourteenth.

As their *lyul'ka* moves past the apartment of the hapless speculator, Bill switches on his phone's flashlight to examine the balcony's underside. It's pristine. No chips, no cracks, no bulges to suggest rusting steel and delaminating layers of concrete. These balconies are firmer than the sum of everything Bill has encountered in the course of his life.

A text from Gwen comes through.

"How is it?"

"So far, so fucked"

It feels good to hear from her. Feels like a broadcast from the Voice of America, a missive from the outside world. It feels good to see an English-language text, too. In Bill's life, English has always been the language of reason; Russian of insanity.

"Hang in there"

"Believe me, I'm hanging"

Bill resolves that if this excursion fails to produce two bloody Russian flatbreads and a story worthy of six o'clock news even in South Florida, he wouldn't worry about stepping on other people's balconies. They are, at least, an improvement over dangling in a *lyul'ka*.

He will try not to worry about being an accessory to a crime. Because, of course, a crime will be committed. Why else would Melsor Yakovlevich Katzenelenbogen be involved?

At least no state lines will be crossed.

Bill starts to feel more or less comfortable in the *lyul'ka*, examining the balconies as they creep by, lulled by the wind and his father's raving about the Château's criminal BOD.

His comfort is bolstered by the fact that they are at opposite sides of the *lyul'ka*, at least ten feet apart, a safe distance.

Gwen texts again, probably driving her bright yellow Remorse distractedly.

"What's your sense re: Zbig? Is it a book?"

"Dunno. Saw the spot of splat. Got nothing."

"Spot of Splat: SOS for short? How is your father?"

"Batshit. Talk later . . ."

Bill is studying the underside of the nominally fourteenth-floor balcony when he feels a cold steel object the size of a quarter press hard beneath his chin.

An old man's voice comes next: "Halt! Who goes there?"

Bill is in no position to respond as Melsor pushes the button, causing the cradle to stop with a jolt.

The elderly sentry adjusts the position of what Bill is now able to recognize as a machine gun.

"Oh, Johnny, it's I. Melsor. What are you doing with the cannon, Johnny?"

"Well, this is a pleasant surprise. Hello, Melsor. Thought someone was coming to rob my place or throw me out. No one rides these things at night."

"No, we just go past your place on way down."

"Okay, suit yourself. I still see shapes pretty good, even in the dark. There are two. If you are one of them, who is with you? Who do I have my gun on?"

"Guy on who you point your gun? He is my son."

"I thought you said you had no son."

"I sometimes don't, so to say. What have you? Kalashnikov?"

"Bushmaster XM15-E2S. The best."

"Automatic?" Melsor is in the rhythm of the conversation. Bill never knew his father had any knowledge of—let alone appreciation for—firearms. The Melsor he knew was at least somewhat interested in literature and his frauds were always nonviolent.

"Semi. Some people don't like semi. They want to spray all over the place."

"Right. You put on pants one leg first. You walk one step in a time. You fire gun one bullet in a time. Just pull trigger faster. What's the problem?"

"I know a guy who can convert it to automatic for no charge, as a favor, but I don't bother."

"Could you please get the muzzle away from my neck . . . Sir . . ."

"Certainly! Pleasure to meet you. What's your name?"

"Bill."

"Come on through, my friends."

"Not this fast. I want to hear your cannon. Shoot one round for me."

"Happy to oblige."

"Shoot into sea, Johnny, like you did when we drank vodka, one year ago."

"You aren't standing in front of me? I see okay by day, but not by night anymore."

"No. I am on right."

"And your son? Not directly in front of me?"

"No. He took step to left when you lowered gun. He ducked down right now."

"Don't want to take a chance on hitting the wrong person. My eyesight took a beating in the war, and it just keeps getting worse."

The old man points the semiautomatic in the direction of the ocean, toward the brightly lit contours of a cruise ship on the horizon.

The sound is muffled, not as loud as a shot should be. Perhaps Bill's hearing is to blame—the cumulative impact of high altitude and winds blasting into his ears.

"You killed shark."

"Yeah, funny, Melsor. Where you gentlemen heading?"

"Under you. To your friend."

"The Evil Dwarf? Help yourselves to the gun if you want. Might as well bump him off while you are at it."

"No thank you; not yet. He is not there. This is why we go."

"Oh, that's right, his sister died. He must be back in Buffalo planting her."

Melsor pushes the button and the *lyul'ka* lurches again. Bill doesn't panic. He clenches his teeth and grabs onto the *lyul'ka*'s railing. His nausea returns.

As they pass Johnny's balcony, Bill walks to the center of the *lyul'ka* to ask: *"Chto eto za muzhik?"* [Who was this?]

"That was Johnny Schwartz," Melsor shouts in response. "Good guy. He lied about his age to go to fight Hitler. He is almost ninety, has prostate cancer, is behind on special assessments. They want to throw him out to street. In Florida we have expression: 'Outlived his money.' "

"Where was he in the war?"

"He once said in Belgium. In 1944."

"The Battle of the Bulge?"

"Something in that spirit. But it wasn't bad until later. He stayed in the army till Germans surrendered."

The *lyul'ka* drops down to the level of the twelfth-floor balcony, slamming not-so-gently into its side, and releasing a few handfuls of concrete and aggregate.

"*Priyekhali,*" Melsor announces. [We've arrived.]

This is how it works: you say *poyekhali* when you set out. You say *priyekhali* when you arrive. Russian verbs of motion are a bridge of fools; they exist to torture students. The elder Katzenelenbogen grabs onto the balcony's railing and pulls the *lyul'ka* to its side.

"Do you have belt?"

Bill pulls off his belt and hands it to his father. The old man ties the *lyul'ka* to the balcony, then, grabbing the railing, rolls over, stepping onto a narrow iron chaise. Bill follows. His feet are now upon another man's property. He is here with no knowledge or authorization from the apartment's lawful owner. This constitutes a clear-cut case of criminal trespassing, or is it breaking and entering, a felony for sure, even in Florida. Knowing Melsor, it's not going to stop at this. What will he do next? Smash through the "slice" door? Break the windows? Douse the place with kerosene and set it on fire?

Honesty and ethical restraint were the two features that separated Bill's life from his father's. This was the order of things: the elder Katzenelenbogen defrauded the public. The younger Katzenelenbogen defended the public from people who intended to defraud it. By defending the public from his father, Bill also defended himself.

It's hard to characterize this as a win-win-win. Just as easily, it can be lose-lose-lose. What's Bill doing in this *lyul'ka*? Why is he trespassing on the balcony and why is he on the verge of breaking into an apartment of a man he doesn't know, a man who, by default, has to be more trustworthy than his father?

Is it the vodka?

He didn't have that much.

Is it the Florida sunshine?

He stayed in the shade, took cabs, wore his *W* baseball cap.

The profit motive?

He has nothing at stake, nothing to gain.

Boredom?

He has an investigation to conduct, and this, clearly, has nothing to do with that.

Not a single explanation holds water, leaving only one— maybe. One he isn't ready to admit.

Melsor slides the slice door open. It's unlocked. Why would it not be? There are no adjacent balconies. Who would possibly enter the twelfth-floor apartment from the outside? Under normally foreseeable circumstances, people don't dangle in *lyul'ki* with twelve-inch rulers in their pockets. This likely holds true even in buildings with substantial Russian populations.

The curtains in the apartment are thick and tightly drawn. While Melsor goes straight after the computers and the telephones, Bill—who has no agenda—looks around the apartment. It's indeed worth examining. A massive hutch decorated with large painted hearts exudes great greenness, a relic of Mitteleuropa by the Florida seaside. Usually these things are filled with small trinkets—thimbles, steins, boot-shaped cups painted in an array of nauseating colors.

The contents of this hutch are surprisingly restrained. There are three sets of finials one usually sees on Torah scrolls; six finials altogether, ranging in height from five to eight inches. Each is decorated with small silver bells.

Torah breastplates are leaning against the back of the hutch on the shelf below. There are five altogether.

Bill opens the door of the hutch to run his fingers over one of the breastplates. A chain is attached to it, waiting to be hung on a scroll that appears to have gone missing. An index finger is all you need to distinguish a genuine object from a fake. Bill doesn't know enough to determine the age, but his gut says mid-nineteenth century, maybe a bit older. You make these determinations by instinct, by touch. You run your finger over the breastplate's surface. He touches one of the breastplates— it is what it looks like. He couldn't prove it, but he is certain.

Behind one of the breastplates, he finds five small velvet bags. These are usually used to store tefillin, the phylacteries, basically two leather boxes containing small scrolls, with narrow belts attached. Bill picks up one of the bags. It feels a bit heavy. He stands in front of the breakfront, mesmerized. Opening the drawer, he finds kiddush cups, all of them in silver, all showing wear and oxidation. The drawer is deep. He sticks in his hand, making the cups part, and causing two to be displaced and fall overboard. There have to be at least a hundred.

In the other room, Melsor is cursing. He is done with whatever it is he set out to do.

Bill is half in shock when he and Melsor pile back into the cradle. Beyond apprehension, beyond fear, he can think of nothing other than the objects he has just touched, objects that spoke to him in a way that Zbig did not when he touched the Spot of Splat.

"Who lives there?"

"*Svoloch'.*"

That word again, wafting in Florida air, becoming one with the ecosystem, like filthy felt, like sewage pumping into Biscayne Bay.

"Is he a Judaica dealer?"

"No. Lawyer. He was, what's that word? Means *vypizzhen.*"

"Disbarred. Sort of."

"Disbarred. *Spasibo.* Now he steals from us."

"How did he happen to acquire this collection?"

"His wife got it from her father."

"Was he a rabbi?"

"No—Nazi. Did you take anything?"

"Of course not! How can this dwarf you describe . . . What's his name?"

"Greenstein."

"*Greenstein?* He's a Jew!"

"So? Fascists can be Jews. Why not?"

Bill considers his father's words.

"I suppose that's true. And it's becoming increasingly true by the day."

"After war, her father worked for Ford in Detroit. He had box of gold teeth under bed whole time after war. When he died, his daughter took teeth from box and melted them, sold broth, and bought this apartment."

"Broth?"

"Gold broth."

"You mean bullion?"

"Yes, bullion. Gold bullion. Not broth. This was in one of the times when oil was high, dollar low, and gold very, very high. Next they will melt silver, I guess."

The *lyul'ka* reaches Melsor's apartment balcony.

"*Priyekhali,*" Melsor announces. [We have arrived.]

Nella is still on the balcony, still smoking.

"Nu, postavili zhuchka vashego?" [Have you planted that bug of yours?]

"Da, batareyki na nedelyu khvatit." [There is enough battery for a week.]

"Nu tak bol'she i ne nado." [You don't need more than a week.]

"Why not?" asks Bill.

Would they need to perform this trick again? If he were honest with himself, Bill would have admitted to mixed feelings about that experiment in felonious conduct.

"In one week, we have election. Now we must know what he thinks, what he plans. Next week, it will not matter—unless you are federal prosecutor."

Bill goes into the kitchen and emerges with the bottle of Grey Ruse.

"Good idea," declares Nella, raising a glass. "You think correctly. Well brought up child."

"Za nas s vami i khuy s nimi," says Bill, raising his glass. [To all of us and fuck them.]

It's a traditional Soviet toast, which Bill appears to have missed more than he realized. He knows that the toast applies to the situation in which he now finds himself. He just doesn't yet know how.

After a long, drunken evening where not much of substance is discussed, Bill is told that he would be staying in the "other apartment," one that belongs to Nella and is used mostly as storage for her art business.

"You will take freight elevator, and if you run into anyone, which you will not, because they are all sleeping, you will not say a word in Russian."

"Do you think they are also bugging *you*?"

"No."

"How would you know?"

"They are soft. And also . . . you will not say to anyone that I am your father. Johnny Schwartz is okay—no one else! Don't answer questions. Tomorrow I will tell you more. We will meet at Broadwalk and talk in fundamentals."

Melsor's English seems to have improved since their conversation at the Kings County Supreme Court. You could sense that Katzenelenbogen the Elder is on the verge of experimenting with articles, sometimes definite, sometimes indefinite.

"The English word is 'boardwalk.'"

"We say 'Broadwalk.' It has no boards and is broad. *Shirokiy*."

"Well then . . ."

"You will walk out of Château at five forty-five A.M. Don't talk to anyone, and—this is very, very important—don't speak Russian. Give guards in booth angry look. You will pass Aquarius, Trump Tower Hollywood, and Wave. Turn right, and you will see Magnolia Terrace street. Five blocks from here exactly-exactly. Wait for me. I leave Château at six A.M., and we rendezvous at six ten. We will be on Broadwalk before these soft-bellied *shtetl gonif*s wake up."

Bill considers correcting his father's Yiddish—plural of *gonif* (crook) is *ganovim*, not *gonif*s—but thinks better of it. You could ask him how and why he knows this, but this will not be useful. Bill knows many things; usually, he has no idea how or why.

Perhaps the father and son Katzenelenbogen are still in competition. There is no fathomable reason to acknowledge it.

Isn't it better to just win?

7

AMBULETTE

Nella's one-bedroom apartment, located on the thirteenth floor passing for the fourteenth, is filled with canvases, all of them couch-sized, all of them stacked on the floor.

There are obligatory paintings of Paris cafés, of two-mast ships in the storm, multiple nauseating paintings of angels, paintings that blasphemously combine portraits of rich, or rich-enough, formerly Soviet Jews with works that—deservedly—hang at the Tretyakov Gallery in Moscow and the Hermitage in Saint Petersburg. You could see that this is the part of the business that moves. The canvases are all waiting to be packed and shipped.

In the bedroom, Bill finds a stack of paintings he actually considers intriguing. These are based on the erotic eighteenth-century poem *"Luka Mudischev,"* whose hero is endowed with a penis so large that it's lethal. This series of paintings is done with a straight face, with text reproduced on the canvases. Clearly, several artists were involved in painting this series, each of them bringing his own brand of naughtiness.

This was actually more than a mere wall hanging—it fits into Bill's definition of art. Drinking vodka with these painters would likely be as pleasurable as it would be suicidal.

After a self-guided tour of Gallery Nella, he spots a bottle of vodka on the kitchen counter—it's a super-cheap brand, in a plastic half-gallon bottle with a handle. This type of bottle is called a "handle," perhaps because it features a literal, physical handle, or perhaps to suggest that its consumer may be losing his grip. There is a dancing Cossack on the label. The stuff is called Kozachok, but it's made in Philadelphia.

Bill takes a sip from the bottle. In Russian, this manner of drinking is called "*iz gorla,*" from the neck.

The plastic bottleneck feels warm. Vodka at this point in the evening stops being about pleasure. It's an obligation, a compulsion, a *mitzvah* even.

He has no assignment, no deadline, no editor—just emptiness. If there is mystery in its infinity, it eludes him. This flavor of infinity is devoid of wonder. His hands long for purpose and a keyboard. He picks up a television clicker. There were screens in the newsroom, but someone else tended them. At home, he had no functional television set, having forsaken recreational use of the medium circa 1995.

The technology—or at least the number of buttons—now present in the clicker mystifies him. The thing is busier than his smartphone. Experimenting, Bill pushes a button near what looks like the front of the thing, causing the screen on the wall to light up. Good guess. The screen is split into sections, and the largest of these sections, on the left side, is displaying what seems to be a fragment of a television show.

It seems to be completely idiotic. It displays a coffin draped in black cloth. On top of it sits a pair of red, ultra-tall pumps, the kind that scream porn, or at least the kind that used to scream porn. He doesn't know any women who wear that sort of thing. Maybe Gwen would have, in her gonzo days, at Style. Or now, perhaps. He has no idea.

The show is called *Merry Widows*. Reality television, it's called, complete with "contestants" matching the dearth of shame and brains in pursuit of valuable prizes. He keeps track of that sort of thing when it gets filtered through *The New York Times* and *The New Yorker*. The show is a work in progress—coming soon. What could the prize be? A contract on the husband? Can't be. He is already dead. He had it coming.

He turns off the television set, steps out onto the balcony, walks up to its edge, and takes another gulp of Kozachok. It's room temperature, a solvent.

He looks at the lights of the South Florida coast. He owes Gwen a call. What's he to do, ask her how her day went? Pretend that they are a couple? They were together once, a decade ago, before her fraud. Does he have to confront her? Does she get to confront him back? Does everyone need to confront everyone else? Give it a break . . .

He did not come to South Florida to make peace with his father. No need for that. He had been to Miami before, report-ing stories, speaking at a conference—two of them, actually—and never did he consider calling Melsor.

Neither of them is gravely ill. Melsor has the powerful look of a geezer who will one day crumble like a mighty oak, obviating the need for peacemaking. It will be unforeseen, unless the state-ment above could be classified as foresight. Peace is overrated.

Bill peers over the railing.

"Jump," the impulse screams.

"Fuck you," he responds out loud.

A deep gulp of Kozachok from the plastic bottle . . .

This is nothing like hammering TBs at Martin's. He imagines the fall. He has seen the videos, watched obsessively for days, felt them beckon. How long is the fall? He grabs onto the railing, grasping, squeezing till pain sets in, till knuckles whiten. Is the free fall the point? Not yet, not to him. The edge is a state of consciousness, a state of being.

Will Kozachok give him the courage he lacks—the courage Zbig seems to have had, unless it was an accident? Is determination of the truth among the goals of an existential investigation? Is negation of the truth—exaltation—an even higher goal?

You can calculate the seconds, the fractions of seconds the drop takes—it's a simple formula; sixth-grade physics—but what of the feeling, Zbig's feeling? What secret of the universe did he come to grasp? Can words express his final knowledge?

The phone rings. It's Gwen. He lets it ring.

Bill sets up the cot near the stack of Luka Mudischev paintings. Stretched out fully dressed, he pops open his laptop, sets it on his chest, and searches for "BASE." Before, he looked at BASE jumping videos as he tried to fathom the idea of unencumbered flight. It was art, really. Now, he is considering chutes as something real, as equipment, as something that can be acquired and—yes—used.

Jumping with a parachute somehow seems easier than using a flight suit, but even jumps with chutes aren't recommended for people who haven't completed hundreds of skydiving jumps. Bill's number of jumps is zero, plus he has a complicated relationship with heights.

Stories he reads warn about extreme dangers and illegality (you have to trespass), which only eggs Bill on. Some say that even experienced skydivers need to work with mentors when they move on to BASE. Drunk and getting drunker, he is amassing information with the zeal of a science writer—his zeal.

He finds an info-graphic summarizing the causes of death of BASE jumpers, and he finds a cool epidemiology study of injuries, nice work by a Dr. Omer Mei Dan, an Israeli-born orthopedic surgeon who practices at the University of Colorado and BASE jumps a lot.

Of course, it makes sense that as a BASE jumper you face double jeopardy: slamming into the ground and slamming into the object you are jumping off. This is why a round chute used by skydivers isn't the thing you need. You need something called a "ram-air chute," a rectangular canopy that lets you maneuver.

Bill couldn't have done a better job of gathering information if he were sober, though if he were sober, he would have stopped short of pricing the chutes. New ones cost $3,000, give or take, but a used one can be picked up for $1,700, still way the fuck too much, considering Bill's financial handicap.

Also, sober, he wouldn't have called the seller in California, telling him that the chute should be packed and ready to use, and he wouldn't have used his *Washington Post* credit card or put down the Château as his mailing address.

It was a self-correcting problem though. Surely the card has been canceled and the charge will be declined.

A call comes in: it's Gwen.

Bill picks up.

"I've been thinking about you, worrying a little," she says.

"Good to hear your voice."

"How many years have we known each other?"

"Fifteen? A bit more, actually."

"I never thought of this before. All the Russians I know are named Alex. You are not really William, are you?"

"No. It's Ilya. I slapped on the *W* and the *M* when I was young and stupid."

"May I call you that?"

"I'll answer to anything."

"Nice name: Ilya. What does your father call you?"

"Nothing. He just says 'You,' and I respond. His wife is a 'you' when spoken to and a 'she' when spoken of. We don't use names in my family."

"Is this something Russian?"

"No, just something warped."

"Now, Ilya—this sounds good—your father, I imagine him as a tough gangster sort, muscular, lots of gold—Miami."

"You're closer than you know."

"What's his name—is it Alex?"

"Melsor, actually. Melsor Yakovlevich Katzenelenbogen."

"Which means . . ."

"Katzenelenbogen means 'cat's elbow' in German. There is a ton of spelling variations outside the Fatherland. No idea how the name became Jewish and why a cat's elbow and not, for example, a dog's."

"And his first name . . . Melsor?"

"It's an acronym: Marx, Engels, Lenin, Stalin, and the October Revolution. Children used to be slapped with ultra-patriotic names in the 1930s."

"Melsor . . ."

"He could just as easily have been named Elrad, as in electricity and radio, or Tractor, as in tractor. It's a remnant of his father's extreme Bolshevism."

"Why didn't he change his name here, like you did? A name like Mel would be less fraught. Or Alex."

"I asked him that years ago. He said the name Melsor makes him a monument. All Russian poets dream of monuments—Pushkin, Akhmatova, Vysotsky even. But Melsor is already a monument, many monuments, in fact. To totalitarianism, true, but they are monuments nonetheless."

"I look forward to meeting him in a few days. Will I?"

"Careful what you wish for, Gwen. There could be remorse involved."

They hang up eventually, and as Bill tosses on the cot, sweating, memories, dreams, reflections visit him. The most important of these stems from the Kings County Supreme Court.

Properly used, ambulettes are as benign as any other van with a driver. The fraud involving them is so simple that it might as well have been invented by Gogol:

You find a doctor to determine that a Mrs. Cohen is not well enough to take a regular taxi when she goes to her physical therapy appointments. Instead, she needs an ambulette. A bus costs two dollars; standard car service costs twenty dollars; an ambulette charges Medicaid sixty dollars or more.

The scheme works optimally when no one goes anywhere:

- Mrs. Cohen, the patient, gets ten dollars in cash from the ambulette service to stay at home, which she prefers to do anyway.

- The doctor gets ten dollars for prescribing the ride, and
- The ambulette fleet owner keeps forty dollars, which goes even further, because he doesn't own an ambulette and employs no driver.

Some foolhardy operators own physical ambulettes, which invites trouble, because a physical ambulette can be followed by undercover investigators, even reporters.

Melsor's metaphysical—nonexistant—flock of ambulettes was not vulnerable to such primitive surveillance. Alas, when his reckless competitors were caught, they ratted out Melsor.

He was indicted on May 1, 2001, the day he subsequently called "My Personal Holocaust."

During a court hearing, the situation was compounded by the fact that the lead prosecutor was Bill's former colleague from *The Duke Chronicle,* the student newspaper. The dude's name was Jon Abramowitz.

This connection came to light in the hallway, when the prosecutor greeted the son of the accused with a friendly shout, "Hey, Bill, dude, what the fuck?"

Recognition caused Bill to roll his eyes and the prosecutor to chuckle.

"I didn't know you were Russian," he said, and Bill chose not to respond.

The elder Katzenelenbogen observed this exchange from his wheelchair. Things moved beyond awful when Melsor demanded that Bill do two things in the name of the family ties. Bill was expected to:

- Explain some key points to the prosecutor as part of an off-the-record "gentlemen's conversation," and

- Hang on to a suitcase stuffed with hundred-dollar bills until the matter blows over.

Bill said no and no.

How could Melsor even consider dragging his son—a man whose career is grounded in honesty—into the sewer that he inhabited?

"Predatel'!" Melsor shouted in Russian from the wheelchair pushed by his second wife, the one who stayed a few months and whom Bill didn't get to know. [Traitor!]

"Sorry you feel this way," said Bill in English, and left for Washington before the trial concluded.

This was a distasteful event. Even without obstruction of justice, prosecution was halfhearted, and most of the already reduced charges were tossed out by the judge, who cited the defendant's courage and past contribution to the struggle for human rights. In addition to being wheelchair-bound, Melsor claimed—through his attorney, of course—that he engaged in the ambulette fraud in order to pay off the medical bills incurred when his wife was dying of breast cancer. This was technically correct.

The penalty was irrelevant. Melsor Yakovlevich Katzenelenbogen had to promise to refrain from conducting unsupervised business with Medicaid for five years. Prosecution must have realized that Melsor's stash was so well hidden that they saw no point in looking for it. Does anyone care about fraud perpetrated by an immigrant who ambulates in a wheelchair and respires with the help of an oxygen tank the size of a small WWI torpedo?

Melsor wasn't "disgorged."

The day after the verdict, Melsor's health improved. He

junked the wheelchair, returned the rented oxygen tank, and bought a condo in Florida.

Since Melsor gave up his crooked-doctor accomplices—including the asshole whom Bill blamed for killing his mother—the government pressed the sexier charge of conspiracy against the docs who prescribed the ambulette rides in exchange for kickbacks.

The doctors were disgorged, lost their licenses, and the most obnoxious member of what was described as a "ring" may still be a guest of the federal government.

The *New York Times* reporter who broke the story about the ambulette fraud—Gardiner Harris—was actually a friend of Bill's, or so Bill thought.

Though the two spoke often, Gardiner disappeared for a few months, but on the day the story on the ambulette caper ran, Gardiner sent Bill a two-word e-mail: "Sorry dude."

Bill responded with a one-word e-mail: "fucker."

Gardiner wrote the story with the flourishes intended to get you on the front page. His tone sucked, too. He was taking an elitist, detached posture, gently ridiculing immigrants as they fight for survival.

Fortunately, the initial story ended up on page eighteen. The final story—the trial—was buried even deeper.

Bill gets up from the cot, undresses, and, stretching out, utters a phrase his father will neither hear nor comprehend:

"I am fine, Dad. My career, which meant everything to me,

is completely, irrevocably over. I am fifty-two years old. I have no personal life to speak of, and I am oh-so-close to the edge."

At this point, Bill switches to Russian: *"Plokho mne, okh khudo."* [It's tough, very much so.]

In English, he adds:

"Thank you for asking, you narcissistic prick."

8

ART OF DEAL

It would be incorrect to describe Bill's morning-after condition as chipper. On the morning of January 12, his eyes are puffy and, should he look in the mirror, he would notice that they are bloodshot as well.

The back pain is intense, a reminder of his encounter with a crooked cane.

At dawn, Bill struggles to power through these challenges and climb out of bed.

His fashion choices that morning: a pair of cargo shorts and a bike jersey. He doesn't own a bike anymore, but he likes having three massive pockets at the small of his back.

Stumbling over paintings, he makes his way out the door, taking a freight elevator. Bill is never late. Usually, he is a little early.

He exits through the valet parking area, the place closed off with the Dumpsters.

Florida is bathing the street with entirely too much light for his hung-over, uncaffeinated comfort. The rounded curb is so white that the rays it reflects are wreaking havoc directly in the center of his cranium. Mrs. Kisel' is, of course, gone from the curb, as are her bags and her furniture. The *Dzhuyka* wan with the driver from mental health must have made a curbside pickup.

Surely her stuff is resting in the Dumpsters. Bill is so certain that he resists his natural urge to climb up and check.

At the guard's booth on the corner of the building, Bill sees the same Slavic-looking man he saw the day before. He looks up as Bill gives him his quasi-military salute.

"Poor, pathetic fucker," Bill says to himself.

Turning right on Ocean Drive, Bill heads toward the "Broadwalk."

His back pain is persistent, dull. Why is he getting himself sucked into someone else's intrigue? Is he so desperate for parental approval? Is he, at age fifty-two, a good boy? As a reporter, Bill knew where to draw the line, even when family members were involved. But now, as a God-knows-what, he is God-knows-where, and this state of affairs somehow seems appropriate. He has what he deserves.

Bill stands on the appointed street corner, checking his e-mail. Nothing even remotely interesting. Flacks pitching stories.

He returns the phone to the back pocket of his bike jersey. His right arm lingers atop the bruises on the impacted spinal disk and beneath his shoulder blade.

Ocean Drive is coming alive with buses and taxis. Flowers he doesn't know the names of are in bloom. Bill looks up, marveling at the rapidly approaching object on the horizon. This is

Melsor. He remembers that the man always hopped up slightly when he stepped on his left foot. It's the signature Melsor hop. A thousand years earlier, when they were a family, before emigration, before things went completely, spectacularly to shit, Bill's mother teased Melsor over that hop and even tried to reeducate him.

He never learned to walk like a human, and, if anything, at eighty-three, his hop is more pronounced, faster, higher, arthritically automatic.

"Fucker," says Bill, watching his father approach.

Again, no handshake, just a nod.

"I walk fastly. If you can't keep up, we talk later."

"Good morning."

"Speak English. I don't have practice here, except reading. I need English for, so to say, *paskvils*. I don't want to slow. You can wait in café, I don't know where there is one."

"No problem keeping up."

It's a lie. He is keeping up, but this pace is unnatural, startling, faster than a walk, slower than a run, a geriatric marathon.

"Nella says Roza Kisel' hit you across back yesterday?"

"I am told it's my own fault."

"In Florida, you don't slow down and yawn. In Florida, you have to be assertive, because if you are not, someone will hit you across back."

"That's what I hear."

"You are guilty yourself."

Melsor didn't always require the underpinnings of reality, but there were times when said underpinnings found him.

His campaign against the Soviets—which resulted in the family's emigration—was, without doubt, based on a solid ethical foundation. And the ambulette scam, criminal though it was, produced results. Ill-gotten, but tangible, quantifiable, concealable, probably not bankable, but obviously undisgorgeable.

The previous night's journey on the moving scaffold, though unsafe and criminal, didn't result in deaths or arrests. Melsor Yakovlevich Katzenelenbogen was easily underestimated, and from this his power stemmed.

Bill had never misrepresented himself to a source, never broken into an apartment in search of clues, never hacked into anyone's computer system. But that was Bill on his own turf—the solid matter of his own creation. Now the turf is his father's, and on Planet Melsor the laws of physics are not the same. The laws of economics and especially ethics aren't the same, either.

They walk past a cluster of motels, past a parking lot, toward what appears to be the promised Broadwalk.

"Are you still writing poetry?" Bill asks, trying to be civil.

"Yes, but only for political purpose."

"About your Donal'd Tramp?"

"About *svolochi* on condo board. For now."

"Poetry about the condo board?"

"Why not? I wrote about Communists . . ."

"Are you publishing?"

"Yes, on Web site, stihi.ru, and in *Machta*."

Stihi is poetry. Has to be a Web site for poets, amateur and professional. *Machta* is a mast, the thing on a sailboat.

"*Machta* is a local Russian newspaper, I presume?"

"Shopper. They have ads for Russian stores, doctors, lawyers.

They don't pay anything, but they publish everything, and everyone reads it."

"It's okay. The First Amendment applies, you are fully protected."

Bill looks up at a cluster of aging high-rises. Scaffolding cradles hang on two of them. Bill considers them with a quiet sense of achievement.

"I will give you poem to translate. I brought it. You can translate on back of same page when I go to bathroom."

"Sounds reasonable."

"I have to put it on leaflet today."

There is a dune to their right. It's 7 A.M.—too early for bathers and even some runners.

The sidewalk shifts to the left, and the father and son walk past a rack of rental bikes and encounter a low fence on the ocean side.

"I walk from mezuzah to mezuzah."

There is a presumption—an erroneous one—that Bill grasps the meaning of walking from mezuzah to mezuzah.

Melsor walks up to a wire-mesh fence, touching the back of a rotting fence post and proceeding to kiss his middle and index fingers. The act of touching and finger-kissing has the look of a cultist sex act, a mechanistic, ritualistic observance, as far from passion as you can get.

"From mezuzah to mezuzah, two and half miles, what I have walked is one mile, so it's seven there and back."

Bill doesn't know what to make of this, other than that someone—probably a black hat—had secretly attached the mezuzah, a small tube containing a Hebrew scroll, to the back of a fence post.

Why anyone would do that is beyond Bill's ability to comprehend. A two-quarters Jew, he isn't observant. But in places where he often found himself—Northwest D.C., Bethesda, Maryland—a mezuzah is standard equipment.

Bill can see how one would nail the thing to the doorpost. He can even see the rationale for nailing it to a gate leading to a Jewish home. But the idea of affixing a mezuzah surreptitiously to the entryway of a public park constitutes a secret, even mystical, incursion on a secular public space, an act of kabbalistic expansionism. What happened to separation of church and state? What happened to the distinction between yours and mine? Fuck that, what about the distinction between you and me? Why would someone like Melsor—a man who owns no indoor mezuzah and has no idea what is written on the scroll that goes inside it—(a) be cognizant of the secret outdoor mezuzah and (b) feel the need to touch said mezuzah?

Observing Melsor kiss his own hand doesn't surprise Bill. Poets are prone to such conduct. Bill is gathering the courage to ask his father the questions he intended to ask him for decades—at least three, perhaps as many as five.

"I think of poets as people who suffer—a lot. But you don't suffer at all."

He is making a path for his ultimate question: Hey, Dad, how do you reconcile being a poet with committing fraud? This is rich in subtext: just because New York State and the feds didn't have the *beytsim* to go after you all the way makes you an unconvicted felon, guilty as sin, but, for some absurd reason—i.e., unjustly—free and insulated from consequences of your felonious actions.

Does Bill want to see his father behind bars? What kind of idiotic question is that? Yes, of course, he does—yes!

"Ya sebe ne vrag." [I am not an enemy to myself.]

Then in English:

"I make enemies to suffer."

"What about the things you did that were of, shall we say, disputed legality?"

"After your mother died, I had no choice. I had debt, and that doctor gave me excellent opportunity. I took it."

"Did you like doing what you did?"

"I did it well—and money was the best."

"I can see that."

"Are you specialist in insurance?"

Bill responds with a nod. Insurance is gambling and gambling can be a crime. The rest is regulation, law, procedure. A reporter who doesn't understand insurance well enough to love it is not truly a reporter.

"Imagine you buy insurance for apartment. Then you walk out and don't lock your front door, and thief comes in and takes your new Samsung television. Will insurance give you money back for it?"

"I think it will. You insure against stupid shit like forgetting to lock the door."

"Okay, maybe, but it absolutely shouldn't pay in this situation!"

"Why not?"

"Because you commit—tributary negligence."

"Contributory negligence."

"Yes. If you don't protect valuables and someone takes them, is that stealing?"

"Yes."

"Taking Samsung from unlocked apartment is same as taking garbage from trash can."

"Are you arguing that Medicare and Medicaid assets are, in effect, abandoned property?"

"Yes. Government commit tributary negligence."

People are starting to come out on the Broadwalk.

They walk in groups of three or four, with the majority of groups speaking Russian and a few speaking English. All the solitary walkers speak loudly into their cell phones. Bill looks into their faces. Regardless of the language they speak, all the passersby exhibit a similar range of scowls. Some are glum, others angry. A few appear to be only mildly disaffected. Bill keeps looking for smiles, but sees none. Perhaps happy idiots are destined to stay in cold climes, in subsidized housing. This form of retirement, these modes of alienation are the provenance of the chosen few—the best of the best.

"I stop at Margarita Will. They have bathroom."

"Margaritaville?"

"Yes. You need to go?"

"No, but thanks for asking."

Melsor reaches into his pocket, produces a crumpled piece of paper, and hands it to Bill.

"Here. Translate. I will be long time. You have pen?"

"Always."

Though not a poet, Bill cares deeply about poetry, especially Russian poetry. Alas, Melsor's poem has a certain slapped-together propaganda look, a bubbling brew of threats and innuendo. Does he actually expect Bill to *translate* it? Does it need to exist in English? Had that thing been actually good, Bill would have been honored to spend the time, deciding whether to preserve the meter, the rhyme, or the meaning.

As a teenager in America, he was once forced to hand-print his father's CV. The Katzenelenbogens didn't yet own a Latin-script typewriter. He remembers being strong-armed to translate court filings, business letters, film scripts—Melsor called them "scenaries," from the Russian word *scenarii*. There was a time when Melsor penned television commercials, and Bill's attempts to convince him that no one anywhere would have any use for this work were met with commands to shut up and write.

"Yaytsa kuritsu ne uchat," Melsor said at that time. [Eggs do not teach a chicken.]

Sometimes Bill executed translations while holding his nose. This was expected of him, ordered really. He had no choice. Is it any surprise that being relegated to service as his father's writing tool made Bill's Inner Child exceedingly angry?

Perhaps it was this upbringing that made Bill the reporter he was. He was not an obsessive broomstick-armed pursuer of *the truth*. He was an obsessive broomstick-armed pursuer of *reality*, which, of course, constitutes a target even more fundamental.

If you want to fill the world with guys like Bill, make more guys like Melsor.

Melsor's propaganda screed could be given its due in the exact time it took Melsor to work his eighty-three-year-old prostate. He sends a copy to Melsor, and, for the hell of it, a blind copy to Gwen.

"You finished?"

"It's in your e-mail."

"Give me original."

Melsor takes the paper and stuffs it in the pocket of his shorts. Taking the translation as his due, he sees no reason to say thank you.

"Tell me about the demographics of your Château."

"Half Russian. Half American."

"All Jews?"

"About ninety-five percents."

"Okay. They, I mean, you, hate each other?"

"*We* don't hate Americans. They hate *us*—zoologically."

"Why would anyone hate us? We are such nice, trusting, honest, sincere, easygoing people . . ."

"We are completely different people. We go on Broadwalk in early morning, they sit in their units and read newspaper. In afternoon, we swim in ocean, they don't swim at all. They sit near swimming pool under umbrella, smeared with lotions. We are brown. They are completely white."

"You stay away from the pool completely?"

"Usually, but when we use pool we jump in."

"Different esthetics, too?"

"They say we want things done cheap."

Melsor deliberately stretches out the word "cheap," making it sound more like "che-e-e-ep," with an upward inflection.

"They say Russians want things chip-chip-chip. They shout at us when we speak at North Pool: 'This is public space—speak Russian in your unit.'"

"What about this Johnny Schwartz, of the Battle of the Bulge, the one who almost blew me away with his Bushmaster? He is American."

"Yes, he is with Russians. He has no money. His unit is almost in foreclosure."

"It's a porous divide then."

"He is exception. Everything else is rule."

"Do the Americans have more money than the Russians?"

"No. We have about same. Look at foreclosures list: half Russians, half Americans."

"Interesting."

Lists of foreclosures are the sort of thing Bill would seek out as well. His geezer is many things, but stupid he is not.

"In a week, we have election. Future of Château will be decided."

"Seems fitting. We just decided our country's future."

"That was good, with Donal'd Tramp. Except our situation is completely different."

"Hmmm. What's the problem here?"

"Special assessments. BOD want to spend nineteen millions more to knock down balconies. Our balconies are excellent!"

"So why knock them down?"

"Because of *otkat*. What's English word?"

"Kickback."

"If you are on BOD and support them, ICII give you three-year lease on Lexus."

"What's ICII?"

"I call them ISIS. They are construction contractor."

"How does it work?"

"BOD has five people. You need three members to win."

"I saw that in the *paskvil*: something about having two members in one's pocket."

"Our ruling block is led Greenstein, whose apartment you saw yesterday."

"Greenstein is the board president?"

"No! Greenstein is *vice* president. He is too smart to be president. Nobody wants to be president. President signs all papers. If there is forensic audit, he goes to prison. You take biggest idiot you have and make him president. If he is crazy, they can't persecute him, they can't disgorge him. Woman who hitted you on back was for two terms president."

"So whom does Greenstein have in his pocket?"

"Two Russian guys: Roytman and Kushman."

"Greenstein is American, and Roytman and Kushman Russians?"

"Yes."

"So it's not exactly broken along Russian-American lines?"

"It's more about kickbacks, and Americans like *otkaty* as much as we. They vote: start to break parking lot. They break parking lot, then they don't finish, and go on to break South Pool, then, after that's broken, they will break North Pool."

"Don't they get permits?"

"No."

"Are there deadlines specified in the contracts?"

"Clever boy. They have deadline, but contracts are given as change-orders to ISIS. In this way, there are no competition bids."

"I see . . ."

"You add one year and one year and one year, and it becomes accumulative."

"You could sue, I suppose. You've sued people before, God knows, you know how."

"I sue only on contengincy."

"Contingency?"

"First meeting is always free. One lawyer, old Jewish man, explained to me: 'You could sue. You could get lawyer, not on contengincy, to argue that it is violation of Florida law and Declaration of Condominium.'"

"Okay."

"Yes, and if I lose, I will have to pay for my lawyer *and* condo board lawyer. And if I win, it's even worse. If I win, judge will say: 'Yes, I agree, condo board violate Florida statue, shame on you, break up what you built and make it the way it was. What condo board did is very, very bad, but penalty is nothing.' So, it cost us to build, then it cost us to destroy, then it cost us to build again. Judge will not tell you to fire contractor. So, if I win once and ISIS win three times: they build, they demolition, they build again!"

"Does anyone actually *like* your BOD?"

"Widows."

"Why widows?"

"Their husbands left them more money than they have brains to know what to do with."

"Is there anything you can do?"

"I run for BOD right now."

"Do you stand a chance?"

"I think I may . . . It will take miracle, but I, so to say, believe in miracles."

They walk in silence for a few minutes, passing a mixture of eateries and motels.

They pass a building that looks mildly Italianate in that Las Vegas sort of way, then they enter what looks like a park, complete with low trees.

"They have two mezuzahs here," says Melsor, stepping off the path and transferring kisses to both.

Bill toys with the idea of reminding the old man that he is half Armenian, but thinks better of it. If Melsor self-identifies as a Jew, a Jew he is. Bill self-identifies as (a) a Homo sapiens,

(b) a small-d democrat, and only then (c) culturally a Jew. You don't have to be born Jewish to be the kind of Jew Bill is.

"I read Donal'd Tramp's memoirs, *Art of Deal*. He is philosopher—people don't understand. I want you to see what he writes."

He pulls out a phone and hands it to Bill.

"Make it bigger. I took picture for you."

Bill pushes apart the words on a photo of page sixty-three of *The Art of the Deal*:

"Money was never a big motivation for me, except as a way to keep score. The real excitement is playing the game . . . If you ask me exactly what the deals I am about to describe all add up to in the end, I am not sure I have a very good answer. Except that I've had a very good time making them."

"I am happy for him, less so for this country . . ."

"They don't like him in Washington—or Hollywood. Not this Hollywood; other Hollywood."

"But they like him in Moscow well enough. I am afraid we've just elected a Russian agent to the White House."

"In White House, he replaces agent of International Islam! Putin did right thing. He helped Tramp—yes, but he didn't make up anything. He didn't forger letters from our fool Debbie Wasserman Schultz, my congresswoman, so to say. He knows how to do business."

"True, he wants Crimea, he takes Crimea. He wants Washington, he takes Washington."

"You are probably one of people who call him tug."

"True, I have, on occasion, called him a thug."

"You can say Tramp is tug, Tramp is crazy, Tramp is stupid, Tramp is narcissist, Tramp is fascist, but if you read him with open mind, he is like Albert Camus. If you want to understand me someday, you should read Tramp."

"I didn't cover this election. I haven't met any Trump supporters—until now. No one I know voted for him, of course. Most of us are in mourning for our country."

"All your friends have been to college in America. All professors are leftists. In November, this country was saved by people who didn't have this, so to say, education. They didn't learn political correctness."

"I am grateful."

"Common sense must always beat political correctness."

"You were once a leftist professor; remember?"

"That was in Moscow."

"Yes."

"In Moscow I was for capitalism. Communists were on right. That put me on left."

"The world turned around for you?"

"Tramp reminds me of me. I didn't believe it was impossible to leave Soviet Union, and we left Soviet Union. He didn't believe it was impossible to become president, and he became president."

The walk ends with Bill doing something he hasn't done before, even as a teenager: he asks Melsor for the car keys. (When he was young, the family didn't own a car.)

As Melsor hands him a fat key to a Toyota Prius, Bill reminds himself that upon return to D.C. he really should obtain a valid driver's license.

9

GUCCI

The stroll on the Broadwalk is refreshing: seven miles at a brisk pace is more than Bill would do at home.

Upon reaching the Château (they return separately, as per his father's instructions), Bill needs to remind himself why he came to Florida in the first place.

At the apartment, he clicks on the 911 recording describing Zbig's hard landing at the Grand Dux. He tries to focus, which first and foremost entails recapturing the emotional component of focus. Bill does have emotions. They are slow, granted, but they are present.

He looks through the list of contacts on the iPhone, only to realize that he doesn't have Zbig's home number. He calls the cell phone, feeling odd, knowing that he is calling a dead man.

What is that Hindu custom of wives killing themselves to be cremated with their husbands? The Brits didn't appreciate that custom when they ruled India. Was he expecting that Pani Consuela Ramirez-Wronska would kill herself to be cremated alongside Zbig? He is building up to another absurdist concept: Should cell phones be cremated with their owners?

He dials and gets a recording. Not Zbig's voice, but standardized call-has-been-forwarded shit from the phone company. He calls Zbig's office, but also gets the-number-you-have-dialed-has-been-disconnected.

The White Pages offer nothing of value. Bill decides to find the house by memory. He hasn't been there for seven years, but he remembers the style as Bauhaus-on-Acid. The place was white. There seemed to be a hot tub on the terrace, and a view of Miami.

The Prius prances silently southward on Ocean Drive, Bill takes in the peninsularity of the place. It's predominantly north/south; no east/westness of any significance. If you are unable to find a house on so thin a grid, you are, as Mr. Trump might say, a loser.

Bill turns left, then, through the windshield, silently takes stock of new construction, the old placeholder buildings, the dilapidated motels, the ultra-tall high-rises for the ultra-rich.

He has difficulty recognizing Lapidus's Fontainebleau Hotel, the landmark of landmarks. There is a tower next to it. Why? The place looks expanded, bifurcated. Has the stairway to nowhere survived this desecration? Bill has never been inside; never got around to it. Too late now.

Continuing his southward trek, he starts to encounter the beautiful, more modest Art Deco structures, a Bauhaus haven, painted in shades of coral and chartreuse green. The Prius seems to know what to do, drifting silently past the base of the viaduct to Miami, then on to the roads that hug the eastern shore of Biscayne Bay.

The place is in a gated community, because of course.

Bill shows his D.C. press pass, and the guard surprises him by waving him through.

Inside, he notes a cacophony of architectural styles, from genuine Spanish Colonial mansions, to Disneyized Spanish Colonial, to porno-Italianate, to Narco Deco, to Deco Proper, to Last Wednesday's Mish-Mosh with an Obscene Fucking Roofline. Bill is looking for Bauhaus-on-Acid.

He follows his instincts as impressionistically as he can, but this gets him nowhere. The only house that seems vaguely familiar is painted a light shade of green. It has to be the wrong place, because Zbig's house was definitely, aggressively white.

A text announces itself. It's from Lena, the ex-wife, who is technically his current wife:

"A REMINDER: The separation agreement unambiguously stipulates that you are responsible for paying all the fees associated with the final divorce proceedings. I know you don't like your lawyer, but my lawyer agreed to complete this for $2,500— flat fee. If this is agreeable, please make a wire transfer to me ASAP and I will disburse it downstream."

Lena hasn't bothered Bill for some weeks. Lots of people stay separated for years, decades even, not because they hope to reunite, but because they can't get around to spreading the ashes. Why is she bothering him now? What changed? Maybe she heard about his firing and wants to make sure that she gets the last—albeit nonexistent—$2,500? What should he tell her?

He will deal with this later.

He looks for phone company trucks—with the right story those guys might give you the address—but none can be found. Finally, he decides to find a house—any house in the approximate neighborhood—knock on the door, and act lost. This trick works only with houses that don't have servants who open doors. If you chance upon a friendly, ditzy busybody, you will get the help you need.

Now, Bill is looking for cars and license plates. Not New York. Not New Jersey. Not Maryland. Maybe Virginia, people are friendlier in Virginia. He spots Kansas—perfect! A Cadillac Escalade, big enough for grandchildren. Beige.

The house is new. It displays no identifiable architectural style other than rich. The place is a little smaller than the neighborhood average—not large enough to employ a butler. It's still worth something in the millions, of course; Bill has no way of telling how many. The door is painted turquoise—not a Florida shade, but friendly to a fault. Bill spots an oversized mezuzah. Colorful, Israeli.

A trim, petite woman in her seventies opens the door.

"I am looking for . . . ," Bill begins, but the woman interrupts. *"Ya ne govoryu po-angliyski,"* she responds in Russian.

Even better. Switching to Russian, Bill tells a version of the truth: he is lost, looking for the house of his friend Zbig Wronski.

"Tot chto razbilsya?" asks the woman. [The one who fell to his death?]

Again, Bill tells the truth, and the woman points him to the greenish house he remembered as white.

He doesn't need to wonder what a Russian-speaking older woman is doing at a Miami Beach mansion with an Escalade with Kansas plates. In twenty-first-century America this question is absurd. Is it not possible that her son—or daughter—had purchased green cards for the entire family by investing $500,000 or more in a U.S. company and creating jobs? Can anyone suggest a better method for laundering money than, say, buying into production of alternative fuels in America's heartland, or building high-rises in Hollywood? And if you have a few gold bars to spare after that, why not buy a mansion?

There is no answer at Zbig's house. Perhaps Consuela Ramirez-Wronska has decamped for Rio or moved in with a lover or lovers. Consuela is Brazilian, a former model who posed in and out of swimsuits. Bill met her only once, the last time he saw Zbig. While he tried to strike a conversation, she sat silently staring into her drink and her salad, running out the clock.

As he returns to what he now knows is the right house, Bill vows never to doubt his wondrous combination of memory and instinct. Has he not become a sleuth of air, a marathoner of clouds? Inspector Luftmensch!

After ringing the bell repeatedly, Bill looks in the window, seeing a lot of modern white Italian stuff. No trace of humans. Heading back to the car, in front of the garage, he spots a large box with the words "Salvation A." written with a black marker on its side. The box is hard-sided cardboard, probably from a light fixture.

Bill opens a flap to realize that he is staring at the sole of a loafer. The rest of the box is filled with men's clothes. He places the box in the back of his father's Prius and drives off.

Under normal circumstances, he would take Collins Avenue, also known as US-1, and keep going till the Château shows up on his right.

This time, he feels the urgency to get the hell out of there and takes I-195—the viaduct—to I-95.

As he heads back, Bill glances at a billboard in the vicinity of the I-95 North ramp.

A billboard-sized doctor in a white coat, looks handsome, professional. A stethoscope around his neck attests to his goodness, or at least legitimacy. The doctor is on the corner, superimposed on a photo of a beautiful bikini-bottom-clad woman on white Florida sand. She looks up, smiling, exposing her white teeth and, to a lesser extent, her breasts. But the focus of the photo is the woman's behind.

The question, posed in massive block letters: "ARE YOU PERFECT THERE?"

A red starlike shape provides an addendum: "Make No Payment till August!"

The doctor is broad-shouldered, handsome. His facial features are broad, Slavic, familiar. His name is Zbignew Wronski, MD. The woman looks familiar, too. Her name is Consuela Ramirez-Wronska.

Meanwhile, at the Château, all three elevators display a new *paskvil'*, titled "Ode to Condo Board on the Occasion of Upcoming Election."

In this *paskvil'*, the English and Russian texts are displayed side by side:

Губернатор Вам не страшен,
Президент Вам нипочем,
Здесь миллионные расстраты
Поощряют Лексусом.

Во Флоридском нашем кондо
Невозможно стало жить.

Наводнение в Мейн Лобби,
Исколеченный Сауф Пул.

Но проделкам Вашим наглым,
Верьте мне, пришел конец!
Да, приехал гость желанный—
Федеральный прокурор!

Будет здесь 'фарензик одит,'
Мы вернем свое добро.
Не забудьте Вазелинчик
Захватить с собой в тюрьму.

You don't fear Florida Governor,
And the President, to boot.
Squander millions, and as kickback,
Get a prepaid Lexus lease.

There's no room for joy and laughter
In our beautiful Château.
See the flooding in Main Lobby!
Behold the crippling of South Pool!

But your profligacy's over,
Yes, I know of what I speak!
Yes, a welcomed guest is here:
An inspector with a badge!

Upon a forensic audit,
We'll reveal your foul crimes.
Wearing stripe, in federal prison,
You will take it in the ass.

Publication of this poem on these pages should not be construed as an endorsement of either artistic value of the original or faithfulness of translation.

The *paskvil'* is cited in full to demonstrate that Bill made some telling choices in his translation. In the original, we do not see "an inspector." Instead, we encounter a *"federalnyy prokuror,"* a federal prosecutor.

Bill takes the liberty to translate this as "inspector," as in *The Inspector General,* a comedy by Nikolai Gogol. Bill rereads it every few years. It's a classic comedy of mistaken identity: a young man arrives in a small provincial town, where corrupt officials mistake him for an inspector general from Saint Petersburg, traveling incognito with secret orders.

The two closing lines are noteworthy, because the author of the Russian text employs the word *"vazelinchik,"* a diminutive for the word "Vaseline," a lubricant sometimes used in sexual encounters.

The translator, in contrast, goes straight to the point, which in this case also constitutes a threat: upon a forensic audit and prosecution, the once-pampered, esteemed members of the Château's BOD will have to face the harsh reality of prison life.

At the apartment, Bill reaches into the box of Zbig's clothes, pulls out the loafer, and slips it on his foot.

It's dark blue. It's suede. It has a gold buckle—a horse-bit-like buckle in the spot where Bill is used to seeing worn leather laces, or, on more formal occasions, pennies. It's Gucci. It fits perfectly.

He and Zbig borrowed each other's stuff all the time when they were at Duke. It feels good in a strange way to know that they still can.

A text from Gwen:

"That poem—WTF?"

"A faithful translation of my father's work"

"Seriously?"

"I let him rave"

"Non-confrontation?"

"I don't care anymore. He is not I"

Bill reaches deeper into the box to find the loafer's brother. He slips it on as well. He rolls his feet. The feeling is akin to standing barefoot on a yoga mat. He takes a step, observing his feet, which no longer feel like his own. Is that not a burst of Zbigness radiating upward, toward his consciousness, something that was absent when he pressed his palms against the marble floor at the Grand Dux?

Is this box not a treasure trove of clues that would have eluded an investigator more earthbound than our Inspector Luftmensch?

Returning to the box, Bill spots a bit of blue, tufted silk. He pulls on it. This produces an odd-looking sport coat. Burberry.

He is aware of the look: sockless Gucci loafers, a Burberry sport coat over a T-shirt, a prickly, unshaven face. Now that look is his, seamlessly so.

Surely there would be jeans in the box—black.

With these finds, Bill feels ready for Art Basel.

He is about to rifle through the pockets of the remaining clothes when he receives a text from his father.

"MIT MI HIR IMEDIAT!" Melsor commands in all caps. "URGEND!!!!"

10

THE INSPECTOR
GENERAL

While Bill is proudly a Luddite, Melsor is not. His *kabinet* is filled with gadgets, most of which have the bulky look of obsolete recording devices that cost a fortune in their day.

The computer is new—a massive aluminum-clad Apple desktop.

"*Slushay, vot . . . Eto o tebe,*" says Melsor. [Listen. This is about you.]

He clicks on the "Play" arrow, and a crackling recording of a conversation between two men fills the room. The bug Melsor and Bill had planted the previous night is cranking out intelligence.

One of the people on the recording is young and Russian, clearly the guard Bill encountered at the gate the day before.

The other is Greenstein, "the Evil Dwarf," the chief Jew-Nazi of the Château, the *obersturmbannführer* of bloodsuckers, the *crème de la svoloch',* the sort of Jew who has no problem living in an apartment purchased with gold bars obtained by means of melting the teeth of Holocaust victims, some of whom could very well have been his cousins.

How many teeth per square foot does it take to get to South Ocean Drive? Should the previous owners of those teeth reconstitute from ashes, arise from the golden sands, and, with guns in hands, seek restitution? And what of those Torah breastplates Bill saw in the Greenstein apartment? Where did the scrolls go? That's the problem with fascism: it's messy, it leaves traces even after the last tooth has been melted. Has Inspector Luftmensch acquired a client? Has he become an agent of the dead? Should he jump back into that *lyul'ka*, liberate the Nazi loot, and, under cover of darkness, drop it off on the doorsteps of the closest Holocaust museum? There must be one in Miami . . .

The security guard's name is Stepan.

STEPAN: Mr. Greenstein, someone I haven't seen before just went in here, into complex when you weren't here.

GREENSTEIN: Who?

STEPAN: Looks like someone in official capacity.

GREENSTEIN: Young?

STEPAN: Comparatively.

GREENSTEIN: Meaning?

STEPAN: I estimated him at fifty, but still hardboiled, thin. Had Halliburton bag.

GREENSTEIN: Where did he go?

STEPAN: That's worst part. To Katzenelenbogen.

GREENSTEIN: Maybe his son?

STEPAN: I thought he always said his son was dead. And they don't look alike.

GREENSTEIN: This indeed doesn't smell good, Stepan. Think it's FBI? Or is he one of the Florida agencies? DBPR?

STEPAN: I don't know, but I feel something wrong. He's not one of us. Clearly doesn't speak Russian.

GREENSTEIN: Did you try to speak with him?

STEPAN: No, we didn't speak. Later, he walked around lobby, looking at damage in details.

GREENSTEIN: So, you looked through the camera as he splashed around in the lobby. You should have come up, asked him to show documents.

STEPAN: I could, of course, but got scared. I don't have document myself, no work visa, no Green Card.

GREENSTEIN: You are a loser and a slave, Stepan. I should have driven you out a long time ago. You don't have a visa and a Green Card because people like you don't deserve Green Cards. Take my word for it, Stepan, when Trump sends visas and the National Guard to get you, I will not stand in their way.

This is followed by another call, several hours later, in which Stepan reports the contents of the tasteless poem affixed to the elevators' walls.

The poem contains the following lines:

Но проделкам Вашим наглым,
Верьте мне, пришел конец!
Да, приехал гость желанный—
Федеральный прокурор!

"Read it in English," orders Greenstein.

But your profligacy's over,
Yes, I know of what I speak!

Yes, a welcomed guest is here:
An inspector with a badge!

Greenstein thanks Stepan for the report and hangs up. Melsor looks away, pours himself a glass of Grey Ruse, and downs it. Bill pours himself a glass as well.

"I don't like that poem," says Melsor, looking out at the ocean.

Father and son Katzenelenbogen are sitting on the bright white leather sofa. Bill is staring at the horse bits on his Gucci loafers. Amazing things happen when blue suede catches Florida sunshine. It's entirely too early to start drinking vodka, but what's done is done.

"I couldn't do that poem justice in the time allotted."

"No, it not you. It was too long. Americans don't like long things. Tramp uses Twitter—one hundred forty characters—and he is in White House! I need new format. I wrote something Americans will like. *Chastushki*. I will write them, you translate, and we find singers to perform them at political rally. I will publish them in *Machta* without pseudonym after that."

Here we go again, the same mechanism: just as Bill starts to feel more or less safe, just as he thinks it might be okay to talk about the loss of his mother, the fucker pulls his next insane stunt.

Chastushki are four-line Russian folk poems, sort of rhyming, limerick-like, usually obscene, often sung by women in traditional costumes. They have been used for political purposes, too.

"I wrote the first in the cycle—here," says Melsor, handing Bill three pieces of paper with an old man's shaky-handed scribbles.

"Holy fuck," Bill says to himself after looking at the first rhyme. It's—fuckfuckfuck—about him, sort of:

К нам приехал ревизор—
Сволочная гадина.
Ни хрена он не найдет!
Всё уже украдено.

An inspector has arrived,
Poisonous and bastardly.
He won't find a single thing,
All was stolen long ago!

Imagine this performed in English by Russian women in native garb. Holy Mother of God! Even whatshisname, Donal'd Tramp, as he is known around these parts, might have a better grasp on reality.

Bill has three serious questions for God, and he is starting to believe that he is entitled to some answers:

- Why is it that all narcissists in your Creation ultimately get their due, while this narcissist—mine—continues to exist, indeed thrive, in blissful isolation from the world you created?
- Are you perchance sending your angels to hold back sword-wielding hands that so appropriately and deservedly aim for Melsor's back?
- Why, my Lord, have you not done the same for me, your sometimes-faithful servant who until recently lived strictly by your laws as reflected in journalistic ethics?

The remainder of this cry of Bill's Russian soul consists of extreme obscenities that can be easily imagined by the reader and thus need not be reproduced. The old man is just getting going with his *chastushki*. With luck, he will get distracted.

After this silent meditation, Bill asks his father for more information about Greenstein.

He got a law degree in night school. He represented manufacturers of dietary supplements, but ultimately was disbarred in a sting operation when, on behalf of a client selling amazing cancer cures, he handed an envelope stuffed with hundred-dollar bills to an FDA inspector. Through bungling on the part of the DOJ, Greenstein escaped conviction, but was disbarred. Now he serves on the BOD of the Château's condo association and drives a 2017 white Lexus GS, one of the cars Bill catalogued in the parking garage.

Not much needs to be said about Stepan; he is obviously a run-of-the-mill thug, except he is a thug with an endearing quality: his sense of self-preservation.

"I need you to help me. I need you to walk around complex and say nothing. When they speak to you in Russian, say you don't understand."

"What the fuck for?"

"I will explain. They think you are from FBI. They think you could also be from DBPR, undercover. They think I am working with you."

"What's DBPR, by the way?"

"Florida Department of Bribery and Profitable Relations I call it. They think you are inspector."

"What is it really?"

"Department of Business and Professional Regulation."

"Not a bad plan, actually."

"They will come to you. They will come and be your best friend and you will get what we need—*kompromat*."

"*Kompromat.*"

"Yes."

"Meaning what?"

"*Kompromentiruyuschiy material.* Must be English word for it."

"Compromising material."

"Sounds right. They give it to you, and you will turn it to me."

"Why would they give me anything?"

"To make deal with persecutors, you do it early, get on ground floor, prevent unpleasantness. I did it in Brooklyn, which is how I kept all this!"

"You were charged. Remember? Felonies?"

"Details . . ."

"And what do I get for taking part in this demented charade?"

Melsor doesn't respond. Likely, he sees no need to.

PART II

‖‖

There are people—I categorize them as life's losers—
who get their sense of accomplishment and achievement
from trying to stop others. As far as I am concerned, if
they had any real ability, they wouldn't be fighting me,
they'd be doing something constructive themselves.

—DONALD TRUMP
The Art of the Deal

‖‖

11

|||||||||||||||||||||||||||||||||||||||||||||||||||||||||||||||||||||||||||||||||||||||||||||||||||||||||||||||||||||||||||

THE WATERS OF
THE CHÂTEAU

A hardened, yellowed, fat-stained strip of paper is attached with thick, clear packing tape to the elevator wall.

The paper is decades old. It's yellow, crumpled—about a quarter of a standard page, cut unevenly with scissors, a corner ripped off by hand.

It's a warning scribbled with a ballpoint pen in an old person's shaky handwriting:

Stop throwing Orange Peels Over Balcony.

There is a dichotomy out there, in the world: people are divided into those who throw orange peels and those who rage about this practice.

Maybe it's not strictly a dichotomy. There are also bystanders, wallflowers. Bill has not thrown a single orange peel over a balcony railing since getting to Florida. In fact, he has no recollection of having thrown orange peels over balcony railings at any point during his life. But neither has he ever felt outraged by peel-throwing on the part of others, and he has never attempted to threaten or hunt down the peel-throwers.

A question: How can you be certain that the object dropping past your balcony is, in fact, *orange* peel thrown by someone above you? Do you extend your hand and catch it?

Bill briefly considers detaching the note from the Formica wall of the elevator and saving it as a document of the time and place, but ultimately leaves it undisturbed.

Rows of white concrete planters create the feel of a grand white alley leading to an intensely blue speck of water. Amid the oversized paisley theme of the Château, this pool is a basic rectangle, decidedly non-Lapidus; post-Lapidus, anti-Lapidus even. It's "other," like a cold, tempered steel blade in your side.

The designers of the obviously renovated South Pool appear to have made a miscalculation. The planters are too small to sustain vegetation. Vegetation exposed to direct sunlight and imprisoned in small containers has to be watered continuously. In Florida, even that may not be enough. Grand as this alley was intended to look, every palm tree and fern lining it has withered. On a scorcher of a day—and January 13 is very much that, even at 10 A.M.—you can hear the crackling and hissing as the leaves of the palm trees take on brittle rigidity, transitioning from green to brown, from succulence to death.

In this temple of defoliation, the pool conjures the archetypal memory of oases Israelites encountered during their forty years in the desert. Discomfort of that memory may explain why there is only one person in the vicinity of the South Pool. Dressed in International Janitorial Blue, he is fishing a large brown palm leaf out of the pool's dead center. Bill mutters a greeting, but, avoiding eye contact, the workman lowers the dead, soggy leaf into a yellow caddy and proceeds to wheel it toward the building.

An architect like Lapidus would have sought mercy killing had he seen this pile of architectural horseshit dropped on what was once his project, but a client like Benito Mussolini would have found this alley esthetically pleasing, even soothing.

Exposed in the middle of a plaza, Bill looks up, forming a visor of his right hand to block out the sun (he forgot the fucking hat), scanning the balconies of the towering Château. He doesn't suspect that someone is staring; he knows someone is. Several people, in fact. Seeking color, his eyes home in on American flags—there are four of them fluttering above, like kites in the wind. On a ninth-floor balcony, he spots a shirtless, rotund man in enormous bright red swim trunks, a septuagenarian surfer. In their endless summers, the Russian people—men and women—gravitate toward loosely fitting Hawaii- and California-themed surfer garments.

As Bill looks up, the man lowers what looks like a pair of black military-style binoculars.

Bill tries to guess this observer's backstory. He could be a re-fusenik who wouldn't be denied, another ambulette fraudster from Brooklyn, a gasoline-tax scammer from Jersey City, a lucky winner of a medical malpractice or employment discrimination suit anywhere in America, a Donal'd Tramp supporter, a Josef Mengele son-in-law. Those gold teeth can buy a lot of Florida real estate.

On the top floor, three balconies away from Melsor's, Bill spots a woman and a man. Both continue to stare even as he re-turns the gaze. They, too, are dressed for water recreation. The man wears massive sky blue trunks. The woman's Zeppelinesque figure is jammed into a leopard-print one-piece bathing suit. Her hair is out-of-the-bottle red. Do they believe they had made themselves invisible and thus can stare in an unimpeded fashion? Or do they simply not give a shit?

Bill is far from sure about what his father wants from him and how firmly that task is based in reality, but if he is to gauge the attitudes of the natives, he has to accept that (1) he will stand out and (2) the barren, scorched white plaza framing the South Pool is not the place to start.

The North Pool, a larger body of water, is nevertheless a more intimate affair. Real estate ladies might call it "dated." Translation: untouched by the dehumanizing bulldozer of renovation that makes all things the same.

Bill is pleasantly surprised to see that the mosaic on the deck sports Lapidus's oversized paisleys, coral and chartreuse. The pool, too, is in the shape of a very large paisley. It's deeper than you would expect from an apartment building or hotel pool. A large, upright, paisley-shaped tower at the deep end suggests that the pool was at one point used for diving.

Though some folks sprawled out to broil atop plastic lounges might self-identify as swimmers and divers, from the liability point of view, it is generally considered imprudent to enable 280-plus-pound objects to drop from great heights into deep water. In a wise move, the diving board has been removed, neutralized, and the entrance to the whimsical diving tower barred.

Bill first considers the chaises. These are mostly plastic, Costco-bought, with older aluminum-frame pieces mixed in. In the corner of the deck, he spots a pile of broken-down outdoor furniture. These pieces are of a different sort. This is Richard Schultz, the original stuff. Not a surprise. You expect to see a pile of crippled Schultz chaises on the deck of a château where Plattner and Baughman pieces rot, rust, and mold in the dungeons.

Schultz's "contour chaises" offer few sitting positions. A contour chaise doesn't recline, because why should it? Bill had seen those things in photos, but had never experienced one.

The chaises around the North Pool are replaced with more democratic models, but the tables are still Schultz. Alas, some barbarian—surely a *Homo Sovieticus*—had painted them with a rough brush, cheaply, viciously, in accordance with the traditions of the Gulag. This was done repeatedly, year after year. Bill snaps a picture of the pile of Schultz lounges and texts it to Gwen.

"OMfuckingGodJesus!!!" Gwen shoots back.

In this case, "OMfuckingGodJesus!!!" is an exclamation pregnant with meaning, teetering on the edge of bittersweetness.

Schultz's furniture surrounded the swinging-singles swimming pool where, in another lifetime, pre-Remorse Gwen purported to have overheard the conversations that ended up in her ill-fated Style piece.

You'd think people know when they are plagiarizing *Franny and Zooey*.

Two dozen Châteauites of different ages are assembled in three distinct groups.

Bill walks up to the pile of Schultz lounges, picks one that looks more or less stable, and sets it down between two of these clusters. Even beat up, at the North Pool of Château Sedan

Neuve, a Schultz lounge looks like a sleek Concorde supersonic airliner surrounded by a fleet of B-52 clunkers.

One of the groups—the English-speakers—immediately switches to a whisper. The other—the Russians of Jewish variety—continues to communicate at high volume, shielded by the secrecy of their language. These are people of Melsor's generation, those who fought their way to freedom and prospered rapidly. In some cases, even legally. Bill believes he recognizes the man in red trunks who was studying him through binoculars earlier that morning.

The third group consists of four very pregnant women whose high cheekbones and demeanor of quiet aloofness scream of their tribes of origin—Slavic beauties, who, were they not very pregnant, would be Trump's type, the Trumpettes, presumably the type he has bragged about grabbing by the whatchums. They are wives and girlfriends of the so-called "New Russians," men with enough money to send their pregnant wives to the U.S. Children born in the U.S. automatically qualify for U.S. citizenship, which gives them the option to escape when things go bad.

Schultz could well have designed the Contour Chaise with Bill's contours in mind.

Another text from Gwen: a link to a catalog where a Schultz's Contour Chaise can be had for $2,164, quite a bit more than Bill's net worth.

The rest of her text: "I think I need 1 for my terrace! Shd I get 2?"

"Hmmm . . ." Bill writes, then reconsiders pushing "Send."

He reaches into his bike messenger's bag and produces Melsor's dog-eared copy of *The Art of the Deal*.

———

Bill limits his exposure by going through the lines his father has underlined.

For starters, there is this insight: "I believe in spending what you have to. But I also believe in not spending more than you should."

Abstracted, this looks almost okay, and it gains in the Russian translation, which is penciled in on the margins. Leafing through, Bill spots another highlighted pearl: "I like thinking big . . . To me it's very simple: if you're going to be thinking any-way, you might as well think big"—an idiot's riff on Goethe's "Dream no small dreams for they have no power to move the hearts of men."

To his credit, Melsor scribbled "Goethe?" on the margin, in Russian.

Another passage, marked and translated with reverence:

"One thing I've learned about the press is that they're always hungry for a good story, and the more sensational the better . . . The point is that if you are a little different, a little outrageous, or if you do things that are bold or controversial, the press is going to write about you."

And this: "You can't con people, at least not for long. You can create excitement, you can do wonderful promotion and get all kinds of press, and you can throw in a little hyperbole. But if you don't deliver the goods, people will eventually catch on."

This selection and underlining tell a story, and it's not the story of Donal'd Tramp, but the paradox of the intense appeal of authoritarianism to a man like Melsor, the boy whose very name says Stalin, but who nonetheless grew up to despise Stalin and Stalin's heirs.

Unlike self-described progressives like Bill, Melsor actually fought against authoritarianism—fearlessly at that. What does Melsor Katzenelenbogen see in this Donald Trump? Wouldn't a quote from Stalin, radiating surefooted certainty of a shiny-booted barbarian, feel at home in a book by Donald?

If Trump's meaning can be stretched into a philosophy, Stalin's is more in the realm of stand-up comedy. His stakes are high, shades dark, phrasing blunt. History is on his side, too. His lines always get a laugh, or at least a smirk: "The death of one man is a tragedy. The death of millions is a statistic." Also: "Ideas are more powerful than guns. We would not let our enemies have guns, why should we let them have ideas?" And there is this: "Death is the solution to all problems. No man—no problem."

There is a reason Bill remembers all this. Decades ago, in Moscow, Melsor was famous for quoting Stalin's pronouncements. He did this with a faux Georgian accent. This was a parlor trick of sorts. And now Melsor is adoringly underlining, translating, embracing the latter-day dime-store version of the dictator he once despised.

Hearing the stomping of feet followed by a thunderous splash, Bill looks up in time to see a broad figure submerge in what can best be described as a modified belly flop. The sight is reminiscent of the dive of a Typhoon-class submarine.

The four pregnant Russian girls look up. They are sitting on the side of the pool, soaking their feet, drinking water out of large plastic cups. They are young, beautiful, and their pregnancies make Bill hold his gaze longer. All four appear to have gone to the same stylist. Their hair is shoulder-length, completely straight. One might jump to the conclusion that Bill's attention to them bespeaks his primal wish to procreate, because at this stage it's increasingly unlikely that he ever will. Perhaps he is drawn by the look of detachment on their faces and the electricity of their aloofness that is surely generated by friction with their beauty.

Red Trunks executes a lap in a powerful, splashy butterfly style, and, still grunting rhythmically, pulls himself up on the edge of the pool, rubs his belly in a rounded, spontaneous, Buddha-like gesture, and starts humming an unrecognizable Soviet march.

This has to be the man who was studying Bill through binoculars earlier that morning.

Red Trunks walks past Bill, returning to the chaise. The flat sheet of plastic visibly gives beneath his weight, straining heroically, bowing a bit, resisting, but in the end it remains structurally sound, upright, true to itself.

Red Trunks stops humming the instant he settles into the plastic chaise.

"Revizora nashego videli? Polyubuytes'," he announces loudly to the group of Russians around him. [Have you seen our inspector general? Behold!]

Men like him have only one volume level—all the way up. No dial is provided. With the volume being the message, this determines the character of the conversation that follows.

Bill is six feet away, his face stuck in a book so moronic that it would benefit from being held upside down.

"Eto Melsor Yakovlevich yego vyzval?" asks a woman in a zebra-print bathing suit, presumably the same one Bill spotted on the eighteenth-floor balcony a few minutes earlier. [Did Melsor Yakovlevich summon him?]

"A chto eto za mudak? FBR?" asks a woman in a black bathing suit. [Who is this fuckup? FBI?]

"Kak znat'? A po proiskhozhdeniyu on kto?" asks a man in blue trunks. [What do you think his ethnicity is?]

RED TRUNKS: *Irlandets, Anglo-Sakson khuyev. Oni vse v FBR takiye. VOSPY. Ni khera v nas ne razbirayutsya—on ni khera i ne poymet.* [Irish, some fucking Anglo-Saxon. They all are at FBI. WASPS. They don't understand a fucking thing about us.]

Who are these people?

Bill understands their language, but they are nothing like him. Their speech is deeply uncouth, not because of its vulgarity (vulgarity can be a positive), but because of complete absence of intonation. Properly spoken, Russian is operatic, its song soaring and dropping like an aria well performed. Here, there is no up, no down. Bill understands all the words, all the grammatical structures, but he has to struggle with the sense.

ZEBRA-PRINT BATHING SUIT: *On tyt, govoryat, inkognito.* [He is traveling incognito, they say.]

BLACK BATHING SUIT: *Da esche s sekretnym predpisaniem.* [With secret orders.]

At least these people are able to quote from the opening scene of *The Inspector General.* This is not necessarily a sign of great erudition: most people of their generation are able to remember parts of that play.

Gogol was skewering provincial officials and the culture of corruption in nineteenth-century Russia. These people appear to be skewering the investigator taking on latter-day corruption.

The play Bill finds himself in appears far more sinister than *The Inspector General.* This is more than a case of mistaken identity. These people are dismissing any efforts to stem corruption, challenging him to teach them a lesson, to defend the honor of the Federal Bureau of Investigation.

BLUE TRUNKS: *Trampa chitayet.* Art of Deal. [Reading Trump. *Art of Deal.*]

BLACK BATHING SUIT: *Oni yego boyatsya. On priydet, i ikh v sheyu pogonit, chtob bisnesu ne meshali.* [He will come in and throw them out, to keep them from getting in the way of business.]

ZEBRA-PRINT BATHING SUIT: *Chto oni, eti FeBeRovtsy ne ponimayit chto etot Katzenelenbogen avantyurist, moshennik prostoy?* [Don't they, the FBIniks, understand that Katzenelenbogen is a simple crook?]

BLUE TRUNKS: *Professional'nyy dissident. Chego s nego voz'mesh?* [A professional dissident. What do you expect from him?]

BLACK BATHING SUIT: *A im to chto? Im by tol'ke den'gi v settlementakh kachat' da disgorjmenty delat'.* [What do they care? They just want to get their settlements and disgorgements.]

Bill has never heard any Russian émigré describe dissidents as cranks who should be disregarded, avoided.

True, his people migrate to the right, but in the past, Republicans, even Republican wing nuts, have always sided with the dissidents. This was somewhat incongruent, to be sure: the very people who oppose civil liberties at home wanted to export them behind the Iron Curtain. And now they simply don't give a shit. Is this what convergence looks like? Has the world become a big crooked condo board?

Bill is generally inclined to sympathize with anti-Melsor sentiments. But Melsor's dissident past is actually something he admires; it's the reason, the only reason perhaps, to give him the benefit of the doubt.

That's what the judge did, and for the first time, Bill starts to think that—maybe—the judge was right to let the old man walk and keep his stash.

ZEBRA-PRINT BATHING SUIT: *On v vodu ne idet. Yego Roza Kisel' po spine svoeyy palkoy yobnula. Sinyachische gromadnyy navernyaka sozrel.* [He is not going in the water. Roza Kisel' whacked him on the back with her crooked cane. A big bruise is ripening, for sure.]

BLACK BATHING SUIT: *Pizda staraya.* [Old cunt.]

ZEBRA-PRINT BATHING SUIT: *Federal'noye prestupleniye FBRoshnikov po zhope khuyakat'.* [It's a federal crime to whack FBI agents on the ass.]

BLACK BATHING SUIT: *Yebanatikam vsyo mozhno.* [Crackpots may do as they please.]

BLUE TRUNKS: *Ladno, a chto vy dumayete oni zdes' naydut?* [Enough on that. What do you think they can find here?]

RED TRUNKS: *Obychnoye delo, sami znayete. Otkaty, da ne to chtob ochen' bol'shiye, v meru.* [Nothing unusual, you know yourself. Some kickback, but not too much, well measured.]

BLUE TRUNKS: *Kak umnomy cheloveku ne vzyat'—ny kak u Gogolya skazanno—kogna samo v ruki plyvet.* [How can a smart man not accept things that—like Gogol had it—swim into your hands.]

RED TRUNKS: *Kak v* Revizore, *u Gogolya, khmyr' govoril, "Ya beru vzyatki, no tol'ko Borzymi schenkami. A eto sovsem inoye."* [Remember in Gogol, *The Inspector General,* one of the men says, "I take bribes, but I only accept Borzoi puppies. And that's a completely different thing."]

ZEBRA-PRINT BATHING SUIT: *A Lexus to u tebya kak?* [How's the Lexus running?]

RED TRUNKS: *Normal'no, chego tam, kak i tvoy.* [Normal, just like yours.]

BLACK BATHING SUIT: *Slushayte, muzhchiny, vy-b k nemu*

podoshli, potolkovali, mozhet vy s nim snachala dogovorites' kak obychno, chtob nam bez disgorjmenta kak-to, poka Tramp ne priydet. [Listen, gentlemen, what if you were to come up to him, had a man-to-man conversation, as it's always done, so there'd be no disgorgement, until Trump comes.]

RED TRUNKS: *Nu my sobstvenno tak i sobiralis', tol'ko davayte prismotrimsya.* [That was the plan. Just let it play out a bit while we take a look.]

Bill shifts his attention to the Americans.

They seem to be roughly the same age as the Russians. They spring from the same *shtetlekh*, have the same ancestors, snooze in the same synagogues.

They can easily be each other's first cousins, but if that's the case, they are cousins separated by history, cousins who hate each other's guts, squabbling over inheritance, holding eternal grudges. Some years ago, in the 1970s and '80s, these very Americans displayed "Free Soviet Jewry" signs in front of their houses of worship. They did this because that's what the rabbi wanted, so who gives a shit. Now, they would happily display a big neon-lit "Take Them Back" sign in front of the Château.

An older woman and a grandchild walk through the doors and settle down in the American group. The woman is petite, her hair permed, painted a shade of beige.

The Russian women don't seem to be impressed by the strategy she's employed in the preservation of youth and pursuit of beauty.

"Obezyana," mutters the redheaded woman in the leopard-print bathing suit. [A monkey.]

Her comrade in the black bathing suit is equally unimpressed. *"Smotri kak morda natyanuta. Spit s otkrytymi glazami."* [Look at how tight her face is. She sleeps with her eyes open.]

Meanwhile, the child, who seems to be around two, takes off in the direction of the cluster of Russians, heading straight toward a large bag, and grabbing onto it. Surely he thinks the bag contains toys, buckets and such.

Red Trunks lazily grabs the child by the arm, pronouncing him arbitrarily an *"ublyudok"*—the product of indiscriminate sexual activity—and waiting for the monkey to pick up the now-screaming child.

As the grandmother comes up, Russian conversation grows louder, to drown out the screaming, physically restrained child.

The woman's name, Bill overhears, is Martha.

In conversation, she is described as a "Chicago cunt." [*Pizda Chikagskaya.*] Conversation related to Martha now focuses on Botox, sundry other cosmetic interventions, even a suggestion that the child's grandmother purchases sexual services of young men on Craigslist.

Walking slowly to pick up the child, Martha throws an angry glance at each of the Russians individually.

"This is a public place!" she declares. "This is America! We speak English here! Speak Russian in your units."

The woman in the zebra-print bathing suit responds for the entire group: "We don't afraid you. We speak what we want!"

"Svoloch'," interjects one of her comrades.

At the beach, the waves make swimming a challenge.

Bill looks around. There are six groups milling here, elderly men and women standing in circles of five or six, speaking in an agitated manner. He walks slowly past two of the groups, long enough to determine whether they are speaking Russian or English. The English-speakers immediately switch to a whisper or complete silence. The Russians—all of them old Jews—continue to converse loudly.

Bill places his towel on the sand. He is now positioned between two circles—Americans and Russians. From here he can focus on whatever shreds of conversation come his way.

At the beach, all conversations revolve around the pending $19 million special assessment that the BOD is about to impose on the Château's 360 unit owners. There is also some discussion of Melsor—nicknamed *"Dissident"*—running for a seat on the board.

One shred of conversation, in translation: "Some say he is insane, but it's not that simple. He becomes agitated when the world fails to operate in accordance with the rules he believes must apply."

Bill regards this as an astute analysis, but says nothing.

One of the Russians, a short man with a goatee, breaks away from the group and approaches Bill. He is dressed for extreme leisure—light-blue plaid shorts and a faded yellow T-shirt that reads "Glasnost," a long-abandoned Gorbachev-era slogan.

The man looks remarkably like Lenin, not the heroic Lenin of Soviet posters and paintings, but a real-life Lenin, the little guy you see in photographs.

"We have proverb in Florida," he says with a thick accent that seems vaguely French. Bill has seen this before: for reasons that he is unable to fathom, some Russians affect a version of a French accent, which grows in both Frenchness and fauxness as they drink.

"You know why it's good to be on beach?"

Bill smiles, but says nothing. He wants the guy to keep talking.

"Because on beach you are surrounded by idiots on only three sides."

"And on the remaining side you have what?" asks Bill.

"Sharks," says the man, pointing to a small figure bobbing in the waves. "This is Herr Doktor of Jurisprudence Greenstein, king of . . . How you say *otkaty*?" he shouts to his group.

"Kickbacks!" shouts the woman from his group.

"Dura, eto-zh ty po-angliyski yemu vykriknula," says her friend. [Idiot, you just shouted it in English.]

"Nichego, puskay ponimayet," she said. [It's okay, this way he will understand.]

Bill looks up to the top floor and sees his father, presumably holding binoculars.

His plan is to get out into the waves, toward the small bobbing figure. Alas, the man who ensnared him is not ready to let go.

"Call me Alex," the man offers.

"Bill . . ."

"My nephew works at Department of Justice—Antitrust Division? Have you heard? Washington? He is Ilya Vilner; my sister's stepson; she raised him. You know him?"

"It's a big place."

"The world is *shtetl*; everyone knows everyone; always good to ask. He is investigator also."

"Okay."

"Lives on Connecticut Avenue, near famous bookstore, Politics and Prose, but closer to Calvert Woodley, liquor store; both on same side of street."

"Sounds good."

"Russian Standard was almost seventeen dollars for seven-hundred-fifty-milliliter bottle at Calvert Woodley when I visited."

"Hmm."

"I am used to less. I keep track of such things. I finished Historico-Archival Institute . . . in Moscow. They teach you that history is under your nose. History in Kremlin and White House is same history in your flat, which is same as history in your street, and your condo, in this situation. You understand concept? You want to know anything about Château, come to me. I have original sales brochures. You play chess?"

"Badly."

"Better badly than not. Means I will win. Chess died because of computer. My grandson shoots at tanks all day."

"It's a skill. May become necessary."

"I even have elevations signed by main architect, Lapidus himself! It's always same thing: they throw away history to keep control—I rescue it. It's war, people's war—eternal. When it will end, everyone will die. Or it will end after everyone dies. I don't know yet. Erosion of truth is same as erosion of sand on beach. You don't win, but you fight."

"Historico-Archival?"

"They destroy records—I save records. It's like game: cats-mice, *koshki-myshki*. I *am* history in exactly same way that you are history. Not like their Tramp—he is narcissist—everything rotates around his belly button, he is whole world."

"Does that mean Trump is history?"

"No. He think he is history, but he is not history. We saw this before."

"Well put."

"We are different: what we do it's not for us. It's for truth, it's for mankind, to establish record, to preserve. Truth is best weapon against fascism."

"Hard to disagree."

"The guy who they say helps you, Melsor Yakovlevich, they say he is crazy, but I say no. He is potentially most effective person here, who is not completely crooked. I repeat so you will understand subtle point: he is not *completely* crooked, only *partially* crooked, which in our situation creates hope. Sometimes he is one of them, sometimes he is one of us. Problem is, crooked people are effective, and we need help."

"Everyone does."

"Melsor Yakovlevich is offended at me. He and I were almost friends when I come here. But then he showed me his poems and I said—not to him, but to common friend—that I used to have dogs in Moscow, Scottish terriers, and when they took shits, their shits were better than poems by Melsor Katzenelenbogen. I called him a *grafoman*. How do you say that?"

"The condition is called graphomania, compulsion to write."

"So, he, so to say, learned that I said it, became very offended, and he doesn't say hello to me when he sees me. If you talk with him, tell him Alex Bogomolov didn't say any of it, about graphomania and dog shit."

"I'll try to remember, should I talk with him. But you did say it?"

"Afraid so. Guilty. There are big lies in world. This is little lie. Innocent lie. Thank you for being here. You know, their next special assessment—nineteen million dollars—means I lose my daughter's apartment."

"Sorry to hear that."

"But it's not me. Individual is besides a point. It's about place. This place is like nothing else. They should make it historical monument instead of fucking it up more and more and getting rich on *otkaty* . . . kickbacks. Architect, whom I already spoke about, was very famous. Morris Lapidus! You know about him?"

"Yes, I actually do."

"Lapidus is father of Miami Modernism current. Developer fired him from this building halfway through design. He wasn't making it French enough, they say, I have letters. It says: put in more French symbols, the lilies, but he says—no—paisleys. They say paisleys are from India, but he says, no, no, and no. You know how this ends. Swimming pools; you've seen? They destroy South Pool already; it's nothing to see—dead. North Pool will be destroyed next. It will be crime. You were there?"

"Yes."

"You know why it's deep?"

"No."

"Ah, this is fascinating. It's deep, because water was used to work as air conditioner for whole building. It was quietest air conditioner in the world. It was separate utility, you paid for it every month. It was candidate for inclusion in American Pavilion in World's Fair in Montreal. It was nominated; I have letters. They were going to make a to-scale working model of it to put on truck to Canada for exhibition! Even now we have kilometers of pipes in walls, they don't know anymore where it leads or what to do with it. If you have questions, run fast to me, I am in unit 215, like Philadelphia. Easy to remember: 215; 215—Alex. Alex—Alex Bogomolov."

"Thank you."

"Don't go in water—there is shark there."

Alex points again at the small figure bobbing in the waves fifty meters offshore: the esteemed Herr Greenstein, vice president of the BOD of the Condominium Owners Association of Château Sedan Neuve, the man whose apartment Bill and Melsor had surreptitiously visited via *lyul'ka*.

When he reaches Greenstein, Bill is up to his rib cage in water, jumping up in the waves.

He has no plans to initiate a conversation, only to give Greenstein the opportunity to do so. He knows what Greenstein looks like, a short, beefy man with broad shoulders, dwarfed by his wife, a woman who maintains herself aggressively fed, permed, and dyed.

The picture Bill saw showed Herr and Frau Greenstein at a formal event of some sort, with him in a plain black tux, and her in what looked like a shining blue tarp, balancing her mass on remarkably high heels. In that picture, they seemed to be held together by an unbreakable bond. She had the height, the mass, the territory. His body was proportional enough to rule out dwarfism, but while he was corporeally minimal, he was projecting inner power, looking like someone who will not be moved, someone feared by lesser men.

Did Frau Greenstein's father approve of his daughter's choice of husbands? Was he a true believer in racial hygiene? Was he a simple soldier who followed orders, or a bureaucrat embracing the technical challenge of making Europe *Judenfrei*?

As an amateur shrink, Bill is far from good enough to hypothesize.

Greenstein comes out at Bill from up high, his big face emerging through the middle of an oncoming wave, but as the wave moves toward breaking, Greenstein hangs back, paddling backward, his intense gaze focused on Bill.

That face makes up for what he lacks in body size: it's meaty, with a unibrow, which becomes all the more prominent because his head is completely shaven.

Bill's Yiddish-speaking grandfather—he had only one Jewish grandfather—had an expression: *a yam potz*. A sea prick. It's used to denote men so peerlessly awful that two of them haven't been known to exist. We know of sea horses, sea urchins, sea birds, but no sea pricks. Yet Greenstein is a *yam potz*, emerging from the waves, unifying the literal with the figurative.

"I think I can save both of us some time," says Greenstein, accidentally gulping and spitting out seawater. "There is no shortage of stories here."

Bill doesn't respond.

"It's terribly entertaining, but they are all unsubstantiated rumors," Greenstein continues.

"Rumors?"

"Malicious, delusional—ubiquitous, unfortunately."

"Ubiquitous?"

"Some of it is actionable, assuming you are desperate for something to do. Not the sort of thing you build a case out of. I am an attorney—I can assure you. This is a waste of time. Nobody wants a goat parade."

Bill is out of uninformative responses. "Hmmm" is genuinely the best he can do.

"I would be happy to go through it point by point. The rumor about the contractor being hired based on willingness to pay kickbacks is completely false. Murthy is a brilliant engineer, whose bids always come in lower than those of any two competitors.

"The people spreading rumors want to do business the Florida way. You know how it's done: three contractors gather on a yacht twelve miles offshore, determine their bids, and decide who gets which job. So they decide a priori.

"So, let's say, you get the Neptune contract, your associate gets the Mermaid, and his girlfriend's company gets the Wave. I am not talking about specific places. I am just using these names to illustrate the point. You know the drill, but it's all collusion outside territorial waters, so there's nothing you can do.

"This contract is not like that at all. It's all completely aboveboard, completely transparent. I can justify every little piece of it.

"And the urban legend about Lexus leases. That's just insane. I will not dignify it with a comment. I know you've been listening to that dissident, Katzenelenbogen. He is completely unreliable, a disturbed individual, completely out of touch.

"Can you imagine him in court? Even in his fraud case in Brooklyn, the ambulettes, with his life on the line, his lawyer didn't dare let him take the stand. They made it look like he was about to die, I am told, and the judge used to be a Soviet Jewry activist. He is viewed as a hero, though God knows . . .

"Pathetic—it had to be like hauling in Sharansky for shoplifting."

Bill throws in a "Hard to imagine," and indeed it stokes the flow.

"Look, I am just trying to save you the embarrassment. You are free to dismiss anything I say when you write your . . ."

"I don't know what you mean."

"Of course, I am sorry. It's not Americans versus Russians. Two of my most steadfast allies on the BOD are of Russian Jewish descent.

"When Wilfreda and I moved here, this was a friendly building. People said hello to each other, people invited each other for drinks, people went to dinners with each other. Now, it's just name-calling.

"The vice president has two members in his pocket . . . Ridiculous. I don't care what race you are, what country you are from. I just care whether you are a nice person."

With this, Herr Greenstein, JD, wades in to shore.

Bill is done here.

He shoots a text to Gwen: "Can someone in your crisis mngmnt firm run license plates? I may need several."

"Easy-peasy," Gwen responds.

12

COMRADE KOZACHOK

Sometimes in life there are moments when we wake up struggling to reconstruct the series of events that led another individual to appear on the adjacent pillow. This moment of uncertainty can occur after a night of unbridled revelry, or—just as easily—after a quarter century of production of offspring and acquisition of property.

One morning, more than a decade earlier, after an office party that went longer than planned, he woke up staring at a bare shoulder he recognized as possibly belonging to a woman younger than himself—presumably Gwen. Not a good thing. She wasn't out of her twenties at the time. He was in his early forties. She had once been an intern he worked with; a student, basically. Yes, she is an adult now, a journeyman reporter, the princess of Style.

The rule he broke that night was more the stuff of the unspoken code of conduct than the stuff of the employee handbook.

Bill's left hand spent the night—or at least a portion thereof—between small breasts that he would have estimated to be consistent with Gwen's. As his fingers brushed past her breast, the woman turned toward him, revealing, at last, that he had guessed correctly.

"I don't sleep with guys in the newsroom," said Gwen. There was a smile on her face.

"Of course not."

"Did we fuck?"

"Tried to, probably."

"I want us to try again."

That night is a memory now, left behind with nothing but a smile and pleasantness of a shared history.

Bill's night of guzzling room-temperature Kozachok out of a large plastic bottle and contemplation of falling from great heights seems to be different. It seems to have produced a tangible reminder—a large box addressed to "Bill c/o Melsor Katzenelenbogen." The box hails from someplace in California. If the sender's compounded neologism of a name is an indication, it's something techy.

It seemed possible that a plastered Bill had ordered an industrial-strength router. He could have bought toy cars, buses, and Caterpillar tractors for his Inner Child to play with. It wouldn't take a big shopping spree for his net worth to dip into negative numbers. How much did he spend?

Melsor is unavailable. Nella explains that he is preparing for a colonoscopy. In the old days, before he decided to insulate himself from the consequences of his father's decisions, Bill would have inquired about symptoms that would classify the procedure as diagnostic. If no symptoms were present, Bill would have pointed out that, as per recommendations of the U.S. Preventive Services Task Force, men of Melsor's age—over eighty—shouldn't get screening colonoscopies if they are at average risk of developing colon cancer. Today, he chooses not to go there; too much complexity.

"I was expecting this," Bill lies to Nella, lifts the box—it's surprisingly light—and takes the thing downstairs to find out what it might be.

At the apartment, he makes a quick incision on top of the box, finding a packing slip and a handwritten note. A document indicates that Bill's American Express card ending in *2002 was charged $1,850 for a "Canopy" and a "Container," whatever those may be. Expedited next-day shipping, at least, was free.

What American Express? He no longer has an American Express card. He had one when he was at the *Post*. Did Comrade Kozachok cloud his consciousness so profoundly that he charged nearly $2,000 to the fuckers who had just fired him?

The handwritten note, scribbled on a thick piece of paper and ripped out of a spiral sketchbook, reads:

> *Hey Bill,*
>
> *It was a pleasure to speak with you. Here, as discussed, is a Canopy and Container that belonged to a good friend of mine. He never used it, so it's not technically "used," though I priced it that way—happy to provide a "good deal" for you.*
>
> *My friend is in a "Better Place" now, and his wife sold his unused equipment back to me. Tell me if you need anything else, Knee Pads and a Helmet for example. His fly suit is the only thing I can't offer. (You understand.) This is not a "safe sport," like golf, as you well know.*

As I said, I am passing this one "at cost." I packed the Canopy into the Container, as per your instructions, so it's "jump-ready."

From what you told me, sounds like you're an experienced jumper. Surprised our paths haven't crossed before.

Fly safe!!!

Your friend,

Jason

You might surmise that Bill would immediately recognize the magnitude of his transgression. You might think he would stop right there, seal the box, ship the canopy and container back to Jason, his new best friend. You might also expect that he would call American Express and the *Post* and apologize: there was a misunderstanding, it's dealt with, please cancel the card.

Inspector Luftmensch does nothing of the sort. With entirely too much excitement, he opens the box and pulls out the canopy-bearing, "jump-ready" container—it's a backpack, really—and slips it on.

It feels good, like a well-tailored sport coat. He walks out onto the balcony and, adjusting the buckles of a dead man's chute, takes in the expanse of the ocean, the low clouds. Bill doesn't actually know this, but he surmises that the world is a different place if you carry a gun. In presumably the same way, a man with a chute experiences heights differently than a man without one.

The clouds suddenly feel within his grasp, and as he conquers the clouds, one more mystery of the universe will have been eroded.

Achtung! William Melsorovich Katzenelenbogen, Inspector Luftmensch, is in the midst of an existential investigation, perhaps the first of its kind, perhaps the last.

———

Now there are two big boxes in the apartment.

One, hailing from California, has provided Bill with the container and canopy that are now on his back. The other, a larger one, is filled with clothes that once belonged to Bill's friend Zbig, the Butt God who fell from the sky.

Bill dumps out the clothes. The pile is big. He has gone through it in a cursory manner a bit earlier. Now he is on the lookout for the usual dross people generate in the course of a normal day: receipts, keys, key cards, business cards, hand-scribbled notes, phone numbers.

There is nothing in the Burberry sport coat, nothing in the black jeans of a variety he has never seen: Ermenegildo Zegna (he thought Zegna only made yellow ties that famously appealed to Bill Clinton's paramour Monica Lewinsky). The jeans feel less comfortable than Bill's proletarian Carhartts. But with Gucci loafers and a black T-shirt, the ensemble clicks. The pockets, alas, are empty.

In the box, Bill finds two more pairs of Gucci loafers, which he admits he no longer holds in contempt, as well as a pair of Ferragamo loafers, which to him look like bedroom slippers. A Moschino shirt looks Hawaiian and thus is not his thing. Also, there are two black and vaguely silky Versace T-shirts (not manly, he determines), a light blue Brioni suit (maybe okay, if suits are your style), a Brunello Cucinelli leather jacket with wide lapels and a profusion of zippers, a pair of Tom Ford dark indigo jeans, two pairs of Dolce & Gabbana blue jeans, and a bottle of cologne (also by Dolce & Gabbana).

Bill goes through every pocket, finding nothing. Some items—the jeans and the Brunello Cucinelli thing—still have price tags. Nobody has just one Brioni suit, Moschino shirt, etc. Where there is one there are a dozen, where there are a dozen there are fifty. This box is just one of many that are now making their way to the Salvation Army donation pile, and—unless, of course, it's the last box to depart—there will be more.

There is nothing in any of the pockets. Zbig is guarding his secrets. He didn't yield a single clue as Bill's hand touched the exact spot where Zbig's cranium popped, spilling its jelly-like stuffing onto the white terrazzo tile. This was the spot of the meeting of the spheres, Zbig's cosmic opportunity to communicate with Inspector Luftmensch.

On the bottom of the box, Bill finds two items that seem out of place. One is a pair of well-worn Levis. In the front pocket, he finds a package of terazosin, an alpha-blocker used to control high blood pressure. Two condoms, in packages, cling to it.

Beneath the jeans, he finds an old rucksack. It looks like something from World War II. The memory of that bag returns suddenly: it was bought at a military surplus store in Georgetown, near Key Bridge.

The bag was of unknown military provenance, but it was solid. It seemed some idiot took a ballpoint pen and gave it a new past, writing in block letters across the back pocket: RAF No. 303 Polish Fighter Squadron. This was not a disingenuous act by a ruthless militaria dealer. The forgery was too obvious for that: there were no ballpoint pens during World War II. The idiot who bought this bag at Sunny's Surplus for (he still remembers) $12.99 was none other than Ilya "William" Melsorovich Katzenelenbogen. This was a birthday present for Zbig. The year was 1985.

Something about Zbig reminded Bill of the brave men of the RAF Polish Fighter Squadron. Sure, they were Catholics—probably just about all of them—but spiritually, they were the brothers of people Bill identified with—the fighters of the Jewish ghettos.

This is the bond—the polarity—that unites Bill and Zbig even now, death notwithstanding.

See it meander through history, watch it boil down to a hard, solid sediment—an existential fundamental, if such a thing is more possible than firmament of the clouds.

Zbig's family was not in London during the war. His grandfather was a fighter in Ludowe Wojsko Polskie, the Polish regiment of the Red Army. (Bill's grandfather was fighting nearby, as part of the regular Red Army.) Zbig's father, a doctor, had three families—serially—and Zbig was the sixth and final child.

The family's move to London, and later to White River Junction, Vermont, had little to do with politics. The elder Wronski wanted to become the best cardiologist he could be. They are dead now: Dr. Janusz Wronski of old age; Mrs. Carol Wronska, a Vermont potter, of pancreatic cancer; Dr. Zbignew Wronski of a fall from the forty-third floor of Hotel Grand Dux on South Ocean Drive, here in Hollywood, Florida. A woman named Consuela Ramirez-Wronska is, by default, the guardian of a rich heritage, which she is now packing into large boxes and shipping off to Salvation Army.

And here is Bill, reclaiming it, getting his gag gift back. Zbig used that bag through Duke and presumably through medical school (Dartmouth) and residency (University of Miami). At Duke, it seemed Bill would become a reporter, one of the best. With his passion for bringing out the truth, was there even a possibility of a second best? Zbig would probably join Doctors Without Borders. It seemed possible that they would meet up at some tent hospital in Africa and spend the night drinking vodka, Polish, of course, and talking about shit that matters.

Bill's career is over, ended in dismissal, and here he is, in Florida, camping out on his stepmother's cot, surrounded by juvenile paintings. Zbig's path is a mystery, too. Instead of joining Doctors Without Borders and saving mankind, Dr. Zbignew Wronski devoted his life to serving the cash-on-the-barrel–paying rich and insecure. It's possible that rumors of patient fucking were true—usually they are. This is as far as you can get from Doctors Without Borders. Zbig joined the ranks of Doctors Without Boundaries.

Bill reaches into the bag. Nothing in the big cargo bay—the place where medical books once lived. Again, no clues. But in one of the smaller pockets he finds a crumpled piece of paper with the words of Volodya Vysotsky:

I'll water the stallions,
I'll finish the song,
I'll stand on the edge for a moment more!

The handwriting is, of course, Bill's, a package of chills from another time. Bill now is not Bill then; Zbig is no more; but the edge, it never changes.

Bill unstraps the container, sets it carefully on the nearby armchair, and, unparachuted, stares out the window at the rushing waves below.

Can a terrestrial investigation (the Château) mix with the existential (Zbig)?

Is the realm of Inspector Luftmensch contaminating the realm of the inspector general or vice versa? On the Château matter, the terrestrial front, Bill needs to talk to Melsor, if only for a few minutes while Katzenelenbogen the Elder is devoting his day to drinking chalky milkshakes and dealing with their consequences.

He imagines that the Zbig book would be a lot like a news story, only longer.

The Zbig story—the Zbig book—is the reason he is in Florida.

However, something at the Château emits that unmistakable smell of wrongdoing. The Château investigation looks like it may actually pay the bills—somehow, maybe. At the very least, it's undeniably his path to free rent while he pursues the Zbig quest. There is no problem with any of this. Bill is not the first investigator to use one job to finance another. All he needs to do is keep his methodology sound, and keep his facts in isolation from his obsessions. If anyone in God's creation has the capacity to keep these tasks—these universes—bifurcated in a manner consistent with recognized and accepted best practices in the field of mental hygiene, that man would be none other than William Melsorovich Katzenelenbogen.

Nearly two days have elapsed since Bill's landing in Florida. On past visits, three days in Florida produced specific suicidal ideation. This time, possibly thanks to Comrade Kozachok, those buggers visited him on Night One. If you accept the notion that nothing in life is accidental, you may see deeper symbolism in Bill's ownership of the container and the canopy. You might think of them as his shield from suicidal thoughts, his protection from height, his flying blankie.

Bill is on the twelfth floor. He has no idea whether that's

enough height for the chute to open. The trick is to avoid slamming into the side of the building.

"Gucci-*shmucci*-Versace," Nella comments on his getup.

Melsor is in the kitchen, eating green Jell-O out of a cup.

"*Ty chto, gomikom stal?*" he asks. Rough translation: Have you gone gay?

The wide lapels of the Brunello Cucinelli jacket, combined with the hyper-tropical Moschino shirt, slinky dark indigo jeans, and slipper-like Ferragamos (Ferragami?), represent a significant departure from Bill's Washington journalist's wardrobe.

"*Yesli-b stal, ya by tebe nepremenno soobschil,*" he responds. Rough translation: Had I gone gay, you'd absolutely have been the first to know.

"This is all they let me eat before procedure. Chemicals. She bought twelve, one for each apostle."

"And you are Christ, no doubt. Can you get away for a few minutes?"

"I took drug. Must stay close to toilet."

"Do you think you have twenty minutes before you have to go?"

"Not possible to know. I don't want to take risk."

"Fifteen minutes?"

"What's urgent?"

"I want you to go to the parking lot and point out the cars of the BOD members."

"How does it help me?"

"You could trust my judgment, perhaps."

"If they say trust me, it means don't. Read Donal'd Tramp! He says it better than anyone."

"Let's go."

"I will go, but you will go to Klub Susanna—put it in GPS—and find their singer to sing my *chastushki*. Offer her eighty dollars in beginning, but go as high as one hundred twenty. You will translate them to English."

"What is Klub Susanna?"

"Restaurant. Near here. Everyone goes there, my eightieth birthday was there. You don't remember."

"I wasn't invited."

"Yes."

"Is there a specific singer you know there?"

"They are all same. Long legs. No voice. Tragic stories."

"Just want to make sure. You want them to sing *chastushki* in English? How does that work?"

"The way you sing anything. Anything is song if you sing it."

"Fine. Give your damned *chastushki* to me."

"I need to put on different clothes. Wait."

Bill glances at the *chastushki*. He recognizes immediately that even for his father, these little songs represent a new level of contempt for the world as it is.

Also, he recognizes that being in Florida is making him grumpy. He has to get out—soon.

Sitting on the porny white sofa while his father changes costumes in his *kabinet*, Bill recognizes that these are not ordinary *chastushki*. (The poetic form is especially well suited for description of genitalia, sexual acts, often al fresco, often while intoxicated.) These *chastushki* are about Florida, about the Florida condominium laws, practices, and traditions, and about specific individuals involved in governance of Château Sedan Neuve, i.e., specific members of its BOD.

In the old days, Bill would have protested. Sure, he would have said, the Russians would understand this poetic form. But even in Russian, what political purpose would that accomplish? Congratulations, you've just ridiculed the BOD Château Sedan Neuve Condominium Association. So what?

Does Melsor believe that the scoundrels who sit on the BOD of CSNCA would feel intense shame, recognize the errors of their ways, and step down one by one? Has he not heard poolside conversations? These people have no conscience. Is he applying his old methods—ridicule of the Soviets—as a way to demonstrate that he doesn't fear them, that their secret police is powerless before him, that Melsor Yakovlevich Katzenelenbogen is bigger than Gulag?

The idea of translating this and singing it in English lies beyond the boundaries of this universe.

Как во нашем да во борде
Разгулялись АЙСИСы.
Разломали наш Шато
Сели суки в Лексусы!

How would Americans, especially those Bill saw at the Château, even begin to fathom it? They would require an hour-long lecture on *chastushki* as a poetic form as well as a brief history of *chastushki* and their use for political purposes today. (Putin uses them, for example.)

It would be the sort of lecture you could get away with at a place like Middlebury, but probably not Duke. How does Melsor expect the cranially calcified, recto-cranially inverted, Lexus-driving, entitled geezers to want to get any of this? Don't they already know everything worth knowing? Have they not eased into lives of applying their vast knowledge to new circumstances? Has Bill not heard one of them admonish those loud Russians for speaking their language in public?

Even assuming the unassumable—i.e., that anyone sits still for a long lecture—the rhymes Melsor has concocted would remain untranslatable. You might get the sense of what he is after, but getting pleasure out of it is beyond feasibility.

In English, this *chastushka* would have to be something like this:

On the board of our condo,
We've elected ISISes,
They have wrecked our Château
And got their Lexuses.

When he was young, Bill made great efforts to explain the world to his father. His failure rate was so high that he started to feel like he had no place to go, no place to put himself.

On one occasion, in the mid-1980s, when Melsor believed that he was entitled to a job at a Russian-language journal called *America Illustrated,* published by the United States Information Agency, he composed a fifty-page legal brief that he wanted to bypass the lower courts and be presented directly to the U.S. Supreme Court. Melsor felt entitled to a job. He wanted justice, he wanted it to be big, resounding, and what's a bigger place to get justice than the U.S. Supreme Court?

Bill, who by that time had taken eleventh-grade civics and was eyeing a career in law, attempted to explain to his father how the courts work. Melsor's brief, no matter how well argued and translated—even if it began with a quote from Thomas Jefferson (which was the case)—would not be considered by the U.S. Supreme Court. It would have to begin as an actual lawsuit, it would have to go through lower courts, and even if questions remain unresolved, the Supreme Court gets to decide which cases end up on its docket. What if the justices don't give a rip about Melsor's fate? Imagine that . . .

Besides, Bill had homework, and a fifty-page translation would interfere with his efforts to practice writing essays for college applications.

Melsor called his son a traitor—*predatel'*. Melsor called him *svoloch'*. Melsor used his favorite Russian proverb: "Eggs do not teach a chicken." After an hour, their standoff was not showing signs of running out of energy.

Bill stood up, and, shouting *"Mudak!"*—a word that falls into the range between a loser and a clueless motherfucker, but stems from a folk word for testicles—bolted in the direction of the closest wall. It was a strong, fully committed headfirst dive. Impact brought relief, the wall parted, drywall crumbled, wiring moved, a two-by-four stud was next to his ear, and there was light. Bill's head was now in a neighbor's apartment.

"I am sorry," he said to the neighbors.

The January 13, 2007, issue of *Machta* features the original Russian text of Melsor's *chastushki*, which appear side-by-side with a quarter-page Russian-language advertisement of a range of delicate procedures that can be performed by Regina Y.

Karasik, MD. The name of one procedure—**Vaginal Rejuve-nation**—is set in large font, boldfaced, and underlined, which would suggest that it's a specialty of the house.

Below Melsor's *chastushki*, in another quarter-page ad, a puffy, bespectacled, bearded gentleman named Viktor A. Vinokur, JD, is offering a broad range of legal services: criminal defense, accidental falls, wrongful death, real estate transactions, wills, and immigration. A one-sentence testimonial describes Mr. Vinokur as—large font, underlined, boldface— **The King of Green Cards**.

Clearly, *Machta* is a shopper with a mission: it is entertaining its readers with faux *chastushki* while helping them become permanent resident aliens with sturdy vaginas.

13

FUCK THEIR MOTHER

"Okay, you will walk me through the parking lot, and I will write down the license plate of every car belonging to a BOD member or a former BOD member."

Bill's reporter's notebook is ready.

"I don't have time."

"Do you want me to help you?"

"What will you do with this?"

"This is Investigations 101."

"What is that?"

"Sorry. You didn't go to college here. It's how college courses are designated, or were: Economics 101, elementary econ, or English 101, introductory English."

"I went to better university than that. Moscow University is like Princeton. And I was adjunct professor here. What did your Duke get you except debt?"

"We can have this conversation later."

"You could have gone to University of Maryland and gone

to officers' program that pays for everything. It's same degree, there was no war, and they would have paid for law school. You could be lawyer."

"I could be lawyer, sure, unhappy one at that, but we are past that. I am fifty-two. Is that why you didn't give me a dime for my college education?"

"You had other possibilities."

"True, you didn't have money then. But a few hundred dollars, even symbolically, would have been nice."

"I brought you to America. You should be full of gratefulness for that."

"I didn't start this conversation. I need you to identify the spots where BOD members keep their cars."

"The cars you want are in spots 394, 302, 249, 173, and 117. I have to go to crapper."

"Thank you, Father."

Aside, he whispers: "Fucker."

Why is it that the Old Bill never called his father Father? He didn't call him anything but "*ty*," "you." He would have preferred to call Melsor "*vy*," the formal version, because the formal address would push the bastard further away.

In Moscow, Bill was proud of his father, the man who stood up to the Bolsheviks, who didn't fear being in contact with the American press, who appeared at demonstrations in front of the Moscow synagogue, who didn't give a rip about getting arrested. When his father's poetry was read by announcers at the Voice of America, Radio Liberty, and the Voice of Israel, Bill was a proud boy.

In America, he came to fear that his father would one day appear at the private school that gave him a scholarship and provoke a fight with the headmaster.

———

In the midafternoon of January 14, the Wronski residence looks as uninhabited as it did two days earlier.

This time, Bill doesn't ring the doorbell.

Instead, he heads straight to the garage, the spot where he had earlier picked up the box of clothes intended for the Salvation Army.

The garage door is partly open; perhaps off its track.

It's heavy, but it lifts, and as it reaches Bill's shoulder, he realizes that he has made a mistake, a bad one.

He sees blinding lights, and with them a camera crew, a rolling camera, and in front of it all, Consuela.

She runs toward him, shouting questions he doesn't wish to answer:

"Why are you here?"

"Why are you wearing my husband's clothes?"

"Who sent you?"

"When will you stop bothering me?"

He is caught, he has no legitimate business in that garage, he is trespassing, wearing a dead man's clothes, and now whatever he says, whatever movement he makes, will be captured on camera.

Bill begins to stammer.

"I am your husband's friend . . ."

"You are a reporter. I know you! He is dead! When will you stop bothering us?"

Bill turns around, and, moving slowly, with a camera following, gets in the Prius and drives off.

———

Bill looks up at the familiar billboard at the I-95 North ramp. Zbig is still there, larger than life, holding forth about beauty, looking down at the motorists as his wife displays her buttocks.

"Dude . . ." Bill says to his dead friend.

Zbig is still there all right, as is Consuela, but the billboard has changed. Zbig's presence is now rendered nebulous, see-through, ghostlike. Consuela, by contrast, is unchanged, except a large orange-colored arrow is now pointing at her exposed buttocks.

The purpose of the billboard has changed, too.

The original question is still posed in massive block letters: "ARE YOU PERFECT THERE?" Yet someone has painted over it in fat, lime green brush strokes: "MERRY WIDOWS—Watch it on VIVA!"

This is not a defacing of the old, cheesy billboard—it's a relaunch, an upcycling.

So that's what the camera crew, and the confrontation. That's why Consuela didn't want to part with any information about Zbig's life and his death. She got a part—a big part—on reality TV.

You might say she is feasting on Zbig's carcass, and if you are especially devoid of charity, you might add that Bill has been outmaneuvered.

Bill's hands shake a little as he drives up to Klub Susanna. Getting busted does that.

He attempts to put his situation with Melsor in perspective. Though financial details of their arrangement haven't been worked out, Melsor is, in effect, Bill's client. A professional is defined as a person who puts client interests above his own.

Same might hold for acting as a member of a loving family, but Bill wouldn't know much about that.

As a reporter, as an investigator, Bill always believed that his client relationship was with the public. Now, all he has to do is drop in his father's full name—Melsor Yakovlevich Katzenelen-bogen—in place of the public.

A psychiatrist is trained not to take it personally when her delusional patient calls her a whore. Similarly, an attorney representing a difficult client doesn't necessarily resign when said client is resistant to taking considered advice. Sometimes a professional has to allow events to play out, which is what Bill is going to do on his father's behalf right now.

Of course, these *chastushki* are not Bill's idea of what it takes to bring about change at the Château or, for that matter, any-place else. Bill would no sooner write a *chastushka* than he would attempt to submit a grievance directly to the U.S. Supreme Court. It should be noted that after the blowup and the wall-ramming incident, Bill did translate that thing, and after it was mailed out, Melsor forced him to make multiple telephone inquiries to the clerk's office. After forty years, the matter is still pending, it seems.

Klub Susanna is located in a strip mall a few miles inland from Collins. At one point, the space might have been a Costco, a Petco, or a BJ's. Judging by the fact that the front doors are still locked at 4:30 P.M., Klub Susanna does its business late at night. Bill looks in through the glass front doors, sees no one, gets back in the car, and drives around to the back of the mall, where the loading docks should be. He gets around several trucks as their cargo is being unloaded at the adjacent food store, and as he approaches the dock of Klub Susanna, he sees a large white Mercedes 500 and an even whiter Bentley convertible.

Bill parks Melsor's dirty white Prius next to them.

He knocks on the heavy steel door.

"Eto kto?" asks a woman's voice. [Who is it?]

Never in his life has this question given Bill pause.

In the old days—which ended less than a week ago—he could identify himself as a reporter with *The Washington Post* and take it from there. On most occasions, the doors would open.

What should he do now? How should Bill identify himself and the matter that brings him to the loading dock of Klub Susanna?

He could say that he is looking for someone to perform two pages of satirical *chastushki*—a couple dozen stanzas altogether—first in Russian, then in English. He could say that he has prepared a translation. (He was, indeed, getting started on a translation.) This being a Russian establishment, the person or persons inside will not ask what *chastushki* are.

This project goes against his better judgment, Bill could add, lest they think badly of him. These *chastushki* are about the goings-on of a particular condo board, and, no—said BOD will not be paying for this performance. In fact, the crooks who run the BOD aren't expecting this. They are the target of satire here. They will hate it, or should.

It's really guerilla theater: the singer or singers will be escorted in past the guard desk, but they should be prepared to be bodily removed sometime during the performance. They will be paid, of course, admittedly not very much: $80. However, the honorarium could go as high as $120. (He is instructed to try to get it done for $80, and wouldn't mention $120 unless he finds himself being laughed at.)

When *chastushki* are performed, it's better to have at least two singers taking turns. It's conceivable that if multiple singers are involved, they would have to split this modest fee. Bill would have to check on that. He could also acknowledge that he is not sure that everyone in the audience will understand what's happening. Some of these folks are Americans.

Again, Bill could reemphasize that he doesn't believe in this project. He is acting on behalf of his father, being professional about the whole thing.

"*Ya ischu pevitsu,*" he says instead. [I am looking for a singer.]

Inside, someone starts working the locks—there are three.

The steel door opens and an unusually tall, painfully thin woman steps out onto the loading dock. As Bill walks in, she walks out and looks cautiously to the left, then to the right.

At six feet, Bill doesn't expect women to tower over him. She does. They are of the same height, but her pumps, which are strikingly tall for something worn in midafternoon, make her taller.

Her hair is jet black, her getup remarkably patriotic: a short, gauzy, red-white-and-blue dress paired with white fishnet stockings. She is in her midthirties, not the gym-toned midthirties of Gwen, but hardscrabble immigrant Russian midthirties. Hers is not the Russia of Champagne and caviar; it's solvent-grade vodka and Salems. Her God-given beauty is crashing tragically, visibly, rapidly, loudly, leaving a crater.

Does he introduce himself now? Does he shake her hand? Kissing her hand would be bizarre, but it might be what she expects—fuck if Bill knows. Should he speak English, which to her is the language of power, or should he speak Russian, their common tongue?

"*Mogut v lyuboy moment voyti,*" she says, slamming the heavy door and sliding in one of the deadbolts. [They can come in at any moment.]

"*Menya zovut Ilya,*" he says. [My name is Ilya.]

He hasn't used that name for four decades, but in this situation, pursuing someone else's agenda, the name Ilya became his nom de guerre, protecting his real persona and his professional standing from this thing he now finds himself in the midst of.

"*Znayu, zhayu . . . Marina,*" she says, not looking back. [I know, I know . . . Marina.]

"*Ochen' priyatno.*" [Nice to meet you. (Literally: very pleasant.)]

Ilya follows Marina to the corner of a massive room—it's clearly backstage, a place for dumping props.

He notes two halves of an oversized Fabergé-style egg, both studded with pieces of colored glass. Presumably you can use these to lower performers onstage. Each half comes up to Bill's waist. Next to the eggs stands a similarly oversized *matryoshka* doll—it's taller than Marina on heels, he notes. Next to that, there is a cage large enough for a lion, or perhaps for a stripper or two.

Two plastic palm trees stand next to the cage. A bright circle—symbolizing Florida sunshine; what else?—hangs above them, as does a three-headed dragon, probably from a fairy tale–themed number. He could imagine that number, a version of Ballet Russe, *Daghiev Does Vegas*. The small hut perched on chicken legs, which stands next to the cage, beneath the dragon, is the oddest bit of all.

As they near the cage, Marina abruptly turns around and kisses him. Her tongue reaches deeply, aggressively into his mouth. Surprised by this turn of events, Bill doesn't reciprocate. He is letting his mind run through the moral and ethical implications of the situation. Gwen . . . Are they in a relationship? Not yet, and who is to say that they will ever be? They haven't slept together in a decade, and while that relationship is "reheating," the only conversation the two of them have had on the subject of exclusivity ended with Gwen saying that, as he departs for South Florida, a hometown girlfriend is the last thing he needs. It was said in jest, sure, but it was said.

As Marina's hands reach down to grab his penis, Bill—or is it Ilya?—reminds himself that he is at Klub Susanna for a reason, a business reason, you might say, if you stretch the definitions of "business" and "reason." Nonetheless, his lips begin to move, perhaps out of respect for the young lady.

Every sexual encounter Bill has ever had was grounded in a relationship of some sort—at least one drink, at least one conversation, sometimes even a movie. An e-mail, too, is better than nothing. It had been several months—five—since his last encounter, two years since his last relationship.

Had you asked Bill whether he has any interest in out-of-context sex, his answer would be "probably not," but here, at Klub Susanna, with Marina's hand in his Ermenegildo Zegnas, his body is starting to disagree.

Bill likes women—a lot. But Russian women are a mystery. He has never dated in Russian, never made love in Russian, never even thought of it in Russian. He knows all the words that pertain to sex acts and all the body parts that can possibly be engaged—he would do fine at an anatomy lecture, at an autopsy, or in the streets, but in bed he would be lost.

Out of the corner of his eye, he notices the colored glass in the Fabergé egg catching the light of the dim light bulb at the door to the loading dock.

Marina breaks away for an instant, and, taking him by the

hand, leads him toward the egg. There, she turns around, pulls off her Russian flag dress, and faces him head on, wearing a thong that, Bill notices, is decorated with gold embroidery of a two-headed eagle.

Her breasts are small, nipples pink. After turning a little to the right and a bit to the left, thus providing Bill with the opportunity to appreciate the two-headed eagle, Marina pulls down the thong and, stepping out of it, bends over, grabbing onto the edge of the oversized Fabergé. The pumps and white fishnets stay on, held up by a garter belt, which, Bill now notices, is similarly patriotic Russian red-white-and-blue. There is a tattoo on the small of her back—again, a Russian flag and a two-headed eagle.

He is behind her now, inside her. An observer—should there have been one—might have concluded that, judging by the sound of it, Marina is experiencing the most electrifying, most fulfilling sexual encounter of her life. Bill is more dutiful. He moves in silence, biting his lower lip.

She slows down, casting a glance over her right shoulder.

"Ilya, mne chto, podruzhek pozvat'?" [Do you want me to call my girlfriends, Ilya?]

Bill says nothing. Her friends wouldn't assuage his hesitation, it being rooted in deep-seated preference to keep sex a behind-closed-doors activity. She senses his hesitation.

"Esche za tysyachu baksov mozhem tebe zolotoy dush ustroit' . . ." [For just a thousand dollars more they can offer you a golden shower.]

A thousand bucks more? More than what? Bill wonders, but says nothing. What could that possibly mean? Her girlfriends? Are they here?

The space is massive. They are wide open, in full view of anyone who might walk in. Is someone watching, God forbid? Is a film being made?

*"Govoryat vash Donal'd Tramp za etim syuda khodit . . . Teper'
pochemu-to vse zakhoteli . . ."* [They say your Donal'd Tramp comes
here for that. For some reason, everyone wants it now.]

She is still on the golden showers bit. This is not helpful.
Bill didn't ask for any of this, and the prospect of involvement of
third, fourth, or fifth parties doesn't help. Marina's kind offer
of having her colleagues piss on each other, or—worse—on
him, and, of course, the very idea of Donal'd Tramp is even less
appealing. To chase away these thoughts and images, Bill wills
his mind to turn to Gwen.

This is more a meditation than a remembrance, oblique,
stripped of graphic content, yet generating far more heat than
the situation in which Bill currently finds himself. He closes his
eyes, imagining, and if the sounds emanating from Marina are
to be believed, the thoughts revive him.

"Davay konchim v tvoyem Bentli. Ya vsegda khotela," she says,
meeting his thrusts. [Let's finish in your Bentley. I've always
wanted to.]

"Net u menya nikakogo Bentli." [I have no Bentley.]

"Kak?" [How is that?]

"Vot tak." [Just like that.]

"Etot Mercedes tozhe ne tvoy? A kto ty takoy?" [Is the Mercedes
not yours also? Who are you?]

She slows down, moving her hips forward to make him slip out.

"Menya zovut Ilya. Ya na Priuse priyekhal." [My name is Ilya. I
arrived in a Prius.]

Quickly, she leans down to pick up her thong, stretching it
over her pumps, then pulling it up her long legs.

"Ty ne tot Ilya?" [You are the wrong Ilya?] She grabs her
dress and slips it on.

"Eto zavisit ot opredeleniy." [This depends on definitions.]

"Ty nikto?" [You are a nobody?]

"Tozhe zavisit ot opredeleniy." [This, too, depends on definitions.]

"Chto ty tut . . . zachem ty syuda?" [Why did you come here?]

"I was looking for someone to sing my father's songs," Bill responds in English while trying to make himself decent.

"A ya zhdala nastoyaschego klienta." [And I was waiting for a real client.]

"Tozhe Ilya?" [Also Ilya?]

"Tozhe." [Also.]

"I will pay you. What was your rate?"

"Pyat'sot baksov?" [Five hundred bucks.]

"Let me see what's in my wallet . . . I have a hundred . . ."

Indeed, he has five crisp, fresh-from-the-ATM twenties, which he hands to Marina. She takes the money, and as Bill heads toward the door, he hears the familiar sounds of a Russian woman bawling.

As the Château gates open to receive the white Prius, Bill realizes that he is not mentally or spiritually prepared to either see his father or be alone with Comrade Kozachok, another half-gallon bottle of which he has located.

In the elevator, he presses the second-floor button and knocks on the door of Apartment 215—like Philadelphia.

"Ah, my friend!" says Alex, extending his right hand and thoughtfully stroking his goatee with his left.

The Frenchiness of his "ah" suggests that he has been drinking. It's past 3 P.M.

Bill is delighted to note that Alex is playing a recording of Aleksandr Galich. Bill grew up listening to his poetry, his cries of moral indignation done to guitar.

Galich's heyday—like Alex's and Melsor's—was in the 1960s and 1970s. Galich was then a middle-aged man reciting tales of prison camps and the utter absurdity—criminality—of life in the USSR. Those were glorious days. The truth was as easy to spot as it was when we shot at Nazis and they at us, or at least this is how Bill sees this.

During his Moscow childhood, Bill learned a lot of Galich.

While Alex looks rather like Lenin, the apartment décor is decidedly bourgeois, vaguely pre-revolutionary. The massive Europeanish breakfront—representing a fantasy of what a nineteenth-century antique would have looked like when it was new—is filled with the detritus of a prosperous life.

Yet, some of its veneer has popped off and the doors have warped enough that they remain only partly closed. The sofa, too, looks like it's from someplace else. Its wooden frame and size are reminiscent of a Venetian gondola, and its fabric features young shepherds and shepherdesses frolicking blissfully through the Renaissance. The painting on the wall depicts a hilltop castle in the distance. All of this was intended to engender respect, and in another setting—a suburb built up with McMansions—it would have.

Alex is playing Galich's "Kaddish," a musical selection that fits Bill's mood entirely too well. Back in the USSR, Galich was not officially recorded or published. He sang at "apartment concerts," and in the end, people gathered donations that enabled him to continue—and continue he did.

His "Kaddish" is a massive composition about the Polish doctor and educator Janusz Korczak, who operated an orphanage in the Warsaw ghetto, first trying to save his charges from starvation, and later preparing them for death. The song goes on for over forty minutes. Its length, its complexity, illustrate why most of the Galich songs could not be performed after his death in 1977. No one else seems to have the capacity to handle his material. If you want to listen to Galich songs, you have to listen to Galich on old recordings.

"This is very special song," explains Alex, pouring Bill a glass of Russian Standard.

This is exactly what Bill craved: a Lenin look-alike playing Galich, while speaking with a faux French accent in a faux European apartment, pouring Russian Standard as the waves of the Atlantic break on the shoreline beneath.

"It sounds pained," says Bill, faking a lack of familiarity with Galich. He is, after all, with the FBI, or DBPR, or some such.

At this moment, Galich is at the point of the orphanage's departure for Treblinka.

И дождаться доложить не может сволочь
Что сегодня Польша Юденфрай.

And the *svoloch'* cannot wait to report
That Poland is *Judenfrei.*

"This is by Aleksandr Galich; very obscure. My generation."

"Not to me," Bill would have said in an aside had such things been possible. He does his best to look clueless.

"I once heard him in Moscow, at apartment concert. That was 1970. Hostess was nice woman, I think it was Inna Semyonovna Baser."

"I hear the word '*Judenfrei.*'"

"You hear correctly. His point—when he is at his best—is there is no difference between bolshevism and fascism. He—I love this Orwellian English word—'conflates' Hitler's Auschwitz and Stalin's Kolyma."

"On purpose?"

"On purpose, on purpose. Galich is dead forty years almost. Never needed him more than today. Their Putin and our Tramp is same person. It's all same. And main question of Russian literature never changes: *'Chto cheloveku delat?'* What's man to do?"

As Russian Standard finds his soul, Bill concludes that it beats Kozachok every time.

Alex continues:

"This is not conspiracy. Conspiracy unites finite groups of individuals. It's limited, it can be exposed, stopped, its members convicted, executed, so to say. This thing is big stinking swamp of criminality that threatens to engulf all that was ever decent and noble. Polarity is much, much, much more bad than conspiracy. From polarity there is no escaping. There is no East, there is no West. No up, no down, and this is how it always was—illumination of this point is just starting to, so to say, penetrate the lead shield of our skulls. Donal'd Tramp is not external. Donal'd Tramp is internal. He lives in your closet, he lives in your head, he lives in your soul, and there—in those places—he always lived. It doesn't matter which part of approaching darkness you confront. In Spain, fascism could be stopped. Now, victory—cure, so to say—cannot be goal. Palliation is only treatment possible. You fight to defend capacity to look at yourself in mirror, to defend human attributes, so to say, when others around you surrender theirs! They cheer as they surrender, by the way. They always do. Surrender and cheer. We would be happier if we join them."

"What's that toast? *Na zdorovye?*"

"Yes, famous Russian toast. We have better toast: *Chtob oni sdokhli!* Translation is 'They should drop dead.' "

Shouting *"Chtob oni sdokhli,"* Bill and Alex drain their glasses.

"One more time, with feelings!" shouts Alex, wiping his mouth with his fist.

"Chtob oni sdokhli!"

"They don't hear us!" says Alex with feigned disappointment.

"Fuck their mother! Is that another expression you have?"

"We say, '*Yob vashu mat*'.' Should really be '*Yob ikhnyuyu mat*' " Fuck their mother."

"Yob ikhnyuyu mat'!"

With this they drink again.

Alex has no playlist on his computer. He goes to YouTube and runs searches in Russian.

After "Kaddish" grinds to its ending (Dr. Korczak and the orphans die, and there is much discussion of Communist Poland being a for-shit place), Alex fishes out another perennial favorite of the Moscow intelligentsia, the song about Solomon Mikhoels, the actor and artistic director of the Moscow State Jewish Theater, who was murdered on Stalin's orders.

The ending of this *chanson*:

> *Наш поезд уходит в Освенцим—*
> *Сегодня и ежедневно.*

> *Our train is leaving for Auschwitz—*
> *Today and daily.*

As much as he agrees with the message, Bill congratulates himself on reserving just enough sobriety to enable refraining from singing along. (Bill's Englishing sometimes suffers upon blottorization, he might say. Actually, it becomes funnier, less gravity-bound—more improved.)

An evening with Alex boosts Bill's resolve to fight the good fight, but falls short of lifting his spirits. Somewhere along the way, the two reach consensus that communism has adapted, mutated, recurred, shedding some of the collectivist ideas that once wrapped it, providing an excellent cover for criminality, naked authoritarianism, xenophobia, imperialism, and if that's not fascism, what is? This kind of communism stands poised to unite seamlessly with right-wing movements worldwide.

Fascism has adapted, too. No matter what happens, the fact that "Donal'd Tramp" was not laughed out of the Republican primaries on Day One and continued to gather strength, finally overcoming a better-financed, albeit uninspired, adversary, means that the range of socially acceptable discourse has broadened sufficiently to enable convergence.

"We have Russian word: *konvergentsiya*," says Alex.

"Sounds like our word 'convergence.'"

"What is infinitive form of verb? Convergate?"

"Converge."

"I have slogan then: 'Criminals of all countries convergate! Proletarians fucked up!' It's good slogan I composed; no?"

"Criminals of the world converge!" Bill responds, topping off his shot glass.

"No, drink to entire slogan: Proletarians fucked up!"

"Proletarians fucked up!" Bill repeats slowly. "I think we should make it 'Kleptocrats of the world converge. Proletarians fucked up.' Let's do that one now."

They shout in unison, a roaring crowd of two:

"Kleptocrats of the world converge! Proletarians fucked up!"

"Powerful," says Alex. "We should make banners of this slogan, hang it on buildings."

"Let's start with the Château."

"Start with Château. You are right. Sorry there is no herring, no pickles."

"Who needs that . . . Okay, Alex, you finished Historico-Archival Institute, as you say. Until now, we were talking about historical fascism, historical communism, as you say. What do you make of Trump?"

"There is no Tramp. There is Putin."

"Concurred. What about your local fascism, at your Château Sedan Neuve? How do you see it?"

"From inside; how else?"

"From inside?"

"I am BOD member; president, actually. You didn't know? What's your question?"

"You? A board member? President even?"

"Absurd; yes? They urged me to ballotate. Doesn't sound right. What's right word?"

"Run."

"Run. I am in perpetual opposition on BOD. I am president, was chosen last year. Greenstein is vice president. He has two members in his pocket. I have nothing. President job traditionally goes to member who knows least."

"Whom does the vice president have in his pocket?"

"You saw them at North Pool, when you were sitting on chaise in front of them, I saw you when I walked by. You are big celebrity here, you should know."

"Hmmm."

"On BOD, you always need three. Nobody cares what remaining two members think. I am one of the ones no one cares about. Russians mostly hate me."

"But they voted for you?"

"No one knows how anyone votes. Greenstein's wife cooks election results. They want me because I am ineffective."

"What about the effective ones, the pocket members?"

"Their names are Igor Roytman—the big one who was in red swimming suit—and Sergei Kushman, the one in blue swimming suit. They and Greenstein do everything together. He gives orders, they stretch out and salute!"

"Who is the fifth member?"

"Old American guy Johnny Schwartz, who gets drunk every night and shoots at ocean from machine gun. He can't see at all, so he wrecked his Lexus even! He is perfect BOD member, shows up once for first meeting, talks about Battle of Bulge, then doesn't come to single BOD meeting in eleven months."

"Why should he, if all decisions are made by triumvirate? Greenstein and the members in his pocket, as you say?"

"Not all decisions. Main decisions are made by Greenstein and people he meets once a year on yacht twelve miles away in ocean.

"It's where everything is decided. They say, 'Break balconies,' and he breaks balconies. They say, 'Destroy South Pool,' and he destroys South Pool. They say, 'Give me nineteen millions,' and we announce special assessment and take loan from bank—and people lose apartments and take loan on, so to say, subprime rate, because president of bank is on yacht also."

"And you really know this, about the yacht?"

"Yes, I know about yacht."

"Have you been on that yacht, seen it?"

"No. But I know."

Bill tops off the vodka in his glass: "To Historico-Archival . . ."

"Fuck your mother!" Alex responds joyfully.

At this point in the deliberations, Bill bids adieu and departs to continue to meditate on these and other weighty matters in seclusion.

"This place is a fucking ashram," he says as he pushes the elevator button and the contraption commences verticulation, toward the twelfth floor. "An ashram with vodka."

People shouldn't laugh when they are alone, but if something strikes you as this outrageously funny when you happen to be in solitude—let's suppose you find yourself in an elevator—does anyone have the moral authority to judge you for laughing?

Bill breaks the seal on another half gallon of Kozachok and, handle in hand, takes a deep, soul-targeting gulp.

Maintaining your capacity to look at yourself in the mirror is, indisputably, Step One. But shouldn't Step One be followed by Step Two? What is Bill's role in this struggle? Has Bill's father become one of them? If so, this betrayal is bigger than the biggest, most brazen ambulette fraud on earth. Or could it be that Melsor has taken an evolutionary leap ahead of his son, adapting, surviving?

Finally, Bill's mind turns to the subject he has been struggling to avoid: the sexual encounter at Klub Susanna. That act, if you could call it that—which you could and should if you are to be honest—brought on a separate cascade of bad memories.

Bill takes another gulp.

A woman has just parted his borrowed robes and fucked him, albeit inconclusively, so to say, pardon his English, entirely by mistake. And what was that about the Bentley? It's too easy to dismiss this as a case of mistaken identity and wash your hands of the whole thing. Did he have an obligation to avoid this misidentification by stating more clearly who he was and spelling out the nature of his business, convoluted though it was? Should he have left without offering to compensate her financially instead of leaving her bawling in dark seclusion? Further, does he owe Gwen a disclosure?

How would life be different if his mother were alive? Maybe he wouldn't have drunk so much tonight, would be ashamed to. This is not the drinking he was indulging in at home in the not so distant past—less than a week earlier, much less.

That form of drinking involved a bartender, a liquid he could taste. Adverse sequelae weren't lurking around the corner. He was in no physical danger—at least no more than the next guy.

When your hands hold on to the plastic handle and your lips close around the twist-off spiral of the bottleneck, you enter a different universe, and if this isn't your cue to run home, nothing is.

Falling asleep after all that is not among Bill's problems. The ceiling above him spins insistently. The room spins, too, albeit in a different direction.

Bill wakes up at 3:20 A.M. He remembers to text four license plate numbers to Gwen. The fifth car, the one belonging to Johnny Schwartz of the Battle of the Bulge fame, turned out to be unsuitable for blind driving, and therefore was totaled.

Gwen, at her crisis management firm, has access to all the right databases and can run that check easily.

He thinks about his obligations again. Should he disclose the events at Klub Susanna?

Even in his drunkenness at 3:24 A.M., he recognizes that the prudent answer is no.

After Bill falls asleep again, he dreams of being upright, walking past a stack of paintings, bumping into them, watching them fall to the floor, being vaguely amused by this mishap. He is aware of Luka Mudischev staring at him from below. It is a dream, something about the fucking penis; isn't everything always? He steps on one of the paintings angrily, breaks through the canvas, but presses on. He is past the kitchen now, wishing he had coffee; something drops to the floor, something breaks, and he is careful not to step on the shards. He thinks he feels sharp pain in the arch of his left foot, but no matter, he will press on, he will not be delayed.

He needs air, urgently, to fight off this suffocation. Is this how Dr. Korczak and his orphans felt in their Treblinka-bound cattle car? Except they didn't get air. They got Zyklon-B, or some such. Well, not in that exact moment, not in that cattle car, but soon thereafter. After a brief struggle with what in these parts is known as the "slice door," Bill forces it to slice out of the way, letting the air pour in.

What is it about the Nazis? What makes them so relevant to this place, to his dream here? He is outside, walking. But there is a fence. He must . . . get . . . over . . . this . . . fucking . . . fence. He must get to its outer side, where there is more air, where the air is fresher, freer, and maybe his mother is there, who knows? What is she doing there? Dancing with Dr. Korczak? Teaching

English to the orphans? English; a lot of good it will do them in Treblinka.

He must get there, and he would, if it weren't for his right leg. His left leg is on the fence; perhaps if he could use his body as a counterweight, he could roll over, like a pole vaulter, sort of, just roll, it takes a single push. It would be easier if only the fence weren't so cold. Why does it feel so hard, so—aluminum? And why is his face wet? Why is the wind gust so un-dreamlike, so this-worldly?

"Fuck," he says as he wakes up atop a balcony railing, staring at the ocean thirteen floors beneath. This is unmistakably real. He is one very real jolt away from falling. Were it not for the wind driving sheets of rain toward him, he would have taken that final unwitting, sleepwalking jolt.

It's possible that the driving rain brings him back sooner. It is certain that it saved his life.

Sometime later, inside the apartment, Bill pulls a piece of porcelain out of the arch of his left foot, cleans up the shards of the broken teapot, and restacks the Luka Mudischev paintings, carefully hiding the one he destroyed while sleepwalking.

As he closes the slice door, Bill briefly considers wearing the canopy and container to bed. This would require him to sleep on his stomach. The idea strikes him as mildly amusing.

Bill's list of injuries now includes bruising from the crooked cane, the punctured, bleeding arch, plus whatever damage he has done to his liver.

The call from Gwen, which comes in at 6:29 A.M., January 15, feels almost like another in a series of jammed transmissions of a Voice of America broadcast to a Soviet citizen during the Cold

War. A missive from the outer world, an indication that someone out there gives a rip.

"Glad you picked up. Having a bad feeling about all this; you know it?"

"Would love to see you."

"I'm just dropping in for a conference with NFL folks."

"But you have time for dinner?"

"That and you can drive me to the airport—yes. I had someone run the license plates. Are you sure all these cars are in possession of condo board members?"

"What do you mean by 'in possession'?"

"The cars are leased by a third party—all of them."

"All of them?"

"Every single one. Leased by International Construction and Implementation, Inc."

"ICII. My father calls them ISIS."

"Yes. That's what I hate about this: every car you gave me is a Lexus, and they are all leased by this ISIS, and, based on what you tell me, given to members of this Château Blahblah Neuve. They give you a car for being on the board of directors. And other things, too, presumably."

"It's careless—yes. How do you get from fuckup to sinister?"

"They don't give a shit—that's what's sinister. People don't behave like this, flagrantly violating every rule, unless they're certain the entire game is rigged. Everything! This is flagrant. The cartels behave like this, Putin behaves like this—that's about it."

"Trump behaves like this."

"He'd like to, but it won't fly."

"You are so Washington. Here in Florida every man is a cartel unto himself."

"I pushed you out of Washington, to write the Butt God book. Have you done anything on that book?"

"Yes, just getting going . . ."

"I feel responsible for you. I don't want you to come back in a box."

"I'll try not to."

"Can you handle the truth?"

"Try me."

"I liked that kiss. It felt right. I want another—tomorrow. I get the feeling you are in real, physical danger. Take nothing on faith. Trust no one."

"Sure."

"Bill, acknowledge what I just said!"

"Yes, yes . . . yes, I understand."

14

ISIS

Later in the morning—it's January 15—Bill receives an e-mail from his father. The subject line: CURIOS CONVER-SAISHON—ABOUT YOU. Bill clicks on the attached audio file.

"He just left," says a man with a Russian accent.

The previous evening of vodka and Galich had left Bill with the feeling of longing for home.

America is fully his home, too. Alas, America (1) has nothing that could be regarded as equivalent to Galich and (2) has a fundamentally flawed attitude to vodka. Vodka is not a libation! It is not a moral and ethical equivalent of gin! It is not on the same continuum as whiskey! Vodka is a Platonic ideal. Vodka is—vodka!

The second man in the conversation takes a deep breath, the sort one takes when a problematic friend or, worse, a problematic parent, calls in the middle of the night with urgent shit to report.

"Remind me . . ." It's Greenstein.

It's not entirely clear why this conversation hits Bill like betrayal. The two men are on the condo BOD together. Of course, they have official business, they have their own agendas.

ALEX: Are you familiar with *Inspector General,* Mr. Greenstein?

GREENSTEIN: Federal agencies have them, HHS, DOD, but that's high ranking. This guy is low on the totem pole.

ALEX: No, no, not federal agencies—the play! By Gogol.

GREENSTEIN: No. But I am busy now, please state your business, Alex.

ALEX: Inspector general, traveling incognito, with secret orders. I am quoting, almost. Except, of course, he is not inspector general. Corrupted officials believe that he is.

GREENSTEIN: Would you like to talk tomorrow, when you are sober?

ALEX: I am fine now! I am here to tell you that this inspector, he speaks Russian—and, worse, understands Russian culture—deeply!

GREENSTEIN: I find this hard to believe. He looks like a simple flunky investigator, trying to blend in, pretending to be a friend of the lunatic poet.

ALEX: I tested him. I played music only certain people, from certain stratums, would know, and I can tell you—definitely—he knew it! There is also good language training for FBI, I am told. He was drunk, and when lines came up, his lips moved in all right ways. He understands our culture! *Really* understands. In all nuances! Also, can you say *ikhnyuyu*? Like in "fuck *their* mother"? It's toast we drank. I said it first, but he said it with me—no problem. You try to say *ikhnyuyu. Ikhnyuyu.* Even I have hard time sometimes, even now . . .

GREENSTEIN: No, thank you, Alex. What does it matter that a drunk's lips move correctly? I really must go . . .

ALEX: You know, we have expression: fisherman sees other fisherman from far. I tell you, he knows us and is pretending not to! When FBI sends agent who speaks Russian and understands Russia . . . This is complicated situation.

GREENSTEIN: What does that change?

ALEX: He clearly sang the lines from song: *"Nash poyezd ukhodit v Oswentcim / Segodnya i yezhednevno."* Which means "Our train is leaving for Auschwitz / Today and daily."

GREENSTEIN: Auschwitz . . .

ALEX: I didn't mean it as insult. Sorry.

GREENSTEIN: No offense taken.

ALEX: He also knew what "graphomania" means. It means he understands literature.

GREENSTEIN: So?

ALEX: So? It's high-level investigation, with big geopolitical implications! For them to send Russian expert . . .

GREENSTEIN: Of course, if I were to accept the premise that they did. He doesn't look like an anything expert to me.

ALEX: Yes, expert is relative term.

GREENSTEIN: A dim bulb is a dim bulb.

ALEX: This information, about the investigation, is valuable to you?

GREENSTEIN: Not at all.

ALEX: Does it mean expulsion is still going? Even though I bring you this . . .

GREENSTEIN: Yes. This changes nothing.

ALEX: I have nothing left. How am I to pay? You sucked it all out with your special assessments. Can I at least keep Lexus till lease ends?

GREENSTEIN: I will inquire with the sponsor. You have my promise on that, but it's conditional on your behavior. Goodnight, I am hanging up now.

ALEX: Goodnight.

Were it not for the previous night's near-fatal encounter with the balcony railing and the equally sobering conversation with Gwen, Bill would have reached for a bottle, early hours notwithstanding.

How can a man who plays Galich's songs while cheerfully serving his guests drinkable vodka turn out to be a two-bit *suka*? (The word translates as "bitch," but means "snitch.")

Was Alex a *suka* in the former USSR?

Probably not.

How can anyone speak of maintaining dignity, honor, and the ability to look at oneself in the mirror, and then, a few minutes later, beg Herr Obersturmführer Greenstein to delay eviction, or is it deportation, and—please, please, please—allow him to keep that ill-gotten Lexus till the lease runs out?

Is this what it takes to survive? Is evolution pushing us into becoming a lower life form, devoid of ethics, esthetics, dignity? Has Alex—like Melsor—adapted to this Pax Mediocritatem? Or is it a Bellum?

The malaise that hits Bill next is not of the existential sort, nor is it of the variety that can be found in the Diagnostic and Statistical Manual of Mental Disorders. It's questionable whether it's a disorder at all: after a rough day and a rougher night, he simply has nothing to do.

For the first time since he got to Nella's unused apartment, Bill opens the refrigerator. It's full, in a way.

There are usual staples of the Russian émigré diet—Georgian sauces, marinated vegetables. The iconic eggplant caviar in an equally iconic Soviet-era five-hundred-milliliter jar has grown a thick layer of white mold.

Bill looks in the freezer. There, he finds a loaf of Borodinski bread, an intense pumpernickel, probably several years old. He hasn't had it in at least fifteen years, long enough to work up a craving. Though the bread is chocolate brown, its outside is white, frost-bitten.

His phone emits a ding. It's a text:

"SECOND REMINDER: My lawyer needs a payment to finalize this. Your behavior is irresponsible. You should consider yourself fortunate that I didn't make a support claim."

"Sure, go ahead," he mutters. "Make a fucking support claim."

He takes the brick-shaped loaf, raises it high, hitting the kitchen's low ceiling, then swiftly slams it against the counter. This breaks apart the frozen slices.

As the smell of toasting Borodinski bread wafts through the apartment, Bill goes through other frozen foods—all Costco, stuffed this-and-that. No, thank you. However, he also finds a garland of thick wurst, stuck in a sealed plastic bag. He opens the bag, and with a deft pull, breaks off two thick links. In Moscow of his childhood, these were called *sardel'ki*. It's a superfood that can go directly from your freezer to a pot of boiling water. Bill gets the water going, and, while waiting, runs a Google search for ICII.

Investigations have rhythms of their own, and sometimes they need to slow down, even sleep. At those moments there is only one thing to do: look for an angle you haven't explored— get your ass out there—and shake it up.

He returns to the refrigerator. Mustard would be good. Alas, there is no mustard. He will have to settle for the Georgian plum sauce called Tkemali. The thing is contained in a ketchup-like bottle, but ketchup it's not.

A text from Melsor comes in as the water starts to boil: "ISIS takes battle position. Look across street."

Funny, he was just looking up ICII—a sign from the gods! Based on what he sees, ICII looks like any other construction company. It's registered as a Florida corporation. Obviously, it has a corporate fleet of Lexuses, as he has learned elsewhere. Would be interesting to find out whether the BOD members declare them as income . . . On the other hand, fuck that, let the U.S. government worry about tax revenue—Bill has enough problems, thank you very much.

He walks out onto the balcony, only to realize that he can see but a small corner of the across-the-street parking lot owned by the Château condo association. He returns to the kitchen as the water starts to boil. Bill drops the frozen links in, turns off the stove, and leaves. They will have to cook in his absence.

Overnight, while the Château slept, ISIS had installed two office trailers and perimeter fencing at the Château's unused parking lot across Ocean Drive.

Guys in hard hats are scurrying about in the dust, punishing sun, and exhaust fumes. Their movements are economical, soldierlike. They are dressed like an army—black polo shirts with ICII embroidered in yellow over the heart, on the left. The yellow lettering matches the hard hats.

Three tractor trailers are dropping off their loads. One is carrying a massive generator. Another bears a half a dozen front-end loaders. A third is laden with scaffolding. The gates are locked, the fence topped with razor wire.

A group of residents gathers at the gate, looking in helplessly. Melsor is not among them, but Alex is.

Alex is looking in on the arriving equipment, his cheerful demeanor gone.

Two yellow front-end loaders are building a pile of scaffolding on the opposite side of the chain-link fence.

Bill and Alex shout over the roar.

"Rough morning?" Bill inquires.

"Looks like Bagram Air Base!"

"A lot of money being spent. Has the BOD approved a big project?"

"Board doesn't matter. This is *psikhicheskaya ataka,* psychiatric attack, to tell all of us that our votes will not count. Election results will be counted, but differently, like in USSR. You know Gogol, *Inspector General?* Don't lie, you do!"

"Okay, I do."

"That was cleaner time, nineteenth's century Russia. Crooks had fear there and then, so to say: they turned each other in. You know difference between then and now, there are here? Now and here nobody will turn in nobody. They aren't afraid. They don't care—and I don't care anymore. We lost everything—even before next assessment."

"We?"

"It was my daughter's apartment, she put it in my name before her husband went to prison."

"A hidden asset?"

"Your colleagues trapped him. All urologists take kickbacks, but he was caught. They had wire. They taped him, convicted him, disgorged him, mostly, except this apartment, which they couldn't find. Or it was more trouble than it's worth."

"They look for vulnerabilities."

"Apartment was paid for, but we didn't count on special assessments."

"Can't you sell it and move someplace else?"

"Tell your people they can take it now. Tell them Alex Bogomolov doesn't care anymore. No one buys apartments here, so it's not important. You can't pay assessments, you can't sell apartments, you are prisoner. They take your money and do what they want. It's triple fuck-your-mother: Fuck your mother! Fuck your mother! Fuck your mother!"

Another tractor trailer, spewing a cloud of black smoke, pulls up to the gate. Bill starts to cough.

When the cloud recedes, Alex is gone.

||||||||||||||||||||||||||||||||||||||||||||||||||||||||||||||||||||||||||||||||||||||||||||||||||||||||||||||||||||||||||

MY CONTRACT WITH THE CHÂTEAU

Checking his e-mail, Bill finds a note from his father.

The subject line, in English: "Your *Washington Post* email bounce-backed."

Why is this in the subject line? Should Bill acknowledge that his career is over, perhaps weep on Melsor's shoulder? That might make sense in another family, with another Melsor, on a different planet.

Bill moves on to the text of the e-mail: *"Perevedi pozhaluysta."* [Translate please.] The very existence of this document in English—i.e., the fact that it will appear below—indicates that Bill was, again, a very good boy, or trying to be one, which is the same thing.

Upon reading, you will recognize places where Bill would have proposed revisions—toning down reference to the Third Reich, for example—but, in a bow to expedience and conflict avoidance, didn't.

Preparation of this document was a three-step process:

(1) Melsor writes the original in Russian;

(2) Bill prepares a translation in the nonconfrontational manner he learned while preparing Melsor's Brief to the U.S. Supreme Court (importantly, he does this while eating *sardel'ki* and the Borodinski bread he had located in the freezer earlier in the morning); and

(3) Melsor carries out the final review, which involves restoring aggressive use of Capitalization, ALL CAPS, <u>underlining</u>, **bold face**, *italics*, font, and exclamation marks!!! All of these were present in the original Russian and reoccur in the translated version.

The decision to break the document into subsections—stanzas—must be attributed to Melsor.

This document would have looked different had it been bounced back to Bill for the final-final edits. He would have declared it way-the-fuck-too-long, meandering, and fundamentally unreadable—the Unabomber Manifesto.

Nonetheless, with the English mostly corrected, Melsor's declaration of candidacy for the Château's BOD is significantly more of-this-world than even his finest English-language *paskvil'*.

This thing even has articles, some definite, some indefinite:

MY CONTRACT WITH THE CHÂTEAU

By Melsor Katzenelenbogen

I, Melsor Katzenelenbogen, hereby Formally Announce My Candidacy for the Board of Directors (BOD) of the Château Sedan Neuve Condominium Association (CSNCA).

I RUN AS A LIMITED GOVERNMENT CANDIDATE.

Why do I run?

I run because I believe that the Fundamental Governing Documents of the CSNCA <u>and</u> Florida Statute 718 should be respected, studied, obeyed, and be considered in **EVERY RELEVANT DECISION** of this Condominium Association.

Fundamental documents are called "fundamental" because they <u>are</u> *fundamental*.

This is precisely *how* My Limited Governance will be Fundamentally Different from our past BODs—and **especially our current BOD!**—the Members and Vice President of which egregiously flaunted and continue to flaunt all legal constraints that should instead govern their conduct.

Here is what distinguishes me from *all other candidates*:
I—and no one but I—will ratify a **CONTRACT WITH THE CHÂTEAU:**

Should I at any point violate any obligation set forth in said Contract, I will—upon review of evidence by an impartial body—give my *a priori* consent to be <u>automatically recalled</u> from the BOD.

This Unilateral Contract automatically becomes Bilateral upon my election by Unit Owners and subsequent election to the **Post of Vice President** by my fellow Members of the BOD.

In the unlikely event I am NOT ELECTED to the BOD and appointed Vice President by its Members, I will RESIGN from the Board altogether, because under this Governance Structure there is no point to being in the Minority.

About Me:

I am a Russian poet, a veteran of the Struggle for Freedom of Soviet Jewry, a noted literary scholar and critic, and an American healthcare entrepreneur.

My past works of poetry are published by American Student Council for Freedom for Soviet Jewry [**PESNI O SVOBODE** (Songs About Freedom); Ann Arbor, Mich.: 1974]. My later works are published by the noteworthy Amazon.com and are exhibited prominently on www.stihi.ru, an important cultural website, where they are found side-by-side with acclaimed Masters.

I suffered from a long dry spell as a poet, but recently the "flood gates" opened, and I returned to writing.

"Why is Melsor setting aside important creative work for the sake of the administrative?" you might ask.

I answer:

"I run because I realize that—unless <u>fundamental</u> change occurs—I would not be able to live calmly and write here in this perhaps final stage of my Creative Career.

I have met with considerable success in my current work, as I finish a cycle of satirical folk rhymes dedicated to subjects all of us should regard as—yes—**Fundamental**. You may be treated to a benefit performance of these in the near future.

Today, as the very existence of Château Sedan Neuve is in

danger, as a Citizen, I have no choice but to set aside my poetry and turn my gaze to three Fundamental Documents:

- Declaration of Condominium,
- Condominium Bylaws, and
- Florida Statute 718.

I beseech you to join me in reading and studying these Fundamental Documents, because an *Informed Constituency* is the only proven safeguard against *Tyranny* and a mighty antidote to the *Culture of Kleptocracy!*

OUR BOD VICE PRESIDENT, THOUGH A JEW, LEARNED TRANSPARENCY FROM <u>HITLER'S REICH</u>!

Florida Statute 718.113 (2) (a) requires that "75 percent of the total voting interests of the association must approve the alterations or additions."

In the interpretation of the Florida Court of Appeals, approval is required for any effort "to palpably or perceptively vary or change the form, shape, elements or specifications of a building from its original design or plan or existing condition in such a manner as to appreciatively affect or influence its function, use or appearance."

This is The Truth! There can be no Disagreement with this Interpretation!

But our current Vice President Greenstein has declared: *"I am the Condominium!"*

We must shout back: *"No you are not!"*
He will shout: *"Yes, I can!"*
We must shout: *"No, you can't!"*

How do we **MAKE THE CHÂTEAU GREAT AGAIN**?

It will become great after We, the Unit Owners, <u>*break the back*</u> of his regime on this BOD.

The deeper you read our Fundamental Documents, the more convinced you will become that—like the Brezhnev Power, to which I courageously spoke the Truth—people to whom we are entrusting authority live exclusively by the laws they happen to like, discarding and ignoring the laws they don't like.

Today, our situation is very complicated, even **dangerous**:

Two Members are in Vice President Greenstein's pocket, one Member is a weak man who is on the verge of eviction because of Unpaid Dues, and one, whom I respect, is so disgusted that he doesn't attend meetings. (There is no reason to name names.)

I have always been a Limited Government advocate.

During the 2015 election, I posed a single question to all candidates: "Do you plan to be guided by Paragraph XIX of our Declaration of Condominium, which states that "Improvements and alterations costing in excess of $14,999 shall not be made without the approval of 2/3 of the entire voting power of the membership of the Association?""

No Candidate answered in the affirmative. All others REFUSED to ANSWER! **They IGNORED ME!**

Now you can see the consequences—without your approval or even your knowledge!—the South Pool Deck, formerly an Oasis, was turned into an uninhabited Desert where all dies.

Today, our contractor ICII—**like its near-namesake ISIS**—stands poised to warm its hands on a $19 million project!

Replacement of windows alone—how can you not call this a "material alteration?"—will cost more than $8 million!

One thing is Certain: the current BOD of CSNCA will not ask you to approve these changes!

- **LET'S Not Wait Anymore!**
- **LET'S <u>Ratify</u> my Contract with The Château!**
- **LET'S MAKE THE CHÂTEAU GREAT AGAIN!**

—Melsor Katzenelenbogen
January 15, 2017

Getting out his message and being noticed puts Melsor in an elevated mood. He loves the document enough to actually call Bill and compliment him.

"Tonight, we celebrate," he declares in English.

"Celebrate what? You haven't won."

Bill is in an irritable mood, irritable because he is doing nothing, not because he is lazy and wants to do nothing, but because there is genuinely nothing to do. At home, he was always busy, even after his job started to suck.

At the moment the phone rings Bill is watching a video in

which three bird-suited young men are flying off a cliff somewhere in the Far East. The music is irritating in a heroic the-devil-may-care sort of way, so Bill turns it off, relegating the young men to flying in radio silence.

"I no longer see situation where I don't win," Melsor continues, making Bill appreciate the advantages of watching videos of daredevil adventures while communicating with his father.

"I've seen enough surprise defeats," Bill continues, still watching. "First Bernie, then Hillary, more recently. I don't believe in celebrating early."

"I made reservation at Tbilisi—at six. We walk in just before end of early bird special and get free salad and free dessert."

"You and Nella?" Bill skips a few moments of the flight. He can repeat it later. Sure, this is all extreme, but he realizes that it's edited, curated. Bird-suited men die in real life, but on these videos flight is pure and life eternal.

"No, Nella hates Tbilisi. You and I. I pay for dinner, but if you drink, you pay for that. They can separate bills."

"I have dinner plans—sorry."

Melsor pauses. One of the young men on the laptop screen before Bill flies perilously close to the cables of a gondola.

"Is it woman?"

"Yes."

"What woman? Someone you met here?"

"Someone I've known for years—in Washington."

"How old?"

With a flap, or is it a turn, of his wings, the young man on the video averts collision with a gondola. Bill imagines what the collision would have looked like, especially to occupants of the gondola. The young man flies by safely and the gondola continues its climb.

"Maybe thirty-seven."

"Thirty-seven is good. Still hope, but self-reliance—more self-reliance. For how long do you know her?"

"Fifteen years."

"You are intimate, of course?"

"Depends on your definition of intimacy. She is young, too young maybe."

"There is such saying: 'You are as young as your youngest mistress.'"

The flight on the screen continues past otherworldly rock formations, toward peasant huts and rice paddies that look like they may be five hundred feet beneath. Looks roughly like the altitude equivalent to the forty-third story of the Grand Dux Hotel.

"Is she here for long time?"

"No, she just flew in for a day. Meetings."

The chute opens as the first of the three bird-suited men glides downward. The other two follow.

"Is she journalist?"

"Was. Now she runs a crisis management firm—public relations, sort of, with a tinge of private investigations."

That flight; it seems easy.

"Smart! I want to meet this one. I will call Tbilisi and change reservation to three. But we must walk in before early bird special or price goes up."

Bill hangs up, and before more images of yet another wingsuit flight appear on YouTube, he recognizes the magnitude of the intrusion he has just allowed to take place. He should have been on guard. Surely he knows that even blinking is hazardous when dealing with Melsor. An uninterrupted meeting with an emissary from his former life was the only thing Bill craved more than a proper—i.e., non-Kozachok—drink.

Now, Melsor has forced his way into his evening of sanity, perhaps even into his life. Why the hell did Bill have to admit that he was meeting a woman?

16

TBILISI

At the appointed time—5:45 P.M.—Melsor shows up wearing a double-breasted blue sport coat with the insignia of a yacht club that has only Ralph Lauren for a member. The pants are pristine white, as are the belt and the loafers. The polo—make that Polo—shirt is hot pink, the ascot an especially electric shade of lavender.

"I will drive," he declares. "Give me key."

Melsor gets behind the wheel, the white Prius turns on silently and lurches into the nearby white Cadillac Seville.

Paying no attention to the damage—it's quite a jolt; there has to be some—Melsor shifts to Drive, commanding the Prius to lurch forward.

"That's why God created bumpers," mutters Bill.

Their destination is Restaurant Tbilisi. Gwen would join them there sixish. Melsor has been assured that as long as two of the three people in their party walk in before six, the early bird pricing will apply.

"You wrote about science?" Melsor asks.

"On occasion."

Silence.

"Do you think they would have cured her if she got sick today?"

"Hard to say, but things wouldn't have gone the way they did. She didn't die of her disease. She died of treatment, and that treatment is no longer performed."

Why spare this tyrannical geezer from having to confront his role in the travesty he had orchestrated? This cop-out—this lie—is worse even than Bill's maintaining the fiction of his continuing employment.

Could his mother have been here, in this well-bumpered white Prius, sitting in the front seat *right now*?

Not likely, but possibly. Bill would have been happy to take the backseat, be the kid again.

"Did you find singers for *chastushki*?"

"Afraid not. Talked to one woman, she wasn't interested."

"Just as well. I think I have."

"Can I ask you what happened after my mother died? I understand insurance refused to pay for the transplant. Is that what started that ambulette business?"

"I had sixty thousand in debts to hospital, technically, and I was prepared to announce bankruptcy, but Alter said I didn't need to. He said, 'You are respected in Russian community—just see all these people who came out to cemetery.' So, I stopped working for pittance and started ambulette business, which he co-owned with me, secretly, of course."

"It was not entirely legal . . ."

"What I did was not so wrong. I didn't write prescriptions for ambulettes. Alter did."

"Is he still living?"

"Living, living. Should be getting out of prison in about a year.

"Enough unpleasant conversation! I do only pleasant conversation. Imagine big, stinking garbage truck going by. I don't look at it, I don't smell it. I let stream of consciousness take me away to pleasant things: I am in mountain stream, I am surrounded by daisies.

"That's the difference between you and me: you choose to smell garbage, I choose to smell flowers."

Tbilisi is a massive, brightly lit joint. The cuisine is nominally Georgian, but *zakuski* are Russian, salty, fatty, smoky—excellent.

The drink Bill craves is of the sort no self-respecting painter would use for cleaning brushes. A real drink, the kind that gives strength to confront, or at least evade, adversity. A real drink, not swill, not rotgut. A real drink, not Kozachok.

He wants a TB—badly.

Just as badly, he wants to avoid discussion about the physician Melsor was once enamored with. Werner Bezwoda was the name. The fucker indeed was later found to be a fraud. He collected no data—it was all falsified. He had no regimen. He made shit up and put it on slides. But it's over, who cares—she is dead.

The waitress has a pad and a sharp pencil. She stays on message, offering minimal guidance and no recommendations: "It takes the kitchen thirty-five minutes to make kabobs."

"Can you please ask whether they have Tito's and Bombay?

Tito's is a vodka. Bombay is a gin. I want it mixed one to one, shaken, with an olive."

She offers to check at the bar.

The tables at Tbilisi are configured in a way Bill has never seen before. Usually, at least in Washington, a table for twelve is a rarity. Here, a table for twelve would be laughably small. He sees a few tables for groups of four or so, but the bulk are set for enormous banquets. Eyeballing, Bill sees a table for thirty and a table for sixty. A third table, which takes up a corner of the restaurant, seems to be set for at least ninety.

The waitress returns with a tray with two small carafes, one of which contains one hundred grams of vodka, the other one hundred grams of gin—presumably Tito's and Bombay.

Also on the tray, there is an empty five-hundred-gram carafe, a soup plate full of ice, a salad plate with an assortment of olives, and two lowball glasses.

"Do you have a way to mix them?" Bill asks.

The waitress looks at Bill vacantly, shrugs, turns around, and leaves. She did her best.

Bill's thoughts of the logistics of TB-mixing are quickly thwarted by Melsor, who drinks all the Tito's, leaving only Bombay behind. Bill sets aside his Washington nostalgia, drinks up the room-temperature gin, and orders a 750 of chilled Russian Standard—because fuck it.

After doing what he did to his mother—after insisting on the worst, most brutal, and completely discredited treatment—how can Melsor see himself as a medical maven?

He placed his trust in Werner Bezwoda. Now he places his trust in Donal'd Tramp.

Introspection was always a luxury Bill couldn't afford. Tuning out, walking away for years, seemed less perilous—and was.

The Katzenelenbogens gave up on Washington and moved to Brooklyn in 1985. There was no point in staying. The U.S. Information Agency had no plans to employ Melsor. The language schools at the Department of Defense and the National Security Agency were still hiring people who could teach. Alas, Melsor wasn't being offered employment. It's possible that the U.S. Supreme Court filing, which Bill translated against his will, went from the clerk's office to be filed in a dossier kept by another arm of the U.S. government.

On one occasion, Melsor did get as far as a voice test at the Voice of America. He had to read some stuff into a tape recorder. According to a story whispered to Bill by his mother, Melsor read a paragraph, then added: "All of you know that I can speak Russian, that I speak well. So why don't I read you a few selections from the works of Akhmatova, Gumilyov, Tsvetaeva, Blok, and Mandelstam—and, of course, myself."

This quickly turned into a recital of Melsor's works in Russian and English, spilling from the cassette's Side A to its Side B. In the end, Melsor sang. His song was Georgian: "Suliko," a favorite of Stalin's. Did Melsor believe that he was responding to the prompt?

But why wouldn't he discern the opportunity to do better than the prompt and, if the gods smile upon him, seize the day?

After the move to New York, Melsor edited a Russian shopper, sort of like the South Florida *Machta*, which he mostly filled with unauthorized translations from the *National Enquirer*.

To keep his mind agile, he adjuncted at Hunter College. Rita had an office job at an insurance company that was making inroads into the Russian immigrant market. She didn't seem especially bored.

Her diagnosis came down on June 8, 1999: stage III breast cancer; four positive nodes, a motherfucker. A doctor, whom Melsor found through Russian contacts, said that high-dose chemotherapy with a bone marrow transplant was her best bet for long-term survival.

Bone marrow transplantation made sense logically: (1) you harvest the bone marrow and set it aside, then (2) use a massive dose of chemo to kill the disease and the remaining marrow, and finally (3) reintroduce the marrow you had reserved.

There were anecdotes of success and anecdotes of failure, but the procedure made so much sense logically that few women agreed to join randomized trials.

Sixteen and a half years later, at Restaurant Tbilisi, Bill is reconstructing that spring's events.

"She has breast cancer," Melsor told him over the phone.

Bill was in the newsroom at the time. There was no pause, no time to adjust to this devastating bit of news. Melsor jumped straight into what he planned to do about it: "I have excellent doctor who promises to cure it, Jewish man, orthodox: Alter. He is follower of South African doctor who found best treatment."

Bill listened:

"The most important thing is finding highest dose that doesn't kill patient. Alter, her doctor here, told me that this doctor Bezwoda, Werner Bezwoda, used Negro women to find it. Then he started giving it to white women. Now Alter has license to use exactly same treatment as Bezwoda.

"It's difficult regimen, but she is strong."

Actually, Bill knew quite a bit about Dr. Bezwoda and his amazing cancer cure. A week earlier, he was in Atlanta, in the front row at the plenary session of the American Society of Clinical Oncology, watching a presentation of four studies that showed that bone marrow transplantation provided no better survival than conventional chemo. Also presented that day was a study by Werner Bezwoda, the guy who developed the most toxic regimen of all.

While four studies screamed "Don't do it," Bezwoda cheerfully presented results showing that the treatment was just great.

How would Bill explain all this to Melsor? Hasn't he already made up his mind?

Bill heard his mother crying in the background. He knew what was transpiring in that apartment; he felt as powerless as he did the day his father forced him to translate his Supreme Court filing.

Melsor's choice of treatment may be indefensible, but there is logic to it. With him in charge, why would anything other than high-dose chemo with bone marrow transplantation rank high enough to be considered?

All the elements were present:

- The chemotherapy regimen was strong and crude. If that battle-ax wouldn't teach cancer a lesson, nothing would.
- Racist ideology was present, too, at least in Melsor's mind. The therapy was allegedly tested on *untermenschen* in South Africa—without their knowledge, and with good results.

- A conspiracy theory completed the package: the establishment is out to destroy Bezwoda. Why are they out to destroy him? Ha! Imagine the money that could be lost by hospitals and drug companies if breast cancer were cured.

Bill's first question was to himself: Does it make any sense to argue with this guy? Will he be able to recognize that the world that exists outside him doesn't always operate in accordance with his rules, that it's far more complex than it would have been had Melsor been its God and king?

His mother was about to get a brutal—murderous—treatment. Should he have made an effort to inject reality into this situation?

He did make an effort: "I know quite a bit about this treatment. I want you to be careful. I was there, in the front row, in Atlanta, when group after group of top-tier researchers presented the data from randomized clinical trials—that's the gold standard. Their data showed that this is a barbaric, killer therapy."

"They have jobs to protect."

"I know these people. They are honorable. Your Bezwoda was there, too. I saw him up close, presenting results that were diametrically different from everyone else's."

"They were ordered to sabotage trials. Insurance companies will go bankrupt if they keep paying for Bezwoda's cure."

"There was something odd about Bezwoda, a certain kind of smile on his face. You learn to trust this instinct when you do this long enough . . . Please don't do it."

"He will win Nobel Prize after they prove him right. I am absolutely convinced that this is right thing to do. There is nothing you can say that will dissuade me."

"You know, after these randomized trials, insurance companies are refusing to pay for transplants."

"I don't care. We must save her. I will fight with them later."

"Can I speak with my mother?"

"No. You are going to try to convince her not to do it."

"And you will kill her. For nothing."

"They will start procedures tomorrow. You will not speak with her until it's over and she is cured."

Bill didn't get to say good-bye to his mother.

Rita Katzenelenbogen was a 10-percenter, one of the casualties of the procedure. She developed a killer infection after the harvesting of her bone marrow. She slipped into a coma, and died before Bill could get to her bedside. He arrived in time to see her body wheeled out of her hospital room.

What would he say to her if he had a chance? You fucked up, you trusted your husband—my father—following him as he ignored another in the series of red lights he'd ignored in his life?

Bill attended the funeral. Standing silently before his mother's grave at the Mount Carmel Cemetery in Queens, he fought the admittedly Freudian/Shakespearean urge to avenge her death by killing his father and the Great Humanitarian, Dr. Mordechai Alter, the asshole who administered the cure.

He could imagine the headline in the following day's edition of the *New York Post*: KADDISH PICKAX MURDER; WASH-INGTON POST JOURNO HELD.

He could have beaten both Galich and Ginsberg in the "Kaddish" game. He could have owned "Kaddish."

Bill looks up and sees Gwen enter the restaurant.

In heels and a white dress, she looks like a swan making a pond landing. He waves, she waves back.

There is a hug, a quick kiss. An introduction to Melsor leads to a courtly kissing of the hand. She expects nothing less, clearly.

Melsor holds her hand in his a little too long for Bill's comfort, but apparently not hers. She flashes a delighted smile in Bill's direction.

Melsor raises his glass as Bill pours vodka into Gwen's.

MELSOR: I have toast! TBL!

BILL: Which means?

MELSOR: It means: to beautiful ladies!

BILL: *Oy vey.*

GWEN: Why didn't you tell me your father is cute?

MELSOR: Thank you for making my son happy.

GWEN: I don't know whether anyone or anything can accomplish *that* . . . Are you happy with the outcome of the elections?

MELSOR: Donal'd Tramp?

GWEN: Trump; yes.

MELSOR: Very, very happy. I live in America since end of Carter, and things always get better. With Reagan they got better, with Bush they got better, with other Bush they got better again. Now, finally, they will get very good. Only Donal'd Tramp can end political correctness.

GWEN: I don't understand that.

MELSOR: That's because it's everywhere, like air. You don't understand air until you start to cough. Political correctness needs to be taken out, like poison from atmosphere, and only Tramp understands that.

GWEN: So, Trump is like an editor with a red pen? Everything that smacks of what we call the pursuit of equality and social justice, he will take out with a stroke of his pen. Do I understand you?

MELSOR: I know this country. I lived in Washington, I lived in New York, I was editor, I was writer, I was businessman. This country is built on strongness of people and free market. Everything else sucks its blood.

BILL: You are starting to sound like you are a fan of Putin's, actually.

MELSOR: What's wrong with Putin?

GWEN: Meddling with our presidential election?

MELSOR: In this world, everyone spies on everyone. Why is this spying worse than other spying? Because it was effective? Because it helped Donal'd Tramp?

GWEN: I don't want to put you on the spot, but do you think you would have left Russia now?

MELSOR: No. Definitely not. I would have become oligarch. Probably in health. I would build best hospitals in biggest cities and instead of patients going to best hospitals here, best doctors would go there and give best treatments.

BILL: A medical entrepreneur. A hospital oligarch. Of course.

Waking up from silent reflection, Bill turns to Gwen: "How did your meetings go, Gwen, not to change the subject? It was NFL—right?"

GWEN: Team owners. You know, I do crisis management. Well, the players have been beating up their girlfriends a lot lately, and the press has been eating it up.

MELSOR: Managers of football teams? American football?

GWEN: Owners . . . Yes . . .

MELSOR: What did you tell them?

GWEN: The only thing you can do is cut and run. Don't defend the indefensible. Women don't ask to be beat up. Express remorse—and move on as fast as you can. In this climate, you can't afford to look like you are defending this kind of behavior. Violence against women has to have consequences. A wise friend once told me: "Nobody has ever gone wrong by taking too much responsibility. Own your guilt, own your unmooring, reach for more, more, more."

MELSOR: The players who beat their girlfriends, are they black?

BILL: You didn't hear that. I would strike it from the record.

GWEN: Never thought about that. An abuser is an abuser—pigmentation doesn't matter.

MELSOR: Woman is the most perfect creation of nature . . .

GWEN: And?

MELSOR: Feminists take it too far. Let me give you example: an old Jewish man who had sport team, in basketball, not football. He had affair with young woman. She made recording of their conversation in bed, publicized it on Internet, and government makes him sell his basketball team! What kind of country we have if you can't speak honestly in bed with your lover?

GWEN: Hmmm . . . Interesting . . . Isn't wife-beating still considered more or less okay in Russia?

MELSOR: There is saying in Russian villages: "He who beats his wife loves his wife." It means you have to love woman enough to beat her. If you don't care, you will not hurt her when she hurts you. I never beat anyone. Never loved anyone enough, maybe.

BILL: This is not going anyplace good.

GWEN: What's actually happening here, in this restaurant? I don't think I've ever seen tables this long, or this many people at the same table.

MELSOR: You don't understand?

GWEN: Not at all.

BILL: Neither do I.

MELSOR: These are birthdays—eightieth mostly. Mine had forty people three years ago. It was in Klub Susanna, which is better. It has show.

BILL: That table over there will bill ten thousand dollars, maybe more.

MELSOR: That's why they put tips on bill.

GWEN: Who pays? The birthday boy?

MELSOR: No. You invite people, they give you one hundred dollars, and you do deal with restaurant to give you good menu that still costs less than one hundred each. What you don't spend you keep.

BILL: People paid you to attend your birthday party?

MELSOR: You bring checks and maybe postcard. I had forty people and ended up with five hundred dollars left after tip.

Usually at Russian restaurants you worry about the havoc wrought on your food by heat lamps and microwaves, but the Tbilisi kabobs are spectacular, not dry at all.

Alas, with this conversation, Bill will not be able to swallow another bite.

Bill's mother would be eighty now. It would have been nice if she could have seen her sixtieth birthday. It would have been better than being killed by a two-bit crook at a community hospital in Jersey.

Bill looks at the faces of the old people around him. Maybe these folks are happy inside. It's possible that they are rejoicing at their friend's eightieth. But if they are, their faces do not reflect their exaltation, or, for that matter, much of anything at all. No one seems to be talking to anyone. The age spread seems to be from seventy to ninety, give or take. Where are the children, grandchildren, great-grandchildren? Will there be toasts, the wishes of health and happiness to the birthday boys and girls? Or is everyone just waiting for the musical numbers to begin? Will there be anyone around to say good-bye to them when they die?

GWEN: Sorry to eat and run. My flight is at nine forty-five. I can take an Uber.

MELSOR: No, no, I'll drive!

BILL: Actually, no, I will.

MELSOR: Are you sober?

BILL: This is relative. Thank you for your concern.

When the check arrives, Gwen grabs it, but Bill deftly wrests it away. Melsor makes no gesture to reach for his wallet.

There is another kissing of the hand as Melsor is dropped off at the Château, and Bill and Gwen take off for the airport.

"I have two things to say," Gwen begins.

"Shoot . . ."

"First, this was the most silent I've seen you—ever."

"And second?"

"Second, I don't know what to make of your wardrobe upgrade. What happened?"

"Complicated."

"Let's see, you are fucking an eighty-five-year-old widow who dresses you up?"

"No. Can you miss your plane?"

"Can't. A meeting tomorrow morning. Going after the NFL business."

"I am getting used to making out at curbs."

"I can return this weekend, if you want me to. We need a door, perhaps even walls."

Parked at the curb, they make out like teenagers until a police officer, using his cruiser's PA system, suggests discreetly that they get a room.

Gwen gets out of the Prius, straightens her dress, shakes out her hair, and leaves for Washington.

FRAU MÜLLER-GREENSTEIN'S BIRTHDAY

On the way back, Bill gets a text from his father: "Be here at 9:30."

"Why 9:30?"

"Birthday of Greenstein wife."

Is Melsor throwing a party for the wife of his nemesis?

When Bill comes in, Melsor and Nella are listening to the "transmissions" from the Greenstein apartment.

There is a call from the front desk: "Mr. Greenstein, two gentlemen are here to see you."

"So, it's true!" shouts Nella.

"So, what's true?" Bill asks.

"Rumor is—he pays two men on her birthday!"

"Pays two men for what?"

"What do you think?"

"I called Johnny already," says Melsor. "He will like to listen to this. It will keep him from shooting his Bushmaster at ocean. Pour vodka in bottle!"

"And get *zakuski*, I know. You think I don't know?"

Melsor is giving orders, ever the corsair, Captain Blood or Captain Bloodsucker, depending on where you happen to be in relation to his blunderbuss:

"Get vodka!"

"Cut herring!"

"Call comrades!"

"Turn on generator!"

"Find ruler for opening slice door!"

Nella's growling is muffled, its message always the same: "I don't need your damned commands. Don't shout! I know what to do. Better than you do."

If this isn't a partnership, what is?

Johnny Schwartz looks like he ran through the hallway and up the stairs. He wears Desert Storm camouflage fatigues and an orange Miami Dolphins T-shirt depicting a dolphin jumping either to the sun or through a ring of fire. Tall, lanky, muscular, he looks like he spends a considerable amount of time at the Château's gym.

MAN ONE: We are from Craigslist.

GREENSTEIN: Come in, please.

MAN TWO: Who are you?

GREENSTEIN: Think of me as a director.

MAN ONE: Director? We don't do filming. I don't want filming! It wasn't in the deal! What if my wife sees it?

MAN TWO: The Craigslist ad said: Casual Encounters: "mm4w," which mean two men for woman. There's nothing about film. Film is more money, and we don't do it.

Nella returns to the kabinet, *carrying a bottle of Grey Ruse, four shot glasses, and a plate of pickles and tomatoes.*

NELLA: What did I miss?

MELSOR: Two men walk in . . .

NELLA: From escort service?

MELSOR: From Craigslist, maybe escort service also. They are agreeing on price.

MAN ONE: Right, and with another "m" here it's "mm4mw." That's not what was advertised. You need somebody else. You'll find it.

MAN TWO: That's right— "mm4mf" is two men for couple. We don't do couples.

GREENSTEIN: I will not be joining you, no worries.

MELSOR: Are they Mexicans?

JOHNNY: *Schwartzes.*

BILL: Please . . . Terrible word . . .

JOHNNY: What's so terrible about *schwartzes*? Means black. Like my name: Schwartz. Want to call me a racist? Call me a racist.

MAN ONE: Okay. We don't give our price on Craigslist, but our regular price is three eighty. We can do three fifty. For one hour.

MAN TWO: You can be in the room if you have to.

MAN ONE: That's another hundred bucks, usually, but you can be there. But don't try to put nothing up my ass, cause if you do, I'll turn around and slug you. I don't like it, and it's not part of the deal.

GREENSTEIN: Your full three hundred eighty dollars is in line. But I want each of you to take this. One for you, and one for you.

JOHNNY: What do they want?

MELSOR: Who? Men? They want money. Herr Greenstein wants Frau Greenstein to get satisfied by two men, I think.

NELLA: Shhh!!! Quiet!!!

MAN ONE: What's this?

GREENSTEIN: It's Viagra.

MAN TWO: I don't take no Viagra. I have high blood pressure. Fortunately, I don't need none, haven't yet.

MAN ONE: I took it when I agreed to be filmed once, for a screen test. It looks like a little blue football with sharp edges. This one's red and round and has a *C* and a star in the middle.

GREENSTEIN: It's a crescent, and there is a little star that looks like a dot. It's the same Viagra, but it's from Turkey.

MAN ONE: I don't care. I am not taking it.

NELLA (TO JOHNNY): He wants her to get satisfied by two young men. When I heard rumors, they said he doesn't stay in room. He sits in living room and reads newspaper or watches Fox News.

JOHNNY: Why can't he do it?

NELLA: He has micropenis.

JOHNNY: Does it work?

NELLA: I don't know. He has a *protez* . . . How do you say it?

BILL: Prosthesis.

NELLA: It makes him look normal. But his *prostite* falls out. I saw it fall out of his bathing suit and float in ocean.

JOHNNY: I don't understand. Does he have a *schlong* or doesn't he have a *schlong*?

NELLA: They say he does, but it's micropenis—small.

JOHNNY: Small like rabbit-small?

NELLA: I don't know. I didn't see it. But he wears rubber penis, like lesbian. Look in literature. And it floated to surface when I talked to him when he was swimming in ocean.

JOHNNY: It floated away?

NELLA: I don't know. He looked like he didn't notice, but after I left he caught up with it, if he swam fast.

JOHNNY: Caught up with it and put it back there?

NELLA: If he caught it. I am sure it's expensive.

JOHNNY: I hate him as much as the next guy, but I don't see what the big deal is. When you get old, things fall off. How is it different from, for example, dentures?

MELSOR: *Sha!* I want to listen!

MAN TWO: Are you telling us she is so ugly that we need this Turkish stuff to get going?

GREENSTEIN: This is different. It's a natural product. It will not hurt you.

MAN ONE: In the e-mail you said MILF . . .

GREENSTEIN: Beauty is in the eye of the beholder.

MAN TWO: A MILF would have to be your daughter's age. Is she your daughter or something, because if she is, I am going home. I am not going to be a part of this, unless she is of legal age or older. I don't even know how Craigslist's calling this . . . Man gets off on watching two studs ram his daughter.

MAN ONE: And I am not taking any of this Turkish stuff, either, even if she isn't pretty. I say blindfold me and I'll think about my wife.

GREENSTEIN: No . . . She is not my daughter. She is my wife. And she is of legal age.

MAN ONE: So it's straight mm4f, not some weird-ass mm4mf shit, with guys doing shit to us we don't usually do?

GREENSTEIN: Accept my assurances.

JOHNNY: What is that word, MILF? I've been seeing it for eight or ten years.

BILL: Since the McCain-Palin thing in 2008?

JOHNNY: Something like that.

BILL: It's an abbreviation for Mother I'd Like to Fuck. It's a demeaning term for middle-aged women who look good.

NELLA: Wilfreda Müller-Greenstein is not MILF.

MELSOR: Quiet!

NELLA: Aren't you recording?

(Melsor nods.)

MAN ONE: Okay, I'll take this Turkish stuff. You seem okay.

MAN TWO: Okay, I'll take it, too, may need it, from what you are telling me.

GREENSTEIN: I am letting you in on something of a family tradition. There is something of a play involved: I take her out to an early dinner at a German restaurant.

She goes to bed to take a nap while I pretend to watch the news. Then two men walk into the bedroom, and she opens her eyes slowly, and you take it from there. Can you do that?

JOHNNY: After we helped mop up the Battle of the Bulge, we pressed on. I was a mortar man in the Seventh Army Forty-fifth Infantry Division. We went up and down and around Munich, liberated Dachau and a bunch of its satellites, one camp after another, and, believe me, I got to see that country as well as anyone. So correct me if I'm wrong: he has hired two guys and he wants them to do his wife while he is watching?

NELLA: I don't think he sits and watches it.

JOHNNY: My buddies and I had a one-word explanation for all this . . . Just one word . . .

MAN ONE: You want us to wake her up?

GREENSTEIN: Yes.

MAN TWO: Okay, we'll do well by you, man.

GREENSTEIN: I have full confidence . . .

NELLA: I can't tell what's going on in bedroom.

JOHNNY: Seems kind of quiet. Not a good sign.

BILL: Ominous—concurred.

MELSOR: What do you expect? Screams? The girl is having good time.

NELLA: Girl? She is grandmother! I tell you what's going on. She is in bed, pretending to sleep. They walk in on their toes, really quietly, they pull back blanket by a little, and she pretends like she is waking up.

JOHNNY: Is she buck naked?

NELLA: No! This is not like that. They start slowly, but then things go faster. Normal, except there are two of them.

MELSOR: How do you know?

NELLA: I have friend whose husband treated her like that once a year after his *prostitektiny.*

BILL: Prostatectomy.

NELLA: Greenstein is vicious animal to everyone else, but to his wife he is considerable.

BILL: Considerable may not be the right word.

NELLA: What word is right?

BILL: Considerate, maybe.

NELLA: What's the difference?

JOHNNY: If he were considerable, he wouldn't have to pay two guys to do her. He has a micropenis; right?

BILL: Actually, considerable in this case would refer to size, not performance. It could be large, but not seaworthy.

NELLA: Considerate, considerable, I don't care which one it is. He is animal to everyone else, but he loves her.

MELSOR: And she him?

NELLA: And she him.

MAN TWO: Hey, my buddy just passed out!

GREENSTEIN: What happened?

MAN TWO: He was mounting her from behind while she was working on me up front, and he just fell back.

GREENSTEIN: Is he breathing?

WILFREDA (*shouts from the other room*): Yes, he is breathing, he started up again.

MAN TWO: Call the ambulance! What if he dies? He is barely breathing, but his thing is still strong. What was in that Turkish stuff?

GREENSTEIN: Natural ingredients. Nothing that will harm you.

MAN ONE: Hey . . . What happened there . . .

MAN TWO: You went out cold. How are you feeling, bud?

MAN ONE: A little woozy still, did I just pass out? Hey, let's get the fuck out of here . . .

MAN TWO: Hey, dude, look at his eyes, they are bloodred, he's blown all the capillaries in there.

GREENSTEIN: I see no point in continuing then. You are free to go.

BILL: Okay, I get the idea.

NELLA: Sh-sh-sh. I am listening.

MAN ONE: What about our money?

GREENSTEIN: What money? You failed to perform.

MAN TWO: But he passed out, almost fucking died, all because of that Turkish shit you gave us. Now that I think of it, I am feeling light-headed, too.

GREENSTEIN: You were paid to perform a service, and you failed to complete it.

MAN ONE: But we got going, man.

GREENSTEIN: You were paid to provide a complete service. Getting started is of no value whatsoever. It's detrimental, even. You don't buy three-quarters of a surgery, or a quarter of a car, or half a cat.

MAN ONE: We'll report you, man.

GREENSTEIN: To whom? The vice squad? Craigslist? FDA?

WILFREDA: Thank you for your efforts, now get out of here.

MAN ONE: Hey, the cunt has a gun. What the fuck!

GREENSTEIN: It's a Glock 43, and my lovely wife knows how to use it.

(The door slams.)

JOHNNY: Now are you ready for a one-word explanation for all this?

BILL: Yes, why not . . .

JOHNNY: Just one word says it all, from one who's been there . . .

GREENSTEIN: Thank you, gentlemen.

BILL: Shoot?

JOHNNY: Germans . . .

Wilfreda's rant—in German—follows. Amused as everyone else in the room seems to be, Bill doesn't understand anything about what he has just heard. He catches a few German words that sound mildly intriguing, but, ultimately, who cares?

Wilfreda is a mystery. She is in her seventies. Septuagenarians fuck—yes. Bill can easily accept the notion of Wilfreda having an affair, sanctioned or illicit, with, say, the octogenarian heartthrob Johnny Schwartz.

But the thing he hears transpire makes no sense to Bill. It's as puzzling and undeniable as Florida itself: yet another form of exploitation; yet another form of devastation—Bill hears it, as do others in the room.

"Germans . . ."

That one-word explanation is good enough for Johnny, but not for Bill.

Marriages are complicated things. Fascism is more complicated still. You do either for a while, revel in happiness or in the glory of Deutschland-first, Russia-first, America-first, and then you pay and pay and pay, for decades, for centuries. Bill finally gets around to his vodka.

Here in Florida nothing is what it appears to be. Rubber cocks float into the ocean, husbandly duties are not husbandly duties, fiduciary responsibilities are not fiduciary responsibilities. Folks pay one hundred dollars to attend eightieth birthdays out of fear that no one will come to theirs. Casual encounters are not casual encounters, mm4w is not mm4w, idiots are not idiots, Viagra is not Viagra, Grey Goose is not Grey Goose, everyone has an angle, everyone has a fraud.

Bill reaches for a pickle to deactivate what by now has become the familiar taste of Kozachok.

At least a pickle is a pickle.

18

PANI CONSUELA RAMIREZ-WRONSKA

Gwen broke no laws when she fabricated the open fly and the Washington parties, and being summarily, humiliatingly fired by the *Post* dealt with the matter completely.

Bill's misdeeds at this point are, any way you look at them, classifiable as felonies of the sort that may require atonement at one of the facilities operated by the Florida Department of Corrections.

After eavesdropping on the Greensteins' sexual episode, Bill consults a table on the Web site of the Reporters Committee for Freedom of the Press. He clicks on a summary of Florida laws covering recording. Florida Statute chapter 934.03 reads: "All parties must consent to the recording or the disclosure of the contents of any wire, oral, or electronic communication in Florida. Recording, disclosing, or endeavoring to disclose without the consent of all parties is a felony, unless the interception is a first offense committed without any illegal purpose, and not for commercial gain. These first offenses and the interception of cellular frequencies are misdemeanors."

Planting a bug in the apartment of his father's rival candidate for a seat on the condominium board of directors is an act committed for commercial gain. It's a felony.

As a guardian of the public interest, Bill appears to have crossed to the enemy side. He acknowledges this. It's possible that this is temporary and that there is a way back. It may very well matter that the couple he eavesdropped on was the enemy, that he was doing to them what they would without hesitation do to him, that this was an element of broader struggle, an experiment in using criminal tactics to fight crime.

Kozachok continues to go down smoothly, likely because Bill has relocated it to the freezer.

Scribbling in his reporter's notebook reads: "Journalism = Eunuch at a gangbang. You observe, you don't do. I want to do." The fact that only four pages in this notebook contain any writing or drawing makes this entry significant. Here is all that exists:

Page 1—The question-mark drawing done in the course of his flight to Florida,
Page 2—The table listing the makes of cars he sees at the Château parking lot,
Page 3—Zbig's street address/license plates of the Lexuses belonging to the Château board members/addresses of Klub Susanna and Restaurant Tbilisi.

The observation about eunuchs is on page 4.

It should be noted that the entry continues:

"Task 1—Find meaning in Zbig's death. Task 2—Stop ISIS. OK to use criminal means to stop criminal activity."

Now there is decidedly nothing to do. Bill picks up a pen and composes a poem, his first in Russian:

> Резиновый пенис ушел в океан,
> Его подхватила волна.
> А я наливаю водки стакан—
> Как много на свете говна!

Not bad for a debut. The English translation is admittedly imperfect:

> A rubber penis went off to sea,
> It was picked up by a wave.
> And I am filling my vodka glass—
> There's so much shit in the world!

Like a mule who knows how to get his drunken peasant home, the computer takes Bill to BASE jumping videos.

In Washington, he thought of himself as the guy who trained bartenders at Martin's to produce perfect TBs.

Now, alone, surrounded by porny oil paintings of Luka Mudischev, compulsively watching videos of people jumping from great heights, chugging ice-cold Kozachok straight from the bottle, Bill focuses on the design features of the bottle at—or, more precisely, *in*—hand.

On a video, a young woman in a bathing suit prepares to dive off the side of a Norwegian fjord. Clearly, she is not seasonally dressed.

Bill's mind continues simultaneously on two tracks.

On Track One, he wants to know why it is that half-gallon containers of milk have handles while half-gallon plastic bottles of vodka usually do not.

On Track Two, he zeroes in on the young woman's preparation for a BASE jump—her commitment to the jump.

Taking a swig of Kozachok, on Track One, he acknowledges the thoughtfulness of the men and women of Kozachok Distillery Inc. of South Philly, who cared enough about their clients' convenience to decant their product into a handle-enabled container.

On Track Two—the video—the young woman takes a leap into the abyss. What follows is of little interest to Bill.

Bill scrolls back, making the image freeze at the instant the jumper's beach-sandaled feet part with the edge of the cliff, her breaking point. This is it—the precise point of departure, the point of commitment, the point of *doing,* as opposed to the point of *writing. No mas* gangbang eunuching!

He notes that these are questions he wouldn't have thought to ask had he remained in Washington, the place now referred to as "the swamp" in Trampenese.

The moment of departure—this instant of commitment to the leap, this breaking point—has to be the principal element of his obsession with watching these BASE-jumping stunts, this irresistible draw of the eye candy of death.

How could he have not thought of it?

The phone rings. It's Gwen. Fuck it! She isn't entitled to know what he is about to do.

Inspector Luftmensch reaches for the car keys.

It's 1:30 A.M. and not even a stray Lamborghini can be spotted on Ocean Drive. The white Prius tentatively piloted by the undeniably inebriated William "Ilya" Melsorovich Katzenelenbogen is the only moving object in sight.

Police cruisers await, poised to attack from the canopies of flowering bushes and palm tree groves of shopping centers. Bill sees them all, or at least believes he does. He remains calm. The word "philosophical" might be used, given his pre-Prius intellectual journey, the one that produced a debut poem in Russian and derived a monolithic theory that unified journalism, the packaging of vodka, gangbangs, eunuchs, and commitment to BASE jumps into a single entity.

A handle of Kozachok rolls gently on the floor of the front passenger seat.

Yes, police cruisers await, and within them danger lurks, but a wheezy hybrid doesn't make their list of top targets. A gentle weave can be observed in its trajectory—granted—but this is South Florida, officer, be pragmatic. In these parts, everyone has a cause to weave, with explanations falling into a complex cluster of categories of etiology: geriatric, psychiatric, emotional, neurologic, pharmacologic, and multifactorial. If you start pulling over everyone who momentarily deviates from the tyranny of white lines, you will be stopping every soul on Ocean Drive, especially at this late hour.

It's 2:07 A.M. and the lights at the Wronski home are out.

Bill rings the bell, but there is no answer. Consuela isn't home, or she would have at the very least yelled at him, thrown things at him, or made good on her threat to call the police. Fuck it! Bill doesn't care.

This is not just another stiff. This is Zbignew Stanislaw Wronski, M.D., the Butt God of Miami Beach! His college roommate! His friend! Why did he fall into that abyss, forty-three floors below, through the atrium's glass ceiling? Did he fall, or was he pushed? Why? Why? Why? No one, no one is more committed to this story, more entitled to it. This is Bill's leap and his alone. This is his boundary, his end of the old, his beginning of the new, his vote of confidence in his pack and his canopy and every meter of string packed inside it. In jumps, in falls—in everything—all you can do is summon the courage to make your feet abandon the edge. The rest is up to the winds, up to the gods.

Bill sits down on the white marble steps of his late friend's home, grabs onto the plastic handle, and takes a modest-sized swig of Kozachok. God bless South Philly. Sleep, if sleep is what it is, descends slowly, invisibly. He lets go, ascending to the universe of chutes, fly suits, great heights, protruding boulders.

Bill is awakened by a tap on his nose.

The object is inanimate. It is, in fact, a stiletto heel.

"You are drunk," says Consuela.

She is in a black silk sheath dress. It's so classic that the word "short" is all you need to describe it. She seems to wear no jewelry other than a wedding ring.

"Afraid so."

"You had to be drunk to come back—after that scene. With you playing paparazzi. What do you want?"

"It would be paparazzo. Singular. I was alone."

She doesn't look like the paragon of sobriety, either, but Bill is clearly worse off, bad enough to correct her Italian.

"I am here because I want to know what happened to my friend."

"That night?"

"And before."

"Do I even matter to you?"

"You? Yes."

"What do you think about me?"

"You are very beautiful."

"Come in," she says, opening the door. "Bring your bottle. We will need it."

The living room of the Wronski home is aggressively white, cliché white: white marble floor, white furniture.

It's not clear why Bill recognizes the two white leather sofas as the Charles, by B&B Italia. He looked it up once, when he was covering a story about the offing of a lobbyist in his home in Chevy Chase. (The brains, alas, ruined that sofa.)

Bill went through catalogs for that story. It's simple: to begin to understand the stiff, esthetic choices are a good place to start. Objects guide you into the inner world of their owners. It's Anthropology 101, or something like it.

At the Wronskis', a massive painting of a nude woman reclining on the beach hangs over the sofa. At first, Bill thinks it's a photograph, then realizes it's a painting. Super-realism. Bill respects super-realism.

"Do you think it's me?"

"Is it?"

"Could be. Or not. Zbig talked a lot about you, about your friendship."

"Which aspect of it?"

"He said you understand stories the way no one understands stories."

"I am flattered."

"You were the one who told him that a shape is a story, shaping is storytelling, reshaping is, too. He credited you with shaping his career. What were you drinking?"

It's her in the painting, of course. The purpose of art is to provoke. Bill hands her the bottle.

"Out of the bottle?"

Bill nods. She takes a swig, grimaces, takes another.

"This, too, tells a story: a rough remedy for a rough time. What did Zbig tell you about me?"

Bill thinks back. "Nothing, really."

"That's a story in itself. Do you think I am, say, Argentine?"

"Are you?"

"I could be. Do you think Ramirez is my real maiden name? I could be Slovenian for all you know. My name could be Malaria."

"Is it? Are you?"

"Possibly. Did he say I was his patient?"

"Were you?"

"I could have been. Did he say I was a model?"

"Were you? Are you?"

"Could be true."

"Are you going to tell me anything?"

"No. Not now. I never told anyone anything. What they don't know, they make up. I don't talk. Not even the homicide squad."

"They were involved?"

"Maybe."

"Why are you agreeing to be on that idiotic reality show?"

"Because they invited me. Others didn't. Zbig was pushing me to do it, said it was good for business. *Real Housewives* said they already had a plastic surgeon's wife, the wife of the Boob God. And now it's gone, and Zbig is gone."

She takes another swig.

"Are you going to tell *me* how Zbig died?"

"No."

"Forget me—you might owe *him* the truth, unite him with his story."

"It's not useful to pressure me. I will do what I will do—on my terms."

"Have you told the story on this *Merry Widows* thing?"

"Not yet, but I might. Should I?"

"Stories are for telling. I think. I believe—or believed."

"What if they—the audience—aren't equipped to understand?"

"That's not your problem. Your responsibility is to come up to the edge of the cliff and leap. The rest is up to the gods. That's Rule One of storytelling."

"What about the truth? Does it matter?"

"The truth is the thing that sets you free. At least that's what I've always believed."

"Do you believe this still?"

"I think I do. Maybe."

"Why do you waver?"

"Because lies bring victory. Look at Trump. He lied. It worked."

"Hillary never lied? Like George Washington?"

"Hillary lied—but it didn't work. Imagine what Hitler could have achieved if he had social media. You no longer have to imagine."

"Are you getting lost, Bill?"

"I might be—blame the vodka, always blame the vodka. All I am saying is, let me formulate it . . ."

She hands him the bottle.

He takes a swig.

"The truth doesn't fucking matter—not anymore. Do you accept this notion?"

"Yes."

"It is our duty as human beings, as citizens, to be truthful. A 'virtue' is the old word for this. Do you accept?"

"Maybe."

"So: the act of telling the truth is predicated on our rejection of the truth's irrelevance. Think of it as an act of civil disobedience. Am I talking out of my ass?"

"A little."

"Okay, you might extend it to say that telling the truth in the pre-Trump world was already a Fuck You to the system. Yes? Now, in the Trump world, it's a bigger Fuck You—a Fuck You, Fuck You, Fuck You. A triple salute. Are you with me?"

"No."

"I am shitfaced. Sorry."

"No apologies warranted. I needed to hear all this . . . I think. Thank you. You may have helped me more than you know."

"I hope so, but I don't believe I helped you one bit. Or myself, for that matter."

"Rest assured. But I am tired now—ciao. You can sleep on the sofa, if you wish."

"I'll make it home; I am good. The Prius knows the way."

Bill turns to leave but pauses and turns again to face her.

"Does it mean you'll tell the story, anywhere, ever?"

"I might."

19

||||||||||||||||||||||||||||||||||||||||||||||||||||||||||||||||||||||||||||||||||||||||||||||||||||||||||||||||||||||||

THE FORUM

The Gulf Stream Room was mostly spared in the past deluge or deluges that had devastated the Château's lobby. It's a former library—former, because the books are almost entirely gone. The shelves that line the four walls stand bare.

In better days—four decades ago—someone had applied thought here. The floor is the same paisley design, except here it's smaller, the shades of marble lighter. With Lapidus at the helm, this was not some stuffy high-goyish men's club library.

Before he ensconced himself in Miami, Lapidus did many commissions in New York and Chicago—including, in fact, shoe stores. He knew many things, and shelves were among them.

These shelves are white, laminated, with little paisleys that remain as gold as they were the day they were made.

The ceiling tiles in the Gulf Stream Room, alas, are gone. Only the steel grid remains. Since there is no natural light—which is just fine for a library—Lapidus used Poul

Henningson PH5 fixtures—eight of them—to provide peripheral light. In the center, he used a Henningson Artichoke chandelier.

Bill snaps a photo and sends it to Gwen, causing a predictable exclamation: "I want!"

It's 6:30 P.M., January 16. Folks begin to trickle into the Gulf Stream Room for the start of the annual ritual of election to the BOD of the Château Sedan Neuve Condominium Association. The stakes this year are unusually high, but power is locked in. Election is two days away.

The math is simple: five seats on the board, a three-vote majority required to make *any* decision involving the Château's $4 million annual budget, and a virtually unlimited ability to levy special assessments.

It's all about candidates.

Vice President Greenstein is running again, for his sixth term. Micropenis aside, he is a lucky man. Had the misdeed that led to his disbarment also led to a felony conviction, he would have been precluded from serving as a fiduciary of a condominium association.

Two board members in his coalition are unchanged—Igor Roytman and Sergei Kushman.

Greenstein-Roytman-Kushman is an undefeatable coalition of Russians and Americans. Theirs is the perpetual winning ticket.

When Roytman is not engaged in water sports, at least one item of clothing he wears is always red. Today he wears red shorts. This choice of color is a play on his last name: red man. He is a former licensed construction engineer who lost his license for a misdeed no one at the Château has taken the trouble to investigate. There is no reason to look into this. The loss of a professional license, even for cause, doesn't preclude you from serving on the BOD.

Kushman wears black, mostly in order to distinguish himself from Roytman. He is a chemical engineer who once produced paints and furniture lacquer at a facility staffed by prisoners—a Gulag enterprise. Like Roytman, he was a deeply satisfied Soviet citizen who nonetheless took the opportunity to get the hell out as soon as this became possible.

He did end up with a minor felony conviction—paints, fraud, Jersey—but his civil rights were restored more than five years before he was duly elected to the BOD.

Some years, the board is completely harmonious—i.e., all five members vote with Greenstein-Roytman-Kushman. In recent years, as special assessments mounted, troublemakers got as many as two members to the board. With three being the magic number, the presence of two naysayers on the board can do no harm.

It should also be noted that no one knows what happens after all the votes are cast and tabulation commences behind closed doors. By decision of the BOD, this process is entrusted to Frau Müller-Greenstein, the wife of the vice president.

The fourth member of the board—President Aleksandr Bogomolov, a historian—is being forced to relinquish his BOD seat, because he has fallen into delinquency. He has attempted to trade information for dues forgiveness—something Greenstein has reportedly done in special cases in the past—but in this case the vice president saw no point in making a deal.

Though disgraced, BOD President Bogomolov is in attendance at the candidates' forum, sitting in the corner, his arms crossed. It is not publicly known whether he is present in order to bear witness or out of masochism.

The fifth member—Johnny Schwartz—keeps getting elected because he is popular with the ladies. He is also popular with men who go to the gym, where he freely dispenses workout advice. Schwartz hates the Greenstein-Roytman-Kushman triumvirate, but doesn't attend BOD meetings, having determined that this activity is pointless.

But this year, as has been established, the order is being challenged by one Melsor Y. Katzenelenbogen, a former dissident, a poet and retired "medical entrepreneur."

Naturally, this naysayer, this nutcase, this professional renegade, this out-of-touch boob, this narcissistic pariah, has no chance of being elected. Frau Müller-Greenstein will see to that.

No surveys of the Château have ever been taken, but based on observation—Bill's—the voters do not split strictly based on their country of origin. Americans seem to vote for the ruling troika, even though two of its members are Russian. Conversely, Johnny Schwartz may be receiving more than half of the Russian vote—the women.

It is often noted that Schwartz is a doppelgänger for Sean Connery. This is correct, though, absent rigorous polling, it is unknown whether Johnny Schwartz actually gets the votes of *all* women or just the vote of Frau Müller-Greenstein, which could well be the only vote required for ascent to the BOD.

If you wish to find Bill in a room—any room—face the audience and look in the direction of the leftmost seat in the back row. He is either sitting in that seat or standing behind it. This is an instinctive preference, his pursuit of journalistic Feng Shui, perhaps. Also, nothing beats standing up inconspicuously and getting the fuck out. Bill takes his customary back-row-leftmost-seat position. Alas, being the youngest person in the room by two or three decades precludes him blending in.

Rumors that identify him as an agent of an unspecified agency—perhaps FBI, perhaps DBPR—make him even more noticeable—the inspector general, traveling incognito, with secret orders.

Having lost his actual authority, Bill is starting to find himself at ease with the fictional.

People continue to arrive; two and three at a time, arranging themselves in clusters—the Russians, the Americans. Melsor plans to make his entrance in the middle of Greenstein's opening remarks. This would demonstrate his contempt for the existing regime. Nella is in the room, in the front row, across the aisle from Wilfreda Müller-Greenstein. Her mission is to text Melsor and give him the entrance cue.

Four tables are set up in the front. These are the same Milo Baughman tables that can be found crippled throughout the Château. Each is roughly thirty inches by thirty inches by thirty inches—perfect little cubes.

The ruling triumvirate is in place. Greenstein in the center, Roytman on his right, Kushman on his left. Mrs. Roytman is next to her husband, Mrs. Kushman next to hers. To consolidate the GRK bloc, both wives are running for the BOD. Under Florida law, a husband and wife can serve on the same condominium board if they own more than one unit. The Roytmans own three. The Kushmans own five and are preparing to put in a bid for the soon-to-be-vacated Bogomolov unit.

Johnny Schwartz shuffles in like a superannuated GI. His fatigues are pressed; his Dolphins T-shirt, too. Either Mrs. Roytman or Mrs. Kushman stands poised to replace him on the board. Whether you support the GRK bloc or oppose it, Johnny

Schwartz is so ineffective on the BOD that he will not be missed when the GRK bloc transforms itself into the GRRKK bloc.

No place is reserved for Melsor Katzenelenbogen.

"Thank you, and welcome to the 2017 candidates' forum. I am Jonah Greenstein. I am a six-term vice president of the Château Sedan Neuve Condominium Association, and I once again humbly seek your support.

"I am happy to report that, in addition to our proven leadership, we have a new, reinvigorated slate of exciting candidates. You will hear from all of them tonight. This has been a very positive campaign so far, and with your unwavering support, I plan on all of us working together. Together, we will make the Château great again!"

Greenstein pauses—it's a cue for applause, and Wilfreda Müller-Greenstein applauds as expected.

"Though this year has brought setbacks, such as three separate floods that have devastated our lobby, our able contractor, Dr. Murthy, has been able to mitigate the damage," Greenstein continues. "I remind you that these are acts of God, something none of us foresaw or could foresee. Nonetheless, we have completed the rebuilding of South Pool and have improved the South Pool deck. We have begun removal of the antiquated and inefficient cooling system and the spaghetti-like clusters of pipes that were installed four decades ago.

"First, we want to make sure that you hear what all of us— your BOD—have done for you."

"You got more rich!" shouts a rotund woman in the third row. She is shorter than an average twelve-year-old, her hair out-of-the-bottle red. She wears a sheer tropical-print muumuu over a gold-colored bathing suit. "Answer questions about your nineteen-million-dollar deal with ISIS! How much they give you?"

Others—Russians—echo her questions, with all of this being blurted out at once:

- "You signed contract in secret!"
- "It's our nineteen million, not your nineteen million!"
- "When do we get copy of contract?!"
- "Did they give you second Lexus?"
- "What will you tell to DBPR when they come to investigate?"

Greenstein retains his composure. "I can confirm that a contract is on the table, and that following this meeting this board will decide on its ratification," he says. "We have an absolute right to ratify the contract and the financing package, and until such time when the contract is duly ratified, we will answer no questions. You are welcome to comment, but we will answer no questions. Does anyone have any opinions?"

Hands shoot up, but no one seems to see any reason to wait to be recognized.

- "Did you have competition bidding or did you just give it to ISIS, as always?"
- "How many contractors bid and how much did they want?"
- "Did you meet on yacht outside U.S. territorial water?"
- "Did you bid the rigs?"
- "What will you tell to FBI when they come?"

"First, these were all questions. And second, I assure you that this board is committed to the principles of transparency and that we did not, as you say, 'bid the rigs.' Your duly elected board doesn't rig bids! I want everyone here to recognize that we are all in it together, I want everyone to be friendlier, or at least more polite. And that's the problem here: no one smiles!"

"Thanks to you!" shouts the woman in a muumuu. "You smile when someone stick big knife under your ribs!"

Greenstein looks directly at her. "No, Mrs. Falk, I can't imagine you smiling, or even being courteous, like a normal retiree."

"Glad you understand," shouts a woman next to the muumuu-clad Mrs. Falk. She is somewhere between seventy and eighty, short, zaftig, wearing a peach-colored velour warm-up suit with matching-tinted glasses.

A tall, bespectacled man next to her shouts: "How can we have opinions when you don't give us documents and say *Don't ask questions?*"

Muumuu says, "It's from Kafka!"

"A lot of angry faces here," Greenstein observes. "This makes me sad, truly. I guess there are no comments. All we heard was questions. Since not everyone here speaks English well, let me explain: an opinion doesn't end with a question mark. A question does. Again, we will not be taking questions at this time. Does anyone have any opinions?"

At this instant, Melsor Katzenelenbogen walks through the double doors, producing a double-loud slam.

He is wearing checkered green-and-white trousers and a double-breasted jacket with what appears to be an emblem of a yacht club. The polo shirt is canary yellow.

MELSOR: Enough!!! It's time to drain swamp! I am candidate for BOD! Where is my seat at table?!

GREENSTEIN: We expected nothing less than sloganeering populism from our opposition candidate. Please make space for Mr. Katzenelenbogen . . .

Stepan and his two security guards do not budge.

GREENSTEIN: Excuse me, we should all scoot over one seat to make room for my friend.

Still, no one budges.

MELSOR: Then I will stand! I don't want to be on pictures sitting at same table with you!

Melsor moves to tower over the seated Greenstein and Roytman and Kushman.

MELSOR: With crooks like you, I *prefer* to stand!

Greenstein and Roytman turn around, look up at Melsor, exchange nods, and move apart. Johnny Schwartz grabs the extra chair in the audience and inserts it between Greenstein and Roytman.

Though a chair has been made available for him, Melsor remains standing.

"Sit down!" shouts someone from the audience. It's Wilfreda Müller-Greenstein.

Melsor settles into his chair and lets his gaze look over the audience, making eye contact or at least seeking it.

MELSOR: I believe the future former vice president was speaking. His time ended, but I will let him make farewell address! And, to his lovely wife, I hope you had enjoyable birthday.

SCHWARTZ: I join Melsor in that hope. Wilfreda, I hope your birthday was filled with love, joy, and excitement.

Half of the Americans in the audience show no emotion. The other half show disgust. Half of the Russians roll their eyes. The other half applaud enthusiastically.

GREENSTEIN: I am here to lament. This used to be a friendly building. People greeted each other with smiles, stood up for each other, were neighbors in the best sense of the word. Now this has changed.

WOMAN IN MUUMUU: Thanks to you!

STEPAN: No interruption! *Ne perebivat'!*

GREENSTEIN: That's right, we can have you removed.

WOMAN IN PEACH: And evict me? So your satraps will buy my apartment chip?

MELSOR: Now let's watch Mr. Greenstein's tugs remove this grandmother. Think about it when you vote.

GREENSTEIN: It's "thugs." Th . . . Not T. We say "thugs" in English, Mr. Kazenelenbogen. Tugs are boats.

MELSOR: Yes, tugs!

GREENSTEIN: What happened to politeness? Decorum? What happened to all of us? I wish all of us could take the high road! What would it take to make the Château flourish as the jewel it once was? I think our first step is recognition that we are in it together. I don't care what country you are from, I don't care what race you are, I care what kind of a neighbor you are. I want to see more smiles!

WOMAN IN PEACH: You want us to smile as your tugs throw us out?

GREENSTEIN: We have hard choices to make. Millions of dollars will need to be spent . . .

NELLA: How is Lexus running?

MELSOR: You say you want to make Château great? Here is what you do: abduct!

GREENSTEIN: Are you trying to say "abdicate"?

MELSOR: Your time is over, villain! I do not afraid your tugs! What's the difference between Greenstein and Katzenelenbogen? Greenstein has tugs that will throw you out. Katzenelenbogen has singers who will sing for you! Give it up for South Florida Russian Women's Folk Choir! Let's go, girls! *Davayte, devochki!*

The doors swing open again, and three old women in Russian folk costumes—headdresses and all—burst into the room.

One of them has an accordion, another a balalaika, the third two wooden spoons, an authentic, widely used percussion instrument. The singers take position in the middle of the aisle, between Nella and Frau Müller-Greenstein.

Now Melsor shouts over the sounds of soft-playing accordion: "ISIS is on our doorstep. Their machines will start demolition—demolition that these crooks, these adventurists, will make you pay for!

"In my first act as your vice president of your BOD, I will fire ISIS! Together we will defeat ISIS! No more destruction! No more kickbacks! No more Lexuses! Together we will make Château great again!"

WOMAN IN PEACH: Melsor Katzenelenbogen, you will not be elected! The commandant's wife decides who get elected!

MELSOR: Their time is over! Let's shout, all together: Make Château Great—Again!

No one shouts. The accordion plays on, providing soft background music. The audience—the Russians and the Americans—look on in bewilderment. Greenstein is on his feet; his coalition members, too.

One of the singers—the wooden spoonist—emits a guttural sound, the sort that makes *chastushki* what they are. She begins to sing:

Гринштейн гонит в ад из рая
Нас по адской лестнице.
Как оброк с нас собирает
Спешиал ассесменты.

All three women carry sheets of paper, which they throw at the audience, like propaganda leaflets from a plane.

The second woman, the one with the balalaika, takes a turn, singing the English translation:

Greenstein shoves us from heaven to hell,
Down the Devil's staircase.
Like a ransom he is collecting
Special assessments.

She makes room for the accordionist:

К нам приехал ревизор—
Сволочная гадина.
Ни хрена он не найдет!
Всё уже украдено.

Now, the spoons player steps in with a translation:

The inspector has arrived,
Poisonous and bastardly.

He won't find a single thing,
All was stolen long ago!

"Podpevayte!" beckons the accordionist. Then in English: "You sing, too!"

"Remove them," shouts Greenstein as the Americans and a large number of the Russians look on in catatonic silence. However, about half of the Russians, including Nella, Alex, and the woman in peach, pick up the *chastushki* song sheets and sing along:

Протекает в лобби крыша,
Дуба дал эар кондишен,
Здесь нам братцы не до песен
Расползлась повсюду плесень.

The Americans aren't singing, but some of the Russians are, even in English, wooden as it is:

Roof is leaking in the lobby,
Air conditioner has kicked off,
We have no time to sing
Mold is climbing on the walls.

The security guards have their orders, but they seem to have no idea what to do. You can remove one lunatic, but not dozens of people as they sing along in what has the look of a cultist observance.

Что Флоридский нам закон?
Нет на нас здесь правил.
Без балконов и окон
Жить нас борд заставил.

Florida law means nothing here,
There are no rules for us.
With no balconies and windows
The board made us live.

As the guards stand in confusion, Bill notices a drop of water appear on his notepad. Another drop lands on his arm, another on his forehead. Is it raining? Indoors? The singers are undeterred.

На борду сидят подонки
И отдачи требуют.
А нам хочется скорей
Чтоб их больше не было!

Lowlife sits on condo board
And demands a kickback.
And all we want
Is for them to go extinct.

What the fuck? Has someone turned on the sprinkler system? If so, why is the water coming out of air ducts? Has something gone completely, wildly awry? The singers don't care . . .

Мой милёнок не убийца,
Мой милёнок не бандит.

Он не просто так ворует—
В кондо борде он сидит!

My beloved's not a killer,
My beloved's not a thug.
He doesn't need to pick your pocket,
'Cause he sits on condo board!

The water comes down in streams, and some of the folks—
Russians, Americans—are trying to fight their way to the doors,
but it's slow going. The singers' costumes are getting soaked,
people are rushing past them, but they keep going:

В гараже у нас давно,
Мыши-крысы бегают!
Оставляют нам говно,
Вот как нас преследуют.

In our garage for a long time now
Rats and mice are running amok!
They are leaving us their turds
That's how we are persecuted.

Bill gets out of his chair to snap some photos, but before he
is able to capture these events, he feels excruciating pain across
his upper back, in the exact same spot where he was hit before
the onset of all this madness, on his first day in Florida. Has she
been released? Does the *Dzhuyka* Loony Bin release its inmates
so soon after admitting them?

Bill gets out of the way just in time to evade a second
blow, which crushes on the chair. The old woman in a soaked

nightshirt regroups and runs toward the candidates as they scramble to evacuate. Her crooked cane poised, she runs past the singers.

Her battle cry hasn't changed after days she spent as the ward of *Dzhuyka*:

"*Fashisty! Svolochi!*"

The room is emptying fast, but the singers are oblivious to the flood and the attacking old woman.

Раз в неделю в лаундремате
Забирают доллары,
А в козну их не сдаёут—
Воровать здесь здорово!

This *chastushka* is especially heinous in translation. Bill cringes, but he has no one to blame.

Once a week at our laundry,
They take the money
But it doesn't go to the condo—
Stealing's so easy here!

The final *chastushka* is actually the only one Bill likes, sort of. Just two lines:

Есть у нас четыре бида
Перестроить пирамиды.

We already have four bids
To replace the pyramids.

The existence of these *chastushki* in the English translation constitutes strong evidence that the New Bill—as opposed to his Inner Child—is very much in evidence in Hollywood, FL. As an adult now, Bill has the capacity to pick battles, and this capacity is what distinguishes him from a child.

Did Bill actually translate these?

He did.

Fuck the Inner Child.

The water makes a swamp of the rug, then, in gentle waves, escapes into the taupe and white marble floor of the hallway, hiding in every seam, seeping into walls, where, in the damp darkness of wooden studs, it will unleash the spread of mighty black mold. The damages could cost millions; the kickbacks, even more.

The more vigorous of the hundred or so people in the room walk out rapidly; others hobble as water keeps pouring out of the air ducts, rising to shin level. The singers press on, wet, loud, diving deep into their repertoire, improvising. Melsor is dancing. Bill has never seen or even imagined Melsor in any situation that even tangentially involves music, yet here he is, undeniable as life itself, stomping away like a drunken peasant.

As water keeps rising, the singing stops, the accordion grows softer. They sound like partisans at a bonfire, enjoying the well-deserved respite after a glorious day of Nazi-killing.

The old woman with a crooked cane is the first one out. Bill imagines her running with the glee of madness, a crooked-cane-bearing majorette leading a hobbling procession.

The board members are presumably directly behind her. Fortunately for them, the presidium table was close to the doorway.

Somebody slips and falls. It's the Russian woman in the muu-muu. Bill is in intense pain; two strikes of an aluminum cane will do that. Why does she choose him? Is it madness, or is it a dare, or is it both? He bends over the woman in the muumuu and extends his hand. She is prostrate, helpless, but she grabs his hand, grabs it hard. She is too heavy for one man to lift.

"Oy, spasibo vam," she says to Bill, and he pretends not to understand that he is being thanked, profusely at that.

In English, he tells her to place her feet against his, then to sit up, and as she struggles upward he wonders what his mother would look like now, at eighty. He was unable to help her, to save her from *her* Great Flood, from murderous high-dose chemo, from Hurricane Melsor—but he will help this woman, and he will help her now.

"Careful, walk slowly," he tells her, and they wade forth.

Theirs is a slow, stumbling, grumbling procession that moves with the speed of the slowest walker-assisted burgher.

"Thank you," she says as they reach the elevator door. The floor is wet here, too, and water keeps coming. He grabs a chair and places it in front of her, to stabilize herself as she awaits the elevator that will evacuate her to the dry land of a higher floor.

She switches to Russian, adding that she has heard people say that they know why he is here and that she is certain that he is able to understand her.

"Vy iz FBR. Vy nasha yedinstvennaya nadezhda, poslednayya, yedinstvennaya. Spaside nas. My praymo stonem ot etoy korruptsii. Kak v plenu zdes' zhivyom v etoy proklyatoy Floride."

He understands her perfectly: "You are from the FBI. You are our last hope, our only hope. We are groaning under the weight of this corruption. We live like prisoners in this cursed Florida."

"I am sorry, I don't understand you," he replies, turns around, and wades back through the stream rushing over the marble floor.

On the way back, he runs into Johnny Schwartz helping a stooped man with a walker reach dry land. Not a surprise: surely, the Battle of the Bulge had lessons to teach. You don't abandon the wounded and the vulnerable.

"We must help them even if they voted for Donal'd Tramp," Bill says to himself, then, recognizing the thought for the cheap shot it is, perishes it.

After saluting Johnny, Bill returns to the flood zone.

The room is empty. The singers are gone. The dancing Melsor is gone, too.

The air vents have run dry.

After the flooded forum, there is a vodka-drinking (*vodkopitiye* is the term playfully derived from *chayepitiye*, a tea party) at Melsor's. The apartment is filled with people—maybe fifty, most of whom now look vaguely familiar to Bill.

Six bottles of super-chilled Grey Ruse stand in formation in the center of the table. Plates of herring, sardines, heavy spreads from a Russian store as well as odd, salty items from Costco are positioned around them.

Bill spots the only person who doesn't speak Russian—Johnny Schwartz. He stands alone beneath an especially large oil painting of waves breaking on a rocky and therefore un-Floridian shoreline. He has the look of a man sizing up the scene.

Though he is presumably looking for just the right younger woman, he greets Bill with a warm "How do you do, young man" and a handshake.

He places his hand at the corner of his mouth and motions to Bill to bend toward him.

"Your father came back to see me the other day," he whispers. "He told me not to mention to anyone that you are related. What's that about?"

"He didn't explain?"

"No."

"He wants everyone to keep thinking that I'm an FBI agent or some such, staying at his place, at his beck and call."

"Are you?"

"I could be."

"I really love your father, not in a *faygeleh* sort of way, but as much as one man can love another."

"Careful there."

Bill catches shreds of a conversation between the three *chastushki* singers, septa- or early octogenarians, obviously Jewish women in Russian peasant garb.

He lobs a question at Johnny—"I understand you fought in Germany . . ."—while continuing to listen to the women.

They are discussing the report that President-Elect Trump had a team of hookers perform "golden showers" in his hotel suite in Moscow.

"We trained for jungle fighting," Johnny begins. "At first, they were going to ship us to the Philippines, but I guess they needed us in Europe more . . ."

Bill engages in one conversation while simultaneously listening to the other.

"A chto oni vidayat etikh zolotykh dushakh? V chem tut prelest'?" [What do they see in those golden showers? Where is the delight in it?]

"I was young—seventeen—I lied about my age, but others weren't much older. I was the only Jew in my unit."

"Oy, Olya, dazhe ne sprashivay; ne ponimayu—muzhiki. Chert ikh znayet." [Oy, Olga, don't even ask. Who knows what they like—men.]

"Vot by my mogli dlya nashikh samodeyatel'nost pokazat'. Tol'ko vot pomerli." [We could have shown our husbands some action. Except they died.]

"Ne govori." [Don't even say it.]

Johnny opens a can of Budweiser. "What are they talking about? Do you understand Russian?"

"Golden showers," Bill whispers.

"I can't hear so well anymore. You have to speak louder . . . The Battle of the Bulge . . . We were fresh troops, young, the grass was green, got there at the very end, mopping it up after all the hard work was done. After that, they sent us toward Munich. They didn't tell us jack shit about Dachau till we found it."

"Ty znayesh, ya pryamo tri mesyatsa prazdnuyu." [I've been celebrating for three months straight.]

"Ya tozhe. Pomog nam Putin. A ya o nem tak plokho dumala." [Me, too. Putin helped us—and I once thought so badly of him.]

Meanwhile, Johnny's story proceeds to the concentration camps. "I saw a shot-down Messer, and I salvaged the camera from its wing. It survived the crash. All I needed to do was fill it with fresh film."

"Kak mne eta Obamacare ostopizdela." [I am so sick of their Obamacare.]

"Nelzya ikh vsekh k vracham vodit', Negrov, nelegalov." [They needed to take them to doctors—the Negroes, the illegals.]

"A nam v ocheredi zhdat'." [And we have to wait in line.]

"There was a guy from Iowa in my unit. He hated Jews, but by the end of it, after he saw what he saw, it got under his skin. There was one time we lined up all the SS at a camp. They surrendered, but we shot them one by one anyway. Are you listening?"

"I am," Bill responds truthfully, more or less.

Listening to two narratives in two languages is not for the meek.

"Vy znayete, ya ran'she ne verila v evolutsiyu. Dumala chto my proiskhodim ot inoplatetyan." [You know, I used to not believe in evolution. I thought we were brought here from visitors from other planets.]

"A teper' poverila?" [Have you started to believe?]

"Da, u nas u vracha recipshonistka sidit. Negritynka. Nu pryamo obez'yana." [At my doctor's office, there is a receptionist. A Negress. I look at her and think: an ape.]

"It was my friend from Iowa who did the shooting. It changed him, the awful things he saw. Then a lieutenant showed up, made us stop. Took my camera, never saw it again."

"What do you think of the election?"

"Not much."

"Does it remind you of anything? You've actually been there; others are imagining, fantasizing."

"What? The war? Nazis? No . . . I don't know much. I was dodging bullets. They shot at us, we shot at them. I got back and voted a couple of times."

"Who was the last guy you voted for?"

"Last guy . . . I voted for Ike. You know what, there are women here. I think I am going to find me a widow—you should, too."

The three singers are basking in post-performance bliss. So much so that they haven't bothered to change out of their wet costumes.

The ensemble was started by a woman named Faina Fainberg, an ethnomusicologist, who once collected folk songs in Russian villages. Faina was a perpetual adjunct professor in the U.S., living on a modified starvation diet—until she was diagnosed with advanced breast cancer.

She was advised to sue the guy who did her last mammogram a few years earlier, and she won big. Now she lives in a condo in Sunny Isles.

"You can teach anyone to sing Russian folk songs, engineers, even FBI agents," she says to Bill flirtatiously.

"I don't know about engineers," Bill retorts.

"Actually, my two ensemble members. Bella was a civil engineer, Natashka was chemical."

The appalling conversation he heard between Bella and Natashka—the two widowed Jewish engineers in Russian folk garb—was not okay, but it was an overheard conversation. He was not a party to it. Nothing he could say, nothing he could do.

There was something deeply attractive about Faina, and that something was her art. What he saw in that performance wasn't a clowning Jewish intellectual or a professional entertainer pretending to be a Russian peasant.

This wasn't Soviet-era "folk" adapted for stage. Condo board content, the setting (the Gulf Stream Room), and Bill's idiotic English translations notwithstanding, this performance had the sound of genuine folk music.

He approached Melsor from the side and whispered in Russian: *"Ty byl prav. Gde ty ikh nashel?"* [You were right. Where did you find them?]

"Na Craigsliste—120 baksov." [One hundred twenty bucks on Craigslist.]

With this, Melsor drains his glass of Grey Ruse and bows.

———

On January 17, at 6:49 A.M., Bill gets up in time to watch the sun rise over the ocean. A thin rose-colored stripe appears beneath blue clouds, growing, reddening, its boundaries cutting through the grayness of the water. He notes that for the first time since his arrival he isn't hungover.

What happened last night? It seems he imbibed sparingly, slowly sipping Kozachok posing as Grey Goose, then again sparingly, under its own label. He recalls being amused by seeing Johnny Schwartz slip away with Faina, the ethnomusicologist.

After the party, he surfed the Web, catching up on the latest golden shower cheap shots and Trump's absurd pissing match with the civil rights icon John Lewis, who'd had the gall to question his legitimacy. (Bill has met Lewis at many Washington events over the years and regards him as a prince of a guy.)

He recalls dipping into Florida condominium law and speaking with Gwen. They both noted that their conversations are acquiring the feel of a budding long-distance romance. The Princess of Style has blossomed into the Queen of Remorse, and their dance has changed. The moves are slower, more intense, less comedic—a different feel altogether. Their airport curbside makeout sessions at National and Fort Lauderdale felt different, too. Is that what "right" feels like?

On the morning of January 17, before resuming his duties, Bill decides to go for a run.

No one seems to have bothered to rope off the Gulf Stream Room and the surrounding hallway. Since Lapidus never foresaw repeated flooding, he didn't spec any floor drains and about an inch of standing water remains in the Gulf Stream Room. The artichoke chandelier is on the floor, bent, destroyed by streams of water that came down through the air ducts. Three of the six PH5 lights are destroyed, too.

This had to be an awful lot of water. There was no rain. It had to have come from somewhere. Bill turns around and heads toward the elevator. He is back on the second floor, walking through the plaza toward the South Pool. The pool has ceased to be a speck of intense blue in the middle of a fascistically grand plaza, that bit of other—that unmistakable touch of Benito Mussolini in the realm of Morris Lapidus.

The pool is still there, but the water is gone—every drop.

At the curb, Bill sees a gondola-shaped sofa. A massive breakfront rests on its side, one of its glass doors broken. The sofa-sized seascapes are still in their heavy gold frames, prostrate on the pavement. Massive black trash bags are piled up on top of each other—a lifetime of treasures steaming inside them, family photos, china, crystal, documents—everything.

It's not the sacking of the Winter Palace. It's the sacking of Alex Bogomolov's apartment.

Alex sits on the sofa, looking as comfortable as he did on the night when he and Bill pounded Russian Standard and expressed deep thoughts. In fact, a bottle now rests on the pavement next to him.

"Please join me in the final toast," he says, pouring vodka into a stemless crystal champagne flute and handing it to Bill.

Bill takes it from his hands.

"Chtob oni sdokhli," says Bill, raising the flute skyward like a sacred chalice. His Russian is clear, as Moscow as the church bells of the Kremlin.

May they all drop dead.

We know who they are—nothing is hidden. Everyone knows who they are. Even they know who they are. Especially they.

Has a more perfect toast ever been made?

The truth feels satisfying. This never fails.

"When did they throw out your stuff?" asks Bill.

"Last night, when I was at Melsor's party, they came and threw my things in street."

"I am sorry. Where did you spend the night?"

"Here, on mattress."

"Where do you go next?"

"Ne znayu, no mne pora." [I don't know, but the time has come.]

"Uvy," says Bill, switching to Russian. [Alas.]

"A ty smozesh eto opisat'?" [Will you be able to describe this?]

It's from Akhmatova, loosely; the prologue to the *Requiem*: she stands outside the Kresty prison in Leningrad, trying to get a food parcel to her son Lev, who is inside. Injustice has no motherland. It has no time limit. It is a constant, a polarity. Theft is a polarity, too, as is betrayal.

"Dumayu, chto vste-taki smogy." [I think I can.]

"A otomstit' smozhesh?" [Will you be able to avenge, too?]

"Postarayus'." [I will try.]

"Thank you," says Alex, getting up slowly. "I don't know who you are, but I believe you."

He nods to Bill, and begins a long descent down the ramp of Château Sedan Neuve.

PART III

|||||||||||||||||||||||||||||||||||||||||||||||||||||||||||||||||||||||||||||||||||||||||||||||||||||||||

I play to people's fantasies. People may not always think big themselves, but they can still get very excited by those who do. People want to believe that something is the biggest and the greatest and the most spectacular. I call it truthful hyperbole. It's an innocent form of exaggeration— and it's a very effective form of promotion.

—DONALD TRUMP
The Art of the Deal

|||||||||||||||||||||||||||||||||||||||||||||||||||||||||||||||||||||||||||||||||||||||||||||||||||||||||

20

|||||||||||||||||||||||||||||||||||||||||||||||||||||||||||||||||||||||||||||||||||||||||||||||||||||||||||||||||||||||||

THE REICHSTAG

As we reconstruct Bill's activities, the remainder of January 17—the entire blessed day—comes up utterly blank. Yes, there is a curbside morning shot of vodka from a crystal flute, a farewell to Alex, an acknowledgment of his Russianness. There is an attempted run on the Broadwalk, but after the run—nothing. Not a big, dark, secret nothing—those are honorable—but an even more malignant nothing: small, empty, the sort that masks the utter absence of pursuits of any sort. Not reading, not writing, not drinking even, the sort of nothing that drains the soul and by comparison makes a bender acquire redeeming qualities. An entry in Bill's reporter's notebook can likely be traced to that day: "Jesus, have I retired? Am I a Floridian now?"

On January 18, a note, written on a hardened, yellowed, fat-stained strip of paper, is taped to the elevator wall:

(so ignorant)

Don't throw Anything Over Balcony.
Security Informed
(orange peels etc.)

Unspecified objects are being tossed. These may be food-related: a smattering of peels, rinds, seeds, shells. Containers that had formerly encapsulated edible items, and, of course, bottles, may be thrown over balconies as well. Possibly also items of clothing, pieces of furniture, television sets, other electronic devices. Some of these objects could have been ignited prior to being thrown. The author is silent on this point.

"(so ignorant)" bespeaks contempt, but may also suggest that the thrower was careless in selecting items for throwing and has therefore unwittingly provided clues about his or her identity. Was an addressed envelope or a credit card statement among items tossed? If so, this was a cry for help, and help is on the way: the authorities have been informed.

"(orange peels etc.)" may tell us about the author's interpretation of the psychodynamics of this form of aberrant behavior: the perpetrator begins by throwing citrus peel over railings. This may be done innocently, out of laziness or for thrills, but this act sets the thrower on the path of an insatiable pursuit of the pleasure of watching shit drop. Orange peel is then a gateway projectile.

Tomorrow, on January 19, 2017, the thrower and the critic will cast their votes in the election to the BOD of Château Sedan Neuve Condominium Association, CSNCA. And on January 20, a gentleman whom many of the Château residents call Donal'd Tramp, the presidential candidate who received enthusiastic support here, will be sworn in as the leader of the free world.

This note differs from the one that Bill saw on this elevator wall before. The first one bespoke defeatism, futility. This one has the law-and-order swagger of America First. It trumpets our triumph—greatness regained.

A day and a half after the flood, the marble in the Château's lobby is still submerged under an inch of water. The wall-to-wall carpet in the Gulf Stream Room has turned into a purple paisley swamp. The few cardboard tiles that remain encased in the suspended ceiling are sagging under the weight of the waters that had rushed through the air-conditioning vents the day before.

Water from the pool doesn't ordinarily travel through air vents, but the Château is a place of many pipes; anything can happen. The timing, of course, is odd, and Bill wonders, "Could it be sabotage?"

As Bill stands observing this devastation, a single sagging tile drops heavily to the floor, unwieldy like a plastic tub of water, sloshing in its clumsy descent, joining its fallen brothers on the drenched floor eighteen feet below. There is no glory in this sound. It is the sound of prostration. Inner corruption has completed its journey.

The light fixtures are destroyed, all but two of them are dead on the floor. Most of the tiles have landed on the floor as well, but some are draped like wet pillowcases over chairs.

Bill picks up a soggy tile and hangs it over the lectern. Call it an installation, call it a composition: it tells the story. The lectern is a symbol of pompous, empty promises. A wet, dislodged ceiling tile is a symbol of falling Zbig-like from great heights. The Confederacy fell thus. The American democracy is making a heavy, creaking, waterlogged sound as we speak.

Bill snaps a picture, then runs a quick search for "hollywood fl television news," and www.local10.com pops up.

It's an ABC affiliate, and as the name suggests, its Web site oozes with local Florida news: grainy black-and-white surveillance videos of home break-ins, images of snakes in toilets, alligators in the sewers, blood-soaked pit bulls who have been very, very bad, and interviews with folks who thought they really knew those three freshly arrested teenagers who took a fun new designer drug called Bath Salts, gouged out the eyes of an elderly neighbor named Fisch, and ate his tongue raw over sushi rice. On a related note, you can look up restaurant inspections—by county!

Bill sends his staged photo of the lectern and the tile to the news tip desk. His note: "hey, just thought you might want to know: there was a flood at the Château. pool drained into this meeting room—through the ducts!—during [here the phone switches to all caps] WILD CONDO BOARD MEETING"

Bill lets the caps stay. He happens to have a sketchy address with a name he uses when contacting sources whose browsers might get searched as part of a leak investigation. Everybody needs an alias sometimes. His is "alex," followed by a long string of numbers and letters, @mail.ru.

He doesn't want his name associated with this piece of shit. He isn't even sure why he is doing this. His initial plan was to go jogging, as he did the day before, and he believes he still will.

After brief reflection, he adds: "I hear the VP of the board is a disgusting crook—will make good TV, I promise."

Which phone contact should he give them?

"You should contact Melzor Kazzenelenboggen (I can never get the spelling right; name too long). He is trying to unseat corrupt board and has all the dirt."

Bill taps in Melsor's cell phone number, hits "Send," and,

without giving the matter further thought, walks out into the dark, chilly morning.

Bill passes the security gate at 6:17 A.M.

He is not the first inhabitant of the Château to step out into darkness.

Three others—sad-faced men circa seventy-five, plus/minus ten—stand outside the building, waiting patiently as their little white dogs contemplate emptying their tiny bladders and bowels.

There is a joke about such men:

Why do Jewish men die before their wives?

Because they want to.

It's possible that these men are goyim, but the joke still stands. Goyim are people. This is about dogs. These dogs aren't dogs. All three—no, wait, there are four . . . All four are well under the weight limit of fifteen pounds specified in the condo "dos and don'ts" Bill noticed on the Web site. He happened to click on "pets"; he has no idea why.

These dogs don't apprehend tiny bad guys, they don't sniff out little explosives or baby cadavers, but they do have a mission: they substitute for the grandchildren who don't come to visit.

They aren't especially good at breathing, which is why they sometimes ride in baby strollers. They spend their days listening to complaints, about "mommy," about "daddy," about the sadly deteriorating physical and (allegedly) mental health of both, about doctors who overcharge while failing to acknowledge the obvious signs of mini-strokes and myelodysplastic syndrome, about Obamacare, about unappreciative, rude family members, and, of course, about crooked condo boards. *Svolochi* . . .

The dogs listen and they wheeze. If they could kill themselves, they would. When you are smaller than a cat and lack opposable thumbs, it's hard to pull the trigger.

Why do these dogs get Prozac?

Because they need it.

Bill runs past the silent, scooper-wielding sentries at the Château's gates and heads north on Ocean Drive.

It seems all the buildings around him are shedding their balconies. Steel rebar protrudes from their sides, awaiting encasement in concrete.

Imagine replacing all the balconies on one of these forty-year-old high-rises. You don't do it through competitive bids. You do it pursuant to local customs. Deals are concluded on chartered boats 12.1 miles offshore, outside U.S. territorial waters.

Bill has done his homework. He has enhanced his considerable prior knowledge with assistance from Messrs. Google and Kozachok. He has read up on local business practices and, what do you know, Melsor's stories check out. Out there, in open sea, with only Flipper as their witness, contractors harmonize to make a $2 million job into a $6 million job with another $3.7 million hiding in change orders. You can make a lot on the main job, but don't neglect the change orders. You don't bid out those; they are a layer of cream on the pasteurized dullness of milk.

New balconies that have replaced the old shine with chrome and glass—airborne aquaria. The logistics and, for that matter, economics—and let's not forget political economy—of balcony replacement are transparency itself.

You knock down the old balcony, you jackhammer the floor inside the apartment to bury new rebar, you leave it up to the folks inside to refloor—if that's a word. The windows get pitched. Time to refenestrate. The storm screens get shit-canned, too. Half of them don't work anyway. With this simple maneuver, you have just spent $80,000 on the balcony and forced the poor bastards in every apartment to spend at least another $40,000 on floors and windows.

With the subprime credit line the condo board took out (without anyone's approval) from a friend at a local bank, the out-of-pocket for each apartment is $150,000, depending on how long the board decides to keep the credit line gushing—and how much it wants to spew out.

With all the multipliers accounted for, with all the line items considered, Bill has just run past a couple billion dollars' worth of economic activity spread over less than a linear mile of Ocean Drive.

Let's say you devoted your life to screwing other people. You break no more laws than you have to. You avoid being disgorged. You build up a goodly stash. You move to Florida. You get fucked by your condo's BOD. Your stash gets drawn down. You try a new fraud, but it fails. The world is changing; you are losing your touch. You move on to a lesser place, or you start whacking people across their backs with your crooked cane until *Dzhuyka* carts you away. You might die in the middle of it. You might want to.

You will make room for fresh, idealistic sixty-seven-year-olds to take their turn at the good life by the sea.

Sunrise this morning makes the ocean purple. It's orderly, well-behaved, a good boy, waiting in its proper place, separated from the Broadwalk by one hundred feet of sand.

A tractor drags a sand plow to groom the beach much like one brushes the little white dogs Bill just saw ambulating, wheezing.

The Broadwalk lies a foot above sea level, maybe two. One big wave and this Hollywood Health Spa, which happens to be a Russian bathhouse; this Hollywood Grill, an Armenian restaurant that actually looks intriguing; and this Italian joint called Sapore di Mare, will wash away into said *mare*.

Bill tries not to blame the glum-faced people around him for having triggered a host of political disasters, the most recent of which is the rise of King Donal'd I, who tomorrow will be crowned. Forget xenophobia, forget the wall, forget making fun of the handicapped, forget the FSB prostitutes, forget the golden showers, whether or not they flowed! Here is the biggest incongruence: Floridians voting for a climate change denier are akin to concentration camp inmates embracing the ideal of racial hygiene. At least that's what Bill thinks, and his beliefs and his speech are protected by the First Amendment.

Massive towers are rising along the oceanfront, some bearing the Trump name. Twenty-story buildings like the Château were once thought to be tall; now, forty floors is about right. These towers contain apartments costing tens of millions, money that seems disposable to so many people. Do they recognize that they are building in the path of something far more ominous than the biblical flood?

That flood came and went. This one will come and stay.

There was a story Bill read in *The New Yorker* a bit more than a year earlier, in December 2015. The point: Florida is Ground Zero of global flooding. It sits as low as Kansas—about six feet above sea level. A drained swamp, it is cursed with a high water table. Its buildings, big and small, sit atop water-soaked limestone, and it takes pumps to keep this territory from drowning.

Bill read this piece in Washington. He read it the way most of his elitist friends read it, all of whom reached the same conclusion: let the fucker sink. With their chads hanging, they gave us George W. Bush, who gave us the invasion of Iraq in search of imaginary weapons of mass destruction. That was before *this thing,* this Donal'd F. Tramp. Let the waters come down, God, flood the place at your earliest. Maybe swimming with the fishes will make these *kakers* realize what they have done. Make sure you extract proper repentances before they drown. *Oh Lord!*

But now Bill is here, in Hollywood, running on this preposterously named Broadwalk. Should he hate the people who are starting to show up in this under-caffeinated darkness? Can he hate the red-haired grandmother who shouts in Russian into her cell phone? That word again: *"Svolochi!"* It's omnipresent. Might as well make it English.

Can Bill hate this life-battered, middle-aged couple emerging from the place Melsor calls Margarita Will? They were born Caucasian, presumably, but their skin has acquired the texture of distressed cordovan leather. They stand silently, staring at the ocean, dragging on their Camels, getting their early-morning pick-me-up, saying nothing. They are a bit older than Bill, or at least they seem to be. Theirs was a one-night stand or a thirty-five-year marriage; either way, nothing to talk about. If they couldn't drink, they would all go insane.

And here comes an overweight gentleman on a rusted, squeaking, folding bike with little wheels!

In the past, people came to Florida to die. They still do, but now they insist on stuffing the planet into the coffin with them. If death is boring, the end of the world is the most boring thing imaginable.

Bill is unable to blame these people for getting distracted by something else, anything else, even this Donal'd Tramp.

Every night in Moscow, Bill's parents took walks. This was their escape from the communal flat on Chkalov Street, at its intersection with Karl Marx Street, on the Garden Ring. The place is called Zemlyanoy Val, the Earth Berm.

They walked past the Pokrov Gates—Pokrovka, named after the shroud, the one thrown over still-dead Christ. These nightly journeys through the heart of Moscow were his beginning, his Jerusalem. Sometimes they walked farther, past Arkhipov Street, where the Great Moscow Synagogue stands. It wasn't their destination, at least not in the beginning.

Bill listened the way only children can: intensely, like a finely calibrated recording device, immortalizing the turns of phrase, the details. He was too young to understand every aspect of everything he heard, but he learned to recognize the importance of it all.

His parents spoke about the government's attacks on the intelligentsia, about disasters at work. When you teach Russian literature at the college level, as Melsor did, it's hard to keep from being reported to the ideological hacks. How do you cover the Decembrists' revolt without bringing back the echoes of contemporary dissidents? Can you steer away from the political minefields of today when you teach Akhmatova? That's even if you don't mention her *Requiem,* which you can't.

His parents spoke about the political trials—Yuli Daniel and Andrei Sinyavski, Aleksandr Ginzburg and Yuri Galanskov, the Leningrad poet-parasite Iosif Brodsky, the Pushkin Square Demonstration, the incarceration of Alik Esenin-Volpin in an insane asylum. They spoke about the Six-Day War, the invasion of Czechoslovakia, the Red Square demonstration, the tax on education levied on Jews who seek to emigrate, the Leningrad airplane hijacking. He grew up amid the evening crackle of the BBC Russian Service, the Voice of America, Deutsche Welle, Radio Liberty, the Voice of Israel. There was a world out there, pulsating with its separate life, watching his country with concern. Increasingly, his parents spoke about emigration, especially in the early '70s, when the synagogue on Arkhipov Street came to life with protests.

The U.S. embassy was nearby; he often went there by himself, to linger near parked cars. One Chevrolet—it was a Bel Air—became a vector in his escape fantasy. It was long, wide, golden. He contemplated its dashboard, imagining being inside.

He didn't root for the USSR, didn't refer to its sports teams as "we." Instead, he plotted desertion, mutiny, treason, defection, emigration. War fantasies set in well before he was ten: he is in the army, the USSR is at war in Europe, and Americans are involved. He crosses the battlefield—he surrenders, switches sides. They take him: he is already one of them.

He understood the meaning of the expression *figa v karmane*. *Figa* is the Russian version of a "fuck you" sign. You keep it in your pocket. With a *figa*, you are ready to listen to nonsense of any sort. It can't touch you.

It's all here, hardwired into Bill's skull as he runs on this Broadwalk, pondering the shroud of darkness that is about to descend on his new land, the land he loves—his first experiment with that face of love. He served this land valiantly by—pardon newsroomspeak, which is not a cliché—empowering its afflicted and afflicting its powerful.

Of course, he became a reporter because of those conversations on those nightly walks to Pokrovka. He is who he is because of those Moscow conversations that imprinted on his soul.

Melsor has changed in America, hardened, mastered the craft of deception. Perhaps America was gentler on Bill. He didn't have to change his orientation from honesty to fraud. He became a reporter, he kept the struggle alive. And now he is a reporter no more. It's possible that he will not be able to root for America in the next Olympics. It's almost a certainty that a *figa* will once again take up residence in his pocket.

In Moscow, he had a place to run, but not here. This is the end of the line. He is no longer passive. Observers observe. He will resist. Act. All those jokes about emigrating to Canada—he finds them offensive, cowardly. This 240-year-old democracy is worth fighting for. He will act alone if he has to. He will become a soldier-poet, a soldier-storyteller, an army of one. He will fight by all means at his disposal. He will correct every wrong in his path, in this Florida, at this Château, even in Washington, upon return.

At 7:48 A.M., when Bill returns to the Château, he sees a television truck with the Local News 10 logo on its side. The truck's antenna is up.

Achtung: state-of-the-art South Florida journalism is being practiced. Someone is being unmasked, confronted, chased. Of course, it might also be an animal story: alligator eats *svoloch'*, or, more likely, *svoloch'* eats alligator.

After a contemplative seven-mile run, Bill has momentarily forgotten that he had anonymously, blindly reached out to his colleagues at this Local News 10, giving his father's name as a contact for a flood story.

Perhaps he should have consulted with the old man.

"Oh hell," Bill concludes with abandon you would expect from a cultural Slav. "What's done is done."

Melsor is in the midst of an animated conversation with a reporter, a big guy of roughly Bill's age, whose name is also Bill—Bill Boyle. Bill had glanced through his mini-profile earlier that morning.

Sometimes Bill thinks that he should have stayed on the police beat all his life. The cop beat always goes to the young, but seasoned reporters like Bill Boyle, who make it a career-long pursuit, do it with the sort of grace that comes from deep knowledge. Bill—Bill Katzenelenbogen, that is—should have switched to television, too. There, the chase is raw—gushing blood, foamy brains on the gleaming white terrazzo. Freed from the bog of words, it's all visceral, all important. Sometimes you need a specialist—a board-certified sleazeologist—especially in South Florida.

For the first time, Bill K recognizes that his father gives good TV. Being a dissident poet was good media training, it seems.

"Off record . . . ," Melsor begins, "I do not exclude such possibility in which crimes of this condominium board are getting investigated by government at *highest* level."

What a fucking lie! Does he actually believe it?

Four decades earlier, an American with a camera—a kid who lucked into an important documentary about the Soviet Jewish movement—had come to their apartment in Moscow, and Bill watched his father recite poetry in Russian. That performance was staged—it's now on YouTube, probably.

This performance, today, is impromptu, in the moment, full of give and take.

Nella stands six feet to the side, near the glass doors to the apartment building. Bill nods silently to his father and steps behind her.

"We are *on* record, Mr. Katzenelenbogen," Bill B notes without much enthusiasm. "Am I pronouncing your name correctly?"

It's basic housekeeping. You want to make sure that you are talking to the right weirdly named dude and that he knows that all the shit he spews will be hung on him.

"You may call me Melsor. You have my permission to broadcast everything I say then. Just cut film where I say 'off record.'"

It's hard to miss this trick. When he says "off record," he is making sure that the point will, in fact, get on the record. "Don't go there" means "Go there."

It's a little clumsy, unnecessarily desperate, but what the fuck, it works. Bill K would have simply noted the point off the record, off camera, and told his colleague how to get the rest of the story elsewhere.

Being manipulative is too much work. It's easier to be up front. But Bill Katzenelenbogen is Bill Katzenelenbogen and Melsor Katzenelenbogen is Melsor Katzenelenbogen.

"Could you repeat what you've just said, this time on record?"

"I do not exclude possibility, Bill, that crimes of this dishonest condo board are investigated by *highest* government authorities."

"Do you *know* this?"

"Ask yourself question: Would serious person like I say it if he does not know? I fought against KGB. I won. I was persecuted by Justice Department in America. I won. Now I tell you: yes, there is investigation."

This is pretty good: he is planting innuendo, and watching it take root. Would the old man have done even better on camera had Bill—Bill K—remembered to give him a heads up?

Alas, for television, especially South Florida television—this is bullshit. No pictures, no story. Real stories are being missed. Cops are shooting black guys, fires rage, floods flood, pit bulls, boa constrictors, and alligators are on attack. The camera is about to stop rolling, the antenna outside will come down, and this van will drive away.

"Two night ago, at forum for candidates for condo board, these tugs endangered lives of unit owners. They *deliberately* caused swimming pool to break and pour into Gulf Stream Room through air ducts, costing unit owners hundreds of thousands dollars in damage and almost killing hundred old people! I can take you there in one minute. People of Florida must see this dangerous situation!"

"Are you saying they *deliberately* flooded the meeting room in the middle of the candidates' forum—to scare you?"

"No. I don't say this. I don't know exactly *why* they did it, because I don't speak with them. I am ballotating against them in election today. I don't expect to win. This system here is rigged, too. The night of forum—*during forum*—water from swimming pool started to pour into Gulf Stream Room exactly as I was speaking! I am saying—for quotation!—'Follow money, Bill.' It's for their advantage to have swimming pool break, because they now have excuse to get bigger kickback from contractor."

"I see," Bill B cuts in. "Do you have any information to indicate that they are getting kickbacks on construction contracts? On insurance money?"

"Of course, insurance money counts toward kickback!"

"But deliberate sabotage—come on . . ."

"You should see Gulf Stream Room. You will see devastation from flood!"

"We will do that in a minute. Just making sure, you are saying that this was a *deliberately set* flood that endangered the lives of senior citizens living in this building? And they did it in order to scare off dissent?"

"I'm not able to exclude this possibility."

"And you are saying that a high-level federal investigation of activities of this board is under way?"

"I am not at liberty to answer, Bill. You should ask them. I am told to say that I have no comment. FBI will say they can neither confirm nor deny existence of federal investigation. It's standard practice for them, except if your name is Hillary Clinton. Here, I have telephone, you have telephone. You can call FBI, or I will call chief tug here at Château: Obersturmführer Greenstein! I will call him in front of you."

This is getting better, but it's still just a garden variety condo board brawl—not a story.

"Are you calling the president of the board?"

"No! I am calling Greenstein, *vice* president of board. He is too smart to be president of board. President of BOD is fall guy. President goes to prison, president gets disgorged. *Vice* president is man with real power!"

Melsor sets the phone on speaker. Amazingly, Greenstein picks up. Melsor must have had his identity masked.

"Hello . . ."

"Villain! I have Channel 10 here!"

"Melsor? How did they get past security?"

"*I* got them through. They are *my* guests! I can still have visitors in your concentration camp!"

"No comment."

"Your chief tug—Russian—dived under security desk when he saw camera was filming. He is undocumented alien; yes? You should be careful with Donal'd Tramp becoming president in one day!"

"I am not going to dignify these unsubstantiated aspersions with a response."

"Sir, this is Bill Boyle, I am a reporter with Channel 10 News. Would you come out and talk to us?"

"Bill, I've seen your stories."

"Would you be willing to come down and talk with us, sir?"

"No."

"No?"

"If you are speaking with Katzenelenbogen, you are engaging in fake news."

"Then you should come down to the garage and set me straight."

"I said no."

"Are you declining to comment, sir?"

"I am going to comment: according to articles of the condominium of CSNCA, to be considered legitimate, *any and all* communications must originate from the board of directors. I would not put it beyond this splinter group of malcontents to sabotage this building."

"Are you making an accusation, sir?"

"Not yet."

"Is this all you are going to say?"

"If you are speaking with that indicted criminal, you are fake news."

"Is this your comment?"

"You are fake news. You don't deserve a comment."

With this, Greenstein hangs up.

The quality of sound of that conversation is as bad as it gets, traveling through the air from the wheezy cell phone to the microphone of a television camera. You could probably still rescue it if you absolutely had to—but why would you?

This is a brawl like any other in South Florida. Walk into the lobby of any of these balcony-shedding high-rises, and you will see exactly the same thing. Laws are easier to enforce when you have deviations from the rules. Here in Florida there are no rules. Here in Florida there are only deviations.

"Now you see how criminals operate!" shouts Melsor.

Bill K, had he been a television reporter, would have given the photographer the kill signal long ago.

It's possible that there is something captivating—"mesmerizing" might be the word—about Melsor's ravings. Having grown up with them, Bill K is in no position to know.

"It's very, very simple. This is very typical tactic for which fascists get credit. It's called Reichstag fire. Nazis themselves burn down German Reichstag and blame Communists so they get applauded, so to say, when they go kill Communists. Anyone can do it. This is how Putin came to power, they say. I do not exclude possibility that he had his secret police blow up two houses in Moscow so he could blame Chechens and start war. It's good, tested *tryuk*."

"*Tryuk?* What's that?"

"Lie."

"Oh, a trick . . ."

"It's standard tactic. They do it and blame us, malcontents. Reichstag fire is very, very effective tactic. I do not exclude possibility that this is something Donal'd Tramp will do in four years, if he is smart. And he is very, very smart. I will recognize it, of course, but will not tell you."

"Interesting. You two will have a secret."

This is a cluster of wild, unsubstantiated aspersions, sure, but Bill B is having fun watching his feisty geezer trample European history in a heavy-hoofed gallop. But this is Local News 10! Flashing lights and snarling animals are their stock in trade, and this shit—whatever it is—will not cut it. Time to go . . .

A mighty sound, heavier than a head-on car crash, but with a flash, makes all heads and the camera turn north, toward Fort Lauderdale, toward the spot where the swimming pool's hulking sarcophagus-like bottom rests atop the parking deck.

A cloud of smoke and dust dissipates quickly, drowning in a stream that rushes out of a long crack, a broken seam, bursting like an improbable constellation of fire hydrants uncapped, spewing out a white, chlorine-scented torrent. An eight-foot chunk of concrete drops squarely on top of a white Lexus, pinning it to the parking deck. Water comes down with flash-flood force, aiming it point blank at another white Lexus, an SUV, which begins to budge, smashing into a white Lexus sedan, then making a beast o' three backs with a silver Mercedes convertible, and on, and on, and on, a man-made pileup triggered by a man-made flood. Bill K, Bill B, Melsor, Nella, and the camera-wielding photographer press against the side of the building, watching the mad demolition derby, as cracks in the pool widen, and the waters gush until there is no more—until sunlight comes through the missing section of the pool's bottom.

Bill B breaks the silence.

"Holy fuck! Did you get that?"

The photographer, a young Hispanic guy, nods. He has seen many unbelievable things here in South Florida. And now this.

21

THE USUAL

Bill is pleased to see that the warning to the thrower of projectiles is still taped to the elevator wall. Someone at the Château cares passionately about justice.

He attempts to make sense of the morning's events:

It's possible, of course, that the South Pool had spontaneously drained into the Gulf Stream Room. But the timing—during the forum—is highly suspicious.

The Greenstein faction could have arranged the draining of the South Pool to point the good burghers toward thinking that this was the work of the Katzenelenbogen faction.

The Katzenelenbogenites could have started it, too. Their goal would be to make it look like the Greensteinians were trying to make it look like the Katzenelenbogenites were making it look like the Greensteinians did it.

Two general principles are observed in this war of illusions:

- **LEVEL ONE:** The Katzenelenbogenites want the Greensteinians blamed, and the Greensteinians want the Katzenelenbogenites blamed for the *actual acts* of destruction of the Château's pools.
- **LEVEL TWO:** The Katzenelenbogenites want the Greensteinians blamed for *creating the illusion* that the Katzenelenbogenites had committed the acts of destruction and, by the same token, Greensteinians want the Katzenelenbogenites blamed for *creating the illusion* that the Katzenelenbogenites had committed the acts of destruction.

This is classic. Not much time is needed to unpack it.

When you consider the collapse of the North Pool, events gain nuance quickly. Statistically, it's remotely possible that the North Pool would burst spontaneously the day after the draining of the South Pool into the Gulf Stream Room.

However, it's fallacious to assume that the collapse of the North Pool was facilitated by the same faction that triggered the draining of the South Pool. The copycat effect cannot be ruled out, i.e., hypothetically, the Greensteinians could have caused the draining of the South Pool and the Katzenelenbogenites could have busted the North Pool. Or the other way around.

Assume for the sake of argument that the collapse of the North Pool is spontaneous: after forty years of dedicated service, the pool's wall bursts. But what are the odds of this happening in front of rolling cameras not quite two days after a mishap involving the South Pool?

The sound of a blast that preceded the collapse of the North Pool raises questions too. Yes, it could have been the sound of rebar bursting and concrete cracking. Bill hasn't seen anything of the sort before. An explosion seems more likely, or so they, whoever they are, want you to think.

Wasn't Melsor talking about the Reichstag fire, praising it as a method of seizing power? And then—presto—the North Pool bursts! Does this make Melsor a suspect, or does it make Greenstein a suspect?

The right answer seems to be both and neither.

Bill's initial analysis assumes two possible groups of perpetrators. What if there are others? And what if some of them are acting in unison? Oy . . . He might need to do something he has never done before—put up one of those ridiculous whiteboards and cover it with notes, clippings, and photographs. There is no better way to get bogged down in bullshit.

Would anyone even investigate the swimming pool collapse he has just observed? A fire truck showed up, sure, but there was no fire and thus nothing to do. By then, the Channel 10 crew was gone. They had great stuff and needed to process it. The cops showed up as well. They spoke with Melsor for a few minutes and moved on, their demeanor saying, "Fuck it."

Technically, a crime or crimes have been committed, but if you want to find out whether explosives were used to blow up the North Pool you will need to load a wheelbarrow with little pieces of wet concrete and rebar and send them off to the FBI lab in Quantico, Virginia. You'd need to convince the FBI that you are dealing with a suspected act of domestic terror. The two police officers on the scene at the collapse of the North Pool show no signs of desire to make this case.

There was a fucking massacre at the Fort Lauderdale airport two weeks ago. Now *that's* a real case! Grainy images, corpses on the terrazzo floor.

And what do you have here?

Here you have people with strange accents saying crazy shit. Let them figure it out, settle it among themselves. It's tribal. Sometimes an investigation is just not useful. Even if they are blowing shit up.

The pools will be reconstructed, water damage corrected, mold removed—again. Bids will be rigged in open sea, and kickbacks will accrue to the board without regard for race, color, religious creed, national origin, ancestry, sex, sexual orientation, age, genetic information, military service, or disability. Fuck all that! All the more reasons to get on the board!

Bill returns to the apartment, takes a quick shower, and puts on his naturally distressed Carhartt jeans, his time-honored Top-Siders, and his fully depreciated Duke T-shirt, which doesn't look a day over thirty.

He is in no mood to play South Florida dress-up.

He is feeling the urge to get home, to Washington, to the world, to figure out his next step, to start his life anew.

The word "Resist," which has popped up on social media, resonates within his soul.

He is fucking nowhere with the Zbig project—doesn't even know whether there *is* a project. And now there is shit to be done here, at the fucking Château. He can't just leave; can he?

Not today at least.

He will crack this fucking case, thinking globally, acting locally—resisting. What was that thing Martin Luther King said: "Injustice anywhere is a threat to justice everywhere"?

It's true.

He will right these wrongs, and then and only then will he leave.

Bill has a couple things to check out, urgently. Alas, his first step would be to talk with Melsor.

It might say somewhere in the Diagnostic and Statistical Manual of Mental Disorders that Melsor Katzenelenbogen should be avoided for at least two hours following television exposure, and that four hours is probably safer.

"Do u have time 2 talk?" Bill texts his father at 8:59 A.M.

"*Menya v Machte opublikovali,*" Melsor responds. [I was published in *Machta.*]

Not exactly a response.

This is a fine morning for Melsor. He is already on to his second narcissistic event.

Three dots flash ominously on Bill's screen. A "request" is coming, and Bill knows it. It's more like an order, of course:

"*Novyyee chastushki. Srochno nuzhen perevod.*" [New *chastushki.* Translation urgently needed.]

"Why urgently?"

"*U menya repetitsiya. Devochli poyut.*" [I have a rehearsal. The girls are singing.]

The dots flash again. Shit! Melsor has more to say.

"*Vot link Machty. Perevedi. U tebya eto poluchayetsya.*" [Here is a link to *Machta.* Translate. You do it well.]

This is—what?—a compliment? From Melsor Yakovlevich Katzenelenbogen? The first? No . . . Is the fucker well?

Bill follows the link to *Machta,* which has indeed published *chastushki* by Melsor Katzenelenbogen, composed on the occasion of the impending inauguration of Donal'd Tramp.

Bill reads the first *chastushka.* It's not too awful, actually, in that certain post-apocalyptic way, which on the eve of the coronation strikes the younger Katzenelenbogen as appropriate:

Нам, ребята, не страшны
Мусульманскиые орды.
Трамп теперь нас в бой ведёт.
Заряжай! Стреляй! Вперёд!

Bill copies it, and—maybe it's because he doesn't give a shit—the translation emerges quickly:

Don't you worry, don't you fear!
Muslim hordes stand no chance here.
Long live Donald! Hooray Trump!
Load your AR-15!
Onward! Watch them fall! We win!

The second *chastushka* has the consistency of a parody, which it probably isn't, strictly speaking, but with humor being the bedrock of this genre, there is no way to know:

Ай да Вовка, ай да Путин,
Дал нам президентика!
Никогда бы Трамп не выиграл,
Подсобили хакеры!

Bill isn't embarrassed by this one. He actually agrees with the message, albeit from the opposite end of the political spectrum:

Way to go,
Brother Putin gave us quite a president!

No way Trump would have won,
FSB hackers got it done!

The third *chastushka* is even better than the one that preceded it:

В Вашингтонском да в болоте
Крокодилы плавают.
А народ им говорит:
Будем с Путиным дружить
И болота здесь сушить.

Bill has two simultaneous, interrelated points to make:

- It's too early for Kozachok, either in its own bottle or in
  the Grey Ruse disguise, and
- Occasional poetry always sucks, because it does.

However, these *chastushki* keep getting better, which makes
translation easy:

The Potomac swamp of late,
Big green crocodiles populate.
Our Putin and our Trump
Will soon drain that stinking swamp.

The final *chastushka* is sort of okay, too!

Как в Техасе-Аризоне
Вырастет рубеж-стена.
Хорошо нам станет жить

Рассветёт моя страна!

Bill gives it what it deserves; no more, no less:

Soon in Texas-Arizona
Border wall will rise from sand.
Life will get much better then,
As our country flourishes!

Bill shoots the translations over to his father—the whole thing takes twenty minutes tops.

He opens the window—the physical window, that is—to let a warm breeze enter the apartment. The wind is stronger than it was when he ran on the Broadwalk. Bill's gaze sweeps over the ocean.

What will the end of the world look like? We could be mowed down in a single event, or it might come in gentle waves. Like these, below. Pelicans may still be overhead, and they may or may not be on fire.

A cruise ship may be on the horizon, a small plane may be dragging a banner advertising an all-you-can-eat special at some god-awful joint.

Actually, the world could be ending right now, and Bill is growing increasingly certain that it is.

If it's comforting for you to believe that he is going mad, be my guest.

Bill would be of no use in helping with this determination.

Like the rest of us, he would see no reason to distinguish madness within his skull from madness around him.

Bill calls Gwen.

Is she still coming here, to Florida, tonight?

He gets voicemail and one of those fucking "I can't talk to you right now" bounce-backs via text.

Bill knows how his parents survived in a totalitarian state.

They had each other, they had him, they escaped into their lives. It's less clear to Bill how he will survive today, in this transformed world, with his mother gone, with his father bowing to King Donal'd.

They say Jews don't bow to anyone but the construct they call "G-d," but a vote for America First, a geriatric goose step, and a crypto-fascist salute are obviously within the range of possibility.

Whom does Bill have today, as darkness descends?

Gwen? Maybe, kind of, sort of.

He wishes she were here, in Florida, in a large bed, sleeping peacefully.

Is she his Beatrice now?

He has had relationships, but never with Beatrice.

Maybe now . . .

Stealing a girl from Dante is a risky move, granted, but maybe Beatrice will be his just when he needs her—now.

Bill arrives in Melsor's apartment at 10 A.M., as the last of the *chastushki* singers leaves and Melsor settles onto the porny white sectional to watch MSNBC.

"What? No Fox News?" Bill asks in English.

"I watch MSNBC. I want opposite point of view. I already know what I think."

"Oh . . . I need to interrupt you nonetheless."

Rachel Maddow says something truly scary about Trump: the link between his close associates and the Russian banks. She laughs nervously—who wouldn't?

"*Ona lezbiyanka. Ostromnaya baba,*" says Melsor. [She is a lesbian. A humorous broad.]

"That's what I hear . . ."

"*Yevreyka. Po dedushke.*" [Jewish, on grandfather's side.]

"I really do need your attention for a moment."

"I am listening."

"Do you remember that rant, where Greenstein's wife chased out the two guys from Craigslist—where she screams in German?"

Melsor looks quizzically at Bill.

"Do you have it recorded?"

"Yes, I record everything from transmissions."

"Can you give it to me? Now . . . Please . . ."

"*Zachem?*" [Why?]

"I thought I heard something useful. My German sucks. I want someone else to take a listen."

As Melsor gets up to get the right recording off his computer, Bill changes channels to the ABC affiliate.

"We interrupt this program to bring you a special bulletin: a deep swimming pool cracks open at a luxury ocean-side condo in Hollywood!"

The anchor, seated at the news desk, is dark-haired, young, leggy.

"Our reporter is on the scene."

This is followed by images of water bursting through a widening crack, a chunk of concrete dropping on top of a white Lexus, and rushing waters creating a pileup of Lexuses and a Mercedes.

The deep, heavy thud and Melsor's equally explosive words are picked up, too: "Reichstag fire is very, very effective tactic. I do not exclude possibility that this is something Donal'd Tramp will do in four years, if he is smart. And he is very, very smart."

"Our reporter, Bill Boyle, was on the scene. Bill, what did you see?"

"To be honest, Claudia, I was focused on an unrelated story. Suddenly, there was what sounded like an explosion."

CLAUDIA: Explosion? Is it terrorism?

BILL B: Could also be the sound of the swimming pool collapsing on its own.

CLAUDIA: We have a graphic here. This was a very deep aboveground pool that is essentially embedded in the parking structure. How were you able to film it, Bill?

BILL B: As you can see, Claudia . . . Could you run it again? As you can see, the stream is very narrow at first, but the pressure is extreme, because of the sheer depth of the pool. It was more like a powerful fire hydrant than a flash flood at first, and then—you see here—a section of the swimming pool drops out and lands on top of this car. It was very concentrated still. You can see it sweep other cars—at least a dozen of them—out of its way.

CLAUDIA: What was the story you were working on?

BILL B: Just basic condo board turmoil, the usual in South Florida. Accusations of malfeasance flying back and forth. These are basically multimillion-dollar enterprises that operate without any fiscal controls.

CLAUDIA: The usual turmoil then?

BILL B: The usual.

As a child, Bill knew that his father's outbursts started softly, with a hiss.

"*Sv-volochi . . .*"

Melsor spent time with that son of a bitch, that idiot reporter, gave him an interview, explained the Reichstag fire even. What he got for his efforts was a story that described his struggle—his struggle for justice!—as "the usual," something that you might as well accept!

Imagine that: Melsor Yakovlevich Katzenelenbogen was being trivialized!

"Yego kupili, tvoyego Billa." [They bought him, your Bill.]

"He is not 'my Bill.' I don't know him. And, for what it's worth, what he did was anything but unprofessional. He had unique images of the swimming pool collapsing, causing a flash flood in the garage—destroying some really expensive cars—before your eyes. It's amazing footage. I'd do the same thing."

"This is dishonest! He could show injustice! Lawlessness!"

"That guy is not a *svoloch'*. He is a pro."

"Then you are *svoloch'*, too."

"Thanks for the insult. You might want to try to see the world as it is, just this once. You were trying to sell him on a story, and you were upstaged by a big bang. There was an explosion! Or whatever the fuck it was. That's it! Nothing else to it! Collapsing swimming pools will always trump a struggle for justice, if that is what it is."

"Don't bring Tramp into this . . ."

"I didn't. I said trump, like in cards. Did you hire some asshole to blow the thing up? Did you have it done?"

"If I said I did or no I didn't, you wouldn't believe me! Would you?"

"No. I certainly would not."

"And if I did, would you turn me in to your FBI?"

"It's not *my* FBI. I am not with the FBI, as you know."

"You are a conformist!"

"You are a narcissist!"

"You are unemployed. I called and found out."

"First time you gave a fuck about me. Thank you, Father."

"You are ungrateful."

"At least I am not a felon!"

"Neither am I."

"You are guilty as fuck, and you know it."

"Don't pretend that you understand me!"

"Theft! Fraud! Snitching on your accomplices! No remorse that I can see. And a stash of ill-gotten money very much intact. Look at all this! It's all built on fraud! I wouldn't know how to explain it in a way that you would give a fuck about. I'll fucking do it anyway . . ."

"Fuck, fuck, fuck. Do you know more words than 'fuck'?"

"I've been called many things. *Svoloch'*, for example. By you! I don't give a fuck about that. If you want to insult me, tell me I am not a gentleman. Tell me I am not behaving as a decent human being—the way you used to. In Moscow. Remember? Moscow?"

"You were child!"

"You made me into who I am, and then you stopped being who you were! How is that fair? What did this fucking country do to you?"

"Fuck, fuck, fuck . . ."

"What made you give up on decency? You threw it out like a used condom. What made you so smug? Do you even understand what I am saying?"

As Bill leaves, slamming the door, a familiar epithet is the last thing he hears:

"Predatel'." [Traitor.]

"You still don't understand, do you, asshole?" Bill mutters in the hallway. *"You* are the traitor."

As Bill slams the door, he believes that he will leave this place and not speak to the fucker for another decade or two.

Maybe it's better this way.

Strike the "maybe." It is better this way.

When he checks his e-mail a few moments later, he has received a recording of Wilfreda's rant.

It comes through—sans message—just as he enters the apartment.

The geezer is softening, accepting the notion that standoffs aren't always in his best interest.

This could also mean that the other side—the Greenstein assholes—is guilty of wrecking the building. Or that his side—the Katzenelenbogen assholes—is.

Somebody is feeling secure about their smoke screens, or halls of mirrors, or whatever you call rat-fucking in this new America.

Maybe at some point Bill was thinking of helping his father, repairing the things that went wrong, but no more. Now his loyalty is to the truth.

Whatever it is, Bill will find it.

He will—what is it our president-elect says?—he will drain this swamp. And if he finds real, indictable fraud, he will burn them, all of them. He taps out a quick e-mail to a friend who once covered Germany, before being shit-canned by the *Post*.

This dude was the best reporter Bill ever met. Let's call him Subodh. A Brahmin who grew up in India, he used "Subodh" as a pseudonym when calling sources at the White House a generation ago.

The name somehow got out into the newsroom, and it stuck.

Subodh is freelancing now, mostly for *Bethesda Magazine,* or maybe *Washingtonian.* Bill reads neither.

A text message from Gwen announces itself.

"Can't wait to see you."

"Mutual."

He does want to see her—that's true.

He thought about her last night, tossing on his cot, finally getting his computer and turning to videos of bird-suited jumpers launching themselves off cliffs and tall buildings.

"What's on your mind?"

"What's a man to do?"

"????"

"Fundamental question of Russian literature."

"Relevant here/now?"

"Relevant as fuck."

"Brooding?"

"Brooding."

"Gotta run. A sweet deal about to come through. Drawn to you."

"Mutual."

"Let's stay sober this time."

Bill walks up to the refrigerator to look for something edible, and by the time he is done toasting frozen Borodinski bread and smearing it with something that purports to contain cream cheese, an e-mail from Subodh comes in.

It's like a gentle breeze bringing the comforting scent of home:

Bill! Dude!

Nice to hear from you, you old sheep-plugger. Heard about your shit-canning. For insubordination! You de man. Go team! Hope vicissitude sits lightly on your shoulders.

Hearing from you brought back pleasant memories of broomsticks shoved. You still have the scale; right? Now, with this new White House, it will be possible to shove entire brooms without anyone noticing! I hate Bezos as much as the next guy, but the Post *is producing excellent fodder for SNL these days.*

Having considerable difficulty imagining you in Florida, even for a day, even for an hour.

As you know, I am blessed with free time, so I was able to give you ultra-quick turnaround. You will find the transcript and the translation in separate attachments. It's disturbing on more levels than I can count.

I realize that you are not asking for advice. Still, I suggest that you bring in the constabulary. At the very least, notify the nearest Holocaust museum. I can guarantee that when you deal with this shit, guns are involved somewhere down the line. Stay safe. You owe me a TB at Martin's. Make it two—or, hell, three.

Yours,
Comrade Subodh

P.S. Never mind advice . . . You will do what you will do.
P.S.S. Is this a book? Dude!

Bill first clicks on the German transcript and reads the thing. Yes . . . just as he thought. It's amazing how far you can get with a little Yiddish and having watched *The Marriage of Maria Braun* and *Das Boot* with subtitles multiple times while your brain was forming.

FRAUENSTIMME: *Du knauseriger, perverser Scheisskerl! Kannst du nicht an irgend etwas anderes denken als an deinen kleinen Schwanz? Glaubst du wirklich, dass ich mir zum Geburtstag wünsche, von zwei fremden Männern gefickt zu werden? Mit zweiundsiebzig Jahre! Stell dir vor mit siebenunddreißig ...*

Ich hätte dir nichts erzählen sollen! Höre zu: "Wenn ich drei Mal nächtlich hätte vögeln wollen, hätte ich keinen Mann ausgesucht, der ein Stück Gummi in der Hose trägt!"

Glaubst du, ich möchte wirklich Verkehr mit einem ganzen Zug haben? Oder geht es eher darum, dass du insgeheim von all diesen Männern gefickt werden möchtest? Oder glaubst du, dass alle Deutsche so etwas wollen? Willst du mit mir abrechnen dafür, was meinen Vater getan hat?

Er rettete das ganze für uns. Er kämpfte am Fließband gegen einen Hungerlohn und verkauften keinen einzigen Zahn.

Nur zur Kenntnis: Ich will Schmuck zum Geburtstag, du mieser, perverser Hurensohn! Ich will einen Ring wie Ida Kruger und alle anderen jüdischen Frauen haben. Ein Jubiläumsring von Tiffany!

Du muss es nicht unbedingt von Tiffany kaufen, du kleiner, schwanzloser Untermensch! Du muss dir nicht vom Geld des Sponsors unbedingt trennen!

Nimm noch einen von dieser kleinen blauen Taschen, entleere das Gold, und lass Dir wieder eine Stange fertigen. Worauf wartest Du? Du bist ja siebenundsiebzig Jahre alt! Du leidest unter Herzschwächen! Ich überlebte Krebs zweimal. Nur Gott weiss, welche Krankheiten ich sonst habe.

Du, Schwein, nimm diese Tasche! Nimm sie in deiner Hand! Geh zu einem deiner Juden! Lass es schmelzen! Und kauf mir was ich tatsächlich will!

MÄNNERSTIMME: *Ja, Geliebte.*

Just to be sure, he clicks on the English translation.

WOMAN'S VOICE: You cheap, twisted bastard! Can you think about anything beyond your little dick? Do you really think I wanted to get fucked by two men on my birthday? I am seventy-two years old! Maybe at twenty-seven . . .

I should never have told you anything! Listen to me: "If I wanted to be fucked three times every night, I would not have chosen a husband who wears a piece of rubber hose in his pants!"

Do you think I really want to have relations with a platoon? Is all this happening because secretly *you* want to be fucked by all these men, or is this what you think all Germans want? Are you getting even with me for what my father did, you ungrateful rat?

He saved all this for us. He struggled on his assembly-line salary and never sold a single tooth.

Just so you know: I want jewelry for my birthday, you cheap, twisted son of a whore! I want a ring like Ida Kruger and all the other Jewish women have: an anniversary ring that they have at Tiffany's!

You don't even have to get it from Tiffany's, you little, no-dick subhuman. You don't even need to part with the money from the sponsor!

Just take another one of these blue velvet bags, empty out the gold, and have them make you another bar. What are you waiting for? You are seventy-seven years old! You have a heart condition! I had cancer twice. God knows what other disease I have now.

Here, swine, take *this* bag! Take it in your hand! Go to one of your Jews! Have it melted! And buy me what I actually want! For once.

MAN'S VOICE: Yes, beloved.

ŠVEJK

By 10:30, the video of gushing water slamming a white Lexus broadside into its sibling, then slamming both into a Mercedes convertible, is trending on Twitter.

How often do you get to see a deep pool collapse, making a Rube Goldberg spectacle out of expensive white cars? The fact that the video made it possible to suggest that terrorists were involved makes the thing sweeter still.

When Bill K calls Bill B, he has no idea that the latter records suspected crank calls, nor does he care. A transcript of their conversation follows:

BILL K: Hey, that was quite a story.

BILL B: Thanks. Who is this?

BILL K: Bill Katzenelenbogen. I used to be with the *Post*.

BILL B: The New York *Post*?

BILL K: The Washington *Post*.

BILL B: Sure. Name sounds familiar. Any relation to that lunatic I spoke with?

BILL K: Son.

BILL B: I am sorry. I bet he is pissed about the story.

BILL K: Furious. He doesn't understand that the flood is the thing.

BILL B: True. The flood is the thing.

BILL K: I was the guy who sent you that e-mail. Worked out well for you, dude.

BILL B: Now you are going to say I owe you one?

BILL K: I am!

BILL B: Shoot!

BILL K: Tell me what you know about the plastic surgeon who went splat.

BILL B: The Butt God?

BILL K: Zbig Wronski.

BILL B: What's it to you?

BILL K: He was my college roommate. Thinking about doing a book. Did you cover his death?

BILL B: I did, just one story. We had a computer simulation. Sick. The cops closed the case, called it an accident. Pervert shit, so weird you can't touch it. Never learned what the fuck it was. That's really all I have. Except . . . I think the cable TV assholes were pimping a tape—his wife's interview on some reality show.

BILL K: Can I have it?

BILL B: If we have it, it's under an embargo. Our word of honor. I can't be caught at it, but—shit—I owe you one. Checking, checking, checking—yes, it's here!

BILL K: Can you show it to me?

BILL B: Heading out on an overturned vegetable truck story. Tossed lettuce all over southbound I-95. Want some salad?

BILL K: Not that kind . . . Fatalities?

BILL B: Two or three. We actually have a video of that thing *happening*. You see the driver fly out headfirst and hit the pavement—instant death! Then you see lettuce fly. Call me on my cell in two hours.

Four calls are all it takes to locate Roza Kisel'. There are only so many places for the Jewish community of South Florida to store its demented indigent brethren.

Bill ventures a guess, then another, and thirty minutes later, he parks Melsor's Prius in the parking lot of the Beth Shalom Home for the Aged.

The place has the look of a small hospital.

His initial guess is that Mrs. Kisel' would be kept in a rubber room, where she surely belongs, but as he introduces himself as her nephew, the middle-aged woman at the desk looks at him with approval.

"It's so nice to have a young person visit," she says, and points him to the hallway. "Mrs. Kisel is in room 312. Take the elevator around the corner, hon."

The first time he saw Roza, she wore a housecoat, carried a crooked cane, and screamed about *svolochi* and fascists. She had a point, as Bill now knows.

Their second encounter, in mid-flood, also entailed physical pain. His shoulders and his back hurt still, especially in the early mornings, when he begins to contemplate getting up.

Expecting to get whacked again, Bill is surprised to see Mrs. Kisel' seated in a chair, reading a Russian translation of Jane Austen's *Emma*, a book Bill regards as ghastly. Roza is dressed in a comfortable blue pantsuit and sensible sneakers, the sort nurses wear. She looks up over her thin reading glasses, exuding a sense of comfort, like a professor holding office hours.

The picture on the wall looks vaguely familiar. It's clearly Washington; Georgetown, in fact. The C&O Canal. There used to be a restaurant there. Port O' Georgetown it was called—few people remember it, but it had a killer terrace.

Clearly not a personal item, clearly not Roza's, that painting has nothing to do with anything. Eye candy for the demented, it's a part of the room, the representational counterpart of a hospital bed.

"Mrs. Kisel', thank you for agreeing to talk with me," Bill begins in English.

"*Oy, eto vy! Prostite, chto ya vas dvazhdy udarila,*" she responds. [Oh, it's you! Forgive me for having whacked you twice.]

Bill shrugs. It's a painful motion, thanks to her. Compared to other setbacks in his life, being whacked across the back with a crooked cane by a madwoman is a minor inconvenience.

With that motion—the shrug—he has blown his cover—fuck it. Yes, he speaks Russian, and very well at that.

"*Eto ya vas tak dlya maskirovki, prostite uzh starushku. Vizhu, krasivyy molodoy chelovek—kak palkoy ne udarit'?*" [I did that for cover, forgive the old lady. I see an attractive young man; why would I not hit him?]

Madness is gone from Roza's eyes, and how does she know that he speaks Russian? Thanks to Melsor's propensity to see an enemy behind every tree, his Russianness was to be kept secret.

"*Nu eto nichego,*" he responds with a slight wave of the right hand, a dismissive gesture that reveals something they can't teach at the FBI academy—the Russian body language. [It's nothing.]

"*Prezhde vsego, kak vas zovut?*" [First of all, what is your name?]

"William."

"Vil'-yam? Da bros'te vy. Kakoy vy tam Vil'-yam? Khoroshiy Moskovsky mal'chik, khorosho vospitannyy. Nevooruzhennym glazom vizhu. Kak vas vpravdu zovut?" [Vil'-yam? Please . . . What kind of a Vil'-yam are you? You are good Moscow boy, well brought up. I see this with the naked eye. What is your real name?]

"Ilya."

The sound of his real name rolling off his tongue feels as comfortable as wearing his own Carhartts after days of masquerading in Florida costumes.

His mother would be Roza's age now, give or take a year or two.

"A po otchestvy vas kak?" [And what is your patronymic?]

"Melsorovich," he replies with hesitation.

"Melsorovich. Nu togda vsyo ponyatno. Nu, mozhet ne sovsem vsyo, no mnogoye. Nash Melsor—tot chto zhulik?" [Melsorovich . . . Then it all becomes clear. Maybe not all of it, but many things. Our Melsor, the one who is a crook?]

"Roza Borisovna . . ." He pauses long enough for her to appreciate that he knows her patronymic.

She nods.

"U menya slozhilos' vpechatleniye, ves'ma vozmozhno lozhnoye, chto vy v etom ikhnem Shato basseyin v zal spustili," he says softly, Russianly, letting his Moscow elocution kick in. [I have formed the perhaps false impression that you are the person who flushed the swimming pool into the meeting room of that Château of theirs.]

She smiles.

Had this been her apartment, she would be pouring tea into those orange made-in-Czechoslovakia polka-dotted cups, the ones Bill saw smashed up, in bags, on the curb, during her eviction. In better days, there would have been sweets in a colorful cardboard box depicting roses, the Kremlin, or both. He should have brought her one of those boxes, he realizes. He is certain you can buy them at a place called Matryoshka, in Sunny Isles, God knows. Maybe he will make a stop there before he leaves. He wants to.

"*A vy kto po spetsial'nosti?*" she asks. [And what would your profession be?]

"*Byl zhurnalistom. Teper' ne znayu.*" [I was a journalist. Now I don't know.]

"*Mozhno skazat' vam doveritel'no, Ilya Melsorovich?*" [May I respond in confidence, Ilya Melsorovich?]

This question, short and to the point though it may be, bears unpacking.

Admittedly, "in confidence" is a weak translation of "*doveritel'no.*" "In trust" would be better, as it conveys respect, the sort of respect he hasn't felt since Moscow.

There is something wonderful about being addressed formally as "*vy,*" as opposed to "*ty,*" by an older person. This would be the manner in which a Moscow professor would address her students. Having left as a boy, Bill was forever familiar—"*ty.*"

Holy shit! That's what's missing in this fucking Florida: respect.

Would it be too late for Bill to abandon his American nom de guerre and resurrect his former self—Ilya?

As Ilya, he would start from scratch.

He nods. Of course, Roza Borisovna, you can respond in confidence.

"*Po sekretu, na ushko?*" [Secretly, whispered into your little ear?]

He nods again.

"*Chest'yu poklyatnites', pozhaluysta.*" [Swear upon your honor, please.]

"Chest' shtuka vazhnaya, osobenno seychas, v nashe idiotskoye vremya," he responds. [Honor is an important thing, especially in this idiotic time.]

"Imenno po-etomy ya vam takoye usloviye stavlyu." [That's precisely why I am setting these conditions.]

"Da," he says. *"Chest'yu klyanus'."* [Yes. I swear upon my honor.]

"Nu, togda—da, vy pravil'no vycheslili. Ya flexible payp vrezala nedaleko ot nasosa basseyna—s odnoy storony, i v vozdushnyy dakt s drugoy. I basseyn, predstav'te sebe, zaprosto spustilsya." [Yes then. Your calculations are correct. I cut a piece of flexible pipe into the swimming pool drain, near the filter, on one side and the air ducts on the other. And the pool—imagine that—simply drained."

"Tak—eto Severnyy Basseyn. A Yuzhnyy?" [So, this takes care of the South Pool. What about the North?]

"A etot ya dinamitom." [I did that with dynamite.]

"Kak vy yego dostali; dinamit?" [How did you get it, the dynamite?]

"Kak, kak . . . U menya chetyre funtika posle raboty ostalos'. Ya zhe vzryvnik." [I had four pounds left over from work. I am an explosives expert.]

"Professor v Gornom Institute . . . V Moskve . . . A do togo, inzhener-vsryvnik v Soyuzvsryvprome," Bill adds. [A professor at the Mining Institute in Moscow. And before that, an explosives engineer at Soyuzvsryvprom.]

She looks at him quizzically, and he explains that Roza Kisel' is an uncommon name, and that it figured on the list of refuseniks. The Orwellian name of her former employer, *"Soyuzvsryvprom"* is from that list, too. It stands for "the enterprise of explosion-making."

She wants the details. How did Bill get that list, that bio?

He called the YIVO Institute for Jewish Research in New

York. The place has an excellent archive and, more importantly, excellent archivists. In this case, he scored a direct hit: a
list of refuseniks put out by the Anti-Defamation League. Roza
was in the 1982 edition—one of the longest: almost one thousand
names.

Next, he ran a pedestrian Google search, and her name
popped up again in the *Las Vegas Sun* in 1998. It was in a piece
about a Russian restaurant that was opened by a former Moscow engineer, an explosives expert who by then spent more than
a decade working for gold mining enterprises in Nevada.

Cirque du Soleil performers regarded that restaurant as their
home away from home. The story was about a bunch of clowns.

For that crowd, the place had to be very good.

"Rasskazhite mne pro vashe . . . kak eto skazat' delikatno . . ." [Tell
me about your . . . how do I put this politely . . .]

"Moyo buynoye pomeshatel'stvo?" She smiles. [My violent insanity?]

"Ono samoye." [That very thing.]

"Ilya Melsorovich, vy so Shveykon znakomy?" [Ilya Melsorovich,
are you familiar with Švejk?]

Is Bill familiar with *The Good Soldier Švejk?*

Švejk is his hemoglobin! Švejk was read to him before he was
old enough to handle a book that thick. It was the yellow tome
with illustrations—and don't forget those cartoons, those incred-
ible cartoons.

Melsor is wrong. It's Švejk's creator, Jaroslav Hašek, not
Donal'd Tramp, who is the oracle of our times—and he lives on,
producing recipes for dealing with madness. "I have the honor
to report that I am a complete idiot," Švejk states with a salute

that bespeaks mental health in the feebleminded world blown apart by the Great War.

Švejk stands shoulder to shoulder with Don Quixote, Young Werther, Onegin, and Huck. Švejk is immortal. Brecht extended Švejk's adventures into World War II—literally. Joseph Heller did the same, but figuratively. Without Švejk, there could be no *Catch-22*. Even *M*A*S*H* stands on Švejk's blocky shoulders.

Bill's mother wouldn't part with that well-worn yellow tome. It traveled to America in a suitcase, next to a stack of the Katzenelnbogen family photos. Surely the brave soldier exists in a box in Melsor's apartment. Bill should dig him out, liberate him on the occasion of the encroaching reign of King Donal'd I, the Sun King who ate Washington. Actually, fuck it. Bill knows Švejk by heart—the parts that matter.

Švejk's mystery is what matters: is he genuinely extremely feebleminded, or is he pretending to be extremely feebleminded in order to liberate himself from the feeblemindedness around him?

"*Da, so Shweikon ya znakom,*" Bill responds. [Yes, I am familiar with Švejk.]

No shit.

"*Togda vy vsyo ponimayete?*" [Then you understand everything?]

"*Nachinayu . . .*" [Starting to . . .]

"*Smotrite, yesli vy skazhete khot' komu-nibud' ob etom nashem razgovore, vam prosto ne poveryat. Skazhut, chto eto vy psikh.*" [You see, if you were to describe our conversation to anyone, you will not be believed. They will say that you are the one who is insane.]

Bill nods.

"*Po-etomu, poymite, drug moy, ya sovsem ne volnuyus' o tom, chto vy znayete o moyey podryvnoy deyatel'nosti. Vy im vyskazhite vsy pravdu, a oni vas v yebanatiki zachislyat.*" [So, my friend, you understand why I am not worried in the least about you knowing about my sabotage, my work with explosives. You could tell them the truth, but they will say that you are the one who is insane.]

"*Da. Eto absolyutnaya zaschita,*" Bill agrees on reflection. [Yes. This is an absolute defense.]

"*Ona samaya. Chto-b vy ne skazali, oni vam otvetyat, chto Roza Kisel' psikh, yebanatik—ya slyshala, chto tak menya v Shato nazyvayut.*" [Indeed, absolute. No matter how you frame it, they will tell you that Roza Kisel' is a psychopath; a, pardon me, fucking lunatic they call me at the Château, I hear.]

"*Vy znayete, molodoy chelovek, mozno vas poprosit' sbegat's k kontsu korridora i prinesti mne Ginger Ale iz mashiny etoy proklyatoy. I zaplatite pozhaluysta, u menya posobiye esche be oformili,*" she says. [Please, young man, may I ask you to run over to the end of the corridor and grab a ginger ale from that cursed vending machine. My subsidy here hasn't been determined.]

A few minutes later, laden with four cans of ginger ale and an assortment of vending machine offerings—he got the entire lineup of sweets: M&Ms, Hershey bars, Three Musketeers, Oreos, and Reese's—Bill returns to Roza's room.

He has a point to make on the subject of Švejk.

Švejk didn't demonstrate much initiative during the Great War. He was moved around, passively, and much of the time he was simply lost and looking for his regiment.

The good soldier didn't flood any meeting rooms, didn't blow up pools with dynamite. Bill couldn't remember whether Švejk ever discharged his rifle. One of his war buddies gets shot in the ass, Bill recalls. Does Švejk have a "fuck you" sign in his pocket, like all the people Bill loved during his Moscow childhood?

Hašek provides no answers, because, clearly, he doesn't want to.

"Ya ne sovsem s vami soglasen naschet Shveyka. On idiot, a vy, sobst-venno, terrorist," Bill counters. [I am not entirely in agreement with you about Švejk. He is extremely feebleminded, and you are, essentially, a terrorist.]

"Chisto teoreticheski, ya, konechno, za neprotivleniye. No eto zhe fash-isty, grabitely, svolochi! To u nikh special assesmenty, to u nikh zuby. Mimo etogo prokhodit' nel'zya." [On the purely theoretical level, I am all for passive resistance, of course. But these are fascists, robbers, *svolochi*! They have their special assessments. They have their gold teeth. This cannot be ignored.]

"Ah . . . Vy tozhe pro zolotyyye zuby znayete?" [So you, too, know about the gold teeth?]

She nods.

"Znayu, znayu. Vot vam i, kak govoryat v narode, quod erat demon-strandum. *Fashisti. Svolochi."* [I know, I know. And so, to use a folk expression, *quod erat demonstrandum*. Fascists. *Svolochi*.]

QED indeed.

One last question: *"Kak vy tuda, v Shato, dobirayetes'?"* [How do you get there, to the Château?]

"Ahhh, oni zdes' dumayut, cho menya plemannitsa k vrachu vozit. Na samom dele u menya net nikakoy plemannitsy—eto moya studentka byvshaya." [They think that my niece takes me to the doctor. Actually, I have no niece. It's a former student of mine.]

Bill glances at his watch. It's time to go, but Roza disagrees.

There is a book-sized chess set—she saved it from her eviction. It's no use to lie to her, to argue that he doesn't know how to play.

Ridiculous! Good boys like Ilya Katzenelenbogen know how to play chess, and even now, in her golden years and in the care of the South Florida *Dzhuyka,* Professor Roza Borisovna Kisel' will not be beat.

23

MERRY WIDOWS

It takes an hour for Bill to lose one chess game and, surprisingly, win another. It's 12:30, dammit. On the way out, he calls Bill B:

"Dude . . ."

"Meet us in front of Juicy Gyro, 6900 block of Collins. We're in front, in a van. You're buying."

"Sure, it's not far, get the food now. Give me fifteen."

"What do you want?"

"Shwarma and diet something."

"Suit yourself. Their gyros are better."

"Remember the ground rules—you can't tell anyone. An embargo until this piece of shit airs."

Bill nods. Sure. How would he, a fired journalist, break an embargo? With what?

Stepping into the van, Bill hands a twenty-dollar bill to the photographer, the same young guy who filmed the swimming pool collapse.

"Give him another five," says Bill B, clicking on a file on the screen in front of him and taking a big first bite out of the gyro. It is, as advertised, a juicy one.

There is some video static, followed by the image of Consuela, long-legged, resplendent, in a little black dress and dangerously tall pumps, reclining on the shrink's couch.

It looks like she is in a real shrink's office, in real analysis, with the patient on the couch, facing away from the analyst. The analyst is straight out of central casting; poor man's Freud.

Freud argued that laymen could be analysts, but that was before reality TV. For all anyone knows, today he might have argued that, with public exposure being the norm, it would be fine to Webcast analysis to the people. And with judges and doctors (especially plastic surgeons) playing the reality TV game, why should shrinks be left behind?

In any case, shrinkage is what's being done, here, now, for the benefit of Consuela Ramirez-Wronska.

They seem to be somewhere mid-session.

BILL B: Look at those fucking legs!

ANALYST: You were saying, Zbig was hypertensive . . .

BILL B: So fucking what?

CONSUELA: He was. It was under control. He took drugs for it.

ANALYST: Did that create problems with your lifestyle?

BILL B: "Lifestyle" . . . always a loaded word. Do you think they are real?

PHOTOGRAPHER: Legs—yes. Boobs—no.

CONSUELA: It did. He was unable to take enhancing drugs that he needed if he were to have a vigorous sex life. We could still have sex—when it was just the two of us. But he wanted more.

ANALYST: And you?

CONSUELA: I did. But when we wanted to have others in bed with us, well . . . he would have needed some . . . help.

BILL B: So that's what the cops were saying . . . Shit . . . How do you like your shwarma?

BILL K: Good. Did we get any fries with that?

PHOTOGRAPHER: No.

ANALYST: How did it make you feel? Having sex with multiple people?

CONSUELA: I never thought about it. It's just what we did. Some people are straight, some people are gay. This was our thing.

ANALYST: Did he find a way to deal with this problem, this need for a substitute for these drugs? Some people take these drugs anyway. And some people swear by nutraceuticals.

PHOTOGRAPHER: Are they going to talk about fucking iguanas next?

BILL B: Them and boa constrictors. Reptiles are the thing.

PHOTOGRAPHER: Gross.

BILL B: Why gross? They are reptiles and they consort with reptiles. It's godly.

PHOTOGRAPHER: Fuck you.

CONSUELA: He found something better than drugs. Danger. Heights.

ANALYST: Do you like it, too?

CONSUELA: One day, in Colorado, he took me by the edge of a gorge. It was very nice.

ANALYST: Fear, pheromones, adrenaline—there could be a link. At least many people think there is.

BILL B: Do you think he's doing her, the TV shrink?

PHOTOGRAPHER: Sure, why not? I don't care.

CONSUELA: It was bigger for him than it was for me. Sometimes we would get a room on the top floor of the hotel, and he would use the balcony to . . . I told you already.

BILL B: I hope they made the estate pay for fixing those glass panes at the Dux. That was reckless behavior, in my book. Standing on the railing with his dick hanging out. Unnecessary.

ANALYST: I see, he stood close to the edge of the balcony and looked down?

CONSUELA: That, and sometimes he would let his hands go and stand balancing on the railing.

ANALYST: Fully dressed.

CONSUELA: Not always.

ANALYST: How did that help?

BILL B: Remember the time they found a sixteen-year-old kid hanging by the neck on a playground swing, with his pants down and, on the ground in front of him, a photo of two broads fucking a guy?

PHOTOGRAPHER: Yeah. I was on that story. What's it called, that thing they do?

BILL K: A ménage à trois?

PHOTOGRAPHER: No! I know that one!

BILL K: You mean what the kid did?

PHOTOGRAPHER: Yes, that.

BILL K: Autoerotic asphyxiation.

CONSUELA: It helped by giving him a powerful, lasting erection—the closeness of death . . . I am not a doctor . . .

ANALYST: But he was . . .

CONSUELA: But he was . . .

ANALYST: Did this work?

CONSUELA: Yes. I can tell you that.

ANALYST: So what happened that night?

PHOTOGRAPHER: What's auto-erotic asphyxiation? I forgot.

BILL K: Constricting the flow of oxygen to the brain to get a more intense orgasm. If you do it in a noose and you pass out, you fucking die. It's not suicide. It's an accident. I heard of cases, in small towns, where they call it murder—and they go out searching for the killer. And sometimes they make arrests. That's the scariest part.

PHOTOGRAPHER: And you know so much about this because . . .

BILL K: Because Fuck You, that's how.

CONSUELA: We were in a hotel room . . . On the forty-third floor.

ANALYST: Who is *we*?

CONSUELA: The three of us—a patient of his was with us, and Zbig walked out on the balcony.

PHOTOGRAPHER: Was there a golden shower? Who does he think he is?

BILL B: Who *did* he think he *was*?

ANALYST: This is a violation of medical ethics, of course. The patient . . .

CONSUELA: Her husband didn't mind.

ANALYST: Hmmm. And . . .

CONSUELA: And what?

ANALYST: What happened?

CONSUELA: We made love, then realized that he wasn't there. And I got out of bed, and he wasn't on the balcony any-more.

ANALYST: Could you see the atrium panels from up there?

CONSUELA: No. It was dark, but I could see the ambulance driving up, with lights on.

ANALYST: Dr. Wronski was prominent here in South Flor-ida, as are you. Do you see any meaning in what happened that night? Any lesson learned? People want to know.

BILL K: What a great fucking question!

CONSUELA: What do you mean?

ANALYST: Is there anything this big life of this big man, Dr. Wronski's, can teach the rest of us? Is there meaning?

BILL B: Give me a fucking break . . .

CONSUELA: Zbig lived for beauty, he gave all he had.

ANALYST: And that's all?

CONSUELA: That's all.

BILL K: That's all? This is not even an answer! Where is the mystery? Is there anything left? Just porn? Threesomes, four-somes, hookers, golden show-ers?

I thought she was okay for a while. But she's like Trump in a skirt. Better legs, I give you that.

BILL B: Don't forget the butt. *Much* better than Trump's.

PHOTOGRAPHER: You seen Trump's?

BILL B: I needed that—thanks, asshole.

BILL K: The man lived, the man died. There has to be more to it.

BILL B: I can tell you the only meaning I derive from this shit: It's going to take quite a dance number to get this on the news.

BILL K: Even in South Florida?

BILL B: Even in South Florida.

24

|||||||||||||||||||||||||||||||||||||||||||||||||||||||||||||||||||||||||||||||||||||||||||||||||||||||||||||||||||||||||||||||||||||

THE TREASURE OF
THE CHÂTEAU

Bill K says good-bye to Bill B and his Sancho Panza. Their ca-
maraderie, the zingers they let fly as they watched the embar-
goed preview of that preposterous interview, made him fathom
the magnitude of his loss. What a horrible time not to be a reporter.

It's akin to missing your boat to Spain, leaving the fascists
unopposed. Here today, with Democrats having neutralized the
progressives, the battle lines have been drawn: the rampaging
dinosaurs vs. the press. It's us versus them, the lying white men
in suits versus defenders of justice, accuracy, and truth.

Bill loves the drive on Collins Avenue—always has. And he
is probably not the first man to ponder fascism along that route.

It feels like Tel Aviv, just bigger, and still very Bauhaus. Very
German, but good German. Our German.

There was a time when Holocaust survivors—folks with
numbers on their forearms—lived here. Isaac Bashevis Singer
walked these streets, exchanging nods with people he knew,

speaking Yiddish, Polish, English, taking Nobel Prize–worthy notes, thinking Nobel Prize–worthy thoughts, muttering Nobel Prize–worthy mutterings, and, in addition to all this, trying to get laid.

Here, on the right, is the Fontainebleau, a landmark now encumbered by an extra tower, that appendage that annoys Bill. The great white Fontainebleau, a creation of the great Morris Lapidus, who had a vision of building castles up and down this strip—castles that included, less famously, Château Sedan Neuve, the castle fated to fall.

Bill really should stop and go in, to see the Fontainebleau's lobby, to marvel at its curves, its whiteness, its Staircase to Nowhere. Of course, he should do it because good design is good, but also because a design nobly executed is a weapon against fascism: a Katyusha.

Piloting the white Prius north on Collins, he is a man in a hurry. Whatever it takes, he, William M. Katzenelenbogen, must get on that boat, he must join this fight, he must strike anywhere and everywhere, fighting by all means at his disposal.

Bill knows exactly what he can do.

In the eternal fight against fascism, "can" equals "must."

It's 3:30 P.M., the Russians have left the ocean, and only a small figure—a man—is bobbing in the waves.

Bill walks up to the chaise—the only chaise on the beach—picks up a pair of black-and-purple plaid shorts, reaches into the pocket, and finds a set of keys and a cell phone. The figure out there, in the ocean, starts a journey toward the shore, and seeing no reason to conceal his actions, Bill turns around and walks toward Château Sedan Neuve.

He walks up the steps, past the scorched, dry, empty pool, finally entering the building from the pool deck. He pushes the elevator button to the ninth floor and heads slowly along the corridor to the Greensteins' apartment.

There, he walks up to the disgustingly painted breakfront, opens its doors, and—one by one—takes out the velvet bags. There are six bags altogether. There could be more, he should look around, but time is short. He reaches inside one of the bags—it's gold. Crowns. Taken out of the mouths of dead Jews, or perhaps Jews still living.

Chills run up his spine and down again.

Greenstein can't be far behind. It doesn't matter. If Herr or, for that matter, Frau Greenstein gets in his way, he will kill them with his bare hands. Hands in which the Treasure of Château Sedan Neuve is now safe.

"Ruki vverkh!" commands a man Bill recognizes as the Russian security guard.

"You really should be using German," Bill says calmly. "Repeat after me: *Hände hoch.*"

Then, for good measure, he adds: "Asshole."

There is a gun pointed at him. Bill doesn't know his calibers and doesn't give a fuck. If he is ordered to give up these bags, he will do no such thing. After years of humiliation, they are in his hands, safe. This is it.

"Hey, in English we have an expression. You may not have heard it, so pay attention: Fuck you."

Dropping five of the bags on the floor, he takes the sixth, and, swinging it, whacks the gun-wielding guard across the face.

"Yob tvouy," the man shouts, and reciprocates by throwing a

left, getting Bill under the chin, then following up with a whack with the handle of his pistol.

Bill falls to the floor, his body shielding the five bags. He is thinking of the right word to describe what's just happened . . . "Pistol-whipped." No hyphen, one word: "pistolwhipped." That's what he is, pistolfuckingwhipped.

He has no idea how long he has been out, but he is comforted to realize that the five velvet bags are still beneath him. He has not been moved.

Good thing—he will not let these bags go. If he can't liberate them, he will sanctify them with his blood. Looks like he already has. He doesn't want to move . . . The bags. He must protect the bags.

Somebody throws a bucket of water on him. Fuckers. He will kill them, or he will try.

"So, you went for it . . ." It's Greenstein. "You give us no choice."

"How do you know I am not with FBI?" Bill responds, thinking of the bags.

"Because you are not. I did some research—not much is needed these days. A few little guesses, face recognition, this and that. It's not nice to waste FBI agents, but you are not an FBI agent. It's not good to kill reporters, but you are no longer a reporter. You are a *former* reporter. Your father might care, a little bit, but frankly that, too, is uncertain.

GREENSTEIN: Stepan, would you make this gentleman disappear?

STEPAN: How?

GREENSTEIN: Do I need to explain?

STEPAN: Shoot him here, now?

GREENSTEIN: Not in my apartment, idiot. He will ruin the rugs.

STEPAN: I can take him in bathroom and shoot him in back of head.

BILL: You will need to move me. And take these teeth.

WILFREDA: These are my father's teeth.

BILL: No. They are actually *Jewish* teeth. Your father was a Nazi.

WILFREDA: My husband is a Jew!

BILL: So?! You can be a Jew and a Nazi. Why is this so fucking hard for people to understand?

WILFREDA: I want my teeth!

STEPAN: I need clear orders.

WILFREDA: Kill him!

BILL: Go ahead, see if I give a fuck.

GREENSTEIN: Hold off on that. What will we do with the body?

STEPAN: Can I kick him at least?

BILL: Be my guest. I am not moving.

STEPAN: What if he screams?

BILL: Wouldn't you? That's the problem with you Nazis. You talk a good game, but when it comes to implementation, you fuck up big. Look at Franco. Look at Mussolini. Look at your Hitler. Your Trump will fuck up, too. And we will remove him.

GREENSTEIN: Pistolwhip him again, this time for real, and carry him out in a big duffle.

STEPAN: Do you have one?

BILL: See what I mean? Implementation.

STEPAN: Give me bags now. I am warning you.

BILL: Fuck you.

Pain is the last thing Bill remembers, together with this thought: "They killed me. Cowards."

When consciousness returns, he is covered with shards of glass, as is the room. He checks whether the teeth are still there, and they are. He has not been moved—means he has not been out long.

"How are you, *bubbie*?"

It's Johnny! The blind man with his Bushmaster.

"Molodetz!" It's Melsor. [Good lad.]

Good lad? Please . . .

The shards around and on top of Bill are from the "slice door," as sliding glass doors are known in the dialect of Château Sedan Neuve.

BILL: Johnny, I want you to take these bags. All six of them. You will take them to the Holocaust Museum. Can I trust you?

JOHNNY: I liberated Dachau. You know that.

Bill looks at Greenstein.

BILL: I know. And, you, Herr Greenstein, it's time for us to talk. You almost killed me, you Nazi asshole Jew. Would you like to be arrested on charges of assault with intent to kill—and, while you are at it, disgorged?

GREENSTEIN: What do you want?

BILL: The envelopes with the condo board ballots are being steam-opened right now. I know the results.

GREENSTEIN: What are they?

BILL: There was a write-in campaign, it appears. A move-ment. Frau Greenstein, write this down.

WILFREDA: Yes, dictate.

BILL: The winning slate: Roza Kisel', president. Melsor Katzenelenbogen, vice president. Nella Katzenelenbogen, board member. Alex Bogomolov, board member. Johnny Schwartz, also a board member.

And I want Roza Kisel' brought back here in a fucking black stretch limo. No, make it white. This is Florida.

WILFREDA: Yes?

GREENSTEIN: Yes. What choice do we have?

STEPAN: I have to go now.

BILL: Indeed, you do—you'll catch the next plane to Russia, douchebag. God save the czar!

25

BEATRICE

Gwen comes out of the gate wearing a polka-dot dress and an unbuttoned green Barbour coat, a messenger bearing greetings from a different universe.

They embrace, her hand running over the bruise on the back of his head.

"What happened to you?" she asks, pulling away for a moment. "You're bleeding."

"Nothing to worry about. Just pistolwhipped."

"Should we turn around and return to D.C.? I want you alive."

"In a couple of days, yes, let's return, maybe."

They kiss again. Gwen is here—his, for him. They will survive this in each other's arms, he is certain of this, like his parents did, taking walks through the darkened city—theirs.

She pulls back again.

"Were they trying to kill you?"

"They were. They failed."

"You didn't kill anyone . . ."

What can Bill possibly say to this? How is it relevant? I found my Don't Give a Fuckness, I stared down a gun without flinching, defanged the Evil Dwarf, restored justice in a corner of South Florida. And, yes, I got the girl; did I not? Is this not worth killing for? What difference does it make whether I did or didn't?

"I don't like this pause—please say no."

"No. Let's just say I won—and they lost."

It's 7:05 P.M., January 19. The burghers of the Château are in a meeting, feverishly counting the ballots. When it comes to ballots, Frau Wilfreda Müller-Greenstein is an exceptional, experienced cook. There will be no surprises—no reason to babysit the meeting.

Bill doesn't have to manage that thing anymore. He can be here, at the airport, holding Gwen. If such measurements had been taken, it would be revealed that they stay joined in an embrace longer than any other couple upon that gleaming terrazzo floor over the preceding three and a half hours, and those other contestants were much younger, indeed neither was of legal age. Also, they were boys.

They part, but his right arm remains on her, held in place by her left hand. He feels her beating heart. He feels the possibilities—all of them at once—ranging from the physical—the taste of her mouth—all the way to the existential—his rebirth as a writer, perhaps.

No, this will probably not happen, not with this Zbig thing, but with something else, something urgent, something political.

He stops for a moment in the darkness of the parking garage, and they kiss again, briefly this time, but long enough to chase away the thoughts about the story that brought him here, to Florida.

They kiss again and again in the Prius, and as the car starts silently, his hand drops to her mid-thigh, coming to rest beneath her hem and her hand. He keeps it there.

They drive in silence, drinking it in, looking at the lights.

"How is the book?" she asks as the ramp takes them to Ocean Drive.

His hand is on her knee. It feels to him like a greeting of sorts, the ringing in of an era. What will he do in this new era? Books perhaps, though not about the reptile-fucking rich. He has been looking into this thing, but no aspect of it has drawn him in. You need that if you are to get cranking.

So, no journalism, unless he finds a way in.

Perhaps crime reporting for a television station would be the thing. Opposition research comes to mind, too. Public relations, even that narrow field called crisis management, is clearly not an option the way it was for Gwen. Not for him. He couldn't possibly.

Or maybe he will do what so many others have done—become a PI. William M. Katzenelenbogen, Existentialist Investigator of the Gold Coast, Inspector Luftmensch. You have to admit, there is panache . . .

The pondering of career options when your hand rests upon your lover's knee is frowned upon, even in Washington. But in Bill's case, an exception is warranted. The guy has never had a job. He has had a place in the universe—it was inseparable from other aspects of his existence.

You will see: when this Trump madness subsides, retreats,

dissolves, because this is, after all, America, Bill and Gwen will be together still, made stronger by their adventure.

Readers are encouraged to mobilize their memories or imaginations to reconstruct what happens before dawn. We will skip over all this.

The sun is yet to rise, and Gwen is in Bill's arms.

She begins to talk:

"I haven't had a chance to tell you, that deal, it's big. It's for a PAC. Republican this time, probably channeling money for the Trump organization, on the private side, so it's very hush-hush. There will be more revelations, and they will want me on their crisis team, running it."

Bill takes a deep breath. He sits up in the bed.

"I hope you don't mind."

"What right do I have to object?"

"I hear you thinking: 'A Faustian deal.'"

"No. You are not a reporter—not anymore. You represent no interests but your own."

"And you, Bill? You are not a reporter, either."

"No. I am not."

"What will you be? Are you capable of making a deal?"

"Faustian?"

"Is there another kind?"

"I could become a PI."

"That's Faustian in my book."

"I've been thinking of hanging out a shingle: EXISTENTIALIST INVESTIGATIONS L.L.C. William M. Katzenelenbogen, Inspector Luftmensch."

"Clever. That's you."

"But there is something I must do first. Finish the unfinished business. Understand something big."

"Honor your art?"

"My former art."

His Carhartts, his T-shirt, and his Top-Siders on, Bill leans over the bed and kisses her brow.

EPILOGUE

At the Château, Melsor's parking spot is occupied by a new white Lexus GS F with temporary plates.

On his cell phone, Bill looks up the starting price: $84,000.

Melsor's payoff arrived the morning after the election. Not a bad way for returns to start trickling in. As the vice president of the CSNCA BOD, Melsor Y. Katzenelenbogen is entitled to a first-class ride. The good men of ISIS have seen to that. ISIS works fast.

Bill leaves the dirty little white Prius in front of the gleaming white Lexus.

He needs to run in for a moment, to get something. He does get that something—two items, to be exact, and as he leaves, he notices an ISIS eighteen-wheeler unloading scaffolding in front of the Château.

Regime change or not, the balconies will come down.

————

Back at the Grand Dux parking lot, Bill considers drafting a note to his father, but quickly rejects the idea. Has he not expressed his thoughts on multiple occasions without being heard?

Fuck it, Melsor is the only family he has. He starts drafting an e-mail, but stumbles immediately. In previous e-mails—there were few—there was no need for salutations. It was all business. You would think that after a half century the Katzenelenbogen men would have ironed out the problem of salutation, but it is what it is, or, to translate a Russian expression, "When it's fuck your mother, it's fuck your mother, but when it's fuck your mother, it's fuck your mother."

It's all in the inflections. Isn't everything always?

A text comes in as Bill exits the elevator on the top floor of the Grand Dux:

"Bill, you are uncooperative! This is your THIRD AND FI-NAL REMINDER. Why are you dragging this out? Just let me go!"

He starts on a response, weighing the idea of answering, and as three dots surely blink on Lena's phone, he keys in "GO!!!" but erases it.

On the rooftop of the Grand Dux, the alarm, in winding, howling waves, braids with the wind. A light cloud has descended, grazing the roof, a smoky tangent. The wind is oceanbound, the cloud is its ward.

Winded from the run up three flights of stairs to the roof—the forty-eighth floor—Bill waits for his heartbeat to settle. His T-shirt sleeves flutter, like banners, like petite blue wings. His *W* cap begins to move, the wind has entered it, an unseen wedge inserted, it quakes. The hat, it takes its leap. The hat, it rises. The hat, above him, a flying instrument with buoyancy all its own, the visor down, like a parachutist—a jumper—beneath the canopy, his sail. It rises, turns a somersault, then, in a leap, surfing the invisible currents toward the sea, disappears completely. Bill may believe he sees it still, but it is out, gone, free.

He looks into the ocean. He turns around, letting his gaze sweep across the inland marshes, high-rises, channels. Pelicans above invite him to join their silent patrol. The wind will show him how silly it was to fear, introduce Bill to the world Zbig fathoms fully, uniting them in knowledge. Roommates again. Absurd, but true.

Infinity is a concept, but it's a feeling, too. It takes a leap—just one. One leap, toward imprisonment or liberation. Commit, commit, and rush to penetrate the spheres. Life/death is a dichotomy of outcomes, and is there anything more boring than outcomes, I ask? Is retreat possible? A stupid question. The edge—that's all there is. It's all about the edge. To fathom Zbig, to catch him by his feet, you grab his final moment, his Zbigness. No other way exists.

They will be here soon—security, rent-a-cops in blue, armed, dangerous even if you are white. He must make his resolutions quickly and act forthwith.

Bill's thoughts:

The cloud's content, its gentle fog. I could attach myself to it, Inspector Luftmensch in his magic dirigible. It's porous, the boundary between the spheres. This is my story. My cloud, my dirigible. It's lifting, lifting fast, and I remain below.

The purple band on the horizon brightens, orange in its core. Dawn nears, my dawn, the first I've ever owned. This narrative is mine at last. I didn't get to choose my material, my smarts and deficits—none of the attributes, mental, physical. I didn't choose those precious intelligentsia sensibilities. I didn't choose those cold, dark streets. I didn't volunteer to be a carrier of my father's criminality, the cancerousness of my mother's breasts.

I was a journalist once. No more of that. I had a Beatrice, I thought. No more. I had a book to write, I thought. I may—or not. It rides on this. The quest is not to understand. It's to explore, which means to feel. There's nothing harder. The method of elimination is all I ever had, I see this now. Commitment to the narrative does not mean having to relate. It is okay, it's noble to bottle in. Inspector Luftmensch has no loyalties, he has no obligations, and he has nothing to explain. With firmament beneath me still, I make my choice with open eyes. What difference do eyes make when there's a leap?

I'll set my gaze upon the rising sun, this orange streak on the horizon. It pulls me, eastward, through air, clouds, ocean. To tell your story, you become it. Inspector Luftmensch knew this all along. Now I know, too.

I haven't seen the edge, the very edge—not yet. Would it be cowardly to stand and peer, to let prior knowledge fuel my fear? I'll see it soon enough; I'll take my leap, my flight. The concept of the final step seems old and quaint. The edge is of no consequence—I see this. The final step—it's of no greater consequence than the first—and damn those stallions. The song— irrelevant. The edge—romanticism of the unknown. What does it matter? Trajectory is my metric now, my neopedestrian vector in my new realm.

I check the buckles on my pack. Where is the rip cord? A brave man never checks; a coward—always. This is not suicide. This isn't what ascetics call mortification of the flesh. Glorification is the word, and it's about meaning, not flesh. There's time to think about the rip cord, about the pilot chute. I will do no such thing.

"Here I come!" I shout, setting my course into the wind, and then I leap.

There is a strip of sand beneath—the beach.

Melsor begins the morning of January 20 the way he begins all mornings. On the balcony, staring into the ocean.

He is not the sort that waits for sunrises or sunsets. He is on this balcony for a reason. Fifty push-ups today, like every day. He used to do these on the concrete floor. He still has the breath, the heartbeat, the musculature, but some errant nerve caused pain. He tried to elevate, doing his push-ups off the edge of a plastic chaise, and that worked fine for a few weeks.

Now, Melsor places his hands on the balcony's aluminum railing; this is hardly a push-up, you might as well be standing upright, but the pain announces itself, shooting up from the small of his back.

Melsor is not the sort that surrenders. He faces south. Up, down, up again, counting. One . . . exhale . . . forty-nine to go . . . inhale. He pauses on top of the second push-up, looking up at the twin towers of the Grand Dux.

Three . . . Forty-seven to go . . . He will do every single one of them, gulping down the pain. Up-down, up again, counting, because life is not a handout. Life is a privilege, life is what you defend, life is the thing you conquer.

Melsor is naked except for his white boxer shorts. Fruit of the Loom; the only brand he has worn since coming to America. To people who inhabit the skyscraper aeries a few hundred feet away, he is a figure bopping up and down anonymously on the balcony. He could do this completely naked if he so chose.

Push-ups on the balcony speed up his blood's journey through his calcifying arteries, his constricting veins. It gushes through, like breath through a whistle. This is his private moment, a send-off to a day in a life that is, once again, becoming public. He was a poet once, a bard of freedom, a voice of moral authority, a weaver of verse on the world's stage. He is a leader now, a vice president, the de facto king of his Château. Has he changed? No. Never. The world is the one who has changed, matured, wizened to the point of accepting his leadership, offering itself to Melsor Yakovlevich Katzenelenbogen. Here I am, Melsor Yakovlevich—I am yours. Take, reap, rule, do as you please.

Melsor has worked up a sweat, enough to wipe off with a cold, wet towel. He had soaked it in the sink and brought it out in a Walmart shopping bag to keep it from dripping on the white tiled floor. It's a sponge bath really, something you learn to appreciate in a cold-water communal flat in Moscow, the kind of place where the corridors are long and where there is no shower. The public bathhouse is too far for daily or even weekly visits—a basin filled with water and a wet towel is all you get.

Melsor runs the towel beneath his armpits, sending streams of cold water down his chest, past his core, down to the band of the boxer shorts, letting it stream through the subtropical jungle of coarse hair behind what is technically known as a "functional fly front."

He walks inside the apartment, pulls on a pair of cargo shorts and a striped T-shirt.

The instant he steps out of the Château's gates, his body takes over, running itself past the glum white men with their glum white dogs. They stay behind him, unaware of their surrender.

Note his elbows, they are bent, a bit arthritic perhaps, but stiffer than granite. Winglike, they speed him up as he rushes north toward his destination—the Broadwalk.

There, at the Broadwalk, he pauses, looks back, past the Château, past the Diplomat, past the Grand Dux. It's a cloudless morning, the beginning of a cloudless day. More than anyone, Melsor knows that sometimes, sometimes you must look back, to measure the distance covered, legions defeated, lands conquered, nations subjugated.

Usually, he can get all these thoughts packed like proverbial sausage into proverbial *kishke* of a single instant. He will touch the mezuzah next. Unlike his *nebesh* son, Melsor is not in the least perplexed by the mezuzah's presence here, its hiding place on the back of a rotting fence post.

Its purpose is to send Melsor on to his daily triumph over age, to protect his launching pad from unwanted intruders. Should some overly eager city maintenance worker find it and pull it off with a crowbar, Melsor will buy a new mezuzah and affix it to another rotting post, and if they dig out the posts, he will use trees, for this is the place that needs protection; screw the apartment. Nella takes care of that.

Before his hand gets to the mezuzah, Melsor pauses, turning around to consider the view, squinting to increase the resolution of the sweeping picture before him—the ever-rising skyline of the South Florida coastline. He lingers a bit, questioning whether he is actually seeing an intensely orange dot pop up next to the Grand Dux. What can it be? A parachute? Sometimes speed-boats drag parachutists along the coast; it's hard to fathom why. Those fools—and fools they must be—are never more than a few meters in the air.

This one is near the building's top, too close to the building to make any sense. There is no boat that Melsor can see. No airplane either. Suicide maybe. Two weeks ago, on Local News 10, Melsor heard about a plastic surgeon, the Butt God they called him, who fell to his death. It was at the Grand Dux. Here in Florida you do what you want. If you are crazy, be crazy. If you want to jump, well, knock yourself out—jump.

The orange dot is gone. Perhaps it was never there. It could have been triggered by solar activity, or—and this is unlikely in the extreme—it's Melsor's mind playing tricks, conjuring images, lying.

Melsor kisses his hand and reaches behind a post, where his fingers find the hidden mezuzah that shouldn't be there, but, the rabbis be damned, is.

ACKNOWLEDGMENTS

The disintegrating hulk of Château Sedan Neuve cannot be found on any map of South Florida. The building is my homage to the great Morris Lapidus, the creator of Miami modernism, whose Hotel Fontainebleau is one of my favorite buildings anywhere.

I urge you to refrain from going on the Web to reserve a room at the Grand Dux Hotel in Hollywood, Florida. Someone may take your credit card number, but you will not get a room. Like the Château, the place exists only in my imagination.

My biggest debt of gratitude is to my father, Boris Goldberg, for not being Melsor Katzenelenbogen.

Boris has taught me everything I know about being a journalist and a novelist. While I am his creation, Melsor is mine. You might say they have me in common, and, importantly, they are both poets. Melsor's principal mission is to help me play out my fascination with dishonesty—political, economic, intellectual, artistic, personal.

ACKNOWLEDGMENTS

I accept full responsibility for the Russian poems attributed to Melsor and Bill. English translations are mine as well. I composed this oeuvre while sitting on my father's sofa in South Florida. I feel obligated to disclose that he declared my poetry to be beyond awful and generously proposed edits, which I rejected.

The idea for this book was tossed to me by Susan Keselenko Coll, a comic novelist whose ideas I took seriously even before we were married. My literary agent, Josh Getzler, thought the idea was a hoot, and my editor, James Meader, suggested that this could be not just one, but a series of novels—a fucking career!

As I dug into the material, I became fascinated by the institution of a condo board. In the context of the United States, it's difficult to imagine a political structure less accountable, less transparent, and more open to abuse. The problem is especially acute in Florida, where laws governing these entities are as weak as the stakes high.

Florida, I learned, is a land of opportunity to defraud thy neighbor. Sunburn notwithstanding, Nikolai Gogol would have struck gold on Hollywood's Broadwalk. (That's Broadwalk, not boardwalk—it's an actual place.) Should you find yourself there, you might want to listen in to the narratives glum-looking passersby pour out into their cell phones. My informal survey suggests that condo boards are their chief complaint, followed by deteriorating health and America's predatory health care system. The inadequate level of attention from children comes in fourth.

As I wrote, I became obsessed with the Russian culture of South Florida. I hung out at Russian restaurants and Russian clubs, navigating rivers of vodka, and listening, listening, listening. Chunks of this novel are lifted from these overheard conversations.

My Washington friends Ellen and Gerry Sigal were generous with their time. Gerry, a builder who knows from Florida, helped me devise the disasters that befall the Château and has allowed me to shadow him at work.

In Florida, I often consulted with my *Duke Chronicle* friends Davia and Jim Mazur. Nina Gordon, a *Chronicle* friend as well, was immensely helpful and encouraging, as was her law partner Arvin Jaffe. I will continue to pick their brains as this thing rolls on.

As always, I turned to my friend and (on occasion) co-author Otis Brawley with questions involving medicine. Omer Mei-Dan, an orthopedic surgeon and BASE jumper, answered my questions about the mechanics of this extreme sport. Kate Whitmore translated Frau Müller-Greenstein's lament into original German. Julius Getman walked me through legal perils faced by those who hold loot from the Holocaust.

The list of friends and family members who offered guidance or looked over the manuscript includes Amin Ahmad, Jeff Altbush, Marilyn Altbush, Peter Bach, Alan Bennett, Joel Berkowitz, Laura Brawley, Ken Crerar, Claire Dietz, Slavik Dushenkov, Anna Dushenkova, Richard Folkers, Graydon Forrer, Vladimir Frumkin, Peter Garrett, Galina Goldberg, Tom Grubisich, Gardiner Harris, Dudley Hudspeth, Jonathan Keselenko, Marian Keselenko, Steven Lieberman, Richard Liebeskind, Julie Lloyd, Patricia Lochmuller, the late Mike Madigan, Harsha Murthy, Amanda Newman, Matthew Bin Han Ong, Alexei Pervov, Caitlin Riley, Gregory Rolbin, Lela Rosenberg, Kara Sergeant, Angela Spring, Jon Steiger, Dave Stephen, Valerie Strauss, and Mel Tomberg.

I've also benefited from advice from the talented younger generation of my wonderful blended family: Sarah Goldberg, Katie Goldberg, Max Coll, Emma Bivona, John Bivona, Ally Coll Steele, and Rory Steele.

After considering thanking the semi-fictional character the Château residents call Donal'd Tramp for giving this book urgency, providing the macrocosm for my microcosm, and inspiring me to write like the wind, I decided to do nothing of the sort.